OTHER TITLES BY THIS WRITER

(alternative titles refer to US and UK editions)

as Malcolm Macdonald

The World from Rough Stones

The Rich Are with You Always

Sons of Fortune

Abigail

Goldeneye

Tessa d'Arblay

In Love and War/For They Shall Inherit

The Silver Highways

The Sky with Diamonds/Honour and Obey

His Father's Son

The Captain's Wives

Dancing on Snowflakes

as Malcolm Ross

The Dukes

Mistress of Pallas/On a Far Wild Shore

A Notorious Woman

An Innocent Woman

A Woman Alone

A Woman Possessed

To the End of Her Days

Kernow & Daughter

Crissy's Family/The Trevarton Inheritance

Tomorrow's Tide

The Carringtons of Helston

Like a Diamond

Tamsin Harte

Rose of Nancemellin

as M. R. O'Donnell

Hell Hath No Fury

A Woman Scorned

All Desires Known

For I Have Sinned

Sons of Fortune

Malcolm Macdonald

Cover design by Abbate Design
Cover photography by Jeff Cottenden
Sourcebooks and the colophon are registered trademarks of Sourcebooks, Inc.

Published by Sourcebooks Landmark, an imprint of Sourcebooks, Inc.
P.O. Box 4410, Naperville, Illinois 60567-4410
(630) 961-3900
Fax: (630) 961-2168
www.sourcebooks.com

Originally published in London in 1978 by Hodder & Stoughton.

Library of Congress Cataloging-in-Publication Data is on file with the publisher.

Printed and bound in the United States of America.
VP 10 9 8 7 6 5 4 3 2 1

Part One

1854–55

Chapter 1

They had never run the blockade at night before. The air, already crisp with the moonlight, was sharpened with the scent of barley-stubble—she had sailed so close to land. The sea was a dark green pasture, billowing hither and thither beneath the slightest breeze. She spread her full head of sail and nosed lightly through those shimmering waters, alert for the least sign of the blockade. Somewhere out there Sir Henry Morgan and the Terrible Turk lay in wait for her. And in her hold she carried dangerous cargo—the most dangerous cargo of all: the croquet hoop from the middle lawn.

She held it behind her, concealing it as best she could in the folds of her skirts. Up the rose pergola she stole, hugging the safety of the rock shoals to her right. At the bend by the trellis the harbour mouth came into view. Almost there—almost safe.

Caspar Stevenson, well hidden in the rock shoals of the azaleas, watched his young sister's childish manoeuvres with angry contempt. She was just a nuisance in this game. "Blockade" demanded cunning, resource, and boldness; Abigail brought to it nothing but a brazen sort of stupidity—and the most violent temper in creation.

"Let her pass! Let her pass!" he prayed silently toward his brother, Boy (alias Sir Henry Morgan). Once Abigail was safely through to the harbour, the game could be played in earnest.

Boy Stevenson had seen Abigail sneaking along the rose pergola. He waited until he was certain she had dumped her cargo before he challenged. There was a universal conspiracy among the children that Abigail must be allowed to win, for when she lost her tantrums made the game unplayable.

"Ahoy!" he called.

Abigail said nothing.

"You—off the port bow!"

Abigail stopped and put her hands on her hips before she remembered to put them back behind her, pretending she was still in cargo. "Starboard!" she said scornfully.

"Starboard bow." Boy accepted the correction.

"Beam," she persevered.

"Prepare to receive boarders. I'm seizing your cargo."

Abigail gave a screech of triumph and, raising both empty hands above her head, began a very unshiplike dance on the lawn. "Empty! Empty!" she shrieked and cackled.

"Then pass, stranger," Boy said, turning with relief to resume his patrol.

"I jettisoned my cargo by the azalea—by the *cliff*. I'm allowed to return and take it in free."

Boy saw with horror that the Terrible Turk, otherwise Nick Thornton, had come right up to the pergola and was standing in the shade of the azalea. "No, Nick!" he began. "Don't!"

But it was too late. Nick was already holding the abandoned cargo over his head. "Prize!" he cried. "Pri-ize!" He made two descending notes of it.

Abigail's shriek of rage made one long rising note. She hurled herself at Nick, bearing him down though he was almost twice her weight. He recovered quickly, leaping back to his feet and beginning to dance in triumph as she had danced moments earlier. "Spoilsport! Spoilsport!" he taunted and laughed.

Abigail's scream halted every scurrying night creature for a mile around. Boy ran to stop her from attacking Nick; at such moments she had no control of herself. Last year she had nearly bitten off one of Caspar's fingers; the tip of it still had no feeling or power of movement.

But, unpredictable as ever, Abigail went as silent and calm as the night the moment she saw Boy. "It's mine," she said. "You challenged and lost. Tell him it's mine."

How he wished he could. "Sorry, Abbie," he said. "The rules of 'Blockade' are clear. Jettisoned cargo is in hazard until…" Abbie began to pant vehemently. "You should just have said, 'I jettisoned,' Boy persisted. "You shouldn't have said where. So Nick was quite within…"

Her howl of anguish, though less fierce than the earlier scream of rage, was broader and more smothering. In its time it had drowned church organs, railway trains, and German bands. Even as it diminished, as she ran away headlong down the pergola, it held the rest of them rooted to the spot.

Only Abigail's sister Winifred moved. She rose reluctantly from her hiding place between the two clipped box trees and placed herself firmly in the path. The conspiracy was that everyone did their best to let Abbie win, but if the plan came apart, she was not to be allowed to oil off into a tantrum. When Abbie was still a good half dozen yards away, Winifred stepped aside and held out a foot to trip her, knowing well that Abbie was never quite so possessed as to lose all sense of self-interest.

Abigail stopped in time but mimed a greater imbalance than she felt; she glowered at her sister and breathed out great, draughty lungsful of air.

"Nick's right—you are a spoilsport," Winifred said.

"I know!" Abigail shouted defiantly.

"You spoil every game when you lose."

"Of course I do."

"We don't want you out here." She could see how fiercely Abbie was fighting her own unruliness. Winifred, pitying as always her young sister's strength of passion, almost relented. Only a memory of the disasters that had followed so many earlier concessions prevented her. "Go to bed," she said sharply. "Bed's the place for babies."

Abigail stalked off into the dark shadow of the house, howling a great baleful sound. Before she went in by the garden door the howls ceased and her voice rang out of the dark. "I can't help being born after all you!"

She slammed the door so hard the glass shattered and fell in ringing sherds to the flagstone pathway.

There was a silence. Then Nick said: "An impressive temper!"

"We ought to make her come back and play properly," said Winifred. "But it would spoil it for you people."

From across the garden came Caspar's shout: "Start the blockade again!" He had worked his way stealthily back through the shrubbery and up the west pergola so that his shout would reveal none of his tactics for running the blockade.

Within moments Abigail's outburst was forgotten, and five legitimate frigates were seeking again to outwit the two pirates and reach the safety of the harbour.

Caspar was not the only one to have watched these events secretly and at close quarters. The "harbour" was, in fact, a medieval watchtower at one corner of the garden, for the Old Manor had once been well fortified. And on top of the tower, enjoying an evening cigar, stood John Stevenson and Walter Thornton, fathers of the two families whose older members were at play below.

"Such energy!" John said.

Walter, standing beside him, leaning on the rusted iron rail that ran along the parapet at the top of the tower, looked down at the unsuspecting children below, and drew a sharp breath in agreement. John stirred and stretched.

"How do we channel all that energy, eh?" he asked. "They'd wreck the world if we let them."

Walter looked at him in surprise. "*Channel* it?"

John was equally surprised at Walter's response. "Of course. It's our duty."

"Oooh…" Walter sounded dubious. "I think that's a fallacy."

"You do surprise me."

"If a youngster knows what he wants, and it's not something criminal or harmful, I'd say a parent's duty begins and ends with paving the way for him. Only if a child is aimless, surely, do we intervene more purposefully. Otherwise we're just playing God."

His conviction obviously worried John. "Do you really think so?" he asked.

Walter laughed. "An easy thing to do from the Olympian heights of this tower, mind you."

"You have me worried now, Thornton," John said, ignoring Walter's light-heartedness. "No one did any directing for me, it's true. But then I started at the bottom. All directions led upward, I suppose…Here's the nub of it now: My children are less free than yours. Young John will take over the business, of course, he'll have to. But the others must take up more respectable professions." His laugh was so brief that Walter could not tell whether it was humorous or bitter. John went on: "This family cannot flout Society forever. If anyone is 'playing God,' as you put it, then it's Society, not I."

Without waiting for Walter to reply, he leaned over the parapet, cupped his hands to his mouth, and called "Bed!" to the children below.

Boy and Winifred looked up in astonishment; none of them had known the two fathers were at the top of the tower.

"Have you been up there all along?" Nicholas asked.

"We have," Walter told him.

"Bed," John repeated.

Some of the younger ones began to protest.

"Silence, sir!" Walter called. "Do as you are bid at once." But his eyes were not on any child of his own; they were on Caspar, now clearly visible in the moonlight. Such hate! And in one so young!

Caspar, trembling with passion, held the croquet mallet—his cargo—before him and snapped the handle in two. He narrowly avoided putting out his own eye with the splintered end. Then he, too, turned and headed for the garden door.

"You might have let them finish," Walter said.

John, unwilling to face the truth of it, turned sideways and went over to the outer rampart.

"Good night, Uncle Walter. Good night, Father," Caspar called when he reached the door. His voice was now calm, even moderate. The other children joined in and John's guilt was drowned in a chorus of farewells.

"Didn't you notice Caspar in the shrubbery?" Walter asked. "He was almost to safety."

"It was but a game," John said. "And Caspar's anger is only a spark. He just hates being thwarted." He looked at the clearing sky. "It will grow even colder soon. We could have a frost." He only half offered this as a reason for having cheated Caspar of his prize.

The clouds above, which had allowed the moon to peer fitfully down, were now breaking into ragged wisps. The whole eastern half of the sky was clear and all the land beneath was soaked in the cold moonlight. Silver-blue trees and hedgerows thrust up from shadows of deepest purple. The two men stood as it were in an arbour, canopied with thin cloud that muted the contrasts of light and shade. They watched the carpet of cold light come sidling toward them over the fields and hollows. Now that the children had gone, the night silence was profound.

"You were talking about Society," Walter reminded John.

"Aye. We have little to do with it, of course. Work. The estates. Nora's own businesses..."

"Quite," Walter said.

"And if the purpose of life is to be useful, to serve God and one's country, to be a good steward of...all that is entrusted to you...and so forth..."

"Quite," Walter said again.

"Mind you, Nora does hunt. She has friends there. Lord Wyatt. Lord David Hardwick. The Marquis of Whitesands. But they are *friends*. And that is very different from the broad and shallow set of mere acquaintances we call Society."

Walter realized he could not say "quite" yet again.

"No," John continued, "Society and we..." He could not seem to finish the sentence.

"Are you trying to say that people are snubbing you?"

"Oh, all the time. Lord Middleton's"—he pointed north, for the Middleton Hunt Kennels were just a few miles away over the brow of the hill—"still blackballs our application regularly. Oh yes, we're being cut all the time. But we expect that. Anyone who starts with nothing and becomes very rich must expect that."

"Then what worries you? Something is obviously worrying you."

"In a word, Nora."

"It would hurt her, of course, more than..."

"Hurt!" John laughed despairingly. "She isn't even aware of it."

"Oh, come!"

"Well..." he conceded. "Yes, she is. She is *aware* of it. But she thinks that those who cut us are not even worth our contempt."

"Perhaps she's right."

"For *us*. Yes, of course she is. We don't give a fig for it all. But what about our children? Society can be most vindictive. Society has an elephant's memory. Is it fair to our children? The boys especially?"

"Come, I'm sure you exaggerate. But look, why not send them away to school, so that they can build their own acquaintance early?"

John nodded and smiled. There was a hint of triumph in his eyes, as if he thought he had led Walter step by step to this conclusion. "That is precisely what I have arranged."

"Ah! And Mrs. Stevenson, I take it, is not enthusiastic?"

John cleared his throat. "She does not yet know."

Walter drew in a sharp breath but said nothing. At last he understood John's fretful preoccupation.

"I've had so little time," John explained. "You and I are off to the Crimea next week. You know how much organizing that has demanded. There was so little time left for...ordinary things."

"My dear fellow, you don't need to justify yourself to me!" Walter said. "How long has it been arranged?"

"Some weeks."

"And Mrs. Stevenson has no idea?"

John shook his head glumly.

Walter whistled. "Then I do not envy *you*!" he said.

Chapter 2

JOHN HAD CONVEYED ONLY THE MOST SUPERFICIAL PARTS OF HIS FEARS TO Walter—and even that had been hard enough to put into words. His deepest worry was not that he had made such important arrangements behind Nora's back, it was how to explain the whole business to her without wounding her acutely.

The problem was that Nora saw herself not as a ragamuffin grown rich but as a member of the ancient aristocracy restored to a rightful inheritance. True, her father had been no more than a handloom weaver. But her grandfather had been a yeoman farmer and her great-grandfather had been gentry—the squire of Normanton, no less. (Sometimes, to shorten the period of her family's decline, she claimed this rank for her grandfather, omitting the "great.") More recently she had set some genealogical sleuths to work and discovered (as who could not discover by going far enough back?) earls and marquises on one side or other of her family's bedsheets.

In short, Nora's contempt for Society's ways was not the sour grapes of the excluded parvenu; it was the amused disdain of the old aristocracy. She did not realize that her membership in that ancient and exclusive set was conceded by herself alone. Her hunting-field friendship with Lord Wyatt, Lord David Hardwick, and company merely fostered the illusion. It never occurred to her for one moment that Society saw things quite the other way around.

But Society did. To all her neighbours, to all who returned her visits with a single card handed in by a footman, to all whose "middle-class" conventions (her words) she flouted with an aristocratic directness that was now going out of fashion even among aristocrats—to all these, to Society, she was a parvenu. She might have the money, the friends, and the panache to carry it off, to force a grudging tolerance of her ways, but in the long run Society was both implacable and invincible. The children would pay the ransom for their mother's victories. Only if the boys got away to a good school now, where they might form those lifelong childhood friendships on which all later access to Society would depend, only then might they escape those penalties.

Now how was John to explain as much to Nora without wounding, perhaps fatally, that sense of self which sustained her blindness through every social encounter? How could he tell her that only by accepting Society's estimation of her as an ex-slut could she prepare the way for her children's acceptance?

Until this night it had been easy to pretend that the problem was remote. The recent dreadful news from the Crimea had crowded out all other thoughts. As soon as word had come through that the army was hopelessly bogged down at Sebastopol and that it could barely be supplied from Balaclava harbour, eight miles to the south over roads axle-deep in mud, John had volunteered his best navvy gangs and his own services to build a light supply railway from the port to the siege lines—an offer the government had gratefully accepted. The necessary organization had filled his days since then: seven steam vessels and two in sail, totalling nearly five and a half thousand tons, laden with nearly two thousand tons of rail, six thousand wooden ties to hold them, and about three thousand tons of other material (fixed engines, cranes, piledrivers, trucks, wagons, barrows, blocks, chainfalls, wire rope, capstans, crabs, sawing machines, forges...) all to be distributed in such a way that even the loss of three vessels at sea would not endanger the venture—all this had occupied his time. On top of that there were the five hundred navvies and overseers to select, issue with kit, to victual, to provide with clerks and surgeons...Oh, these last few weeks John had found little time to worry about the future social acceptability of his children!

In the rush of things it had seemed easy and logical enough to arrange, almost in passing, for Young John and Caspar to go away to school. And in the press of all that organization it had been easy, too, to let each "right moment" for telling Nora slip away, one by one; and now there were no such moments left. The Crimean venture was organized; they'd see the ships off next week and then he and Walter would go overland to Naples, and thence by ship to Balaclava, gaining ten days for the survey. There was nothing now to prevent him from telling Nora—except that all the right moments had been squandered.

"Nora, there's something I forgot to tell you..." "Eay, love! I don't know how it slipped me mind, but..." "Didn't I tell you? I'm sure I did. I could have sworn..."

Oh dear, oh dear! He lay in bed listening to her moving around in her boudoir, waiting for her to come and join him.

❧

Seen through the aura of the lamp she held before her, John was no more than a blur on the white of the pillow. His eyes, following her movement, gleamed back a pale fire borrowed from the lamp. It gave him the appearance of a wary night creature. When she put the lamp on her bedside table and drew back the curtain, the light fell squarely on him. How ill he looked!

He had worked too hard these last weeks. She ought to have paid more attention to him. She ought to have insisted that one of his deputies should do the organizing if John himself was to take charge of the actual work in the Crimea. She knew how he'd throw his heart and stomach into the job once he arrived.

Yet she knew, too, that all this blaming of herself was idle. John looked on this Crimean venture as his personal sacrifice for England—a return for all that England had given him. How, then, could he spare himself?

"If you're not more careful of yourself, you'll wake up dead one morning soon," she said as she climbed in beside him.

He pulled a face. "I'll rest a day or two now. Thornton's a tonic. I'd not feel half so happy with any other engineer."

He was still full of tension, belying the promise of these words.

"You need a month's rest, against what you're going to do."

"I'll try and get it," he promised, "tomorrow and Sunday."

She turned down the wick and extinguished the light. For a while they lay side by side until the immediate dark turned pale in the moonlight. She listened to his breathing. He drew breath easily enough but he held it for a second or two before letting it out. He always did that on the nights when worry chased sleep away.

Why tonight? Was he telling the truth when he said that all the organizing was done? She thought she knew how to relax him then. She propped herself on one elbow and began to run the fingers of her other hand through his hair, avoiding the thinner parts, where it annoyed him to be touched.

He closed his eyes and smiled. "Hmmmm!" he murmured.

She kissed him, gently at first, then with passion. Having intended only to soothe him, she found she was arousing herself. She dug her kneecaps into his thighs and induced an experimental shiver. "Do I take this nightdress off all by myself?" she asked.

He continued to smile. "Hmmmm!" This time there was an edge of complaint.

"Oh, aren't I a terrible woman?" she mocked. "Forcing the poor fellow!"

"'Twill do you no good," he warned in a tired whisper.

She snaked a hand down to the hem of his nightshirt, then up his thighs. More hair there than on the top of his head.

He was limp. "See?" he said. "Gone away."

She smothered his words with her lips and pushed her tongue onto his. "See!" she whispered, moments later. "Welcome back!"

Soon she was drowning in goosedown as his weight bore upon her with that marvellous thrust and pull that was John and only John—and herself and only herself. It was not the greatest love they had ever made, but it was still stupendous. After fifteen years of an often stormy marriage, after eight children, and after such a weary month as this had been, it was miraculous.

But it failed of its original purpose—to relax him into sleep. She awoke—was it hours or only moments later?—to hear that same check in his breathing; and she knew he was trying to lie especially still, trying not to disturb her. His very effort had awakened her, for she could sleep on through all his natural restlessness.

"What is it?" she asked. The words rasped as they cleared her throat.

He sat half up and began to caress her arm; accidentally his knuckle kneaded her breast. "Don't get me going again," she warned lightly. "I'll show no mercy."

He lay back then, absolved.

"What is it?" she asked. "Can't you tell me?"

She saw his lips vanish into his mouth. His eyes trembled, so tightly did he hold them shut.

"I have to tell you," he said. "I'm weeks late as it is."

She almost laughed. The unintended metaphor of the failed menstrual period was so incongruously forced into her mind that his real meaning did not at once strike her. When it did, the edge had gone off the fear it induced.

"When I went to Carlisle last month, I stopped off on the way back and went to Fiennes…"

"What's that mean—'going to fines'?"

"No, Fiennes," he said. "The school. It's spelled f, i, e, n, n, e, s but pronounced 'fines.' I went there, to Fiennes."

"Where is it?"

"Up in one of the dales, near Langstroth. Just on the southern slope of Whernside. It's very remote. But I think it would suit Young John and Caspar very well."

"I disagree," she said flatly. "Another Dotheboys Hall!"

"Not at all. It is a first-rate public school. New headmaster, Dr. Brockman, who was an assistant at Rugby. Excellent man. Keen as mustard. And there's a fine military tradition there."

"Fine for the middle classes," she agreed. "But our boys hardly need it. We can buy them better tutoring than any school can give."

John was already shaking his head. He was not listening. She had to fight down her anger. "But we can!" she insisted. "And then Young John will go into the business. We can buy Caspar any commission he wants in any regiment he names. We can buy Clement his indentures or whatever he wants to do. It's the same for all the children: We can launch them better than any of these middle-class manufactories. Gents made wholesale from tradesmen's sons, indeed!"

"Before you say any more, Nora, you had better know I have entered them. As soon as they are out of quarantine next week they will go."

For a moment she lay frozen, not believing, yet knowing it to be true. It was true that John had taken this most important decision without consulting her. It was true that he now presented her with it, fait accompli. She knew these things to be true from his very tone. Yet still she could not believe it.

He had made himself a stranger. He had made her a stranger to him. When time began again to move, she flung herself on her side, turning her back to him and pulling the eiderdown up over her head. She wished she could sleep. Or scream. She wished for any violent release from this terrible cold bitterness that now filled her.

He pulled away the eiderdown, enough to reveal her ear.

"I meant to tell you straight away but then I got called to the War Office. And then this measles quarantine somehow made it less urgent. And then—well, you know what these last weeks have been."

Her voice, even to her, sounded remote, straight down from the North Pole. "If you had returned immediately and told me, do you think it would have been different? The delay is nothing. What hurts is that you decided without me."

"We have discussed it often enough."

"Indeed. So you knew how I feel about tarring our children with the middle-class brush."

He chuckled. But there was a special note to it, one that was never there when his amusement was genuine. "You'll make a grand old lady!" he said.

"What's that supposed to mean?" she asked gruffly, annoyed with herself that she could not help taking such obvious bait.

"I mean there are certain ways of treating Society that only eccentric elderly viragos can carry off."

She had no idea what he was talking about. She resettled herself and sighed. "I must assume you are very tired," she said.

"In time you will see that the boys will benefit by going away to school."

"Hmm!"

"I promise you will."

"I thought our marriage implied an unspoken promise, at least, that such things would not be settled as you have settled them."

"Oh come, Nora! We should not be quarrelling. I'm off to the Crimea on Monday."

She burst into tears then; but not at the thought he was trying to implant—the thought that he might die out there (though the truth of it only deepened her misery). It was his crude attempt to manipulate her into acquiescence, first with that nonsense about viragos and now with this reminder. She was wounded too deeply to fathom him—that he could think she would not notice his blatant engineering of her emotions and, worse, that he thought she might respond to it.

She lay long awake that night and would not be comforted.

Chapter 3

The tide had turned and was now visibly rising. The Thames, after some choppy confusion, was flowing "upstream" again, flooding the banks of grey mud. Here and there the mud, cracked and glistening like wet elephant hide, clutched at the hulks of abandoned boats. Some were reduced to mere ribs, festooned with estuary weed; others seemed from a distance to be still seaworthy.

"Papa, why don't you take some of your men and make those ships float again?" Boy asked.

"Yes!" Caspar agreed eagerly. "Then we could have our own ship!"

John laughed. "You may be sure," he said, "that if anything could get those wrecks to float again, there's enough skill on either bank of this river to take them to China and back."

"But there may be useful things still on them." Caspar was unwilling to let go his dream.

John tousled his hair. "They didn't last a single low tide. Believe me—anything a strong man and a crowbar could shift has gone long ago." He pointed at the flocks of birds, wheeling and screaming. "They belong to the seagulls now."

One of the officers from the leading ship of the Crimean party came out to join them on the wooden gangwalk that ran around the warehouse at their back. "Your men are almost assembled, sir," he said.

"Couple of minutes more?"

The officer laughed. "Aye, it is fresher out here. They seem a rough lot. I hope you'll manage to caution them to good behaviour on the voyage, sir."

For a while the two men, towering over the boys, looked down at the temporary rivers and streamlets between the sodden banks of mud. The northwest wind cast shivering nets of ripples over the water.

"Have you been to the Crimea before?" John asked the officer.

"Not on the *Mohawk*. I was on the *Vectis* when we carried stores to Balaclava."

"What is it really like out there?"

"You feel no danger in the port, but the muddle is terrible. It's a disgrace beyond my power of description, sir. If your railway moves those mountains out of Balaclava and gets the stuff where it's really wanted, you'll do a lot to win this war."

John smiled at him gratefully. "That is exactly what I shall tell my men. As to their behaviour, you need have no fear there."

They went inside then. John pointed to Walter and gave the two boys a push in his direction. After the cold air on the balcony the heat in the warehouse and the stink of men hit them like a wall; it almost pushed John physically off balance. While he recovered he looked down from the improvised rostrum—a large hatch cover balanced on four sacks—and surveyed his navvies. He could understand the officer's alarm. A railway navvy was a man of legendary strength and violence. It took a year for even the best farm worker or building labourer to put on enough muscle to match the navvies; but the violence that had made them the scourge of the countryside in the early days of the railways had now become quite rare, thanks to the steady work and orderly conditions provided by the big contractors like Brassey and Peto—and, to be sure, by John himself. Even so, five hundred of those huge-muscled, self-reliant titans made an awesome assembly. Even John, who moved among them every day, felt it; and if he had just put his hand to the controls of the biggest leviathan steam engine in the world, he would not feel master of a power half so great as this.

"How many of ye," he shouted, "began on the London–Birmingham line?"

There was a puzzled stir. It was not the way they expected him to start. In the gloom he saw only a few dozen hands raised up.

"Thirty or forty. And the rest of you younger, I'll be bound. Eighteen years is a lifetime in this trade. The reason I ask is because that's where I began—on the London–Birmingham. I made the running at Camden up cuttings that would test the strongest of us still. I near lost a leg on the banks at Tring. I carried the remains of four good men out of Kilsby Tunnel in sacks."

The silence was now absolute. There was no other audience in the world to whom he could talk in such direct shorthand and who would instantly grasp his meaning. Boy and Caspar were thrilled. They loved all his tales of navvy days.

"Aye. There's things about the navvying life that folk outside will never fathom." A murmur of agreement began to rise. He grinned. "Do ye remember how they feared us? There's folk who still hush their young ones with threats of navvies. Ye'd think we were hordes of Tartars. Yet what did we do? We fired a few hedges. We invited the farmers' geese to an early supper." They began to laugh.

"We maybe bloodied a nose or two and broke the odd window. And we left behind a few spare feet for baby boots."

He let the laughter rise and die. "It was little enough to fear us for. Yet if they had known what we were really about, they would have both feared and marvelled." His raised finger and glinting eyes, darting this way and that over the crowd, promised a rich secret.

"For what have we really done? I'll tell you: We've left behind us a land enriched beyond dreams. We've changed the face of this world! Yes, you, and you, and you—you've done it. D'ye remember that time when a bale of raw American cotton in Liverpool docks was sent to Manchester and was back in Liverpool the very next day as woven cloth ready to export? Our metals made that possible. We've given a new bloodstream to civilization. We've made our mark on the face of time! We did that.

"But have ye ever stopped to wonder *why us?* Why not the Germans, eh? Or the French? Why not the Dutch? Why not the cowardly Russians even? Why us, the English? And by English I mean Irish and Scotch and Welshmen, too. Why?" He lowered his voice and leaned toward them. "Because we're *free.* The Europeans stumble from revolution to tyranny and back. The Russian serf dares not call his soul his own; he must slay and be slain without even asking the cause. There's no strength in that. One free man will face down a dozen of them. Free men like us. Free Englishmen, volunteers every man, at full liberty to go or stay as we please. And just at this minute it pleases us mightily to go and fight the barbarian." They cheered at that.

"So! We who changed the face of England now have it within our power to change the course of history. When we've done our task it will be possible for a Russian to die at nightfall, his heart pierced by a bullet that less than twelve hours earlier lay in the hold of a vessel on the Black Sea. We did it with cotton; now we'll do it with bullets and guns. It's never been done before. In the long tide of human conflict no army has had such service behind it as we shall now provide. Think of it, my friends—just five hundred of us, and we are going to make history. Look around you and feel the pride of it. And now let the Russians tremble, for they've cause enough!"

His ending was as abrupt as his beginning had been; it, too, took them unawares. Silently their minds repeated his closing words and then the thought gripped them and they shivered the rafters with their cheers. He stood above them, arms folded, smiling back to give them a focus. Then, while their cheers rang on he jumped lightly down and joined Walter Thornton and the ship's officers.

"Capital speech," Walter said.

Caspar and Boy basked in the glory of belonging to such a father. "Those sailing from Tilbury had better march down to the ferry now," the senior officer said.

"They'll regroup outside," Walter told him. "It's all in hand." His shortness suggested to John that he'd already crossed swords with this officer. Both Walter and John felt extremely protective of their men and wanted it clear from the outset that this was no military expedition and their men were under no kind of military discipline.

No one who saw them strolling and larking through the streets on their way to the jetties could possibly mistake them for any sort of a military crowd, however. They carried Boy and Caspar shoulder high, passing them from man to man, cheering and whooping every near-fall.

"I was rather hoping you'd say something about the need for good order and discipline on the voyage out, Mr. Stevenson," the officer said. "Idle hands, you know. Trying time. On an emigrant ship you can starve them and keep their spirit low. Hardly do that here. Wish you'd said something."

John smiled. "I think you'll find I did."

The officer raised his eyebrows and looked at the motley gangs of men streaming down the road. "You know them, of course," he conceded.

"None better," Walter said. "A hint from John Stevenson is an iron law to any man who works for him. They'll give no trouble."

The two boys went on with the party for Tilbury, across the river, where John and Walter would join them later after seeing the Gravesend party, this side of the river, safely embarked.

The dock whores were being turned off the boats as the navvies went on board. Their departure raised boos and cries of mock agony from the navvies. Impossible offers and wild promises were shouted between the two groups, the departing women and the arriving men. Then one of the navvies, nicknamed Harvest Hog, a strapping young fellow with fair, curly hair poking out all around the rim of his moleskin hat, shouted: "Give us one last look at old mossyface!"

His half-taunt, half-plea was directed at the youngest and least ugly of the women.

"Ye gods, she will, too!" Walter said. He and John were still on the quayside, with the women between them and the boat.

Walter was right. Giggling, the young girl lifted high her skirts and turned to face the ship. Several others, also laughing, copied her action. Finally all the women stood facing the men, holding up their skirts and waving the dirty lace they clutched in their hands. It was an unedifying display of frowsty thighs and poxed and pickled carrion, but it brought a vast cheer from the men on the decks. The cheer fetched the captain above. As soon as the women saw him they dropped their skirts and ran.

A few desultory boos arose but John's upheld hand prevented them from becoming general. Moments later it was over for everyone except Walter; he stood watching the women dwindle to mere dots of colour near the dock gates. The lust in his eyes was frank and joyful. John wondered how long he could continue to extract any delight from those diminutive images, horrendous even at close quarters. Lovingly Walter watched them until the very last had vanished, draining his illusions to the dregs.

"There's still time," John teased.

Walter's eyes even now raked the air that had held the women. "The female gender," he said tonelessly. "I hate 'em." He laughed explosively.

"Hate?" John asked.

"Yes. You could waste all twenty-four hours of the day thinking about them. Don't you think?"

John merely smiled.

"No, but don't you think?" Walter persisted; his foxy eyes glistened in his full-bearded face. He squeezed John's arm, compelling an answer.

"To each his own," John said ambiguously.

"Ooh hoo boo!" Walter made a pantomime of his disbelief. "Old dullard!" His eyes were still searching the docks, as if they hoped the women might suddenly materialize out of the air.

"Have you thought about death at all?" John asked.

Walter giggled. When he saw John's unsmiling face, he laughed. And when John finally did smile, there was no humour in it. Then Walter's laugh ran out of zest and, for the first time, it was borne in upon him that they were headed for a theatre of war.

Chapter 4

Nora made her peace with John. Or, she wondered, had he made it with her? At all events a peace of sorts had been declared between them before, as an end-of-quarantine treat, he had taken the boys south to see his ships steam and sail for the Crimea. Hurt though she was, it would have been unthinkable to let him go on such a mission with bad blood between them. Nevertheless he was in no doubt that her acceptance of the fait accompli was very conditional. As far as she was concerned, this school—Fiennes or whatever it called itself—was on trial.

Her first instinct had been to take Caspar and Boy all the way there in her own carriage. Not that she thought they needed mothering; they were well used to travelling alone by train. But she wanted to see the place for herself. John had been so vague on all matters of the boys' accommodation and the arrangements for their ablutions, laundry, sickness, playing facilities, and so on, she suspected he had never even asked about such details. It was so like him. With every new railway contract he or his deputies took assiduous care to ensure that conditions for the navvies would be (in her view, as the firm's comptroller) palatial; but for himself he took no thought. He'd sleep in barns and wash in cattle troughs or drinking fountains if need be. So, naturally, he'd extend the same carelessness to his oldest boys.

All he had been able to say was that Dr. Brockman believed every boy in the school was due the same care and attention as was traditionally allowed only to the most gifted. That idea was revolutionary enough in itself to blunt the edge of Nora's anger and to prick her curiosity. And that was another reason for her wanting to go with them to Fiennes.

But John's protest, coupled with the urgent pleas of the two boys themselves, persuaded her that she should, however reluctantly, let her children arrive at school like all the other boys, unaccompanied. She compromised by going with them as far as Leeds, where she went east to York while they went west to Ingleton. The York train went first. The Stevenson private railcoach had been hitched to the end of it, so she could stand on the little rear balcony and wave until the curve cut off her view.

"See you at Christmas!" she shouted, not even sure they were still in earshot.

How small they looked—twelve years old and eleven! It seemed ridiculous to be sending such tiny things away to that remote, unknown, and no doubt fiercely spartan place. Many times over the days that followed she had to fight back an impulse to get into her coach and drive the eighty-odd miles that now separated them. And their meagre letters ("Today it is raining...yesterday I got beaten for talking...tomorrow the two halves of our school play football. It is great fun...") were no guide at all to what was really happening.

There were the odd moments over those same weeks when neither Boy nor Caspar would have protested her arrival; indeed, quite the reverse. But they suffered no premonition of those fleeting instants of homesickness as they stood and waved her train goodbye; in fact, they could barely contain their impatience until it was out of sight.

"Come on," Caspar said. "If we change our first-class for third we can save about nine bob each, I should think!"

In fact it saved them ten shillings each.

"Nick says that at Winchester the school grub's not enough to keep a sparrow alive, so if Fiennes is the same, we'll need the extra," Boy said. He was annoyed that he hadn't thought of selling their tickets.

"Don't let on to our father we've done this," Caspar told the ticket clerk. "Or our mother."

The man grinned.

"Why put the idea into his head?" Boy asked crossly as they walked away.

"You know how Papa and Mama talk to everybody in railways."

Already "Papa" and "Mama" sounded like strangers. They had no place in this new, third-class world.

In the open wagon you could put your trunk against the front siding and huddle in its partial shelter against the rushing wind. There, too, the shower of soot and cinders was least. Unfortunately the snow, which began to fall before they were even halfway, seemed to obey a different aerodynamic rule; it curled around in a windy eddy and struck upward at them, reaching into the legs of their breeches and around the turned-up collars of their coats.

From Skipton to Hellifield they sang and stamped their boots and cracked jokes with the cattledrovers and stall women from Skipton market. But as they climbed higher into the Pennines, into a world that grew whiter and colder by the minute, their good spirits died and they huddled their chill flesh into smaller and yet smaller knots and they thought of the footwarmers in the first-class coaches, and the soft plush seats of the first-class coaches, and the oil lamps and curtained windows of the first-class coaches, and wondered that such a paradise could be had for a mere ten shillings. Only their pride—the sense that they were both already on trial—kept them from confessing it to each other.

From Giggleswick to Ingleton they felt it was a miracle simply to survive from each *dee-da, dee-da* of the wheels on the rails to the next. When the train stopped, Caspar was frozen to whimpering and Boy was on the verge of joining him. They could barely move their legs, much less tug their heavy boxes to the gate in the side of the truck. Boy barked his shin in getting down and was surprised to feel nothing.

"Bless me, are you the Stevenson boys?" A stout coachman in half a ton of clothing came waddling down the platform. The fact that they were the only boys to get off the train was answer enough to him. "Happen ye'll dress for it next time," he said. "We're not your London tropics here, see thee."

"Nay, we're from these parts," Boy told him, using a Yorkshire intonation but not the full dialect.

"Then thou 'ast no more gawm than Old Man Fuzzack," the coachman said, grinning with all the superiority of righteous contempt. He gave a brief, piercing whistle and his horse raised its head from its nosehag and ambled down the platform, pulling a small carriage behind it. The coachman still grinned at them, the grin of a man whose world constantly rearranged itself to his convenience.

"Dr. Brockman's very own equipage," he said. "A rare enough honour. Allow me to introduce myself: Percy Oldroyd, known as Purse. Coachman, gardener, gasworks stoker, rodder of drains, ratcatcher, kitemender, breeder of fighting cocks, cistern unfreezer, ratcatcher—did I say that?—drink fetcher (at a price) and bet placer (ditto ditto), leaf burner, hider of disasters, fire fighter…" The list petered out; he had been speaking merely to fill the air while he loaded their trunks onto the carriage. "And just this minute," he added, throwing wide his arms and sweeping them beside him down the platform toward a tavern at the station gate, "reviver of two cold tykes who think they've seen and felt the worst of the Yorkshire dales. But have they? Have they? They have *not*!"

An hour later, mildly drunk and very warm, they came out of the tavern, pulled the blankets from the horse and, huddling in their warmth, climbed up one on each side of Purse. Their revival had cost him nothing; each of their ten shillings had shrunk to nine. But they felt wonderful. It was a true privilege to buy the drinks for a splendid fellow like Purse.

There was a sharp climb out of Ingleton; they all got off and walked to lighten the load on the horse, who, even then, barely managed it. Over three hundred feet they climbed in less than a mile. It was a transition from the sheltered, tree-lined streets of the dale to the moaning winds on the old Roman road below Raven Scar. They climbed back beside Purse and looked around, in the fast-fading light, at a landscape as bleak as any they had ever seen. To their right, southward, reared Ingleborough summit, its vast gritstone cap perched on deeply fissured cliffs of weathered limestone—a dirty-coloured mass in a white world. A mile or so farther on, with the day almost done, they came to the crest of a shallow ridge that ran across the valley, cut only by the waters of Winterscales Beck. Before them and to their left the land sloped away, treeless and desolate, until it rose once more to the massive coffin shape of Whernside, some three miles away.

"There's the school now," Purse said.

Without the aid of his pointing whip they would not have noticed the gaunt pile of stone huddled in the snows to the south of Whernside; it was a mere darkening of the deep lilac grey with which the late twilight painted the distance. Under these snows the only prominent feature of the moors was the network of drystone walls that ran up and over the mountains. Where the walls came to a "scar"—a small limestone cliff, deeply etched by wind and rain—they would halt at its foot and run onward and upward from its head. They were black and angular, like straight-run cracks in white porcelain. With the coming of night the lights of the town of Langstroth began to twinkle.

It was a landscape that its makers, the serfs of Yorkshire's great medieval abbeys, would have recognized in almost every detail, for little had changed since their time.

As they went, Purse told them something of its mysteries—of streams that vanished into gaping ghylls, some so small you could slide down into them before you saw them, others large enough to swallow a village; of clints, vast stretches of barren rock so eaten by wind and rain they looked more like the exposed brain of a giant sheep than anything made of stone; of holes that wormed their way down deeper and farther than any man dared go. Once a farmer from over

Yockenthwaite way had tried to explore one of these caves; he had been gone a month and had come back by another hole six miles away, singed bald by the devil's flames and yellow with the sulphur. He had "never from that day forth talked to no man."

"There's whole secret kingdoms under here," Purse told them. "And a deal of work to do! There's a farm at Bruntscar—ye may see it well from the college—where if ye put an ear to the rock, there's a *thrum-thrum* as never ceases. Idle folk'll say it's a watter fall below ground, but"—he gave a wink—"*we* know better!"

What a privilege! thought the two tipsy children. To travel beside such a splendid fellow as Purse and to *know better.* Happily they wandered, guided by him, through secret grottoes and measureless caverns, by winding tunnels and subterranean causeways in fairylands of dwarfish industry, scorning the earthbound folk above who did not know better.

By the time they reached Langstroth dale they were almost sober and beginning to feel the cold once more. Fortunately the wind here was a mere breeze compared with the blasts that had chilled them on the train. The looming bulk of Whernside, now black against a near-black sky, sheltered the whole dale from the northeast wind.

Later, when they came there by daylight, Langstroth town would seem quite ordinary, a market town huddled in its dale, shrinking from contact with the peat bogs and moors around it. But that night the dark and the blanket of snow gave it enchantment. Every leafless sapling was part of a larger but unseen stately tree. Every candlelit cottage window marked the invisible façade of a substantial house, invisible but there. The silent and deserted alleys seemed about to fill with people on their way to a splendid entertainment. Yes, they thought, Langstroth was a splendid town full of splendid houses—doctors' and lawyers' and cornmerchants' houses.

Just as they were about to leave the market square Purse pulled up the horse.

"Where's the pair of ye to mess?" he asked. "I'd forgotten ye'd be in Old School. Ye'll need a mess in Langstroth."

"We don't know," Boy said. "No one said anything about that."

Caspar giggled; he always thought it fun when bits of the grown-up world crumbled.

"Eay, there's that many changes now," Purse grumbled. "I thowt as ye'd be in one o' the new Houses. They don't mess in the town."

"What's 'Old School,' Purse?" Boy asked.

Purse laughed grimly. "I'd not put swine in it," he said. "Ye'd best mess by me and Mrs. Oldroyd, then. It's five bob a week, now: laundry, a room between ye, and a good savoury tea, and dinner Sundays."

"Four and sixpence," Caspar said.

"Nay!" Purse laughed. "Fee is set by College, see thee. I can't abate it. College pays us, see, and your father'll pay College."

"Boots to be cleaned then," Caspar persisted.

Purse chuckled and nudged Caspar with his elbow. "We'll see," he said, conceding without announcing the fact. He clucked the horse into motion again and turned down an uneven lane leading uphill from the square. There were only a dozen or so cottages before it gave way into the moor.

"You're nearest the school of all the messings," Purse said. "Young Bell messed here till last week, but now they've lodged him in one of the new Houses."

The Oldroyd cottage was the last on the left, the nearest dwelling to the school. It was stone built and, like most daleshouses, tiled with stone slabs. Mrs. Oldroyd, roused by the noise of the horse and carriage, opened the door a crack, poked her head out, saw them, shouted, "Be quick, it's that cold!" withdrew again, and slammed the door.

"Mrs. Oldroyd, as ye'll find," Purse said, "has a tongue she could hire to a tinsmith. But a champion heart. Depend on it."

When they were at the door, Mrs. Oldroyd opened it again, plucked them in out of the cold, and slammed it at once, leaving Purse to unload their boxes in the dark outside. They stood blinking owlishly in the light, though it came from but a single candle and was feeble enough. The kitchen was as warm as a bakehouse; indeed, the most delicious smell of baking bread came from the new iron range across the room.

"Well? Have you names?" she asked, looking rapidly from one to the other. "And are you naked under them horseblankets?"

"I'm John Stevenson, but they call me Boy. And this is my brother Caspar, m'm."

They unwrapped themselves from the blankets and stood holding them awkwardly, not wanting to put them down.

"They'd best drape over the horse while we sup," Mrs. Oldroyd said. She took Caspar's blanket and gave it to Boy, nudging him toward the door. "Ye'll eat, if it's not a soft question? I know that man of mine put naught but spirits inside you."

"Brandy, m'm," Caspar said. "We almost perished on the train."

"Oh aye!" Her eyes raked the ceiling with weary, wifely asperity.

Purse came in with a box just as Boy went out with the blankets. "Brandy!" she snorted.

Purse winked at Boy and relieved him of the blankets.

When both boxes were in the spare room, Mrs. Oldroyd brought in a new candle. "See it lasts the week," she said. "If ye want more, buy for yourselves."

"Where's the bed?" Caspar whispered to Boy as Purse came in.

"Where do we sleep?" Boy asked him.

"In Old School," Purse said. "I told ye. They lock ye in come eight of the evening and ye stay locked in till half-past-six tomorn."

"Then what do we want this room for?" Boy asked.

Purse laughed richly. "Oh, ye'll want it right enough! Never fret. Every evening ye'll hang in here until one minute of eight and then ye'll streak like hares for that hell over the bog. Come here." He beckoned them to the tiny window in the back wall. When he had scratched the frost off one of the panes they could see a number of lights, which could have been two hundred yards or ten miles away, mere pinholes in the black evening. "Yon's the school," he said. "And mark me now: Between there and here is four hundred acres of bog. Bottomless bog. Never, never, never be tempted to cross it. Even in summer when it looks dry enough. Always go by the causeway."

"It can't be bottomless, you know, Purse," Caspar said. "The earth is round."

Purse looked solemnly at him. "And it goes all the way through to Australia," he said. "The only time it's safe to cross the bog direct is when there's that many dead kangaroos on the surface ye may step from one to t'other."

They all laughed heartily at that.

"I take it ye've unpacked, then?" Mrs. Oldroyd shouted from the kitchen.

Purse put on a look of exaggerated guilt. "Take only your bed linen and one nightshirt each, and your books and toys. Ye may leave all else besides here."

"And our money? Where will that be safe?"

"Nay, there's savagery enough there, but honour with it. Brass is as safe there as here."

"We'll leave half and take half," Caspar said. "Split the risk."

Purse smiled at him appraisingly. He pointed to some pies and jars of jam. "Take them and all," he advised. "Food fashions friends."

While they unpacked all but the items Purse had mentioned, Mrs. Oldroyd spread a gorgeous feast of cold brawn, hot bread—great brown doorsteps of it—and mulled ale. The bread oozed with salted beef drippings and jelly.

"Don't go thinking ye'll do this well every day," she said, looking her fiercest at them.

Purse winked.

Half an hour later, warm to the marrow, they put their lightened boxes back on the carriage and braved the last few hundred yards of blizzard that separated the Oldroyd paradise from the school. They were almost over the causeway before they became aware of the size of the place—a large, dark, angular group of buildings stretching both ways from the causeway head, it seemed for miles.

Small lights studded the large silhouette; they revealed nothing but minute details of brick and stone within eighteen inches of each flame. The blackness beyond was then made blacker still. Through tiny windows the two boys saw meaningless scraps of interior—the foot of a banister, part of a beam, the corner of a shield or picture.

Next year, Boy thought, *all these bits will mean something.* He wondered what—joy or fear? He was surprised not to feel more afraid. Perhaps it was because the mulled ale had rekindled their tipsiness.

"You afraid?" he asked Caspar.

It was a silly question, with Purse there. Caspar merely sniffed.

"Nay, it's naught so bad," Purse said. He spat the phlegm from his frost-parched throat and added, "Leastwise, not once ye've been drummed in."

The mysterious expression and his reassuring tone—his carefully reassuring tone—were as terrifying as anything their imaginations could serve up.

"Lorrimer," Purse said, pointing at an older boy who stood in the centre of the arched gateway a dark shape in a pool of light. "He'll likely show ye round."

When he could see the carriage well enough to make out Purse and the two youngsters, Lorrimer turned on his heel and walked over the yard to shelter by the open door to one of the buildings. After their run over the snow-muffled causeway the clamour of their iron tyres was especially strident in the cobbled yard. It rang from the stone walls all around, making the new boys feel much too conspicuous.

"Master Lorrimer. The Honourable Patrick Lorrimer," Purse said. He spoke so flatly it could only be meant ironically; it made them wonder if Lorrimer really was an honourable. Cleary Purse and he were no friends.

So much to learn about all these new people! Caspar thought.

"Hold your tongue, you scabby grunt!" Lorrimer said, without humour. "I hope he's given you two no lip. You're the Stevensons, major and minor. No minimus?"

"Still at home," Boy said. He held out his hand.

Lorrimer took it awkwardly. "After I've shown you around, things'll be a bit stiffer. I'm a buck and you'll both be roes. We've got till lockup. Did you bring any fodder?"

"Some pies and a cake," Caspar said.

"That'll do. What you get at trough isn't fit for pigs. Come on."

"Our trunks?"

"That fat grunt will see to them. About the only bloody work he does."

Purse pretended to laugh—a bit edgily, Caspar thought.

"I expect you both feel pretty shent. Where've you come from?"

"London. But we didn't know it was going to snow. We travelled third from Leeds."

"To save the clink? We all do that—you won't be sorry. Food is an enthusiasm here, you'll find. You'll never get enough. Nor warmth."

He led them down some worn stone steps into a sub-basement. Corridors ran to their right and left and straight ahead, visible only by the single oil lamps that flickered at the end of each. The place smelled of badly trimmed wicks and coal smoke. Lorrimer hesitated. "All right, you can come this way just for once. After drumming in you'll have to go around by those outer corridors. This shortcut is just for bucks." He led them along the corridor that ran straight ahead. "The two side corridors meet up again at the end here," he explained.

Boy almost burst with questions: What was behind the doors on each side? What was a "buck"? What did "drumming in" mean? And where could he have a pee? He'd forgotten that at Purse's. He thought it best to ask nothing—keep the head down.

Caspar was slightly less inhibited. "Do we get studies?" he asked.

Lorrimer grinned. "Not in Old School," he said. "We're the last of the old order. There's cupboards down those side passages, which go by seniority. You can hire them from some of the bucks."

At the end of the passage he pointed to a clock set in the wall. On one side, carved in the stone, was the legend *UT HORA*, on the other *SIC VITA*.

"What's that say?" he asked.

"As the hours pass, so passeth life," Caspar translated.

Lorrimer winked at Boy. "Oh, no, it don't," he said. "Here it means 'I'm sick of this life, bring out the whores.'" The two older boys laughed.

"Who has those studies we've just passed?" Caspar asked.

"The pharaohs and the King o' the Barn. And some of the sixth. They're the gods around here."

"I suppose we shall fag for them," Boy said.

"Roe," Lorrimer corrected. "We don't call them fags here; we call them roes. You'll both be roes until some more new 'uns come and relieve you. The pharaohs are your masters."

"Teachers?" Caspar asked.

"No. The teachers are 'beaks.' There's only four of them. You call them 'sir' except your tutor, whom you call 'master.' Our tutor here is Whymper. I'll take you to meet him before lockup."

He saw the strain on their faces as they tried to memorize all this. He laughed. "We're all confused," he said. "Don't worry. Before Brockman came the whole place was like Old School. Just anarchy. Now he's started these new houses and he's trying to 'army-ize' us. In the old days anyone could whack anyone if he was strong enough, and any young 'un had to roe for any buck. Now Brockman's brought in these Houses and appoints the pharaohs to lead them and all the beatings go down in a book and only pharaohs can beat, anyway—except that here we have the King o' the Barn, too. He couldn't get rid of that. Brockman thinks it's a great improvement but no one else agrees. We're still pretty anarchic here, you'll find. The pharaoh system only works where there's a beak living in. There's no beak lives in Old School. Come on, the Barn's up here."

To one side of the clock there was a narrow, winding stone stair, dangerously worn. It led up into a large hall, dimly lit with flaring fishtails of gas. "Everyone's in public school," Lorrimer explained the apparent desertion of the place. "This is the Barn. It used to be *the* school in monastic days—I suppose you know we're a monastic foundation?"

They nodded.

The air was thick with smoke from the fire. It made their eyes water.

"We three-quarters bunged up the chimneys," Lorrimer explained. "Otherwise the draught makes it hells cold, especially in the passages. The boot room over there is the old monks' washroom. The initials over the door"—he pointed to some crudely carved letters: WIGG—"mean Wash In God's Grace. They were not carved by Wigg, who's a buck in this house at the moment. Carving anything is a school-beating offence; we're not barbarians like at Eton and other places. Anyway, you'd better know the pharaohs' names. There's Swift, who's head of pharaohs. The pharaohs are Deakin, Malaby, and Shortiss. And Blenkinsop is King o' the Barn. Each of them has two roes—one for boots and one for clean collars."

"What's 'roe' mean?" Caspar asked.

Lorrimer chuckled as if he had hoped to be asked. "Less than nothing," he said. "It comes from 'zero'—half of zero: roe, d'you see? And believe me, it's right. Less than nothing."

One end of the Barn was crammed with old refectory tables of solid oak. When they drew close the boys noticed that the tops, which were a good six inches thick, had bowl shapes scooped out of them.

"Do we eat out of those?" Boy asked.

"We don't say 'eat' here, not for school meals. We say 'trough.' We *trough* the school grub—all it's fit for. We *eat* the fodder from home. And at mess in Langstroth." He pointed to the hollows in the oak. "Those are the troughs."

There was a noise from above. They turned and looked up, realizing that the hall had two galleries running its full length. Three doors let off each gallery into rooms beyond—rooms that had no windows between them and the gallery. The noise was made by Purse, carrying their trunks along the upper gallery. He was puffing and groaning.

"Less noise, you stupid grunt!" Lorrimer called.

Purse, who gave no sign of having heard, disappeared through the central door. "Those are the two dorms," Lorrimer said. "You're in the junior dorm, which is called 'Squint.'"

He saw Caspar looking at the ancient roof timbers. "You admire the hammerbeam roof?" he asked.

Caspar looked at him. "Not hammerbeam," he said. "It's stiffened collarbeam."

"Caspar!" Boy said sharply.

But Lorrimer laughed a long time, as if Caspar's correction had been exquisitely funny. "I'll tell you some more language," he said when his laughter died. "Grunts are college servants. In the Houses they call them 'churls.' A villain is anybody outside the school or not connected with it; even the lord lieutenant is a villain. The masters are called 'beaks.' I told you that. We call the head man 'chief,' but not to his face, naturally. The bursar is called 'Bully'—he used to do most of the school beating, because the chief before Brockman hadn't stomach for it. He didn't last long!" He studied their reaction closely. "Of course, a school beating is rarer than a house beating."

They took the good news in glum silence.

"A Barn beating is commonest of all," Lorrimer added. "Or perhaps a dorm beating. You lose count. It depends on the whim of the pharaohs and the King o' the Barn. Blenkinsop, now, is hells fierce. By the way, you shouldn't do up the bottom button of your waistcoat—very bad form. It's worth a Barn beating."

He spoke to Caspar, but both boys hastily loosened the offending buttons. Lorrimer, encouraged, began to look them over more critically. "Your bootlaces," he said, "should be crisscrossed, like mine. Only pharaohs can wear them ladder-fashioned. And your boots look bloody shent; you'd better give them a good blacking before you go and see the master. Whymper's an uncommon enthusiast for boots, fingernails, and earholes. I hope you realize how kind I'm being to you two."

"Indeed we do, Lorrimer. Thank you most dreadfully," the boys said.

"That's all right. You can share your pies with me later," Lorrimer said.

"What's drumming-in?" Caspar asked.

Lorrimer grinned a secretive grin. "It's after lockup, when the master's gone for the night."

He would tell them no more. "Public school ends soon," he said. "Time to go and see old Whym." He pointed to the boot room.

"Where's the boghouse?" Boy asked. "I'm pretty tight for a pee."

"Me, too," Caspar said.

They were both quite, quite sober again.

Algernon Whymper was a tall, elderly man with a shock of black hair, just turning grey at the sides. From his ears dark hair shot stiffly, like a childish line-drawing of an explosion; it straggled in wiry curls along the line of his eyebrows; it peeped from his flaring nostrils like twin black caterpillars in sanctuary; it stuck out at his collar and cuffs like straw from a hastily assembled scarecrow; it carpeted the backs of his hands and the stretches of skin between his knuckles. The boys' alternative name for him was Esau.

He was a man of large, impressive menace; even his friendliness was menacing as he swayed above the two Stevenson boys, drilling them through with his eyes. He inquired about their journey. Boy told him they had grown very cold but were now warmed through again.

The news appeared to alarm the master. "Not *comfortably* warm, I trust?" he asked sharply.

Both boys shook their heads vigorously. *Certainly not,* they implied.

"A comfortable warmth is very enervating," he said. His own pupil room was as hot as a linen cupboard. "Er—to a boy's frame," he added. He poured them each a sherry, large for himself, small for Boy, and very small for Caspar. "As with all unseasoned timber," he explained, "warmth sweats up a lot of sticky nastiness in a boy. A lot of wet sullenness. D'ye take my meaning?" He looked hard at Boy, who, filled with ignorance, looked uncomfortably away. "I see you do, sir. I see you do. Well, none of that here, sir. We'll cool it out of ye." He looked at Caspar. "You, too, in time. No warmth here."

There was a long silence. The fire crackled merrily. The sherry slipped down with a pleasant, sweet afterburn.

"Are your ears clean, sir?" he suddenly asked Caspar.

"I've washed them, master," Caspar said.

"Show!" Whymper looked into them critically and grunted, satisfied. "Too young for much nastiness yet," he said. Then he turned to Boy, who sensed he had been kept until last. "But you, sir. Show me!" He gripped the proffered ear and peered into it with fanatic interest. "An amazing organ, the ear, young man. All the good that'll ever get into a boy goes in by the ear; all the bad in him comes out that way. Wash them well, I say. Twice a day is not too much. Twice a day. Twice a day. You'll see the filth pour out and you'll feel the good of it. Do you know you're full of filth? Look at those pimples! It's bursting from you."

"I washed them as well as..."

"Answer the question, damn ye! Do you know you're full of filth?"

"Yes, sir—er—master." What else could Boy say?

"Good!" Whymper's satisfaction seemed abnormal. "Then ye know the problem. And until you know the problem, you can't begin the cure. What money have you?"

They handed over their official money: five pounds for contingencies and their train fare home; and a florin each to be doled out at threepence a week for the remaining eight weeks of term.

"No more?"

"No, master." Both boys were shiftily effusive. The master looked at them, they at him. A thrill stole over both of them simultaneously as they realized not only that they were going to get away with the lie but that the master knew they were lying and didn't care. Even more than that, he expected them to lie—was almost glad they had lied.

It was their first step toward understanding that they were now entering a system where the pretence that a certain form was being followed was vastly more important than the reality. It had been an initiation test and they had passed it.

"Now," he said. "I am your tutor. It is I who will write your end-of-term reports to your parents." He drilled them again with those black eyes. "It is I whom you must satisfy of your progress here. But that progress, little fellows, is not in my hands. It is in yours. We do not molly-coddle young milkysops here. No hothouse here, sirs! You will do fifteen half hours of public school each week and the rest of the time at tutorial lectures and private study. Have you a mess in the town yet?"

"At Mr. Oldroyd's, master."

"Good. Good. You'll do most of your private study there, of course, though I believe there are some old cupboards about the passages here where you may lock yourself away with a candle and a book."

"Do we study with each master, sir?" Caspar asked.

"Indeed, young fellow." Whymper's friendly smile was more menacing, somehow, than his stern face. "With all four of us. And as there are four hundred and thirty-two boys all told, you may be sure that little learning is imparted in the hours of public school. You have the headmaster for divinity. Mr. Carter for unseen translation and construction. Mr. Cusack for Euclid and mathematics. And myself for composition—which is Latin elegiacs, Latin theme, Greek hexameter (all original, of course), Greek iambics from Shakespeare, Greek prose translation from Robertson, and Latin prose from *Spectator*. You have these books?"

They nodded. The course here outlined by Mr. Whymper was a direct continuation of the one they had already begun at home under their own tutor, Mr. Morier-Watson. It held no unknown terrors for them.

"It's pretty sharp work," Whymper went on. "But it's too wide and general for mere talent to carry you. Only the true sap may triumph in the end. So take heart! The prize is for every boy here. Hard work can always snatch victory from under the nose of lazy brilliance." He smiled benignly. "Good. I can see already that we shall rub along famously. Keep your ears clean. Keep your fingers—*fingers!* Show me your fingers."

Twenty clean fingers poked at him, feathering themselves prone and supine, gleaming an unnatural pink.

"Good, good. Ears clean. Fingers clean. And boots clean. Work hard. Play the man. And you can be proud of yourselves and we can be proud of you."

"Do you know how he gets such hairy hands?" Causton asked. He was an unprepossessing boy of about Caspar's age. He was watching Caspar unpack his things into an oak locker beside his bed. Each of the forty beds in the dorm was separated from its neighbour by such a locker.

"How?" Caspar asked.

"He fiends himself all the time. He's always at it. It puts hair on your hands."

Caspar had no idea what Causton meant but he looked instinctively at the backs of his own hands to see if any hair grew there.

"Yah!" Causton crowed. "Caught you! Caught you!"

Caspar looked at him in puzzled surprise.

"You fiend yourself, eh?" Causton taunted. "Caught you!"

Caspar shrugged.

"Made you look. You had to look." Causton was disappointed in the response.

Caspar unpacked his greatest treasure—the Dart, a toy steam locomotive with a brass chassis, copper boiler, and two oscillating cylinders. The dormitory was lit by a single gas jet high on the wall, but even in that uncertain light it gleamed.

"I say!" Causton exclaimed. "That's a beauty! May I?"

Caspar handed it to him in a pantomine of caution; Causton took it as if it were made of crystal. He sniffed the firebox, spun the wheels, blew down the funnel, and nodded approvingly. But his tone was disparaging. "Oscillating cylinders," he said. "Of course, you only get steam on one stroke."

"I'm saving for a slide-valve engine," Caspar said.

"I'm getting one for my birthday next month. Let's race them!"

Caspar nodded and put the engine away in the back of the drawer that pulled out from under the bed.

"You're a quiet 'un," Causton said. "You won't be so quiet after lockup. At your drumming-in."

Caspar did not reward him with any display of feeling. Causton seemed strangely torn between an impulse to friendship and the desire to crow over the tortures to come.

Boy, unpacking on the far side of the dorm, beyond the long line of trunks and boxes down the middle of the room, heard Causton's taunt and felt his own guts turn over. He wished someone would tell him what drumming-in meant, but he certainly wasn't going to ask.

"Come on, where's the scoff?" de Lacy asked. Boy was going to sleep between him and another fellow called Carnforth.

"Scoff?"

"Grub. Tuck. Those pies you told Lorrimer about."

"We promised to share them with *him*."

"I'll join you. I'm not fussy."

"Let's eat them when he comes." Boy wanted to keep his food as long as possible; he was still full of Mrs. Oldroyd's good bread and brawn. Anyway, de Lacy was already friendly enough; no need to buy him with pies.

De Lacy looked exasperated. "Carnforth and all the rest will be back from their messes, too, then. You won't be so casual about food this time next week. Wait till you've endured four or five troughs!" He began to wheedle. "Come on—I can have my share now."

"I'd rather wait for Lorrimer. I did promise."

"Nyah, nyah!" de Lacy taunted. "Wait for Lorrimer! Lorrimer's just a piece of shit. You needn't worry about him."

"All the same..." Boy began. The look on de Lacy's face halted him. The fellow was frozen, his face a mask of fear. Boy followed his gaze and saw Lorrimer, standing in the gloom by the end of the pile of boxes.

"I was joking, man," de Lacy said, attempting a laugh. "I knew you were there."

There was a long silence. "Right," Lorrimer said at last and turned to go. Over his shoulder he added to Boy, "See, this is what I mean. In the old days I'd have thumped de Lacy for saying that."

At once de Lacy sprang to his feet and ran after him. "God, man, I was only joking. Honestly! You have my pie. I couldn't eat it anyway. You have it."

Lorrimer watched him in disgust, saying nothing, not moving.

"Not toe-taps! Please! Please, Lorrimer, don't tell Blenkinsop. I can still hardly walk. Please not toe-taps!"

Lorrimer turned and walked away, out into the gallery. A picture of despair, de Lacy scuffed his heels all the way back to Boy's bed. "Fick, faec, fock, and fuck!" he said without heat. "God, I hate hate *hate* this place."

Boy did not risk a word.

"You'll hate it, too," he said to Boy. "You'll think drumming-in is bad enough. You wait until Blenkinsop comes with his toe-taps!"

"What is drumming-in?" Boy asked.

"You'll see! Any minute now."

At that moment Lorrimer returned; de Lacy backed against the wall, shivering. Boy had never seen anyone in such a funk. He began to despise de Lacy and to wish he were next to someone else. It was an opinion he was quickly to revise.

"I disagree with your description of me," Lorrimer said casually, even pleasantly. "I have a little practical lesson for you." He held out a crumpled sheet of paper. "Have a taste."

De Lacy took the paper and brought it near his lips; suddenly he dashed it to the ground.

Lorrimer merely smiled—at least, his teeth gleamed like pebbles in the gloom. "Perhaps Blenkinsop can teach you."

De Lacy burst into tears but he bent with much greater speed than anyone expected and retrieved the paper. "You sod!" he said. "You utter sod!"

"That's better!" Lorrimer spoke gently as he sat down on Boy's trunk and began to unlace his right boot.

De Lacy, still sobbing, now obeyed Lorrimer's original command. Then he hurled the paper to the floor once again.

"Now—just to ram home the difference," Lorrimer said. He pulled off his sock with a smiling, theatrical flourish. "Lick here." He pulled up his big toe.

Utterly broken in will, de Lacy bent down, took Lorrimer's foot in his hands, and gingerly licked a small streak of toe. Lorrimer stood up suddenly, forcing de Lacy to the floor, mashing his face with the naked foot.

Boy could stand no more of it. Until then he had been at least in part on Lorrimer's side—a diminishing part but enough to stop him from interfering. Now, thinking to do no more than lift Lorrimer's foot off poor de Lacy's face, he stooped, caught up Lorrimer's ankle, and abruptly stood upright. He knew he was no kind of match for the older boy, but he was quite prepared to take the most fearsome lathering if only to prevent the total humiliation of de Lacy.

But Lorrimer was taken completely off balance. He fell back like a statue, stiff with the surprise. His eyes were wide as his head struck the brass corner of Boy's trunk. Pupils and iris vanished in those final inches to the floor. Then the eyes closed. He lay, awkwardly cramped and very still, between the chest and the bed.

Boy's first thought was for de Lacy. Shock had stifled the sobbing at once, its place taken by a wide-eyed admiration tinged with fear.

"God, he'll kill you," he said to Boy as he got up.

Causton, followed by Caspar, ran around the boxes and stood aghast over the unconscious body.

"You cut along," Boy told de Lacy. "I'll stay and face him." It seemed an easy boast to make, with Lorrimer so still; certainly he would be in no state to fight.

"Is he breathing actually?" Caspar asked.

They all stared down, not daring to touch someone so dangerous.

"He isn't breathing," Causton said. His quivering tone almost began a panic.

Boy knelt down and listened at Lorrimer's open mouth; he touched the unmoving chest; he felt for a pulse; then he looked up at the others. *I think he's dead,* he thought; he could not utter the words.

"We must all say he slipped," Caspar said. He turned to Boy's box and picked up a bar of soap. The others, unwilling to follow the implications of Boy's silence, watched dumbly.

Caspar looked at the body and the chest, put the soap on the floor at a carefully chosen spot, stood on it, and did a half-skating movement but leaning back so that the soap skittered away from under his foot and spun against the next bed, bouncing off and finishing, still spinning, against the wall. The motion was so violent that Caspar only just prevented himself from falling on top of Lorrimer.

Causton giggled nervously. "Yes!" he said. "That's what happened. We'll tell them that and show them the soap." He dashed forward to pick up the bar.

But Caspar was quicker. He darted forward, putting himself between Causton and the soap. "Leave it," he said. "Let them find it."

Causton looked at him blankly for a moment, then grinned. De Lacy was quite open in his admiration. "By God, young 'un—you've a head and no mistake!"

But Caspar was not flattered. "That?" he asked contemptuously, looking at the soap. "What else could we say?"

"We can tell the truth," Boy said. "We must all tell the truth."

But de Lacy shook his head vigorously. "Won't do," he said. He repeated the words several times, as if allowing himself time to think. "If he is dead, you'd blacken him forever. His people are ever so up, you know."

"No one would thank you for the truth," Caspar said.

"Yes, you couldn't do that to his memory," de Lacy confirmed.

But Boy was unshaken. "We are not in this world to get thanked. Nor to tell lies. We are here to do our duty and tell the truth." It was a decoction of many hundred sermons but he made it sound from the heart.

"I won't support you," de Lacy said.

Boy looked at him until his eyes fell. "I still won't support you," de Lacy repeated stubbornly.

A tall, thin boy, no more than a knobbly silhouette, stood at the doorway. "Brace up!" he shouted. He was about seventeen, almost a man to the youngsters in the dorm.

"Blenkinsop!" de Lacy called. "There's been an accident. Lorrimer's beastly quiet here."

No one else breathed. The silence and de Lacy's urgency communicated their terror to Blenkinsop. He breezed into the room and scrambled over the boxes, a house-beating offence unless you were a pharaoh or the King o' the Barn. He looked at Lorrimer's body, then at the solemn faces all round. "Christ!" he said.

He bent down and repeated all the tests Boy had made. "For Christ's sake!" He looked up. "He's dead!"

"It was an accident, Blenkinsop," Causton said.

"I did it," Boy said. "It was not an accident."

Caspar looked at de Lacy; neither said a word.

Blenkinsop looked from one to the other, too worried even to think of throwing his weight around. He stood up. "I'm going for the master before lockup." At the door he paused. "Don't touch Lorrimer."

Boy looked down at the sprawled body. Lorrimer, who had shown them around—only moments ago, it seemed—who joked about whores, told them the slang, invited himself to a share in their pie…*dead!* Lorrimer, who had been so beastly, so bestial, to de Lacy, so fierce and terrifying…*dead!* One minute there, more frightening than anything; next moment, because of one slip, one chance, one too-violent meeting of brass and bone, gone. Gone where? What had happened to all the *busy-ness* that had been Lorrimer?

"His foot just twitched," Causton said.

"It did not," Caspar replied, equally certain.

"It did."

"It was a trick of the gaslight."

"Chickens do that," de Lacy said.

"Do what?"

"Twitch. After they've had their heads chopped off. They run around, too."

"Have you seen it?" Boy asked. He was watching Lorrimer's foot, hoping it would twitch again—if indeed, it had twitched.

"Bet you've never seen it," Causton said.

"Not actually seen it. But all the servants'll tell you."

"Servants'll tell you anything," Caspar said.

"I *saw* it," Causton repeated.

"A chicken running around with no head?" Caspar asked.

"No! His foot. It definitely twitched."

Boy watched dumbly and wished he could have the last ten minutes over again. He looked around the cold, barely lit room, at the forty identical beds like lidless coffins, at the ancient limestone walls, at the miserable faces of the others, and thought *I will always remember this. Whatever happens next, I will always remember this.*

By that mysterious, wordless telegraph which galvanizes all human communities, the rumour of Lorrimer's death spread through the Old School. In dribs and drabs, by ones and by twos, they slipped through the door and collected silently around the body. If they spoke at all it was to ask the same repeated questions—is he dead? what happened?—hardly expecting more answer than a shrug from de Lacy or a raised eyebrow from Causton. In fascination they stared at the two new boys, one of whom had already made such a monstrous mark upon the school.

One, more adventurous, stooped and touched Lorrimer. "Not cold," he said. "Warmer than me."

"It's warmer still where he's going," someone else said.

No one laughed; they steeled themselves not to turn and look at this wit. The embarrassment grew acute.

"Couldn't we cover him with…something?" one lad asked.

Boy plucked a sheet from his bed and covered the body. It was an awesomely final act. He felt himself about to burst into tears. Would the others grudge him that luxury?

"Out!" The shout came from behind them. They all turned to see a stocky, curly-haired figure in a tail coat, arms akimbo, framed in the doorway.

"Swift," de Lacy whispered to Boy. "Head of pharaohs."

Everyone shuffled mutely out, except the original four.

"Well?" Swift shouted. He still had not moved from the door; everyone had had to squeeze past him, squirming and apologizing, and confirming his authority.

"We were here when it happened, Swift," de Lacy said.

"When what happened?" He came around, not over, the boxes. "He slipped and struck his head, you see," de Lacy said.

"Just there." Causton pointed superfluously to the shrouded body.

"I pushed him," Boy said. "Why try to pretend? I did it."

Swift looked quickly at the three who had spoken, then at Caspar. "One more to vote," he said.

"He fell," Caspar said, looking steadily at Boy.

"That's what I want to hear," Swift said, also looking at Boy. "Let's just have one simple story."

"He was...doing unspeakable things to de Lacy, and I pushed him away," Boy insisted.

Caspar made a disgusted noise, threw up his hands, and turned his back.

Swift looked from one to the other. "You're the new roes. Stevenson ma and mi." It was not a question but both nodded. "The word of one Stevenson will be enough, I think. You can vanish." He nodded at Boy.

Just then Lorrimer's foot twitched. They all saw it.

"See!" Causton said triumphantly. "I told you."

Boy's relief was overwhelming. "God!" he said leaning over and pulling the sheet off Lorrimer's face. He grinned sheepishly. "God be praised!" But Lorrimer was still apparently without breath. Boy was just about to straddle the body and apply the resuscitative massage he had once seen his father do to a seemingly dead navvy overcome by bad air when Swift kicked his backside lightly.

"Stow the gratitude, young 'un," he said. "If he's alive there's nothing to stop the drumming-in. And look..." His sharp eyes beckoned them all into a conspiracy. "Since he is alive, I think we'd all prefer to understand he slipped rather than"—he frowned at Boy—"whatever you were hinting at."

"The truth is the truth," Boy said.

Wearily Swift rose, grabbed Boy by the hair, bent his head down, and thrust him along the gangway at the foot of the beds. "Do as you're told, sir. Go and get ready for your drumming-in. Piss your bladder dry and shit yourself empty—we don't want any accidents. Your drumming-in is in ten minutes. And you," he turned to Caspar, "will follow."

Boy had no choice but to obey. And after the dread of what he had done to Lorrimer, the ordeal that lay ahead could, he imagined, hold few extra terrors. That conviction fell apart when he returned to the upper gallery ten minutes later. It was now thronged with excited boys who looked at him with a mirth that was part-truculent, part-shamefaced. He knew two things now about drumming-in: It involved the whole house and it happened on the upper gallery.

Back in the dorm he found that Lorrimer, whether dead or alive, was no longer there. Nor were Caspar, Causton, and de Lacy. Only Carnforth, his other dorm neighbour, remained.

"You didn't kill Lorrimer," Carnforth said after introducing himself.

Until that moment Boy had shared the same belief; but Carnforth spoke so shiftily he began to doubt again that Lorrimer was alive. One twitching foot seemed little enough proof. And it was true about chickens.

"Your bro will be back soon," Carnforth said. "Come on, get your clothes off. Quick as you can now."

"Do what?" The bottom fell out of his stomach.

"You have to do it naked. Everyone has to."

"I will not!" But even as he heard himself say the words he knew the determination was empty.

"If you don't, they'll come in here and tear your clothes off. It's what they're hoping for. Blenkinsop will really tear them. I mean shred them. Even after he's got them off. I've seen him."

Suddenly Boy stepped out of his clothes, down to the underpants. He had no idea the night was so cold.

"Everything," Carnforth said.

Boy felt gooseflesh grate against gooseflesh as he pulled off his underpants. The cold shrivelled his penis to a little acorn. He wished he could stop shivering; everyone would think—would know—how terrified he was. He grinned weakly at Carnforth. "We should do this in the summer," he said.

"It wouldn't work," Carnforth said stolidly. "We'd know each other too well by then. What they're getting ready for out there you could only do to someone you didn't know." Then, realizing perhaps how unfeeling his answer had been, he added as he half-pushed, half-steered Boy toward the door, "You're lucky really. You'll have a rope. Until two years ago they used to do it without ropes and a boy was killed."

Just before they reached the door it was pushed open and Caspar and Causton came in. Caspar's eyes went wide with shock as he took in Boy's nakedness. Boy saw the terror follow, "Bear up, young 'un," he said and walked swiftly out to the gallery.

Thus Christians to the lions—the sense that every eye in the universe was upon you, and every defect of your body and character made plain. A great hoot of derision greeted his appearance. A boy in a tail coat, not Swift but obviously a pharaoh, strode toward him holding a length of rope. With a practised flick of the wrist he threw a loop in the rope and tossed it over Boy's neck; for an instant Boy thought of a hanging. "And your arms," the pharaoh said crossly, annoyed at Boy's lack of response. "Shove your arms through."

Boy obeyed. Suddenly he had an inkling of all that was to follow, for when the pharaoh stood aside it became clear that the rope snaked out over the iron rail of the gallery, over one of the beams—a stiffened collarbeam, as Caspar had told Lorrimer—over the next beam, and back to the gallery, where it was made fast to the railing. He was not left guessing for long.

"All you do," the pharaoh said, "is jump up there"—he pointed to the first of the two beams over which the rope trailed—"and fetch that book back here. If you fall, the rope'll save you."

Boy could barely make out the words over the excited barracking of the rest of the house. The book lay dusty at the exact midpoint of the beam.

Blenkinsop joined them. He had a head like a caricature of a phrenology cast—every normal bump, lump, and protrusion, including the Adam's apple, was too prominent to seem real. Boy found himself imagining phrases such as LOVE OF FAMILY, CRIMINAL TENDENCIES, BASER APPETITES written one upon each bump, as in all the books on phrenology. All he saw were the shaven hairs of the beard, tightly extruded and bristle-blue on the sallow skin. Blenkinsop's eyes were supernaturally shiny as he scanned Boy's naked body.

"Is this what you call drumming-in?" Boy asked.

"Ho ho ho ho, no no no no!" Blenkinsop said. "But if you do that"—he pointed at the beam—"fast enough, you can spare yourself the drumming-in." He laid a mock-kindly hand on Boy's arm. "No need to tremble," he said. "Yet!"

"Come on," the pharaoh said crossly, as if Boy had been doing all the talking.

Boy looked at the beam again. He could not stop trembling as he walked toward the rail. When he touched it he almost knew he was not going to be able to climb up and over onto the beam. He looked around in his terror. A hundred—it looked like a thousand—gloating faces. He tried to imagine little Caspar standing there ten minutes from now. He could not bear the thought, and he needed the pity of it to save him from his own terror.

"Listen," he called. There was a momentary hush. "My brother cannot stand heights. He will certainly fall. Let me do it twice—once for him."

There was an uncertain murmur until Blenkinsop, who now held the other end of the rope, gave it a tweak. "Come on!" he shouted. "Your heroics don't impress us a bit."

The rope tweaked Boy forward, almost toppling him. Gusts of laughter resolved themselves into a chant: "Come on! Come on!"

Caspar and Causton, still in the dorm, heard all of this through the open door, though Caspar still had little idea of the ordeal awaiting him.

"Is that true?" Causton asked. "Can't you take heights?"

"*He's* the one with no head for heights. They terrify him."

"And you?"

"I don't mind."

"What a sterling brother!" Causton said.

"I can look after myself," Caspar told him. "I wish he wouldn't interfere."

Outside Boy was beginning the sickening climb over the railing and onto the lower of the two curved stiffeners. What Caspar had said was quite true: Even the view from the lower branches of a tree would give him vertigo. But the words of his father, words he had heard a hundred times, rang in his memory: Never flinch. Never show fear, and you'll master any group of men. Show no fear and there's naught you may not lead them to—no dangers you may not brave together. Show no fear.

So this was not the first time in his life he had put an ice-cool face upon the world while he seethed with terrors inside. It was not as bad (he told himself) as, for instance, dropping down into the blackness of a tunnel ventilation shaft with one foot in a noose at the end of a rope. If he could ignore the scorn of the others, it was not as bad as that.

He slipped his arm through the decorative rose cut between the stiffener and the collarbeam and then inched his way up the centre of the strut, testing each toehold, each new hand grip, up, up, until he could swing a leg over the beam. The mob watched in what—so soon after their catcalling—seemed like silence.

He straddled the beam, not daring to glance down. Here a second stiffener, above the beam this time, ran up to form, with its partner on the other side, a semicircular arch of wood beneath the apex of the roof. It effectively prevented him from standing.

How should he go now? He was sitting the wrong way, facing the crowded gallery, his back to the book he had to collect. Could he turn around without looking down? He decided he could not. He would have to inch himself along backwards.

"Boo!" someone shouted when he began. "Do it twice? You won't even do it once!"

Laughter turned to derision. Still struggling to keep his outward calm, he looked from one pitiless, gloating face to another. Some eyes could not meet his, but most stared back with savage glee as they shouted fake encouragement at him.

The beam was filthy. His hands were at once black with soot and dust—the black, oily dust of gas jets. So, too, he imagined were his buttocks and scrotum. Steadily he worked his way back until he felt the book touch the base of his spine. He breathed out his relief and sat upright, reaching a hand around for the book. The movement unbalanced him.

For a moment his legs flailed wildly and he knew he was going to fall. The gallery shouted *whoo-oo-op!* and parodied imbalance to one another. *God, let me fall where the rope will be shortest,* he begged. His ears were filled with a great wind. He saw the apex of the roof turn and tilt at a crazy angle. He saw faces, laughing—hooting with laughter. He prepared himself for the tug and burn of the rope about his chest.

Then there was a searing pain at his ankle. It had caught a notch checked into the beam by a carpenter, perhaps to house the calipers when the beam had been lifted up here. If it would hold! If flesh would not protest too much! If it would only hold! His fingers spidered over the top of the beam. Then over the edge. Now he had two holds—two bits of flesh to divide the agony. Arm and leg muscles took the strain. He was going up. He was not going to fall. More strain. Surely a bone must snap or a tendon wrench free from its attachment? The pain was intense. How could he stand such pain? But slowly he was recovering his position on the top of the beam. The hooting and the barracking did not for one moment let up.

Inch by torturing inch he regained his balance. When finally he sat upright he was bathed in sweat. Ironical cheers greeted the achievement. He looked around that cruel sea of faces and could not help smiling his relief. More carefully this time he felt behind him. No book. The book was not there!

"Fly, man!" a boy cried, giggling and flapping his hands. He jumped up and down on the spot. Others joined in, jumping and flapping their arms, laughing. "Fly!" they chorused. "Fly!" He could feel the tremor of their jumping, shaking in the beam, as he frantically groped behind him for the book.

"Fly down!" one boy cried and pointed over the gallery rail.

Unthinkingly Boy glanced down. There was the book, battered and open, on one of the oak tables. It was all he saw, and he saw it for only a flash; but that was enough. The entire hall spun in a shower of flying black darts, swirling in a maelstrom about his head. Mindless now of the scorn of others, he hurled himself forward and clutched at the beam, eyes tight shut against the black whirlpool that sought to suck him down.

Again the chorus of boos—and this time, something more: missiles. Books, rocks of stale bread, rolled-up clothing, a kale stalk, bits of kindling, whizzed past him or struck him hard where he clung for dear life to the beam. Someone out there was a wizard with a peashooter, too.

It will not do, he told himself. *You must face them. You must see it through.*

Caspar, sick himself with pity for his mad, brave brother, followed his progress by changes in the tone of the shouting and derision.

"It's to do with going out on one of the beams, isn't it?" he told Causton.

"I'm not allowed to say."

"You have no idea what torture that would be to my brother."

Out on the beam Boy was slowly but resolutely raising himself upright again. A book caught him across the nose with a flash of searing light and a salty, hollow sharpness in which his head rang. Two images of the hall spiralled over one another. But still he went on raising himself upright.

When he made his first move back he discovered what all new boys who tried to go along the beam at the straddle discovered—he was going against the grain of the wood. A long splinter of pitch pine pierced the heel of his right hand, another his left thigh. He had no choice but to kneel or get turned into a pincushion of splinters. He began another painful move to the new position. The sweat now made him feel deathly chill.

Everyone had been waiting for the discovery: they howled with laughter and pricked one another's bodies with imaginary splinters. Boy searched for one kindlier face in all that unrelenting mob and found none. What he did find made him freeze halfway up into the crouch: Blenkinsop was unfastening the tethered end of the rope!

Moments later the free end swung loose, a whippy pendulum, from the neighbouring beam. Boy was paralysed, one foot in the crouch, one still hanging down. He could not move; he could hardly breathe. His eyes bulged.

Now the silence was complete. Blenkinsop looked around, grinning, ready to ward off a shower of laughing congratulation. He faced nothing but blank, horror-stricken silence. Boy realized that he had not been alone in depending on that rope; it had been every fellow's licence to mock and jeer. But now, to a man, they sat-crouched-hung there with him, appalled at his danger, willing his muscles to move until their own ached.

"You blithering fool, Blenkinsop!" Swift hissed in that straining silence. But there was nothing he, or anyone else, could do to retrieve the loose end now. Boy had to make it back to the gallery alone.

No one looked at either of the senior men; no one could take his eyes off Boy, still rigid in the middle of the beam.

"Come on, Stevenson. You can do it!" someone said.

"Yes, come on, man!" Several took up the shout.

Boy opened his eyes then and saw smiling, fearful encouragement on every side. He saw, too, that someone in the hall below had dowsed the gaslights in the lower gallery and the main body of the hall. Only the upper gallery was lit. The height, the sickening, headwhirling height, had gone.

This beam rests two feet above the floor, Boy told himself. *Stand up!*

He stood. He could smile. He smiled at the silhouettes that thronged the rails, knowing they were smiling, too. One, two, three, four easy steps brought him to the safety of the upper stiffener, but now he did not pause. He swung himself around it and, thrusting an arm through the rose-shaped hole, made the easy leap for the railing, catching hold of it without difficulty. If the move had been made upon the ground, no one would have turned to watch; yet now a great roar of relief rang from every throat there. Boys clustered around to haul him in over the railing and slap him on the back. "Well done, man!" they cried.

Over, Boy thought, close to tears. *It's over!*

"You'll only get a light drumming-in after that," Swift promised.

"What?" Boy was incredulous. *More? After that?*

Swift laughed, not quite wholeheartedly. "Oh yes. That"—he pointed airily at the beam—"was a fraud. No one escapes a drumming-in, however well they do the beam."

Several lads around giggled at the trick, but the mood was friendly.

Only Blenkinsop looked peevish as he came forward to Boy.

"Come on," he said roughly. "Get that rope off. It's time for your little bro."

"Let me do it again," Boy said. "In place of him."

Swift shook his head. "Can't be done, young sport."

Blenkinsop was very rough in getting the rope off. They swung the loose end over the beam, fished it in with one of the poles for opening the upper windows, swung it over the next beam, fished it in again, and tied it to the railing. Swift checked the knot and then looked at Blenkinsop as if he had needed all this time to reach a decision. "You'd better come and see me in my study when this is over," he said.

From the change in the hubbub outside, Caspar guessed that his turn had come. He stood, with pounding heart and lost stomach, and dropped his blanket. Causton stared at his tiny erection.

"Why that?" he asked, his eyes wide in disbelief and delight.

Caspar looked down and blushed. "That always happens when I have to think about cruelty. Like whipping slaves and things. Doesn't it with you?"

"I should say not! Not thinking about *that*, anyway!"

With only the upper gallery lights on there was too much shadow for many to notice Caspar's strange condition. But Blenkinsop saw it. He brushed his hands down there many times as he tied the rope. In the end he was quite excited. Caspar was more bemused than embarrassed. He kept looking at the beam, working on how best to clamber up the stiffeners and walk along it.

Someone thrust a book into his hands. *Eating Exercises* it said on the cover; the spine, more truthfully, said *Latin Exercises*. "Take it to the middle of that beam and put it down. Then come back," Swift said.

"Leave it there?"

"Yes. If you do it fast enough, you'll escape your drumming-in."

Right, Caspar thought. *This isn't so bad.* His erection fell. He clamped the book between his teeth, knowing exactly the route he was going to take.

He sprang up onto the broad wooden handrail that capped the gallery railings, steadied his balance in a trice, and then made a further diagonal leap straight onto the collarbeam, crouching down at once to get under the slope of the rafters.

There was a gasp from those who saw the move from the side where he made the leap. Fractionally later, so quickly had he moved, there was an answering gasp as those on the other side saw him appear, miraculously, above their heads.

He barely paused, moving forward and rising as the slope allowed. When he reached the upper stiffener he leaped again, landing at a crouch three feet up; in the same move he dropped to his stomach and swung his legs down under the curve of the stiffener. He had judged it perfectly, for his feet came to rest on the midline of the beam. He swung the rest of himself under and once more crouched, this time beneath the curve. Again he went forward, rising as the curve rose until he was standing fully upright and sauntering out to the middle of the beam.

People were excited now, clapping and cheering and shouting encouragement. Caspar was as lithe and delightful to watch as an acrobat. Where he bent over to place the book exactly in the centre, a great sexual *whoo! whoo!* went up, almost unnerving him.

He stood again, smiling, and returned, almost exactly reversing the routine he had used in getting out. Just under thirty seconds from starting he was back again on the gallery, fighting off Blenkinsop, who had his hands all over him, trying to get off the rope. No one had ever walked the beam so quickly. Boy watched, regretting his jealousy but unable to master it as the congratulations showered on Caspar.

But there was already a move to form the gauntlet along the gallery for the drumming-in. Eager lads lined up, at three-foot intervals, legs apart to make a long tunnel. "*Drum drum drum drum...*" they began to chant in a gleeful monotony. Grinning, they looked over their shoulders and invited Boy to go to the head of the tunnel.

Drained now of all feeling, he walked mechanically to the end of the gallery. Caspar watched him pityingly, still believing himself to be saved from the ordeal by the speed he had shown on the beam.

"You too," Swift said.

Caspar looked up at him in astonishment. "But you said…"

Swift smiled. "Don't worry. No one has ever done it fast enough. But they'll let you off very lightly. Cut along!" He pointed to the end of the gallery, where Boy was beginning to crawl on hands and knees through the tunnel of trouser legs. As soon as his head was out of danger the rest of him became fair target; but the slaps he was getting were mere tokens—except from Blenkinsop, who had taken off a shoe and gave Boy two good belts with it before he had reached the sanctuary of the next fellow's legs.

Caspar's treatment was even milder, more like slaps on the back plus several quite tender caresses, especially from Blenkinsop.

But both the young Stevensons ended up with skinned knees and toes; all the goodwill in the school could not make the floor less abrasive.

Twelve minutes later, aching, sore of skin, but freshly bathed at the tap in the boot room and glowing in the sense of having gone through the fire, they fell into bed and settled to sleep. The gaslamp was never turned off, day or night; Boy lay watching it in those last drowsy moments of wakefulness, still doubting that Lorrimer had survived and wondering why no one but he seemed worried by the fact. In a frightening way that terrible business was beginning to appear almost normal in this place—too normal for the mind to dwell upon for very long.

Downstairs all the bucks had piled their mattresses at one end of the Barn and were raucously playing at what they called "Olympic games," which involved leaping and somersaulting into the soft pile, the most agile being favoured with loud cheers from the rest. Less energetic souls read tales of blood and thunder aloud by the firelight. The lucky ones grilled chops and lumps of sirloin over the fire. The mouth-watering pungency of sizzling fat penetrated every corner of Old School, reminding most how hollow their guts were. The joke was then to wait until the lucky one sat down, with his chop between two trenchers of bread, and then to shower him with "squibs" of flaring lucifers; a chop in the hand could not honourably be snatched, but one dropped or put down while, say, part of a burning nightshirt was extinguished was fair booty. Not a boy there who would not far rather nurse blisters and the toothsome memory of the meat than go to bed unburned and grieve for its loss.

In Boy's exhaustion the aroma of grilling meat delayed his sleep only by moments.

"*I* put out the downstairs lights," de Lacy said, "when you were on the beam."

Boy nodded as he fell asleep, hoping de Lacy had noticed the gesture.

Moments later, it seemed (in fact, it was almost forty-five minutes), he was awakened by Blenkinsop, who had come into the dorm to "see if Caspar's knees needed any treatment." The inspection had entailed several minutes' groping under the blankets. Then he had remembered Boy.

He shook him roughly awake; Boy came spiralling up through seven hundred layers of sleep. The shallower he got, the more he ached.

"How dare you drop off to sleep, Stevenson ma?" Blenkinsop asked in a gentle, almost conversational tone.

Boy blinked, unable to keep his eyes open. The words and the darkness spun around him.

"How dare you?" the senior repeated. "You needn't think that we've forgotten the way you tried to blacken poor Lorrimer's name. A man slips and falls and you, trying to make yourself out no end the hero, you accuse him of 'unspeakable things.' Well, we've had quite enough of your heroics. We'll just see how heroic you are."

Boy was not jolted fully awake until Blenkinsop, swift as a snake, darted a hand under the blankets, grabbed the nearest ankle and jerked the foot—Boy's left foot—out over the side of the bed. In the same quick move he pirouetted round and sat down on the leg, imprisoning it. Boy's foot now lay pinioned, toes up, between Blenkinsop's knees. A great knobbly hand held it painfully bunched and vulnerable. The toes already wept and smarted where the skin had rubbed away on the gallery floorboards.

He saw Blenkinsop's other hand, its fist in clenched silhouette against the gaslight, rise above the dark cliff of the shoulder. It floated in an unreal space, remote from him. It fell.

The world exploded in a riot of pain; his foot became a gulf that swallowed everything. He vanished, dissolving into that vast, molten anguish where his toes had been. He could see nothing in the sudden, searing light.

There was a thud. A voice, de Lacy's, said, "You utter sod!" Blenkinsop's weight vanished. De Lacy had clouted him with a boot swung by its laces.

The dorm began to return. The pain was still excruciating but no longer all-embracing. He was somewhat separate again from his agonizing toes. There was an argument going on. De Lacy was saying, "No you're not! Swift's chucked you out. You're just an ordinary buck now. This isn't the old days. If you lay a finger on any one of us again, we'll go straight to Swift and you'll get a house beating. And shan't we just gloat!"

"You'll be sorry you said that, de Lollipop," Blenkinsop threatened. "I'll be King o' the Barn again yet. Then I'll show you what toe-taps can really do!"

But at least twelve boys stood around him, all holding impromptu weapons. Through the pain Boy found time to wonder that de Lacy, who had been so petrified of Blenkinsop as King o' the Barn, now stood up to him so calmly when the title was stripped away. Then he fell back to sleep.

Chapter 5

IN GAMES OF CRUELTY NATURE HOLDS ALL THE TRUMPS. HER GIFT OF OBLIVION allowed Boy to awaken not knowing he was at Fiennes, not remembering the savageries of the previous evening, his conscience wonderfully clear of all the uncertainties about Lorrimer's death or survival. For several seconds the blissful state persisted. It was odd, because he had not awakened spontaneously. The cries of the pharaohs still rang around the room: "Come on everywhere! Stiffen up! Out o' those chariots!" It was half-past six and dark as midnight inside the almost windowless dorm.

One pharaoh, Malaby, the one who had tied the rope around him last night, gave Boy's toes a friendly tweak. "You, too, Stevenson ma."

The pain, sudden and fierce, brought back all the rest: Blenkinsop, the beam, *drum-drum-drum*...and Lorrimer. What was the fate of boys who killed boys? Or even half-killed them?

"We're all going for a little run."

It was a new tradition at Fiennes that all the boys, from the meanest roe to the pharaohs, as well as the two younger masters, Mr. Cusack and Dr. Brockman (the bringer of this new tradition and its staunchest proponent), ran up the winding sheep paths to a cairn placed exactly one thousand feet above the school and a mere three hundred and twenty feet below the summit of Whernside; only on Sunday were the celebrants of Holy Communion excused—which went far to account for the school's reputation for piety.

"Go in your vest and trousers," de Lacy advised.

Boy hobbled painfully downstairs in the general crush from junior dorm. Nobody said that dreadful punishments awaited the last man back from the run but he had already been at Fiennes long enough not to need telling that sort of thing.

Going down the stairs, where the windows were at eye level, he saw that the dawn was, in fact, well advanced. Caspar joined him in the passageway that led to the yard—the old cloisters.

"How's the foot?" he asked.

Boy shrugged. "It will heal."

"I'd love the chance to hurt Blenkinsop. My toes are raw."

"Did he do the same to you, before me?"

"No." Caspar coloured. "He keeps trying to tickle my wetty. I hate him. His breath smells."

"What's going to happen about Lorrimer, I wonder."

"It depends on how idiotic you are," Caspar said, thinking that Boy was merely asking about which story they should all tell.

The sun was just rising as they came out into the yard. They could not yet see the globe itself but it struck a pink sheen across the cold, lichen-eaten stones of the school buildings. The sky was a russet grey, hovering between the purple of night and the red of sunrise. Not a cloud was in sight. It was very cold and still. Everything, even little pebbles that normally would have kicked loosely away or wobbled underfoot, seemed to have been cast in a single block of iron and painted to resemble a frozen world. The exit from the schoolyard onto the moor lay through an arch flanked by four giant stone troughs, filled with water and capped with thick sheets of ice.

"We dip in those on our way back," de Lacy said. "It's best to work up a good lather coming down, then you can be in and out without cooling off much. If you go in cold, you'll stay cold all morning."

Boy wondered how they were to dry off. No one had brought towels and none were to be seen around the place. He and Caspar joined the scattered throng of more than a hundred boys in every variety of dress, trotting through the arch. He found a way of running that did not hurt his toes too much.

"There's chief," de Lacy said. "With Agincourt today." He pointed to a crowd of about forty boys running toward them over the moor; in the thick of them was a tall, chunky, well-built man with curly blond hair. "Agincourt's his own House," de Lacy added.

The whole world was white. Bog, marsh, moor, pasture, and scree were reduced to one appearance. Only the forms of the dalesides provided any relief; they were like pictures of the tops of clouds as sketched by balloonists; above them towered two giant masses: Whernside—a daunting climb even from here, halfway up its side—and Ingleborough, several miles down the valley.

On its way to Ingleborough the moor rose gently to a broad crest that obscured any view of the coastal lowlands beyond; it exactly symbolized the remote, own-worldliness of Fiennes.

Both Boy and Caspar, in imitation of their father, loved to look at landscapes and talk with knowing superiority of the geological forces that had shaped them.

"Glacial," Caspar said.

"It's colder at the top," de Lacy told him.

The two Stevensons exchanged amused glances. "Until it carved its way out through that limestone ridge the water must have formed quite a lake here," Boy said.

"The bog must be the remnant," Caspar replied in bursts of breath. The hill was growing steeper and talk less easy. The weaker runners were dropping into a plodding walk until the chief or some senior fellow would shout, "Brace up!" and then the walk would take on the veriest tinge of a trot. At the steepest places these fainthearts made parallelograms of muscle, hands pushing on knees to make the climb tolerable.

The higher they went the more dales came into view—it was surprising what a difference even a few feet could make: Cam Fell, Oughtershaw, Foxup Moor, Fountains Fell, and more distant humps rolled in folds under the pale blue snows. Here and there the black, yet-to-be-frozen waters of upland tarns mottled the otherwise unbroken surface.

"Gordale Scar is about twenty miles that way," de Lacy said. "It's really sublime."

Another boy, overhearing, turned round and mocked: "Sublime! Oooh hooo!"

"Pox your bum, Randall, you fiend," de Lacy said evenly.

Very few boys were talking.

"In milder weather you can stay asleep from your bed to the top and all the way down again," de Lacy said.

No one lingered at the top. De Lacy had been right: It was much colder there, on the ridge, where the lightest breeze from any direction was whipped around the breastlike pinnacle of the summit. Running down was easier but less comfortable, especially for Boy, who had to try to run on the side of the foot Blenkinsop had mashed.

"I'd really like to hurt Blenkinsop," Caspar said again. He felt he owed Boy something for that offer to walk the beam twice last night.

By the time they were halfway down, Boy had drawn well ahead. Caspar then found a way of catching up by sliding down the steepest bits on one boot.

"You'll wear out your boots that way," Boy told him. "Mother will know it couldn't be normal wear and she'll be mad!"

Caspar pulled a face but did not repeat the trick.

Chief was first into the trough, after a furious sprint against several pharaohs for the privilege of breaking the ice. For a while they larked about in the water, catching up the ice fragments and dashing them against the walls, where they shattered in tinkling sherds, leaving scintillating white blisters adhering to the stone. They ducked each other, too, with great bull roars while the younger lads laughed and cheered in piping treble around them.

Chief pulled his trousers on before he left the yard. Once he and Cusack had gone the atmosphere changed. The ostentatious manliness vanished and four hundred naked boys piled through the stone troughs as quickly as muscle could carry them. Boys who had pubic hair and lived in the Houses (where there were female domestics) were obliged to pull on cotton drawers; but everyone else, including boys of all ages in Old School (where one ill-paid old man was supposed to do all the domestic work), simply picked up his own clothes and ran hell for leather back to the dorms.

As de Lacy had said, if you went in hot, you came out at least warm; and if the run to the dorm didn't dry you off, there was something odd about you. In that brief, naked run back to the dorm, Boy and Caspar saw hardly one backside that did not bear the mark of the cane or the slipper.

Despite the horror of the icy water, Boy had to admit that he felt splendid by the time he slipped on his clothes; they had a strange new silken texture. But there was no time to luxuriate in the sensation. It was fifteen minutes to first trough and in that time they had to clean a pharaoh's boots, lay out his clothes, and tidy his study. Caspar was boot roe to Deakin; Boy was clean-collar roe to Malaby. They would remain so until released by a fresh crop of newcomers. The pharaohs all went back to bed until five minutes before trough. Then, in one frantic rush, each aided by his two roes, they got up, washed, shaved, and dressed, ready to file into the Barn looking as if they had been up for hours. God help the roe who crumpled or dirtied anything or presented it the wrong way around or fumbled too long with a button.

First trough was at half-past seven. At twenty-five-past the grunts began ladling out glasses of thin beer and setting them on the four tables. At twenty-seven minutes past they started to dole out a glutinous mess of shredded flannel and bobbin grease called "porridge and treacle." The roes took turns to run a shuttle service of intelligence between the Barn and the pharaohs' corridor; so Boy and Caspar found themselves running and shouting things like "twenty-six and a half minutes past, beer on three tables...twenty-seven past, porridge on one...twenty-eight and a quarter past, porridge on half the top table...twenty-nine past, the master's egg's in...bell in twenty seconds..." and so on, right up to the bell.

On a good day the shirts went on, the collars and cuffs were studded, the ties knotted, and the boots laced, each exactly as the beer or porridge reached its appointed tide mark in that inexorable filling of tables. On a bad day, each piece of intelligence brought fresh oaths from the pharaohs and the blows would rain down on the heads of the luckless roes.

Today, it seemed, was a good day. They filed into the Barn in perfect order—roes, bucks, Trench (the new King o' the Barn), and the four pharaohs. Then the master, bursting with hair at every orifice.

"*Benedictus benedicat*," Whymper almost sang.

Everyone could smell the master's egg, a strong, rich note over the insipid steam that rose from the "porridge." In three minutes the porridge was gone. In four minutes the egg, too, was gone, its delicious aroma already a fading memory. All stood. There was a fart from third table. Some boys giggled, some cried with overloaded disgust. There was a scuffle, silenced by imperious looks and shushes from top table.

"*Benedicto benedicata*," Whymper almost sang.

Then they filed out again, pharaohs first this time. All the boys carried glasses of milk, which were set out, one to each boy, during the meal. At the door they each collected three twisted cones of paper containing tea, sugar, and cocoa—the complete ration for the day's brews.

"Time for a brew before chapel," de Lacy said. "Stevenson mi can come too, as long as you've got those pies."

The coal fire in the Barn and the four gas burners in the outer corridors were all occupied by the time they got there, so they had to kindle an impromptu fire of sticks and a broken packing case in a corner of the corridor. This made them late for chapel. And, in any case, the pies were much too delicious simply to gobble down; neither Boy nor Caspar could remember any food half so tasty coming from the kitchens at home before.

Fortunately, a large number of boys were late that day, enough to form a battering legion and charge their way through the pathetic rank of three beaks trying to block the entry. Only one latecomer in ten got marked down, neither Boy nor Caspar among them.

As they trotted back from chapel to house—everyone trotted at Fiennes until the end of school at half-past three—Boy began to feel that life wasn't going to be so bad. This mood was shattered when Malaby called Boy into his study, just before school was due to begin. He pointed at the floor. "What's that?" he asked.

"Your carpet," Boy said, wondering what was wrong with it. He had brushed it furiously and was certain that not a speck of dirt was left upon it.

"Oh, is it! Then why the hell don't you treat it like a carpet? I thought it was some old rag you'd found, you've thrown it down so carelessly."

Boy stared down again in bewilderment; not a crease or fold was there in it.

"Do you live in these conditions at home? What is your guv'nor—some sort of tradesman, is he not?"

Boy stayed silent, knowing he could not say the words that sprang into his mind. But even his silence felt like a betrayal of his father.

"Do you tolerate servants who chuck carpets down like that?"

This time Malaby obviously expected an answer.

Boy coughed up a pleading little laugh. "Honestly, Malaby, I see nothing wrong with it."

"Nothing wrong! My dear young fellow, they've obviously sent you to a decent school in the nick of time. Down on your knees, please!"

His heavy cajolery, delivered in the lightest tone, filled Boy with foreboding as he obeyed.

"Oblige me," Malaby went on, "by drawing your finger along the line of the floorboards." Boy did so. "Good. Now, while you try to hold the memory of that line in your tiny little brain, kindly trace out the line formed by the edge of the carpet."

Again Boy obeyed. Malaby's drift began to reach him: The two lines were not precisely parallel!

Malaby saw the understanding as it dawned in Boy's eyes. "Oh yes! Horror of horrors! Not parallel, as old Euclid so quaintly phrases it. Those two lines don't meet in the hereafter; they meet somewhere in this bloody room! They subtend an angle greater than zero—are you familiar with these mathematical arcana in your tradesman's palace?"

Boy nodded miserably.

"Because if not, I'll teach you. I can already see I'm going to have to teach you quite a bit. You obviously strolled in here thinking you needn't give a hoot about old Malaby's comfort, you can sling his rug down any old how."

Boy, who had slaved extra hard, he thought, to make the study pleasant, felt the injustice of Malaby's scorn fiercely; but again he held his tongue.

"You've just earned a Barn beating. Now get out!"

"What's a Barn beating?" Boy asked de Lacy.

"Oh, Malaby's always in a wax when he's behind with his prep..." de Lacy began; but he had no time to explain a Barn beating because at that moment a buck poked his head into the passage, nodded at Boy, and said, "Whym wants you. Five minutes ago."

Boy's heart fell to his boots. The Lorrimer inquisition was about to begin. Barn beatings and tongue lashings from Malaby would soon seem very small beer.

Mr. Whymper did a lot of breathing and staring before he spoke. "Last night!" was all he said.

Last night? Did he mean Lorrimer? Or the drumming-in? Or even Blenkinsop? So much had happened last night. Boy was determined not to resolve Whymper's ambiguity for him.

"Yes, master?"

"Well?"

Boy shrugged, nonplussed.

"Answer the question, dammit, sir!"

"I'm sorry, master. What is the question?"

"You know full well 'what is the question'!"

"About the drumming-in, master?"

Whymper's nostrils flared until Boy thought they would disgorge the two black caterpillars. "Drumming-in! Drumming-in? There is no such thing, d'ye hear! This school tolerates no such rituals. If you hear of it, if you hear so much as a whisper, you are to come at once to me and we shall extirpate it, eradicate it, root it out."

The word "root" must have tripped the schoolmaster's equivalent of a hair trigger in his mind, for he at once added: "What is the derivation of the words extirpate and eradicate?" Then, no doubt remembering that their business was much too serious for pedagogical games, he said gruffly, "No matter. No matter. You understand what I was saying before?" He glared at Boy, challenging him to so much as mention the drumming-in again.

"Do you mean Lorrimer, master?" Boy longed to ask if he were alive or dead but did not dare.

"Yes, I mean Lorrimer, sir. I understand that three people who were there say he tripped and fell. But you, for reasons best known to yourself, persist in blackening his name with some wild talk or other, incidentally casting yourself in an heroic mould."

"That is true, master."

Whymper's attitude certainly didn't suggest that Lorrimer had died, but how could you tell with someone who obviously knew that the drumming-in ceremony went on and who yet denied it so blatantly? And to one of the victims within hours of his experience of it? There was such a puzzling gap in this place between what people said and what they did.

Without looking, Whymper reached behind him, into a nook between the chimney breast and a bookcase, and fished out a stout malacca cane. In crude assertion of his power he laid it on the faded leather of his desk; the fine wire binding around the end of it gleamed fiercely in the multicoloured sunlight that fell between them from the stained-glass window. "What is true, Stevenson? That is what I wish to know. That is what I intend to know."

"It is true that three people say he slipped."

"Including your own brother."

"Including him. And I say he was bullying de Lacy and I merely…"

"Bullying?" It was obviously not the word Whymper had expected. "But you said 'doing unspeakable things'—that is very different from mere bullying."

Boy took a deep breath. "He was making de Lacy lick his toes. Lorrimer was making de Lacy lick Lorrimer's toes. Then Lorrimer stood on de Lacy's head. And there was worse than that. I call it unspeakable, master."

"And *I* call it unspeakable to blacken a boy's name—an honourable name, from a family far more ancient than the Stevensons, I may say—when there is a perfectly reasonable alternative explanation."

Boy was silent.

"What do you say to that?"

"I say that they will have to swear it before God and I know that at least one of them, being a Stevenson, will not then be able to maintain the lie, master. And I trust the same is true of the others."

Whymper looked puzzled at this.

"Surely there must be some kind of inquiry…" Boy began.

Before he could say more the door opened and a tall, powerful man walked in. His fair, curly hair, released as he lifted his mortarboard, gave his rugged face an almost boyish look. Only then did Boy recognize him as the chief.

"Good morning to you, Whymper," he said; then he looked at Boy with a stern, guarded sympathy—a conditional promise of sympathy, Boy thought. But Boy was on the lookout for sympathy that morning.

Whymper had risen at once. "Good morning, chief. This is Stevenson major. Stevenson, here is your headmaster, Dr. Brockman."

Brockman held out a muscular hand—a big bunch of squabby fingers, which closed right over Boy's paw. "I sent for you a good thirty minutes ago. I trust you weren't skulking somewhere?" Something in his tone let Boy understand that a partial rebuke was aimed at Whymper, for not sending Boy at once.

"I was with Mr. Whymper, sir," he said.

Brockman smiled thinly at the master.

"We were discussing Lorrimer," Boy added, thinking it no harm to get at once to the matter.

"Yes, how is young Lorrimer?" Brockman asked.

Boy looked in relief from chief to master. How *is* Lorrimer? The question answered his own unspoken one. The whole day grew lighter. And Whymper's answer put the seal on it: "He has taken nourishment and is sleeping."

"Good, good," Brockman said with conventional cheer. "A nasty shock. Now, m'boy, I wish you to come with me."

Boy followed, walking on air. Lorrimer was alive! *Alive!* The most beautiful pair of syllables in any language. He found he could even picture Lorrimer's face again now—something his mind had shrunk from in dread of the pallor, the white eyeballs, he had feared to discover. Now he could imagine Lorrimer talking, laughing, sneering. He could even rehearse again that dreadful fall without cringing in his flesh and cursing his own impulsive nature.

"Stevenson ma." He caught the undertones all around as he trotted beside the chief, who, striding in flowing gown and crimson hood, swept a miraculous swath through knots of boys on their way to tutorials. He was surprised to find that he and the chief were hand-in-hand. He had heard little of what the man was saying but understood, vaguely, that it was to do with the age of the foundation and the many changes it had seen since the days of the monks. In the end, just as they reached the gate of the chief's garden, he became aware that Brockman had halted and was looking at him, as if waiting for an answer to some question.

"What is it, m'boy?" Brockman asked at length.

"I wasn't sure whether Lorrimer was alive or dead, sir."

Brockman continued to look at him long and hard. "I see," he said. "Then you have heard very little of what I have been saying."

"I'm afraid not, sir." Boy smiled ruefully.

They went through the little garden, directly into the chief's study. Caspar, who was already there, stood up as they entered. A large elk-hound lay sprawled before the fire. It looked up but did not otherwise stir. Boy was motioned to a leather chair next to Caspar, on the side of the fire away from the window. Brockman took the matching chair and became a silhouette whose features were barely lit by the small flames that flared now and then from the glowing coals.

"I was talking to you about change, m'boy. Change and permanence. Change in order to achieve permanence, if you will, in an old foundation such as this is. Do you know how old it is?"

"Pre-Reformation, sir?" Boy suggested.

"That stained glass in Mr. Whymper's pupil room is among the oldest in Yorkshire. To bring change to such a place, m'boy, is no easy matter!"

"No, sir," Boy said, since some comment seemed to be called for. He saw the chief smile, a shade dejectedly, and realized he would have to do better. He looked at Caspar and shrugged.

"Your father, now—he is, of course, the Stevenson who is building this siege railway in the Crimea?"

"Yes, sir." Both of them answered at once. "It will be over forty miles before he has finished," Caspar added.

"A great achievement. You will both be very proud, to be sure. It is a great thing to do for one's country."

"My father says he is pleased enough to repay his country, which has done so much for him," Boy said.

"Of course. It applies to us all, I hope. Your father is fortunate in one respect: The great opportunity presented itself. And all honour to him for grasping it so firmly, I say. But those of us not so fortunate should not grow discouraged when no great opportunity presents itself. We must make all the more sure to seize the smaller ones that come our way."

Boy nodded, thinking this was a very simple homily to digest. Caspar, taking the cue, nodded as well.

"In my work here, for instance. How do you, Stevenson major, think I might best serve our country?" His eyes rested on Boy, who looked up in fright. It was surely not his place to offer suggestions.

"What small opportunities may come my way?"

Boy took his courage in both hands. "I suppose, sir, that each one of *us* is—er—a 'small opportunity'...in a way."

Brockman leaned suddenly forward, his voice full of enthusiasm: "Jove,

I'm sure you are right, m'boy!" He looked at both as if he suddenly had great hope of unsuspected wisdom in them. "But in what way? An opportunity for what?"

Boy merely breathed a couple of times.

"Come, m'boy. You're no fool. I've met your father, remember. I know your stock. You can answer me well enough, I feel sure. Only diffidence prevents you." His glance took in Caspar.

"An opportunity to educate us, sir?" Caspar said; he had been waiting to speak.

"And what may that mean? What is 'education,' do you imagine?"

"To turn us into Christian gentlemen, well grounded in the classics?" Boy said. That was an easy answer. Their tutor at home, Mr. Morier-Watson, had always said that was the purpose of education.

It was the right note. He could see that in the chief's gleaming eyes. "Yes!" He leaned back and put large, spade-tipped fingers together. "I suppose it is open to each of us to hope to leave behind some monument, a single achievement, great or small, to the glory of God and for the benefit of one's country, or one's fellows. Your father, if he does nothing else—though, indeed, I'm sure his life will be both long and distinguished, but if your father does nothing else, I say—he will have his Crimea railway."

He looked sharply at Boy, almost begging him to supply the obvious extension.

"And you, sir, would have the school," Boy said.

The chief smiled. "Will I, Stevenson? I wonder." There was a long silence before he added: "And what *is* a school?" Now he looked at both of them equally. "Could it, for instance, exist with no boys?"

They laughed, but chief's monitory finger halted them.

"No, no," he said. "I do not jest. Could I and my assistant masters, could we, call in a builder and set out so much bricks and mortar—dormitories, refectories, schoolrooms, and so on, as well as playing fields and fives courts, and everything that goes to make what the vulgar might call a school, you follow? A school at holiday time, y'ou might say."

They nodded.

"Would you call that a school, either of you?"

"No, sir."

"It has everything except…"

"Pupils, sir." They grinned. It was as exciting as finding a new passage in Socrates, where Plato has him making an absolute fool of someone.

"Exactly! You are *kind* enough to say that this school may be my monument.

But will you be *good* enough to make it so? For, as you have just proved to me, without pupils there is no school." He smiled. "Will you?"

"Yes, sir," they promised, easily and eagerly.

"Will you strive at all times and in all things to be industrious, pious, chaste, sober, athletic, and God-fearing—true, muscular little Christians?"

"Yes, sir." It was not quite so easy a promise to make. They began to feel uneasy that chief meant every word of it quite literally.

He weighed them up before he spoke again, apparently deciding they were worth the words. "Many things here are unsatisfactory. I do not conceal it from you. Three years ago I found this place a relic of Georgian barbarism; it was almost as bad as Eton in my boyhood. And Old School, where you now find yourselves, is, I fear, as close to the infamous Long Chamber at Eton as you might find in all the world. It will be a remarkable boy—remarkable for purity and strength of character—who will pass unscathed through Old School. I hope that you, and others like you, but especially you, are such boys. Because I mean to change it—and without such boys I cannot do that." He leaned back and put his fingertips together again. "Are you of the company?" he asked.

"Sir?"

"Or will the old barbarism claim you in its turn?"

"No, sir," Caspar promised brightly.

Boy thought well before he answered: "I cannot truthfully say, sir. Not yet."

"Hmm. An honest answer, m'boy. Well, you may both go now. Major to private study until my divinity class at noon. Minor to Mr. Cusack's geometry class."

As they reached the door to the garden, Brockman spoke again: "Remember, m'boys—*patientes vincunt*, the patient conquer, as Piers Ploughman says. And we have a very long furrow to plough!"

"What did old chiefy say to you?" de Lacy asked when Boy returned to Old School.

"I couldn't understand it," Boy half-lied.

"The usual rot? 'Help me change the school, m'boy'?"

"That sort of thing, yes."

"Ignore it. Rubbish! This is a damn fine place as it is."

Boy secretly marvelled that the demotion of one bully could turn a school that de Lacy claimed to "hate hate *hate*" into a "damn fine place."

"Let's go out and start a snowman before it all melts," de Lacy said.

Chapter 6

Cossack—as Mr. Cusack was inevitably called—was a young man, bordering on not-so-young, with an earnest, sober face that nevertheless hinted at a sort of red-cheeked, watery-eyed dissipation. He had not a hair on his scalp. It shone like wax beneath a dome of glass. Yet he was not a hairless man. He had muttonchop whiskers that ran around to a shelf of beard beneath his chin. As soon as he saw Caspar he beamed with delight and cried out: "It's new!"

A raucous laugh, full of anticipation, went up from the rest of the class—a hundred and twenty-eight boys, for this was public school, not a tutorial.

"A new specimen of pond life! Let it come to me!" He beckoned Caspar into his open arms. The laughter redoubled. Caspar walked up to the podium.

"Does it have a name?"

"Stevenson mi, sir."

"Is that what its mother calls it, I wonder?"

Caspar drew close and said, in an undertone, "Caspar Stevenson, sir." Already he felt that a Christian name was somehow girlish and shameful.

Cossack lifted him bodily onto his lap. "Casparius, *filius Steveni*. Or are you a big family, hmm? Are you a legion? Is it *filius Stevenorum*?"

Caspar smiled weakly. Cossack had peppermint breath, with a hint of whisky behind it. He knew the smell of whisky from the way Mr. Morier-Watson sometimes smelt.

"Slow," Cossack judged. "It's a slow specimen. Cold-blooded, I shouldn't wonder. Perhaps it goes faster in the fine weather." He turned to the class. "They do, you know, these cold-blooded things in the pond." The class grinned and giggled, glad it wasn't them.

"But where does it swim in the pond? In the scum at the top, hmmm?" He glared at Caspar; his hands round Caspar's waist were growing hot. "Or in the dregs and sludge at the bottom?" He glowered at the class, who roared back their delight. "Pockets, sir!" someone shouted.

"Yes, look in his pockets," others took up the cry.

Cossack looked sternly at Caspar. "What does it keep in its pockets?"

"Nothing, sir."

"Nothing! Nothing? I expected at least a million pounds. But let us see… ahah!" And his hand pulled forth from Caspar's jacket pocket a greasy string of bacon rind. It surprised Caspar far more than it did the beak, who grinned knowingly. "Nothing, eh? Except its lunch—which it has brought to school with it!" The class roared again.

The next thing to appear was a broken top, then a large humbug, covered in fluff. "And its pudding!" Cossack said. "So this is how our new rich eat!" Then there was what looked like a marble but was, in fact, a glass eye. It rolled lugubriously on Cossack's desk, staring at the whole world impartially. Each item was held up for inspection by the class—"Nothing!…More nothing!" and so on, easy sarcasm. The class howled back their simple delight.

At first Caspar thought that Cossack was producing these things the way a conjuror pulls ribbons and pennies from people's ears and lapels; but soon it was clear that everything was, indeed, being turned out from his pockets. He looked around the class and realized: They had put these things there. In that confused mêlée in the Barn, just before chief had sent for him, hand after hand had dipped into his pockets, each depositing its pretext for Cossack's ridicule. He remembered thinking that the horseplay had been rather too exuberant. Of course—it had been a cover for their planting.

Cossack knew it, too. Caspar could tell that from the way the beak held up each item and accepted their laughter. Thank God, he thought, there was nothing but a handkerchief in his trouser pockets. He'd surely have felt it if they'd put anything in there.

The last item in his jacket was a folded page cut from a magazine. Cossack carefully unfolded it. His hands were covered in down, like the hairs between a pullet's feather stubs. The page was from a fashion journal; it showed a lady in a new patent hoop—with some crudely added modifications. Caspar saw, and also sensed in Cossack's sudden rigidity, that this was a new feature of the pocket-picking ritual. It bordered on the impermissible. For a long moment the beak hovered between the game and an outburst of rage. The game won, but only just. However, having decided to go on with the game, Cossack threw himself into it with all his former relish.

"And what has it in its trouser pockets?" he asked, plunging both hands firmly in.

To Caspar's relief there was only the handkerchief. He watched it emerge with reptilian slowness, tugged inch by inch in Cossack's fastidious thumb-and-finger grip. It was almost free when another folded sheet of paper fell out. He knew he had not put it there. For a moment both ignored it. Cossack's other hand was warm and heavy on Caspar's thigh. The fastidious hand plunged back into the other pocket. Both hands lumbered heavily around in those narrow confines, seeking further booty. Cossack's breath howled in and out through the labyrinth of his nostrils and sinuses, very pepperminty. Close up, Caspar could see each scarlet vessel on the man's cheeks and nose. The colour was intense.

He tickled. "No holes, hmmm?" Caspar squirmed and giggled under the fevered probing of those huge hams, closing over his thighs and slipping down into his groin. "No secret little ways, hmmm?" The class laughed; this was obviously the climax of the show.

"Bit of paper dropped, sir," one lad called.

"Read the paper!" several others chorused.

The fastidious hand went on delving while the other dangled, ape-like, to the floor and retrieved the folded sheet between two knuckles. The single hand unfolded it and laid it flat upon the desk. The message was upside down. Caspar turned it around. It said: *Why doth the Cossack so chiefly go about to undermine our trouser pockets?*

Caspar gulped and tried not to breathe. Cossack read the message several times, until the entire class had fallen into a hush. Only then did he look up. His eyes raked the ranks and files of boys; their eyes dropped as corn before the scythe. This time there could be no doubt: Someone really had gone too far.

"Swift minor," Cossack said, his eyes resting on one boy.

The boy looked quickly up and down again, trying not to smirk.

"Yes, I thought so. A poor piece of homage to your illustrious namesake, Swift, if I may say. Let me give you something better. From *Gulliver's Travels*, I adapt slightly: 'You are the most pernicious race of little odious vermin that nature ever suffered to crawl upon the surface of the earth.' Well, Swift, is that not more apposite!"

"Yes, sir," Swift mi grudged.

"Or *ibidem*: 'I am amazed'"—he transferred the paper from his ape hand to his fastidious one—"'how so impotent and grovelling an insect as you could entertain such inhuman ideas.' Is not that more to the point, Swift?"

"Yes, sir."

Hail fellow, well met
All dirty and wet:
Find out, if you can,
Who's master, who's man.

"From *My Lady's Lamentation.* Are you, by chance, in any doubt, Swift, who in this room is master, who is man? Because if you are, we may easily arrange for my young man's lamentation!"

"No, sir!" Swift hastened to reassure him.

Cossack tipped Caspar unceremoniously off his lap. "Down there, sir, where I may see you." He pointed to an empty seat in the front rank and then returned to Swift. "Since you seem so fond of that illustrious man—who had the misfortune to bear your name, but the fortune to die before you came along to besmirch it—you will come to my chambers before lockup and I shall give you his *Imitation of Horace*, one hundred lines of which you will put into Latin iambic dimeter."

"Yes, sir," Swift said miserably.

Cossack began again to quote:

I've often wish'd that I had clear,
For life, six hundred pounds a year...

His voice petered out and his eves strayed toward, then lingered on, Caspar. His lips smiled but his eyes were cold.

"You can't ever get the better of Cossack," Causton later told Caspar. "He knows everything. He's a sod, though. Literally, I mean. He'd bugger you as soon as beat you. Blenkinsop used to be a great favourite."

Caspar had no idea what this meant, but he stored the incomprehensible facts away.

They had only two parts of public school that day. The idle boys liked public school. Since the classes varied between one and two hundred in number, any individual was unlikely to get singled out too often. And, naturally, the masters would concentrate on their more able pupils—all except chief. In thirty minutes of divinity lesson, he could fire off fifty questions to as many pupils, striding among them, cracking his fingers, pulling ears, shouting, "Mmm? Mmm? Eh?...

Come on, m'boy, come on!" No one dared to feel the luxury of neglect in chief's class.

The rest of the day was taken up with private work-study and tutorials. For study periods boys in the Houses went back (naturally) to their studies, while those in Old School went to their messes in Langstroth. So, too, did the hundred and twenty boys in Hospice, which was identical in every way to Old School except that its members were housed in a different building, the former monastic hospice.

All tutorials were private—that is, parents were billed for them as extras and boys were, theoretically, free to choose which tutors they attended. In practice the end-of-term report hung over them all, severely qualifying that freedom. Tutorials, where the classes were down to a manageable thirty or forty boys, were held in the pupil rooms; in summer they would sometimes be held out on the moor. There were two tutors who were not on the public school staff. They had come as private tutors accompanying individual boys at some time in the past, had picked up a popular following because of the high quality of their lectures, and had stayed on after their original charges had left. Mr. Cheetham was called Chiz; Mr. L. St. John Peach was called Sinner. Chiz had a small stipend as warden of the Hospice, now a mere sinecure; Sinner had no official standing. Both relied entirely on tuition fees, which, in turn, depended absolutely on the size of their classes. The fee was three and a half pence per boy per tutorial, or £2. 11*s.* 6*d.* a term, of which two guineas went to the tutor, the remaining 9*s.* 6*d.* being kept by the school for the hire of the pupil rooms, coals, gas, etc. The four established masters (chief, Whymper, Carter, and Cossack) also held private tutorials under the same system and charges.

Without these extracurricular lessons no serious learning could have been imparted at the school—at least, to boys of an average laziness. Yet the ten poor boys from Langstroth who attended by right (and after all, it was for their supposed benefit the school had been founded and, at the dissolution of the monasteries under Henry VIII, endowed) had only the fifteen half-hours of public school to rely on their instruction, though it was their presence alone that justified the name "public" school.

Caspar fell in with one of these lads, Ingilby by name and a year his senior by age, as he went back over the causeway, intending to do some private study in his mess. He had a feeling that Ingilby had been waiting for him.

"What do you think of Cossack then?" Ingilby asked.

"Hells scaring," Caspar said.

"See who can throw a snowball farthest!"

The competition ended with their pelting one another around Langstroth market square, only becoming allies again when a miscast snowball struck a farmer in the back. They both ran, laughing and fearful, up one of the alleys. Ingilby pulled him into one of the cottage doorways.

"I live here," he said.

They peeped out into the lane. No one was following.

"Come on in. Our dad wants to meet you. He knows your guvnor."

"My guvnor?"

"Aye. He called here, that day he came to see chief. Our dad used to work for your guvnor before his accident."

"Wipe feet," Mrs. Ingilby said mechanically as they crossed the threshold. The kitchen was identical in layout to the Oldroyds' and almost identical in its contents, except that Mrs. Ingilby was obviously a cheesemaker on more than a domestic scale, for two cheese presses, one iron and one of wood, both on wheels, stood near the back door.

At the moment, though, she was baking havercakes—large, soft pancake-like rounds of oaten bread. She was in the middle of separating one from the hot "bakstone" with a knife. Then she lifted it with the shovel-like baking spittle and turned it in swirling wraiths of aromatic steam. When Caspar opened his mouth to introduce himself, a fountain of saliva shot half across the room.

Ingilby was sidling innocently toward the cake stool before the fire, where a havercake stood drying. But his mother well knew what he was at and caught him a sharp whack with the baking spittle before he could break off a chunk. He yelped, more with indignation than pain.

"Everything comes to them as waits," she said with a smile, not taking her eyes off Caspar while she dealt the blow.

"I'm Stevenson minor, m'm," Caspar said, wondering if the townsfolk recognized such names.

She certainly recognized the Stevenson part, for her smile doubled.

"Oh, you're very welcome, Master Stevenson." She wiped her floury hands on her apron and then did not know whether to offer one to be shaken.

Caspar stepped to her, holding out his hand. She shook it uncertainly; her skin was warm and soft.

"Your master was here..." she began, and then laughed at her mistake.

"Father!" Ingilby sneered, unfortunately drawing attention to himself just as he was trying again for the cake. Still laughing, she clouted him even harder and pushed him toward the back door. The handle of the cheese press against his hipbone doubled his punishment. He ran out of the back door rather than let Caspar see the tears he could not suppress. Outside someone was hitting at wood with a mallet.

"You may 'ave some cake, Master Stevenson," she said.

"Oh, no thank you, m'm," he answered politely.

Her face fell. "Oh well, suit yourself," she said, not understanding the convention. Then she saw his disappointment and, smiling again, broke him off a corner of the cake that lay drying on the stool: "Thou near lost that," she said. "Offers aren't doubled hereabouts!"

The cake made a delicious, crusty porridge in the saliva around his tongue.

"Good an' claggy!" she said, watching him chew the glutinous mass. "Aye. Thy father were 'ere—eay, two month back. My man were a Stevenson man, thou knows." She lifted the cooked havercake on the spittle and draped it from the "flake"—a sort of horizontal drying rack just below the ceiling near the back door. "They don't bake it this way in these parts." She wrinkled her nose at Caspar as though joining him with her in something not quite proper. "But I'm from Wensleydale, so it's my way."

Wensleydale was half a day's walk away.

"Go and see 'im," she said, nodding toward the yard, where the hammering was still going on.

A snowball stung his cheeks and eyes as soon as he poked his head out the door. Through the ringing of his ears he could hear Ingilby's staccato giggle. That was to teach Caspar for seeing him cry.

"Nay!" A roar came from the shed across the yard. A stocky, raven-haired man with a full beard came to the doorway and shouted something in a dialect so thick that Caspar, who could understand anything said in the East Riding of Yorkshire, could not decipher a single word. Ingilby turned huffily and leaned over the wall of the pigsty to scratch the sow.

"Master Stevenson!" the man said with a smile that was shrewd rather than broad. He held out his left hand for Caspar to shake. "Come in out the cold."

The shed was a carpenter's workshop, so well organized it seemed twice as large inside as out. A gluepot mewed and gurgled on a small coke brazier near the window. Mr. Ingilby—for it was obviously he—guided Caspar to a space beside its warmth. Only then did Caspar notice that he had no right hand. Instead his right forearm was bound up in a leather harness that had all kinds of straps and bindings, one set of which now held fast a mallet; when the man had stood at the door Caspar was certain he held the mallet in his hand.

He saw Caspar's fascinated stare. "Art right-handed?" he asked.

"Aye," Caspar said, flexing the fingers of his right hand as if that proved it.

"Did'st ever think as how the right hand is the idiot of the pair?"

"No!" Caspar said; nor could he believe it.

Mr. Ingilby smiled knowingly. He took up a scrap of timber and clamped it under the bench holdfast; then he laid a round mallet and chisel down beside it and wafted Caspar an invitation. "I'll prove it to thee," he said. "Cut me a square pocket in that wood."

Amused, Caspar picked up the tools. "How big?"

"One chisel-width will serve."

Caspar placed the chisel as perpendicular to the edge of the wood as his eye could judge it and set to tapping with the mallet, cutting cross-grain first.

"Now, see thee," Mr. Ingilby said after Caspar had made several cuts. "Which hand is doing precision work, and which is doing slave's work?"

Caspar thought and then chuckled in disbelief of his own eyes. "Maybe you're right, sir," he said as he laid down the tools.

"Aye," the other affirmed. "Happen I am."

"Did you lose your hand…?" Caspar began. "I mean…how?"

"Aye." Mr. Ingilby answered the unspoken part of the question. "On a Stevenson job. The very last week in Bramhope Tunnel. Eighteen forty-nine. A runaway wagon, it was, and me the fool that stopped it! But not before it had squandered that bit of me." He waved the vanished hand with a flourish. "But I have a Stevenson pension to be thankful for. To see me out. And Missus, if she overlives me." He began to tighten the straps that bound the mallet; then he stopped as if a new thought had struck him. "Thy father"—he spoke like an oracle—"is a great man. But even rarer"—now he looked searchingly at Caspar—"he's a good man, too. I've known men would die for 'im." He looked away. "Nay, I'd die for 'im."

Caspar felt tears pressing at the back of his eyelids, and a lump grew in his throat; this tribute was so unexpected. Mr. Ingilby had perhaps said more than he intended. At all events he now caught some of Caspar's embarrassment. He cleared his throat. "Anygate," he said, "I've a deal of respect for thy father. If I may do aught for thee by way of service, thou needs but ask on. I'll do it gladly." Fussily he resumed the work he had been at before Caspar and his son arrived, a plain coffin of deal boards.

Caspar had once heard his mother say to his father, "I never see a crow fly overhead without thinking 'how may I put that crow to our advantage'!" The moment the words left her lips he knew he was of the same company. *Yes!* he had thought. *That's the way to be. That's me too!*

So now he thought feverishly for some service Mr. Ingilby could render him. All he could think of on the spur of the moment was that he might need a good, stout study cupboard; but even before the thought was complete he turned it down. Study cupboards were of little use to a roe, for as long as he was in the place he remained at every pharaoh's beck and call. No, he'd think of something.

Then suddenly, with no thought at all, he heard himself say: "Teach me to carpent."

"You what?"

"To be a carpenter." He laughed nervously; now he had said it he didn't even know if he wanted to be able to "carpent."

Mr. Ingilby broke into a slow smile. "Aye," he said with decision. "By God, so I will! I don't know what thy father would say, but if such is thy wish—so be it. When?"

"How long d'you work?"

"Till seven as a rule. It all depends."

"From half-past six, then, to seven, three times a week."

Mr. Ingilby tousled Caspar's hair in delight. "Eay! So I've gotten a 'prentice, and 'is name is Stevenson, son to Lord John!"

Only Stevenson men were allowed to call his father "Lord" John, which had been his nickname in his navvying days. Caspar felt all at home, and the feeling was warm.

As he left, Mrs. Ingilby pressed a flake of havercake smothered in blue-milk cheese into his hand. It was a banquet. How he envied young Ingilby, too, as he trudged back across the causeway for Latin theme. It was a thousand-mile walk.

He was barely through the yard gate when someone dealt him a vicious thump in the back. It almost sent him sprawling.

"Hi!" He turned around, snarling, and threw a punch before he even knew who his attacker was. It turned out to be Swift mi, who had put that enigmatic note in his pocket for Cossack to find, and had got a Latin impost for his reward. Soon they were fighting as hard as the slippery cobbles and the snow would allow.

Before they reached any resolution, however, Swift major, head of pharaohs at Old School, came upon them. He pulled them apart by their collars, effortlessly. "Barn heating for both of you," he said as he let go. He walked on without a backward look.

Swift mi smiled at Caspar, as if there had never been the slightest animosity between them. Caspar smiled back; he had enjoyed the fight as far as it went.

"Sorry," Swift mi said, watching his brother all the way down the cloisters. "He can be hells decent at home, you know."

"So can my bro," Caspar said. It seemed to give him a bond with Swift mi. "What's a Barn beating?"

"Oh, a light paddling with a hairbrush or a slipper by the King o' the Barn. Only it's in front of all the other chaps."

"When?"

"That's the worst. No set time. They can send for you any time between seven and lockup. Perhaps Trench'll be decent, seeing it's his first day. If you want to fight, by the way, all you do is call out 'Ring! Ring!' at the top of your voice and everyone gathers around and forms a ring. Then you may fight. They can't beat you for that. That's legal. But what we were doing was plain ragging and really we ought to have got a house beating for it. We're hells lucky, really."

They were lucky, too, that Trench came out and called, "Baaaaaaaarns!" very soon after seven that evening, so they hadn't long to stew. Everybody ran indoors and found something in or near the Barn to busy himself with. The tradition was that although a fellow was beaten in full view of everyone, nobody watched. Instead they all sat and pretended to bury their heads in a book, or a letter home, or making a model—any other business but watching the whacks. In reality they found every way to peep without being seen: peering through fingers, staring at concealed bits of looking-glass, beetling their brows, and straining their eye muscles. A casual onlooker would be astonished that thirty or so boys could be so indifferent to the torture of several of their fellows, until he learned that to be caught openly watching was to join the tortured boys, bending bare-bottomed over the top oak table.

Today five bare bottoms gleamed palely in the dark of the winter evening. Five boys bent over, resting on the oak, mutely waiting. Again Caspar had that embarrassing erection, but beneath the table; no one, he thought, would notice. The beatings went from left to right. No one had ever worked out whether it was better to go first or last. The first victim got it over with quickest but the King o' the Barn's hand was then freshest. The last got the whacks from the tiredest arm but had to endure the sounds—and the sight, for they were not allowed to look away—of all the previous assaults. The argument was endless.

So, too, was the argument about which was worse, hairbrush or shoe. Opinions pro and anti varied, depending mainly on which weapon the protagonists or antagonists had sampled last.

Caspar was to be whacked third. Boy (for failing to reconcile Malaby's carpet and Euclid) was last. And Trench was to let them sample the arguments in favour of the hairbrush. Caspar was soon glad not to be next to Boy, for there was one further refinement to the ritual. Before each thrashing Trench called out "Turn!" whereupon the boy about to get it turned to face the one whose thrashing would come next. And there they lay, present and proximal victim, eyeball to eyeball, proximal seeing in present's face an augury of his own punishment, blow by blow.

A Barn beating was a standard four whacks, unless the offence would normally have merited a house beating and only the caprice of the pharaoh had made it otherwise; then the boy got six. Today Swift mi and Caspar were getting six, the other three would have the regular four apiece.

"Turn!" Trench said.

Caspar saw a flurry of hair beyond the back of the head of the fat boy next to him. The whacks sounded very distant. The victim made no sound.

The hammering of his heart at the pit of his neck drowned everything. Surely, he thought, it must be ringing around the Barn? Surely, at the very least, it must be making the table shiver? His midriff felt very cold without the trousers.

"Turn!"

The fat boy turned, looked in mortal anguish at Caspar, then shut his eyes so tightly they vanished into twin craters of puckered flesh. Was it worse to be whacked if you were fat? Were there more nerves? Or was it better because of more padding?

Whack! That didn't sound distant. And if the fat boy's response was any guide, it was worse to be fat. "Hooooo!" He let out a draught of foul breath into Caspar's face, stopping him from daring to inhale for a moment. As the other three blows followed, Caspar saw him blanch, bite, and bare his teeth like a death's-head, shiver, and rise to the edge of whimpering. Caspar could have done with someone bolder to his left. How he wished there was some magic phrase that would make the clock slip a bit. *Please,* he thought, *I don't want to escape it, but I do want it to be so that I'm walking away, rubbing my bum. Please! Now!!*

"Turn!"

Swift's face. Swift mi. Swift winked. He winked back. *Youch!* Pain, pain, pain. A stinging radiated from high on his right buttock. Nothing existed now but the skin on his bottom. It strained for the next. His ears, too, strained for every little clue that would tell of the descent of that fierce arm. Couldn't there be some way of—*eeek!* That was worse, that was worse. Lower down, same side. The stinging area was doubled. Concentrate on your hands; they're not in pain at all. Lucky hands. Think of them. Lucky, lucky—*wham!* Oh my God, what has happened to time?

The whole of his right buttock was like flesh in the aftermath of wasps. If his had been an ordinary offence, the next whack would have been the last. But this was only halfway! For the next three he lay as still and unreacting as possible, deliberately thinking of nothing, concentrating on staring blankly into Swift's mask—which he purposely put out of focus—and on not twitching a muscle.

Trench laid them the same way—top, middle, lower buttock. Not a square inch of skin there did not shriek its protest as he walked away. Trench then stood where Caspar had bent, and gave Swift his six.

Down in the study passages Caspar was surprised how soon the sting went. It wasn't so bad, really—except for those actual moments and the waiting, bent over and bare. "A light paddling"—Swift mi was right, actually. He wasn't a bad sort, Swift mi. Caspar began to feel brave. Nothing at home had ever prepared him for this. His father had never raised a hand to them; he could be terrifying enough without any violence. So all this hitting and pain had been novel and frightening. He thought he had come through it rather well.

Then he saw Blenkinsop standing in the open door of his own study and smiling. "Hello, young 'un. You took it pretty well, I thought."

"Did you see?" Caspar asked. He felt very manly to be talking so to a senior fellow.

"Every stroke. How d'you feel? Does it hurt much?"

He was being very pleasant. For a moment Caspar forgot how bestial Blenkinsop had been to Boy. "It stings a bit."

"Ah!" Blenkinsop gripped his arm and pulled him into the study. "I've got the very stuff for that. Rub it on now and by this time tomorrow there won't be a mark to show."

"No, honestly, Blenkinsop. I'll be all right. Don't bother."

"No bother at all, young 'un. As a matter of fact, I've taken a liking to you. A great liking. So it'll be a pleasure. Let's see now."

Caspar stood awkwardly, wishing he could just turn and run away.

"Come on!" Blenkinsop squatted jovially in front of him and began undoing Caspar's flybuttons.

The young boy giggled in embarrassment. "I'll do it," he said. "You're tickling." He turned around and finished unbuttoning himself.

Blenkinsop tore his trousers down and breathed heavily inward between his teeth.

"Is it bad?" Caspar asked, trying to crane around and look over his own shoulder.

"It will be if we're not quick." Blenkinsop swept a pile of books off the table. "Lie down here. No, no. Face down!"

For the second time in less than an hour Caspar found himself face down on oak and wondering exactly what was about to happen. He wasn't a bad chap, Blenkinsop. It was jolly good of him to take all this trouble.

Blenkinsop tipped something cold and creamy out of a bottle onto his buttocks and began to rub it in with a slow, hypnotic relish. It was very soothing, Caspar had to allow.

"Tchah! Trench puts them all over the shop," Blenkinsop said scornfully. "He's no craftsman, I'll vow. I can lay down six and not vary it by the breadth of a hair. You'd have a six-week shiner if I'd done this."

"I'm lucky, then." Caspar giggled.

"You ask Gordon what I did to that boil on his bum!" Blenkinsop was relishing the memory. Then he came back to the present. "Oh, I wouldn't hurt *you*, young 'un. I'm hells fond of you." He massaged on into the silence. Caspar thought he could detect a shiver in him, in his hands and voice, just the same as under the blankets last night. When Blenkinsop spoke again his tone was a lot softer. "Did you get stiff today, too, eh? Did you get the bone?" When Caspar didn't answer, Blenkinsop laughed. "I see you did. Your little bottom is blushing, you know. Have you got a bone now?"

"No," Caspar said.

"Do you know how to get one?"

"I don't want to know. I wish you wouldn't talk about it so. I don't like it one bit."

Blenkinsop gave a tolerant laugh and patted him on the bottom. "I thought you'd be grateful to me for stopping these bruises. Go on, up you get!"

Caspar stood, now feeling sheepish. He didn't want to seem ungrateful. "It's kind of you, Blenkinsop. I am grateful, really."

"Perhaps you'll do me a little favour, then?" Blenkinsop asked casually.

"If I can."

"Cut over to Crecy and give this book to a chap there called Garrett, would you?"

Caspar was delighted to get out of Blenkinsop's study so easily; he had feared something more was about to happen, though exactly what he could not say.

"It's hells cold out. You'd best take my scarf, young 'un."

It was cold outside. Caspar had to ask the way to Crecy and was told to go through a small triumphal arch, past the boghouse, and over the games field. He found his way easily enough; the snow brightened everything outside. Crecy was nothing like Old School. Everything looked clean. Everyone had studies. It all seemed very organized.

He felt the hostile, polite gaze of the Crecy boys upon him as he stood inside the door and waited for someone to fetch Garrett. Like bees in the same apiary, the boys did not venture any depth into neighbouring hives. He marvelled that he had so soon become an Old School man; if he and Boy hadn't been delayed by the quarantine, they might have been in Crecy, perhaps. Then they'd feel like this about going inside Old School. What made people one thing or the other like that? Could you tell one person he was a…a *glash*, say, and another that he was a *glish*, the deadly foe of all the *glashes*, and would they then fight each other? That would be quite funny.

Garrett came and took the book, looking at it a little mystified. He told Caspar to thank Blenkinsop. Caspar ran all the way back over the snowy playing field, dancing, leaping with sheer *joie de vivre* that he had survived so much and felt so good. Even old Blenkinsop wasn't so bad, really. It was hells kind of him to do that thing about the bruises.

He was rather surprised to bump into Blenkinsop just as he was about to skip through the triumphal arch.

"Hello," he said. "Do you want your scarf?"

Blenkinsop shoved him roughly back into the dark. "You know what I want," he said. He gripped the little boy firmly by the arm and hustled him over to the boghouse. *Christ,* Caspar thought. *Am I going to get whacked again? What for now?* He felt like giving up all attempt to understand.

When they reached the boghouse Blenkinsop shoved him just inside the door. "Here," he said. "*There's* a bone for you!"

He guided Caspar's hand to his—well, it was more like gristle than bone, Caspar thought. Hot. And gristly-slippery. And lumpy. And very big. Huge.

"Go on, then!" Blenkinsop said.

"Go on what?"

"Move your hand, you fool! Fiend me!"

Caspar let go.

"No! Like this!" And he showed him how to fiend.

Caspar obeyed with fascinated curiosity. The effect his action was having on Blenkinsop was very weird—the noises he made, the change in his breathing, the way he swayed, the jerks of his hips. Feeling nothing himself, Caspar listened and observed these transports in the other.

And that was when he remembered his vow. If ever he could hurt Blenkinsop... well, couldn't he just hurt him now! He almost giggled aloud.

With the same gleeful curiosity he reached both hands over and, with all the force he could muster, bent that long, gristly stick double, this way and that, just as you would try to break a green branch off a tree.

Blenkinsop's shriek rang out across the field—a thunderclap of pain and rage that Caspar did not wait to hear out. Its dying fall reached him as he leaped through the triumphal arch and ran to find Boy and bear him the joyful tidings.

The story had a greater effect than Caspar had dared to hope. The two older boys—de Lacy was with Boy—seemed able to imagine the pain much more easily than Caspar had. In fact, its intensity had surprised him. But he only had to tell them what he had done and then at once began to mimic Blenkinsop's agony, doubling over and saying "Christ!" and "Ooooh!" and—with great relish—"the poor sod!"

"You'd better keep out of his way for some time," de Lacy warned.

"I know how to deal with him," Caspar said. "Swift mi told me."

But de Lacy's warning was too late. Blenkinsop was already coming down the passage, shouting "Stevenson mi! You little vermin!" at the top of his voice. Caspar darted behind a cupboard, waiting his time. Blenkinsop halted at each cupboard, sure that Caspar was in one of them. He kicked them and yanked open the doors in mounting fury, until at last he reached the one that concealed—though it did not enclose—Caspar. He had been waiting for the moment. He darted out, taking Blenkinsop sufficiently unawares to slip past him and race away to the Barn. Blenkinsop recovered quickly, though, and was almost out of the passage before Boy said, "Come on. He'll kill him if he catches up with him."

When they reached the Barn, Caspar was backed firmly against the bootroom door and Blenkinsop stood over him, panting hard and in no hurry to strike. Boy thought Caspar was going to try to duck at the last minute, making Blenkinsop smash his hand into the door; but Caspar's scheme was even cleverer than that.

As soon as Blenkinsop drew back his fist, Caspar cried "Ring! Ring!" and ducked out beneath the surprised Blenkinsop's arm. At once he took up the stance of a bareknuckle pugilist and waited for Blenkinsop to follow. Grinning at this show of pluck—or cheek—the others began to cluster around and form a ring.

"Come on, Blenkinsop," they cried. "In the ring!"

For a moment Caspar feared he would take the challenge, and then the whole bright plan would shatter. But in the nick of time Blenkinsop realized how ridiculous he would look in a ring with a boy nearly eight years his junior, and so, scowling, he walked away. Caspar had sense enough not to dance and crow.

"Don't ever let him get you alone," de Lacy warned. "He'd scatter you abroad!"

Chapter 7

Since neither Boy nor Caspar suffered any deformity, nor laboured under any physical infirmity, nor had his uniqueness stamped upon him in any remarkable way, both settled very quickly to life at Fiennes. A week after their arrival no stranger could have singled them out. They spoke of grunts and villains, beaks and roes, they troughed and said the food was shent—or even hells shent—as if these words had always been plain English. And whenever a pharaoh bellowed: "Roe!" they were not always (as they had been in the beginning) the last to join the line that quickly formed—for the last roe was the one who did the pharaoh's bidding. Sometimes the pharaoh would want the roe to pick up a fallen book, or open a window, or brew tea; at other times it was "Get me a quart of beer from Ma Webster's" or "Take this wager to old Purse—and don't let the beaks catch you." On the coldest days they would send a roe to go and sit on a bog seat to get it warm before the pharaoh came and used it.

All of this the two boys accepted as part of the natural and universal order of things. It was at least as natural as the endless round of Caesar and Livy and Pliny and Tacitus and Greek verbs and Euclid that filled their official hours. But they grew increasingly aware of the deep gulf between official school, both public and private, and the unofficial sort of school that thrived out of sight of chief and the beaks. The difference was probably less marked in the Houses, where each boy had his own study and slept in his own cubicle in the dormitory and where the hours of seven to nine each evening were passed in supervision.

But in Old School and in Hospice, beaks were rarely seen after seven, and their absence was certain from lockup at eight until six-thirty the following morning. That hour before eight, when boys were still at liberty to go to Langstroth or walk about the courtyards, was filled with a rising sense of excitement. For years Boy could never see gaslights loom out of the mist without thinking of that moment when the grown-up world could cease to exist. All his experience became tuned to it, everything referred to it, however trivial or everyday—even the crunch of gravel underfoot or the playful shout of a fellow hidden in the dark, over the wall, in another quadrangle, running on the moor; or the chime of the quarter-to-eight bell, rolling over the wet wastes between Langstroth church and the school, drawing boys magically inward...All of these were vibrant with a promise of those glorious hours when outside rules would crumble and ancient traditions supersede them.

For at eight the King o' the Barn became a primeval Lord of Misrule. Pharaohs and roes all but ceased to exist as boys naturally sorted themselves into the brave, the foolhardy, the merely willing, and the outright cowards or weeds—categories that cut through all divisions of age and official status.

A born scholar could lock himself away in one of the cupboards in the outer passages, which he could either inherit by seniority or hire from a less bookish inheritor. There, with a "candlestick" (fashioned from a bent book cover, holed at the ridge thus formed), he could do his Latin and Greek for as long as he could endure the intense cold and damp—and as long as he could tolerate the happy shrieks of his fellows, the smell of grilling chops and cheese, and the sweet, hot aroma of mulled ale.

But few were so steadfast when Olympic games called. The run up the Barn, the heel-hard launch from a mattress, the mad head-over-heels light, and the cushioned landing in the twenty other mattresses piled against the wall—Homer had no such thrills. And when that game palled, there were buck-buck, piggy-back jousting, build the human wall, kill you, where's Jonah, Jacob's ladder; the variety of ways to get dirty, tear clothes, bleed, sweat, and laugh and laugh was endless. There were crazes and fads, too. For a couple of weeks that term there was a craze for sliding on one's back down a flight of stairs holding two brim-full pots of beer—trying not to spill a drop, of course.

For quieter moments there were ghost stories, told around the dying fire. Several of the fellows could make the blood run cold, but the doyen was Randall, of the lower dorm; he could even frighten himself. In fact, that was his trick. He appeared to be discovering the twists and turns of the story in the very moment he told it. In that way he kept every muscle in every body in his circle of hearers screwed up to a barely endurable tension as they watched him discover terror upon terror, and followed him into that dark. His true greatness lay in the fact that in all his stories—whether about a headless dog upon the moor, a disembodied hand in a vicarage, or a beautiful but deadly ghost-child seen only on bright summer days—the person so haunted or plagued would apparently triumph; the ghost would vanish, its manifestations cease…and *then!* Randall knew a hundred different ways of saying "then" and rolling his eyes piteously and implying such terrible compassion for the hapless victim, who must now be unmanned, unnerved, and demoralized, whose hair must blanch, whose blood curdle, while nameless horrors were loose once more around him. Randall made boys glad to flee to beds in crowded dorms and pull the blankets down hard over their heads, for flickering gaslight got every shadow pregnant with numinous fears.

And there were surprising evenings when nothing happened, no special games, no great spinning of yarns. Especially as the end of term and Christmas drew on, evenings of this sort grew more frequent. Boys would sit in groups of ten or so around the fires (either the proper ones or "tramps' fires" built here and there on the stone floors) and talk of home and the adventures of last summer—visits to Egypt, Greece, the Alps. Boy was popular on these occasions, and his stories of the railways his father had built were always in demand. They loved to hear of quaking bogs subdued, of holes drilled through mountains, of valleys spanned by soaring arches and estuaries ringed with causeways of stone; of the strange customs of the navvies and their extraordinary capacity for labour; of how the French bourgeoisie rode out in their carriages from Rouen to watch the mad English workers moving prodigies of earth and rock; of how tunnels could be driven from opposite sides of a hill to meet not an inch out of line; of steam piledrivers that could crack a nut under a ten-ton weight yet leave its kernel intact; of rolling mills where men with tongs could catch the leading end of a red-hot ribbon of rail, moving at the speed of a galloping horse, and bend it around for a second pass through the rollers that had disgorged it; of machines that punched rivet holes in iron plate in the most complex patterns, controlled not by men but by sequences of holes in little metal plates no bigger than playing cards; of rascally foreigners who wouldn't pay, and the devious and often terrible ways that Stevenson's used to extract their dues.

For many at Old School these were their first, informal lessons in geography and modern history—indeed, in life itself, for what could the sons of gentry and aristocrats and clergymen know of that vast commercial world which now sustained them all? And for Boy's part, he soon saw the justice of Carnforth's unthinking remark, the first night, that you couldn't put anyone you knew, friend or not, through the torture of drumming-in. Those nights of misrule welded bonds between boy and boy that time itself could not sever.

And that made the official House beatings all the more remarkable. House beatings were at the fixed hour of eight, immediately after the callover that followed lockup. They had been instituted by chief to allow the pharaohs to keep House discipline without undue reference to the beaks; the system had been imposed, willy-nilly, on Old School and Hospice, though both places lacked the organization to sustain it. In the Houses there were deep divisions between juniors and seniors. Juniors were as scullerymaids; seniors were lords of the earth. The sort of discipline inherent in the pharaoh system came naturally with such divisions. But in Old School a pharaoh might find himself called upon to thrash a boy after callover, when half an hour later they would almost certainly be ragging together, sharing toasted cheese, sitting side by side swapping yarns, or fiending in some cupboard or corner. In practice, it meant that some beatings were fairly perfunctory while others were needlessly savage, depending on the relationship between the pharaoh and his victim; and since, according to the ritual, each stroke was given by a different pharaoh, a beating could consist of any permutation of stingers and ticklers.

In fact, since flesh is quick to mend, the ritual was worse than the caning. Immediately after callover, the day's tally lined up outside the head pharaoh's study to sign the beating book, wherein were recorded the offence, the time it was apprehended, and by whom; and there was a blank column where the number of whacks was later filled in. No boy knew how many he was to get until he had got them. There was no set scale; the offence that drew two whacks one day might get four the next. A boy who squirmed or gasped or cried out always got more than one who was rock still and manly about it.

On signing the book the boy had to say: "I admit this offence and accept the punishment." There was provision to appeal to chief, but only *after* the beating. "There'd be no point in going before, would there?" Malaby said. "You'd have nothing to complain about." When all had signed they went up to the Barn where the most junior of them had to shout "All out of the Barn!" All the lucky ones then went to the passages, where they could lurk and listen; but to be caught watching was to join the next day's quota. That was the only good thing about a House beating: None but the pharaohs saw it; even the other victims had to turn their backs.

Once the Barn had emptied, the boys about to be thrashed had to pull all the tables and chairs to the sides of the room, leaving the centre free for a good run. They had to put a single chair facing the wall at one end and then go to the other end, take off their trousers and underpants (if they wore them), and wait, also facing the wall. Soon—though it could be anything up to five minutes—the four pharaohs, each carrying a cane, came up from their studies. The King o' the Barn was also there, to spy out strangers and to invite them to the following day's ceremony.

The head of pharaohs called the waiting boys out for thrashing one by one, not in their order in the book, not in seniority, not in alphabetical order, not in any order a boy could predict. When a boy's name was called, he turned and floated through a half-real space and time to the chair at the far end, hung his trousers over its back, bent over it, and grasped the farther pair of legs as low down as he could without lifting his feet off the ground. Usually a pharaoh stood there to whack his wrists with the cane if he didn't bend taut enough.

Then a pharaoh would take a run at the bending boy and deal him one fierce thrash. The others would watch closely to see if he squirmed or puckered up the flesh of his buttocks. If he did, they added to the previously agreed tally of strokes. One by one each of the pharaohs, going in strict rotation of their seniority, took his run and gave his thrash. They were actually allowed to run the full length of the Barn but rarely did so—only for truly dreadful offences like cheeking a pharaoh or publicly bringing odium upon the school in front of villains in Langstroth. In any case, the long run added nothing but more terror to the ordeal, for even in a short run a hefty pharaoh could get up enough swing to "tap the claret," as it was called.

The thrashes were not regular. Sometimes three or four laughing pharaohs would come down like wagons in a train, right, left, right, within the twinkling of an eye. (This fashion had started when some pharaohs had watched six men with sledgehammers piledriving the stays for a circus tent at Ingleton Fair, at the rate of four hammer blows every second. For a while after that every boy got four thrashes, whatever his offence, until the pharaohs had perfected the technique.) Sometimes the pharoahs would stop and gossip or tell a joke between strokes; and woe betide the boy who, thinking his punishment was over, stood and stretched while this happened.

Three or four was the usual number of whacks—far more commonly doled out than five or six, or one or two.

During that first term Caspar got House beatings for fighting without a ring (three times), whistling (twice), singing annoyingly, pretending to smoke a pencil, trespassing on pharaohs' corridor (in fact, he bent to pick up a book that had dropped just inside the imaginary line dividing pharaohs' from common corridors, so technically only his fingertips had trespassed), and failing to soak himself well after morning run. He got Barn beatings for wrong buttons, ostentatious tie knot, smiling in prayers, humming, running upstairs when not on a pharaoh's errand, having both hands in his pockets, and inking an anchor on his forearm. Canes, slippers, and hairbrushes fell upon his naked buttocks eighty-six times between that first Barn beating and the last full day of term. Blenkinsop never again offered his balm.

Eighty-six was not an unusual number. Boy got ninety whacks for very similar offences. In a way, it hardly interfered with their ordinary school life. They grew used to sitting on blood scabs and bruises of baboon-like hue. That extrasensitive pluck of blue-black flesh when the muscle beneath it grew taut became normal; they would have missed it far more acutely than they noticed its presence. They quickly learned that the sting of the cane was short-lived; Caspar even managed to recite the nine-times table right through to himself, without a break in the rhythm, during one House beating of four whacks. And the ritual of looking at and displaying to the rest of the dorm a particularly fine set of "cuts," as the bloodlined bruises were called, became one of the fun parts of the day.

The juvenile mind is so wonderfully adaptive that it was to be many years before the oddity of all this became apparent to Boy and Caspar. The offences they were beaten for were committed between the hours of six in the morning and lockup at eight. Yet after lockup such offences vanished from the criminal calendar; they might be indulged with impunity—often encouraged by the very boys who, moments earlier, had solemnly and sternly punished the identical acts! You might as well wonder why, on a day when you had broken, say, three commandments, God might still send the sun; while, on a day when you were exceptionally pious, the skies might open and the blizzards howl. Justice at Fiennes was every bit as capricious as all the other myriad forms of retribution which flow from mighty but ineffable systems.

But this is not to say that the hours of school were all dour while those of lockup were all excitement. School had its pleasures, too. Having been privately tutored so long, both Boy and Caspar were ahead of all but the most bookish of their fellows. As latecomers they had taken care not to shine too brilliantly and so had a lot of scholastic capital left to fritter; in short, it soon became clear to them that they could pretty well float along for a couple of terms while they tasted all the delights the school could offer and which no home could ever supply.

Hours that might have been—that ought to have been—spent in private study in their mess at Purse's were spent helping "Mrs. Purse," as they called her. She took in washing from several of the beaks and it was the two young boys' delight, on a cold winter afternoon, to stoke up the fire under the copper and watch the linen bubble in the grey suds or see the swirling wraiths of steam hurtle at the ceiling when they lifted the clothes up for a dunking. And every splash sent droplets outward in steaming ballistic arcs, like the smoking fragments of an exploding mine.

If Mrs. Purse caught them at such play, she would haul them roughly about the outhouse as if trying to jerk one of their limbs out of joint. And all the while they would shriek with laughter at her harmless ferocity.

"Oh, Mrs. Purse," Caspar would say, "you do cook the most sumptuous tripe!" And he would lift out a shirt of Cossack's or one of Whymper's drawers.

"Be off! Be off!" she would shriek back in a frenzy, fetching him a vicious blow that missed by careful inches.

"Honestly," Boy would chime in, "all the fellows would rather have that than our breakfast porridge. You should just try it!"

And she would run after them in a howling frenzy, pausing to catch her breath whenever it seemed likely she might catch them.

Later, when they came back for their savoury tea, she would call them "ill-thriven tastrils" and set the food before them as malevolently as if it were poison. And when they wolfed it down, for every day it was the most succulent food they had ever had, she would say they were "all gob and no gawm" as if she spoke a judge's sentence. They should be "skelped with the spell of a chair," she would threaten with glowering eyes as she pressed havercakes of treacly parkin into their pockets and watched them run back over the causeway to school.

Only once did Blenkinsop try to waylay Caspar—in the town, for he knew that in the school Caspar would only call for a ring. Caspar had been hanging around the market, helping to beat the cows from pen to pen, and was hurrying back to a tutorial class when Blenkinsop stepped out from a gateway, saw him, and stood so as to block the path.

The house within the gate was the doctor's, so Caspar guessed that Blenkinsop had not deliberately waylaid him; this meeting was sheer chance.

"Changed your mind about me, young 'un?" Blenkinsop asked. His tone was friendly enough.

"How, Blenkinsop?"

"That was pretty shent what you did."

"I only did it because of what you did to my bro."

"Ah! So you won't do it again?"

"No!" Caspar cried.

Blenkinsop grinned. "That's the lad!" he said, walking away. "See you after dark, same place."

Caspar let him get some way away and then shouted: "I won't! I won't fiend with you. Ever!"

Blenkinsop turned, looked at Caspar a long time, then shrugged and walked away. This lack of open threat was somehow even more menacing than any straightforward vow of revenge. For days Caspar went in fear of meeting Blenkinsop at some place where a cry of "ring!" would be useless; every blind corner held the dread of it. But nothing happened and, as day followed day, the fear subsided.

For Caspar there were his "apprentice hours" at Mr. Ingilby's workshop, too.

"Do'st thou want to knock together one or two knickle-knacks?" he asked Caspar right at the outset. "Or learn the trade from A to ampersand?"

"Learn the trade," Caspar said without second thought.

"Five year," Ingilby warned. "Five year to get the rudiments." He saw the boy's face fall. "Happen thou'll frame to it sooner," he said comfortingly. "Being son to Lord John."

Caspar just knew he would. But by the end of his first lesson he was less sure, for he spent the entire half hour down in the pit at the dusty end of the saw; and all they had to show for it was two eight-inch planks of elm.

"We'll cut sapwood off tomorn," Ingilby promised.

Caspar groaned and wondered if strength and voluntary movement would ever return to his arms.

"Nay, see thee," Ingilby warned and patted the two bits of elm with the stump of his hand. "Them's thy masters now. Thou'll stick by them while they're worked up into aught to be proud of. Thou'll know every bend and twist of grain, where they're kindly an' where they're stunt. They'll learn thee! And be glad they're not oak."

And so it was to be, lesson by lesson. Ingilby's bible was *Nicholson's Guide to Carpentry, General Framing and Joinery*, from among whose patterns Caspar chose to make a simple Jacobean-style occasional table. Its only joint was a tenon, stopped and haunched for the top, tongued and pegged at the legs. It took him all term to make and polish. Then he looked up its price in Ingilby's other bible, *The Preston Cabinet and Chair-maker's Book of Prices Agreed upon July 1802* and found this table was worth but five shillings and sixpence.

"That's not much, is it, Mr. Ingilby?" he complained.

But Ingilby only smiled. "Now, now," he chided. "That's no way for a master's son to be thinking." And his eyes twinkled as he spoke.

*

Their times in Langstroth filled only a portion of their free hours at Fiennes. With their schoolfellows they spent many afternoons rambling over the dales; their compulsory morning run up Whernside did nothing to blunt their appetite for those wild, open places, swept with the keen, clean air.

In fact, in connection with that break-of-day run Caspar had the honour of founding a new school tradition that very first term. He fretted at being so slow to descend Whernside after he had reached the cairn at the top of the run. Being athletic, he could run uphill quickly enough, but the way down was so steep that mere length of leg could always carry the race, and the wheezing and panting boys he had passed on the way up could, if they were taller, easily regain their advantage on the way down.

Then one day—this was during his third week at school—he was hanging around the gasworks shed, hoping to cadge a raw carrot off Purse as soon as he had finished filling the gas retorts with coal. Caspar loved the pungent, tarry, sulphurous smells of the place and often wished there was a pudding with just such a flavour. (Once, on one of Stevenson's workings, he had watched some scaffolders heating a drum of coal-tar creosote, and one of them had told him the dark liquid was their pudding. He had been mortified when they had failed to invite him to share it, for no pudding had ever smelled more appetizing, and the truth had almost broken his heart. Now, all his life, he knew he would be haunted by a lost, never-attainable gastronomic delight.)

He dipped the corner of his handkerchief in the tar that floated on the water that sealed the gasholder. Tonight, he thought, already savouring the pleasure, he could lie in bed and sniff at it through the cloth.

"Thou'rt fond o' yon tar, I can see," Purse said.

Caspar noticed that Purse was about to put some beautifully curved pieces of wood on the retort fire. "What's those?" he asked.

Purse looked at them. "Staves off an old barrel. The hoop's rusted, see thou."

Until that moment a barrel had always been just a barrel to Caspar; his mind's eye had never dismantled it into hoops and staves. He held out his hands. Purse gave him the stave he had been about to burn.

Delighted with its shape, he turned it over and over in his hands, marvelling at the skill that curved and formed it. And then it suddenly came to him that this was exactly what he needed to get quickly down Whernside of a morning. He begged three of them off Purse—one to mess up, one to get perfect, and one to spare—and ran all the way to Ingilby's, where he drilled a hole in the toe of one and threaded it through with stout hemp cord.

Next morning he was delighted to find that it took very little practice to go skimming—or "staving" as everyone quickly called it—down the slopes that led back to school. The best way, he found, was to stretch one foot ahead as a sort of brake; light sideways flicks with the heel of this foot would also correct the course if need arose. It took both hands to haul on the cord and keep the toe of the stave from digging into the ground and sending the "staver" tumbling headlong.

"Wheeeee!" he screeched as he staved down through thickets of stumbling legs.

"Whee-hee-hee!" he cackled as runners leaped aside and stood and watched and marvelled and cheered.

And "whooo-oa!" he called in an altogether different tone as he saw himself headed for the tall, blond, burly frame of the headmaster, standing legs apart, arms akimbo, right in his path.

"Can't stop, sir!" Caspar yelled, longing to shut his eyes against this nightmare, but not daring even to blink.

Chief was prudent enough to step aside before Caspar could scatter him like a solitary ninepin. Caspar came to a chill, dusty halt about five yards beyond. He turned to see chief's beckoning finger curling and straightening with ominous deliberation.

His approach was as curved and as sidelong as the stave he held in his hand. Chief stretched forth his vast pink paw; the piece of wood seemed a mere toy when he grasped it.

He turned it this way and that, looking at the cord, then at the slope, then at Caspar. Meanwhile a knot of boys had collected around.

"Don't ban it, sir," one of them pleaded, a boy called Spier, from chief's own house.

"Yes, please don't, sir!" several others joined in. Soon the chorus was quite general.

Chief patted his palm with the stave. Suddenly his free hand shot out and grabbed Spier by the arm. Grinning fiercely, he began pulling the boy to him and then thrusting him away—back and forth, back and forth—a favourite trick of his.

"I won't ban it, Spier!" His tone was vehement, as if they had all been begging him to impose a ban. "D'ye know why, Spier?"

"No, sir," Spier gasped, being almost tumbled off his feet with each thrust and pluck of that brawny pink arm.

"Because, Spier, when your team played mine last Saturday, Spier, it was the most lacklustre, Spier, spineless, Spier, bottomless, Spier, puny, Spier, wet,

Spier, performance I have ever seen, Spier." He let poor Spier go and began to grab indiscriminately at others in that laughing, squirming pack, which grew larger by the second. "It seems, Boyce, that our new system, Boyce, is producing, Wilkinson, young gentlemen, Wilkinson, of no fibre, Moss, no spirit, Moss! Mmmm, Aylsford, what say, Aylsford? And so, Aylsford, a few knocked heads, Fowler, a few grazed knees, Churley, a broken arm or two, Davies, a cracked skull or so, Abercrombie, may teach ye that pain don't signify! Mmmm? Say?"

The conclusion was drowned in cheers as boys dashed off to the stone baths, eager to get through their ablutions and chores so that they could scour the place for barrel staves. Within two days every spare stave within five miles (and many more that had not exactly been spare) was at Fiennes. Never had boys climbed Whernside with such vigour, nor descended with such élan. And it was as chief had said—grazed knees, twisted ankles, even a broken arm (though, fortunately, no cracked skull), but none of it daunting enough to send the stavers back to the old pedestrian way of life.

Even Lorrimer, who was back in school three weeks before the end of term, joined in with glee. When he met Boy for the first time after he was up and about again he walked by with a wink. Boy thought it uncommonly decent of him.

On Saturday afternoons the whole school played football if the state of the ground permitted. It was a vast, sprawling, anarchic game that covered almost the whole length of the Whernside valley, the "goals" being medieval walls about four miles apart. Chief and Cossack were the team captains (and referees) but they saw their main function as "levellers"—that is, they would trap the ball away from older boys and make sure the younger ones got their share. House pharaohs acted as whippers-in, allowing no strays or slackers. When the ground was too boggy, boys were free to go on walks or runs over the countryside.

Boy was never to forget his long walks over Whernside, Widdale, Baugh, Abbotside, and a dozen other fells, during these times. The unseasonable snows of late October had soon given way to an equally unseasonable warmth. Almost always Boy went out with de Lacy and a fellow from Agincourt called Moncur, whose parents had sent him a copy of Charles Kingsley's new book, *Westward Ho!* The three would go out to some sheltered hollow—a dry ghyll or a shallow cave in a scar—where, when the sun shone, they could almost imagine it was spring. And there they would take turns reading aloud, spellbinding one another with the amazing adventures of Amyas Leigh and his crew.

"And it's all true!" Moncur would swear. "Kingsley's a professor of history, you know."

They became a new Brotherhood of the Rose and spent long evenings, before lockup, drawing plans of the ship and charts of her voyage.

They wept when Rose herself was killed—not one of them could read the chapter through without suffering at least a certain huskiness of voice. How they came to hate the very name Spaniard! How eagerly they rechristened their ship *Vengeance!* How stirring it was to be Protestant! How grand to be English! They ran screaming up and down the fells, brandishing bright swords of gorse root, and taking it in turns to be the Inquisition and get killed.

Secretly Boy took the white girl raised by Indians, Ayacanora, into his lonely fantasies. He saw her always sprawling drowsily in tropic groves banked around with gaudy flowers whose soporific perfume (which was also, somehow, her perfume) made the zephyrs heavy and excitingly perilous. He tried to picture her Indian-English skin, her eyes lustrous and huge; but she was too dangerous to imagine all at once. Only bits of her. An ear lobe, clear and sharp, with blurred hair, soft jawline, slim neck, shining eves, and again the perfume of her. An elbow—the inside of it, the soft part—and next to it, the sheen of skin that rippled softly over her ribs, and above it, fruits of flesh, lemons of all softness. Two. The thought of them could spurt through him like incendiary blood. And at climax, the thigh lifting from thigh. Where did the rest of her go then? Just thigh, lifting, away from thigh, in a black tropic jungle. The black marked the space between heavenly thigh and heavenly thigh. What is in that space? But before he could see, there always stole upon him that delicious, melting, throbbing ending, and it didn't matter any more. The images had done their magic and could be put away, along with their dark mysteries, for another night. "Ayacanora," he would breathe, thrilling himself to drowsy sleep again. "Ayacanora. My girl, girl, girl." He came to love the word *girl.*

"I shall be a soldier," Caspar told Causton and Swift mi one day. "My poor bro will have to see to family affairs, but I shall cover our name with glory."

He never talked of business or trade, always "family affairs"; chaps at Fiennes were not keen on commerce—even Causton and Swift mi, both of whose people were in trade, never spoke of it.

Causton's people had been amazingly careless about the matter of a career, so, though he was all of twelve years old, he had not yet the remotest idea of what he should be in life. He decided that he, too, might as well aim at the army. Swift mi knew he was going to the East Indian part of the family's tea business, but the idea of soldiering suited him better at this stage, so he joined Caspar's army, as well.

No one could quite explain why it was Caspar's (or, rather, Stevenson mi's) army. As its youngest member he ought, by all the rules of a place like Fiennes, to have been the very last to claim it as his. And, to be fair, he never once called it "my" army—always "ours." But everyone else knew it as "Stevenson mi's." Perhaps it was because, thanks to his father's playful training, Caspar could draw a map that looked a dead copy of a real one from the Ordnance Survey, right down to the puzzling little compass roses and strange messages like *Mag var 19° 33'* that decorated the borders. Maps like that gave everyone confidence.

Perhaps it was that Caspar made the best medals. For a while that term there was quite an enthusiasm for making gorgeous medals, cut out of ticket card, and then awarding them to one another with grand ceremony. Caspar had discovered the scene painter's trick of dabbing in bold highlights and shadows, giving a powerful effect of sculptured relief to his designs; his crosses and stars looked as solid and chunky as the real things. He made a whole chestful and often stood before the boot-room looking glass frowning sternly; as he saluted himself in the styles of a dozen armies. (This particular enthusiasm waned when Barley, the fat boy who had shared Caspar's first Barn beating, took to awarding himself such ridiculous decorations as The Most Noble Grand Cross of the Thibetan Buttered Beauty, fifth class, and The Purple Liver, with the motto *For Soaks* across its face.)

Or perhaps it was just that Caspar always seemed to fit best at the centre of things. When there was a charge to be led up the sheer face of a scar, Caspar always broke the skyline first; his restless body, nimble in its speed, demonic in its energy, always drew the eye. Without a weapon of any kind he put so much vim into his wars and made them so blood-curdling that there was a special thrill to the climax of every battle as, naturally, he and his regiment overran the defenders' lines and took no prisoners.

And when wars grew weary, Caspar always had his treasured Dart to bring out and steam. In the half-dark of the gaslights, when its steam hung in wreaths on the evening air, it looked especially realistic and always drew a great crowd, which often included pharaohs.

In the last week of term Causton got his new slide-valve engine, the Achilles, and at once issued a challenge to Caspar. Its double-acting cylinders gave full power on both forward and backward strokes of the piston, so without a handicap it would have beaten Dart every time. it took two days to establish what the handicap should be. Blenkinsop, despite his dislike of Caspar, was a great enthusiast of steam engines and helped both youngsters to push theirs to the limits of their safety valves. It was he who set the final handicap for the big race, which was held on the next to last day of term. And it was he who, on that day, helped Caspar to fire up the Dart. Caspar was delighted that Blenkinsop had at last forgiven him; his one great dread had been that the senior boy would regain some official position in the House or school and so be able to make his life intolerable.

News of the Grand Train Contest spread through the school. Chaps came to the Old School cloisters from every House to watch; over a hundred and fifty had gathered by the time the races began. Someone said that more than £300 was laid in bets, with Achilles the favourite. Blenkinsop told Caspar he himself had a fiver on the Dart, which quieted Caspar's last lingering suspicion that Blenkinsop's real game might be to make Dart lose the race.

It was quite dark when the time came for the first of the three runs that would decide the contest; Dart was to go fifteen paces, Achilles twenty-one. Swift ma was the starter. On the first run he delayed so long that Dart's safety valve began to weep and tremble, and Caspar thought his neck would twist off, what with turning back to watch Swift and forward to look anxiously at the hot little bomb whose wheels he held in check.

At last there was Swift's cry of "Off!" The wheels thrashed the air, spun on the stone, gripped, and the Dart was away, true to its name. After that Caspar could not touch it except to correct its direction with a sideways poke of his stick. A great roar went up from the boys who stood on, sat on, leaned on, or peered through the cloister balustrade.

"On Achilles! On! On!" they howled.

"Forward now, Dart! Keep forward!" they bellowed.

And Dart kept forward. Swift's delay, by raising the steam pressure to its very limit, now stood the little engine in good stead so that it reached the finishing line an easy two seconds ahead of the more powerful Achilles and still had steam to spare. The cheer was deafening, but Causton was not the least put out; he grinned broadly as he picked up the laggard (and now clearly misnamed) Achilles.

"Beginner's luck," he scoffed. "The next two are ours. We are about to reverse the legend."

"Words!" Caspar sneered.

"I'll give you ten to one."

"He's up to no good," Blenkinsop said, worried now at Causton's confidence.

Caspar ought to have delayed his "ready" signal until the safety valve began to tremble once again, but impatience led him to guess the pressure was almost there and to give the signal early.

Again they were off. And again the Dart surged ahead of the Achilles—or was that a false impression, fostered by the six-pace handicap? Surely not. Caspar, looking beneath his arm, watched the gap narrowing, narrowing, narrowing. Quicker than last time? He skipped in frustration on the flagstones and blew futile draughts down at Dart, whether in hope of fanning its fire or just generally wafting it forward he could not have said.

By the three-quarter mark it was clear that, barring a miracle, Achilles was set to overhaul Dart well within the distance. As indeed she did, exactly reversing the margin by which Dart had taken the first round. The cheer, now running with the money, was even greater.

"A fine handicap you set!" Caspar said bitterly to Blenkinsop as they went back for the third and final run. Blenkinsop merely grinned. "Got us the right odds, though," he answered. "And I've a trick yet to serve. You wait—you won't lose."

"What odds?" Caspar asked. "I haven't bet anything."

"More fool you, then." Blenkinsop knelt beside Caspar as he blew into the firebox to raise the steam more quickly. "Giddy?" he asked.

Caspar nodded.

"Let me," Blenkinsop said as he edged Caspar aside. Every breath laid an incandescent gold on Blenkinsop's strangely knobbled face. He blew and blew until the safety valve wept and shivered.

"Shall I give the ready?" Caspar asked, certain of a "yes."

"Just one more thing." Blenkinsop drew a number of wooden spills from his pocket and popped them in his mouth, rolling them around like a humbug. Then he spat them out and poked them swiftly into the firebox.

"Hey, they're wet!" Caspar protested.

Blenkinsop winked. "You've enough steam now and they'll soon dry. Then you'll just see!"

Caspar, delighted at this stratagem, turned to give the "ready" to Swift.

"Here, you must hold it." Blenkinsop handed him the engine.

"Off!"

This time there was no doubt. The Dart thrashed away as it had never thrashed before, not even on its hardest trials. It was actually going as fast as

Achilles, despite the difference in power between them. Caspar danced and skipped in triumph as the distance between the two held and Causton began to look really worried.

Blenkinsop's ruse with the damp firing worked, too. Caspar saw the now-dried kindling flare into life, hotter and brighter than any of the gas flares along the cloister. It gave a hellish, flickering joy to the cheering faces that thronged the balustrade, and it punched Caspar's dark, exultant shadow on the vaulted arches above.

Suddenly there was a deafening explosion that left the cloisters ringing with a painful high note. A burst of sparks replaced the Dart. A broad, vicious crack split the paving slab on which it stood—or had stood, for there was now nothing there but one bent wheel and a few small sherds of unrecognizable copper and brass.

Where was the Dart? Even Caspar in the depth of his shock knew these few bits were only a tenth of that once magnificent machine. It had simply vanished into the air.

He laughed. What else could he do? It was that or tears. Everyone laughed then as Achilles steamed on through and collected the prize.

"Hard lines!" Causton said, holding up the triumphant Achilles, letting its wheels thrash the air to exhaust the steam. He was genuinely disappointed at Caspar's bad luck; it was not the way he had wanted to win. "Where's the rest of it?" he asked, looking at the cracked stone and the few scraps left around it.

"We'll have to search tomorrow," Caspar said, looking vaguely out through the thinning crowds and into the dark of the courtyard.

And then he froze. And his heart rose up into his throat. And his stomach lifted and turned over. For there on the far side of the courtyard he saw that the window of the pupil room, the window with some of the oldest stained glass in Yorkshire, was shattered beyond any repair. And Cossack was at that moment in the act of opening the remains of one of the frames. Even that careful movement was enough to send several more once precious fragments clattering down, no more valuable than the cheapest coloured cullet.

"Who is the culprit?" Cossack's voice boomed out over the courtyard.

"I'd better own up," Caspar muttered, full of dreadful fears.

"And Blenkinsop," Causton said. "He's in it, too. Where's Blenkinsop?"

The cry went up: "Where's Blenkinsop?"

He was nowhere to be found.

On feet of lead Caspar walked over the courtyard to the beak. When he stood before him he could see no feature inside the intense black of the silhouette, but he could sense an almost ungovernable fury in the way the man breathed and swayed.

"I'm extremely sorry, sir. The pressure built up too much and it just exploded," he offered.

Only that terrifying breathing.

"I'm sure my father will make what financial reparation may be..."

"Silence, sir!" Cossack barely spoke. His voice was threaded precariously on a tremble. "You! You think...you think that money—can...Well, you come here, sir, and I'll show you! I'll show you, sir. I'll show you. I'll show you indeed. I'll show you what money can't. I'll speak to you in your own ruffian tongue." He could hardly get out some of the words.

Miserably Caspar turned and began the long trek around the cloister, through the courtyard, the Barn, the passages, and so up to the pupil room. All the way people patted him on the back and commiserated. "Hard lines, mi!"..."Hard cheese!" But all Caspar could think about was the three sharp cuts still on his bottom from a House beating a few days ago; Cossack would surely see the marks and lay his own on top, where it would he more painful.

For Cossack hated him. Caspar knew that. He was always picking Caspar out in sarcastic asides. He would say, for instance, in giving out a sum: "A man buys lands at seventy pounds...or, in your case, Stevenson minor, seventy thousand pounds..." Caspar was at a loss to understand why Cossack did it, for the sarcasm never brought much of a laugh; it bewildered the other boys as much as it did Caspar. Money was not made much of at Fiennes. But these constant digs left Caspar in no doubt that Cossack hated him. He had often wondered why Cossack never thrashed him. Well, he was going to make up for it now!

In the last of the passageways he met Blenkinsop, who smiled at him broadly.

"Oh, Blenkinsop, thank God! You'll come and see Cossack with me, of course?"

The smile grew even broader and more reassuring. "Don't worry. I've just seen him and explained everything; you'll be all right, young 'un!" Playfully he whacked Caspar with an imaginary cane.

With much lighter heart and tread Caspar went up to the study door. Only when he heard the beak's dreadful "Come!" did his confidence in Blenkinsop's reassurance begin to fade.

One look at Cossack was enough to shatter the rest. Whatever Blenkinsop had said, it had done nothing to improve the man's anger.

"I'm waiting," he said before Caspar was even inside the door.

"Sir?" His voice sounded like a stranger's.

"I'm waiting to know why I should not flog you within an ace of your life, Stevenson minor." Anger made him slur the words.

"But, sir!" He felt panic beginning to claim him. "Did not Blenkinsop explain? The wood? The damp wood, which he put on the..."

"Enough! Do not seek to shift the blame, sir!" Cossack boomed. His voice alone was a physical assault. "I am talking of *this*." He held forth a shattered fragment of the Dart. "What is this?"

"My engine, sir. I was saying, did not Blenkinsop explain that he..."

"This, sir! This!" Cossack's unsteady finger pointed to the safety valve, half-buried in the mangled copper plate of the boiler. "This!" He thrust it inches from Caspar's nose. "What is your explanation for this!"

"It's the safety valve, sir."

"And in it, sir. What is in it? What is that...*stuff*, inside it?"

Caspar peered into the recess and his bewilderment only increased. There was something in the safety valve. Greeny-white stuff. Limestone fur? Had the boiling water deposited it there? Was that why it had exploded? "I don't know what it is, sir."

Cossack smiled thinly, a ghastly, disbelieving grimace. "It is blotting paper. And well you know it."

"I, sir?" Even Caspar could hear how insincere his terror was making him sound.

It merely confirmed all that Cossack knew, or (in his drunkenness) thought he knew. "Enough, sir. You shall take your medicine. But first you shall know what illness you are to be cured of. What you have done this evening is more heinous than anything any boy has ever done. Oh, yes! Don't look s'prised! You have cheated in the vilest way, because you could not bear the thought of losing. Oh, you may wipe that puzzled frown from your face. That angelic innocence does not move me one jot."

"But, sir—"

"Silence, sir!" Cossack thundered, almost falling over. "Every word you seek to interpose from this moment forth merely augments your punishment. You sought to win a large sum of money by the vilest of underhand means. By plugging this—this safety-thing"—Cossack grew even darker in his fury at lacking the right word and thus losing the authority of his "proof"—"you sought to win by a fraud. You are the sort of cheat to whom money is more important than honour—if you even know what honour is!" He reached for the cane with the gleaming silver ends. "You are one of this new breed of modern men for whom money is a god. 'I'm sure my father will make financial reparation'!" he quoted with a sneer.

Anger began to replace Caspar's fear. He stood still as a stone carving, but his eyes no longer meekly avoided those of the master.

Cossack saw the change and was startled. He began to bluster, trying to regain his former total ascendancy; he wanted Caspar's eyes rooted in his boots. "Your father!" he snorted. "He may think money a god, too, for aught I know. He may have taught you that all means, fair or vile, are sufficient to gain it—God knows, it's a common enough belief nowadays. He'll probably be proud of you for this evening's foul...underhand...Yes! These new moneybags!" Still those piercing eyes would not lower themselves. "You Stevensons are just moneygrubbers!"

"You may be sure, sir," Caspar said, "I shall take the earliest opportunity to acquaint my father..." At that his courage ran out.

He forgot how he had begun the threat and so did not know how to end it. Only his dumb, seething anger remained. He began to plot exactly how his father would tear this odious tyrant apart.

Cossack took his silence as victory enough. "Do so!" he sneered. "The last boy I flogged as I'm about to flog you ran away snibling"—he struggled—"sniv-el-ling home. And he came back with a ticket round his neck reading 'Same Again!' and signed by his mother."

Perhaps it was the memory of that, or the sight of Caspar staring up at him defiantly, speechless in anger, but something in Cossack snapped at that moment. Shivering in a lunatic fury he thrust Caspar down over his leather-topped desk, not bothering to take down his trousers.

It was a mercy too small to weigh.

Outside, the cloisters were crammed with boys, gleefully watching through the hole once barred by the oldest stained glass in Yorkshire. A unique chance, for there was no rule (there had never needed to be a rule) forbidding anyone to watch a beak's beating from the cloisters.

"Aaach!" Blenkinsop cried in disappointment. "He hasn't even made him take his breeches down!"

Others laughed. They counted the strokes aloud to begin with. At eight they began to tail off into a whisper. By twelve no one counted aloud any more, not even Blenkinsop, whose voice had been the last to tail off.

In fact, they lost count as they watched that appalling torment of one of their smallest go on, and on, and on. And on. Some said it was twenty-eight. Some said thirty. One swore to thirty-five. Sometime near the end Swift ma broke free from the trance that had gripped them as they watched Cossack's bloated, implacable face and heard the repeated swish and thwack of the cane.

"I've got to stop this," he said.

But before he reached the broken window, satiety must have claimed the beak, for he halted and then stood, looking in seeming bewilderment at his hand, at the cane, and at the motionless frame of the little boy bent over the table.

"You may go," he said gruffly.

Caspar did not move. He heard the words. He knew vaguely that the most terrible thing in the world had stopped. But another pain, even more terrible, now crept in under it. He could not move.

"Enough of this shamming!" Cossask grabbed his collar and yanked him upright.

Caspar trembled like someone in an ague. His muscles would not heed him; like every other fibre of his mind and body, they clamoured to be elsewhere—anywhere. He would gladly have changed with the meanest and second most wretched of the earth's creatures at that moment.

"What can I do?" he asked in a voice that meandered through an octave. "What can I do?" His arms would not drop to their sides.

If Cossack had any idea that he had done something truly monstrous, he gave no sign of it. "Do? You may go down, sir. Go down from this place and reflect on the vile trick that brought you to this retribution. God is not mocked. He found you out!"

When Caspar still did not move, Cossack looked uncomfortably away. Then he reached in his pocket and pulled out a sixpence. "Perhaps I was a mite hard," he allowed. "Here, take this and cheer up!" Roughly he thrust Caspar out through the door.

For some reason the movement brought not relief (relief was a dream beyond dreaming) but a kind of hot-cold numbness that was different from the outrage that racked every shrieking angle of him. Beyond the door stood Boy, and Swift ma, with de Lacy just behind. Swift caught Caspar under the arm. "All right?" he asked.

Caspar looked at him. "What can I do?" he implored. Then, for the first time, he burst into tears.

Swift made a bitter, determined grimace as he gently passed Caspar on to Boy and de Lacy. "Take him up slowly," he told them. "Christ! His skin is frozen!" He himself went straight into the pupil room, not even bothering to knock.

When they reached the top gallery Caspar's trembling was so violent that he seemed on the point of shaking himself to bits.

"Caspar!" Boy cried out in alarm, as his brother slipped from his grasp for the umpteenth time. "Please, Caspar!"

Caspar looked piteously at Boy, as if he might know some trick for stopping this dreadful palsy. Then, mercifully, he passed out.

Mercifully—for the first thing they had to do was to lay him face down on his bed and gently peel off his trousers. Had he been conscious, they would never have managed it. Every boy in the dorm who saw Caspar bare cried out in pity and covered his eyes—and these were veterans of savage floggings who had boasted and gloated over their and others' wounds for years.

Boy now found himself trembling almost as violently as Caspar, but with rage. He went at once to his bed, took a hammer from his drawer, and set off for the gallery. It was Lorrimer who barred his path. "What are you going to do?" he asked.

"What d'you think I'm going to do! I'm going to pulp Cossack's right hand. He'll never do this again."

Lorrimer shook his head and put out his hand. "Leave him to Swift," he said firmly. "Give me that hammer."

Anyone but Lorrimer, Boy would have hit. He gave up the hammer and broke down into tears.

"Save that until you've helped your bro," Lorrimer sneered. The scorn was enough to jerk Boy out of his crying fit and send him back to Caspar's bedside.

They bathed him gently and rubbed him with goose grease. He did not wake.

Swift came back. In his hand he held the fragment of the Dart that Cossack had thrust under Caspar's nose.

"He's drunk," he said. He gave the broken engine to Boy. "Says your bro had fifty quid on the race and bunged up the safety valve with blotch." He pulled a face. "Even so…"

Everyone knew what he meant. By the standards of even ten years ago what had happened to Caspar was only a little excessive; but those ten years had seen a subtle shift of feeling in such schools as Fiennes. By now such a thrashing seemed almost barbarous.

"He wouldn't bet fifty *pence*!" Boy said. "He wouldn't even think of it."

"All the same he did bung up the safety valve."

Boy looked at the irrefutable evidence of this in the fragment he held in his hand. It puzzled him; he wouldn't have thought Caspar capable of such cheating. Yet Caspar did love to win—that couldn't be denied.

De Lacy took the broken engine and looked into the safety valve. "Is it green?" he asked.

"What?"

"The blotting paper."

No one could be sure in the dim light; they had to bring a candle and have a really close look. But they all agreed it was green.

"Then that's who did it!" de Lacy said triumphantly.

"Who? Who?" they asked.

"Well, for Christ's sake, who uses green blotch?"

"Blenkinsop!" someone said.

And then everyone remembered and agreed, even boys who had never seen Blenkinsop's blotting paper, that he did, indeed, use only the green.

Swift went out to the balcony. "Blenkinsop!" he roared without actually checking that the boy was in sight.

But within the minute a frightened and sheepish Blenkinsop stood in the doorway of the upper dorm. "I didn't know Cossack was going to do that," he said defensively. He made no attempt to deny what he had done. "I thought he'd just get an ordinary swishing. Just to pay him out."

"But why the hell did you bung it up?" Swift asked.

"He wanted to blow it up," Boy said. "That's obvious."

"He had fifty quid on it with me," Lorrimer said.

"So!" Swift's disgust was heavy. "That lie has the same signature." He grabbed Blenkinsop's arm. "You're coming back to Cossack with me—if he hasn't drunk himself sodden by now."

When they had gone, Boy suggested sending out for the doctor. But Lorrimer said no, let Caspar sleep on. The doctor could see him tomorrow. Boy was about to argue when Moncur, of Agincourt, came into the dorm. He stopped just inside the door.

"Can I see him?" he asked.

No one said yes, but no one made any move to turn him away.

"A lot of us saw the flogging," he said. "Chaps from Agincourt. And Crecy. We're going to barricade chief until he agrees to change things." He looked around, finding a sympathy that fell some way short of open support. "We're fed up, being flogged all the time like common soldiers," he added.

Boys at Old School knew how fierce life was in the new Houses, without the compensations of unsupervised lockup to lighten the harshness of the new discipline. But what had they to gain from a rebellion? Chief might ease the load a bit, but he'd certainly demand that the rebels submit to a thrashing before he conceded—otherwise he could kiss farewell to good order forever. In spite of what had happened to Caspar, this was not really their fight.

Moncur was about to redouble his argument when Boy lifted the sheet from Caspar.

"Christ Almighty!" Moncur had to steady himself against the pile of boxes. When he had recovered somewhat he looked at Boy. "Surely you agree, Stevenson?" he said.

In a general way Boy did agree; but he saw this affair as Stevenson *vs.* Cossack, not as a spur for a general school rebellion. And, in any case, he wasn't going to be the only boy from Old School to get caught up in such a rising.

"I'm going to settle with Cossack," he said. "I'll see chief on that account."

Lorrimer broke in. "I'll bet Swift's on his way there now. And Cossack and Blenkinsop. They wouldn't dare keep chief in the dark."

"Well…" Moncur shrugged, not too crestfallen. "I suppose we'll go on without you. We're going to try and drag chief into the gasworks shed; he'll like that less than being locked up in Agincourt."

Mossman, another boy from Agincourt, came sauntering into the room at that moment. "Don't stir," he drawled sarcastically. "The rebellion's off. The sixth has pissed on the fireworks. They're going to chief with some ideas for next term. Everything's fizzled."

He looked at Caspar, then at Moncur. "This wasn't our fight, anyway."

He left before they could throw something at him.

Boy sat at Caspar's bedside, intending an all-night vigil; but in the small hours he nodded off to sleep. Caspar woke just before five. For a long time he had no memory of who he was, much less of where he now found himself. But when he stirred, the most terrible pains racked his legs and ran up his back. This pain restored to him his sense of person and place. He remembered, too, how movement had helped last night and, thinking anything would be better than the present agony, decided to get up and walk about. At least those convulsive shiverings had stopped.

He moved with monumental slowness so as not to awaken Boy or anyone else. He could not face company. Even so, he was whimpering at the pain by the time he had got dressed.

The movement did not help him as much as it had last night, but now that he was up he could not go through the torment of undresssing again. Gingerly he hobbled out to the gallery and began the painful descent to the yard.

The cold, damp air moaned over the rough stone of the walls. It tugged at his hair and winnowed his neck and cheeks. There was no suggestion that other humans were nearby. He might have been the last person left on earth. He was glad now to have come outside. The pain had given him no sense of being alive, but the chill air now bid to revive him.

Then, on the only morning of term on which the climb was not compulsory, he turned his face to Whernside and began the ascent.

His way led past the gasworks shed, where Purse was shovelling the first of the day's two rings into the retorts. Purse neither heard nor saw Caspar as he passed the open door, only feet away; but moments later he caught a glimpse of some movement through the dust-shrouded window. He came to the door and recognized Caspar at once.

"Stevenson?" he called. "Eay, young man!" But when Caspar gave no sign of having heard, he scratched beneath the brim of his hat and went back to his shovelling.

In the cloisters, Caspar's foot struck a wheel from the shattered Dart, but he did not pause to pick it up, nor even to look at it. He took no care to be silent as he went through chief's garden at Agincourt. He cared for nothing. As he let himself out by the upper gate he saw that a lamp was being lit in one of the bedrooms. He was only a few paces out into the freedom of the moor when he heard chief's voice cry, "Boy! Come back, m'boy!"

The waning moon, still almost full, came out from behind a cloud. It must have shown Brockman the figure of Caspar, walking slowly and steadily away, not even pausing. Caspar knew he had been seen but his disobedience left him unmoved. He was wondering if there was anything left about which he might possibly care. There was absolutely no sign of the coming dawn.

Chief's cry was heard by one other at least. In the gasworks shed Purse laid down his shovel, put on his overcoat, and walked out into the dark, following the path Caspar had taken.

When Caspar was halfway up the hillside the last of the thin, ragged clouds passed down into the sky below the moon, which now rode out, almost painfully bright, into a clear, inky vastness. It was hard to believe all that brilliance was borrowed. The light showed every stalk of sedge, every heather leaf, each prickle of gorse; it was even bright enough to show their colours, sable and purple and green. Deliberately he walked into the gorse. Only his skin felt the stab of those myriads of needles; only his skin winced.

A cow, straying from its pasture, stared and breathed at him over a limestone outcrop. The whites of her eyes burned with a supernatural brightness. She backed away on legs that the steepness had converted to stilts. She trampled through a sheet of ice that groaned and wheezed before it shattered. *That's how cold it is*, Caspar thought, not feeling any cold at all.

It seemed no time before he was at the very summit, over thirteen hundred feet above the school. But he did not look down. Nor did he remember any of the dashing charges that had so often won him and his army this eminence. From here he could see the entire system of Yorkshire dales, black and royal in the burnished moonlight. The clouds were now no more than a vanishing scumble on the skyline, hinting at the approaching dawn. Indeed, a tinge of green already suffused the eastern rim.

That's where his home was, in the east, over the dales, down into the Vale of York where his mother hunted with the York and Ainsty, and up again into the Wolds, where Lord Middleton's hunt would not accept his mother at any price. Why were people so against them? Like Cossack.

He and Boy would be home tonight, back there over the horizon in lovely Thorpe Old Manor, in the wolds. No he wouldn't! Of course, this Christmas they would all be down south at Maran Hill, their other home. He thought of the long tedium of the journey, almost to London; his sudden dread of it was the first non-physical feeling he had had since waking.

"Young boy!"

Chief's voice. No need to answer, somehow. There was a lantern swinging below. And a man, very lithe and powerful, coming quickly up with short, springy steps that were almost a run. Some way behind him came Purse, a more laborious climber. Chief was not out of breath when he arrived.

"Stevenson minor? I thought it would be you." He drew close and put down the lantern before asking gently, "Why have you come here?"

The question puzzled Caspar. He pointed over the dales, spreading his arms theatrically, as if it were an answer.

Brockman turned and looked where Caspar had pointed. He stared at the sleeping dales for a long time, nodding his head. Then he looked down at the school; Caspar had forgotten it was there.

"You can even mark the individual stones, see!" Brockman said. He turned to Caspar. "I hope you will one day be able to love it as every boy should." He waited for a response. "And…forgive it," he added.

Caspar nodded. Those ideas were so remote: love, forgiveness.

"It *will* be different now, Stevenson."

Caspar opened his eyes and saw…the stove in Purse's kitchen, blazing merrily, and Mrs. Purse—smiling! Smiling anxiously. And it was bright sunshine outside the window.

"There now!" Mrs. Purse said. "Just look at them apples for cheeks! Thou'rt hungry, I'll be bound?" He could sense a great bewilderment in her. It banished all her protective ferocity and left her as vulnerable as he.

"What has happened?" he asked.

"Dr. Brockman and Purse carried you down." She touched his cheek. "Poor mite! Poor mite!"

Her fingers were a lovely warmth. Suddenly he knew all that had been missing, not just since last night but all these weeks: tenderness! Gentle, sweet, lovely, warm, precious, feminine tenderness.

He reached up and caught her fingers as she was in the act of withdrawing them. And he pressed them against his face just as softly as she had laid them there before. The room shivered and dissolved in a hot ocean. He blinked, and two fat, hot, sumptuously hot, tears rolled down his cheeks and vanished among their entwined fingers.

"Oh!" she cried, now as overcome as he was. She fell to her knees beside him and threw her arms about his tiny body.

"My little lamb! My poor little lamb!" she said between sobs.

He snuggled and pressed himself into that ample bay of softness and wept and wept for sheer happiness.

Chapter 8

Caspar had never seen his mother so angry; it was hard to keep remembering that the anger was not at him but against Fiennes. When Nora saw what that school had done to her little boy, she almost screamed aloud, first with shock, then with anger, of such intensity that it seemed to expel her from her own body. She became, as it were, a livid bystander of herself, angry in her own right and angry by proxy. Her fingers kneaded and pinched her brow; she felt the pain of their pressure and she felt her fingertips as if they touched a third party. She could not look twice at Caspar's wounds; yet, looking once, she could hardly take her eyes off them.

Caspar was as yet too young to play the complete man; in another few days he would have healed enough to be able to choose between laughing it off or accepting every crumb of sympathy going. But now, a bare twenty-four hours after the flogging, his wounds were at their most severe. To surrender to the full intensity of his mother's solicitude—even to increase it by fanning her anger—was a luxury he could not forgo. Gasp by gasp, between tears and hugs, she got the story out of him.

From all over the house came the other children and the servants, to look in horror, to listen agog, to add their share of compassion. Soon Caspar was convinced of two things—that what had happened to him marked a new depth in man's inhumanity to man, and that it had been worth it.

Winifred, the eldest, looked at his wounds and cringed to Nora's side. "They're horrible, horrible people, Mama," she said. Like her mother she hated the sight yet could not look away. She also knew well her mother's opinions about "gent manufactories" as Nora called the schools.

Clement, who would one day be "Stevenson minimus" and was already imagining what it would be like when he joined Boy and Caspar at Fiennes, was appalled. "I wouldn't let them do that to me," he said, with more bravado than conviction.

"Try and stop them!" Boy sneered.

"We'll do more than try!" Nora said vehemently as she rocked Caspar back and forth. "Wait till your father gets back." But even as she spoke she knew it would be no good waiting for John; his return was all in the air. She would have to deal with Fiennes herself.

Abigail, who would be nine that Christmas Eve, was, outwardly at least, more shocked than any of them. She stood apart, in the middle of the room, and stared in terror at the marks on Caspar. Then, her hands writhing in fruitless contest with the air, she shouted: "I think people are just horrible. People are stupid!" ("People" in her vocabulary always meant adults.) The inadequacy of these words in the face of those monstrous wounds angered her to bitter tears. She stood alone in the middle of the room and shook the floor with her grief.

It was one of those displays that hover between the pathetically comic and the deeply moving. In the circumstances of that place and moment, the potential comedy was apparent to no one, except perhaps to Boy, whose own anger had found its scope with time. But for the rest, Abigail's unequal battle between words and feelings touched them all. It kindled among them, adults and children alike, a communal anger and pathos that might soon have grown into a general hysteria if Nora had not, quite by accident, said the one thing that stopped this progress in its tracks.

"Never fear, popsie," she promised Caspar. "You will never go back there again!"

Caspar froze in mid-sob. Mr. Ingilby's workshop…Purse's winking, smiling face…Mrs. Purse's food and all her lovely anger…the other fellows…life after lockup—all that fierce, free comradeship…the sky…the wind…Never again! Never again?

It was unthinkable.

He looked straight into his mother's eyes. "But I must go back," he began. And now his tears were at the fear of all he stood to lose.

But Nora, not knowing that, was smiling serenely now that the decision was out in the open. She shook her head, thinking to comfort him out of a hateful obligation by removing all sense of it from him.

Panic began to take him over. "Yes, yes! I must," he insisted. "I love it there. Don't you see?" He wanted to pull away from her but that embarrassing thing had happened again—the erection. It hadn't happened since his first week in Fiennes, not since he had discovered the real purpose of the funny stiffness. At least, it hadn't happened any longer in connection with cruelty or pain. But now, here in his mother's boudoir, what with his trousers down to his ankles and being dressed in among her skirts and surrounded by all that hot female sympathy, it had happened again. He burned with shame, not that it had happened but that she might notice it. Or Winifred, still beside her.

He ought to pull away from her so that he could oppose this terrifying notion with the vehemence it demanded. Steeling himself not to wince, he stooped quickly and grasped his trousers, snatching them up around him as he rose. He almost managed it. Or did he? Did she see? Naturally the trousers didn't slide up around him swiftly as they would have done without his embarrassment. He dared not look at her, or at Winnie, until the last button was done up again.

"Your behaviour is pretty shent, mi," Boy said quietly.

It wasn't quite the proper idiom but Caspar knew instinctively why Boy had used it—to make outsiders of everyone else in the room. Fiennes was under attack. Fiennes, not Cossack. They could not allow that; they must rally round.

Suddenly their family had become "villains."

With more fortitude, with a greater indifference to pain than he thought he could muster, Caspar nodded his acceptance of Boy's rebuke and turned to Nora. He stepped away from her, peeling her unwilling fingers off his shoulders and arms. "It wasn't the school," he said firmly. "It was just Cossack."

"He was drunk," Boy added. "And he doesn't like us."

"The school is all right," Caspar insisted.

Nora, always alert for an insult, rounded on Boy. "Doesn't like who? All the boys? Who is 'us'?"

"Us." Boy shifted uncomfortably. "Us Stevensons. He doesn't like us." He wished he had not started this hare. "It's only him, you see. Not the school. Only Cossack's to blame."

"Why does he not like us? I don't think I even know the fellow. Cossack? What sort of name is that?"

"It's not us," Caspar said. "It's money. He doesn't like people with money. He's always being sarcastic about it." How could he possibly convey to his mother, to anyone in that room except Boy, the quality of that sarcasm! Home and Fiennes might have been on different continents. "He thinks Papa is a parvenu."

"His real name's Cusack. We just call him Cossack because he's so fierce."

"He…what?" Nora stood abruptly. Now she was in a new kind of rage, one whose edge was no longer blunted by compassion for Caspar. For a moment Caspar thought she really was angry with him. "A lot of the fellows give out against parvenus," he said, hoping to make Cossack sound less unique and his crime, thereby, less heinous.

Of course it had the opposite effect. Her rage now towered so great that she no longer trusted herself to stay in speaking distance. She swept from the room, still radiating a fury that made them quail. "Put him to bed," she told the night nurse out in the passage. "Dust those sores with calomel."

Mademoiselle Nanette, her lady's maid, followed her without needing the bidding. She had been Nora's maid for the past seven years; she knew that Nora would never rest until she had been to Fiennes and faced down these *monstres barbares*. In her mind she was already sorting out which clothes Nora would be needing for the journey and which would best suit that angry confrontation. Black and yellow? A wasp?

As they went through the boudoir into the bedroom Nora heard Abigail say: "I hope Mama will hurt and hurt that man!"

Even in her rage Nora could not suppress a fleeting smile. There were times when Abigail was possibly the most infuriating infant in the world; but she had her moments. Like everyone else, Abigail knew Nora would be going directly to Fiennes.

It was too late that night to command a special train for the journey. Nora had to content herself with dispatching a man to the station with two messages to be sent over the railway telegraphs.

One was to King's Cross, ordering a special train (with their own private carriage and a flatbed wagon to take her coach) to be cleared through to Ingleton tomorrow. The other was to the stationmaster at Ingleton; he was to go, tonight, to Langstroth and to inquire into Dr. Brockman's intended movements—if the headmaster was expected to be away tomorrow or the day after, the stationmaster was to telegraph back and save Nora the waste of the journey.

There was some use, after all, in being wife to a director of, and large shareholder in, a couple of dozen railway companies!

Then she went downstairs to dine with Winifred and Young John.

Boy was annoyed that Caspar had made so much of his cuts. It gave people at home a distorted view of Fiennes. Of course, he understood his mother's anger. After all, less than twenty-four hours earlier he had been on the point of doing Cossack far greater harm than she would be capable of, whatever she might say to chief. But he could place his own anger in the full context of Fiennes; to him it was a complete anger. Hers was very partial—a mere multiplication of the annoyance with which she had accepted their entry into the school, for she had been unable to conceal it from them.

All through dinner Boy tried to tell them about the other side of Fiennes, but everything conspired against him. The costly Spode off which they ate, the deeply waxed mahogany of the table, the gleaming silver, the fine candles, odourless and smokeless in their graceful candelabra, the soft carpets, the warm fire, the shuttered windows and the quiet world they enclosed, the silent and unobtrusive service, the rich food...how in such surroundings could he hope to convey anything of the quality of Fiennes! Everything he tried to say was snapped up by his mother—and by Winifred—as further proof of the complete depravity of the place.

"No plates! You mean you eat out of hollows scooped in the *tables*?" they said, with vastly overloaded disgust, as they complacently fingered their own china and plate.

"Locked in from eight till next morning? And no grown-ups at all?"

"And anybody just builds fires wherever they like?"

"And are you telling me you can't wash or clean your teeth after this 'lockup'?"

"So the only hours you are actually compelled to attend school are the seven or so hours of public school each week! For the rest you may please yourselves, just as long as you can please your tutor at the end of term? It seems to me, my lad, that you have been sliding along on the benefit of Mr. Morier-Watson's teaching this term—and that your good report is more due to him than to anything you have gleaned at Fiennes."

"It sounds as if all the real care you get is thanks to Mrs. Oldroyd—who has no connection with the school at all. As far as Fiennes is concerned, you boys in Old School could as well be rotting in some old woodshed. Has anybody from the school, to your knowledge, ever inspected Mrs. Oldroyd's, or any of the other places, to see that they furnish suitable messes?"

"Messes! It's the word right enough!"

Boy grew more and more annoyed. The women were right, of course—but only from their outside point of view. Fiennes was sloppy and negligent and unfeeling and cold and dirty and barbarous and all the other things they called it. Yet it worked! It suited boys, or most boys. For him and Caspar it was a marvellous place.

He told them about the new Houses that chief was trying to bring in. Everything there was just as his mother and Winifred would like it. Yet all the boys who lived under the House system, even the pharaohs, envied the boys who lived in the anarchy of Old School and Hospice. But it was no good; neither of them would, or could, see the point.

Then Caspar came down, trembling from the pain each step cost him, a frail ghost in a nightshirt. It shocked Nora and Winifred, whose sarcastic greeting to each utterance of Boy's had turned into a comic, unfeeling game.

"Popsie, you must go back to bed," Nora said, getting up and running to him; but she pulled him in front of the fire and rubbed his shivering arms. "Why aren't you sleeping? And where's your night nurse?"

"I want to be sent back to Fiennes," he pleaded. His lip trembled as he begged her with his eyes.

"After this! How can you say it?"

"You see!" Boy told Winifred. She pouted.

"I want to, that's all," Caspar said.

"I'm going there tomorrow. I want to see what sort of place could do that to a child for accidentally breaking a window."

"But you won't take me away? Please! Oh, please!"

Nora stared at him in bewilderment.

"Please don't. Please, please…" His desperation alarmed her. She didn't want to be blackmailed into a promise she might regret, but she wanted to offer him all the comfort she could. Against better judgement, she said: "I won't keep you at home if I find it at all suitable."

As soon as the words were out of her mouth she knew it had been a mistake to make even so conditional a promise. Abigail, the born pessimist, would have taken Nora's words to mean the worst. Clement would have decided either way—worst or best—but would have changed his mind in half an hour. Young John and Winifred, her two level-heads, would have been guardedly relieved. But Caspar had a grasp on human nature which, in her more honest moments, she had to admit came straight from her. He now behaved in every way as if she had promised unconditionally that, come mid-February and the start of the new term, he and Boy would go back to Fiennes. She had given the emotional inch, and he, true to his blood, had taken the full span; from now on he would allow no question but that she had promised.

"You promised, Mama!" She could already hear the plaintive whine, see the bitter tears sprouting, the frank reproach of his gaze. Mercifully those blandishments lay two months away as yet. John might be back by then.

Chapter 9

NEXT DAY, AS HER TRAIN SPED NORTHWARD, NORA TRIED TO COMPOSE HER thoughts and feelings about the school. Word had come from the stationmaster at Ingleton to say that Dr. Brockman was expecting her arrival. Young John's defence of Fiennes had made a deeper impression on her than she had realized at the time. She had thought his enthusiasm rather jejune, his judgement all out of proportion. She had watched the frustration grow in him, the way it grows in all youngsters when a grown-up cannot see what they are driving at, and she had longed for him to hit on something she, too, could imagine herself enjoying, so that she could respond—as much as to say "You see! There are things I can share."

But the more he said in praise of Fiennes, the more deplorable the whole place sounded. True, their tutor's reports had been excellent (though Whymper's comment on Caspar, written well before Cossack's onslaught, had been unfortunate in the circumstances: "The little fellow has come out extraordinarily this term," he had said. But how could one trust reports, good or bad, from such a dreadful place? She would have to get Mr. Morier-Watson to examine them both after Christmas; that would show what sort of progress they had really made.

And then, just as Young John's account of the school had confirmed all her worst fears about the place, Caspar had come downstairs in such extremes of agony, not because of what Fiennes had done to him, but because he might not be allowed back! Young boys were extraordinary creatures. She had lived in poverty herself, in a turf hovel near Manchester, after her father had died. Over the last sixteen years she and John had built a fortune, in large part so that their children might be spared the terrible experience of poverty. And now here were her two eldest boys revelling in the sort of life young orphans in a slum rookery might lead—airless rooms, blocked chimneys, no supervision, no washing facilities, loathsome food served with less taste and care for cleanliness than in any workhouse or prison; and when they were not praising all this, they rejoiced in the degree of civilization to be found in the humble cottages of coachmen and carpenters! And, if that were not enough to have to swallow, she and John had to pay for these delights merely because a certain proficiency in Greek, Latin, and divinity was conferred in those conditions! It was insupportable. John simply could not have seen the place—or else he had been hoodwinked by being shown one of the new Houses.

Of course she would withdraw them from the school, and Dr. Brockman could whistle for his fees in lieu of notice; she didn't think he'd want the conditions at his school to come out in court. The press would make a jolly picnic of it. And, naturally, John would support her, once he understood how he had been deceived. As soon as she reached that point of resolution she closed her mind to any thought of her encounter with Dr. Brockman; there would quite simply be no argument. The boys would leave and that would be that. In fact, this visit was mainly to persuade John that she had not made the decision lightly but had travelled all the way to Yorkshire and had given the school every chance to vindicate itself.

She fell to worrying about John. She had had a letter from Arabella Thornton saying that Walter had written to tell her how furiously John was throwing himself into his work in the Crimea. It worried Walter and it worried Tucker, the Stevenson agent out there. And, naturally, it worried Nora, too—the more so in that she was not there to see it, so her imagination served up nightmares that were probably worse than the real thing. She had known from the start that John was going to make himself ill on this job; it was his form of patriotism—a form common enough among men who, for one reason or another, do not wear uniform yet who burn to serve their country.

On their first contract, Summit Tunnel on the Manchester & Leeds, he had been able to work eighteen or twenty hours a day without harm to his health. But that had been sixteen years ago. Five hundred contracts ago. Four million pounds ago. Command had been new, the work new, every problem new. Every day a new face and a new challenge. Now? There wasn't anyone in the business he didn't know, hadn't worked for, or who hadn't worked for him. No type of rock he had not cut, bored, or blasted. No kind of terrain he had not beaten. No weather he had not survived. No timetable he had not met. No treachery he had not outdone. No challenge he had not mastered. The Crimea would offer nothing he had not faced and beaten in a hundred disguises. What challenge did it leave him but the formidable adversary of his own constitution? And he would defeat that, too. She could do nothing except worry and hope he would spare enough of himself to savour that ultimate triumph.

The seasons were upside down. October had dealt the snows that belonged to Christmas, and here was December looking like March. It was a surprise, almost, to see no lambs in the fields. After Leeds the train rattled around the edge of the dales through fierce, blustery showers of hail and slushy rain that beat almost horizontally. She could see sheets of water hanging in slanted festoons from ink-black clouds. Between showers the sky would clear to an azure blue across which raced wisps of cloud too thin to dim the sun. In these intervals the fields and woods seemed to smile and relax.

At Ingleton she thanked her engineer and fireman and told them to be ready to steam back to Leeds at about five o'clock. It was now after lunchtime. She would hardly need the whole afternoon to set a flea in Brockman's ear, but it was best to allow for any unforeseen difficulties. Then she went to pay her respects to the stationmaster. He told her that while he had been at the school the previous evening, in response to her telegraph, he had run into Dr. Brockman and had thought it best to say straight out why he was there.

"How did he take the news?" she asked.

"Not happy," the stationmaster confessed.

"Well, I'll not improve that mood. You know what he did to our boy?"

"Aye, m'm. It's the talk of Langstroth."

"What are they saying? Does that mean such a flogging is uncommon at the school?"

"Nay, I'd not say that. But the lad is known here and there in the town, and seemingly well liked. But that place is noted for hard floggings."

By the time she returned to the platform her coach had been lifted down and two horses from the local livery stables were being coupled to it. They were fresh enough to take the hill without requiring anyone to dismount. Mademoiselle Nanette peered glumly out at the gaunt landscape they were now entering, made even more gaunt by the fact that the lush pastures and woods of the lower lands were still in sight, less than a mile away but already far below.

"There is nothing like it in France," she said with a theatrical shudder. She spoke in French. She and Nora always spoke French when they were alone. Nora owned a lot of property at Deauville, which she hoped one day would become a fashionable seaside resort. Also she and John had friends and connections in France, chiefly in iron and in railways. There were many reasons for keeping her French more polished than most English people would have considered proper or necessary.

"There is," Nora contradicted. "The Dordogne. Parts of it are like this. And Pic du Midi."

Nanette gave that eloquent French shrug which involves eyes, eyebrows, lips, jaw, neck, elbows, and hands as well as the shoulders. "I don't know them," she said.

Nora smiled to herself. Of course Nanette knew them; she had been to both areas with Nora on several visits. What she meant was that those places were not really France. For her, France began and ended in lower Normandy.

"Poor children! The English are mad!" Nanette said. Her word for it—*fous*—was an explosive Last Judgement where the bland English word "mad" would have been a mere comment. Nora looked out at the sheep-razed slopes, the cold stone walls in whose barren crevices nothing had lodged or rooted in five hundred years, the bare stone caps to the hills, the dispirited boggy land to their left, and she thought, *The girl is absolutely right! We must be mad to banish our boys to such a limbo as this.*

A heavy shower caught them as they entered Langstroth. People vanished from the street. The town closed its doors and windows and huddled against the stair-rods of water that gushed down out of the skies. The coachman pulled into a narrow street, sheltering somewhat in the lee of the houses. But it was soon over and moments later they trotted along the causeway looking in astonishment at the school.

The bright sky glistened on every slate, stone, and cobble. And the place was huge—much bigger than Nora had expected. Her sneer to John about "Dotheboys Hall" had conjured up a decrepit academy, the size of a vicarage, built against a workhouse, which, in turn, abutted on an ancient abbey. What she saw was a haphazard arrangement of ancient buildings, ecclesiastical and secular, for all the world like the lopped-off remnant of a medieval city huddled on the vast flank of the hill.

Their arrival was obviously expected. No sooner had they entered the arched gate than Purse stepped forward, touching his hat. Nora pulled down the window.

"Percy Oldroyd, m'm," he said. "I'm to conduct you to Agincourt."

To his surprise she got down from the coach. "I'll walk with you," she said. "I've heard champion things about you. Purse, isn't it?"

He smiled, "So they have it, m'm."

"It was your wife who first tended young Caspar. I owe you both thanks for that."

The smile vanished. "We never wanted thanking less, I tell thee."

She relished that friendly "thee." He had heard the Yorkshire in her. He continued: "When I fetched him off yon brow"—he nodded toward Whernside—"I near went to that Cossack..."

"Where?" Nora interrupted. "Why did you fetch him off the hill?"

"Did'st thou not know? Morning after it happened, the little fellow climbed yon brow. Five in the morn, it were. He couldn't rest, see thee. Dr. Brockman and me, we carried him off it. That's how he come to in our house."

Nora looked up at Whernside with new eyes. She tried to imagine how it might have been that morning...dark and windy, perhaps. Wind moaning around the stones and soughing through the heather. And little Caspar, racked beyond endurance with the pain, struggling up there in the dark and cold—it looked forbidding enough now, what had it been like at five of the morning? Her anger returned with all its primal force. Oh, she would make some dent on this place in the next hour!

But she had done enough battling in her life to know that a hot head needs a cool mind for a tenant if either is to win. So, outwardly calm, she turned back to Purse. "Well, now tell us, Purse, what has been happening here since? Is this Cusack man here? He's the one I really want to see."

"Nay, m'm!" Purse said with relish. "He were out on his ear that same day. He's gone for good, he has."

"And Dr. Brockman?"

Purse was puzzled at this. "Doctor's still here..." he began.

"Yes, of course," she interrupted impatiently. "I mean how...has he changed... has he said anything?" She floundered. How could Purse know the answers to these questions? "Did he say aught that morning?" she asked. "When you..." She pointed at Whernside.

"Well now he did say *one* thing." Purse spoke as if he had just remembered it. "He said, 'This'll never happen again!' Aye, that's a fact. 'This'll never happen again!' I didn't know, like, if he said it to me or to the little mite. Not that he could hear him, being passed out like. But them were his words—'never happen again.'"

"D'you believe him?"

"Oh, I do, m'm. It's my opinion he were right shocked, Dr. Brockman."

This brief talk with Purse in no way dispelled her anger but it did blunt the very sharpest edge of it—enough to prevent her from getting off on a disastrously wrong foot with Dr. Brockman. Also, more subtle influences had been at work as she and Purse had walked among the school buildings. The ancient walls, the worn steps, the pleasantly protective cloisters and yards, the stone water cisterns—she saw them all with a mind's eye that had been softened by Young John's eulogy. It was not hard to understand how such a place could grow on you.

Brockman did her the honour of coming to his gate as soon as he heard the carriage approach; he was embarrassed to see Nora walking ahead of it, so that he had to meet her cool gaze all the last thirty paces of her approach, from the moment Purse turned back to show the coachman where to take the horses.

"Mrs. Stevenson? I trust you had not too uncomfortable a journey," he said.

She took his hand for the briefest moment. "I've had very little comfort, Dr. Brockman. Young Caspar has had less."

"Indeed!"

She could see his eyes appraising her—not as men's eyes usually appraise a woman and as she was used to seeing men's eyes appraise her. Brockman's saw into her, seeking something within to weigh and to judge. "May I offer you some refreshment?"

He spoke as casually as if she had merely called upon him while on an errand elsewhere; she was not going to let him turn this into some chance meeting. "My time is short," she said. "And I wish to see this school before I go. It will be best if we walk and talk." She turned and faced the way she had just come. Nanette was getting out of the coach.

"As you think best," Brockman said curtly. "And your companion?"

"Since she is neither a defenceless child nor legally in your care, I assume she will be safe from assault under your roof, Doctor?"

It was a prepared rebuke but she had not imagined herself smiling as she said it, not even an acid smile. She did not know why she had smiled.

He did not smile. There was now a tight-lipped wariness in his attitude toward her. She asked Nanette, in French, what she preferred to do; Nanette answered that she had some letters to write. Mrs. Brockman had come halfway down the path when her husband opened the gate to let Nanette through. He introduced his wife to Nora, though Nora was clearly her junior. Nora then presented Nanette as her companion.

"What did she say?" Mrs. Brockman asked.

Nora thought Dr. Brockman would translate, but he turned to her. She grasped then, with something of a shock, that the headmaster had no French.

"She has some letters to write," Nora explained.

"I hope you will return and take some tea with us, Mrs. Stevenson," Mrs. Brockman said.

"I hope it may be possible," Nora answered, not yielding an inch.

As soon as they set off for Old School, Brockman came at once to the point. "Of all the troubles sent to plague a headmaster, Mrs. Stevenson, I make no secret to you that parents are usually far and away the worst. But in this case I have to confess I stand, as it were, at your shoulder. I look around at this place, which is and will be the work of my life, and I feel for it some of that loathing which you surely feel."

"I doubt it..." Nora began, annoyed with him for grasping this initiative.

"Oh, more keenly, I assure you, since I am the more deeply involved."

"It's an odd word, 'involved,' from a man who locks up two hundred boys at eight each night and never goes near them till next morning...who lets drunken bullies flog the flesh off ten-year-olds. 'Involved,' Dr. Brockman? If you drew a line at neglect, where would it run!"

He was silent for a while. "How may I put it?" he said at last. She could sense a frustration in him. His great hand squeezed at the air near her elbow, as if he would rather squeeze her arm to force his view upon her. "When your husband's firm builds a viaduct, now, do the men not...?"

She flared up at that. "Don't you dare patronize me, Dr. Brockman, with your simple parables. If you've a straight reason for what you did to my son, you'll tell me straight. If you've none, there's an end to it, and we'll waste no more of each other's time." She was glad to have back the initiative.

He was silent again but his restlessness was even more intense. They had almost reached Old School before he spoke. "Then I will not tell you," he said. "I shall show you. You shall see it all with your own eyes. And then I'll attempt to explain."

He showed her over Old School then. Even with Young John's praises to forewarn her she found it shocking. But Brockman did not try to excuse it or to modify her judgements—indeed, she grew annoyed at the way he agreed with and even surpassed them in severity.

"Small wonder," he said, showing her the pathetic study cupboards that littered the dark, dank, cold, outer passages, "that they take themselves off to messes in the town!"

"Over which you appear to have no control," Nora added.

"Only the ultimate control of expulsion. The messes do no harm to the young ones. Indeed they somewhat bridge the gulf between home and...these barracks. But the older boys find they may keep money there, and spirits, and they bring in wenches. And then we must expel them, if they are found out. Now, I think that is a disgraceful way for a school to fail its pupils—to force them upon the town, to expose them to temptations, then to wash its hands of them. It shames me."

He spoke of everything in that vein until Nora, thinking she saw through the stratagem, said, "Tell me, doctor, suppose you were headmaster here. How would you change it?"

She had wanted him to take offence but he merely smiled, somewhat grimly. "Ah! You, too, think it is easy. I wish I could tell you how many parents actually approve these arrangements. Eton, I promise you, is very much worse than this. When I was a scholar there—the very month I arrived—there was a rebellion against Dr. Keate, the headmaster. To crush it he flogged every boy on the school list from the letter A to the letter Z—some eighty boys. It went on from ten till past midnight. And when he retired to his bed, the whole school, from A to Z, lined up and cheered him. And the boys of that generation are now, like myself, parents. I dare swear that most of them—deplorable as it may sound—most of them would approve of what happened to Caspar."

Seeing the incredulity in her face he beckoned her outside. "Come and see my new Houses," he said. "They are everything Old School is not. And you will not believe the opposition I have met in trying to establish them. Opposition from the Trust that nominally manages Fiennes (though most of them never set foot here). Opposition from parents—some parents, who object to the greater fees. From my colleagues—and, of course, from the boys." He looked shrewdly at her, sidelong. "If I were a sporting man and wagered that your two boys, after less than a term here, have already told you how preferable is life at Old School to life in the new Houses, would I lose?"

She had to allow that he would not.

"The sad truth is," he said when they were outdoors again, "that you and I, Mrs. Stevenson, are not a majority."

Nora marvelled that she and he were suddenly on the same side of the fence, but she was interested enough in what she sensed was coming to make no more than a noncommittal noise in reply.

"And the more I have my way with Fiennes, the less it will resemble other leading schools." He smiled at her as he went on. "If you will permit me just one 'simple parable,' what should we say to a farmer who neglected to drain his land and who let weeds flourish, and yet who could find in an acre of wheat perhaps a dozen ears of prize quality—and who offered them as proof of the value of his method of farming! Of course we should laugh him to scorn. Why then do we not laugh to scorn all our leading schools—for that is precisely their principle!"

They were crossing the playing field and had to go aside to avoid a marshy patch. Brockman laughed. "You see! I cannot even drain my land!"

Nora could not help warming to him. At least her dislike was softened to the extent that she was prepared to admit his heart was in the right place. But that did not change the basis of her problem. Very well, he was not an evil man, merely a weak one. But neither kind of man was fit to have charge over her sons. "You say parents approve?" she prompted. She wanted to judge just how weak he was.

He nodded sadly. "For most parents, and for most teachers too, education is an obstacle race. A school is, for them, a place where a boy is provided with opportunities, and slight encouragement, to excel. But no extraordinary effort should be made to reach the laggard, the slow, the wayward, the indifferent. It is, as they see it, a sink-or-swim world. And school must mirror it."

"It *is* a sink-or-swim world," Nora said. "But we do not throw newborn babies into deep water on that account!"

He stopped and looked at her with some excitement, forgetting himself so far as to grip her arm, just as he gripped every boy he talked to. She became aware then what a very physical man he was, to need this contact in order to feel he was communicating. Yet it was true. The passion of his convictions was there in the way his hand trembled. "How I wish I had said that," he told her. "These are *not* young men!" He raised his voice as if to shout down an argument held in the very air around him. "These are children! And we throw them together in conditions where ninety men in a hundred could not be trusted. Then we whine over breaches of trust."

He saw her wince under his grip and at once fell into a stammering, blushing confusion. His embarrassment could not have been greater, she thought, if the assault had been indecent. To prevent him from shrinking out of sight, she said, "Let me repeat my earlier question, doctor, in a different spirit. If you were headmaster and had absolute powers here…I mean, what will the school be when you have had your way?"

"This is Crecy." He held open the gate, glad of this activity to rescue him from the confusion he still felt. "Mr. Carter's house. The Carters are in Dorset for Christmas so I'm sorry you will not meet." Then he stopped halfway up the drive and grew thoughtful. "My school," he mused. "My ideal school. Hmm.

My ideal school"—he watched her keenly now for her reaction—"will devote as much effort and expend as much of its resources on the least promising boy as on the most. Every boy will feel he is a person and is *known*." A few drops of rain began to fall but Nora made no move toward the door, only yards away; she sensed that Brockman's words were very close to the core of his convictions. At that moment the last shreds of her animosity toward him fell away. She was even prepared to concede that he was not a weak man.

"Every boy," Brockman went on, oblivious of the raindrops, "must feel impelled—and I say *im*pelled, not *com*pelled—to give of his best. His intellectual best in the schoolroom. His physical best on the playing field. And his moral best in all his dealings with others. Of the three this last far outweighs the former two. I would be happy for indifferent scholarship and moderate athletic prowess to flourish here if every boy showed moral excellence."

The rain was now falling so heavily that even he noticed it. They ran to the shelter of the porch. Again he apologized in confusion, just as when he had gripped her arm.

She saw then that there was something of the boy still in him. For all his impressive size and handsome masculinity, for all the scholarship he possessed, for all the moral passion that burned in him, there was something endearingly immature in his lack of social ease. Suddenly she could imagine him among the trustees whom he scorned so deeply—worldly aristocrats and bluff, foxhuntin' squires no doubt, of a type she knew so well. She could see exactly how bad he would be in such company, he would rub their fur the wrong way, most of all by assuming they had a common interest in the school. To a man they would prefer Old School, where the premium was on courage, tribe loyalty, self-reliance, and indifference to pain or discomfort, if the school accidentally turned out a few scholars, well and good. But Brockman's ideal of a well-rounded athletic Christian scholar as the standard boy would be anathema to them. She was surprised he had survived a single term; he was certainly no weak man to be headmaster still after—what was it—two or three years.

Now she wanted to know all about him and his methods. "Those are your principles," she said, cutting once again through his confusion. "They do not run square with what Young John has told me of your system, Dr. Brockman."

A servant opened the door, saw the headmaster, and pulled it wide to let them pass. She noticed that Brockman thanked the man.

"Machinery, machinery, machinery!" the headmaster said as he led her toward the boys' part of the House. "The perfect school will leave nothing to chance.

It will never rely on the merit of this or that teacher. The machinery, the arrangements, must secure excellence. The governance of the school must be liberal—by which I mean each boy must be given unlimited trust in his actions. It must also be protective—by which I mean suspicion must permeate the very fibres of the system. It must also be individual—each boy must feel his honour is indivisible from the honour of the House and the school."

They were in a light, cold, airy corridor, windows all down one side, doors all down the other. "These are the studies," Brockman said. "One to each boy in the House. It is here that boys are prevented from becoming a mob—the sort of mob, I fear, we still have in Old School. You see what I mean—machinery? The only difference between the boys here and the boys of Old School is"—he pushed open a door—"the individual study. Machinery!"

It was a very plain little room. A table, two chairs, a bookcase, a cupboard; no fire, no gas ring. Still, she thought, the gaslight was probably enough to heat so small a room.

"There is one other difference," he added, taking her the full length of the corridor to a large common room. "All the boys in the House, except the pharaohs, do their evening study here under Mr. Carter. Now if you were to witness it, you would probably think it a very commonplace matter of teaching and intellectual guidance. And so it is. But it also means that between seven and nine—the two most dangerous hours of the twenty-four—everyone is under a master's eye." Up went his finger. "Machinery!"

"And the pharaohs?"

He gave a bitter laugh. "I could not hope for a better example of my difficulty, Mrs. Stevenson!" He led her back along the corridor toward the dormitories. "I intended the word to be *pharos*." He spelled it out. "The pharos was the legendary lighthouse at Alexandria—a wonder of the ancient world. My idea was that the boys so favoured were to be as beacons to guide their fellows. But my 'beacons' came up under the old barbarism. It is they who have perverted the spelling to 'pharaohs' [again he spelled the word out] the hated slavemasters and pagan idolaters of the ancient world. Fortunately, in a school each generation is short. From your son's generation, now, I hope to rekindle my beacons and banish my slavemasters back into the dark where they belong."

The cubicles around each bed in the dormitory were high enough to cut off each boy from his recumbent neighbours but low enough for any master or pharaoh to see over. "Machinery! Machinery!" Brockman said yet again, waving his big hands vaguely toward the honeycomb of partitions; but this time he did not elaborate. Then, determined that she should see all, he took her down to the kitchens.

As they walked back over the field to Agincourt, Brockman's House, she realized that John had not been deceived and that Brockman was far from being a weak man. She also began to understand that Fiennes, once it approached his ideal school, could indeed give her sons something they would not get at home—a magnification of everything the best of homes could provide.

"You must build your other Houses as soon as possible, Dr. Brockman," she said.

He snorted and stopped. "I could build them all tomorrow," he said.

"But?"

His eyes resumed the audit they had practised when she and he first met. "Tell you straightly, you said? Very well, Mrs. Stevenson. When I came here the headmaster had a monopoly of boarders. You see, your sons—the boys in Old School and in Hospice—are not, strictly speaking, boarders. They are scholars, the last vestige of that medieval band of students who once camped hereabouts and studied at the Abbey school. D'you know that at the peak of its fame the Abbey had thirty thousand scholars—from all over Europe! That was when the celebrated Aloyis was teaching here. It is hard, looking at the valley as it is now, to imagine thirty-thousand camped out there. And how could one man have taught them?" He lifted his hands in ironic answer to his own question. "Your sons, as I say, are scholars rather than boarders. And when I came here, the headmaster had a monopoly of boarders. The result was that the other teachers were mere migrants—birds of passage. Good fellows maybe, but only by accident. They had no stake in the school—no sense that here was, or could be, a permanent home for them. Mr. Cusack was such a man. Well, I determined at once that if I was to put my ideas into practice, I had to gather around me a corps of masters who shared my aspirations and who had at least as much stake in Fiennes as I. So I broke my own monopoly."

"That was brave," Nora said admiringly.

"Futile, rather. My 'corps of masters' consists of Mr. Carter. And to persuade him to build Crecy I had to guarantee him two hundred and fifty guineas a year—which is the full extent of my own income. And I had to guarantee a loan of three thousand pounds to build the house—which is the full extent of my capital. I am a younger son. There will be no more. So there, Mrs. Stevenson, we lodge. And I hope if I now repeat that I share your horror at what happened to Caspar, you do not doubt me."

Nora had a fleeting suspicion that the whole afternoon had been deliberately engineered toward this conclusion—like a well-constructed begging letter. But she was a rich woman, and the rich have many opportunities every week for such suspicions. In practical terms it hardly mattered whether Brockman was cunning or just ingenuously lucky. Indeed, if she was now to get financially involved, it would be better if he were cunning.

"Why can you not turn Old School into a House as it is?" she asked. "You'd save the building costs."

He clasped his forehead. "We have not covered one hundredth part of my beliefs touching education," he said. "A House of a hundred boys would be a monstrosity. I will permit no House of more than forty boys. A class of one hundred boys is also a monstrosity. I would like no class of more than thirty. And the school will never hold more than four hundred and fifty boys. That is as much as any headmaster could deal with properly—in my view."

They had now reached the gate of his own House. He let her pass and then, as they went up the drive, he said: "I dearly wish to abolish the distinction between public and private tuition here. I think all boys should receive thirty or so hours of formal classroom instruction each week in classes no more than thirty strong. But for that I need twenty masters—not four. And I would have to abolish the free places and instead give scholarships for the boys from Langstroth. Money, money, money, you see, Mrs. Stevenson. I cannot pay the masters until I have put up the tuition fees. I cannot raise the fees until I have the masters to justify it."

He came past her to open his front door. In doing so he took her arm, this time knowingly, for his grip was feather light. "But we shall do it," he said. "Make no mistake of that. I shall do it despite the Trust. I shall do it in the teeth of the boys' opposition—and that of some of their parents. I shall do it no matter how skeptical my colleagues here may be—and no matter what it costs in personal sacrifice."

For a moment she glimpsed through his boyish bravado an intense weariness. She knew then, as if the experience were her own, what it must be like to have pledged all his capital and mortgaged all his income to achieve Crecy, after his own Agincourt. And there were nine more Houses to build—nine more battles to fight, to win, to commemorate! How could she ever have imagined him to be a weak man?

She reached a decision. "I'll stop here tonight," she said. "And we'll puzzle how you may achieve it in under one lifetime, doctor. I have a certain way with money—as you may know."

It took him completely aback. His surprise was so spontaneous that she knew she had guessed wrong. He had not schemed to trap her into helping; at most he might have hoped for some trifling donation.

"But…I…ah…you cannot possibly…that is, I cannot allow…you to give money—good heavens, madam, that was not my intention in telling you…"

Now it was she who laid a hand on his arm. "If you knew me," she said with a laugh, "you'd know how comic that last remark was. Me—*give* money! Give! No, doctor, I smell investment here, and that does to my blood what the smell of chalk and slate probably does to yours."

"Investment?" He seemed bewildered.

"You pledged two hundred and fifty guineas to Mr. Carter if his House failed to provide that income?"

"Yes."

"Has he taken up your pledge?"

"Indeed not. In fact…" Brockman hesitated.

"In fact, he's earned above your guarantee." She supplied the words for him.

"He has." Brockman's loyalties were being strained.

"*Well* above?" Nora pressed him.

He did not answer. But his silence did not worry her. Two hundred and fifty was over eight percent gross return off the three thousand he had mentioned. That was all the incentive she needed. And she was going to offer Brockman the prospect of getting his Houses the moment he was ready for them. Every man had his price.

No, his silence did not worry her. Before the evening was out she would know the school's finances down to the last brass farthing.

She was up early the following morning, but Brockman was up before her. She saw him and a handful of boys making the morning run up Whernside; they would be boys whose parents, for one reason or another, could not have them at home this Christmas. She could not see their stone cisterns from her window, but she could imagine them all splashing around in the icy water, gaining in manliness by pretending to have it already. The mere thought of such a plunge made her shiver.

The sight of the runners also added to her understanding of Brockman as a person with strong beliefs and a willingness to endure anything in order to put them into practice. Even if no boys were left in school for these holidays, she had no doubt he would be making the same run and splashing in the same cisterns all by himself.

As she dressed, she reviewed the agreement she had reached with Brockman the previous evening. Not quite as good as she had hoped. He had insisted that the housemasters should have some financial stake in the Houses and that ultimately each should buy out any loan on his own House. To Nora, who always looked for perpetual investment where bricks and mortar were concerned, this was not very satisfactory. Only the knowledge that her own boys would be benefiting (and the fact that the return on the advances would be five per cent) persuaded her to go forward with the scheme at all.

The bargaining that had gone before her acceptance had increased her respect for Brockman. Her fertile mind had put forward half a dozen alternatives as to how the whole scheme might be managed—different ways of timing it, different forms of administration, different provisions for involving the housemasters, and so on.

She had watched him weaving among them, testing each not by the yardstick of profit and loss but by seeing how well it furthered his own principles. From them he would not be budged by so much as the thickness of a single banknote.

His resistance to financial temptation especially impressed her. Here was a man racked by debts and the burdens of guarantees. He was in charge of an institution that, if managed in certain ways—and not bad ways, either—could yield amazing returns on a fairly modest outlay; yet all he thought of was "educational principle"! His school had to be profitable, of course—but only to protect that principle, not to make him rich. Such monumental self-denial left her speechless with admiration.

But it also made her feel wanted! The Brockmans of this world—or, rather, not *quite* of this world—needed the Noras, who were so totally of it.

Breakfast was passed in a very English reticence about yesterday's discussion and decisions. Brockman, his appetite honed keen by the winds of Whernside, put down a plate of devilled kidneys, a bowl of fish kedgeree, two poached eggs, and some cold chicken. As he ate he spoke heartily of his hopes for the school; but his tone was so bluff, so different from his earlier seriousness, that it was as if he were telling them to Nora for the first time—and as if she were a casual visitor who needed this jocularity to capture and hold her interest. She could not imagine why he was taking this new line with her, but she felt the distance it put between them.

Again she saw that unworldly, boyish quality in him, beneath the learning and the undoubted authority he carried as headmaster. Only in their last few moments together, when, clearly, some reference to their agreement had to be made, did his seriousness return—though he said little, preferring, for some reason, for Nora to make the summary.

"I think it best, doctor," she concluded, "if I write to you, setting out these arrangements. And though we do not, perhaps, need a legal agreement, I shall, nevertheless and with your leave, ask my lawyer to look through the letter." When he looked doubtful she added: "And I believe you should do the same."

Then she understood the cause of his doubt, for he said, "When you say 'you,' you mean *Mr.* Stevenson, I presume? Surely you must consult him?"

She smiled. "No, Dr. Brockman. This is not my husband's money."

It was not hers, either, but she was not going to tell him that. In fact, the money she was going to use belonged to a syndicate headed by two German-Jewish bankers named Wolff—two brothers. In the money panic of 1848 Nora had been given exclusive control of their London funds. She had turned their original £180,000 into well over half a million, so no one was going to interfere with her control of the fund now. She could quite safely pledge this tiny fraction of it to Fiennes.

As she spoke, all his embarrassment returned. "But...I had no idea...I mean...I naturally assumed...dear me!" He added something in Greek and smiled, assuming absent-mindedly that she understood him.

"Money has no gender, Dr. Brockman," she chided. "At least, not in plain English. And in Latin I think you'll find it in my camp, not yours?"

He nodded, agreeing with her Latin grammar, but she deliberately took this gesture for a general agreement and a waiving of all objection. She heard him draw breath to add some further point, but she had already passed beyond him. Quickly she spoke in French to Nanette. Then she turned round and told Brockman—still in French—that she really had to be on her way. That was to pay him out for his Greek. He was nonplussed enough to forget whatever thoughts he had been about to pursue.

Later she wondered if this ruse had been entirely wise. Perhaps she should have let him talk it out; perhaps those objections would now fester within him and poison the whole scheme. At all events she would now know just how keen he was to get his Houses. If he let some irrational objection about taking loans from a woman override what he claimed was his dearest wish in life, then he was a small man of no account.

Perhaps, on reflection, it had been best to leave him to wrestle alone with it.

Nanette was disgusted at the way things had turned out. "Money!" she sneered at Nora when they were on the train and homeward bound once more. "One sniff of it and you forget everything else!"

"Money *is* everything else," Nora answered evenly. "At least it makes everything else possible."

"Hah—good! Then poor Caspar is already healed!"

Nora was well used to Nanette's bluntness; indeed there were times when she relied on the girl as a sort of conscience. But this was not one of them.

"Oh, look!" Nora said, pointing at a turf hovel about a hundred yards from the line. "I once lived in a place identical to that. Identical!" An old woman leaned wearily in the doorhole, listlessly watching the train go by. "That could be me," she added. "Old before time."

Nora imagined she had been changing the subject; but Nanette stared at her in bewildered pity and a sort of baffled affection. At last she shook her head at the gulf in understanding that stood between them.

Chapter 10

When she returned home Nora found she could not look her two eldest sons in the eye and tell them exactly what she had and had not done up at Fiennes, so some of Nanette's scorn must have found its mark. She thought this reluctance odd because the two boys would, in fact, heartily approve of what she had done—anything that didn't prevent their return and that didn't give Brockman cause to single them out.

All she told them was that Mr. Cusack had gone. She did not claim his departure was her doing; even if it had been, she would never have told them so. But she used that very fact to allow them to assume that she had insisted on Cusack's removal and that Brockman's acceptance of it had become the basis of a most satisfactory compromise.

But then, the very next day, came news that drove out all thoughts of Fiennes and money and Brockman's Houses. Even Caspar's bruises became trivia. For John was gravely ill. The message did not exactly say his life was despaired of, but the implication was there in every line.

He was being brought back in stages, overland from Naples, resting, recuperating, and then braving a further hundred or so miles by coach or rail. It was a dour, prayerful Christmas at Maran Hill. Then, early in the new year, word came that he had reached Paris and would soon be in Dieppe for the sea crossing to Folkestone.

Nora went at once to Folkestone, intending to take the ferry to France and nurse him until he was well enough to face the crossing. She arrived at the English coast to see a great storm thrashing the waters of the Channel; it was unthinkable for any kind of vessel to put to sea. She sat in her hotel room, looking out through rivulets of rain upon the windowpanes, her eyes raking those shivering, angry wastes of water…for what? Not a boat, certainly. They were all jostling at anchor in the harbour below—ketches, brigs, schooners, luggers, steamers—fretting to be out and away. Their hands, unpaid and idle, were a great nuisance about the town, begging and drinking, fighting and carousing.

There was really no point in her staying at the coast. London was a bare two hours away. The company could telegraph her. She could easily be back before the steamer was made ready. And there was certainly plenty of business to attend to in London.

Twice she told Nanette to pack for the return. Twice she paid their lodging. Once she got as far as the railway station yard; the second time she went no farther than the end of the street before she told the driver to turn around and take them back to the hotel. There she resumed her vigil at the window, peering through the wind-lashed rain looking for the clearing skies that would not come. Nanette did not sneer at *these* changes in plan, for they were of the heart, not the head.

Nora, who had not even seen the sea until she was twenty—almost two years after her marriage—came to know its many angry faces too well now as, over the best part of a week, the gales veered from southwest to north. The sou'westerlies, reaching up the Channel, pushed vast torrents of water before them, making mountainous green breakers that hurled themselves at the chalk cliffs and spent their energy in a seething white confusion on the banks of pebbles between the tides. Along the breakwater these giant waves rose in solid sheets of shimmering, translucent grey. Some of the water thus raised never fell again to the sea but was borne upward on the storm and swept over the masts and sheets of the sheltering fleet to batter the town in a salty deluge.

As the winds went round west and then nor'west the character of the sea changed. The waves, no longer pushed from behind, fell somewhat in height; but the fall was relative—these were still angry and powerful rollers. Now, in the crosswind, they sidled at the coast as if each bit of water elbowed its neighbour for the chance to lead the charge. And the onslaught was no less thunderous, though now the salt deluge swept clear over the harbour and fell in the black shelter of the farther jetty.

Finally, with the wind in the north, the immediate coastline fell into the lee of the land. Half a mile out the storm dipped down off the clifftops and peeled back the crest of every wave. At that distance all their violence turned to beauty—serried ranks of white combers displaying their plumes, the young on the heels of the prime in the wake of the spent. Inshore, shivers of ripples shook the harbour, as the unrelenting north wind turned cold and yet colder.

"If this direction holds and the wind drops, we'll fairly bustle over to France," Nora said.

A telegraph message came from Dover, via the new Channel cable. It was from Walter, saying that he and John were in Dieppe at the Hôtel des Bains, and that John, in their enforced rest, was making good progress. But from what, she wondered? From critically to merely dangerously ill? From ill to convalescent? Unless she knew how bad he had been, she could not tell just how good the news from Walter was. At least it meant John's life was not in danger; this (she could now admit to herself) had been the fear that had kept her in Folkestone when it would have been so much more sensible to go to London.

The day after the telegraph message came there was a drop in the wind, though it still held northerly and now grew even colder. In the harbour there were unmistakable signs of preparation for sailing. Seamen vanished from the streets and began to swarm the masts and spars, unfurling the shrouded sails. The wind tore black smoke from funnels and, within an hour or two, thin plumes of vented steam showed briefly white before the vapour vanished in the cold and now dry air. Nanette packed yet again, confident that it was now to some purpose.

The first time Nora had made this voyage, in the spring of forty-five, passengers were rowed out to the steamer. A storm had been blowing then, too, and merely to reach the ship had been quite an achievement—especially as she had been heavily pregnant with Clement at the time. Now a small steam launch took them out to the steamer in much greater comfort.

The storms had discouraged travellers—never very numerous at this time of year anyway. So she and Nanette had the Ladies' Cabin almost to themselves. Nora was a good sailor but not so Nanette. To keep her occupied, Nora made her read aloud, above the clank and whoosh of the engine, the groan of the paddlewheels, and the roar of the wind. She chose Gerard de Nerval's *Les filles de feu*, especially the sonnets called *Les chimères*, because they angered Nanette and would keep her mind off the heaving of her innards. They angered Nanette for exactly the reason that they delighted Nora: The haunting beauty of de Nerval's language moved both of them, but his subject matter—that strange mixture of private obsession, alchemy, myth, and the occult—repelled the down-to-earth romantic in Nanette just as it excited the ultrarealist in Nora. It showed Nanette herself grossly, dangerously magnified; it showed Nora states of being that she could never aspire to and that she could therefore toy with in safety.

At all events the ruse worked. Nanette felt no nausea until they were standing in the customs shed at Dieppe—and then, paradoxically, it was because the land now appeared to be heaving. The fifteen minutes they had to wait for the customs to appear were the most nerve-racking of the week for Nora—to know that John was within half a mile of where she stood and that only two dirty officials in stained uniforms, jacks-in-office grudgingly torn from their tots of brandy, now kept them apart. As soon as the ritual was over she took a fly to the hotel, leaving Nanette to organize a couple of porters and their luggage.

Every inch held a familiar memory. Here was where she took her first walk on French soil—with John. Here was where they bumped into Tom and Sarah Cornelius. Here was where the four of them had eaten one of the finest meals of their lives—in a dirty fishermen's café you wouldn't have looked at twice. There was the railway station, Stevenson's first contract in France. His work was everywhere; memories of him were everywhere.

She shook herself, annoyed that she could not think of him in more positive ways—as if she feared to believe he might live, as if such belief were tempting Providence. It filled her with foreboding, too, this taste of a world filled with everything about John except his living presence.

Walter Thornton must have known she would be on the first cross-Channel boat into Dieppe. She saw him standing at the window of the hotel lounge, already smiling and waving encouragement, certain that the first fly to draw up would be hers.

"How is he?" she asked before she was fairly through the door.

"Asleep now. He had a fretful morning, knowing the storm was gone and you might be here any hour. We sent to the harbourmaster every fifteen minutes, I'd say!"

"Yes, but how *is* he? Can I see him?"

Walter did not want to say no. She felt a passing anger that this man (whom she had never been able to admire) was coming between her and John. Then she saw how tired Walter was, too, and her anger turned to shame. Their work in the Crimea must have been done in appalling hardship, quite unimaginable to her. And on top of that they had this dreadful journey back, Walter with the added responsibility of a sick friend.

She sat down then, to let him sit too. "Poor you," she said. "You must have had the worst of it."

Walter smiled thinly and rubbed his eyes. "It's over. The worst is over. Thank the Lord he's recovering so well now."

"He *is*, isn't he? You aren't just saying that?"

"Oh, completely. He doesn't need anyone with him now. He's not ill any more. Just exhausted."

"What was it?"

Walter shrugged. "Exhaustion. As I say. Sheer, utter…exhaustion." He could think of no other word. "We ought to have noticed it, Tucker and I, but we're so used to the way he drives himself at the best of times. You know." He raised his eyes skyward and snorted. "And these were the worst of times. I doubt I've ever seen worse."

"You were all at the limit."

Walter nodded his agreement, eyes closed. He kept his eyes closed.

"You must rest now, Mr. Thornton. I'll look after John. You must still be all in."

He revived then, opening his eyes and smiling. "No," he said with self-encouraging vigour, "not any longer. This storm gave us both rest. I think I'll go out and walk a bit. Blow away the cobwebs."

She smiled tensely, trying to appear nonchalant, as though she believed him. Of course he would go directly to the nearest brothel.

She knew him well enough to be sure of that. And he would go at once because to be alone with her embarrassed him—embarrassed them both. For more than fifteen years ago she and Walter had met by the wayside, about three hours before John had entered her life. She had been barefoot and penniless, and Walter had put a sovereign in her pocket, paying for a favour whose memory would forever make it impossible for either to be in the other's company without that particular embarrassment.

They both rose. She put a hand on his arm. "I doubt I can ever say how grateful I am to you," she said. "And John, of course."

He grinned. "It was little enough. I couldn't say which of you I did it for. I'd have done it for either."

It was the first moment of true warmth between them since their original meeting, so long ago. She was glad to have taken the plunge—and so, she could see, was Thornton; they had surmounted something, pulled down a bit of the old barrier.

To be sure, she could not respect him any the more. How could you respect a man who went off whoring several times a week? Especially a man who let his wife devote herself to the rescue of fallen women!

When Thornton had gone she asked the manager where John was. He looked surprised that she should inquire; it was the best room—the one they always had.

She left instructions for Nanette to wait below, or in her own room, and not to bring up the bags until sent for; then she slipped quietly into their room.

The curtains were drawn and it took some moments before her eyes grew accustomed to the gloom. She stood still, feeling a small moment of panic—she could not hear John's breathing. Then he stirred in his sleep and she was afraid she had woken him. Rather than risk that, she turned toward an alcove at the far end of the room, where one small uncurtained side window let in the only light the room possessed.

She stood awhile, staring down at the cold, grey street. A fly drew up. Nanette got out. At that moment Thornton came out of the hotel and spoke to her. Had he been waiting? Nora drew back a little in case she should be accidentally caught watching them, but when they looked up, the window he pointed to was the curtained one away to her left, not hers.

Why, when one saw Thornton talking to any female, did one imagine only a certain suggestive conversation taking place? Nanette liked Thornton, she could tell. Nora watched his greedy, glittering, foxy grin at work on her...could almost imagine his rich, gurgling, basso-profundo laugh...could see Nanette, being flattered, turning coquettish. At this safe distance Nora, too, could afford to admit that the man had attractions beyond the reach of moral sense.

She remembered then that from this same window, after that Olympian meal, she had watched Tom and Sarah Cornelius walk hand-in-hand in the moonlight. She knew that Sarah had been Thornton's mistress for a time after Tom had died. Now, watching him at work on Nanette, she understood exactly what had made Sarah succumb to him—but, after sixteen years of friendship with the Thornton family, she knew just what had ultimately repelled Sarah, too.

"Nora? Eay, love!"

She turned to see John struggling to get up. She ran to him to stop him from rising any further in the bed. In the flurry before he sank into her embrace she caught only the briefest glimpse of him, but it was enough to fill her with horror. She barely recognized him, his cheeks were so drawn, his eyes so hollow, his hair so thin—he gave the impression of toothless senility. Only his body belied that impression. His huge frame had not changed. The muscle he had acquired in his years of navvying was all still there; she clung to it, ran her fingers over it, dreading the moment when she would have to pull away from it and look him in the face again.

"Bit of a shock, eh?" he said. His voice was firm, too; no weakness there.

She gripped him tighter.

"It's been worse. For three weeks Thornton wouldn't let me have a looking glass." He chuckled.

"Oh, John!" She kissed his neck, his ear, his hair, his cheekbone. At last she dared to look at him.

Perhaps the preparation afforded by that first hectic glimpse of him now cushioned the shock, for he seemed less pitiable this time. He was—or had been—ill, very ill. No doubting it. But his smile was strong, his eyes clear.

"We finished it," he said. "Forty-two miles. We did seven miles in the first twelve days!"

"I know. You wrote and told me. And it has been in all the papers." She kissed him, his lips, his nose, his cheeks, while relief from all her suppressed fears welled up within her. He sank back on his pillows and closed his eyes.

"How are the children?"

"All well. Of course, this Christmas was not our brightest."

"And the boys? What about school?"

She did not answer at once; the pause made him open his eyes again. "Trouble?" he asked. "You're not still..."

She smiled. "No. There was a little bit of bother but it's all sorted out. Dr. Brockman and I are the firmest friends."

He lifted his head off the pillow. "You saw him? You went up there? Or did he..."

"I went there." She laid her hands on his shoulders, bearing him down. "You have a gift for finding people. Thornton once said to me—you remember the day we all went on that picnic, and you hired a starving lame fellow we met..."

"Noah Rutt," John said. "He works for us still."

"And I said it was foolish charity to employ rubbish like that, and Thornton told me that cripple'd turn out to be a second James Watt or something."

John began a diffident laugh.

"Because," she insisted, "you have a genius for picking people."

"Picked you," he said, stroking her cheek. "Unless it was t'other way about."

"And you picked Brockman."

"D'you think he's that good?"

"If any man's destined to make his mark on the school system in England, it's him."

He closed his eyes again.

"You sleep now," she told him. "I'll be here."

One eye opened. "I can't manage much," he said. "Ten minutes' talk even and I'm exhausted."

"You'll mend. You'll soon be your old self."

As he sank into sleep he said, "You needn't stay. I'll sleep an hour or so. Don't stay."

She waited half an hour, until she could see how untroubled his sleep was, and then she went out to see Nanette about unpacking their things. *Good*, she thought. *I've told him now.*

But she had not told him. And over the days that followed, while they were together—first in their room, later in walks over the sands—the rest of the story trickled out. The more he heard the less pleased he grew.

She should have left the assault on Caspar for him to deal with; that was his first complaint.

"But I didn't know when you would be back," she said.

The better his health grew, the more he tried to belittle his collapse. He now behaved as if the illness had been a private weakness—something to be ashamed of. It seemed necessary to his recovery now to make light of it—so she could not insist he would have been—indeed was still—too frail to deal with the Caspar business.

"It can't have been all that bad," he said. "Boys are flogged at school all the time."

"And you approve?"

"It's not a question of approval. Caspar is going into the army. I tell you a woman has no idea of the brutalities of a soldier's life. It's not a woman's place to interfere in these things. A woman has no..."

"I'm not 'a woman,'" she flared at him. "I'm Caspar's mother. And when you're halfway around the world, I'm his father, too."

He looked at her coldly. "You will never be that. As I was saying: He will witness—he will even have to order—floggings of a brutality that..."

"John!" she cried, desperate for him to understand. "The flesh on his bottom was cut bare and bleeding. There was no skin left! It was butcher's meat."

"I'm sure you exaggerate..."

"I do *not*!"

"Will you let me finish just one sentence! He is going into the army. He must be tough. He must be tough in body, mind, and spirit. Tougher than you can possibly imagine. You talk about butcher's meat! I saw men flogged in the Crimea with six ribs showing through—the flesh flogged off them crumb by crumb!"

She winced and shut her eyes. He put an arm around her then. "I'm sorry, love," he said, more gently. "It's the only way to get you to see. The boys are in a man's world, now. And you brought a woman's view to it. In the long run, that won't help Caspar—nor even in the short run, either."

"Suppose he doesn't want to go in the army?" Nora asked.

"Of course he will. And if I tell him that's where he'll go, he'll go!"

She smiled, but not at him. "You don't know him at all, do you!" she said, half speaking to the four winds. "The last way to get Caspar to do anything is to command him."

"A soldier must get used to command. And he will be expected to go into the army—especially now that..." He bit off the sentence.

"Especially now that what?"

"Never mind. We've run this subject into the ground."

She knew then that he was concealing something from her. So she went right back, hoping to steer him to whatever it was. "Anyway," she said, playing woman-having-last-word (which she knew would rile him), "the beating Caspar got was so bad that Brockman sacked this Cossack fellow."

"Tcha! He was probably leaving anyway. Brockman just gilded the truth a bit to pacify you."

She could not win. A dreadful foreboding began to fill her. There were times when John became very moody and depressed—"when you're in a valley and see only your own feet," was how he himself put it. When those moods were upon him, nothing could lighten them or make him take a cheerful view. She was terribly afraid that such a cloud was now descending on him; sometimes it could last for weeks. Later, when it was over, he could admit that his fears and angers had been groundless for the most part, but he could never see things so dispassionately at the time. When she reminded him of past occasions he would only say that this time it was different.

She had tried every way to prevent these moods—ridicule, anger, laughter, indifference, tears—but nothing seemed to have any effect; they followed some course of their own, indifferent to every kind of persuasion. And she, being closest, always bore the worst of it, just as she had the best of him when he was in good cheer.

"Funny he should take that attitude," Walter said when she explained to him why John seemed out of sorts. "In the Crimea he was ready to fight a duel with a lieutenant of the Fourth Dragoon Guards who had one of our navvies flogged for insolence."

"A duel? I don't believe it!"

"He didn't issue the challenge, of course. The officer did that. Stevenson took the lash out of the sergeant's hand and wiped the blood on it over the officer's buckskin. I've never seen Stevenson so angry."

"How did it begin?"

So Walter told her. The officer had been out "hunting" a bobbery pack of mongrels he'd assembled from the strays of Balaclava port; it was one of those flamboyant jokes that Guards officers seemed to enjoy. One of his chases led over the line Stevenson's was then laying and the navvies had refused to get out of his way. Their ganger had insulted the lieutenant, who had then sent for an armed flogging party and had actually administered twenty or so lashes before John had arrived and, single-handedly, routed the party. That was when the officer had sent John the challenge to a duel.

"And he accepted?" Nora was still incredulous that John could have hazarded his life, his business, or even (to look only at the most immediate risk) the Crimean railway for something so addleheaded as this bit of foolery.

Walter nodded. "He must have been tired beyond all sense."

"Did they actually fight?"

"Er…military affairs intervened. Another Dragoon Guard had a word with someone on the staff, and the young hothead was sent up the line within the hour. Oh, they can move when they want to!"

"But what could John have been thinking of! If he'd won, he could never have returned to England. And if he'd lost…!" She lifted her hands in despair. "Why didn't you and Tucker stop him?"

He merely looked at her with a knowing smile. "He just said how could he ever take charge of his men again once word got around that he'd refused a challenge. It was a matter of honour."

She almost wept. Men who'd worked for him—and with him—for sixteen years! Did he have to go fighting duels to retain their trust and loyalty?

Walter left for England that afternoon, looking very much better.

"Amazing what a few hours on the old fork'll do for that fellow," John said in a rare spell of good humour. He teased her then. "He was a bit warm to Nanette, eh? Ye don't suppose…"

Nora dismissed the very thought of it; not only did she trust Nanette, she also knew Thornton. "He may lack all scruple," she said, "but that doesn't stop him being a gentleman. He'd never touch a single girl—not a respectable one, anyway. Married women, widows, and tarts—that's his strict three-course meal."

Later when they were out walking on the beach—or, rather, picking a careful way over its chalk and flint pebbles—his black mood descended again and he set about her once more for "interfering" at Fiennes.

His attack was so unfair that she was goaded into saying, "Splendid words—from the man who risked making orphans of eight children and a widow of me, and all for a navvy old enough to fend for himself, I'd say!"

She regretted it at once. Reasoned argument never even dented these moods of his. He was silent a time, then he said bitterly, "So you've told it all to Thornton!"

"You know better than that," she said. "You know me better."

"Do I?"

She shook him urgently. "John! What's the matter with you? Why be like this!"

He looked at her coldly and then resumed his walk, leaving her to catch up.

"We can go home, too," he said the following day. "I'm well enough. I'm back to normal."

Glumly she had to agree that in one very negative sense he was "back to normal." A few weeks earlier, when she had first arrived at Dieppe, he had still been much too feeble to sustain this brooding anger at such a pitch of intensity.

He had enough social grace to feel embarrassed at his anger when Nanette was around; he covered it by pretending to fret at not being back in harness. Nora abetted this deceit by suggesting a further week or two's convalescence with old friends of theirs, Monsieur and Madame Rodet, along the coast at Trouville.

"Rodet would love to see you again," she said. "And he knows everything that's going on in French railways. You could catch up on all you've been missing."

To her surprise he seemed on the point of agreeing; so she added: "And I know I'd love to see Rodie again."

Rodie—Madame Rodet—was her greatest friend this side of the water. Either side, come to that. It would be marvellous to see her again.

But no sooner had she said the words than he began to shake his head. "Too much work," he said. "We can't afford to fritter any more time on our own enjoyment. Besides, I want to see the boys before they go back to school."

She kicked herself for having brought her own pleasure into it.

Chapter 11

THE CHILDREN WERE DELIGHTED TO HAVE THEIR FATHER BACK AGAIN. Caspar's stripes had almost healed; thin lines of dried scab, like old cat scratches, were all that remained—nothing to rouse anyone's anger. And Caspar, of course, was now being very manly about it all, especially as they were due back at school the next day.

"Not too bad, was it, eh?" John said, jovially.

"Oh, it healed pretty well, sir," Caspar answered, all nonchalant.

"And you're looking forward to the new term?"

"I should just say so!"

"Well listen, young man—you'll be a soldier one day, and wounded soldiers don't go tattling to the womenfolk at every little scratch. I thought you would be more manly. You've disappointed me." Then, seeing how crestfallen Caspar became and not wanting to mar his return home for something that was, at bottom, Nora's fault rather than Caspar's, he nudged the boy in a more jocular mood and added, "Besides, you know what the ladies are—how they like to fuss. So promise you won't distress your mother in future, eh?"

And for Caspar, his wounds gone, it was an easy promise to make—and it felt like only a very minor betrayal of his mother, the sort you get in families every day.

The schoolroom was closed for the occasion, of course, and there were rides around the park in the governess cart, and a short play by Winifred all about the return of a feudal knight to his castle; and then when the last muffin had followed the last pancake down red lane, the climax of the day: *The Tale of the Crimea Railway, As Told by Its Builder.*

Children from any other family would have found it a weird story indeed—ranging from stirring military adventures, like the Battle of Balaclava and the bombardment of Sebastopol, down to the most arcane railway technicalities—gradients, curves, tracklaying details, and all. But these were Stevenson children. When their father said one in one-eighty they could see the slope; a two-hundred radius curve would get them leaning inward as, in their mind's eye, they raced around it; say to them "two-inch and under" and they could hear the sound that particular grade of gravel made as it was tipped. Without these details a railway story—even one told by their father—would have sounded hollow, concocted.

This secret knowledge bound them in a private glee they could share with no other children—not even the Thorntons, for Walter had not John's gifts as a storyteller. It gave them great power in their play, too, this knowledge of the real engineering world. For instance, when they made miniature canal systems down by the river, where other children would say, "We must line them with clay," a Stevenson would say, "We'll puddle it with best Leicester blue daub," and immediately the canal was somehow more real—even if what they actually used was a rather leaky Hertfordshire glacial clay.

By the end of the day, nervous energy, buoyed up by the delight of his children, was all that kept John on his feet. Nora could see the exhaustion closing in upon him. But he would not be warned. Every time she suggested he should finish, or at least rest a while, he would brush her words aside and encourage a general chorus of boos at this spoiling of the sport.

Next day, of course, he paid the price of it. He was so weak he could hardly stand. His fingers trembled and could not hold knife or fork. Nora had to take Boy and Caspar to the station without him for their return to Fiennes. It was a week before he regained the strength his one day had cost him. By then all the delight at being home had faded and his dark mood had asserted itself once more.

Nora did her best to keep out of his way, since she more than anyone seemed to have a worsening effect on him; but she could hardly absent herself from their table and their bed. At the end of one especially dour day, when he fretted from sunup onward to be back in their London office, planning a tour of all the current Stevenson contracts to bring himself up to date, he asked her to come to bed early. She hoped she knew why; but she was wrong.

"You ought to be told," he said when she lay beside him. "I don't know whether I should have told you before—or whether I should be telling you at all." He thought for a while. "That man—the officer in the Fourth Dragoons who intervened to stop the…" He cleared his throat.

"Duel?" she said.

He nodded. "Captain Proudfoot. Keith Proudfoot by name. He and I became quite close friends. And he had connections with the general staff. Anyway…from what he said, there may be a peerage for me in the offing. A barony probably."

"John!" She was thrilled. She wanted him to tell her again, a dozen different ways. "How marvellous!"

"Of course, it's far from certain." He began to back away from the idea now it was out.

"You deserve it."

"I don't suppose the army can do anything but advise in the case of civilian honours. Not like a medal."

"When you look at some of the people who get these honours!"

"So it's only a recommendation from—I don't know—Raglan, I imagine."

"I'd say it's an honour that's long overdue." She hugged him, glad not only at the news but also at the chance to show her love. The Right Honourable Lord Stevenson! First Baron—what? "Baron what, have you thought? Eay, John, I'm that glad!"

He barely responded. He lay there, smiling faintly at the middle distance.

"And the children will all be Honourables, too. The Honourable Winifred Stevenson. The Honourable John Stevenson…Oh, John—aren't you pleased? Why are you just sitting like that?"

He came out of his reverie and looked at her; he looked at the arm she had laid across his chest as if he might be a little more comfortable without it there. "Of course you won't breathe a word?"

"Of course not! I'm surprised you feel the need to ask."

"Not even Nanette."

"John!"

She pulled her arm away. Silence fell. "If you're in such doubt you shouldn't have told me," she said, hurt.

"I told you for a reason." For a long while he added nothing more.

"I suppose I may hear it this side of dawn," she said at last.

He breathed in and closed his eyes. This implication that he knew she was going to be angry was, in itself, enough to make her so.

"These honours," he began. "They aren't handed out like prizes. It isn't a…a sum of money that you're free to spend or save or gamble. It isn't just a royal pat on the head."

"It's a recognition," she said.

He looked at her speculatively. "Recognition of what?"

"Services done. Service to the nation. And if that doesn't describe the Crimean railway, then..."

But John was shaking his head. "More," he said. "It's more than that. For services they just hand out orders and decorations—Member of This, Companion of That. When they give a barony it's a recognition of more than services. It's a recognition that we are fit people for other Englishmen to look up to." His gaze turned into an open challenge.

"So?" she asked uncomfortably.

"Not just to look up to, but to admit into good society," he went on.

She grinned then. "Yes! They won't snub us now. Even Lord Middleton's hunt won't dare blackball us any longer—it would be like a slur on the queen's judgement." She giggled with suppressed delight.

"Not just to look up to," he went on relentlessly. "Not just to admit into good society. But to emulate—to use as an example."

"They've far to go to catch us up!" Nora sneered. "There's no man in the realm could follow you—do what you've done, get where you've gotten." She spoke in this way because she now had more than an inkling of where this particular homily of John's was going.

His annoyance was like a reward—he, who had expected her anger. "I'm not talking about example in that sense. I mean behaviour."

"Morally, you mean? I hope you're not implying that I need..."

"No!" he said vehemently. "I do not mean morally either—as I suspect you know. I am talking about behaviour acceptable to Society. I am talking about conforming, Nora."

There was another silence.

"Very well—talk away!" Nora said at length. "I shall be interested to hear what Lady Stevenson may not do that plain Mrs. Stevenson achieved."

"Lady Stevenson will have to be At Home more often. Lady Stevenson will have to take a more prominent place in local Society, pay more morning calls, help determine the shape of Society—or that part of it in which she moves. Lady Stevenson will not be able to hang about the fringes of the City, dining alone with her banker..."

"Are you implying that Nathaniel and I are anything more to each other than..."

"Of course not. I know. And you know—and so, I hope, does Nathaniel Chambers. But Society does *not* know. Society will draw a different inference."

"So Lady Stevenson will have to wash Society's mind for it, too. It won't be the first washing I've taken in."

"Lady Stevenson will have to stop glorying in her past poverty and her noble climb out of its depths. Lady Stevenson cannot entertain portrait painters at her table—nor doctors nor clergymen either."

"Not *Sir* Edwin Landseer?" she asked innocently.

For a moment he was deceived; his mouth fell open. "You mean he's now in your magic circle, too?"

"I only use him as an example. I'm surprised that no lady could seat Sir Edwin, whom the queen..."

"Of course there are exceptions. Don't be so deliberately obstructive. What I'm saying is that Mr. Llewellyn Roxby and his kind would not be fit acquaintances for a baroness. They are not, in fact, fit for Mrs. Stevenson either—but the queen did not select Mrs. Stevenson as a suitable person for other members of Society to take example from."

"The queen won't select Lady Stevenson, either. It will be John Stevenson she'll select. I'll be there by accident—if at all."

He looked at her then and nodded as if she had said something quite shrewd. "Exactly! 'If at all.' If we don't get this peerage, Nora, do you think it will be because the Crimea railway wasn't good enough—deserving enough—or because Mrs. Stevenson's eccentricities make the honour impossible?"

Nora felt her guts drop from inside her. What John was implying was monstrous, yet there was a clever little nugget of truth at the heart of it. Her individualism and neglect of middle-class society (and for Nora the queen herself was the very essence of all that she meant by "middle" class) might not please any of these drab, grey, mid-century administrations who told the queen whom to honour, whom to shun.

"I'm sure all this would have been news to Lady Henshaw," she said, rallying, "who kept that flock of goats to pull her carriage. You've been reading too many books on etiquette—that's your trouble."

"Lady Henshaw was an old eccentric. She did not move in Society. And books on etiquette don't come into it."

"All right. What's the name of that fellow Chambers was telling us about last year? Very rich but can't get into... *Richard!* Mr. Richards. When I'm the Lady Stevenson, I'll behave so properly you won't see me for the ice. And I'll hire my title out to Mr. Richards, be his hostess, greet his guests at the door. Thousand pounds at a time! You know me—I have to make money at something."

John sighed and raked the ceiling with his eyes.

"Why not!" Nora challenged him. "Is that not exactly what Lady Parke used to do for poor George Hudson at Palace Gate? And didn't Society look up to Lady Parke? They certainly flocked to her entertainments, even the Duke of Wellington—that's where *you* met him."

John rearranged the bedclothes in his exasperation. "This is all nonsense, Nora. It doesn't come near answering the question I asked."

She didn't want to answer that question, for the only answer she could make would be as wounding to him as he had been to her. So she tried a different tack: "Can you honestly see me at morning calls four afternoons a week! Can you imagine me cutting someone who interests or pleases me merely because Society—a lot of frightened old hens..."

John exploded one fist in the other. "That's just *it*, Nora. That's exactly what you will have to do. Or would have to do—we mustn't talk as if the honour were certain. Would have to do. If Society decides that Mr. X is beyond the pale, no one cares if that strange Stevenson woman acknowledges him. But if Lady Stevenson accepts him, they cannot ignore it. And you will embarrass them. Mrs. Tomnoddy cannot cut Mr. X, because Mr. X enjoys the patronage of a peeress. So your thoughtless act—some whim to please your own notions of who's interesting and who's dull—could force local Society to tolerate and admit some rank outsider, an out-and-out cad."

"John! Do you actually *believe* this rubbish?"

"How dare you!" He began to tremble with anger.

But she was not going to be cowed now; it had all got too deep. "Equally, how dare you assume I would befriend the sort of person you're...that I would befriend an out-and-outer!"

"George Hudson!" he crowed. "Since you've brought his name up."

"What about George Hudson?"

"You've gone on entertaining him."

"But he's a friend!"

"He's been cut out of Society since his bankruptcy."

"Well, I haven't exactly seen *you* turning the cold shoulder on him."

John was pointedly silent. Nora now stared at him in disbelief. "You mean if you get a barony, you'd start cutting Hudson?"

"I'd have to. Of course I would. That's my point, Nora. A peerage conveys difficult responsibilities."

"Then I say the market in peerages is suddenly looking very bullish from this side of the bed!"

He rocked himself furiously, letting the momentum carry him upright and onto the floor. "I thought you'd say that! You think only of yourself. You'd do anything except answer my question."

"Listen…it doesn't matter now. It's too late. If my behaviour is in question, if my behaviour it going to deny you the barony, it's too late now."

"What d'you mean, 'too late'?"

He was not really going to listen; already he was reaching for his dressing gown.

"I mean I'd have to conform for the next ten years, without one slip-up."

"You would. And you could. If you thought of anyone but yourself. What a feeble answer to my question!"

Seeing now that she had nothing to lose she decided to speak her mind quite openly: "What question? Are you interested in possible reasons for denying you a peerage?"

He was making for the door to his dressing room, apparently not heeding her.

"What about the law of *scandalum magnatum* then?" she asked.

He paused a moment, shrugged, and went into his dressing room. Before he could shut the door she raised her voice: "I intend you to hear this, John, since you've goaded me four times to tell you. It can be for your ears alone or for the whole household to hear. Shut that door and you'll be making the choice."

Angry still, but now with a certain wariness, he came back and stood in the doorway. "More blether?" he asked.

"That law says anyone who spreads scandal about a peer can be fined and imprisoned, *even if the scandal proves true*."

"Very interesting."

"So they don't hand out peerages these days to anyone who might force them to dust off such an embarrassment to modern democrats."

He yawned ostentatiously.

"What I'm saying, John, is that they investigate the origins and background and character and behaviour of all potential peers long before they make any direct approach to the men in question."

He leaned against the doorjamb.

"You," she went on, "began our business with the benefit of a forged letter. You forged it yourself…and Dr. Prendergast, who's now Bishop of Manchester, spotted it. They are almost certainly going to be asking him about you."

"He wouldn't dare! We covered all those traces. He tried it once, remember."

"It may be just the revenge he's waited for. You'd never prove he spoke. Nothing would ever be written down. You'd simply never hear of your barony again."

She could see the thought worried him.

"But it needn't be Prendergast," she went on. "When Charley Eade tried to set two mob men onto me in Manchester that time, they only needed one look at you and they turned into walking apologies for dancing masters—two of the hardest criminals in Manchester!"

He was now looking at her very uncertainly.

"Where did you get five thousand pounds from, John? The five thousand you had when we started this business? I've never asked, but I'm surely not the only one who's wondered. And if there's any serious notion of giving you a peerage, I'll wager there's half a dozen men in Whitehall have already begun to wonder, too—or are about to start."

"Have you finished?" he asked, biting his lip.

"So if you don't get the call to St. James's, love, the reason may just be something other than that your wife has the odd portrait painter to dinner or takes luncheon with her banker once a month. Why play a low card if they hold the ace of trumps, eh?"

He did not even say good night but slammed the door hard enough to rattle the windows. She sighed and lay down. It saddened her deeply to have to do what she had just done. It almost made her cry. But life would become intolerable if the idea were allowed to take root that her behaviour had cost John his peerage.

Besides, if getting a barony really entailed giving up all the pleasant things in life and putting on that dreadful straitjacket of Society, she'd stay plain Mrs. "Mistress" it meant, mistress of your own life. She'd go on having painters and doctors and professors at her table, even if Society frowned at the depravity of it. Such people could often be perfectly respectable—and were a sight more interesting than most of the nincompoops who were *in*.

Chapter 12

Stevenson's new London office was in a modest pair of terrace houses in Nottingham Place, just off the New Road from Paddington to the City—a mere hundred yards from Regent's Park. It had not been intended as their headquarters. They had acquired the buildings, and several others on that side of London, in settlement of a debt. In the normal way they would have put the properties up for sale at once, but last year they had been forced to modify their old premises in Dowgate rather extensively and had moved all except their financial office, which had to stay in the City of course, out to these houses in Nottingham Place. To prevent total divorce between these parts of the firm, the senior people in every department, and anybody with some especial contribution to make on that particular occasion, assembled at banqueting rooms in Holborn every Saturday for a teetotal buffet luncheon.

John's first day back in the saddle had been on such a Saturday. It had seemed sensible to return at the end of the week, with the sabbath break immediately following; and also the luncheon would give him the best chance to meet and talk with all his senior people. The teetotal rule had been broken to allow everyone a glass of champagne cup to toast his recovery and the latest news about the operation of the Crimea railway, which was excellent.

It had been a heartening return to work, yet the very elements that made it so heartening had, for him, a certain amount of chagrin. In short, he had hardly been missed.

At the most abstract level that was a high compliment. In his navvying days and during his rise he had seen many contemporaries who insisted on being one-man bands, who would even sack a man for doing this or that aspect of the work better than they themselves could. Five of his own senior men owed their careers (and often a considerable fortune—for half a dozen Stevenson deputies had country estates above a hundred acres) to such dismissals by others. Inevitably the one-man bands fell into the pit of financial disaster. Not, John maintained, because of any great error on the part of the man himself but because he could assemble around him nothing but yes-sirs and no-riskers, people who were by their very natures made incompetent when competence mattered most.

So, to return after more than two months' absence and find the company as vigorous and healthy as if he had been there every day was a striking indorsement of his skill at picking men. But what would members of Parliament feel like when society was perfected and the last useful law was on the statute book? What would doctors do when the practice of their art had banished disease forever? Or painters when every character, gesture, twig, petal, and dewdrop had been depicted to photographic perfection, somewhere, by someone? What would *everyone* do when there were no more working goals? What was paradise like?

If his mood as he walked alone through Regent's Park that afternoon, after the luncheon, was any gauge, paradise was a very purgatory. He would now have to take seriously his own threats of many years' standing to enter public life, locally or nationally. And if he were honoured with this peerage, that transition would be even more expected of him.

These thoughts led him at once to Nora. He realized—had long ago realized—that his main reason for not playing a larger public role had nothing to do with the demands of his business but rather with the unconventional behaviour of his wife. No man could take any large part in the affairs of the nation—or even of the parish—if his wife refused to play a corresponding part in Society. Why could she not see that? Why could he not bring her to understand it? Nowadays whenever he came near the topic, she would sense it a mile away and put up her hackles like a hedgehog. It was something they simply could not discuss sensibly.

And she could so easily do it, too. All her friendships in the hunting field—if she played on those a bit, she could, in a season or two, find herself at the very heart of London Society. And no one could keep Nora down for long. Very soon she'd be one of the leaders; if she put her mind and heart in it, she could do anything. And then she could indulge these strange tastes of hers for the company of painters and writers and people she called "interesting"; she could even make it a sort of fashion, as long as she kept it within sensible bounds. Why, when he could argue it all to himself in such a reasonable way, could he never explain it to her? Something about her always made him angry first and led him to say wounding things. And then, naturally, she would retaliate.

Like last night. Except that she had now gone much farther than ever before; she had strayed right into the truth! He had to be honest about that. But she'd done it only because she knew the truth would hurt so much; there was a great deal in the past, in his past, that would not stand examination now. But any man who could honestly say otherwise about himself was rare and fortunate.

And Nora had touched on only the half of it. For she did not know that once, long ago, when he was a lad of twenty, he had married (or what passed for married in his circle) a girl named Alice. And for one happy year—the happiest of his life, he now thought—he and she had lived in a little timber cottage at the end of a lane in Irlam's-o-th'Ights, just west of Manchester.

Then, one dreadful day, he had been forced to run for it. Even to have delayed while he explained things to her could have cost him his life; as far as she knew, then, he had simply ditched her. Very common. It happened all the time.

But he had not ditched her. He had come back as soon as the immediate hue and cry was over, though he still was not exactly safe—at least, not safe enough to be making the sort of open and widespread inquiry he longed to be making for her. So, in the end, it was she who had vanished without trace—she and the baby she had been carrying. Where? To the workhouse? Not to another man—he could not believe that of her. To the grave? The house stood rotting, untenanted, bereft of clues.

Despite all the happiness he had once known with Nora, he had never ceased to mourn the loss of his Alice. Nora was a marvellous person; objectively he could see that. But Alice! She had been an angel, a unique girl, the only girl he would ever truly love. If he knew she was alive, he would give up everything—family, money, business, friends…everything—simply to be with her. Or so he now told himself.

Her absence, however, left many unanswered questions. What of his marriage to her? True, it was only "over the anvil" as navvies said, but did that make Alice his wife in common law? And did the possession of a common-law wife make bigamy of his regular church marriage to Nora? Anyway, was Alice still alive? And what of the child? He realized that these were questions he had not been eager to pursue these last sixteen years; but they became very pertinent now, with the peerage in the offing. And Nora had, unwittingly, put her finger right on the wart when she had taunted him in that way last night.

He had even been unwilling to face the possibility of official inquiries. Now she had forced him to consider that, too. *Damn her!*

Memories of Alice—beautiful, gentle, sweet girl—now contrasted very harshly with these much more urgent memories of Nora. Awkward, obstinate, clever, full of self, empty of duty, unfeminine…unfeminine? No, you couldn't say that; but too determined to express herself, too angular in character to be properly womanly. He should have tried to find Alice again instead of taking up with Nora.

Charity Bedfordshire (as the workhouse master had named her) could not have chosen a more apposite moment to come back into John's life. He had first met her one evening the summer of 1850, down on the quays in Bristol, plying the only trade she knew. She was then, at seventeen, such a living image of the Alice he had known eighteen and more years earlier that for a while he had been convinced she was the child Alice had been carrying. His child! Even that possibility had made it unthinkable to leave her there on the streets; he had waited for Walter to finish his horizontal refreshments (which was why John had been on the quays at all) and together they had taken Charity back to Arabella as her first Fallen Woman. Arabella had procured a hysterical conversion of which Wesley himself would have been proud, and ever since then Charity had been Arabella's prize exhibit, chief adviser, and—as Arabella always said—"ever present help in time of affliction."

And now here she was, distraught almost to tears, riding around the southern end of Regent's Park in a cab whose fare she could not pay, looking for a street she half remembered from a visit with Arabella Thornton almost a year ago. Mrs. Thornton had gone into the Stevenson office while she had remained in the cab outside. All she could remember was that it was near Regent's Park and was named after some place in England.

So the cab driver had taken her to Nottingham Terrace, York Place, York Mews, Cornwall Terrace, Ulster Terrace…and now here they were in Brunswick Terrace with the driver swearing Brunswick was somewhere in England and Charity wondering how to explain she couldn't pay him until she found the right street and Mr. Stevenson. What she would do if Mr. Stevenson wasn't in his office she had no idea; the things she had to say were for no other ears but his. And then, suddenly, the whole pall lifted and there was Mr. Stevenson walking along York Terrace, not two dozen yards away.

"Sir! Oh, sir!" she called out. "Driver, that's the man I'm looking for."

"Oh, yus?" He glanced warily down through the trap she had opened. "I thought you was a decent gel," he said. "You're rigged out decent enough. I don't touch this class o' trade, young 'un."

"How dare you!" She tried to say the words as Mrs. Cornelius would say them, but she knew she merely sounded like a servant aping her mistress. Nevertheless, desperation must have lent her outrage some urgency, for, although Mr. Stevenson had not responded to her cry, the driver flicked his whip and in next to no time they were alongside John.

She opened the door. "Mr. S.!" she called. And when he hesitated, thinking no doubt that this was some kind of ambush, she added, "'Tis Miss Charity, from Bristol."

Still cautious he came toward the open door.

"I told 'er—I don't touch this class o' trade, sir," the cabby said in preparatory apology.

John recognized Charity and saw that she was the cab's sole occupant as the man spoke. "Hold your filthy tongue," he said, getting in at once. "Drive on!"

"Where to?"

"Anywhere. Round the park."

The man made no move. "I told yer—I don't touch that trade."

John, at the limit of his patience, leaped out and grabbed the fellow by the arm. It was a grip that had once broken a man's hand. "You'll drive off the end of Vauxhall ferry stage if I tell you," he said quietly.

The man gave one yelp of pain and agreed he would at least take them around the park.

Back inside the cab John saw the mingled relief, gratitude, and admiration in Charity's face. "Was he giving you trouble?" he asked.

"Just starting," she said.

He settled back in the cushions, facing her. She wore a sober green dress and plain collar, like a Quaker girl. Her hair was pulled severely back into a plain, tight bun. She looked the very image of piety. And pious women had always exerted the strongest fascination on him. Add to that her resemblance to Alice—less marked now that she was five years older, but still strong—and she began to have the most disturbing effect on him. He had to look away.

"Why are you here?" he asked, trying to lose his gaze in the network of bare branches of the trees outside. "Where is Mrs. Thornton—or Mrs. Cornelius?"

It was grotesque, but Sarah Cornelius, as soon as she had thrown over Walter Thornton and ceased to be his mistress, had become the closest of friends with Arabella Thornton, had provided most of the money for the Home for Fallen Women and had done most of the hard day-to-day work there while Arabella was away campaigning. Charity was, nominally at least, Sarah's lady's maid.

As soon as he asked the question she became flustered, half beginning a dozen sentences but making no sense. "I dunno who to talk to," she said at last.

"Me?" he suggested. "Did you come up here to see me?"

And then she told him how she'd come up from Bristol that day and all the trouble she'd had finding his offices and how she'd been at her wit's end when she had seen him walking by.

"It was Nottingham Place," he said. "The other side of the New Road!"

Their laughter, and this recapitulation of her relief, made it easier then for her to begin her tale.

"Mrs. Cornelius now, was there ever anything between her and Mr. Thornton, sir?" she asked.

"You mustn't concern yourself with things like that."

She looked gloomily out of the window. "My God, and I wish I never had to! I wish I never seen. Nor heard."

In the silence John thought of a dozen ways he might explain away a seeming infidelity of Walter's—a stolen kiss or something like that. But he knew it would be impossible to deceive Charity; she was no young innocent.

"Oh dear!" was all he said.

"*Was* there anything?" she repeated. "'Tis important to you, too, sir."

"I don't know for certain," he said truthfully. "I…suspected it."

"When she was staying at your place? Not after she came down to Bristol?"

"If there ever was anything, I'm sure it stopped before that."

"'Cos he come this morning, after he went to work like, he come back, not to his own house but up to us, up the Refuge. Now he never *do* come there, never. So I thought well, that's a strange one, right off."

"Were…ah…the women there?"

She grinned. God, but she had a lovely little grin! Fit to knock the feet from under you. "That's why he stays away—too many old friends of his up with us being rescued!"

John frowned. "You shouldn't talk like that, Charity. He's your master."

"And she's his mistress, Mrs. Cornelius," she said, unrepentant. "Come on, sir. 'Tisn't no secret, how *he* is."

"Except from Mrs. Thornton."

Her face went hard. "He isn't worth to touch her," she said vehemently.

"So it would be dangerous—apart from being treachery—to talk in that disloyal way about him."

This reminder halted her. She puzzled something to herself and then turned helplessly to him. "I got to tell you. And I can't tell you without speaking of him that way."

He shrugged and resigned, smiling to show her she could go on.

"I were in the women's work room. Know where I mean?"

He shook his head.

"Anyway, 'tis like a long room between the study room and the wash, and you can't help but hear through the walls. Like paper they are. Then she come in. And him behind her. And he were going on—about you. That's why I listened, see. And he said some old geezer had come to see him, about you. Some bloke asking a lot of old questions. From the government, he said."

"Who said? The 'geezer' or Mr. Thornton?" John was on the edge of his seat now.

"Dunno. This bloke, I suppose. Anyway, it were all under your hat and don't breathe. He said he asked all questions about you. Then Mrs. Cornelius and he, they both fell to talking about you, and mister he said he thought as how it was about making you a lord. And missus she said as how you deserved it. And mister said about how they were looking back into your past life, like, looking for skellingtons or something, I dunno. Anyway...looking to see if they could make you a lord." Suddenly the idea caught hold of her imagination anew and she flashed the sweetest, most radiant, smile. "Eh?" she said. "What about that, then, eh?"

He could not hold her gaze. He hated the effect she was having on him. It was so—shallow, so obvious. A man of any intelligence, a man with the slightest bit of moral fibre, should be able to resist these primitive urges.

She was disappointed at his lack of response. "Anyway," she went on, "then he mentioned me. He said as how he always did think there was more between me and—and you, sir, begging pardon, sir—this is what Mr. Thornton said. He said there was more to it than ever come out. And she said rubbish. And mister he said just wait, and you'd been very strange that night we met and you brung me home to Mrs. Thornton. And missus she went on saying it were rubbish. And then they went on talking about this and that and I wasn't really listening, like, 'cos I was trying to remember that night and how you come to rescue me. And I thought, begging pardon, sir, you *was* a bit...strange, like. I mean you did think but what you knew me."

"I did," John said with lowered eyes, wanting to stop this particular reminiscence. "I did, but it was all a mistake."

"No, but the way you were going on, like, made me think that you...like, you know, in books and that where people find long-lost children?"

John pretended to laugh, pretended it was ridiculous.

"No, but anyway, that's what made me think, and that's why I never heard all what they two said. Anyway, soon I thought, hello, they're talking a bit funny, 'cos I come back to them from what I had been thinking on about. So I had a peek, what with the door being open and all, and I seen they had some of their clothes off and he was taking more off and promising her better than what they'd ever had before! So I thought *oh yes! My my!* And she was just standing, shaking her head and saying no with everything—except not with words. Shivering, she was, and crying."

Charity laughed at the memory but the sound in that small carriage was so loud that she instantly thought how unfeeling it made her seem. So she stopped laughing suddenly and then didn't know what to say next. Nor did John.

Charity had understood why Mrs. Cornelius was behaving in that way, for it was exactly the way in which she would have been responding to what Mr. Thornton was doing. But that was as far as her understanding went; she was not given to self-analysis. If she were, she would not now have found herself sitting in a cab in Regent's Park beside John Stevenson. The steps that had brought her there would not (had she paused on each for thought) have carried the weight.

The moment she had seen Mr. Thornton and Mrs. Cornelius doing that thing, she had known, in the way that does not call for words, exactly what her life had been missing since she had become one of Mrs. Thornton's converts. And that was strange, because she hadn't enjoyed it much during those few weeks when it had been her trade—only the power it gave her over men who were much stronger than she. Aside from that, she had taken their money and done what they wanted, but she had spent most of the time thinking about clothes and dancing and walks in the country.

But five years of continence—or perhaps just of growing older—had changed all that. Unknown to her the pressures had been building until this morning when she had seen them at it and had caught that fierce, predatory look of delight in Mr. Thornton's eyes. That had hit her.

She disliked the man for exactly the reason she had given to John—Thornton wasn't fit to touch Mrs. Thornton. But those glittering eyes! They were something outside all ideas of liking or disliking. They stripped you where you stood; she had often felt that. They gloated. And that loose-lipped smile that lurked in his beard—it could make you shiver at times. And then having to stay there and watch them go at each other! She almost ran into the room to join them—or, better still, to make Mrs. C. run out in shame and then take her place with him. But all she could do was stand there, spellbound, living it all through Mrs. Cornelius and thinking that the woman's earlier crying and parade of unwillingness had been very hypocritical when you considered this exhibition of abandonment.

But even if she had stayed as cold as ice herself, she knew at once that it would be impossible for her to remain under the same roof as Mr. Thornton and to go on being lady's maid to Mrs. Cornelius. She could never have looked at either of them straight again; and they would surely have put things together for themselves then.

That was why she had to escape, of course. She kept repeating the reason to herself. But where? What could she do? Without a character, what could she do? No one would look twice at her, except for *that*. There had even been girls with good references down on the quays. So if she didn't want to find herself back there, she'd have to get a protector. She had only the one sellable commodity, so it didn't take much puzzling to get that far.

There was only one man in all the world who occurred to her: John Stevenson. Funny, whenever she had thought of a husband in these past years, it had always been John. By other names, of course, and in other walks of life, usually closer to her own likely sphere. An imaginary police constable called Henry Turvey—he had looked the image of John Stevenson and had rescued her from a fire that had killed everyone at the Thorntons' and the Refuge. Beautiful tears. A ship's mate called Zachary Hitchens had been smitten with her down in the market and had taken her off to a tropic isle where they had lived a long and happy life all alone, spending the gold that a pirate had left there long ago; Zacky, too, had been the spitting likeness of John Stevenson. And there were dozens of others.

But that was not really why she had now flown to him. She knew from the way he had looked at her that night he rescued her she had that power on him. And since! Every time they met, or, rather, every time their paths crossed, she could see that surprise in him, and the longing. She knew he wanted her, though she never thought anything would come of it.

But that wasn't it either. She knew he wanted her and she only had to make it acceptable, even noble, for him to—no, but it wasn't really that. Now that all the bridges were burned behind her she could at last admit to herself that she loved him. She always had admitted it, but only in a very chaste, secret, admiring sort of way. There was no other man, anywhere, not now, not at any time in her past, she loved like that.

And also there was this threat that Thornton had talked to Mrs. Cornelius about; something to do with her. Mr. Stevenson's past was somehow bound up with hers. She couldn't think how. It couldn't be that she was a long-lost daughter—besides, she didn't want to be his daughter! So it couldn't be that. But what if the government people came and started asking her questions? She wouldn't know what answers would help him best. So if she did nothing else, she had to get to see him and warn him and find out the answers.

That was the missing note of pure altruism which finally spurred her into making the break with Bristol and going to find Mr. Stevenson.

These were not the thoughts that had gone through her mind as she stood eavesdropping on Walter and Sarah. But feelings akin to them had bubbled in her blood, and she had reached that final resolution before the other two had finished.

"Did they see you at all?" John asked, more to break the embarrassing silence than to be informed.

"No," she said. "Of course, they weren't looking for anyone. They thought they was safe there. And so they were, except for me, which they didn't know of. The Rescue girls were gone for the morning along of Mrs. Thornton. And the good girls, they don't go up in those parts. They don't mingle. Not they…good…"

At that moment he saw a most violent change come over the girl. Up until that point she had been telling the story as comedy. Her attitude had been slightly brittle, a bit bright-eyed, a bit garrulous. But suddenly, over those last three words she burst into tears.

And it was not a quiet little cry, either. Bitter sobs shook her whole body, squeezing the last ounce of breath out of every shivering exhalation. She breathed in as though drowning and she begged something from him with great, frightened eyes. It was obviously as unexpected to her as it was to him.

"Come!" he said, stirring uncomfortably but making no move toward her. The thought of being close to her really frightened him. He did not trust himself at all.

She mistook his meaning and half-rose to fall into the comfort she imagined he was offering. But when she saw him sitting on his hands, bolt upright, and looking more scared than she would have thought possible, she realized she had turned to the wrong person, that all her hopes of him were groundless, and that she was as alone, as friendless, as penniless as she had ever been in her awful former life. She flung herself down on the seat and wept even more hugely.

He leaned forward and tentatively grasped a fold of her sleeve. "What is it?" he asked. It was all he dared risk touching.

She shrank from him and redoubled her sobbing.

"Please? Tell me," he said. Now he caught her arm gently. The cloth was harsh but his imagination supplied the softness and youth beneath it. He closed his eyes so that he should not see what he was doing.

"I worshipped her!" Charity said in a rough, salty sob. "That Mrs. Cornelius, she were like an angel to me."

"Well, that was foolish of you," John said. He opened his eyes but did not release her arm. The cloth was no longer harsh, somehow. "She is flesh and blood, like all of us. She is vulnerable. She needs your understanding—not your contempt. Just as you once needed hers. And, I may say, got it."

Charity buried her head in the seat once again; the sobbing resumed with all its previous strength.

Knowing the folly of it but unable to help himself, John moved forward and knelt on the floor between the seats. He pulled at her arm to disengage her hand. Surely he could hold one of her hands between his?

She clutched at him with eager fingers. She was quite a strong little creature, really. A moment later he was to find out just how strong, for she darted that hand forward, thrusting his aside, and clutched behind his neck. Before he could recover from his surprise she had pulled him down toward her and was kissing him with big, bold, passionate abandon.

There was a moment—it lasted perhaps less than a second—when he could have pulled away from her and halted everything between them. She could not have recovered from such rejection, and he would then have gained in moral strength each second that passed. He very nearly seized that moment. It was so real it became almost physically there, as if he could have literally grabbed it as it passed.

But it did pass. He merely stared at it as it went by. He stared as a condemned man in a tumbrel might stare at some landmark for the last time, knowing it to be the last time. The rest of him was too busy discovering that this was not Alice—a safe, dead memory whose image he could cherish in the safety of that supposed death—this was Charity. Soft. Young. Warm. Cinnamon-smelling. It was the unexpected smell of her that finally overpowered him. Not quite cinnamon, but he could think of nothing closer. It was very compelling, very heady.

Then she was sitting up and he was still kneeling. And their lips were still together, but the touch was gentler, less urgent, less fearful it might not last.

Blood and sensation returned to his lips. Hers opened, opening his. Her tongue wriggled through and the whole of him revolved around that soft, wet warmth.

I must not do this, he thought. *I am over forty.* But no part of him felt half so old. No part of him did not rejoice at this delight—which every part of him had forgotten until now.

What is it like to start being in love? If one of his boys had asked him, he could not have told them. But now he knew! He remembered. This was exactly it. This warmth of lovely flesh you crave; the question: "What's it like to be *you*?" and wanting to do nothing all your life except find the answer; this sharpening of every sense, tuning it to the one melody alone, making it flat to every other theme…all this was happening, like a long-silent machine fired in steam once more.

She took his hands from her neck and put them on her breasts, moving his fingers with hers, making them caress her. Strange thrilling softness, different from Nora's. Until now he had not known how far Nora had let herself drift from him.

Her knees moved apart, bringing him even nearer her. "Mmmm?" she made a little, questioning moan.

"No," he said, pulling away from her at last. "We'll go somewhere else."

She nodded, smiling contentedly. A little gesture like that, and it put him all in a turmoil! It was marvellous.

Then she looked alarmed. "Here, I can't go back to Bristol."

He rose stiffly, dusted his knees, and sat beside her, putting out an arm for her to settle into. "Of course not," he said. "Now you're with me."

He thought of asking her why Mrs. Cornelius's one slip had so distressed her when what she was now doing, and going to do, had such an opposite effect—but one look at her, so severely exquisite, so flawlessly lovely, and the question foundered in his throat. What did it matter? Who understood motives anyway!

They drove straight to his office then, where he collected some money and left a plausible message for Nora or anyone else who inquired. She wouldn't expect him home, anyway. The quarrel had bought him a good fortnight, he imagined. His lack of feeling, and even of regret, did not astonish him. There was no room inside him even for astonishment, much less for any more complex feeling. He burst with the sudden realization of all that his life had lacked during these latter years. And now the lack was to be met. It was—marvellous, he told himself again. He kept telling himself.

Still in the same cab they meandered down through the West End, stopping every now and then to buy all they would need to support their role as travellers, man and wife, passing through. Especially she needed a cloak to cover her servant's clothes. Along Oxford Street they went, down Regent Street, through Regent Circus and Leicester Square, and so by St. Martin's to the Strand. Their goal was one of the numberless small hotels in the streets south of the Strand, between it and the river. You didn't even need to hand in a visiting card in most of them.

Impatience did not let them go farther than the first one they tried, a small, clean place in Villiers Street. "Mr. and Mrs. Stenson" he gave as their name.

"See, that's a bad start," she said archly when they were alone together.

"Oh?"

"Yes, you be already less of a man than you were when you met with I up in that park."

"Ho! I'll show you!"

She tried to think it was wrong, and it felt like the rightest thing she had ever done. She tried to feel shame at her nakedness—or, rather, she tested herself for shame and could find none. All those sermons she and the other Fallen Women had heard on the evils of the flesh—they referred to other situations, sordid situations, not to wonderful and rare moments like this. He wasn't shamed either, he was marvellous, doing everything so calmly and with such assurance, and so right. She'd do anything for him, and it would be right. This was what bodies were for. You didn't need words to tell you that. And words that said otherwise were words of the ignorant.

His hands, straying over her, melted everything they touched. Her head and limbs moved only to yield. He could do anything, touch her anywhere, and that part developed a magical sensitivity to him. Five years ago a hundred men had been there and back with her and it had meant nothing; but she only needed to see John looking at her, even at her wrists—or toe-nails—and they tingled. For him she felt peeled. He drowned her. She did not know there was such delight. At its pinnacle it tore her apart, racked her in a delirium of sweetness, left her more whole, more *together* of herself, than she could have believed.

And so it was again in those small hours when even your own name sounds like a comic label and your *real* name is body-arms-and-legs-feeling, and everything tastes slightly of salt, and you are sure you are the only two people in the world. And again—long, slow, lazy again—when dawn said it was the day of rest, and the church bells summoned communicants out of doors.

To John's surprise Charity sprang from the bed and began to dress.

"I forgot 'twas Sunday," she said when she had her chemise fastened. "Come on, you'll be late."

He stared at her, too astonished to speak.

"Come on!" She was already half dressed.

"To church?"

"'Course to church. We'd be in time for second communion. Come on!"

He laughed, embarrassed. "I don't," he said. "I don't go. I mean, I don't go to communion."

She stopped with her bodice half hoisted down over her arms, making him marvel, as he ran his eyes from her elbows down to her petticoats, that fires were left in him to rekindle. "That's terrible!" she said. "But you got to start sometime. Come on now—up!"

"I will not," he said, laughing again.

"I can't go 'lone. Just come and sit by I. No need to go up for the wine and that." She shrugged into the bodice.

He frowned. "I meant to ask you," he said. "Why are you talking like that again? They taught you to talk quite respectably these last few years."

"Dunno," she said. "Didn't sound like I no more, I s'pose."

"I'll come if you promise to talk properly from now on," he said. "If I'm going to pass you off here and there as my wife, you can't talk that 'low Bristow.'"

She leaped on him then and kissed him. "Oh John, oh John! I do love you so!"

He imprisoned her with a hug. "Stay and prove it," he challenged. "I shan't let you go."

She put her lips to his ear and said in a voice that made him tingle—but in her thickest Bristol accent: "Theese dursn't hinder I, sinna, else I'll tell they gov'ment geezers on 'ee!"

He pushed her away, smiling. "Very well! You win," he said.

And to make sure she won, she pulled the sheets off as she stood again.

"Couldn't do nothin' with that wheesh li'l twig anyway!" she sneered.

He looked down and nodded glumly. "And you think a reminder of my religious duty is going to help?"

When they were on their way to St. Mary-le-Strand he returned to the theme. "How can you pass the night as you've just passed it and go straight to the Lord's Supper?" he asked.

"It isn't the worst He has to forgive I—me—for," she said.

"You mean"—he chuckled at her simplicity—"if forgiveness hasn't become a habit with Him by now, it never will."

"Yes," she answered, not seeing that he was being flippant. "Anyway, what about you? Do you think it was wrong? I mean a big wrong? A real sin?"

"Well—two commandments down and only eight to go. And when we get back to the hotel, this being the sabbath, we'll make it three, no doubt."

"I'm serious," she said. "Last night was the happiest I ever spent. If it was a big sin—well, that's a funny sort of Father to His children. That's all I can say. And I'll leave it all to be explained on Judgement Day."

But she must have gone on thinking about it during the service, for on their way back she said, "You don't believe in God at all, do you? You're worse than me—going and not believing."

Her hand rested lightly in the crook of his elbow; he squeezed it with his other hand. "I was laying a line in Anatolia last year with Christian labour—Eastern Christians. And we couldn't make them understand they had to get rid of all the topsoil—that you can't lay a line on topsoil. I tried everything. Then my general manager, Mr. Flynn—you may know him. I think he has called on Mr. Thornton in Bristol?"

"That little Irishman?"

"That's him."

"Oh, I liked him."

"Everyone likes Mr. Flynn—except the lazy and the incompetent! Anyway, he had a word with their priest. And the priest told them it was a mortal sin to leave any topsoil beneath a railway line. And, by heavens, never in twenty years have I seen a working so free of topsoil! So of course I believe in God."

"Oh, that's all right then," she said, as if he had just lifted a burden from her.

They drove out to Richmond for lunch, where he was fairly sure of not being recognized. Then in the afternoon he took her over to St. John's Wood, where one of the properties acquired in the settlement the previous year stood empty awaiting sale. Hamilton Cottage, it was called, and it marked the dead end of Hamilton Place.

It was a more imposing building than the name implied, worth at least four servants. It must have been built in Regency days, when this was all still countryside—the open fields of Portland Down.

It had been recently remodelled to give it a more cluttered frontage, a tower at one end, and broad windows in late Gothic style.

"Like it?" he asked her.

She looked at the house as she had gazed at everything that day—with a tourist's eyes. "Why?" she asked.

"Would it suit you?"

She looked at him and her eyes shone. She looked back at the house. After a time she took the breath she had forgotten when his question hit her. "Could you get me a position there?" she asked, only half believing still.

"A very good position," he said solemnly. "The best."

"Go on! Scullery maid more likely."

"Better," he promised.

"Housemaid?"

"Better."

"*Lady's* maid?" She bounced up and down in excitement.

"Better." He persisted.

She frowned. Her horizon had no better to lady's maid. "What?"

"Mistress!" he said and burst into laughter.

Slowly she grasped what he was saying and her puzzlement turned to laughter too—delighted, fearful laughter. "Missy!" she giggled. "Me! Your missy! Well!" Then she looked back at the house, no longer with a tourist's eyes. "My! I couldn't do that. Not there. 'Tis too big."

"Try it," he said encouragingly. "If it doesn't work, you can move to somewhere smaller. But I've seen you, my darling, dealing with women and the other servants at the Refuge; you've got the makings of a lady who could manage a place like that. And when children come along you'll be glad of a bigger house with a nice garden."

Her mouth fell open. "Children!"

"You must have thought of it. If not, you'd better start now."

She looked at the house again. He saw her breathe in deeply, squaring up to the idea of it. A new doubt troubled her. "If we're not married..." she began.

"Don't worry about the neighbours. Most of them are mistresses. You look at the carriages drawn up outside the houses as we go back—you'll see the livery and badges of half the peerage. All quite open. This is the part of London for that."

"Not—not *houses*!" she said, horrified at the thought she might have come full circle.

"Not that sort. The very opposite. I'd wager this is the last district in London where they'd permit houses of that kind to open."

She looked puzzled still.

"I promise you," he said. "You'll find a respectability here that Mrs. Thornton herself would be forced to admire."

Of course! she thought. If the government was looking to see if John was fit to be a peer, then it would be easier to persuade them he was fit if he already had a missy out here with all the other peers! She could help him. How right she had been to come to him!

"Come on!" he said. "I'll show you how a little twig can miraculously grow into a mighty branch all in half a day!"

On their way back to the hotel and the promised breaking of the third commandment, he said, "About Mrs. Thornton. You must write to her—or she won't rest until she's found you."

"What can I say!" She sighed hopelessly.

"Tell her you had the chance to marry well and that you seized it. Very respectable and worthy man. Low church. Dress it out a bit to please her. But say he'd never understand if he knew your past. Had to run away. Keep it quiet. It all fits, you see." A thought struck him. "Your train fare to London. How did you get that?"

"I had to take it."

"Did they owe you wages?"

"I never had wages. It would be a temptation, they said. But I was never left wanting," she added, thinking her lack of wages made them sound mean.

"I'll give you two pounds to send with the letter. Say your husband's quite prosperous but very careful; and you'll send what you can from time to time, and you'll keep writing." And when Charity still looked dubious, he said: "You won't hurt her so much if you do that."

"She'll still think I've deceived them."

"She'll think worse if you do nothing."

On Monday he asked Flynn about Hamilton Cottage.

"Sold!" Flynn said happily. "Stood on the books long enough!" Then he saw John's disappointment. "Why?" he asked, less jocular.

"Signed, sealed, and delivered?"

"No. Only the contract's signed."

"Who to?"

"Fellow called Banks. Nobody."

"Tear it up, then."

"Do what, sir?"

"A house—purchase contract has no legal force. You know that."

"I do indeed. What I don't know is…"

"I won't beat about the bush with you, Flynn. Known you too long and respect your discretion too much."

"Oh yes?" Flynn looked at him guardedly.

"I seem to have acquired a mistress."

Flynn's surprise lasted the merest moment. "Good man yourself!" he said.

"When I left the luncheon in Holborn last Saturday, nothing was further from my thoughts—well, in a practical sense. I mean, we all have our fancies, I suppose."

Flynn leaned his head to one side and smiled, allowing no confession on his part.

"And now it's Monday and we've already settled her allowance and expenses—and we've set our sights on Hamilton Cottage."

Smiling but wordless, Flynn left the office, returning moments later with a handful of torn paper, which he gave to John.

"Good man yourself, Flynn," John said. "Now listen. I am about to suffer a relapse. I am going to Cheltenham spa and if I don't like it there, I shall go on to Malvern. Nobody—you know what I mean?—nobody is to try to follow me there, to either place. You alone will know that I am in fact either at Hamilton Cottage or the Padbury Family Hotel in Villiers Street. Understood?"

Flynn nodded.

"Now," John continued, "draw up a new contract. Let's say—what are you smiling at?"

"I was just after thinking—Hamilton Cottage, Lady Hamilton, Emma—what she was. It's an appropriate name."

John chuckled. "Anyway, as I was saying. Let's say her father's buying it, as a gift for her. I want her name in the deeds. She'll take the name of Stevenson."

Flynn looked at him sharply.

"Go on," John said. "It's common enough. And I want the children to bear my name."

Flynn shrugged. "And what's her father's name—the man who's supposed to be making this gift of the house?"

"Oh, surely"—John laughed—"only one possible. It has to be Nelson. Let's say Fred Nelson!"

Chapter 13

HEY, CHAPS!" BOY WENT SHOUTING THROUGH THE CLOISTERS. "I'VE GOT MY Honourable! I've got my Honourable!"

It was only mid-March, but news of John's "relapse"—his sudden visits to the spas of Cheltenham and Malvern—had reached Whitehall and prompted the government to curtail its investigations and grant the honour before it became too late.

Boy was looking for Caspar to tell him the good news. Soon there was a whole crowd clustered admiringly around him.

"Have you really, Stevenson ma?"

"Good cheese, man!"

"Bumpers tonight! I'll sell you two magnums, if you like—you won't get any in Langstroth."

"Your pater been made a viscount?"

Boy looked superfluously at the letter from home. "No. A baron. Baron Stevenson of Cleveland."

"Why Cleveland?"

"Because that's where we've got some ironworkings—where the iron came from for the Crimea railway, you see. Where it started."

"I'd have called myself Baron Stevenson of Crimea," one boy said, strutting around like an actor.

"Hi, young 'un!" Boy called, catching sight of Caspar at the far entrance to the cloisters. "You've got your Honourable!"

"What's that mean?" Caspar called as he came running to join the group.

"You get precedence at all future beatings!" Causton said.

Everyone laughed.

The whole school was given an extra half-hol. Or, rather, since nothing from Brockman was ever just given, they had to work for it by sitting through a homily on duty and service to one's country. The school already boasted an earl, two marquesses, a baron, and half a dozen honourables—all but the earl's being courtesy titles. Also there was an Indian prince. But all of these were ancient titles, many granted for reasons that no headmaster would try to build a sermon around. Boy's and Caspar's honours were the first new creations in the recent history of the school. The reasons behind the grant were grist to Brockman's mill—and for half an hour he ground it exceeding fine.

Before he released them to the dales and playing fields he added two nuggets of information, seemingly unconnected with John Stevenson's elevation to the peerage. The school now had sufficient funds, he said, to endow fifteen scholarships. Ten would be only for boys from Langstroth and contiguous parishes; five would be open. There was also a sufficiency, he said, to embark on a much more ambitious programme of changes in the school itself. The boggy land between the school and town would be drained during this term and three new houses, Blenheim, Ramilles, and Malplaquet, would he built there over the next year. The housemasters, Mr. Greaves, Mr. Ducie, and Mr. Treloar, would be joining the staff this term—indeed, Mr. Greaves was already here (Mr. Greaves stood and bowed stiffly); he would be teaching modern mathematics. The new houses would be filled by boys now in or due to enter Old School, which, once empty, would be converted into an assembly hall and classrooms. The boys would, he promised, see great changes at Fiennes this year.

Then he called for three rousing cheers for Lord Stevenson. Boy and Caspar, the title still a novelty, burned with embarrassed delight.

What Brockman had not said (because John had asked him not to) was that the twenty thousand pounds voted to him by Parliament on the creation of the peerage had gone straight into a charitable trust, out of which the scholarships and the conversion of Old School would be funded. The same trust would also fund five scholarships to the school from Stevenstown, the town John was building for the workers in the Stevenson iron and steel mills near Stockton on the river Tees. But those arrangements had not yet been worked out.

"What are you going to do, Steamer?" Causton asked. "Shall we call out the army?"

"I don't feel like it," Caspar said. Ever since the Dart–Achilles race he had been nicknamed "Steamer" Stevenson. "I'm going to try and get that pony at

Ribble Farm and go for a ride." He rubbed his buttocks and grinned. "Didn't get in much riding last hols, for some reason."

"Has he got two ponies?"

"I'll ask." Caspar's tone indicated he wanted to be out alone today.

"I think I'll fire Achilles," Causton said casually as he turned away. It was a last bid to attract Caspar and it failed.

The farmer agreed readily enough, for a fee of one shilling. "I've no saddle to fit yon pony, mind," he said.

"A blanket'll do," Caspar told him. "And a snaffle."

"I've only a double-ring snaffle, for the cart harness."

"That'll do. Tie the reins through both rings. I want to save my legs if I've no saddle," Caspar said. What he mainly wanted to do was to reassure the man he knew his way about a horse.

He saw the farmer smile to himself as he led the pony into the yard. "She's not what ye'd call a properly schooled mount, mind," the man said.

"As long as she goes."

"Aye! Well, if it's a *goer* ye want…" Again that smile.

The pony seemed to smile, too, even more secretly. There was a fierce challenging glint in her eye, a quick, mettlesome flicker to all her movements. She shied at every gesture he made but he could tell there was something calm, calculating, and watchful beneath this surface display of temperament. Caspar rubbed his hands in delight. Here was a challenge now!

"She's not been ridden quite this while," the farmer continued to dribble out his warnings.

Caspar led her forward to face a stone wall. Then, with a tight grip on both reins, he leaped quickly on to her back and gripped with all the strength in his legs and thighs. Every muscle in her stiffened. She trembled. She marked time—double time—but she held her ground.

The farmer chuckled with pleasure. "One hurdle you're over then," he said.

Beyond the wall was a newly ploughed field. "Anything sown there yet?" Caspar asked.

"Nay."

"Open the gate then."

She was fighting the bit; nothing was going to make her accept it. She was prancing on the spot, leaning right, leaning left, like a horse broken a bare half-hour. A thought struck a chill into him—perhaps that's all she was! Perhaps she had never been ridden before! West Riding folk, they'd do anything for a shilling. He determined then not to let her have her head at all. There'd be none of that "co-operation" his mother was always drilling into them in riding lessons, not until this pony knew her master.

He forced her into two fiercely tight turns in the yard, a little ritual that had no taming effect on her at all. Then, when she was pointed at the gate, he dug in his heels and sat deep into her, knowing she would go like a shot off a shovel.

She went! Like a shot from a cannon. For almost a furlong the ploughed field might have been best Newmarket turf for all that it slowed her. Then the far wall loomed ahead. Caspar, judging his moment, began to saw the snaffle in her mouth—not fiercely, just enough to surprise her, slow her down, and make her refusal of the wall a matter of his command, not her whim.

It worked better than he hoped. But what he had not expected was that she would then turn on a sixpence and resume her charge back up the ploughed field. The move almost unseated him. And that, in turn, showed the wily little mare that he could be got off. He knew that was exactly the thought in her mind. And he was ready.

But he was ready for the wrong move—a sharp turn, a sudden four-legs halt, a skid, a slew…anything except a graceful dip of her left shoulder and a barely perceptible slowing of her gallop. He was not ready for that.

Over he went. The field and walls and sky spun one gentle arc and he was left standing bolt upright and stock still, looking in astonishment at the mare. She had halted a dozen paces away, had turned broadside to him, and was now shaking her head up and down. If she had laughter within her, that shaking was its outward expression. But all the real laughter was coming from the farmyard wall, where the farmer and two labourers were standing watching.

She let him come up and jump upon her again without a tremor. Now he understood. She was certainly no newly broken mount. Hundreds—thousands—of hours of being ridden had gone into perfecting that trick with the left shoulder. And look at the way she stopped and let him get back on—she was going to try it again! This was her best fun in weeks.

She let him canter her slowly back to the wall where the three grinning faces, rural red, peered into the field, waiting for more. It was a graceful, collected canter; oh, she had been well schooled at one time. No doubt of it. She was fully on the bit. She stopped dead in two paces.

"You might have told me," Caspar said, grinning to show he was not truly angry.

"What? Spoil the fun?" the farmer answered.

"If I was a novice it wouldn't have been funny."

"If you was a novice, young master, you'd find yon mare the gentlest and most tractable of beasts. Go on—gallop her around ten minutes, get the steam out of her, and then ye'll have a good go up on them tops."

"Will she tip me off again?"

"Aye. She will that."

"How do I stop her?"

"There's a guinea for you if you ever find a way. No other man has."

Caspar cantered and galloped the mare around until he felt the heavy going beginning to take its toll of her. Twice more she tipped him. Both times he landed on his feet, still not sure how she did it. But he was sure there was no malice in the trick; she took such delight in it.

When he felt her beginning to labour he took her out to the headlands, where the going was firmer, and began to collect her, riding her forward into contact, slowing her pace, gathering her up.

At last he had her. Ears pricked, a soft foam on her lips, her hack supple, her legs under her, and every part of her waiting to respond to his command.

"Well done, young 'un!" the farmer called.

Caspar had forgotten he was there; he thought the man had left at the same time as his labourers. "I should be charging you," Caspar said as he came back through into the yard.

"Oh aye!" The farmer laughed. "Try it on Tom Simple!"

As soon as Caspar rode the mare out into the dale he realized the ploughed field had taken the barest edge off her mettle. She was marvellous, forging ahead without any pressure from him, plunging surefooted up the sides of Widdale Fell, over Black Side, skirting Shaking Moss and Sweet Side, and so up to Mossdale Moor—five or six miles, crowflight.

Not once did he relax. Another of his mother's axioms was that trust and suspicion go hand in hand when you're riding; the one should always be as high as the other. But his trusting alertness did not stop him from enjoying the day and the place. There was no sun and very little wind. The clouds were one canopy of bright and dark grey rolling slowly overhead. The turf beneath was soft but firm. There was no point in trying to guide the pony except in the most general way; this was her territory and she knew what paths to take and where the going would suit her best.

There was one novelty he had to get used to though. At home his ponies were hunters. If they came to a gully or bank they'd go awkwardly halfway down the side of it and then leap out to the bottom. But this moorland pony was like a little spider; she'd go down the side as surefooted as a goat. More times than not she'd have three feet on the ground and only the fourth one moving—but all very quick, just like a spider. Even a little dry gully that he was sure she could easily jump she would sidle down and up in no time.

After an hour the fun of it began to intoxicate him. Grand schemes shaped themselves in his mind. They could start a stables at school and his army could convert to cavalry. What charges they could make along Whernside! They could build leaps and have point-to-point steeplechases! They could play polo! Yes, he'd have a word with old Brockman and get him to put chaps on punishment out on the moors with bags of paper and they could have mounted paper-chases…or, if they could get a pack of hounds! Just three couple, you could hunt a boy with three couple, and the keep wouldn't cost too much.

He decided then that he was Lord Cardigan leading the Light Brigade. All he needed to do was imagine that this ridge was actually a valley. Easy! The distance was right—about half a mile. And there were the Russian guns, their terrifying mouths perfectly round and black; he could see the gunners standing ready, the tow kindled and smouldering, waiting for them to come within range, knowing they could cut horses and riders to ribbons before the charge was half done.

He spurred the mare forward to a spine-jolting trot. She wanted to canter but he held her back. This was going to be a disciplined charge. No rabble riot. Soon he could see the astonishment in the gunners' faces as these mad Englishmen came on and still on, riding into certain death. Crash! His brigade came under a withering crossfire from their right. Crash! Then from their left. Men fell all around. Captain Nolan fell, shrieking at them and pointing away to their right. Wounded horses broke ranks and charged ahead or turned and bolted, screaming.

Then, in a mighty ragged roar, the guns facing them spoke. Their quarry dissolved in one bank of white, huffing toward them. He felt the sharp whoosh of grapeshot as it parted the air around him. Men shrieked as they were hit. Horses whinnied and reared. But the line held! Only moments later, as the tumult receded, he could hear the steady, measured trot of his troops on either side.

Time to press forward. Down went his sabre. (Did the Light Brigade have sabres? Never mind!) Down went his sabre. The trot extended. Another squeeze and his great charger lifted into a canter. The blood began to race. The guns spoke again, to the right, to the left, to the front; but now his men were blooded. Not one of them winced as the second fusillade took its dreadful tithe of their company. Five hundred men surging forward in one terrifying machine of death. The Russians could double their kill—treble it—and still that relentless charge would overrun them. Nothing could stop his brigade now. War was glorious! How he envied Cardigan; and how he longed to grow up quickly and become a soldier.

He could see the fright in the cowardly Russians' eyes now. There was no time to recharge their guns. They had to stay and be cut down—or run. They ran. He cheered in devilish glee. His men heard him and took up the cheer—a bloodcurdling, ghastly war cry. The Russians on their flanks had thrown down their muskets and were cheering this supreme act of bravery. Now he could smell the spent gunpowder.

What the devil—he *could* smell the spent gunpowder! He overran the Russian artillery and gained the crest just as the ground before him, about a hundred yards away downhill, erupted in a sheet of fire. Moments later there was a deafening thud—a real thud, this, no figment of his imagination. But if his imagination had not already been at work in that direction, he would never have controlled his pony. She bolted even faster than when she had first shot from the farmyard into the ploughed field.

For a hundred yards or so he concentrated merely on staying with her. Then he began to talk to her and gently to slow her down, step by step, with a series of checks, keeping very calm and steady himself. Soon he was able to turn her, and the knowledge that she was going away from home and back toward that Big Fright, slowed her even more. He made her walk the last hundred yards back, talking to and patting her all the way. She was quite calm again by the time they reached the crest.

And there below him was a railway working! Immediately in front of him they were blasting a cutting through an outcrop on the shoulder of the hill. That was the fiery eruption that had startled his mare. The men who had taken shelter on the far side of the outcrop were now swarming back to start shovelling and loading the muck dislodged by the explosion. He looked around for a warning flag and saw none. His lip curled in a sneer. If this had been one of his father's workings, the foreman would be dismissed for that. These were not navvies. This was a rabble.

He rode forward, down to the cutting.

Funny how you could tell the quality of a working from a distance. Closer inspection only confirmed his judgement. There were four drunken men lying under a tarpaulin, singing. The rock face in the working was much too deeply undercut—half the men were in danger of their lives if the face fell. The ropes were frayed and re-tied, spliced and worn. Two men were sitting on the gunpowder barrels—smoking!

With all the self-righteousness of a lad of twelve (or *almost*, as he would have said), Caspar relished every fault he found, and rode around, setting all to rights, just as his father would. It was much better fun than the Charge of the Light Brigade.

A navvy, shovelling stone that had spilled from a broken skip, winked at him. "Seekin' a job, lad? Fancy a chance on this workin'?"

Caspar pulled a face. "That's no working. It's a *shambles*."

The man's eyes narrowed and he came closer to Caspar. "Shambles?" he said. He peered at Caspar. "I've seen thee afore. Shambles? That's a right Stevenson word. Art thou Lord John's lad?"

The man looked at him with a sidelong smile, making his question rhetorical.

Caspar nodded, swelling with pride. "Aye," he said.

"I knew it!" the man crowed. "And I mind now where I've seen thee. 'Twere on the Crake Hall section last year. Thou come there with thy dad."

Caspar grinned in delight. "Is this the same line?" he asked.

The navvy spat. "This! Nay, this is a private line—from the quarry down to Hawes. Bloody rubbish! I should never have left Stevenson's, that's a fact."

"I'll write to my father if you like," Caspar promised.

The man laughed and turned back to his shovelling. "Nay, thanks, lad. I'll make me own way back when I've earned enough here. Tell thy dad thou met us, though. William Millhurst's the name. Tell 'im I s'll come back soon enough."

All the way home Caspar marvelled at this encounter. There, at the back of nowhere, he had met a man who knew his father and who spoke of "coming back" as if it were to enter the promised land. How glorious to be known and loved like that, and to leave enduring monuments, too, all around the world.

For the first time in his life he felt envious that Boy was going to take over Stevenson's. For the first time, too, the army seemed to offer a less-than-perfect future to him.

Chapter 14

"Isn't it strange, Rocks," Nora said, "I can explain it all to you so easily and calmly; and it doesn't matter a damn whether you understand or not. Yet I can't explain it to Stevenson at all—and to me it matters more than all the world that he should understand my point of view."

"Have an apple," Roxby said, beginning to dismantle the still-life group now he had finished painting it.

"What? After it's stood there for a fortnight!"

"Month," Roxby corrected. He polished one of the apples with a cleanish rag and threw it to her. "It's kept well."

She sniffed it. "My favourite! Apple and turpentine—how did you know?" But she took a bite and ate with relish. "I dread to think what you do at the end of a figure painting from the life!"

He grinned back and dug his thumbs into an orange, squinting away to keep the juice out of his eyes.

"It's all just a wallpaper of words to you, though, isn't it? My telling you all this. A way of keeping an empty mind while your hands get on with the painting."

His hands got on with swilling out his brushes while, speaking around the lump of orange in his mouth, he said, "In any sensible country, what Stevenson is suggesting to you would form part of the criminal code."

Nora put the apple down, only a third eaten. "*That's* why I love coming here," she said. "I know I can rely on you for good, solid, down-to-earth advice. Nothing up in the air! Nothing flippant."

"Criminal," he repeated firmly, beginning to wipe the brushes one by one. "I was going to say, I'm glad artists don't have a Society with rules to live by—but of course we do. Different rules, but, in their way, just as rigid. And compared with yours..."

"It's not mine. Christ—don't you listen to anything?"

"All right. Compared with the one Stevenson wants you to submit to, ours is a lot harder to enter. Yours—I'm sorry…*his*—needs nothing but training to enter; anyone can do it. Ours needs talent. Can you spare us a fiver?"

She came around his easel and looked at his painting.

"You wouldn't miss it," he said.

"Who's this for?"

"Oh, the old firm."

She looked puzzled.

"Fits and Starts, Limited," he said. "You must have heard of them—they employ half the artists in the country. What about my fiver?"

Nora laughed, outraged. "*Your* fiver!" But she toyed with the string of her purse.

He saw the gesture and grinned. "Just a loan, of course."

She had to laugh. "My God, Rocks, you're a real out-and-outer, you really are. Most people on the cadge at least go through the motions of signing a promissory note or an IOU, even if everyone knows they intend to dishonour it. But you…"

"Why exchange one form of wallpaper—as you call it—for another?" His hand was already out. "Oh, come on."

She made up her mind. "Mademoiselle Nanette and I will take you to dinner," she said. "Then I will give you a fiver—which makes a round fifty you owe me—and I'll take this picture to wipe out the debt."

He came and looked at the picture in pretended astonishment. "Fifty! For *this*?"

Her face fell. "Don't start that," she warned. "Self-denigration does not become you."

"Done!" he said, cheerful again.

"Yes, I hope I haven't been."

Still he looked at the painting. "Seriously," he said, "what d'you see in it?"

"Oh…'early intimations of the greatness that was soon to descend upon him.' I think that's what the books will say."

Suddenly—and genuinely—moved, he put an arm around her and kissed her briefly on the cheek. "God bless your ladyship!" he said, devaluing the moment. He still held one arm about her, now dropped loosely to her waist.

She looked steadily at his arm, then at him. "I hope it isn't all promise and no performance," she said.

He could think of no funny rejoinder. He gulped. She smiled complacently and walked out of his mild embrace. "Dinner," she said firmly.

❧

Nanette sat and ate in silence at a separate table in one corner of the room. Nora and Roxby behaved and talked as if she were not there at all.

"Seriously," he said when he was well into the second bottle of claret. "I think you should do as Stevenson suggests. Go into Society. Especially now you're a baroness. You could do me a lot of good from inside the citadel."

She looked at him as if it were a revelation. "Do you know, Rocks, in all the weeks of thought I have given this, that's an aspect that never once occurred to me. I wish you would be serious, as you keep claiming."

He looked at her speculatively, trying to decide whether his idea of seriousness would accord with hers. "Very well," he said at last. "I wouldn't want to say this too often—and I don't think you'd welcome it much either."

He pushed the bottle away from him and briefly rubbed his forehead. "I should have said this earlier." He smiled then, a little-boyish smile, compelling her to smile, too. That seemed to compose him. "You know—you must know—that you are no ordinary woman. Indeed you are extraordinary. I'd go so far as to say you are one of the most outstanding women of this age. Perhaps of any age—I don't know. And for you to incarcerate yourself inside the living hell of the standard social round—to go into Society, with its endless treadmill of card-leaving and morning-calling and who's-in-who's-out games—would be…a crime. That's what I meant earlier. I wasn't being flippant. I just didn't think you'd be interested in my considered opinion at any length."

His seriousness moved her deeply. He was extraordinary in his ability to pass, in a few words, from the lightest to the most serious sides of his nature.

She took his hand and squeezed it, rolling her lower lip into a smile, unable to voice her thanks.

"You're wondering where it leads," he said.

She held up a finger. "Before you say that, let me put to you a defence of Society. I don't necessarily believe it, but it's been put to me and I'd like to see how you answer it. This is how the argument goes. In the days of the Regency, English Society was public. It consisted of about a thousand families and they all met one another in public places and they all knew each other. Now it's a long time since that was true of modern Society. We meet and entertain in private—even on public occasions. Who gives a fig for those once-coveted tickets to public balls! What we now covet are the invitations to Lady Whatsit's dinner beforehand. And look at the numbers involved—it must be tens of thousands of families. So we can't use the old Regency system, which could be informal because everybody knew who was anybody. Hence all our elaborate...well, you can see the rest for yourself. The argument finishes by saying that, far from having *nothing* to do, far from being useless butterflies, Society women perform the vital task of regulating entry to, and ensuring exit from, Society for the worthy and the unworthy. Well?"

Roxby nodded. "I don't quarrel with a word of that. Mind you, as a description of what actually happens, it's a bit idealistic—but aren't we all?"

"Oh," she said, disappointed.

"All I'd say is that there must be ten thousand ladies already at that sort of work, choking every entrance and exit as it is—not to mention two million others just aching to join them. But you! Ah, you could do something unique!"

She brightened. "What?"

"You don't need me to tell you. I don't let anyone tell me what or how to paint. You have a genius. It will express itself. You won't be able to help it."

She was silent a moment. "That frightens me," she said at last.

"Good!" He patted her hand warmly and his eyes twinkled encouragement. His charade gained a new dimension then; he began to speak to her as a toddler. "Who's a clever ickle, miss, then! Come on then—one more step. One more step on your own."

Wearily smiling, she shook her head in fond resignation. "What are you saying?"

"Something frightens you!"

"And you say 'good'?"

"I say good because I think it's the first true statement I've had from you all evening."

She drew herself away from him and sat bolt upright.

"I'll amend that. The first *completely* true statement. Otherwise I've heard nothing out of you but cold logic and impartial-sounding reasoning."

She looked at him guardedly.

"I mean, dear Nora, that people don't make big, important decisions—or have big, important disagreements—on such cool and logical grounds."

"They ought to."

He shrugged. "We all ought to be terribly good. We ought to be charitable. We ought to love-honour-and-obey, some of us. The rest ought to have-and-hold...er...forsaking all others...whatever it is." He giggled and caught up her hand. "Spoiled that! Sorry...should have learned my lines." He hung his head, making her laugh indulgently.

He became serious again. "I drop a hint or two about a possible future for you, and you say it frightens you. I believe that. You talk about a disagreement with Stevenson and it comes out of you like an essay in *The Saturday Review*: 'On Society'…'The Woman Question.' At the risk of offending you, I can't quite believe that."

"But the rest is no business of yours. The emotional side of it."

He lifted his hands to the skies, begging strength. "Of course it isn't, you goose! That's why I'm so keen to hear it. And if it were my business, all you'd get out of me would be words and thoughts to serve my own interests."

She looked at him, lost so deep in thought her face was a blank. His eyes held hers, uncertain she even saw him. Suddenly she laughed, a variant of her earlier, indulgent laugh, but harder and less forgiving. "Rocks," she told him, "you've never done a single act, nor spoken a single word, nor thought a single thought that wasn't absolutely in your own interest. So don't invoice what you cannot deliver."

He pouted and looked away, hurt.

She dug a thumbnail into the back of his hand until he winced and withdrew it. "It was not I who raised the bets on honesty," she reminded him. "What's it taste like? I'll tell you something else: I love John Stevenson, underneath it all. And he loves me. It's feelings I'm talking about—real feelings. I do a lot to vex him and worry him. And he certainly pays me back in the same coin! But I'd never deceive him and I'm sure he'd never deceive me."

He grinned angrily. "But it's nice to *pretend*, isn't it!"

She was unmoved—supremely aloof. "With you, yes. You make it delicious."

He shook his head in smiling disgust. "Oh, Nora, you are a monster of some kind!"

"Yes. The kind with an eye that looks at an apple and sees the colour of the pips."

He laughed, seeing she would let him win nothing. Then, just as he seemed on the point of looking away, shrugging, drawing breath, changing the subject, he rounded sharply on her and jabbed a finger, almost touching her. "What you could do…" he began in some excitement. "What you could do is…" He hesitated, as if the words might prove explosive. "You could play a part in history. You could be talked of, as people now talk and write about…No! As *no one* has ever been written of, or talked about. You could be unique!"

"I thought I already was. Didn't you say that? Anyway, what history? History? What are you talking about?"

"The only history that counts. Not Stevenson's kind…bridges and pfah!"

"Be careful, Rocks!"

"Careful be damned! I'm talking about art. The history of art. What survives longest? Eh? What endures? What of Greece? What of Egypt? It's all art." The words tumbled over one another, scraping his mouth, thickening his tongue. "Damn this wine! You know what I mean. How many women now alive—how many women ever—could attract the choice of artists, the masters…"

"'The choice and master spirits of the age'?" Nora smiled.

"I'm trying not to say that. But all right: Yes! 'The choice and master spirits' of this age. You could be the centre, the light, you know, moths and flames and that sort of thing. Oh, God—come back in an hour and I'll tell you."

She drew breath to speak but he leaped in again. "How many other ladies could…?"

She spoke then: "How many other ladies do you know, Rocks?"

"None! That's what I'm saying. You could…"

"I mean ladies of any kind, in Society? You are comparing me, whom you know, with figments of gossip—people you don't know."

"Listen! A good painting's a good painting. You judge it for itself. You don't trundle in Titian and Michelangelo and Raphael and the rest. For itself, Nora. And you should judge people that way, too. I don't want to know about all these other ladies in order to judge *you*. I know you. And I know this age. Art in this age has sunk as low as art could possibly sink."

She was smiling at him. He reached forward and gently pinched her mouth into a more solemn shape. "Don't mock me," he begged. "Please listen. I swore I'd never say this. I swore I'd let you find it for yourself. But suddenly I feel it's so urgent. You are jolted by this disagreement with Stevenson; you could make such disastrously wrong choices. I have to tell you. I think you are already earmarked by history to play a great role…"

She shook her head. "Be practical, Rocks. You know me well enough. 'Earmarked by history' is pure wind. Talk in practical terms."

He grinned, sharp and brief, accepting her rebuke. "In practical terms, London is dead. It's dead every winter. Where is everyone? Off hunting. Enjoying the country, my God."

"Not quite everyone."

"Exactly. And those who are left don't know what on earth to do with themselves except give sad little dinners, meeting the same dull cliques…"

"But people have to go down to the country. Estates have to be managed. That's why Parliament's gone down."

"Not everyone! *Not* everyone—that's my point. More and more people don't have estates. More and more people are sick to death of the country and the insufferable tedium of what passes for life out there in those damp dells. More and more people want to live all their lives in the city—this city. And they don't want to go on and on and on meeting the same vapid, wearisome, spiritless, upper-class crowd. Can't you feel it? Society is changing—or is on the very brink of change. There's a new tide about to flow. A new Society, or a mixture of old and new, is about to form. All I'm saying is that you—you above all—could be on the very leading edge of that change. You could help to make it happen. You could shape it." He gulped. "Lord, I think I'm sober again. D'you want me to talk about history now?"

"And how I've been dog-eared by it?"

"Earmarked!" he corrected before he realized she was teasing.

She laughed. "Bit of both, I'd say. What you are suggesting is that I should form some kind of salon? A place where Society might mingle with Art and Letters?"

She had to admit to herself that it was not impossible—not one of Roxby's wild, engaging fancies. Of course, it was by no means as simple as he imagined.

"I don't belong to either group," she objected.

He laughed. "That's exactly why you *could* do it, better than anyone. Even Mrs. John Stevenson could have done it. Lady Stevenson will find it that much easier."

Roxby and friends would get free food and wine and a congenial background against which to display and preen themselves. And she might go some way toward obeying John's wishes while not departing too far from her own inclinations. And if Roxby was right, she might exceed all that John required of her or all that she sought for herself. Something for everyone. "I'll think about it, Rocks," she told him.

"Capital!"

"As a matter of fact, there's a house for rent in Hamilton Place—at the bottom of Park Lane, you know. I've longed to take it for some time and couldn't think of any justification."

Roxby smiled in feline satisfaction. "With the Duke of Wellington and the queen for neighbours, that takes good care of the social side. And what with Hyde Park and Green Park all around, half your visitors will feel they haven't left the country!" He flashed her a grin that lasted about a tenth of a second but was broad enough to wiggle his ears. "Don't forget my fiver, will you?" he said.

Chapter 15

Caspar scrounged another pony for Boy and together they went out to re-enact the Charge of the Light Brigade and sneer at the inferior railway working. It was a glorious April day, pretending to be summer, but chill in the shadow. The mixture gave the air a special crispness. Both boys, and their mounts, were glad to be out, free from stuffy classrooms or stables, like four adventurers wondering what lay around every corner and over every skyline.

Their speed pushed fingers of tears back along their cheeks, where the water dried to leave pale streaks of salt, like fading snail paths. By the time they reached the ridge that their fancy had to transform into the valley of death they were sated with air and sun and galloping; they were ready for a touch of magic.

Again the dreadful order came. Again the insolent Nolan waved vaguely down the valley and cried, "There, my Lord, is the enemy. There are the guns!" Again the Light Brigade advanced at a measured trot toward the mouths of the Russian guns, ready to endure the dreadful fire from both flanks, ready to die for England.

"There's Jeropkine!" Boy shouted, calling up the first enemy name that occurred to him. He pointed at a man in tail coat standing among the guns.

"I'll stick him!" Caspar yelled back, advancing to a fast trot. He was playing Cardigan; since he was the one destined for the army, it seemed natural he should be Lord Cardigan and Boy his ADC.

But before they could brave the first fusillade the fantasy departed and they became, once more, two sweating schoolboys bareback on moorland ponies. It happened the moment Boy called softly to Caspar, "Cavey. It's old Greaves!"

"Old" Greaves was all of twenty-eight. He was the first of chief's new breed of housemasters—men with a stake in the school. As chief had said when introducing the master on the day of the half-hol, Greaves taught modern mathematics.

But at this precise moment Greaves, upwind and unhearing, was standing with his back to them, one hand behind him, stuck between his coat tails, scratching with rigour.

Boy giggled. "I bet he got took short out here and couldn't wipe himself properly."

They had overcome their giggling fit by the time he heard them and looked around. His face lit up with unfeigned delight that did more to win their trust than could all the words in the lexicon. "Stevenson one and Stevenson two!" he called out. "Just the fellows. Look at this!"

(He would not use the handles "major," "minor," etc. on the very reasonable grounds that a fifth brother would be something ridiculous like "minissimus," while an improbable but not impossible ninth sibling would be "minissy-issy-issy…mus." The boys had made a song out of that. On the other hand, the sequence one, two, three, four…was—and here his finger would jab around from boy to boy while he hammered the word "what…what…what, eh, boy?" at them until someone gained a mark by calling out "an infinite string of rational, whole, positive, natural integers, sir." Greaves was your man for bringing realism to maths, all right.)

He was inviting them to look at the working. The cutting was almost finished, but even from this distance Caspar could see that the face was still much too deeply undermined.

"One of your father's?" Greaves asked.

Caspar left it to Boy to answer, obeying the same logic that had led Boy to concede him the leadership of the charge. He was astonished then to hear the mildness of Boy's reply. "No, sir, as it happens. His firm has done some work in the same valley but a long way away." He waved airily eastward.

Caspar could not let that go by. "Our firm would never do such slipshod work as this." He spoke more to reprove Boy than to answer Greaves more fully.

But Greaves was onto the word at once. "Slipshod? You surprise me."

Again Caspar waited for Boy to amplify, but all he did was nod and say, "Very."

Greaves looked from one to the other, still waiting. Caspar, having given Boy every chance, explained. First he dismounted and picked up a lump of rock; the ground was littered with them—sharp, jagged fragments.

"This sort of thing, sir," he said, passing the lump to Greaves, "should never be thrown so far from the seat of the explosion. Not in this sort of quantity. They're overcharging every shothole."

"Which is wasteful?"

"Dangerous, sir. It can fracture rock without breaking it, leaving it weak and unsafe."

"I see. Yes, I see."

They all began walking toward the site, and as they went Caspar listed its other deficiencies—the undercut face, the frayed ropes, the drunkenness, the smoking near the powder. Greaves listened attentively and looked from Caspar to Boy with an odd grin, as if he, too, suspected that Boy ought to be the one who was pointing out these things. He gazed at the working then with new eyes. "To think that I stood up there admiring their industry and skill!" He chuckled. Then, without the slightest change in tone, as if he really were wondering aloud, he said: "If that cutting measured twenty thousand cubic yards and it cost four shillings per cubic yard to remove, I wonder what the total cost would be?"

Boy, who had also dismounted, put up a hand as if he were in a class. Greaves made a resigned face and hauled it down to Boy's side again. "Just say it," he sighed.

"Four thousand pounds, sir."

Greaves turned to Caspar. "D'you agree, two?"

Caspar, who had not yet grasped the difference between the stage realism of the classroom and nuts-and-bolts reality, pulled a dubious face.

"What is it?" Greaves asked.

"Well..." Caspar laughed in embarrassment and scratched his head. "It's actually more like seven thousand cubes, sir. And you couldn't get it shifted for four shillings. More like six-and-sixpence...seven bob."

"Caspar!" Boy mocked.

But Greaves, who Caspar had feared might get angry at his correction, held up a finger. "No, no," he said. "This is interesting. So, young man, what d'you think it would cost? Really cost?"

"I don't know, sir. I'm not very good at sums."

"Guess. Estimate."

Caspar looked at the working with a weather eye, smoothing down moustaches he had not yet got—his father's moustaches. Greaves, seeing the father through the son's unconscious mimicry, suppressed a smile.

"Less than three thousand anyway, sir. You'd lose if it cost more than that."

"Hm. Let's try a different estimate. How far away is that hill? The one with the two goats. I've just walked here from there so I've a good idea of what your answer should be."

Caspar warmed to the game. Their father always played it—"What's the radius of that curve…the volume of that embankment? How many hundred pounds a day is this working costing us…?" and so on.

"More than a mile, sir. Less than a mile and a half."

"Excellent!" Greaves said. "'Not good at sums, eh? But sums is only a very small part of mathematics. The rest is quantities and relationships. And more. Much, much more. Life itself, I sometimes think." He stooped and picked up a couple of pebbles. He threw one at Boy. "Catch!" he called. Boy's hand darted out and just managed to hold the stone.

"There!" Greaves said. "You just performed a mathematical operation that would consume sheets of paper and involve both differential and infinitesimal calculus as well as simultaneous equations. And you did it all in a fraction of a second!"

The two boys grinned uncomprehendingly.

"You don't believe me?" Greaves said (delighted that they did not) and then went on to explain, in extreme slow motion, all the steps of eye, brain, and muscle that were involved in the apparently simple act of catching a stone: the ballistic arc ("That's approximately $y^2=4ax$ you know!" with a grin), the intercepting course ("Three vectors, mark you!"), the expected momentum of impact, Newton's laws of motion…and all done in a flash.

"Now try it again," he said. "Here's another stone." He threw it this time to Caspar.

But it was not a stone; it was a pellet of goat dung. The wind caught it and blew it sideways, beyond Caspar's reach. But his hand clutched the air where a stone would have been.

"Memory, too," Greaves said. "That's another element in the calculation. You were catching a remembered stone. Very nimbly, too." He looked from one to the other, pleased at the fascination he saw in their eyes. "I'll tell you what," he said. "Have you ever played fives? Or handball, some people call it?"

"No, sir."

"Well, I've had Purse remove the rhuharb frames and extend the concrete behind the old almonry. It should be well set by now. I'll see you there in an hour. We'll further our understanding of the ballistic arc!"

"He makes it jolly interesting, doesn't he!" Caspar said as they rode back.

Boy chuckled. "I was just thinking: If a maths master has to play a sport, it could only be called 'fives'!"

"Why didn't you tell him about how slipshod that working is?"

"Because *you* did."

"I left it to you first."

"Well, other people aren't interested in that sort of thing."

"He was."

"He's different."

They rode on in silence for a while.

"Boy? Do you *want* to be in charge of Stevenson's when you grow up?" Caspar asked.

"Of course I do. What a question!"

"Why 'of course'?"

"Because it'll all come to me. I have to want to—it's like a duty." He chuckled. "Why, young 'un? Looking for work? I'll set thee on."

Laughing, they galloped off the tops, back down to the farm.

Chapter 16

THE BOY WHO IS ADDICTED TO SELF-POLLUTION BEFOULS SO MUCH MORE THAN he imagines," Brockman said.

His hearers, the entire school confirmation class, Boy among them, sat unnaturally still, filled with unnatural tensions.

"Pollute yourself and you pollute your name. Now, a name is like a thread linking you and all the other members of your family: back to your mothers and fathers and earlier forebears, sideways to your brothers and sisters, and forwards to the wives you will one day marry—creatures who are now and always will be purer, finer, and more sensitive than you—and forwards, still farther, to your own sons and daughters.

"Now, I ask you to imagine a thread, of any material you like, buried in fine, dry, pure silver sand. Imagine that you dip one end of it, a mere quarter of an inch, let us say. No! The merest experimental tip of it! Imagine that tip to be left resting in a beaker of foul, polluted water. See! How eagerly that evil brew soaks into the dry thread! How fast it spreads, carrying its vileness the length of the thread! And beyond—into the sand. Oh, it is not long before that deadly turpitude has invested every fibre of the thread, every grain of the sand.

"And your name is, as I say, the thread that binds you and all your people—dead, born, and unborn. Thus it is no idle, pretty figure of speech when I say that the stain of your self-pollution marks all your family. Nor is it for the sake of mere charm that I remind you of those fine and gentle flowers now mere buds, but whose fruit and fructification will be of your loins. They are, so to speak, your sisters now. They are as your mothers once were. So when lascivious promptings arise within you, m'boys, stealing drowsily o'er you with vile, insidious persuasions, you should see, also rising, behind and above them, the loving images of your mothers and sisters. You should see their hands raised in shock and horror at what you are about to do. You should hear their sweet and tender voices calling you in pious supplication, imploring you to spare them this foul degradation, to let them continue in their tender purity.

"'Impossible!' I seem to hear you say. 'You greybeards know nothing of the strength of these passions. In you the fires are already sinking. The hush of middle life is upon you. To be sure, it must seem easy to you.'"

He paused and smiled. But his eyes, as he looked from boy to boy, were deep and firm. And to each it seemed as if that gaze rested on him alone.

"But we do know—we greybeards. We know what you do not yet know: how long and how hard, how bitterly hard, the struggle will be. But also we know how infinitely blessed, how ineffably sweet, are the rewards to the victor. What noble manliness he may then lay claim to! What iron strength of character! What grandeur of spirit! For he has been tested in the hottest and most hellish of fires and there was his mettle forged. There is literally nothing he may not attempt.

"We also know (and I confess I enter on this part of my talk to you with heavy heart, knowing that among you there may be some already well embarked on a sorry voyage whose baleful destination it is now my dread duty to depict in all its ghastliness)—we also know the other side of the coin: the early and dishonoured graves that await the unrepentant addict. For be sure your sins will seek you out. By your pallid, bloodless countenance we shall know you. By your hollow, sunken eyes, red-veined and rimmed in black, you will proclaim yourself. By your pimples you will number each act of abuse as surely as if you carried a tally-stick tied about your neck. And it were better that tally were a millstone.

"For these are but the first and faintest signs of a disease that will as certainly engulf your body as it imperils your immortal soul. Swiftly the insidious and pleasurable poison saps your very vitals. It invests your nerves and strips them of all power of coherence. Step by step it leads on to paralysis and insanity. Not ten miles from where you now sit is an institution dignified by the name of 'academy.' But it is a very different place from this.

"True, you will find boys there, some no older than yourselves. But never again will they taste the sweet intercourse of family life. In the few dishonoured years—or days—that remain to them, the empty rooms and corridors of their minds will ring to the insistent demands of one unceasing, lewd, disgusting passion. They are so far gone in depravity that even the fond embrace of a dear sister or a loving mother would serve only to kindle a lust that dares not own a name. But no sister or mother, however loving, could bring herself to embrace them. For they have grown quite furious and noisy. They are filthy and bloodless. Lacking all appetite but one, their flesh and strength is mere wreckage. And there they lie in reeking cubbyholes, chattering inane and loathsome suggestions, poor, pale, sightless, hairless creatures, abandoned by all as they have abandoned themselves, waiting daily—some even hourly—on a death as certain as it is pitiable.

"Yet even from those depths I am assured that the love of Christ has effected some amazing rescues. I have been told of a pastor who visited one such pitiable wreck of a human being and, finding him in a somewhat calm mood, talked to him quietly and manfully of Christ's love even for such as him; whereupon the frail creature foreswore all his wantonness and within two weeks was visibly on the road to recovery; within six months he was sane again and restored to full and excellent health."

Among chief's hearers there was a perceptible welling up of relief. His picture of the final stages of sensual degradation had made many of them tremble and sweat. The smell of fear in that hall was strong. Boy was more affected than most. He was still shivering in terror, wiping his palms on his clothing and finding them, moments later, as wet as ever. He had no idea of the dangers to whose brink his light indulgences had brought him. Light indulgences! Dear God, now a veil had fallen from his eyes, the pit yawned ghastly deep at his very feet. Two more steps...one more, perhaps, and he might be tumbling into hell! And his dear mother and lovely sisters, how he had sullied their spotless purity with his vileness!

He looked at his body, his hands, his knees, his dirty schoolboy clothes, his coarse, clodhopping boots and saw, for the first time, how loathsome they were. He felt so utterly unworthy.

An image flashed into his mind: Mary Coen. The crippled servant girl on the Stevenson farm in Ireland. She had been crippled in one foot from childhood. Then there had been a terrible eviction when the police had set fire to a shelter of turf and furze her father had built. And all one side of her face and neck had been very badly burned because, being crippled, she couldn't get out in time. Boy's father had witnessed this appalling visitation of "justice," had rescued the girl and had her nursed back to life, and then had given her work in their house in Connemara. Now Boy found himself—suddenly and unaccountably—wishing that his flesh, too, was as disfigured and slighted as Mary Coen's, so that it carried upon it a visible and outward sign of its own inward degradation.

The image of Mary was so powerful, his yearning so all-consuming, that he missed the next part of chief's preconfirmation talk. "How much more heinous, then," chief was saying, "is the same abuse not in self but in mutuality, for there the pollution spreads not north but south as well, not east but west too, not up but down also. And I say now, I say it to you most solemnly with all the awful weight of a promise made before God Himself, that any boy who is found out in either act, whether solitary or mutual, will be required to quit this school and the company of decent fellows before another sun has set."

Then he read them some passages from St. Paul, speaking of the great virtues and well-being that flow from controlling the spirit—not crushing it. "God's plan," he concluded, laying aside his book, "has never fairly been tried, m'boys. I most earnestly entreat you now to try it. Women were created expressly to help men in their life's work. Now, in our own advanced and elevated state of society, the influence of good women is greater than ever, for they and they alone may lift mankind up to a rarer, purer life. You may think that here, where you are, far from your mothers and sisters, far from all soft influence, they are powerless to render you that pious service. But they are not! They are not! Their influence is so all-pervading that you may help them reach across time and space and pluck you up to a knowledge of your own manliness whenever you think you are about to fall among the beasts. Try it, m'boys, and you will feel their power. As the darkness closes around you, as Satan steals into your fingers, conjure up the image of some good woman in your life—a mother, no doubt, a sister, an aunt, a pious neighbour—and feel her eyes upon you. Let her disgust be yours. Borrow her purity as it were a shield. Beg her take a brush to every unswept corner in you. And I promise you, I promise you, within six weeks you will find abstinence to be your natural order. Self-control will be easy."

"My sister," de Lacy muttered to Boy as they filed out, "is such a vile-looking hag she'd put you off any thought of fructification for life—never mind six weeks. I'll sell you her portrait for a quid."

"I ain't got a sister," said a boy called Capon-Smith. "And I barely see me mater above twice a year. I somehow think Manhole Kate is going to fit the good-woman bill the best. Good for a bit of fructification, anyday!"

"Manhole Kate" was one of the alleged loose women of Langstroth; a hundred fellows boasted her conquest for every one who even attempted it.

Boy left them and walked alone as soon as he could. His mind—his whole body—were still in a turmoil. How could these others treat their own impurity so lightly, especially when it led directly to such terrible things: insanity and death, and the perdition of your soul? And expulsion, too!

Even worse, how could they fail to respond to the nobility that seemed to pour out of chief? What a power that great and good man had. As he had spoken, his every look and gesture seemed to convey to Boy, as flashing directly from one heart to another, a rugged masculine understanding of the trials of youthful flesh. Boy knew how strong were his own dangerous impulses, yet the warnings came from one whose every move and word proclaimed an animal nature as vigorous and as enjoying as his own. Brockman had not spoken out of mere convention of some abstract battle with the senses; that struggle had been felt and suffered and known to every degree.

But that alone had not won Boy over to the army of righteousness. Something even deeper, even less tangible had passed from man to boy in that encounter; a rarer and a high power had worked. Brockman had seemed to radiate an intense feeling for the value of a life. Of any life. Of each and every life. So that when Boy had felt at his worst, at his least deserving, at his most ungraced and ungifted, that stern and tender fire in Brockman's eyes had cast its beam on him and found him wonderfully ripe for rescue. His broad, plain words had given Boy an enchanted glimpse of all he might become, of all that life itself might be.

Why, then, he found himself thinking, *it is infinitely worthwhile to try to be good; chief has found me worthy of that promise. And so I shall be. Lord, help me now!*

Part Two

1859–60

Chapter 17

I'VE SPOKEN TO HER AND IT'S ALL ARRANGED," NICK THORNTON SAID. HE AND Boy were walking around the garden at Thorpe Old Manor, waiting for dinner to be called. The Thornton children had come up to spend most of the summer holiday with the Stevensons—a week first in Yorkshire, then the best part of two months in Connemara.

"She's not too young," Nick went on. "I don't know about you, I don't get on too happily if they're too young."

Boy cleared his throat.

"Older ones are—I don't know—nicer, somehow. Friendlier. Don't you find?"

"Mmmm…er…"

"Anyway, she said she'd let us both do it for five bob. But only tomorrow afternoon." He took a half-crown from his pocket and flipped it. The silver coin shimmered through a steep arc before Nick trapped it between palm and fist. He looked at it. "Tails!" he giggled. "That's appropriate."

He held the half-crown between thumb and forefinger. "Anyway, there's my half-kick. Where's yours?"

"I haven't got that much money," Boy said, only just managing to stifle the relief he felt.

Over the last four years he had manfully waged the struggle for which Brockman's lecture, repeated annually with variations, had armed him. It had not been easy—it still was not easy. Time upon time he had imagined the battle was won, and effortless chastity had seemed within his grasp—only to awaken in the small hours and discover something more substantial there instead. Then, when his intellectual and moral faculties were at their lowest ebb, he would find himself the kidnap victim of his own body, whisked off on a detumescent romp that would last until the dawn came to save him and shame him.

Shame would then bind him at the wheel of carnal slavery for days or weeks while his higher faculties gathered their shattered forces and began their labours again…and yet again. These were always times of fierce desolation within him, times when he remembered as an outcast the great, high days of his near-triumph. He was that rare kind of outcast who knows he has deserved to lose the best of mankind and gain, in exchange, the worst of himself—and so must endlessly dwell on his own abjection.

How he used to hate his own body then. He would go without washing for as long as he could get away with it, rubbing his fingers into stinking crevices of his flesh and sniffing them to fire his own self-disgust. The early saints were said never to have washed. He knew why: the odour of sanctity is the stink of self-made-insufferable—and then suffered voluntarily.

He would walk out on the dales, too, saying his own name to himself—John, John, John…at each step until his mind begged relief from the all-obliterating boredom of it; but he would stop only when he came to some rocky cleft into which he could wedge his head and bear down until the pain made him cry aloud.

And in these ways he would usually elevate himself once again from the depths of sensual sloth to a new season of moral vigour. Always there came a moment when the struggle turned deeply joyful, worthwhile for itself alone. He knew then that before long he would be out of the mire, cleansed again, convinced that this time it was for good.

But there was a corresponding moment at the farther end of that sunny plateau—a moment when the glory began to hurt. Then goodness itself became an obsession, a burden to heap him, a rage. Then he knew that dark forces within were massing for one more assault—that, far from being cleansed, he was merely whited over. Most insidious of all was the cloying siren call of his senses, which became infected with precisely those yearnings he sought above all to suppress. Then anything—quite literally anything: the bark of a dog, paper blowing over the playing field, a merry shout, the smell of horsedung, the sight of his name on a team list—would dry his throat and set his heart a-flutter; a cavernous hollow settled on his guts; his muscles shivered for love. A shrieking for love bore in upon him from every angle of the day and night.

And it was while he stood on the brink of such a descent from the plateau that Nick Thornton had arrived with this loathsome and enticing suggestion. On arrival at York, Nick had slipped away from the rest of his family for long enough to meet this Station Road bedwarmer and arrange tomorrow's assignation.

"I haven't got that much money," Boy said.

"Go on!" Nick laughed. "The eldest son of one of the richest men in England hasn't got half-a-kick!"

"Honestly! A shilling's all I could raise—without my mother finding out."

"How? I don't believe that."

Boy shook his head, glad the talk was straying from its starting point. "You know her. If a farthing was to go rolling by on that highway up there"—he nodded toward the road, which was out of sight over the brow of the hill above the house—"she'd get to hear of it somehow."

"Borrow from one of the servants then. I do that a lot."

"Oh, I couldn't do that. I've never done that."

Nick became agitated. "But you've got to! She won't take me alone for half-a-crown. I tried that. This is a special price for two of us. So you have to. Don't you want to?"

When Boy stayed silent, Nick gave a crafty smile. "Not scared, are you, Boy? Not that?"

"'Course I want to!" Boy answered angrily. "Look!" He held forth a trembling hand. "That's how much I want to. But it's not as simple as that, is it!"

Nick, impressed by Boy's earnestness, did a stage bow. "I say! Let's go up the tower and see if we can peep into the girls' rooms!"

"Not our sisters!"

"No—the servants—fool!"

"Too early for them yet," Boy said unthinkingly.

"Ha haa!" Nick taunted. "You know their times then!"

Boy blushed—Boy, whose many nightly vigils from the tower top over the last few years had but once been rewarded with a glimpse of what might have been a breast (or a shoulder, a hand, a handkerchief, a bowl of starch…something pale, anyway). In the end the greatest wonder had been the persistence that endured such cold and cramps for so meagre a return. The power that forced him to it was frightening.

Nick skipped up the steps of the old tower. Boy plodded behind him.

"Wouldn't Caspar loan it you?" Nick asked before Boy was halfway.

Boy just shook his head. He walked past Nick and leaned against the parapet. The land fell gradually from the dry moat at the foot of the tower; then, a field and a half away, it curved over more steeply so that the bottom woods of Painslack Dykes were hidden. The southerly wind carried the gurgling of the brook to them on the parapet. Strangely, it was a sound you could never hear from the house, not even from the upstairs windows, though it was only a hundred yards or so farther up the hill.

"Oh, I say—lace curtains. That's new," Nick said, looking at the servant girls' windows. "Someone must have noticed you've begun to shave. D'you know there's four sets of stairs go up to their quarters?"

Boy laughed wearily. "Don't you ever think of anything else?"

"Do you?"

Boy punched him playfully.

"And they all creak like pensioners," Nick added.

"What would your mother say, Nick, if she knew what you were planning for tomorrow?"

Nick laughed uproariously, startling a jackdaw out of the ivy that clad the tower. "She'd throw a fit and die, I'm sure."

"But don't her wishes mean anything to you?"

The question left Nick solemnly puzzled. "I don't exactly seek her consent, you know."

"But that shouldn't alter it. You know what she would say."

"Exactly so. That's why I don't distress her by asking."

"What if you should think of her while doing it, though?"

Nick made the sound of vomit. "Are you quite sane?" he asked. "Why in God's name should I do *that*?"

Boy stared glumly over the waving corn. He remembered lovely guessing games with his father up here—and Winifred—in the days of his long-dead innocence. The best of his life was out there.

If only he could explain it to Nick the way Brockman would; but he knew that if he even tried it, Nick would laugh him to scorn. "What about yourself?" he asked. "What about what it does to you?"

"It sets me to rights, of course. Good heavens, Boy, you're like an old woman!"

Boy desperately searched for facts, remembered facts from chief's annual talks. Surprising how few they were. "Each spending," he said, recalling one, "is like a shovel of soil on your grave."

Nick did not laugh; he imitated a deflating balloon. "Tell it to the stud boar!" he sneered. "Ask him who outlives all the rigs! Oh, come on, Boy—it'd be fun. It's what women are there for. It's what *we* are for." He spun the coin again and almost failed to catch it. "It's what half-crowns are for!"

It would be more than mere fun, Boy thought. It would be one of the greatest adventures ever. It would clear away so many mysteries—what are they like down there? What do they feel like to touch? You could run your hands over a hundred marble statues and never know. It would be crossing the Rubicon.

"Very well—I'll borrow another bob off of someone and go solo," Nick said.

"No!" Boy cried, without thinking.

"Ha!" Nick shrieked in delight as the cry of *dinner!* came from the house. "You old fraud!"

Their ostensible reason for going down to York was to meet Nick's father off the mid-afternoon train. Their ostensible reason for going early was that Walter Thornton, being a senior engineer on the Great Western Railway, was apt to borrow engines (on the excuse that they needed a test run) and drive them himself, often arriving earlier than scheduled.

When they reached the station they told Willet, the coachman, to come back at three. Then Boy and Nick told Caspar to wait for them on the platform. "We're going for a drink, Steamer," Nick said conspiratorially. "Keep my pater busy if he turns up early."

Caspar, being a few days short of sixteen, was not thought an adequate companion for this most grown-up of treats.

"He'll be happier watching the trains," Boy said as they went out into Station Road. They both laughed at the juvenile amusements of the young 'un.

The whores were cruising up and down Station Road like ships with overcrowded canvas. Normally Boy pretended not to notice them, though for weeks after he had run their gauntlet he would torment himself with the enigma their presence represented. Today he dared to look each briefly in the eye. They were like circus people—accustomed to the mildly curious indifference of passers-by. *Try! Buy!* their faces said for half a second; then they would quench the come-all-you and fix their gaze on a neutral distance, quick as you care.

"Is she one of these?" Boy mumbled.

"Lordy no! Better than this carrion."

Better! Boy knew she would intimidate him. Even these painted galleons made him feel awkward and clumpish.

"Did you tell your mothers afore you come out?" one of the women asked.

Boy blushed furiously and looked away. But Nick laughed and shouted back over his shoulder, "She'd take the scouring soap to *you*, so be thankful we didn't!"

"I'd need it after you, and all," she shouted back, also laughing.

Boy envied Nick his easy way with them. Of course, Nick was older, but that wasn't the full explanation. The truth was that Nick didn't really care. For him this was exactly what he had called it: fun. But for Boy it was going to be one of the great and memorable days of his life—he just knew it. No explorer in Africa, no climber of unscaled mountains, no seeker after uncharted sea passages, could feel half so tense and excited as he now felt. Somewhere very near him there was a woman he didn't know and had never seen, and he was going to give her this hot, heavy half-crown, and she was going to lie down naked and let him do anything. All those blanks in his fantasies—he could fill them now. It was an amazing day in an amazing world.

Near the end of Station Road, Nick darted into a doorway and pulled Boy swiftly in behind him. "Phew!" he said. "I hate the last few steps before the doorway. I always nearly funk it."

Boy looked at him in grateful astonishment—astonished that such a fearless man of the world should feel that way, too, and grateful that he confessed it. "I'm in a funk still," Boy said.

"I mean I get this strange feeling that everyone else in the street knows me and is writing down my name. I'm sure it's all rubbish, of course."

"Of course," Boy said, disappointed that the fear was so parochial. Then the thought hit him like a leaden weight: She was very close now—actually in this house! What was she like? Could he run? He doubted he had strength for that.

"Upstairs," Nick said.

On the first landing a door opened at the sound of their approach. It framed a dazzlingly pretty girl of their own age—about eighteen, certainly no more than twenty. She was not at all like the fireships outside. Anywhere else you'd have taken her for a modest, charming, lovely young gentlewoman.

Not her, Boy prayed, unable to take his eyes off her, smitten by her beauty. He could never put something so vile as himself against such loveliness.

"'Ello!" she said, smiling. "Two cherries?"

"Cherry ripe!" Nick said, as if it were a very witty reply.

"I'm still 'ere tomorra," the girl said gently, directly to Boy. She knew exactly the effect she was having on him.

He scurried wordlessly after Nick, his scalp on fire.

"This is the door," Nick said when they reached the next landing. He gave a knock.

A tall woman in her thirties answered. She saw Nick and grinned. "I only half-believed you," she said.

Boy felt that her pleasure was more than commercial. She found it somehow flattering that Nick had kept his promise.

"And your friend!" she said. "Hello, Charley."

Boy held out his hand awkwardly. Surprised, she took it and gave a limp shake. "A gent," she said, and laughed.

"You should be used to that," Nick said. "You told me you only go with gents."

"And so I do!" She was suddenly belligerent, as if she resented Nick's words. "And gents who pay more'n a dollar, too. So let's be quick about it!"

She dipped a sponge in soapy water and went to Nick first. Incongruously modest, he turned his back on Boy and dropped his trousers. She washed him and gave him a towel. "That's a sharp 'un," she said. "Mind you don't pierce a hole of your own!" They both laughed. She brought the sponge to Boy.

His stomach fell free. All night he had barely been able to contain his lust. Now it drained from him like water through hot sand. The woman, with her open, pleasant, plain, careworn face, was no more and no less appetizing than ten thousand others seen daily in shops or on errands in the street. No mysterious, dusky, half-Indian maiden, she! The woman might as well have been a new servant inquiring if he wanted a change of clothing.

"Ever been with a lass before?" she asked.

He shook his head.

She wrinkled her nose. "You'll love it. You've got everything it needs." She stood and turned again to Nick. "Now—something for me old age."

Nick gave her his half-crown. Boy did likewise. She went to the door, seemingly to bolt it; but before she could do so it burst open and Caspar came swiftly in. He shut it behind him and leaned defiantly against it. "I'm going to watch you," he said.

"Caspar!" Boy exploded. "Why aren't you at the station?"

"Well, it's the whole of Dame School!" the woman said.

Caspar ignored her. He spoke to the other two. "You thought you were so innocent—asking for money like that," he taunted. "I knew straight off you were up to something like this, especially where *he's* concerned." He laughed and pointed at Nick.

"This wasn't our bargain," the woman reproached Nick.

"No." Nick agreed with her and turned to Caspar. "Piss off, Steamer. There's a good Indian."

But Caspar only laughed, even more pugnaciously. "Not while it's my cash pays for your tickle!" He looked at the woman. "They had to borrow off me to pay you," he explained.

"I don't care if they pinched it off of the Queen of Sheba, I didn't bargain on no voyers. You may bugger off."

"Give me my money back and I will. Come on, Nick—get the money back off of her. There's tons of pross hereabouts will let you two do it and me watch for a dollar."

"Oh, very well," Nick grumbled lightly, as if he didn't care what woman he had (which was, indeed, the case); and he bent to pull up his trousers.

There was something menacingly assured and aloof about Caspar. No one, least of all the woman doubted he meant every word.

"Very well," she said, surprisingly chirpy. "You may stay." She began to undress.

She would not remove her stays, though. "You can't expect more for five bob," she said reasonably. Boy's heart sank. Even from where he was he could see how stained and worn they were.

She flopped diagonally across the bed, her head toward Boy, her business end pointing at Nick. "You first!" she called.

Nick leaped upon her and at once began laughing and thrusting like a madman. Within moments he was finished, lying flaked out upon her in apparent exhaustion, gasping *Oh!* and *Ooooh!* in a delight he had not seemed to deserve.

"I know you youngsters," the woman said. "I bet you could start all over again."

In answer Nick began to jigagig, but she threw him off with a laugh. "No you don't!" she said, and did an athletic flip that put her on the opposite diagonal across the bed. "Now you, love," she said to Boy.

But he was staring in horror at the thing his fantasy had never been able to picture. He had thought of it vaguely as an infolding of skin—ordinary skin. Something like the folds of the little finger at the bottom of a clenched fist. Or perhaps a simple dent like a baby's. Or the pencil line rude boys drew on statues. But…this! A hairy gape, all folded and curtainy, like bungled surgery—a silent, freak snout. He could not go near her.

"No!" he cried out and buried his head in his hands. "Never!"

"You, then," the woman said to Caspar, not wanting the boys to have any case for a refund. She was completely unmoved by Boy's rejection of her.

Caspar needed no second invitation. He climbed upon her and began to make a slower and altogether more gourmet job of it than Nick had.

Consumed with double shame, Boy pulled up his trousers and crossed the room to the window, wishing himself already outside, at the station. He looked at the station.

"Christ!" he called out to the other two. "There's a ten-wheeler there in Great Western livery!"

Nick ran to the window. "Lordy!" he said. "Rothwell's double-bogey. That's the pater. Quick, Steamer, squirt and get off!"

But Caspar was already doing up his buttons. All three boys were now in a blind panic to get out, to get away, to get anywhere before they should be found here. They forgot the woman entirely. And it occurred to none of them how unlikely it was that the pater, or "Uncle" Walter, would make a beeline for this one room and stage a ponderous discovery scene.

Outside the door they faced a further dilemma: They could not go down into the street. He was somewhere there—perhaps. They dared not take the chance.

"The back way," Boy said. "Did you see a back door downstairs?"

"There must be one," Nick said.

"Suppose they blocked it off to make an extra room?" Caspar asked.

They all looked down hesitantly at the window on the back half-landing. Nick was the first to run to it. He threw it open and looked out, both ways. "There's a brick ledge," he called back, "and then a sort of low roof next door."

Caspar looked at Boy. "What d'you think? Feel up to it?"

Boy, unable to face further humiliation, said, "Of course!" and walked briskly to the window. Nick was already climbing out.

"Try not to look down," Caspar said.

"Shut up!" Boy snapped at him.

Anxiously, Caspar watched him climb out and begin to inch his way along the ledge. He saw that Boy was not breathing. "You still owe me that one and six," he told his brother belligerently.

Boy breathed vehemently. "I do not!" he almost shouted. He froze to the ledge.

"Move on, damn you. I want to come out," Caspar said less fiercely. "And I say you do. You had the chance with her and you didn't take it." He was on the ledge now, and beginning to crowd Boy, making him move faster.

"But *you* did," Boy complained, astonished at Caspar's effrontery. "So you had that instead of the money."

"If you didn't want me to be your guest, you should have shouted out before I began." They were almost at the next-door roof. "Anyway, I didn't get the chance to finish, so it doesn't count."

Boy stopped. His mouth hung open in disbelief.

"Go on!" Caspar shouted.

"You had a good eighteen-pence-worth from what I saw," Boy said.

"But my bargain was with *you.* Anything that happened between that pross and me was irrelevant."

"Jesus! If you two could just hear yourselves!" Nick said. "And here's a mess, too. There's no way off this roof." He helped Boy down onto the low retaining wall. Caspar vaulted down almost simultaneously.

"Except through that room," Caspar said, nodding toward a window that let onto the side of the roof where they stood.

"Idiot," Nick said. "That's the house we've just come out of."

"It isn't," Caspar replied. "It's next door."

Nick hit the brick wall beside the window with the palm of his hand. "That, dear boy, is the house we just came from."

"Whatever it is," Caspar said, "it's our only way down from here. Is there anyone in there?" He shaded the glass and tried to peer into the room. "Looks empty."

Nick joined him and tried the window sash. It lifted.

"That's burglary," Boy said.

"It's not," Nick told him. "Burglary has to be after dark."

He and Caspar climbed into the room. It was a whore's room, like the one they had just left: bed, washstand, several mirrors, lace trimmings in abundance, an open cupboard full of sheets and towels, a screen near the window, a selection of dainty clothing hanging upon it.

They looked around, licking their lips, committing it to memory. Boy, perforce, joined them. "Come on," he urged. "The sooner we're out, the safer we'll be."

They tiptoed to the door and listened.

"Someone's coming upstairs," Caspar said. "Better let them go by."

"Better hope they *are* going by," Nick corrected.

They waited.

A man was speaking. Nick turned pale. "Howl!" he whispered heavily. "That's the pater!"

"You were right," Boy said in anguish. "Someone did watch us go in. Someone told him, that's what."

Nick rounded on Caspar. "You!" he said. "They must have seen you."

Caspar did not try to argue. "Let them go up," he said. "We'll have to try to slip down then."

"Let's go back onto the roof," Boy said. "I still think this is burglary."

They were halfway back to the window when the door opened. And there stood Walter with a girl on each arm. One of them was the very pretty girl they had passed on the first landing, about five centuries ago.

"I told you!" Nick exploded to Caspar. Then he turned to face his father.

But Walter was staring at the three of them in open disbelief—from one to the other to the other, in a ceaseless round, as if he thought they might vanish if he could switch his eyes fast enough.

"We were out there on the roof," Nick said in the unthinking hope that the least comprehensible part of the truth might divert his father from his obvious wrath.

Walter turned to the pretty girl, on his left. "Are you party to this?" he thundered.

The girl came back hotly. "That I am not!" she said. "These cherries went up to old Maggie not twenty minutes back—yon two, anyway. That's the first and last I saw of them."

A slow smile of understanding dawned on Walter's face. By the time he turned back to the three lads it had grown broad enough to split his face. "So! You've been playing with my toys," he said with a chuckle.

They all relaxed and laughed then. Indeed, the laughter threatened to become a little hysterical. Walter prevented that by dropping the two girls and crossing the room to the boys.

"Come now," he said and, grasping the scruff of Nick's and Caspar's jackets, he used them as pushers to sweep Boy to the door and out over the threshold. He dusted the other two out as well. "Wait on me at the buffet," he said. "We have some talking to do."

Soaping his hands, he turned back to the two girls. Horselike, he kicked the door shut behind him. The last thing they saw was the pretty girl holding her unpinned bonnet above her head while her hair tumbled down—an image to make them sweat for weeks.

"The old dog!" Nick gasped in admiration as he strained to hear what was happening the other side of the door. "I never thought he had it in him!"

"I'll wager you've never once suspected it of me," Walter was saying to Nick.

It was small brandies all round, now that they were men together. Nick shook his head.

"Truly?" Walter asked, as if he hardly dared believe it.

"Honestly, Pater."

His father radiated delight. "You see!" he included all three boys. "That's how circumspect we have to be in these times. It was not always so, and honest days may yet come again. Who knows? But we of eighteen fifty-nine…" He mimed a cloak-and-dagger secrecy that made them laugh. "Our society is managed by women—by the ladies. And that is right and proper. But it means that all our social arrangements are geared to the needs of women, not of us poor fellows." He stretched luxuriously in his chair. "Yes," he sighed. "I daresay there never was an age, nor ever will be again, in which it was so wonderful to be a woman."

"Are they so different, Uncle?" Caspar asked.

Walter stared at him, seeking strong words. "Absolutely," he said. "Utterly. Different species, in my view, like horses and asses. It's a wonder our offspring are fertile. Men, you see, are made in God's Image. Each of us is like a mirror of God's entire universe—which, as you know, is an eternal battleground between good and evil. You and I are small corners of that battleground. We contain all the contradictions of the universe within ourselves—its highest aspirations and its lowest leanings. Love and hate. Command and subordination. We are the makers of a new world in every generation, yet we also man the armies that destroy it. We can fly higher and sink far lower than any woman is capable of."

He smiled benignly around. "Women are either–or creatures, more limited than we. Their natural state is pure and noble and refined. But once they slip from it there can be no possible return. Once degraded, they are as a broken vessel; the mender's rivets will always show. That is why"—he held up a monitory finger and solemnly lowered his voice—"you must never, never, never degrade a girl of good standing—any girl received in Society, or, indeed, any respectable girl, even one in humble circumstances. I would draw the line even at servant girls. I did not always do so, but I am ashamed of it now." His words, however, conveyed more of the glow of reminiscence than of shame. "No! Stick to your widows, your married ladies, and"—he jerked a thumb at the window—"of course, to our coneys out there." He chortled. "There's enough of 'em to go around."

"Enough for two apiece, even," Nick said, greatly daring.

Walter hung his head, pretending to accept reproof.

"But I say, Pater, it do seem a bit rum, don't you know. Mater fighting to mend 'em, and us breaking 'em every chance we get!"

Walter looked at him with a tender sympathy that extended to include the other two boys. "I used to think so, too," he said. "But we are each of us only a small part of God's great plan. Your mother's part is to offer the gentle hand of a fortunate sister to one in an opposite condition. She is to be as a lighthouse in a storm-tossed sea. Our part is more humdrum—I speak only in this particular matter of sexual regulation. We are here to keep the wheels of the world in motion. Our world. The world as we find it here and now. Not some imagined New Jerusalem—for which, of course, we all must nonetheless strive.

"And our world, it is a sad fact, contains a million surplus women. Simple as that. What are they to do? The natural state of a woman is to tend a man's needs and to keep before him and the world an example of the highest and purest—as your mother does. Ah…and yours, too," he said to Boy and Caspar after a moment's thought. "But if there are a million more women than men—what then? They cannot all take vows or till the fields or be governesses or sew and dust and launder—which are the only natural and respectable occupations for unmarried females. Frankly, I think that working in a factory or coal mine or shop is every bit as unsexing to a female as walking the streets."

The boys nodded as if they had always been of the same opinion.

"So," Walter said. "We are left with one of two conclusions. Either God put a million surplus women on these islands by accident, a slip of the Directing Angel's pen, or He meant it as part of some greater purpose. And when you look at the strength of the lower nature He has endowed us men with, when you consider the at-times-ungovernable force of our passions, I think that purpose is not far to seek."

Nick and Caspar, converts before Walter had spoken his first word to them, nodded sagely; but Boy looked dubious still.

Walter turned and spoke earnestly to him alone. "It's a way of keeping the pure women pure while we sully only the already sullied, don't you see! Man-above-the-waist may look for his inspiration to one kind of woman. But the struggle is hard and it can take a great toll of a strong nature. So man-below-the-waist may seek his relief from another kind of woman. Just consider the alternative, Young John. Suppose we had to look for whore, wife, and mother in the same vessel! Would it not be grotesque! How could you and your wife go into Society, greet your guests, engage in amiable conversation, correct your servants, if every time you looked at her or felt her touch it conjured up the memory of such a romp as we have all today enjoyed?"

Caspar chuckled maliciously. "He didn't!" He leaned his head toward Boy.

But Walter looked sympathetic. "He will one day," he said. "He's probably got more true feeling than both you two young reprobates put together." He turned back to Boy. "No, but you see what I'm driving at? Men encompass and express the highest and the lowest in human nature. Women must be either one *or* the other. That is the way things are."

Boy nodded unhappily. He could see exactly what Uncle Walter meant. He could feel the conviction and force of the argument. He only wished he could think how Brockman would reply. He knew there had to be an alternative different from the one Uncle Walter had just posed, but his own mind was blank of it.

"Mind you," Walter said, issuing one final warning to all of them, "don't let me mislead you into thinking that the pure woman is above bodily passion. It is not so. Such a passion is there, buried deep in their natures, often unsuspected by the girl herself until it is tragically revealed in circumstances that drive her instantly from the company of the pure to the herd of the contaminated. And it is hidden for a good purpose—so that she may cultivate her finer nature quite unhindered by those urges that plague you and me from time to time. But it is merely hidden, not absent. It is there for a husband to awaken at the proper moments in married life—to provide that little honey to sweeten the bitter pill of childbearing. If a man—or a youth—should accidentally awaken it at any other time, why then he faces the supreme test of his manliness, to protect the gentle bud and see it does not flower too soon. For believe me, once it is awakened in a woman, this passion—perhaps from its long dormancy—can grow quite ungovernable, even in the purest. The man who stoops to take advantage of that fact is surely the vilest of creatures. I hope…I know that none of you would ever dream of such a thing? That a decent girl would be as safe with you as if she were behind the stoutest convent walls? And though she implored you to take away the burden of her innocence, and though you shivered with yearning to do it, you would yet remember why men are made strong and women weak?"

They all nodded fervent agreement, feeling very high and noble.

"We may safely pour fresh pitch on that which is already glutted with tar. But we shall not place one microscopic speck on that which is unsullied white." Walter leaned back in his chair. "Is not the world marvellously ordered!" he said. "I give thanks for it to our Creator daily! By the way, Nicholas—come to me when you feel like a tumble. If you spend yourself out of your own money, it could lead to inquiries, eh? Once or twice a month should do you, I would think."

"I say!" Caspar enthused when he and Boy were back home and alone together. "What a stupendous pater Uncle Walter is. D'you think we could ask the guvnor for a fem allowance?" He giggled at the thought.

"Our father is not like that," Boy said crossly. "Running off to those filthy women all the time."

"Just because you funked it!"

"I did not funk it."

"All men are like that. Look at the streets! D'you think there's just one tiny band of rich sex fiends goes around employing all those tens of thousands of surplus women?"

"Chief isn't like that. Nor is our father."

Caspar sneered at the mention of Brockman. "Chief is a professional celibate. I'll bet when he wants more offspring he posts his seed to his wife, all wrapped up in a discarded sermon. And you don't know anything about that side of the guvnor."

"Nor do you."

"Thank you—that's my point. If we hadn't bumped into Uncle Walter today, we'd never have suspected him, either."

"And I didn't funk it. I was just too disgusted. I still am disgusted. I can't think why anything so disgusting is allowed in the world. I'll bet pure girls don't look like *that* down there!" He ran off before his anger could humiliate him to tears.

Caspar watched him go, suddenly feeling a great pity for this poor, tormented brother of his.

Chapter 18

THEY MADE THE JOURNEY TO QUAKER FARM IN CONNEMARA FOR AT LEAST part of every summer. This summer of 1859 was to be the longest holiday they had ever spent there and they were all looking forward to it. Connemara had all the wild freedom of the dales without the constriction of school routine. (True, Mr. Morier-Watson was coming with them this time, and, on the principle of always eating a little plain brown bread with your jelly and butter, he was to give them an hour's schooling each day—but that was merely to provide him with an occupation and to save him from the bouts of paralytic drinking that had engulfed him on previous holidays.)

Either from London or York, the journey to Ireland was one to fill the Stevenson youngsters with pride. From London the rails led to Holyhead over the mighty Britannia Bridge, which had been a Stevenson contract back in 1850. From York they went over and through the Pennine mountains to Liverpool by another piece of Stevenson engineering: Summit Tunnel on the Manchester & Leeds. Less impressive than the bridge, it was nevertheless of much greater importance to the family, for it was the contract that had enabled John and Nora to lift themselves from poverty to riches.

It had meaning for the Thornton children, too. Their father had been the company's chief engineer on the tunnel, his first independent contract; its successful completion—without disaster, on time, and inside the contracted price—had been the first of his surprisingly few steps to the very top of the profession.

Whenever Stevensons or Thorntons were aboard, the engineer was under orders to drive very slowly over the section between Todmorden and Littleborough, which had been John's and Walter's obsession for more than a year of their lives.

This time there were seventeen of them. Apart from Nora, Arabella and Walter, who were to spend only ten days in Connemara, the directors' coach seemed given over to a school outing. The Stevensons ranged from Winifred, now eighteen, through John, Caspar, Clement, Abigail, Hester, and Mather, to Rosalind, now seven. On the Thornton side Nick, soon to be nineteen, led Thomas, Albert, Laetitia, Araminta, and Corinna, now ten (or, as she insisted, ten *and a half*). The four servants occupied an entire second-class carriage. The baggage filled two wagons. Their expedition comprised more than half the train.

Not one of the children had ever walked any of the ground over which the train now dawdled, but its features were as familiar to them as their own gardens.

"There's Pex Hill, and your house, Mama!" Corinna said.

"Two Gables," Nick said. "That's where I was born." In his eyes it gave the house something of the quality of a shrine. "Look, Winnie, I was born up there."

Winifred raised her eyes from her book, Carlyle's *Frederick the Great*, which she had been ostentatiously reading ever since Leeds, and stared solemnly at the house for a few seconds, smiled at Nick, and returned to her book.

Boy watched their interaction nervously. He did not suspect either of them of being soft on the other, but he feared that Nick was out to fish in those waters so directly forbidden him by his father.

The three adults shared a private amusement. They knew that Nick had, in fact, been born in a wood about four miles farther west of Two Gables. Arabella, thinking Nick was not due for at least a month, had been tempted out on a picnic by weeks of hot, enervating sun. Walter and Nora alone knew that the birth had occurred on the very gravestone in a long-deserted cemetery where he and she had completed their brief transaction (he for lust, she for a sovereign) a year earlier. It was the grave of one Nicholas Everett, who "departed this life in the yeare of grace 1672" and whose name Walter had (rather ghoulishly, Nora always thought) given to the son Arabella had borne him there.

"It's not Pex Hill," Caspar said. "It's called Pigs Hill."

This, too, was a standing joke between the two families. Both names were found on the maps but the Thorntons insisted on Pex, the Stevensons on Pigs.

"Pex Hill!" Letty cried.

Clement stood up and walked a cramped circle, holding his nose. "Can't you sbell it?" he said. "Bigs Hill!"

"Clement, dear, that's not nice!" Nora said, but her words were lost in a happy, insulting-defensive chorus of Pexes and Pigses and a forest of dismissive hand waves and finger-clamped noses.

"Rough Stones!" Thomas shouted, pointing to John's and Nora's former house, right above the entrance to Summit Tunnel itself. "*Your* pigsty!" he taunted the Stevenson children.

But it was the Thornton misfortune that Pex-Pigs Hill remained in view for two miles, while Rough Stones was whisked out of sight only a second or so after it came in view. There was no equality of time for Thornton revenge; the next part of the ritual demanded that they should count each *dee-dah* of the carriage wheels upon the rails; and the cry "One...two...three..." began only moments after Thomas's shout. It rose to a crescendo at about the hundred mark and tailed off, breathless and exhausted, to one-thirty-one—or, as some of them claimed, one-thirty-two—for there was a butting of rails exactly at the tunnel mouth.

The grown-ups listened to these childish diversions and pondered all those things they could never convey to their children about what these five miles of England had once meant in their lives. For Nora, whose relationship with John had grown steadily more formal these last five years, this part of the journey had become especially poignant. Here was where she had met the man she had thought would fill her life. There, as the train burst out into the sunlight from the western mouth of the tunnel, was the very place where he had prayed always to remember her as she was then, barefoot and happy...where he had hoped she would "never lose the sunshine in thy spirit"...here he had asked her to wed him.

And now he had lost the sunshine on her. Theirs might as well be the coolest of arranged marriages, for all that it was forged in the heat of a love that had felt big enough to burst them. All those hopes, promises, intentions—nothing was left to her but their debris: a few million pounds, hundreds of interests, four big houses and several lodges throughout Europe, John's seat in the House of Lords, her own leadership of one of London's more interesting social circles, engineering monuments in every continent, a place in history—and, of course, eight wonderful, unruly, different, loving children.

Debris? Was that ingratitude? she wondered. Was it asking too much to have hoped that the heart of it all, the love she and John had once shared, would beat forever? More to the point, if some little creature with supernatural powers suddenly appeared to her and offered to restore that love in exchange for all those material trappings, would she close the bargain? She was honest enough not to know the answer. The "trappings" were a formidable compensation.

In her mind's eye (for she could not look directly at it with Walter there in the carriage) she watched Gorsey Hill and the abandoned cemetery drift by.

Her bodily eye fell on Nick, so like his father before Walter had grown his beard. And, perhaps because of his name, she seemed to see again the exact seventeenth-century curlicues that formed the legend: "Here lyes interred the mortal remains of Nicholas Everett" on the overgrown gravestone up there, in the firmly and deliberately unseen wood to her left. She saw the way the sunlight dappled it, felt again the heat of that August afternoon, heard the relentless buzz of the flies, remembered how Walter had taken off his jacket and rolled it as a cushion for her head...these were all things she had forgotten, or had not once bothered to recall, over the twenty years that had intervened. That was kind of Walter; she had even thought so at the time. She was wearing a threadbare blue dress she had stolen off a drunken girl lying in a stupor on some waste ground down in Manchester. She had the dress still somewhere.

She remembered her nakedness from the waist down and how cool it felt when Walter had thrown the dress up, making a slight turbulence in the air about her. And at once—not then, but now—she was hammered by the most intense carnal longing. Not for Thornton! Certainly not for him—she could look straight at him and feel nothing of that sort. And not for his partial re-creation in young Nick, either. No, it was a hunger for...for what?

And there she was—full circle. It was a hunger for John—not just the giant body of him, for that he gave her still. It was a hunger for all that he now withheld. It was a hunger for the pledge he had made her, here, twenty years before.

Arabella's lilac-gloved fingers rested lightly on her knee. "It was so long ago," she said gently.

Nora looked up in bewilderment. Arabella shed a clean, scented handkerchief from her handbag and passed it to Nora—who suddenly realized she had tears in her eyes. She took the handkerchief and smiled around the carriage, feeling stupid. But of all the children only Abigail seemed to have noticed; she was watching her mother in a kind of eager consternation, as if she both hoped and feared something dramatic was about to happen. Nora soon quenched her expectations. She dabbed her eyes and laughed for Arabella's benefit. "Yes, isn't it!" she said.

She dared not look at Walter. If Walter were an actor and had a part in a play that ran a year, he would still be feeling his way into it when the final curtain rang down.

For Caspar the ship crossing from Liverpool to Kingstown was the highlight of this journey. Perhaps because it had to withstand the eternal pitching and tossing and yawing and rolling of a voyage, the joinery to be found on ships was always of such amazing craftsmanship. Even simple oak or mahogany panels had a special robustness, and the rails were so massive and so firmly anchored on their stanchions. The duckboards were perfect grilles of lap-jointed three-quarter oak, and there was a piece of ornamental carving in the saloon, a trophy of fruit and flowers carved in limewood, of which Grinling Gibbons himself might have been proud. Surrounded by such craftsmanship, he felt safe and at home.

He stood in the very bows of the ship as she slipped down the Mersey; you could tell by the crispness of the bubbles at the ship's throat when the water turned from a tidal mixture to the full salt of the Irish Sea. But this river was not just the start of a little seapath to Ireland; it was a world highway. That excited him. There was everything here, from steamers and great clippers down to tiny coastal luggers. He tried to guess their cargoes—cotton from America; and grain and beef; hardwoods from Africa and South America, tea and spices and silk from the Orient; and soon, according to rumour, frozen meat from Australia and Argentina. You could smell the world from here in mid-river.

He had first seen the port as a giant model at the Crystal Palace Exhibition eight years ago. So now, although he had never been beyond the streets that fronted the harbour, he felt he knew it all—every warehouse, alley, and court. He could imagine all those cargoes vanishing into that labyrinth to be counted, broken from bulk, gloated over by fortunate merchants (or cursed by those who had bought into a glut), and consigned to the four corners of the kingdom. That excited him, too.

Over the past few years he had veered back and forth between his parents' wishes that he should go into the army and his own growing—and by now absolute—conviction that he should do that most dreadful thing, especially for an Honourable: go into trade. There had been a third force tugging at him, too: Mr. Greaves. Under Greaves's guidance, he had discovered more than a small talent for mathematics. True, he was still weak at sums—that lunatic world where people bought and sold apples in blissful disregard of the market price, or dug pieces of land in the least competent sequence, or frittered away their lives in filling and emptying leaky bathtubs in which no one ever sat or soaped himself long enough to think of calling in the plumber. But once he had left that world behind and began to deal in pure number and function and relationship, he made enormous strides.

It fascinated him to discover the inevitable relationships that were seemingly built into the very fabric of the universe. His hair had literally stood on end the day when integral calculus ceased to be a series of mechanical steps upon the page and became a concept, graspable in its entirety and never again confused. And the excitement with which he discovered a simple geometric proof of Pythagoras's theorem…the memory of it could still make him feel taller and the air more sweet.

"You get it from your mother," Greaves had said. He had been discussing Caspar with Brockman, who by now had an unlimited admiration for Nora's financial skills. "Keep up your studies and you'll be senior wrangler with no difficulty."

Caspar pretended to agree that his ability was from his mother, but he knew it was not so. She was best precisely where he was weakest—at sums. She it was who had taught him all the tricks that got him by in plain calculation, like casting out nines, cross-multiplying, division by factors, and so on. But whenever he tried to interest her in the elements that so fascinated him—the relationship between inscribed and exscribed circles on a square, for instance—she would follow him a few steps and then ask what *use* it was.

Guiltily he allowed himself to drift along with Greaves's suggestion that his should be an academic career in mathematics. But he only had to think of the way his blood stirred when he took up tenon saw and chisel in Ingilby's carpentry workshop, or walked into Stevenson's steel mills at Stevenstown, or stood, as now, at the heart of some great scene of commerce, and he knew the academic life could never hold him. What prevented him from making the outright break was his contempt for the rest of the curriculum at Fiennes: an unceasing study of the classics and divinity, with no reference of any kind to the modern world. Only Greaves's teaching of mathematics reconciled him to making any effort with his studies.

It was all very well for Boy, who loved the classics and who would no doubt spend days this holiday walking up and down the beaches and over the bogs, talking Latin and Greek with Winifred—another fanatic for dead languages. Last summer they had even performed *Oedipus Rex* in Greek for the bemused villagers of western Connemara (who had nonetheless cheered the rafters down about their ears). Boy was made for Fiennes and Fiennes for Boy; year by year he ascended ever higher into some never-land where he was kitted out wonderfully to serve at the right hand of Alexander the Great or take down the *Eclogues* as fast as they fell from Virgil's lips, if only someone would invent a workable vehicle for travelling in time. It was certain that Boy himself would never be that inventor; anyone with less practical sense or ability would be in daily peril of ten varied deaths. What sort of mess he would one day make of the firm of Stevenson's Caspar shuddered to think.

And that irked him above all. He, who with all the weight of his almost-sixteen years upon him, felt competent enough to take over Stevenson's tomorrow if anything befell his father, would have to join the colours, while Boy, who had neither interest in nor talent for the firm's work, would take it over and very probably ruin it.

This business of joining the colours was—like his drifting along with Greaves's dream of turning him into a mathematician—another of those issues he was shirking. In fact, it had been years now since he had felt the faintest interest in anything military. A good band could still stir the blood, of course, and there was something impressive and awe-inspiring in the sight of a regiment parading its colours and battle honours through the streets; but he knew now that that wasn't a hundredth part of army life. Almost everything a soldier did was carried through by reference to a manual, or a code, or a law, or a custom. And he just wasn't that sort of person.

He wanted to battle all right. He wanted life to be a fight. He wanted that little edge of fear every day (which was why he knew he would shun the academic life, too). But he wanted the struggle to be such that his own effort and cunning counted more than anything else. He wanted to be in business.

From the stern of the ship he watched Liverpool and Birkenhead dwindle to mere darkenings of the horizon.

He was on his way below when he saw Winifred leaning on one of the rails, near a dinghy stowed inboard. At first he thought she was out there to capture what little romance the dirty sea and anaemic evening sky afforded, but when he came near she turned and pointed to the curved pieces of the clinker-built dinghy and said, "Steamer, how do they bend wood like that?"

It was such an improbable topic for her to be interested in that he knew she was merely working around to something else. But he told her how they boiled the wood in iron pipes and bent it around the ribs before it could set, and she showed a polite interest.

"Are you going to be seasick?" he asked.

"No!" The question surprised her.

"You're very quiet."

"Ah!" she sighed, hinting she had good reason.

He waited and then said, "I'm going below."

"I think I've done something rather foolish," she said, avoiding his eye.

He leaned against the rail, not looking at her, to make it easy.

"What do you think Papa would say to the idea of my working?" she asked.

"But you do work. Sunday school…charity affairs…all the…"

"I mean employment. A *job*, as they say nowadays!"

Caspar mimed a summary hanging, throat noises and all.

She smiled glumly. "That's why I didn't tell him, of course. I knew he'd just say no. Now at least he'll have to discuss it."

"Say no to what?" Caspar was excited. Without thinking it through in any detail, he had a feeling that a rebellion from Winifred might somehow blaze a trail for him, even though his own struggle was as yet so vaguely defined. At the very least he would not be alone.

"I wrote to Miss Beale at Cheltenham Ladies' College. She's the new principal. I asked her for a teaching post."

Caspar's eyes went wide; he had never thought of Winnie as anything so grand. He had never thought of Winnie as anything outside the domestic circle. He had just assumed that, being a woman, she'd come out in the usual way, marry, and vanish into her own home and her husband's life.

"I know it's not much of a school," Winifred apologized. "But it could be made something of."

Caspar smiled, but Winifred, mistaking it for a look of contempt, said, "I'll bet Fiennes wasn't much before Brockman came."

"Nor since actually," Caspar said. "What does Boy think of your applying?"

Winifred shrugged. "I've not asked him."

Caspar filled with pride. She had asked him, not Boy! It was the first time he could remember it. And she didn't say "I've not asked him yet." Just that she had not asked him. Caspar knew why, of course, but he had to hear it. "Are you going to?" he asked.

"There are some things you can't talk about with Boy. He just talks about 'duty' and 'obligation.' He won't discuss things. Papa's the same."

"Tell Mama. She'd agree with you."

Winifred smiled conspiratorially, as if to acknowledge it was wrong to be talking about their parents in this way. "I'm saving her," she said, ambiguously.

"Winnie, d'you think Boy will make as much of the firm as Father has?"

She stared evenly at him, knowing exactly what was in his mind. "That would be asking a lot."

"D'you think he'd even make a good job of it? He gets so…I don't know… dedicated to things."

She laughed. "Who's talking!"

"I mean he doesn't know how to come back when the branch he's on gets too thin. He doesn't know how to change his mind."

"Perhaps Father ought to put the firm into management and train all of us to retire into public life," she teased.

And Caspar, seeing he was going to get no commitment from her, pretended to agree. "It's what most people would be doing," he said.

❧

In the cabin below, Nora was trying to persuade Arabella to stay longer than a mere ten days.

"How I wish I could!" Arabella said. "But I simply have to go to Paris. It is all arranged through Lady Bear and the Female Rescue Society." She smiled apologetically. "Besides, it might be very important. They have asked me to make a study of the Continental system. Those *maisons tolérées*, you know."

Nora nodded. Arabella's lack of reticence in this area embarrassed her. Or, rather, it was her earnestness, her total lack of humour; in Nora's own circle it was a subject of deft wit—a light jab and pass on.

"Do you know anything about them?" Arabella asked.

Nora knew her well enough to say, "I have a feeling I'm about to, my dear."

"Have you *seen* them?" Arabella persisted, with only a fleeting smile.

"I've had them pointed out to me, of course. And I know the ones in Trouville are often used by sailors, and others, as a depot for leaving and collecting messages."

Arabella made an exasperated sound.

"Oh, indeed," Nora assured her wide-eyed, "they seem as natural and everyday in France as public houses in England."

"Ah, but a thousand times more pernicious. Believe me! That is precisely what we fear, you see. Once such houses are tolerated and licensed, the girls all listed and recorded, all inspected by government doctors, all given cards of identity, all made official, you see—then vice has made a nest in the very heart of the state."

"But we have it, too—as if I needed to tell you!"

"Yes! But it is not tolerated."

Nora's eyebrows shot up. Everyone knew that it was, in effect, tolerated, and very widely. Whole districts of London and every other city were given over to it; and the police turned a blind eye most of the time.

"Not legalized, I mean," Arabella said.

"The French say that's just our hypocrisy. We pretend it does not exist, merely because the law does not recognize it. And the girls' incomes are not taxed because the money is not income, it is 'gifts from admirers'! Meanwhile we endure a level of disease that shocks them."

Arabella raised her hands in despair. "You see! How right our fears are! If you, an intelligent and sensitive intellect, can think along those lines (and you a woman), how long before our glorious legislators (who are all men) start translating such thoughts into law?"

"What has being a man or woman to do with it?" Nora asked. Then, seeing the hidden incongruity of the question, she added: "In the matter of reasoned debate, I mean?"

Arabella visibly fought for control of herself, as if Nora's mention of reasoned debate were a rebuke.

"I shouldn't have said that," she allowed. "It's a red herring. There are two issues here. The fundamental, moral issue is that tolerance of vice must not be written into the system of the state. But there is a practical issue, too—and for us it will be a tactical one, I'm sure. If such a law is ever passed, it will be framed, debated, amended, and voted on by men. It will be applied by men. All charges under it will be prosecuted by men, defended by men, heard by men, judged and sentenced by men. If it provides for inspection of the women, even that most intimate act will be carried out by men. You may be sure that all these arrangements will not be made for female convenience."

The argument began to interest Nora. "In what way?" she asked.

Arabella, seeing no opposition, now relaxed. "A French woman is inspected once a week. She could be infected at any time and pass on the contagion to dozens of men. The sensible way would be to make each man obtain a bill of health, which he would have to surrender to the woman. And before he could enter the house again he would have to obtain a further bill of health. And if any man were found unfit, he should be put in a prison-hospital, as the women now are." Nora snorted at the impossibility of it.

"Exactly!" Arabella said. "Men would never stand for it. But they impose far worse conditions on the female parties to the affair—and think it all the most natural thing in the world. Oh, it's *their* world, true enough."

Again Nora opened wide her eyes, but this time in astonished admiration. "Dear me, Arabella, what a long journey you have been since last we talked!"

Arabella subsided. "Reluctant step by reluctant step, I do assure you. Still"—she brightened—"that, as I say, is the lesser issue. The main effort must go in ensuring that the state—our state—never provides for vice under the law."

"Only under the carpet," Nora teased.

Arabella did not rise to it. "That is what I have to go to France for. To collect evidence on the degradation of the state and of our sex. I am to visit houses and prisons and hospitals—and, of course, refuges like our own. I shall talk with the *Police des Moeurs* and with anyone who will listen to me or tell me anything. Do you know, most of the people working for reform are Protestants like ourselves. Is that not comforting! Ours is such a superior Christianity."

Nora patted her on the arm encouragingly. "Yes, Arabella dear, do keep that in mind as you watch the Sisters of Mercy at work in the hospitals you will visit!"

Arabella nodded, apparently chastened, seeming to accept the reproof; inwardly she seethed. There were times when Nora's teasing grew a mite sharp.

Nora wondered if Arabella would come back thinking any differently or if she would simply "discover" everything she was so intent upon finding there.

The moment she returned to her own cabin, however, all thought of Arabella vanished. A far more personal worry replaced them: Boy.

She had looked quickly through the dozen or so books her eldest son had taken on this holiday. The few that were not actually in Greek or Latin might just as well have been, for all they meant to her—books on philosophy and religion for the most part. She never saw him read any of the railway papers, nor the iron and steel journals, nor anything concerning civil engineering. Come to that, he hardly ever looked in an ordinary newspaper.

She just could not fathom him. Once upon a time he had been so interested in all these practical things.

Chapter 19

Connemara was where their lives became joyfully simple. Everywhere else she went, Nora felt on show, even on trial, despite all the pleasures her life offered. In Connemara she returned to the uncluttered habits of her young girlhood—at a greater level of security, to be sure, but she was not above rolling up her sleeves and cooking a meal or turning out a room. That was a holiday for her.

Only three servants were kept at Quaker Farm, or Keirvaughan as the estate had always been known locally. John and Nora had bought the place out of Irish railway profits during the famines, over ten years earlier; together with the Quakers they had consolidated the innumerable small holdings and ended the "conacre tenancies" that had kept the people impoverished to such a degree that they actually lived below the reach of the money system, untouched by any possible reward or incentive, living on thin charity between one potato harvest and the next. Some of the men had taken work with Stevenson's, but most families had accepted John's offer of £5 and free passage for themselves to America. The tenants who were left now farmed above subsistence level and were actually handling cash for the first time in their lives. (Even so, John had not considered the experiment a success until he heard one of the tenants, a man who had been kept alive by relief work until he was thirty, complain of a levy by the parish union for the indoor relief of paupers!)

All of them, Stevensons and Thorntons, realized that if they imported the sort of life and standards they enjoyed in England to this wild edge of the kingdom, the whole point of coming here would be lost. So they brought only three maids and a footman; the footman, with one of the maids, would go back to England with Walter and Arabella in ten days. Laundry girls and extra grooms for the children's ponies were taken on locally, from tenants' families. For the rest the children made their own beds, sorted their own laundry, tidied their rooms, and laid and cleared the tables. It was amazing then how little they found they needed, what lumpy mattresses they could sleep on, how dresses and pinafores might last an entire day, knives and forks serve for two courses, and boots go unblacked until a parent or an older sibling with sufficient authority would drag the offender to the boot locker by an ear or a fistful of hair.

For the older boys this sense of freedom began as soon as they got down from the train in the Galway City terminus. Instead of taking the afternoon horse car to Clifden, the families had decided to stay overnight at Black's hotel and spend the afternoon and the following morning seeing the city. The older children would then go on the public horse car; the adults and younger ones on a private car coming down from the farm that evening. The two cars, public and private, would travel together and change horses at the same places.

Boy knew exactly which of the city's sights he wanted to show Nick and his two younger brothers. Ever since the fiasco in York he had been eager to restore his stock with Nick in some way that did not involve his own participation. So as soon as their rather late lunch was over, and everyone was deciding what everyone else would be doing that afternoon, Boy announced that he and the other older chaps would go out along the beach and see what they could add to the shell and coral collection of their museum at home.

"I know a beach where we can get pocketsful in five minutes," he said as he led them down to the Claddagh, the fishing community to the south of the city—where the attraction was (of course) the women. The Claddagh females were not remarkably beautiful, nor especially available, nor notably willing. The handkerchiefs in which they bound their heads did not add the lustre of a mantilla nor the enticement of a yashmak. The blue mantle and red body-gowns and petticoats they wore were coarse in material and crude in colour; they did not sparkle like silks nor flatter like beige and mauve and tan. What they did do, which made the excursion worth several hours out of the lives of five busy young lads, was finish at the knee—leaving the lower limbs and feet *au naturel* as the guide book put it.

Boy and Caspar, trained by years of watching Barn beatings without being seen to watch, gawped sidelong and beetlebrowed at this permanent and unselfconscious display of calf and ankle; Nick, Thomas, and Albert acquired the skill unawares but fast. Had they been translated into five flies on the wall of the ladies' bath house, they could not have been happier. All the while, too, one or other of them maintained a lofty and highminded conversation on the quaintness of the low thatched cottages all around, the durability of local customs, the indifference of the inhabitants to external influences—and, to be sure, the quality of the fish on sale at the stalls. They nearly bought more fish in those few hours than their combined families could have eaten in a month of meals; it was a wonder they ended up taking no fish home at all. All five of them dreamed of amazing romps that night with the bare-calved, horny-soled women who, by daylight, had stared at them with the amused incuriosity that all fixed communities reserve for the rootless visitor. Next day their return visit to the Claddagh almost lost them the second and final public car of the day to Clifden.

The lands immediately west of the city had once been prosperous enough to produce the sort of surpluses that interest marauders. In fact, the west gate still bore the ancient legend: "From the fury of the O'Flaherties Good Lord deliver us." But the neglect of a remote government (the ultimate marauder), the misrule of a local one, and the consequent unrule of the people had combined to produce the ruin that all the fury of all the O'Flaherties had never been able to achieve. The only increase had been in numbers, thanks to the dependable potato and an equally dependable sequence of soft days. The moment the potato became unreliable, especially in the universal failures of 1846 to 1848, that increase had drastically reversed.

When they had started coming here for their holidays, the young Stevensons, unaware of the tragedies that each empty home represented, were enchanted by the little hovels and shanties of turf and rough rock, clay, and furze that lined the roads like semi-natural doll's houses, inviting play and fantasy. But by now the winds and rains had done their work and few vestiges remained. Within a decade the country appeared—and was—more desolate and uncared-for than it had been in a thousand years.

But the real wildness did not begin until they reached the heart of Connemara late that afternoon, when the Twelve Bens towered over two thousand feet above them to the north of the road. Despite the mathematical promise of the name, none of the children had ever found a map that could actually list more than ten of the "Bens"; moreover, when climbing up to the highest of them, Benbawn, it was possible to count no fewer than twenty-four peaks. These irreconcilables merely added to the magic of the whole area.

It was a land mottled with lakes, littered with vast granite boulders torn by glaciers from Scottish or Norwegian mountains hundreds of miles away—a land barely touched, let alone tamed, by plough or spade; a land whose air came fresh off three thousand miles of ocean, demanding to be breathed in great gulps; a land awash with light. Finally it was the light that held the eye and sealed the memory. Nowhere else on earth did it play such tricks with the land, giving mountain and lake and bog the most temporary appearance. One moment these features would rise or stretch beneath a clear sky, as massive and placid as sunlight could paint them. Moments later they could turn to the thinnest of silhouettes and surfaces, as faint sea wrack drifted between sun and land. And in a short while this new face, too, could dissolve into an infinitely slowed-down version of that shimmering, mystical world found beneath rippling water when the sun strikes through its surface. You could watch this land all day, and in no two periods of ten minutes, taken together or at random, would you find it the same.

On the evening of their arrival this great natural theatre performed magnificently. The last few miles of the road to Clifden, south and finally west of the Twelve Bens, lay under a long carpet of cloud that tailed off with a little southward flourish far over the Atlantic beyond Slyne Head. Above this flick-of-the-tail, rearing into the sun, they could see tower upon tower of cloud, like a stack of cauliflowers. Away to the south the sky was all indeterminate streaks of greys and violets, with the odd patch of muted yellow where clouds emerged from the summer mists. To the north the sky was cool, remote, correct—like the most formal classical painting—pale, thin blue glazes over minutely scumbled white clouds. And above was the fleecy grey of cloud bottom seen slantwise.

But as they drew on beneath it, and the wind carried it inland above them, they began to look directly up into the towers of cumulus, seeing cold gray and warm grey side by side, merging. Between, where the cloud thinned and the sky almost showed, there were patches of a blue that burned. Soon, as the sun began to break beneath the edge of this carpet away to the west, it caught the lowest wisps of cloud and turned them every hot hue from gold to carmine. Then, too, in the thinner towers, the sunlight burned with a lowering, sulphurous yellow that sank beside the blue. It was the sort of scene that makes even those who have never held a paintbrush long to take up painting (and that makes professional painters weep at the unfairness of nature).

To the children it was like paintings that moved. From the oldest to the youngest, they sat silent and spellbound, risking every kind of neck strain and injury as they leaned backward in the jolting cars and marvelled at this infinite panoply of colour and mood, determined to miss no moment of the fleeting drama as the wind whisked it overhead and inland, down into the rising dark.

At Clifden, McGinty, the head of the farm stables, was waiting with a dozen of the sturdy, broad-chested ponies they breed in those parts. This was "the bestest part of the journey," according to Rosalind, the youngest Stevenson. All the youngsters, except Winifred, who considered herself too old, and Araminta Thornton, whose mother thought her too delicate, mounted their ponies and followed the car all the way out to the farm. Arabella considered that her Letty, now fifteen, ought really to be riding sidesaddle; but since none was provided, she made the girl ride at the back. It was a measure of the charm of the place that only five days later Arabella saw Nora galloping up the beach, riding astride, and she laughed at it and called it "great gas and gaiters."

The way out to the Keirvaughan peninsula wound south and west over sudden small hills, past a rushing torrent of water penned so long inland and forced to so tortuous a way down to the coast that, now it had reached the final mile, it seemed determined on a white-lathered sprint to the sea. In the gathering darkness its swirling eddies were richly black among the pale glint of the pebbles. All the way the children questioned McGinty mercilessly, determined to discover that the farm had not changed one iota over the past ten months. McGinty, though he was fifty, toothless, and (after his long wait) far from sober, managed to reassure them that nothing had or possibly could be altered.

After a while the road, though still hilly, began to lead more up than down. The trees became sparser, the hedgerows thinner, and before long, they breasted a rise and saw the whole peninsula stretching westward to the last segment of the setting sun, lapped on both its long flanks by the darkling waters of the ocean. All the land between here and the sea was Quaker Farm. The farmhouse was out of sight beneath the farthest headland, nestling at the inner neck of an awkward little stonewalled harbour; but they could see the lighthouse on Inisharone, its light still pale in the afterglow of the sun.

"That's the nearest point to America on the mainland of Britain," Caspar said.

A chorus of goodnatured barracking greeted the remark. Everyone knew that Ballyconneely point and Claddaghduff were more westerly. Caspar, when much younger, had hated "his" headland to be so nearly the most westerly and yet to fail by a mere mile or three; he had spent an entire holiday insisting vehemently that the others were undercut by secret channels that really made them islands. Now each year he re-established the point with mock defiance.

And so, babbling rapidly, reliving what they had relived dozens of times before, ravenous for the game pie, the buttered eggs, the rich oaten doorsteps of bread that waited them, they trekked down into the dusk, lost in their own sense of enchantment.

And there, waiting to greet them in the farm door, with the warm lamplight spilling out into the garden around her, was dear Mary Coen. In that position she was a mere silhouette, but as soon as all the handshakes and, with the younger children, the hugs were over, she came with them into the light and they saw again the scars that disfigured one half of her face. Nick could not look at her. Boy remembered his fanciful wish to bear such outward marks of his inward impurity—and cancelled the thought at once. To Winifred and Caspar, to all the others, she was just lovely Mary Coen, whose sunny nature and beautiful voice soon made you forget that ugly half of her head.

Without Mary Coen, Keirvaughan would be just like any other part of Connemara; it would not be special.

Chapter 20

Walter, walking back to the farm after a successful morning's fishing, was the only one to see John's coach turn off the main road to Ballyconneely. He did not then know John was inside, but anything more than a farm cart or a customs car had to be headed for Quaker Farm, and he was pleased at the prospect of a lift; the dusty road down the spine of the land was beginning to pall.

"Stevenson!" he cried when he saw John. "We had no message to expect you. How capital!"

"I sent none," John said. "The truth is, Thornton, dear fellow, I'm not here on pleasure. An unpleasant bit of family business."

"Oh dear," Walter held open his bag. "Not a bad catch, eh?" he added, seeing that John was not going to prompt him.

John gave a tolerant shrug. "They soon start to smell, don't they?"

"They'll taste all right. You won't refuse a dish, I'll wager."

There was a silence.

"Everyone's having capital fun here," Walter said.

"Good."

Another silence. They drew level with a small, off-the-beach island that only moments earlier had seemed to be much larger and to lie about a mile ahead. Walter, by now familiar with—but still not used to—the Connemara magic, drew John's attention to it. John merely nodded; for a second his grim, blank face became a grim smiling face.

"Is it something very serious?" Walter asked. "Do you wish us to leave?"

That forced John to laugh, to help dismiss the idea. "Heavens, no! It's serious, all right, but nothing like so heavy. It's just Winifred, as a matter of fact. She appears to have applied for a teaching position at some wretched girls' school."

"Which one?" Walter asked.

John looked sharply at him, as if that were the least relevant question. But he answered: "Cheltenham."

"One of the best in the country!" Walter said.

"Good God. Thornton!" John exploded. "I don't give a fig if it's just this side of the pearly gates. The point is she's applied for a *position.* The Honourable Miss Stevenson has been discussing a wage with a headmistress. It's bound to get out. Lord! You slave all your life for them and they throw it away!"

Now it was Walter who remained silent. John looked shrewdly at him. "I suppose you think it's my fault, allowing her all that education?"

Walter smiled fondly. "No, Stevenson. Never that. I know you too well. I've seen you take the most unpromising people and get pure gold out of them. You couldn't bear to think of anybody's potential lying idle. Let alone one of your own children."

John laughed at the truth of it.

"And the result is impressive, I must say. She and Young John walk around talking Latin and Greek like the best of 'saps'—which I'm sure they are. But it's not much use, is it? Except in the classroom, of course."

"Well done, Thornton," John chuckled. "A neatly turned argument. But it don't signify." He sighed. "Well, I shan't rant and roar, I promise that. But Winifred must come to see that she can't behave like some penniless girl with no name, no money, and no obligations."

Winifred knew, as soon as she saw the coach on the peninsula road, that it could only contain her father. She left Boy at once and ran to find her mother. She had hoped her father might wait until the end of this holiday before he talked to her about that letter she had written to Miss Beale. He must be very angry about it for him to have come directly to Connemara like this.

Nora heard her out, then took her by the shoulders and gave one vigorous shake. A gesture of despair. "You goose!" she complained. "Why didn't you tell me earlier? Why didn't you discuss it with me first?"

"I was afraid."

"Of me?"

"No! I was afraid Miss Beale might turn me down."

"You wouldn't draw a salary, of course," Nora said, thinking quickly.

"I intended not to, but I've been speaking to Aunt Arabella and I've changed my mind."

"Well, for the love of peace, go back to your first idea: no salary."

Winifred looked frantic. "I can't, Mumsie. If people like us don't set the tone, women will never..."

"Don't, don't, don't," Nora interrupted. "If you turn it into a branch line of the Woman Question, you will make no impression on your father. I fear you will make no impression anyway. Is your heart really set on this, popsie?"

The question made Winifred feel deserted. Trapped, she blurted out: "Well, you didn't do exactly what Papa wanted, either. He wanted you to be the usual sort of society lady."

Nora smiled absently. Most of her mind was trying to grapple with Winifred's problem in a losing fight against time. "Your father will always find it in him to forgive success," she said.

"That's all I'm asking for," Winifred said. "The chance to do something that Papa dislikes—and make a success at it, too. Like your salon."

Nora pointed a finger at her. "Mustn't be so sharp, dear. That isn't the way at all. You didn't answer my question."

"Well..." she said unwillingly, "if Papa really stops me from teaching now, I wouldn't mind going to university instead."

"In the land where all the pigs fly, no doubt."

"No. I could go to Bedford College. I needn't board—I could stay with you at Hamilton Place. Several of the professors from University College give lectures there. It's as good as university."

They could hear the coach slowing for the final bend and the sharp descent to the farm gate. Nora looked at Winifred—handsome, brilliant, careless girl—and clenched her fists in frustration. "You've left me so little time! You deserve nothing."

"I'd still rather go to Cheltenham. I think I already know more than they'd teach at Bedford."

"Especially if humility's on the curriculum," Nora snapped.

"I've still got all the humility I inherited," Winifred told her with a cold-eyed smile, unabashed.

Nora, hard put to avoid smiling back, turned away. "At least I know which battles I can and cannot win. I don't blindfold myself and blunder onward, telling no one." She gave a sharp sigh and faced her daughter again. "You must prepare to lose this one, Winifred. Perhaps it could never have been won, but you certainly haven't helped."

The coach was in the yard now. They could hear John and Walter talking. John laughed.

"That's a good sign," Winifred said.

"Is it? I'd say it means his mind is set and he's not even rehearsing arguments or looking at alternatives," Nora answered as she went out to greet him.

Later, however, she was less sure; for John, most uncharacteristically, did not at once come to the point. Instead, he behaved as if this visit were the merest whim, an inspiration for filling a few blank days. He romped on the beach with the younger children and timed their pony races. It was not until after tea that he went out with Nora for a stroll on the firm sand above the falling tide. Winifred, filing a thumbnail with her teeth ("biting her nails without biting them," she called it), watched them go, half wishing she was beside them, half glad she was not.

Around the headland and all along the sandy straight he spoke of the business, of friends, and of a commission of inquiry he had been asked to conduct in India, which would mean leaving in six weeks' time and being away for possibly four months. He almost convinced her he had really come down to tell her all these things, even though she would in any case be back in London in five days.

"There's just one little cloud on the horizon," he said as they reached the rocks and sat awhile.

"Winifred."

He looked sharply at her.

"She came running to me the moment she saw your coach," Nora explained.

John stirred the sand between the rocks with his cane. "I don't want to make a mistake," he said. "I'm not very good at judging the females of this family." He snorted a laugh and she knew he was avoiding her eye. "I made a mistake with you once…insisting you should follow a certain course…and you went your own ways, and proved me wrong."

Nora thought it odd that they should always talk like people who had once known each other rather well; it was becoming almost comfortable to keep that distance. For three or four years now John had behaved like that; at first it was with a sort of guilty reluctance, but now it seemed second nature.

"But what is a teacher at a girls' school?" he said. "A sort of public governess, in my view. In Society's view, too, I'm sure."

"Like nurses were before Miss Nightingale?" Nora suggested.

John looked at her with a doubt that certainly seemed genuine. "Do you think so?" he asked. "Really? You're much more sensitive to these movements in opinion than I am. I was sure your salon would be a social disaster. But now…I know half the people who court my acquaintance are really seeking an invitation to…ah…your place. And these are people who would have kept very exclusively to themselves ten years ago. There's a change. And you were aware of it where I was not. So, what d'you say, love—are teachers and professors about to become acceptable in Society? Shall we all soon be pining for invitations to schoolroom soirées?"

With that final question, his strategy overreached itself. The sardonic joke behind it showed through. She saw that he was trying to win her with flattery and, at the same time, to make her case and Winifred's as different as possible, so that nobody could argue from the one to the other. She was not going to allow that.

"John," she answered, "why are you still so obsessed with Society? I mean so *needlessly* obsessed?"

He stood up abruptly, seeing the discussion was not going as he had wished. "All the children must understand—the older ones, anyway," he said, half to himself.

She rose and set off for home, a pace ahead of him. "It's very kind of you to say people court you for invitations to Hamilton Place. But the fact is that you are a rich and successful man. You have earned the ear and confidence of people in government, whichever party is in. You are considered a very sound fellow. Society may sneer in general at the new rich and make jokes about us in *Punch*; but they will always court us in the particular."

"Ah—which particular?" He was reluctant to pursue her argument, unwilling to dance to her tune.

She shrugged, to lay as light a stress as possible on her answer: "Our particulars, dear. Building railways...gathering a salon of all the talents...making money...perhaps—who knows—being headmistress of the best girls' school in the country."

It almost persuaded him. She could see that the prospect of pulling it off twice—once with his wife, then with his eldest daughter—was tantalizing him. But it was as she feared when he got down from the coach and laughed with Walter: Nothing would sway him, not even a guarantee from the Clerk of the Future that Winifred would succeed in that way.

"I wish you were right," he said, "but they aren't like that. They'll forgive us, because we've come up from nowhere. In a way, it's expected of us. But if our children are perverse, they'll say it's become a bad habit. They'll know we're not sound. Our children cannot earn tolerance as we did. They must earn it by being more conventional than convention itself."

"Too late, love!" she taunted. "They've been contaminated."

"By what?" he asked in the thunderous petulance of a man about to complain that no one ever told him anything.

She stopped and faced him, a cool smile twitching at her mouth. "By us, see thou. By us! We should have boarded them out at birth."

It took him several seconds to learn how to silence this objection inside himself, though he did not attempt it aloud to her. All he said was: "Nonsense! You'll see. We brought them up free, and intelligent enough to understand why they must freely choose this path. You'll see."

She wished he hadn't staked so much of his own credit on this demonstration. She wished, too, that he would not insist on making Young John and Caspar attend this humiliation of their eldest sister, under the guise of correcting all their minds on the subject of their respective roles in life.

John sat facing them, wishing they hadn't all automatically—even Nora—put themselves on one side of the room, leaving the other exclusively to him. First he had to bridge that gulf between them. He sighed. His mind chewed on words that did not come easily.

They sat, tensely watching his every gesture.

"We are not a very…usual family," he said at last. "At the risk of boasting, let me start by reminding you that probably only five or six people in the railway-building business have been so successful that Society has, grudgingly, allowed them inside its ranks. And all of those, like me, had to turn their talents elsewhere, into Parliament or local government—or philanthropy—before even that grudging break was made.

"I'm sure I may justifiably boast of your mother's achievements. To enter the financial world as she has done, and to run circles around most of the men in it, would, in anyone else, lead to banishment from all company, let alone Society. Yet she has, in the teeth of it, founded a salon in London that is the talk of Europe and America. I was telling her less than an hour ago—people in the very highest ranks of London Society court my acquaintance in the rather touching faith that it will secure them an invitation to her table!"

They relaxed enough to smile. Young John even gave a light laugh.

John was glad of that. He had come here determined to have his way, but not as a tyrant. He wanted them to understand. To be sure, Winifred had been very wrong and would have to be punished, but first she must see why. In that sense her punishment would be voluntary—undertaken gratefully, even.

He allowed himself to relax then, stretching his legs out before him and settling back into his chair. "So…we are not a very usual family. Your upbringing, too, all you children, has been most unnatural." The word brought the expected stir of surprise and quickened their interest. "Most children are banished behind the baize door. But you, as soon as you could talk reasonably, have sat at our table, shared our conversation, talked with our guests on all but the most formal occasions. Tongues have wagged against us for it. We have 'spoiled your innocence' people have said—some people. And, to be honest, we could not answer them with certainty. Because, you see, all that licence we allowed you was like an investment in the future; and until that future becomes reality, people can always say you have made an unwise investment—and, of course, you cannot answer them with any convincing proofs to the contrary. Is my meaning clear so far?"

They all nodded.

"Because the time when the wisdom or folly of our investment in you will become clear is now very close for you three eldest. Especially for you, Winifred. Do you understand?"

"Yes, Papa."

"And Young John?"

"Certainly, guvnor."

"Caspar?"

Caspar beamed him an admiring smile. "I never realized how special it all was, Pater," he said.

John looked at him a long time, debating whether to insist upon a cut-and-dried answer to his question. He decided to press on instead. Nora wiped her lips to conceal a smile at Caspar's unflagging ability not to give direct answers when he didn't want to.

"Our reason, of course," John continued, "was that you should gain an early understanding of the ways of the world. Since for most of your childhood we were cut out of Society, we thought of it as a way of redressing the disadvantages for you. There is no doubt that people in Society enjoy access to privileged information and powerful mutual assistance that is simply not available to, or extended to, outsiders. I say 'there is no doubt'—I certainly hope you do not doubt it?" He looked around again. "Winifred?"

"No, Papa. I know it to be true."

"Young John?"

"Absolutely not, sir."

"And you, Caspar?"

"I often wondered why it was so important, Pater."

For once John did not mind the indirect answer. It led precisely to his next point: "I'm glad you see its importance now, my boy. It is of the greatest importance...of cardinal importance to all your separate futures."

He rubbed his hands, smiled around at them, and drew deep breath. "We have created a very big enterprise in Stevenson's. Yet it is not big enough to sustain all of you and all your children in the style you now enjoy. Unless you are also in Society in your own right. Each one of you. Individually. And you must know that Society does not hand out its benefits willy-nilly. It demands in return a very high, very correct, very precise adherence to certain standards of behaviour. In the end, no one can kick against it. Not even someone of the blood royal. There is one younger son of a duke—whose name you may hear whispered but never spoken aloud—who was caught last year in cheating at cards. He now lives in Normandy, in daily sight of England—a country he can never again visit. Not even when his parents die may he attend their funerals. He will be turned away even then. Even then. Not all the royal blood in his veins can restore him.

"Now you may think that is most cruel. I may think so. But it matters not one jot what we think. These are facts. Complain against them all you will—they still govern your lives. Like the law of gravity. So just think of the sort of fate that threatens everyone who thinks he—or she"—he looked especially at Winifred—"can flout Society's conventions. Or even slip past them, hoping to go unnoticed. Now your very liberal, not to say indulgent, upbringing may have led you to think otherwise. And that is no idle speculation on my part. For"—he fished in his pockets—"I have a letter here from a person called"—he consulted the letter—"Miss Beale, who is"—he consulted the letter again—"headmistress, it seems, of some school or other in"—again he looked at the letter—"Cheltenham, who tells me that you, Winifred, have asked for a position there as governess."

Boy let out a gasp of horrified incredulity. Winifred stared in open dismay; in those last few overacted and overstated sentences of her father's he had thrown away all the goodwill his earlier words had achieved. They had been a sham to lull her; the iron-mailed fist could now be heard creaking beneath all that soft velvet. Nora wished on John's behalf that he could take back that disastrous lead-in to the subject of the letter, after so promising a preamble. It belonged to an earlier, more aggressive version of this homily. Caspar saw his own struggle with his father—even though it still lay years off in the nebulous anything-can-happen—take on clearer outlines. He didn't so much care about Winnie's battle for her sake; he wanted her triumph to help him in his.

"Oh!" Winifred said coolly. "I can't believe that Miss Beale would lie to you, Father. But if she chooses to, I can't see why it should be only half a lie. I can't imagine her being satisfied at any half-measures. Are you sure she didn't say I wanted to be a scullery maid?"

"I'm warning you, miss," John said heatedly, levelling an accusing finger at her. "I've been calm and reasonableness itself until now."

"Hear, hear!" Nora said.

Winifred did not take her eyes off his face; hers was as expressionless as she could make it.

"A schoolteacher in a ladies' school is nothing but a governess. A public governess," he said.

"What was a nurse before Miss Nightingale, Father? What was a lady writer before Fanny Burney? If there are ever such shameless things as women bankers or stockbrokers, whom do you think they will hail as patroness?" She looked at her mother and smiled—creating an unfortunate suggestion of complicity between them, which John did not miss.

"Now see here, miss. Here's an end to this. Now I am telling you—you are to put all idea of teaching from you. Now and forever. I say so, and that is that."

"So!" Winifred said. "I am to be like those dainty little silver trowels they give the prince to lay foundation stones with. A fake! A toy kept in a glass case and passed around for admiration once in a blue moon."

"Winifred!" Nora warned.

She moderated her tone, but not the argument. "Well, what was all that education for?" She dug her fingers into her breastbone. "What is this feeling in here, that I want above all else in the world to teach? What's it *for*?"

John smiled, a superior, knowing smile that infuriated her still more. "That's this month," he said. "Next month…next year…it'll be a husband you'll want above all else in the world."

Winifred stared at him, forcing herself to be calm, speaking at last in a voice that was both soft and cold. "Reconcile yourself to this, Father: I shall never marry. However you dispose of my life, it shall never be that way."

She glanced at Boy, as if she expected his support. He blushed and looked down. These were the things they talked about only in Latin and Greek, things they could never put into plain English, things they had to clothe in the decent obscurity of dead languages: the filthiness of the body, the loathsome notion of shared carnality. They spoke of these things in the tongues of Saint Paul and Saint Augustine.

John missed the exchange between the two. He was looking at his daughter and remembering how close they once had been, how he had shared so much that passed through her extraordinary mind. Now she had become a stranger. The thought, begun in sadness, suddenly made him angry. She had changed! He looked at the two boys. "Let's get it all out, then. Are you two nurturing secret ambitions to own a circus or become travelling tinkers?"

"Hardly the equivalent!" Winifred complained, but he ignored her, looking at Caspar instead, believing him to be more malleable because he was the younger.

"I don't know, guvnor," Caspar said. "I don't think I'm old enough to know. Not like Winnie. I mean there's lots of things I want to try at yet."

"Dammit, sir!" John cried. "I tell you it is settled. You shall go into the army. Clement into law. And Mather into medicine. And"—he looked intently at Winifred—"all the girls shall marry."

"Of course, guvnor," Boy weighed in with his full support, "there's a ton of other things I'd rather do than take over Stevenson's. But I recognize it'll be my duty, so"—he sighed manfully—"of course I shall."

John looked to see if he were joking; but all he saw was the simple goodness and trustworthiness that everyone saw in Boy.

"Once you tell me all the rules and things for running it, of course," Boy added, thinking his earlier assertion had been too self-confident.

John's hesitation had lost him the chance of any spontaneous reaction. Winifred, knowing her battle to be lost, thought she might as well twist the knife Boy had inadvertently billeted between their father's shoulderblades.

"Ah, Boy," she said, as if admiring someone infinitely superior to herself. "How I wish I could be like you. I daresay you'd even put duty before the survival of the firm."

"Of *course* I would," Boy said stoutly, and looked for his father's approval. "Wouldn't that be right, Father?"

John could take no more of it. He dared not look at Nora, knowing she would be staring at him in cool mockery. "That's settled, then," he said, making for the door.

Before he closed it Winifred made sure he overheard her say: "He'd do more for Mary Coen than for us."

John returned at that. "That's right, young miss," he shouted, shivering with anger. "Mary Coen knows her place and makes herself happy in it. You—and you"—he included Caspar—"could learn much from Mary Coen's example. And I *would* do more for her than I would for you two ingrates!"

"John, dear," Nora said quietly, "I'm sure it'll do Mary Coen more harm than good to know the intensity of your feelings for her."

John looked pure venom at her and slammed the door behind him.

"Lost?" Winifred asked.

Nora stood, to follow John. "Thrown away," she said angrily.

"I would be right, though, wouldn't I?" Boy asked the world in general.

Chapter 21

How much harm has been done throughout history—certainly in the history of personal relationships—by the telling phrase! Such a phrase is almost always a metaphor of some kind; and a metaphor, once divested of all the nice, self-serving, metaphorical ways of defining it, comes down to no more than a cunning half-truth, served up among sophisticates in the confident knowledge that everyone can separate the half that is true from the half that is not. But for the literal-minded, the ingénue, the *un*sophisticate, a metaphor can turn into their Old Man of the Sea—a hump they cannot shake.

So it was with Boy when he heard Walter's picturesque but metaphorical division of himself (indeed, of mankind) into man-above-the-waist and man-below-the-waist. So much that had been obscure, half-glimpsed, fugitive, suddenly fell into place to form a logical and internally consistent schema in Boy's mind.

The whole trick of life, he now saw with a blinding clarity, is to keep man-below as separate as possible from man-above, in thought and in deed. The hand belonged to the arm belonged to Above; if it started meddling in the affairs of Below, it carried a fatal infection directly to the mind, the heart of Above. That was where all those wretched youths in that nameless academy Brockman kept parading through his lectures went astray. That was why dogs and other animals did not go insane by it—no hands! No short cuts from Below to Above.

And that was why women were so different from men in their temperament and approach to these matters. Their Below began at the neck, making the separation so much easier. Why had nobody seen it before?

For a couple of weeks the discovery restored him to the primal happiness that Brockman's lectures had half killed, and which the York whore had finished off. He even knew how he'd cope with her, now. If she lay the way she did, one foot on the floor, he could stand and fold his arms and concentrate Above on spiritual matters while Below attended to his affairs. But there in Connemara it was not possible to put the whole theory into practice. Below had to rut as fair a channel as possible between belly and mattress, while Above clasped his hands in prayer and sought the elusive beatitudes.

As an application of theory it worked well. As a technique it was laden with disadvantages. It took a long time, so that Above had run out of good things before Below reached any conclusion. It was dangerously noisy. And it left embarrassing marks on the bed and painful blood blisters on Below.

A week after the grown-ups returned to England, Boy found himself (both of himself, in fact) wandering disconsolately in a little wooded dell just off the main road to Clifden, as burdened and shivery as ever. If only it wasn't so dangerous with the hands!

He leaned against a tree that lay at an obliging oblique. He tried it. It hurt. He lay still, then rubbed his forehead on its cool bark. He opened his eyes and looked down.

For a fleeting instant he saw the green-clad woman lying at his feet. (Nature serves up metaphors, too—in breastworks of cloud, in forked boughways, in folded crannies of earth.) She fled, of course, vanishing in the bosky verdure beneath and all around him.

But it was a matter of moments to resculpt her in the soft, damp earth and leaf mould. He worried at his hands taking part in this activity, and he even tried a few bungling attempts to manage with just his feet; but then he decided that his hands did no more here than they did in making the bed.

There was no point in sculpting arms and head. Common clay could converse with the foul and corrupt Below. But Above could find no adequate companion for his spiritual intercourse there. At the last trembling moment his imagination failed him. His memory did not; but in no circumstances was he going to re-create that horror. He had to find out what she-Below was like before the ceaseless traffic ruined it.

Mary Coen! That was when he thought of Mary Coen. No traffic there! How do you ask? If you wanted to compare the palms of your hands, you'd say: "Mary, can I have a peep at your hand?"

"Mary, can I have a peep up your skirt?" She'd run forever.

"Mary, d'you know about artists?"

She wouldn't know a thing about artists.

"Mary, would you ever help us win a bet?" Out of character; she'd never believe it.

"Mary, this terrible foot-and-mouth disease has taken a new turn. Would you like me to make certain you're safe?"

She'd get one of the other girls to look.

"Mary—I'm desperate...please!"

Well, now!

"Mary, for pity's sake...please?"

"Mary! If you don't, I think I'll die. Honestly, I'm desperate. Just look at me. Please—oh, please!"

"Mary, I love you! I've always loved you."

God, it might do the trick! He'd go and try it on her at once.

"Indeed I will not!" she said. She did not even stop in her work of trimming the lamp wicks.

"Oh," Boy said, deflated. Having funked the passion he had opted for the flat request. He stumbled up from the table and went over to the window. A large, hot tear rolled down his cheek. He felt so ashamed.

But, paradoxically, the shame gave him all the boldness his spirit had lacked earlier. He turned and came back to the table, sitting down and drawing his chair as close to her as he could. "Please!" he said. "I'm desperate to know."

She didn't look up. "It's no business of yours," she said.

From this side, her right side, you couldn't see any of her hideous burn scars. She was very lovely, with that natural, sharp-lipped, wide-eyed, bright-eyed, green-eyed, freckle-skinned, turned-up-nose, dimple-chinned, flame-haired Irish loveliness. On the other side, though, her head looked like a clot of chewed-up newspaper plastered thinly on a skull that seemed to be on the verge of breaking back through in a dozen places.

"Please!" He choked on the word and gently touched her arm.

She looked at him then, ready to get angry. But when she saw the tear on his cheek, her eyes softened.

His misery, and the hope he still nurtured in the depths of hopelessness, strengthened him to look at her scarred half without flinching.

She tenderly stretched forth a finger and touched his wet cheek, as if she had to feel the reality of it before finding belief. She looked at the tear on her finger. "Does it mean so much?" she asked.

He gulped miserably and nodded, unable to take his eyes off her.

"Why?" she asked, amazed.

"I don't know," he lied. "It just does."

She took the hand that touched her arm and held it. She looked around her in a quandary, shrugging her shoulders. "If I do," she said at last, "you won't go giving out about it? No one else will know?"

Boy looked shocked at the very idea. "Of course not," he said.

"Why me?" she asked then. "Or will any girl please?"

He looked at her in an honest scrutiny that imperceptibly turned to adoration—an adoration that had already (or was it long ago?) filled his body but that only now spilled over into his consciousness. It was true! She alone would do—but not for his original reason. He loved her! He worshipped even her scarred half-face. Without thinking, he moved his lips nearer hers. She took a deep, blissful breath but did not close her eyes—indeed she watched him like a ferret for any sign of flinching in him.

Their lips moved closer. She turned slightly, so that more of her scars faced him. She was infinitely watchful for any sign of rejection.

But he found himself staring at that veined and polished flesh in mute craving. He loved. He loved it. He loved her all. To touch any part of her was ecstasy. He took her head in his trembling hands and turned it so that only her scarred half showed. Reverently, then, he kissed her eyesocket, her hairless scalp, her sharp and crusty ear, the drum-taut skin, the bone. Pure, ineffable love welled out of him and flowed over her, transmuting all it touched.

They kissed then, lips to lips. She, too, seemed on the point of crying. But she pulled away and began to busy herself once more; having come up through a harder school than Boy could ever conceive, she neither trusted nor tempted luck too far.

"I'll not say yes," she said. "But you know where the road does come up from the second bridge?"

"By the little wood?" Boy's heart gave a lurch; it was the wood where his half-formed earth partner lay waiting.

She nodded. "I'm away to Clifden tomorrow evening to take the venison and things off the car. I'll pass back that way at about four." In her part of the world, "evening" began at two in the afternoon.

"Won't they check on your times?"

"Ah, I'll say I was after meeting Over-the-wall Joyce. He'd tell ye how to build a clock."

"I love you, Mary," he said.

Her hand flew to her mouth and then to cover her eyes.

He left her then because he did not know anything else to say.

Next morning he was awakened by the sound of her singing in the courtyard below!

> Oh were I at the moss-house where all pleasures do dwell
> By the streams of Bunclody or some silent place…

She had a clear, vibrant, girlish soprano that suddenly seemed to Boy the essence of everything desirable and feminine; it made him curl and stretch and tingle for joy. Was he not to spend—what? five minutes? an hour?—with her. Mary Mary Mary Mary…She walks in beauty, like…Thou art lovelier far…And sighed his heart toward the Syrian tents…Clasp'd by the golden light of morn, like the sweetheart of the sun…Five minutes with her would seem an eternity of happiness. An hour! He'd die.

How he survived the eternities of that day until four o'clock, he did not know. In fact, he did not wait so long. At half-past-two he thought, *Suppose she comes back early!* His stomach hollow, his heart bursting, he raced up the hill to the main road and then sat sweating and disconsolate for over an hour. She did not come hobbling up the lane until nearly half-past-four.

"I was after meeting Over-the-wall Joyce," she said.

"I don't want to…uh…any more," Boy blurted out, surprising himself, for he had not intended to say any such thing.

"I wasn't going to let you, anyway." She rested her baskets and stood four-square to him, a cheeky smile on that half of her face capable of any expression.

"Mary…" he stammered, shuffling half a pace toward her. He reached out, almost overbalancing himself, and took her hand. Once he had re-established contact, it was easier to move closer. "I've thought about you all day," he said.

Her lips curled in a sneer that was half deprecating, half aimed to rebuke him. She had obviously intended to be truculent and hard-to-get at this encounter. But then she looked into Boy's eyes. Really into them. And all her truculence evaporated; that mournful, meek sincerity vanquished her. Poor Boy was such an obvious victim of this flood of love that she forgot herself entirely. Suddenly it seemed marvellous to her that she, from whom all turned in embarrassment (when they did not accept her as a neutered bit of furniture), could have kindled such adoration and craving in him. She had always thought of him as impossibly beyond her reach.

The sneer turned into a shy smile.

"I don't know what to say to you," Boy told her.

"Nor me."

Awkwardly they moved together until their heads were touching. This time she put her good half against his cheek. He thought she was the softest, most fragrant, most tender thing he'd ever felt. He wanted to kiss her but was afraid to move, afraid to break contact.

"Boy?" she said in a voice lost at the edge of control.

He put his arms around her. The firm, hot fortress of her body strained against him. "Ah God, I love you," she moaned. "I'd camp in your ear if that's all the room you had for me."

"Oh, Mary!" he said, loving the word. "Mary, Mary, Mary..."

"I'll do anything, Boy. Just you say."

They kissed. And again. They kissed long enough for Mary to remember they were still on the highway. She broke from him and picked up her baskets.

"Don't go!" he pleaded.

"I'll just hang them on the ditch," she said. "We'll stroll in there. We can't stand courtin' out on the road."

Her hand was warm and excitingly sinuous as she limped ahead of him.

"How old are you?" he asked.

"Twenty-three."

He was surprised. He knew she was older than he was but not by six whole years. The family often called her "little" Mary Coen, even though she was by no means small; to Boy it had always made her seem much younger. He had not yet caught on to the fact that when rich people said "little" they meant someone who'd take less than the going rate.

"Too old for these capers!" She laughed.

His face fell.

"What's wrong?" she asked.

"No, no. Nothing's wrong," he assured her. He could not tell her that while he had been thinking about her age, she had unwittingly led them to his earth-wife's grove. Instead he tried to steer her to the farther side.

But she had her eye on the conveniently leaning tree. "Would you look," she said. "Wasn't that made for us!"

She turned and leaned against one side of it, unaware that she was standing between the ankles of Boy's surrogate. "Now!" She waited to be kissed.

He attempted to kiss her while, with his feet, he tried, sweep by sweep, to obliterate the work of his hands.

The magic was not there. She felt it and wondered what was making him shuffle like that. "God, is it ants?" she asked in alarm, trying to remain in a near-kiss while she looked down.

"No!" he cried, equally alarmed, clamping his mouth on hers and bearing her back until leaves and sky and clouds filled her eyes with their shimmering reflections.

He forgot his stupid bit of earth modelling then and lost himself in the glory of being against her. She closed her eyes and sighed as she settled herself deeper upon the tree; in passing, it seemed, she moved her crippled left foot to a more comfortable position on the other side of the trunk. This brought Boy, suddenly, into the firmest possible contact with her, *there*. And it was a contact he could hardly lose, whether he stood up or lay upon her; all movement was Above, all togetherness Below.

He trembled with the intensity of his yearning. He felt hollow. The blood seemed gone from his limbs. He could not remember ever having felt like this before. It was not a mere hunger for her sex, though that was, of course, the burden of it, he wanted to possess all of her and never to relinquish her. He wanted to mingle all of him with all of her. So when he pressed his cheek and the side of his head so firmly to hers, it was half in hope that some miracle of fusion would follow, sinking the one flesh into the other.

It astonished him, too, how just to clasp her waist with his hand or to touch knee upon knee could conjure up the whole of her as an image in his mind. Not a clothed image, either. All there, except…

That…what could you call it? The filthy, schoolboy words didn't even occur to him. That smooth, bony softness…that hard softness pressed him and called up no image of itself. Except that he could see how he could tuck around there and the way everything would fit.

She felt him trembling and clasped him to stillness with her firm hands. "It's all right," she said. "Don't fret so."

"I don't know what to do," he whispered.

"No more do I, I never yet did this."

"I just want to be with you always and always hold you…and love you…and be like this."

"I thought it couldn't happen," she said, also whispering now.

"If we kept our eyes shut," he suggested, "could we take off our clothes?"

"Why with our eyes shut?"

"I don't know."

The whole idea seemed to fizzle out until he felt her hand snake between them and begin to thumb open the buttons of her bodice. He did not shut his eyes. Instead he half lifted himself off her and joined in. She left herself then and popped his few shirt buttons much more swiftly. In the same movement she pushed the shirt off his shoulders. He shrugged out his arms and returned to the last few buttons of her high collar.

There was no fear in it now. Nor haste. It became the most natural, leisurely, lovely thing anyone could do. As soon as they were both bare to the waist and clasped again in each other's arms and tenderly running their hands over their nakedness, Boy was struck at his own lack of disgust or even of hesitation. Both had vanished along with that half of their clothing.

He spidered his hands around her rib cage and closed them over her breasts. She made a little noise and reached her lips up to his. He kissed her and went on caressing with his hands.

They were nothing like the breasts of his imagination. Not that they were softer or harder, bigger or smaller, firmer or squashier. The only word that fully described the difference was "real." Mary's were real. He bent to kiss them and discovered he was ejaculating. The really surprising thing was that it was so joyless and remote, a reflex rearrangement that lacked all hint of passion.

The only course was to ignore it, which was easy enough, especially as it made no detectable impression on his physical state or the intensity of his longing for her.

When her skirt was open, there were only two red petticoats for him to unbutton. They drifted to the foot of the tree, a cardinal splash on the green. She was naked to her boots now. She did nothing to help but lay on the tree looking at him with a fond, almost mesmerized smile as he pulled his trousers down over his boots.

Her skin was white as marble, delicately veined. The burns finished at her collarbone; the rest of her was as perfect as the untouched half of her head. Everything he had ever longed for was now so close—the thought pulsed in him like a magnificat.

"Let me see," she said. "I never yet did."

Her hands sanctified him. All they touched belonged to her already.

"One eye! It's like no animal's." She looked up at him. "See, if you will," she told him.

His eyes dwelled in hers. He thought this empty pressure inside him would force him apart. He rested his palms on the tree beside her head and, gently slow, lowered himself upon her. Thrill was in the warmth in her. Heat! He soaked it from her.

She would not be still with him. She strained. Retreated. Writhed. Arched. Clung. All slow, with immense strength but no vigour. The movement, in both, became too complex for him to follow with his mind. He felt his mind surrender its grip on him, on them, on the day. He drowned in her then, in all the sensations of her. He almost became her.

Where they were soft, where they were firm, where the sun blinded white skin, where eyes held pools of unfathomable black, where heat endured, where breezes harboured cool near them, where hair entangled, lips crushed, blood hammered, throats cried—there she was, there he was, between each eternity and the next. And for all eternity. He wept at her goodness. And they were stilled at last.

"There!" she whispered. "Don't!" She found dry patches on her hands and forearms to wipe his tears away.

"Oh, Mary," he said. She swam before him. "There'll never be anyone else for me."

She blinked. The smile on her lips became resigned. She looked away. She slumped. "That can't be, Boy," she said. "And well you know it."

Until that moment he did not know it. Oh, he had known it in a general way, but he had never thought of including himself in the rule, nor of exempting himself from it. Now, in that dreadful, flat finality of her tone, so swiftly on the heels of the tenderest, most lovely thing they could ever have done together, he knew it to be true.

He looked at her and almost did burst apart this time. His insides yearned hollow for her. She had become all his world, not in spite of her scars, not because of them, but simply with them, too.

"We shall make it happen," he promised. "I would give up everything, except you. I would give it all up for you. I will never give you up for anything."

She slipped from under him and leaped into her petticoats. Seeing her breasts tremble as she leaned over to do up the buttons he craved for her all over again. He caught them up in his hands and bore her back onto the tree. She resisted only a fraction of a second, then yielded.

They kissed, hurting their lips. His heart raced; he could feel hers thumping, too. A little artery in one of her scars flushed, flushed, flushed in time with it.

When they broke apart he spoke urgently into her ear. "You said you'd do anything," he reminded her.

"I will, so I will," she answered, clinging desperately to him.

"Then be in love with me!"

"Boy! Oh…little Boy!" She burst into bitter sobs that would not stop.

"And stay in love with me…and be with me…and be mine as I am yours and always will be yours."

She would not answer—unless the rack of her sobbing was answer. It struck into him with a terminal emptiness. It made him face the prospect of not being with her.

"Why?" he asked when she was calmer.

"Sure you know why," she said, reaching for her shimmy and blouse.

"Nothing could stop us if you really wanted to."

She put her head between her two hands and fought hard not to cry again. Speaking from the safety of not seeing him, she said, "They'd dismiss me without a character. And they'd send you off."

"I'd come back."

Like her, he began to dress again.

"If you went good and hard at it, they'd certify you."

"My people wouldn't do that," he said. Then he thought of his father: He would.

"What!" She laughed, with little mirth in it. "The eldest son of Lord Stevenson courts a penniless Irish drudge who looks…" She put a hand to her scars. "God, *I'd* certify you!"

"We can run away! Now! This week."

She shook her head, not denying him, but in pity. "There's nowhere I could hide."

"We'll get married before they find us."

By now the tone of her replies had gone flat. Her voice gathered normality around them. "I'll not marry outside a Catholic Church."

"I'll become a Catholic," he blurted out, thinking that was her objection.

"You don't know your own father," she said. "He's a big fella. And you don't know the big fellas in our Church, either. They'd annul such a marriage faster than you'd cook an oyster."

Boy subsided in bewilderment.

She smiled sadly and came to him. She put her arms about him, a gesture more friendly than passionate, and said: "Dear Boy, you know so much and understand so little."

"I understand I love you."

"No one ever said that to me. No one ever wanted to know me. No one ever dared kiss my scars. I'll learn to be content at that. And so, my darlin' Boy, so must you." She managed to say it all without a sob, without even a hesitation.

Boy held her away and drew breath to speak; but she stopped him with a finger to his lips. "Not another word," she told him.

She was almost back at the road before he called: "I must see you again."

"If we do, we do," she answered.

He glimpsed her fleetingly among the bushes before she vanished, hobbling up the hill. It was the moment in which he learned that love, which he had always held to be the most selfless of passions, was the most selfish, self-absorbed, self-seeking of all. His would not accept her happiness as the slightest comfort or recompense.

He looked at the leaning tree, or, rather, at the air near it—the air which until so recently had parted to enfold that rare enchantment of her. Everything in this grove, he thought, should be singing, "She was here. We have seen her. She passed this way."

At last the loss of her became real. Not a fear for tomorrow to serve. Not an agony he should prepare to face. She was already gone. He had already lost her. Society and his father and the Church and the meek humility that Life had long ago sowed and harvested in her…these had cost him the deepest joy he had ever known. These had cast him into hell.

Hell is joy denied—but infinitesimally remembered.

"Hell, hell, hell!" he shouted to the air. He kicked last autumn's leaves around him in flying clods of mould.

Boy, who never swore, who would at once leave any group of his fellows in which foul language was so much as breathed aloud, Boy now stormed around the grove shouting: "Shit on people. Shit on Society. Fuck my father! Fuck everything!"

His rampage brought him to his earth-wife, whom he set about destroying with savage gusto. Then, in mid-kick, he froze. His breathing locked. The part he was about to boot asunder was the part he had been unable to complete. *Yet it was complete!* In horrendous detail, too.

For one wild moment he thought this palingenesis had come about of its own accord. Then, realizing the impossibility of it, he stooped to make sure the thing was not some accident of fallen earth or trick of the light. It was not; strong fingers and thumbs had pinched those rilles in the clay; knowing fingers and thumbs had pioneered that fossa into the half-razed tumulus of her belly.

Savagely he resumed his orgy of destruction, but this time with his bare hands. He scattered her torso by the fistful, then her thighs.

Before his final assault he paused, somewhat in awe of his own fury. But as he looked down, planning her final dismemberment, a lugworm, three-quarters dead, nosed experimentally out of the remains. He smashed it with his fist.

His fist sank into a cold, gelid mass concealed beneath the soil. He brushed aside the soil to reveal a couple of handsful of lugworms. Not earthworms. Lugworms. From the beach. They were almost all dead.

He sat there knowing he had come very close to insanity. He pinched worm after worm in two—and then segments of worms—on and on, not noticing if they were alive or dead; not caring.

He knew the invisible worms that fly in the night and that had eaten out the minds of those boys in the other academy were even now at work on him. There was no way to deny the leviathan passion for Mary that now so domineered his body. Between these mighty things he would surely be crushed. Passively he waited for insanity to possess him; in a terrible way it would be a kind of release.

Unheard by him, Nick and Caspar, concealed in the thickets on the far side of the grove, snickered and giggled at this dénouement of their little jape. Then they ran a wide detour through the scrub and galloped and skipped their howling homeward way.

Unknown to Caspar, Nick then went in search of Mary Coen, who had proved herself such a willing little cleaver.

Next day Mary Coen had vanished from Quaker Farm.

Chapter 22

The schools' fives games, in which Caspar was a cub competitor, took place in London halfway through that summer holiday. They were held in the grounds of Lord Westcott's house in Grosvenor Square, only half a mile or so from Nora's house in Hamilton Place. Westcott had become an enthusiast of fives at Eton and had built the largest set of courts—six—in any private house in the country. He was close enough to the barracks and the gentlemen's clubs to have a steady supply of fellow players. His courts were rarely idle, except during early August, when rowing, the turf, and shooting combined to deplete the devotees. That was when he had the idea of offering his courts to the schools in a scratch championship for a plate he himself was offering.

Caspar was not in the running for the plate, however. He qualified for the cub fivers, who had to be under sixteen. By the fourth day of the first match, Thursday, he was into the final, against a fellow called Trentham from Harrow.

Usually after the matches Caspar and Greaves strolled down through Mayfair to Hamilton Place, where they drank lemonade in the pocket handkerchief of a garden behind the house. Greaves had been knocked out in the second round of the masters' competition—by (as he was to point out for months to come) the man who eventually won. He stayed on to coach Caspar and two other Fiennes men; for this week he was a guest at Hamilton Place.

It was a rare honour. The head of a great Oxford or Cambridge college might be accepted in Society, though somewhat patronizingly; but lesser academics were decidedly ineligible. You sometimes saw them, shorn of majesty, standing shyly on the fringes of a Society gathering, being talked to in strained jollity by the kinder-hearted; but you knew they were cadet relatives of someone who was there by right.

There was one exception. The man whose conversation proved witty, absorbing, or elevated enough to beguile an elite that perpetually hovered at the edge of stifling or boring itself to death could quite easily gain access, however humble his origins. That was the principle on which Nora, at Roxby's suggestion, had founded her salon. Hers was said to be the only house in London where you might see tenth-generation peers talking at ease or playing cards with writers, artists, eminent surgeons, and men of science and be sure of the finest wines and food; it was one of the few places where the arts mingled so easily with the sciences, too. And, what with the Royal Academy and the Royal Society just up the street, there was always a sprinkling of RAs and FRSs at Hamilton Place.

Except for musical occasions, these gatherings were without invitation. Nora signalled them in the Russian manner, by placing lighted candelabra in the ballroom windows. Being a mid-eighteenth-century house, Hamilton Place had the most inadequate private rooms. Even the principal bedroom was something less than a modern house would offer an upper servant. So if a guest overindulged, it was not thought seemly to give him one of these cells; he was accommodated in the Russian manner, too—on a pile of blankets in one of the grander corridors. It was all part of the charm of Hamilton Place.

In Nora's early days there, some London wits had tried to make a word play on the fact that Kate Hamilton's notorious nighthouse was at the far end of Piccadilly, in Haymarket. There had been jokes about Nora's Hamilton Place and Kate Hamilton's Place—and the likely difficulty in telling one end of Piccadilly from t'other. As jokes they pleased only those with fairly undemanding standards, but Nora had realized they could damage her for all that. So, from the outset, she had insisted that her salon should be exclusively male. On some musical evenings, female performers were, naturally, present but they never mingled with the guests. (There were, after all, ways for women of humble origins, too, to climb to the very top of Society—but those ways were usually called "unmentionable" despite the fact that they were mentioned by other ladies on every possible occasion. Even to perform in public for money bordered on the unmentionable.)

Dinner parties were quite another thing. There Nora blended the cream of her salon with at most a dozen carefully selected guests of both sexes from the upper reaches of London Society. These were the occasions John had meant when he said people courted his acquaintance in the hope of an entrée to Nora's table. And this was the world into which Greaves, by accident of his and Caspar's common interest in the game of fives, had been pitchforked.

Caspar was soon aware of the subtle shift in relationship between them. Greaves would enthuse over things that Caspar quite took for granted—the fact that, for instance, on almost any evening you could talk with a great painter or poet or one of the foremost physicists of the day. Caspar, in the lazy way of the young, had assumed that almost any decent household could get in such people if it wanted. Through Greaves's wide-eyed enthusiasm he came to appreciate his mother's uniqueness. What astonished Greaves most of all was that Lady Stevenson had none of the ostensible qualifications for her role. With men of letters she rarely attempted wit or aphorism; she did not pretend to understand even the most elementary principles of science; she never dashed off even the slimmest water colour or crayon sketch (in fact, a joke had once gone round about Nora's being "no RA"); she was at best a moderate pianist, nowhere near the league of the performers she hired for musical soirées. Yet among the supreme practitioners of all these professions and skills she was held in something of awe.

"Of course!" he said on his third day in the house, when the light finally dawned on him. "That's it! That's why. She never competes. They trust her. She has that quick, fertile mind that can momentarily follow any line of thought or argument, however abstruse, and, like the stone that is dull, yet make the blade sharper."

Caspar, who could not see how a dull stone might follow any line of argument, shrugged. "She says she knows who to steer together and who to keep apart."

"Yes. That's another reason why they trust her. But how does she know? That's the magic of it. How did she know to steer me toward Professor Thomson last night, whom I have admired for so many years? Did she know we would talk for the best part of an hour and that it would be a conversation I would remember for the rest of my life? Before I leave, by the way, I must tell you what I learned of energy from him. We are very close, it seems, to completing Newton's work; soon the last mathematical mysteries of matter and the universe will be unlocked and the Creator's vast handiwork will be plain for all to see—all who can read his language, that is. My boy, we are lucky to be alive at such a time! And twice lucky to be mathematicians."

Caspar tried to revert to this subject as they strolled into Grosvenor Square after he had won his semifinal. But Greaves had other things on his mind.

It was a blistering August afternoon. Nothing stirred unless it had to. The sun poured down on baking cliffs of brick and stucco and then bounced sideways into the streets, so that straw hats were only half a protection against the fiery sky. Everything seemed drained of its colour, reduced to a shimmering neutrality. Cross babies howled from nursery windows. Ill-tempered cooks bawled through open area doors. Pet dogs lay panting in the shade, raising their heads in dumb hope at every stray breeze. Greaves and Caspar strolled very slowly.

"You go at the game so hard," Greaves said. It was not a compliment. Caspar had thought the master's congratulations on his semifinal win were half-hearted.

"Of course, sir," Caspar said. "Is that wrong?"

"You must remember, fives is merely a game."

"But I play to win, don't I?"

Greaves gathered his thoughts, as if the boy's question had scattered them. "We must distinguish two purposes. The purpose of the game, and your purpose in playing it. The purpose of the game is as you say—to win. But your purpose is larger. Naturally, it includes the purpose of the game; and to that extent it is to win. But not to the exclusion of the rest. And the rest includes the mastery of your own faculties—speed, strength, judgement, tactical sense, estimation of your opponent, and so on—the evenhanded love of the sport (which would lead you to cheer an opponent's good play as heartily as you would a friend's), the honour of your House, or school, or (let us hope one day) your country. And we must never forget the sheer pleasure of the thing. In my view, you go so hard to win that you forget all these other things."

Caspar nodded. It was, by and large, true—all that Greaves had said. And he was too hot to put up even a token defence. "I just like to win, sir," was all he said.

"Of course you do, my boy. You're your mother's son, after all. I suppose neither of you knows how to do a thing without wanting to do it supremely. If you find you are middling at something, you drop it."

"I'm middling at Latin and Greek," Caspar chuckled.

Greaves treated this as pedantry. "You drop it the moment you are able," he said. "What are you going to do in life? D'you know?"

They turned south into Park Street, walking on the western side, where there was some relief in the shade. Caspar debated with himself whether to give some conventional answer or to tell Greaves the full story. (He was so wrapped up in his own view of the problem it did not strike him that Greaves's very question assumed the long-talked-about career in mathematics to be a fiction.) He decided there was no one he would rather tell, and no one whose advice he would value more.

"Lord Stevenson wants me to go into the army," he answered.

"But..."

Caspar could not openly say how rebellious he felt to the idea. "I suppose if he hadn't got the peerage, it would be easier."

"For him? For you? What would be easier?" Greaves hated imprecision.

"He says it'll be all right for Boy to take over the family business, but only in a remote way, as a sort of figurehead."

"A figurehead with no head for figures!" Greaves laughed.

Caspar did not even smile. "It's a joke I can't share, I'm afraid, sir."

Greaves pulled an amused face. "Jealousy?" he asked, thinking it absurd for Caspar to be so solemn, at his tender age. He was surprised at the way the boy bristled.

"And it's a joke they won't share when they are thrown out of work in Stevenstown, either, sir."

"No." Greaves was placatory now. "One can easily forget."

"Boy can," Caspar agreed. "I don't think a day goes by without my thinking of the tens of thousands who depend on our firm for their livelihood. I doubt if the thought occurs to Boy from one year to the next. If it did, he'd distract himself by translating it into Latin in the style of Suetonius."

Greaves laughed uproariously. "What an extraordinary fellow you are!" he said. "So—you want the family business?"

Caspar halted and looked at Greaves long enough and straight enough for the master to be sure he was hearing something important. "I want my own business, sir. Even if I had the family business, I would make it *mine*. I would change it." Then he smiled.

Greaves drew a deep, thoughtful breath and resumed their stroll. He shook his head. "A hornet's nest," he said. "How long have I known you—three...four years? And yet I have never known you."

"Oh," Caspar said, embarrassed now, "I have only lately begun to think like this. I used to want to be another Chippendale or Sheraton!"

"And what does Boy think about it all?" Away from Fiennes, Greaves dropped the "one," "two," and "three" as handles to their names.

"He doesn't! You know him, sir. His first question, always, is: 'What's the rule or custom?' That's why he makes such a good pharaoh. And if the rule is that eldest sons follow their fathers, that's all Boy needs to know."

"He's the one for the army, then!" Greaves laughed.

The words left Caspar thunderstruck. Of course! That was absolutely it! How, in all the thought he had given the subject, had that obvious, simple solution failed to occur to him?

"What's the matter, my boy?" Greaves turned back to face Caspar, who had stopped in his tracks.

Caspar, despite the heat, came skipping up to rejoin him. "It's just that you're so absolutely right, sir. I had never thought of it, but what a topping commander he'd make!"

Greaves basked in Caspar's delight. "D'you think he has enough initiative? He's a very conventional soul, as you say."

"Well, sir, last month, we had a servant girl run away from our place in Ireland and Boy organized the search for her. And in two days he traced her across the Irish sea to Liverpool before the spoor gave out."

Greaves shrugged, as much as to say, *So there you are—QED!* Few others would bother to trace a missing servant beyond the front gate, unless she had taken some silver along with her.

Later, when they were in the comparative cool of the garden at Hamilton Place, looking out over the sun-soaked acres of Hyde Park, Greaves returned to the subject.

"You have the diagnosis now," he said. "But what shall you do for a cure?"

"I must make Boy understand that he truly belongs in the army."

"And you?"

"I must fit myself more for a life in business, I suppose, sir." He laughed. "It's funny. I try to interest Lady Stevenson in mathematics—the sort you have taught me—and all she says is, 'What's it *for*?' And I ask myself the same question about the dead languages. Why are we not taught natural science instead? Or modern languages—why are they taught only to girls? They would be far more useful to me. Shall I ever sell a ton of steel in Greek? Even modern Greeks don't speak it."

Greaves coughed uncomfortably. This was getting too close to sedition. "Do you realize," he asked, "how very forward-looking Fiennes is? You talk to some of the other boys at the tournament—ask them how mathematics is regarded at their schools. You'll find the maths master is ranked somewhere between the porter and the leaf sweeper. You do not yet know it, but next term Fiennes will be the first school in the country to have a carpentry shop and a forge. And there is to be a choir and a musical society. Chief is determined, you see, to 'round out the whole boy,' as he says. But these things cannot be done overnight."

The news delighted Caspar, though it still fell far short of the sort of curriculum he wanted.

"I wish I were there to see it," Greaves went on awkwardly. He spoke so softly that it was several moments before Caspar grasped what had been said. "The truth is, my boy—and this is not to become general knowledge before chief has announced it—I have been offered an assistant headship…er…elsewhere."

"No, you mustn't, sir," Caspar pleaded.

"It was the last thing I wanted. But he made me see that our ideas will never prevail if we all stay huddled at the one school. We must 'go forth and speak unto all nations'—or unto all schools anyway."

"When?" Caspar asked, on the edge of his seat.

"After Christmas."

"I'll have them give in my notice," Caspar said firmly. "I'll follow you to the new school, sir. Where is it?"

Greaves laughed, thinking this no more than an excess of zealous politeness.

"I will," Caspar insisted. "I couldn't stand Fiennes without you—I mean without maths as you teach it."

Still Greaves would not be persuaded to take this boyish outburst seriously. There was no time, then, to pursue the discussion for, at that moment, Nora came out onto the terrace. Greaves stood at once. Caspar, following the master's eyes, saw his mother and stood, too. "Have a good rest, Mama?" he asked.

"Rest!" Nora said, fanning herself. "In this heat! I'll join you in a lemonade, if I may."

A footman brought a glass for her and a fresh jug, clinking with ice. They all sat again. Greaves had never seen *iced* drinks before.

"Your son is probably too modest to tell you, Lady Stevenson, but he is into the finals of his age group."

"Well done!" Nora said. But her tone made it obvious that no other result had been expected.

"I play too hard," Caspar said.

"In this weather that would be very easy."

"No, I mean I play only to win."

Nora looked puzzled from him to Greaves.

Greaves laughed. "He is lampooning me, Lady Stevenson. Socrates says that the spectator at the Olympic Games is superior to the athlete, in that the athlete is an involved partisan but the spectator may cultivate a dispassionate appreciation of what might be termed *pure* athletics. I have tried to tell your son that the athlete, too, can cultivate that same appreciation even in the heat of the game."

"You hear that, Caspar," Nora said. "I'm sure it's true. And what other truths have you arrived at?"

"Your son does not think our modern system for apportioning careers within the family very equitable."

This indiscretion annoyed Caspar intensely. He could fight his own battles, he thought. Nevertheless, he smiled sheepishly, as they expected him to.

"Yes, young man!" Nora said, glad that Greaves was there. Now Caspar could not wriggle off into noncommittal shrugs and mumblings. "That is something I meant to take up with you—and now is as good a time as any. I thought your answers to Lord Stevenson were even more evasive than usual."

Caspar sighed. *Very well,* he thought. *Why not? Tell her all.* But he spoke with reluctance, having no way of knowing whether it was a clever or stupid thing to do. "I have no interest in the army," he said. He waited to see the effect.

His mother raised her eyebrows briefly. "A trifle negative, dear?"

He took a further plunge. "I want to go into business." He paused. "Commerce." Again he paused, watching her closely. "Trade!" He made each sound more reprehensible than the last.

Nora's face was unreadably impassive. "They are not the same, of course. What d'you know of any of them?"

"Enough, Mama, to know they would suit me better than soldiering."

Greaves, his upper lip resting on the point of a triangle formed by his two index fingers, watched them, his eyes flicking left and right like a tennis spectator's.

"And what makes you think you would survive? It is not a very considerate world."

"I think I would."

"And if you didn't?"

Caspar drew a deep breath. "At least if I went down, it would be my own fault. No one would order me to take five hundred men with drawn swords to face heavy artillery on three flanks of a valley!"

Greaves drew in a sharp hiss of disapproval. Nora, secretly pleased at Caspar's answers, dared not show it. She turned to Greaves. "And you, Mr. Greaves," she said, "have made a conquest of Professor Thomson."

"I?" Greaves was delighted at this unexpected tribute.

"He told me that we have nothing to fear for the future if our schools have mathematics teachers of your calibre."

"Yes. Fiennes is very lucky," Caspar said with an absolutely straight face—much to Greaves's discomfiture.

The talk then turned to general matters. Ten minutes later, as Nora was on the point of leaving them, a footman came out, somewhat briskly, considering the heat. He waited for Nora to turn to him and then told her that Mrs. Thornton had called in some agitation and would be grateful for an interview.

Hiding her annoyance, Nora left Greaves and Caspar. Arabella had a tendency to be imperious lately. She behaved as if the rescue of tarts and elimination of masculine ardour were the twin hubs of the universe. Whereas, she thought wryly (and to prepare herself not to be too sharp with Arabella), everyone knew the universe had but one hub, and that was here in Hamilton Place.

Their greetings were warmth itself. Arabella was sure she had called on the least convenient day of the whole year. Nora assured her that the musicians were not due for hours and that she had been bored to distraction until the footman brought the joyful news…and so on.

"Well!" Arabella sat shivering with excitement. She was plainly bursting with some news of especial importance to Nora.

"How was Paris?" Nora asked. "It's a city I never liked."

"Oh, dreadful, dreadful!" Arabella said, waving a hand as if Paris had been a mere incidental in her travels. "Now listen. I was walking along one of the pavements there. One of the advantages of having *maisons tolérées*, I have found, is that the *Police des Moeurs* can take you into them. They don't openly have to pretend to you that such places are not to be found. And the wretched panders who manage the houses have to let you in and answer your questions and show you everything. Well, as I was saying, my dear, one day I was walking along—that is, I had been to see a most singular house in the Cours des Coches, which is distressingly near the English Church and our own embassy. A dreadful house, owned by a Monsieur Calignani, a Frenchman, of course, despite his name." She paused, not knowing how to continue.

"What was so singular about it?" Nora asked, hoping Arabella would soon get to the point.

"Every woman in that vile place—and some are no more than mere girls—is a…a teratism…a nonesuch…a grotesque."

"A freak of nature, you mean?" Nora asked.

"Precisely. The extraordinary thing is that this house is not patronized by low and degraded people, as you might think. The policeman who was my guide assured me that only the most refined "gentlemen" of otherwise exquisite tastes are permitted there. And this was borne out by two of the women themselves. Piteous creatures."

"Really?" Nora said, thinking she would soon have to ask Arabella to come back another day.

"Of course, they dress it up in high-sounding names, with doors to each room labelled Manticora, Wyvern, Dipsas, Hippocerf, Simurgh...and so on. But the names were mere perversity. Perversity upon perversion. For they bore no relation to the wretched ogresses within."

Nora cleared her throat.

"Yes!" Arabella said. "Come to the point: I was leaving—had left that dreadful house and was walking up the foot pavement to the Rue Malesherbes when I chanced to look over my shoulder. Well, my dear, picture my surprise when I saw a certain Herr Porzelijn—a Dutchman who is well known to us. And a man less aptly..."

"Ignaz Porzelijn?" Nora interrupted. "Surely not."

"I believe that is...yes..."

"A big man. A very big man. Gross to the point of obesity?"

"It must be the same. But surely you don't know him?"

"I know *of* him. He appears to be a close friend of a young man who works for me. Bernard Bassett—the young man who manages my London properties. This Ignaz Porzelijn is a dealer in antiques, I'm told."

"And in flesh!"

"Really?"

"Oh, no doubt of it. He is well known to us. One of his tricks is to lurk in a carriage near our Hornsey Refuge and decoy women on their way there."

"Tell me more," Nora said, not knowing when the information might prove useful.

"His main trade is in girls of ten to fourteen, whom he takes to continental houses with forged birth certificates provided by our government."

Nora looked scandalized.

"Indeed," Arabella assured her. "in England our birth certificates and death certificates are never brought together. Herr Porzelijn simply asks Somerset House to supply copies of birth certificates for girls now dead but born over twenty-one years ago. We have records where he handed over five ten-year-old English girls to a Paris house, with certificates "proving" them to be over twenty-one—which they have to be in order to work in any of the continental houses."

Nora shut her eyes in horror at it.

"Oh, and there is worse. Girls of five, torn by monsters—no, I'm sorry. I won't. I won't."

"I had no idea," Nora said, still shaken. "No idea. I always felt Paris was a vicious, rotting..."

"Paris!" Arabella cried. "I'm talking about London. Here! A mile from this house. Every night. Every night, you'll find mutilated little creatures flung into Meard Street from a house there. I have seen it. That is no hearsay."

Nora, who, from her early upbringing in Manchester's cotton mills, had thought herself tough and hardened, looked at Arabella with new eyes. Arabella had once seemed, indeed had once been, a delicate prude, full of vapours and fancies. Now, match her where you would, she was a woman of formidable stomach and great bravery.

"I'm sorry." Arabella smiled grimly. "That has nothing to do with why I am here. I was telling you about the Cours des Coches—what an apposite name! And Ignaz Porzelijn. He was just getting out of a carriage. And! On his arm!... Guess! You'll never guess. Little Mary Coen! She was unmistakable, of course."

Nora was so surprised she stood up. She sat again, abruptly.

"Mary! You are sure?"

"Of course I'm sure—I have her in the carriage outside. She is recovered now. Naturally he had drugged her—that is quite common. She had no idea who I was, or where she was, or who she was. I'm sure she still doesn't know what has so nearly befallen her."

"But how did you get her away from him? He sounds a very dangerous sort of man."

Arabella made a contrite smile. "I had the police with me, remember. And I told a leetle, leetle lie, I fear. I said the girl enjoyed Lord Stevenson's protection. That was enough!"

Nora laughed. "That's no lie, Arabella. He'd do anything for that girl. He saved her life when she was just ten, remember? I don't suppose you do. When she was burned like that."

Arabella coughed delicately. "Er...the word 'protection' can imply different things in different countries."

"I see." Nora looked at Arabella through narrowed eyes. "Or even in different tones of voice or a different tilt to the shoulders? Mmm?"

"I'm afraid so."

Nora laughed. That was rich! The one thing she was certain of was John's absolute fidelity to her. "I'm sure his honour will withstand it," she said, to Arabella's great relief. "But has Mary told you...I mean, presumably you know how she came to be there?"

Arabella put her head on one side, guardedly. "I know in part. She absolutely refuses to say why she ran away in the first place. Something happened there in Galway, but she won't say. Not to me. Perhaps she will to you. I'm certain she came to London looking for Lord Stevenson. She was in some trouble and needed him. She denies it, of course."

"That's very possible. She worships him. We pay her next to nothing, you know—but she won't dream of leaving. Well..." She laughed. "Until this."

"The point is, she *did* see Lord Stevenson, here in London."

"Oh? But now isn't that odd he never mentioned it! And he was very upset at her running off like that."

"But she didn't speak to him. He didn't see her. She saw him get into a cab—this was up near your office in Nottingham Place, the only address she knew. She shouted but failed to make herself heard over the traffic. So, having no money left she followed him on foot as best she could. She ran all through the park, she says, so she must have followed him almost all the way here."

"Here?" Nora said. Her disbelief in the girl's story was growing strongly. "But John never comes here—only for dinner parties. Otherwise never! He always stays at his club."

"Well, she said Hamilton Place. She's quite certain of that. And she told me the name when we were still in Paris. She lost him in the park and she wandered around for hours. And then she saw him again, just as he was leaving this house. Again she was too far away for him to hear her, but she knocked at the door and your housekeeper saw her and spoke to her."

Nora rang for a footman, who appeared instantly. "Ask Mrs. Jarrett to come here," she told him.

"And your housekeeper gave her a little money. And advised her to go to the Hornsey Refuge—which was where Porzelijn was lying in lurk."

Nora was now in something of a dilemma. Arabella had been so kind, in intention and in deed, and was so pleased at the way it had turned out, it would be a poor recompense to demolish the girl's story on the spot. And Nora was sure the story would be demolished, for John would never set foot here when she was away, and Mrs. Jarrett would never part with a farthing in such circumstances.

Nora had to get Arabella out before Mrs. Jarrett appeared. She stood and said, "I'll come to the door myself, my dear. You've been most kind. And, of course, any expense you have incurred..." and so on all the way to the door. Arabella, at first a little startled, left feeling a glowing sense of having done her duty well and truly. Just before she got into her cab she turned back to Nora. "I still have hopes of finding young Charity in this way, you know. Even after almost five years! I'm positive she didn't run off to get married. I'm sure she was inveigled off in just this way." And with a wan little smile she got up into the cab.

Nora beckoned Mary Coen up to the house. The girl, who had already got down from Arabella's cab, gingerly climbed up the marble steps.

"Oh, your ladyship, isn't that a grand house!" she said in awed tones.

"But you've seen it before," Nora said.

The girl looked genuinely puzzled. "Indeed and I have not, ma'am."

"But I thought you told Mrs. Thornton…never mind."

She took the girl back to the drawing room and made her sit down. Mrs. Jarrett was there, waiting.

"Mrs. Jarrett," Nora said, "have you ever seen this girl before?"

"I have not, my lady."

"Have you ever given her money?"

"She has not!" Mary said hotly.

"Indeed not!" Mrs. Jarrett said simultaneously.

Nora looked at Mary in bewilderment. The girl neither looked nor behaved as if she knew her whole tissue of lies was falling apart.

"But you told Mrs. Thornton she did."

The girl was speechless.

"You said you came to this house, and…"

"Not *this* house, ma'am. Sure I never was here in me life. It was Hamilton Place."

"This *is* Hamilton Place," both the other women said together.

Mary looked from one to the other and back. Then she stood up and went to the window, to look up and down the street. "No," she said at last. "'Twas a big house right enough, but never so grand as this." She looked at Mrs. Jarrett. "And 'twasn't you, ma'am. I'm certain sure of that."

"So am I!" Mrs. Jarrett said firmly.

"Thank you, Mrs. Jarrett," Nora said. Something was very wrong here. Mary was either the most brazen liar—which was not credible—or something more was yet to come out. She wanted no witnesses to it.

She made Mary sit again and she gave her a lemonade, which the girl drank greedily. The jug had been on the table all the time but she had made no signs of wanting a drink. Nora realized she had forgotten what it was to live life at such a level that self-effacement of that kind was second nature. To herself and Arabella, life in that house of freak girls seemed the bottommost hell. But to Mary? No one had ever adored her for her scars; would it have been such hell? Then she remembered the terrible images Arabella had implanted in her mind and realized there was an infinite grading of hell, each of which would seem a paradise to those in the one next below.

"Well, Mary," she said, "you are sure it was the master you saw. Not someone who happened to look like him?"

"Oh, 'twas the master, I'll swear," she said.

"And it *was* Hamilton Place—but not here?"

Mary nodded, unshakably. "Hamilton Cottage, Hamilton Place. Though, God, 'twas no cottage at all, but a grand house."

"And the master was in this house—this Hamilton Cottage—for hours?"

"Sure I don't know, ma'am. I only seen him coming away. Didn't I think he was after collecting your rints? I thought you'd own all o' them grand houses. And think of the rints you'd be gettin'!"

Nora could not help smiling at this notion that John might drive around from door to door, collecting rents. But where? Where were all these fine houses? "D'you remember the names of any other streets around there?" she asked.

The girl rolled her eves upward and closed them. "Circus Road...London Road...Grove End Road...Abbey Road..."

"Are you sure it was *London* Road? Not Loudoun Road?"

She opened her eyes in delight. "Yes, ma'am. That was it. Loudon. I didn't know how 'twas said."

"St. John's Wood!" Nora said grimly.

"That was another!" Mary cried. "St. John's Wood Road."

"And what was the—this housekeeper like, Mary?" Nora asked. "Try to describe her." She forced herself to speak calmly—almost languidly—so as not to arouse any anxiety in the girl. Had it been any other part of London, her suspicions would never have been alerted so quickly; but St. John's Wood was always talked about with that knowing smile. Men winked at each other when they said that name. "St. John's Wood—where even St. *Joans* would," one wag said.

At first Mary's description of the housekeeper called to mind no one in particular. Then, possibly because Arabella had mentioned her so recently, the picture of Charity...what-was-her-name...Charity something, came into her mind. She made Mary repeat the description and became even more certain of it. The "housekeeper" was Charity. She had never trusted that girl, had never been entirely happy with John's account of his rescue of her—common little harlot, that's all she was. There had always been a certain *je ne sais quoi*, a certain atmosphere between John and that creature.

And four years ago? Hamilton Cottage...that rang a bell at the back of her mind. She was sure the firm had once owned a house of that name. But four years ago. Too far away for any details to linger—just the impression of a rumpus of some kind. The sale had not gone smoothly.

She knew there would be no rest for her until she had nailed this suspicion down, one way or the other. After all, Charity could very easily be someone else's kept woman out there; and John might have discovered her only recently and might be trying to persuade her to return to Arabella. That would be very like him.

Feeling heartened at the thought, she rose and rang for a footman. "Well, Mary," she said, "I must busy myself now. Tomorrow we shall talk more about this and decide what is to be done for the best."

She told the footman to have her carriage brought over from the mews opposite and then to see that Mary was found a bed for the night.

"You can help out in the scullery this evening," she told the girl.

It was three o'clock before her carriage pulled into Nottingham Place. By then Nora had found so many innocuous reasons for John's visit to Charity—if, indeed, it was she—that she had more than half a mind to turn around and go home. But she knew she would never sleep entirely easy until she had run this particular hare right into the ground, so she decided to go through with it all.

The office was so somnolent, she knew, even before she asked, that Flynn, the general manager, was away.

"He's seeing Lord Stevenson in Westminster, your ladyship," Oates, the chief clerk, told her. "At the India Office," he said.

"Perhaps you can help me, Oates," she said. "I simply wish to look back in the records of our property sales some time about five years ago."

Oates nodded. "I think we still have them down here, ma'am. Five years is the borderline for going up to the attic."

He searched for quite some time before he found the book in question. "Property not being our main line, as you might say, ma'am, it does tend to get pushed aside once it's done. But I think this is the man for us." He opened the ledger. "Which property was it?"

"Somewhere out near Maida Vale, I think. Hamilton Cottage." She did not want to say St. John's Wood. She watched carefully to see if Oates had any special reaction. Rumours and secrets had ways of flying around the enclosed community of an office. Oates behaved entirely normally, she was pleased to see.

"Oh, I remember Hamilton Cottage, ma'am. There was an argument about that; maybe you call it to mind. We had a contract to sell to someone..." He thumbed through the book, quickly finding the page. "Yes. A contract to sell to a Mr. Banks. But in the end we sold to a Mr. Nelson. A better price, too. I daresay that was it."

Nora's relief was indescribable. Nelson! It could be Charity's husband—or protector. At all events it was sold. John had not just kept the house.

"What was your exact question, ma'am?" Oates asked.

"Oh, just an impertinent letter—I suppose from someone connected with this Banks person. I wanted to nail it at once," she said. And then, to throw him even farther off the scent, she added, "I suppose it was freehold?"

He did not consult the book. "No, ma'am. A nine-nine-nine-year lease."

She stood to go. He sprang to open the door. "Thank you, Mr. Oates. You have an excellent memory. How would we manage without you!"

Oates swelled visibly with pride and then, to show how complete his recall could be, he added, as she went down the stairs. "Oh, I remember that sale quite well now, ma'am. Just seeing the page has brought it back. I remember who the house was bought for, too."

"For this Mr. Nelson, you mean? You met him?"

"No, no. That was her father. I never met him. But I know he bought it for her. It was all put in the deeds. He bought it for his daughter. I remember it because her name was Stevenson! Things like that, you know, they stick in your mind. Of course, that must have been her married name. I believe she was a widow."

Nora wondered she could keep this smile on her face and the tremble out of her voice as she turned and said, "Really, Mr. Oates? What a prodigy of memory you are! You probably even remember her full name."

"Indeed, ma'am. Mrs. Charity Stevenson. I remember thinking: There's two words as don't belong together—charity and Stevenson's, you see!" Then, realizing the unflattering implication of his words, he began to stammer confused apologies.

Nora was doubly glad of this. It prevented the man from seeing her own distress, and it gave her something to do.

"On the contrary, Mr. Oates. You are quite right to say it. Every man who works for Stevenson's has the satisfaction of knowing he earns every penny of his wage. There is certainly no charity here!" She turned to go again, but at the half-landing she added: "You've saved me a good day's work with that excellent memory of yours. I would have discovered all this myself, of course, tomorrow.

Please remember that—you saved me a day's work." If it ever came out, she did not want him thinking he had betrayed his master.

He mumbled that it was nothing and went back to the office, slightly puzzled at her choice of words. Moments later he had forgotten about it entirely.

All the way down to the India Office Nora seethed. It was not just that John had a mistress, and had kept her four years. Four years! For four years she had shared him. How many times had he come home with the stink of that little whore still on him? But it was not just that.

In a way, that was too great a hurt for her to comprehend all at once. The wound it dealt her, like all big wounds, left her immediately numb. Instead her mind buzzed furiously around the lesser details. That he should permit her to take the name Stevenson! How dare he—when he had been making the world sick with his endless talk of honour and seemly behaviour! While he was giving his name to that sow…that bitch…that little bit of vermin. How dare he!

And no doubt they had children by now. She almost howled when she thought of his marvellous body rutting away in that—that excrement. The body he had promised to her alone. And the children, too, would no doubt be called Stevenson. Suddenly she saw what a monster she had yoked her life to. If he had given her any other name but Stevenson, not all of Oates's gift of total recall could have harmed him. But he had to put that brand on her. Nelson! She could have had that name instead.

Nelson…Hamilton! Oh—very funny! Flynn must be in on this. Someone in the office had to know. How they must have laughed. Men! Arabella was right. Until now, whenever Arabella had launched into her increasingly virulent diatribes against the perfidy of respectable pater-familiases and the whited sepulchres of middle-and upper-class manhood, Nora had smiled inside herself at the thought of John, who was so far above all that. Through all the vicissitudes of their marriage, she had never entertained the faintest suspicion of him in that way. Well, now who was the sentimental fool, and who the tough, clear-eyed woman!

Oh, yes; Arabella was right.

And the children would be Stevensons, in name as well as in fact. He was that greedy! Well, life was long. If it was ever in her power, she would destroy that woman and her brood. She cared not how. She would do it.

At the India Office Nora pencilled the one word *Urgent!* on her card and sent it in. Even before the pageboy had gone back in through the great portals, John appeared. He must have been standing near a window and have recognized her carriage as it came down Whitehall.

She was still too angry even to notice his anger, until he almost wrenched off the carriage door as he climbed inside.

"It is intolerable that you should come down here hounding me like this," he barked. "How dare you!"

"You speak as if I did it every day," she was stung into saying. "But you must know I..."

"And you must know—you must know your place, ma'am." He spoke just as if she had remained silent. "When a man is on important..."

"Now listen to me!" she interrupted.

But he did not even pause in his sentence: "...business of government, why, the whole country would come to a halt if our wives pursued us down here."

"I have only one thing to say..."

"And I will not listen to you. When you behave like this it is small wonder we have so unruly and rebellious a family. It is the quality of the parents' behaviour that sets the tone of family life."

"I'm glad you've brought that up, because..."

"No, damn you!" he roared. "I will not hear you. This is all part and parcel with your behaviour and the children's behaviour to me at Quaker Farm. If you have something to say"—he descended from the carriage again—"you will raise it at the proper time. I am not at your beck and call."

The carriage window was open but she was not going to brawl with him across a Whitehall pavement.

"Home!" she called to the coachman.

All the way back, along Whitehall, Regent Street, and Piccadilly, she fumed at John's monstrous hypocrisy—"parents' behaviour...tone of family life" indeed!

The carriage was turning back into Hamilton Place before she realized she had not once been even near to tears since Oates had dropped his grenade. She was self-observant enough—just—to realize that hers was a hard, cold anger. Did that mean she no longer loved John in the slightest degree, had not loved him for some time? Could such love die in an afternoon? Undoubtedly a hot, tearful anger, full of self-pity, would mean she still loved passionately. So did this cold, vindictive anger signal a death that had already taken place?

She was glad of one thing: It helped her face the world, being so calmly furious. And she had an important world to face tonight.

~

Nanette unknowingly contradicted these hopes as she helped Nora to dress for her salon. Tonight was to be the last and most important musical evening of her season.

"You must not let this stupidity upset you so," she said.

Nora, astounded, thinking the maid must be a mind reader, asked what she meant.

"This Mary Coen. It is nothing."

"Oh!" Nora laughed. "I had forgotten that."

"So you say," Nanette answered. "But look at you. Every muscle!"

Nora decided then to confide in Nanette, who had shared every other secret—well, almost. She had to tell someone. She had to get those words out of her and into the world. If Rodie were here, she would tell Rodie and not Nanette. But Rodie was in France. So…

"I have just discovered that Lord Stevenson has a mistress," she said.

Nanette did not even pause in brushing Nora's hair; but Nora saw her lips pinch together.

Nanette shrugged. "He is a man."

"I never thought it of him," Nora said. "And don't try to pretend you did."

Already, even the fact of saying it made it sound less dreadful. But to call her—and them—Stevenson; that still hurt furiously.

"It's more natural than not," Nanette said.

"Natural!"

"Normal, then. It's more normal. Sad, yes, but normal. A French woman would not be surprised. She would know what to do."

Nora glanced in the mirror to see a sly little smile on the maid's lips.

"Oh, no," Nora said. "That's not me."

The little smile turned to a sneer. "No, that's not you. You preserve your honour as a superiority. For you it is like capital, yes? You will bank it with Lord Stevenson and take your profit in his guilt. That's *you*!"

"You attend to your work," Nora snapped.

The little smile returned.

Chapter 23

Caspar did not like his mother's musical evenings. At other people's musical evenings you could talk away all you wanted. But not at his mother's. There everyone behaved as if it were a church, with music for prayers and applause for amens. Just as they were about to start Karl Philipp Emanuel Bach's A-major symphony he remembered that tomorrow was his big day and he ought to try to get some sleep. He stole away as the first violin arpeggios rang out. *Chomp and scrape*, he thought.

Ten minutes earlier Mary Coen had finished her work down in the scullery. Everyone had been very kind to her; it was a happy house this, from top to bottom. Down there she had heard nothing of the recital; but as she limped up the back stairs to the attics, those ethereal melodies of the greatest of K.P.F. Bach's great Hamburg symphonies began to reach her. At the final landing she found the green-baize door open, no doubt because of the heat. The sound carried in its full, majestic volume up the great stairwell and pinned her to the threshold in wonder.

She had never heard an orchestra before, much less one of this quality. The sound burst on her with all the soul-shattering impact of a revelation. She could no more move back from that spot than she could command time to cease. Forgetting who she was and where she was, she edged forward to the balustrade and sank to the soft stair carpet.

Bathed in that infinity of music she pressed her cheeks to two of the ornamental-iron balusters and peered over. Two grand spirals of rosewood and marble led her gaze down to the great hallway below. She had no eyes for the rows of listeners who crowded the hall and thronged the lower gallery, all as rapt as herself; instead she looked in astonishment at the twelve players who sat facing the foot of the stairway, unable to believe that a mere dozen men could conjure up such glory and launch it on the air. She wanted it never to stop.

She closed her eyes then, and let the sound possess her totally.

They were beautiful melodies. You could sing them, but you didn't want to. Even choirs of voices could not get that loveliness out of such tunes—not heavenly choirs, either. It was already perfect. She envied those players, whose life was passed so close to that perfection.

An image arose in her mind then: the image of Boy, whom she loved... loved...loved, and never could have. This music was her love for Boy. Its celestial reach was hers. Its great calm and permanence was everything that the world could never diminish from her. Its fleeting passage was the poignancy of all that she had lost in losing him. Its dying fall was the death of her hope. Its memory, on into the silences, was her life. She clung to the banisters as she clung to the music as she clung to the memory of her sweet, tormented Boy. The tears that ran down her cheeks were no more intrusive than her breathing.

Mrs. Jarrett, passing the open door, looked down and saw the dirty little scullery maid sitting out on the gentlefolks' landing, cheeky as you please. "Hey, miss!" she called out sharply. The girl began to stir, as if rousing from a deep slumber.

The call did not reach down to the guests, but Caspar, on the landing below, and opposite where Mary sat, heard it. He looked up and was astonished to see the girl there. He had never seen Mary anywhere but in Connemara, so it was a second or two before his identification became fully conscious. When it did, he sprinted on and up the last flight of stairs to where she sat.

"Psst! Come off out of it!" Mrs. Jarrett was hissing at her through the doorway.

"That's all right, Mrs. J.," Caspar told her. "I'll look after this."

Had it been any other servant, she would have drawn herself up to her full majesty and, ignoring him, have ordered the girl back into bounds. But she stood there uncertain, remembering that the first big, blistering disagreement between the master and mistress—years ago—had been about this girl; the master was known to be very solicitous of her; the mistress had made the girl sit in the drawing room this afternoon, had given her refreshment—and had hastened out of doors immediately after. A housekeeper's job was to peer and pry, she knew; but, she decided, there were times when it was best not to push too hard. Anyway, she could not bear to look at the girl too long.

"Very well," she said, and went, ostentatiously stiff, up the servants' stair.

Mary flashed Caspar a smile of gratitude.

"I'm amazed to see you," Caspar said. "Obviously I'm the only person who doesn't know you have come back to us. Or didn't know."

She could not hear him. The music had claimed her again.

"Do you like it?" he asked.

She nodded, not opening her eyes.

He waited, knowing the music would soon end. These scrape-scrape merchants needed their fizz like everyone else. He took advantage of her closed eyes to scrutinize her face. The unblemished half really was rather serenely good. She'd have been a stunner if she'd got out of that fire a bit quicker.

The outlines of her body were clear beneath her light scullery dress. He remembered how perfect and pale her flesh had gleamed with Boy in that grove. Idly, with little sweat, he wondered if there'd be a chance for him here—though she was a bit old. He looked at her scars without reaction; you could forget them when you knew her well enough. Someone should do that. Someone should marry her. Anyway, it was quite exciting to sit beside her. She was even warmer than the air.

The music finished. She heaved a deep sigh of satisfaction. "God, I never heard the like o' that," she said.

"Once a week all summer," he told her. "Bring me the good tidings, Mary. How are you here?"

She looked at him steadily and for an uncomfortably long time; then she closed her eves and shook her head.

"Poor Boy nearly went mad," he said shrewdly.

He saw the anguish in her eyes. "Ah! Tell him..." she blurted out, then stopped.

"Tell him what? 'Oh yes, and I've seen Mary Coen. Yes, she's in London. No, no particular message, I'm afraid.' Tell him that?"

"So he..." She could not think of the word.

"He's bad, Mary," Caspar said seriously. "He's convinced you ran away because of what he did."

She looked uncertainly at him.

"I know what you and he did," he said, unable to rid his mind of the memory of her nakedness, knowing it was the same nakedness that now lurked only a fraction of an inch beneath the plain brown cotton of her dress.

She knelt up and, walking on her knees, came to sit beside him on the top step. The movement pulled her dress so taut he had to look away.

"Did he tell you?" she asked. Afraid to raise her voice, she put her lips close to his ear. Her hair fell on his shoulder. The smell of her was something...citrus: clean and strong. His neck tingled.

He leaned back, to look her in the eyes. Her blemished side was nearest him; funny, she used to be much more self-conscious about that—always putting herself on the other side. "Of course he didn't! You should know Boy better than that." He looked away. "I saw you both. Boy doesn't know I saw you." He turned to her again. "But I'm glad I did. If I hadn't, I'd really have thought he'd gone mad after you ran off. So...what d'you want me to tell him?"

"Say..." She let out all her breath. "Nothing! I can't tell him." She began to sob. Not violently. Not loudly. But—to Caspar—all the more heartrendingly for that.

He put an arm around her shoulder and squeezed. He forgot his own rather shallow urges and wondered how he could ease her pain. "You must tell someone," he said. "If you want to tell me, I give you my word I'll let it go no further. Come on. You can't keep this...whatever it is...to yourself forever."

Still she sobbed. "Is there anyone you *can* tell?" he asked.

She shook her head vehemently.

He did not know what to suggest next. He took his arm away and moved to sit a little apart from her.

Then she spoke. "Promise not to tell anyone?"

Caspar thought. "If I think Boy is going to do something stupid, I will tell him—or I will tell him as much as he needs to know in order to stop him."

"Stupid?" she echoed.

"Of course! I told you—he's taken it very badly."

"You won't breathe to your mammy, though? Nor Mrs. Thornton—nor anyone?"

"That I will promise."

So she told him.

She told him of the dreadful things Nick Thornton had proposed to her and the night upon night of the remaining holiday he had sketched out for her in libidinous detail—all under pain of exposure of herself and Boy. Once it started there was no stopping her; the story poured out. Her love for Boy. His for her. His impossible ideas about their future. How it all became too much for her, until she fled to the master. How the kind young lady had given her money and told her of Mrs. Thornton's Refuge. Then the big fat man who told her of a country where they'd think her beautiful and would give her, in a day, more money than she'd see in a year, just to adore her. And Mrs. Thornton finding her, and saying the man was a wicked liar and only wanted to enslave her. And then coming back here.

She was quite calm, almost serene, when she had finished. "What d'you think, Master Caspar?" she asked. "D'you think he was lying?"

"Who? Nick Thornton?"

"No," she said impatiently. "The big fat fella. Do you think there is a country where I'd be beautiful?"

Suddenly he felt ten years older than Mary. How could he tell her it didn't matter? How to share with her the insight he had achieved just now—that you forgot her scars when you knew her? He wanted to kiss that side of her face—purely—but he did not dare. Instead he took her hand. "Of course there is," he said.

"Where? I never was told of it."

"We *all* love you, Mary. Boy most of all. We went right across Ireland looking for you. We can't think of Keirvaughan without you. That's the country where you're beautiful."

But when the music started again and he saw her face light up he knew she would never freely go back there again; nothing he could say had half that power over her.

Chapter 24

Stay for some supper, Rocks," Nora said when the last guest had gone. It was not an invitation but a command. Not that Roxby, despite his now fairly dominant position among the country's younger painters, would have refused an invitation. Too much of his bread was still buttered by Nora and her friends.

"I shall never know where you find the energy," he said, "even at the best of times. But…in this heat!"

It was a very light supper: quenelles of plover fillets made with *pâte a choux* panadas, followed by *fanchonnettes* garnished with a fanciful design of pistachios and currants; only two wines—a Montrachet '48 and pink champagne.

Roxby, raising a glass of the champagne to her, asked, "What are we celebrating?"

"My liberation," Nora answered, toasting him in return.

"Is that what the end of a season represents now!" He chuckled. "How blasé we soon become. Time was when every ounce of your…"

"The end of a season," Nora interrupted. "Yes. That is it exactly. Just…a season. There will be others, no doubt."

"To be sure there will," he said, looking at her somewhat sideways. "Nora, you wouldn't be ever so slightly tipsy, would you?"

"Why?"

He looked at the wine coolers. "Because there's two soldiers left to kill—and you surely aren't relying on me, are you?"

"What a strange thing to worry about."

He looked away and coughed. "The fact is…" he began.

"No, Rocks!" Nora said.

"The fact is I was going to ask you…"

"Rocks—no!"

"…could you possibly…?"

"No!" She almost screamed the word.

"A hundred. Just a hundred?"

She looked steadily at him, waiting for his eyes to return to her. They did, but too briefly to communicate anything.

"You wouldn't miss it," he said. Still she watched him. "Guineas, then?" he added. He looked at her then. She smiled and shook her head.

"Why not?" he began to whine.

"Because you don't need it. That's why. You have plenty of money."

He drained the champagne and poured another glass, filling hers, too. "How do you know what I need?" he asked lugubriously.

Her laugh said, *What a stupid question!* "Because, dear boy, you made the mistake of letting me manage your finances."

"*I* did? You gave me no choice."

"Though what sort of 'mistake' it is that gets you from three thousand pounds in debt to…"

"To five thou' I can't touch!"

"…to an income of three hundred, I'm sure is a mystery. And you're earning a good two thousand from your painting."

"Ah well," he said, all cheerful again. He sipped his champagne and smiled at her. His whole attitude said, *It was worth a try.*

"Why d'you do it, Rocks?" she asked. "Especially why d'you try it on me? You know you haven't the slightest need of it."

He giggled. "I don't know. I just feel I have to touch people for a loan. It's just a thing." He buried his face in his hands and laughed silently.

"Go on," Nora said, laughing already. "Tell me."

"I touched Billy Holman Hunt for a thousand last week. I don't know why I did it. I just couldn't seem to stop myself. We were talking about nature and colour—you know, the old problem—and just out of the blue I asked him for the loan of a thou'. You should have seen his face! You know what he's like."

Nora almost shrieked with laughter. "I think it's a disease. Like Lady Hobo, who keeps slipping off with my silver and then doesn't know what to do with them and sends her footman out to pop them back through my letterbox. A disease. There ought to be a name for it."

"Tangomania—the mania to touch people."

"I didn't know it was recognized."

"No, I just made that up. Not bad, is it! I say, am I really earning a couple of thou' a year?"

"You're *getting* it. If your celebrated artistic conscience tells you you are also *earning* it, then I suppose you are. It's still nothing to what you will make before you are finished."

He smiled at her gratefully, then laid his hands palms upward on the table and looked at them in the way that painters tend to look at commonplace objects—with a critical absorption. "These are the fellows," he said. "Not me. I don't earn it. They do." He looked at her with that same absorption, making her shiver. "Half a painter's life, you know, is spent emptying this"—he tapped his forehead—"into this." He held up his right hand and wriggled the fingers. "It's not safe until it's down here. But now, this year, for the first time in my life, I begin to feel this fellow actually knows more than I do."

Nora breathed out, envious and admiring. She took his two hands in hers and squeezed them. "They'll take you to the very top."

Snakelike he flipped his hands away and then trapped hers in his much larger grasp. "Got you!" he said.

She looked down at their hands like a remote spectator. "So you have! But what are you going to do with them?"

She delayed returning her eyes to his, but when she did, her gaze was level and unblinking. A light, amused smile parted her lips.

He stopped breathing. She felt his grip tighten, then waver. His tongue darted out and wet the centre of his lips. She had never behaved this way before.

He made a slight movement of withdrawal. She thrust her hands deeper into his. Again their eyes dwelled in each other's. He cleared his throat.

"Nora," he said.

"Yes, Rocks?"

"Where is Nanette?"

"In bed, I trust."

"Why?"

"Because I sent her away."

He swallowed and stared at her. "Yes," she said.

Not "Yes?" Not "Yes!" Just yes.

"Are you serious?" he asked.

She laughed. "Oh, Rocks! If I were serious, would I have chosen to sup with you! I seem to have caught a different form of 'tangomania,' that's all."

Next morning she rose early, sent Roxby away, and wrote to Winifred to tell her she was to come to stay at Hamilton Place that autumn and enroll at Bedford College. Then she went to find Caspar.

But he was out, riding with Greaves in Rotten Row, so they did not meet until breakfast.

She was glad of Greaves's presence. Caspar was such a self-sufficient and secret-keeping fellow it was hard to pin him down in public, impossible in private. With Greaves there he could not be his usual slippery self, at least not so blatantly.

"I've been thinking about your wanting to go into business, Caspar," she said. "Were you quite serious?"

She chose a moment when his mouth was full of devilled kidneys, to give him time to take stock. She herself ate only water biscuits and apple marmalade at breakfast.

"Don't know, Mama," he said at length. "There's a lot in what you said yesterday. I shall have to give it a lot of thought."

"Well, think quickly. There might just be a very good business opportunity in the offing."

He pretended to be unmoved but she noticed that his ears twitched.

"Small," she said judiciously, "but it could show a good return. It might just suit a young fellow." She did not precisely wink at Greaves but she pulled a complicit face that flattered him into joining her. Both were amused to watch Caspar's nonchalance crumble.

"You mean an *actual* one?" he said. His heart began to race. What could it be? What could he do—still at school?

"What else?" she answered. Her tone implied it was all very natural. "A real business, real goods, real money. And a real disaster if you fail. Which you very easily could. I just want to see if it's all talk on your part."

"How could I do it though?" Caspar laughed nervously, unwilling to believe it. "I mean...staying at school?"

Nora shrugged. "The true business of business lies in overcoming such difficulties."

Greaves cleared his throat and wiped his lips. "Er...Lady Stevenson...I don't think Fiennes School could be used as a place of business," he said diffidently.

"Naturally not," she answered, not taking her eyes off Caspar. "That would be out of the question. But is there any school rule to forbid a boy from partaking in business with another location—if, for instance, all correspondence was directed elsewhere—not to Fiennes?"

"I'm sure I don't know. I doubt, of course, whether it has ever..."

"If a boy went into the town to buy toffee for half a dozen of his fellows and charged them a ha'penny each?"

Greaves laughed. "Oh, that. I'm sure that would happen every day." He raised his eyebrows at Caspar, who nodded his agreement. "But the sum involved is so trifling."

"Or if some young nobleman's signature or assent were needed in a matter of the family estates during term time, he would presumably not be whipped for it?"

"Naturally not, but..."

"Or if one of your young gentlemen held shares and it were advantageous to sell, he would not be rusticated or gated or striped for doing so?"

And Greaves had to allow, reluctantly, that such activity would be quite in order.

"Well, Caspar," Nora said, "it seems your school presents no official bar to business, great or small, so long as correspondence is directed elsewhere."

This exchange had given the boy time to collect himself. "I'd be jolly interested, Mama. I'd certainly give it a fair dose of the old cogitation, don't you know."

"Such locutions!" Greaves interrupted, eager to re-ravel some of his authority. "Cogitation is 'measured,' not 'dosed'."

Caspar accepted the reprimand with a solemn, thoughtful nod. He was glad to have bought back his subordinate position for such a trivial price. "Anyway," he said, "my mind is too much upon the fives finals today."

Nora, who had not hoped even for so much commitment as she had got, was pleased enough. "That's right, dear," she said. "You go and win your little game, and, by the time you come back, I may have one or two suggestions for you."

"The ladies—God bless 'em," Greaves said when he and Caspar were on their way to the fives courts. "They don't understand the importance of sport in a man's life."

"I think, sir," Caspar said tactfully, "you'll find Lady Stevenson was merely supporting your timely warning yesterday not to think I must win at all costs."

If there was anything in this notion of his mother's, Greaves had to go away with glowing memories of his days at Hamilton Place. And if it were in some way against school rules—those vague rules that dealt with activities which were "not quite the thing"—it would be useful to have a master as a passive accomplice. Even more so if he were an ex-master. When Caspar arrived at that thought he realized he must already be quite taken with this new idea of his mother's—if it could turn the bitter blow of Greaves's impending departure from Fiennes into a possible asset.

❧

"I won! I say, Mama, I won." Caspar began speaking as soon as they came through the garden door.

Nora, who was cutting a bunch of roses, looked up in delight. She handed the pruning snips and her gloves to the footman and came to greet them. "Well done, dearest!" She kissed him.

Greaves cleared his throat, as if prompting Caspar.

"Yes," Caspar said. "It was something of a fluke, right at the last. Until then it was very close. Touch and go."

Greaves beamed approvingly. "Trentham was a worthy opponent." he said. "You were well matched."

"Except that I won, sir," Caspar could not help adding.

"Well, Mr. Greaves, you are no doubt pining for your family. I cannot tell you how much we have enjoyed your stay—nor how grateful we are for all you have done for Caspar. Today's win is more yours than his; I'm sure he'd be the first to agree."

"Indeed, sir," Caspar said. "Without your help I wouldn't even have got to the first round."

"You're very kind, my boy. But you are a natural player. I have done little but help you to some shortcuts. And as for your kindness, Lady Stevenson, the gratitude, let me assure you, is utterly on my side. This has been one of the most stimulating weeks of my life."

"How kind you are, Mr. Greaves. I was about to add that if it any time you happen to be passing down Piccadilly and you notice the candelabra in the windows you would be most welcome within."

Greaves, having fired his big guns on the chitchat, could now only stammer his joy and sense of unworthiness.

"Not at all," Nora reassured him. "Professor Thomson is not the easiest man to divert. If you found it easy, you have untapped gifts that make you more than welcome here. Now Caspar, come, I have something to show you."

"I'll come and see you off at the station, sir," Caspar promised over his shoulder.

"I thought we got rid of him rather well," Nora said when they were well out of Greaves's earshot. "I don't suppose he'll come down to London too often, do you?"

Caspar did not know what to say that would not be disloyal to Greaves or that might not unwittingly reveal something (though he could not say what) to his mother.

The "something" she wanted to show him was a handsome-looking brass and cast-iron bedstead standing rather isolated and forlorn in the ballroom. It was merely the frame. There was no mattress or made-up bed to it.

"What is it?" Caspar asked. Then, seeing his mother's surprise, he added, "Well, I know *what* it is, of course. What's it there for?"

"Look at it," she said.

"It's a bedstead."

"Well made? Any faults, would you say?"

"How should I know?"

"You never will unless you look."

Caspar acted the part of a man knowingly inspecting a bedstead, until he felt too foolish. He laughed nervously. "Honestly, Mama. How should I know!"

"You had better find out, Caspar dear, and quickly, because I rather think that selling bedsteads is going to be your business these coming months."

Caspar threw back his head and roared with laughter. Great gusts of it echoed down the room and out into the hall. Mary Coen, who was helping to shroud all the furniture in the public rooms, now that the season was over, heard it and smiled. It was a happy house, this. She was going to like being here.

"Mama," he said in ironic sorrow. "Selling beds! Really! Me?"

Nora nodded an I-thought-so sneer. "Too good for the Honourahle Caspar, is it? All gob and wind, as we used to say. All gob and wind."

"But *beds*!" he continued to protest.

She rounded on him then, and he saw the anger and disappointment in her eyes. "Hark to me," she said. "If you had an ounce of the true business spirit in you, you'd sell matches, or…or dried leaves…or *horsedung*! If the profit was there. You think you've got business spirit. The only spirit in you is the spirit of rebellion."

He expected her to stalk off then in a temper; but she stood and breathed at him, waiting.

She's giving me another chance, he thought. And then the truth dawned. She *wants* me to do this! She wants me to succeed!

He smiled at her, as if she had not flared up at all. "Beds, eh?" he said cheerfully. "Well, ain't that a turn-up!"

He looked the bed over once more, not acting now, nor feeling so foolish. She wouldn't risk all this…she wouldn't risk the hurt to him, if she believed he would fail. "You want me to sell it?" he asked.

"Aye," she said, grinning again. "And three hundred and ninety-nine like it."

His mouth fell open. "Four hundred!"

"Oh, you can add up, too! That'll come in handy. What'll you give for four hundred, then? What price?"

"But I have no money—none I may touch, anyway."

"That's always the second thing to worry over. The first is the price. Without a price there's no market at all."

He stared at her and blinked. "You want me to guess?"

"I want you to find out. Really, Caspar, I'm beginning to doubt your seriousness again."

The full implications of this affair were just getting through to him. "I could sell them, couldn't I! I could sell them entirely through the mail, from school—that's what you meant—from somewhere in Langstroth. Purse's place! Slip him a few bob—use his name. But I need a warehouse. Where? Up there? Or down here in London? Lords, there's a lot to it, isn't there!"

Nora came to him and gave him a huge hug. "You'll do," she said. Then she dug him lightly in the ribs. "But first the price."

"I'll walk back from King's Cross," he said. "I'll go in every furniture shop in Tottenham Court Road and Oxford Street. And then I'll tell you my price."

When Caspar had gone, her blood began to boil at John's arrogance in thinking he knew what was best for the children—without even consulting them, considering their talents, putting them to the test, or even putting his own ideas to the same test. Worse still, the very ideas were not his own; just a shallow repetition of a vague formula laid down by a fatuous Society that didn't give a damn about business anyway. Well, if he thought that bringing up children was a simple matter of applying formulas, like designing bridges or costing earthworks, it was time someone took the contract out of his hands. Her children would never know how much they owed that Charity creature.

"I was in twelve shops," he told her when he had returned. They were eating a light luncheon in the garden. "For three-foot beds like that the price seems to vary from about sixteen to twenty-six shillings. And there's one make of bed, from France, I saw in three shops at three different prices: seventeen shillings, nineteen and eleven, and twenty-two and six. The same bed. Not unlike mine, either."

"Oh, it's not yours yet!" She laughed. "Was there any difference between the shops to account for the price difference?"

"I suppose the top-price one was in a more swell place. But..."

"Swell?" Nora interrupted. "Why an expensive education should produce this love of vulgarisms, I cannot fathom."

"A more helegant hemporium," Caspar mock-quoted impatiently. "The other two were much of a muchness. Or should I say 'a goodly quantity of a goodly quantityness'?"

They both laughed. "I can see you are going to be impossible, Caspar," Nora said. "Especially if you make a success of this."

He was serious at once. "Will I, Mama? D'you think I can do it?"

He saw her eyes soften. He was sure she was on the point of saying that of course he could and other motherly reassurances; and then she withdrew it all and hardened herself. "That, my dear," she said with asperity, "is the whole point of this exercise—to settle it one way or the other."

Chapter 25

Bernard Basset was the man with the beds. To hear Nora, Bernard Bassett was the man with most things. "My young man of many parts," she called him, sometimes adding, "most of them downwind of the law." He had begun life—his commercial life, the only life that mattered to him—as a clerk in Chambers's bank, where he had infuriated his principal with daily suggestions for the root and branch reform of the entire banking system.

That was when he had come to Nora's notice, for she, too, had strong opinions on banking. That was back in 1848, when Nora had begun putting the £325,000-odd Wolff Fund into property, buying about two thousand acres of North London, roughly Camden Town to Holloway, and covering them with middle- and lower-middle-class houses. She had detected a useful greed in young Bassett, coupled with boundless faith in his own astuteness, and a cocky, democratic manner that infuriated all who thought themselves his social superiors—and that included almost all their leaseholders. It was a great advantage. These people would usually agree to anything just to get this chummy, ingratiating, odious fellow to go away.

It was Bernard Bassett who had managed the job of acquiring the land, clearing it as building demanded, and then administering the growing estate of houses and shops. By 1859 the total value had grown to just under five million pounds; of that sum, three-quarters of a million was Nora's, and, because of the way the Wolff Fund had been drawn up, it was hers exclusively, independent of any money from Stevenson's. Moreover, John could not touch a penny of it. Barring disaster, the estate would double its value over the next ten years—Nora's share, too, of course.

In Caspar's estimation "young" Bernard Bassett did not seem at all young. He was at least thirty-five. He also looked mad, with his restless, wet, staring eyes, always seeming on the point of winking, always radiating a spurious reassurance. His lips hung loose, slackly ready to talk, smile, pinch in doubt, round off in wonder, twitch in sympathy—as if they had learned their business in melodrama and could not adjust to everyday life. Even so, Caspar could not dislike him; there was a fascinating awfulness about his transparent insincerity. You wondered how he could bear to be with himself all day.

Caspar asked him first how he came to own these four hundred beds.

"Ah," he said. "A very shrewd question, Mr. Stevenson. At least, in anyone else it would be shrewd, but—knowing your vintage and the vineyard, if I may so put it—then it's no more than I would expect. How do I come to own four hundred beds, eh? The truth is, I don't exactly *own* them—that is, if you want them, I do own them, if you don't, they all go back to their *other* owner. Is my meaning clear, Mr. Stevenson?"

"You're an agent?" Caspar said. "Or a partner?"

"Exactly! Though that isn't quite the case. But exactly put. Yes. Very fair. Yes, I shall have to watch myself with you, sir, I can see."

"But how do you come to have four hundred beds, whether as agent or owner or whatever you may be?"

"I can see you're no fool, Mr. Stevenson. So I won't try and beat about the bush. I'll tell you straight—and it's something you'll learn when you go into business yourself. An astute and clever and smart fellow in business—any business—well, you'd be surprised at the offers as come his way. Every day. You'd be astonished, I say. Some I take up; most I ignore. But of the ones I do entertain, you'd be…er…"

"Amazed?" Caspar suggested, "surprised" and "astonished" having gone before.

"Quite. Yes. I do make quite a success of most. You'd be amazed."

"But not *these* beds?" Caspar asked, worried—not that he believed Bassett, but he did not like this suggestion of doubt.

"I would. Oh, I would." Bassett breathed in deeply, squaring up to his own assertion. Then he paused and looked appraisingly at Caspar. At last he shook his head, like one good-naturedly accepting defeat. "I won't try and gull you, Mr. Stevenson. I could make a success of this. I could make a very big thing of it. But I'm passing it on to you to please your mother. As a favour, yes. I worship Lady S. I owe that great and gracious lady everything I have in life." He paraded a sudden alarm. "When I say 'worship' I wouldn't want you to misconstrue me, Mr. Stevenson. I mean in a most platonistical and distant and businesslike way, I do assure you. Yes. Well now, did you have a price in mind?"

Caspar still looked dubious. He wanted Bassett to offer first.

Bassett tried but failed to meet Caspar's gaze. "Lord, but you're a shrewd one, Mr. Stevenson!" he said. "Yes. I tell you, there's men in business about me twenty years. God's truth this—if your dear mother was here, she'd tell you. There's people know me well who'd have swallowed that one about doing all this to please Lady Stevenson. But not you I can see it, though you're too polite to say it. Yes. Well now, let me put the real facts straight before you. No waiver this time. The truth is, I'm a bit pressed." He winked. "Not a word to your mother about this, now. I know I can trust you. Yes. They're after me—the banks. And…er…other parties. I'm being pressed shocking. You wouldn't believe it, Mr. Stevenson. You. Would. Not. *Believe.* It! People who've known me all my life, behaving as if I can't be trusted one more month. They know I'll pay. Did I ever default? Did you ever hear of it? No. And the favours I've done them!" He was near to tears.

Caspar was embarrassed at the transparency of it all.

"So, Mr. Stevenson! You'll gather I'm strapped down and the men with the hammers are all around me. Yes. Not to put too fine a point on it, Mr. Stevenson, as God is my witness, I'm desperate for a bit of crinkle, I mean the real paper. I've got to slip these dogs. Not that I'm trying to appeal to your pity. I wouldn't insult you, sir. Yes. What I'm saying is that you can really push me hard to a very keen price on this. My back's to the wall, as your dear mother would be the first to tell you, if she was here—which I thank God she isn't. I'll come down ten…twenty"—he gritted his teeth, hating to have to say it—"*thirty* percent. Just to get a sale. Yes." His eyes opened in mute appeal.

"Thirty percent of what?" Caspar asked.

"Yes!" Bassett said with brave decision. "At least that much. Though it hurts. And that's gospel. Those beds were going to be a nice, tidy little nest egg to me. They were going to stand me in good. But…" He smiled bravely. "Well, have we a market, Mr. Stevenson?"

"A hundred and fifty would be a fair price," Caspar said, unable to make any headway through the persiflage.

"Oh, you're very hard, Mr. Stevenson." He sucked his teeth. "Very hard. Yes. A hundred and fifty. Hmmm."

"A fair price I think."

"Well…hard but fair, I think I could just squeeze to that."

Caspar stood and grinned, holding out his hand. Bassett took it and shook. Caspar did not let go. The fellow's hands were cool, bone dry, almost scaly. He'd done no sweating at all. It was all smoke. "More than a fair price," Caspar said. "A good price. And at thirty percent off—a hundred pounds. I'm delighted."

Bassett dropped his hand like a hot coal. "Lord, Mr. Stevenson, I'm never shaking on that. What! A mere hundred! Why, that's less then I gave. I couldn't do that."

"Then you gave too much," Caspar said coldly. "Anyway, I thought you said you hadn't given anything yet."

"Ah! I speak in ellipsis, Mr. Stevenson, as to that. But my associate would never go so low. In any case, thirty percent off of a hundred and fifty is a hundred and five, unless they've changed all the tables since I left Eton." He gave a wink.

Caspar laughed at the thought of this cockney rogue at Eton. "A hundred and five's the highest I'll go."

Bassett, looking highly offended now, stood and shot his lower jaw at Caspar. "I wouldn't insult my associate with that offer, I'm afraid," he said.

"That is your privilege, of course," Caspar said lightly. "A hundred and five's my best offer."

An extraordinary change came over Bassett. He ran toward Caspar and fell to his knees, clutching Caspar's jacket. "Oh, please, Mr. Stevenson, sir! I beg of you. Please raise your offer, sir? A hundred and thirty. They'd retail at nineteen and eleven, easy, them beds. Yes. Easy! You'd show a good whack at a hundred and thirty—you know you would. Why, if they didn't stand you in a hundred and fifty sheer profit, I've never done profitable business in my life. Gospel! Please, Mr. Stevenson! You've no idea how desperate I am."

Caspar waited until the man's grip relaxed. "A hundred and ten," he said. "Against better judgement. Not a penny more."

Bassett stood and walked back to his desk. "I can't do it," he said. "I just can't do it at that."

Caspar almost relented. He knew he could still make a handsome profit at a hundred and fifty, if need be. But Bassett had shown himself unaccountably weak and Caspar didn't want to make his own side of the contest weaker still. In the end, he simply shrugged and walked out.

When his tread reached the halfway landing Nora came out of the inner office and said, "Well?"

"He's all right."

"All right?"

"He's pretty good. I'd not like to work for him when he grows up. Tell you straight."

"You were awful!"

"I know!" Bassett laughed. "How long is it since I've done that sort of business?"

"Eighteen hours, if I know you!"

"Now, Lady Stevenson, I ask you…"

Nora smiled him to silence. "Can you see him through the window?" she asked. "I don't want him to catch sight of me. He thinks I'm at home."

Bassett crossed to the window. "He's on the pavement. Looking like the world's fallen around him. Either that or he's trod in something."

"Open the window and tell him a hundred and fifteen, here, tonight, and he's got a bargain."

Bassett relayed the message.

But Caspar would not budge. "I'll tell you what," he shouted up. "I'll come back here before eight this evening with a draft for a hundred and ten. We'll see if *you're* still interested."

"Don't answer," Nora said. "Just slam the window down."

Bassett obeyed. "Where'll he get the money?" he asked. "Won't he be on his way to you now?"

"No. He has to raise it commercially from a bank."

"No one would lend it."

"Chambers will. I hope he goes there first. Otherwise he'll smell a rat when he finds only Chambers is willing—at fifteen percent!"

Bassett whistled.

"Which Caspar must try to get down to twelve. But no lower. I want that interest to bite. Till it hurts. He's got to learn the difference between borrowed money and capital reserved from income. So you can let him have them for a hundred and ten. He's going to need every penny of margin when he finds out about *you-know-what*."

They both laughed then, thinking the whole thing the greatest joke.

"'Platonistical'!" Nora jeered. "And 'ellipsis'! Where *do* you get such words!"

Chapter 26

Caspar was delighted with himself. He had got his four hundred beds at a knock-down price of a hundred and ten and he had his loan at twelve and a half percent. Neither negotiation had been easy but he had persevered and triumphed. And now he was on his way to Avian's, the swell shop in Oxford Street, where he hoped to sell his first beds for sixteen-to-seventeen bob apiece—a gross return of two hundred percent!

All right—suppose he didn't sell them for sixteen. Say he did abysmally badly and only sold them at about eleven bob each. That was still a hundred percent profit. He had no idea business was so easy and such fun. Perhaps he could astonish his mother, if he sold the lot to Mr. Avian or his buyer! Suppose he pretended to be foolish and let them go at only ten bob; wouldn't Mr. Avian see it as the chance of a lifetime and snap up the lot, so that he could sell them off at their true price of about seventeen, wholesale? Just see her face then!

Twitching with excitement, he told his porters to wait around the side while he went in to see whoever did the buying. The first person he saw was the man he had spoken to on his fact-finding visit the previous day.

"Good morning, sir! May I inquire if you've made up your mind?" the man said. He seemed very pleased to see Caspar again.

Caspar seethed with excitement. "I have! I have indeed. Would you kindly direct me to your buyer."

"Er—byre, sir? I'm afraid I..."

"Your buyer. You know—the chappie who buys furniture."

The man's smile grew thin. "Er...we don't buy furniture, sir. We sell it."

Caspar's face fell. "Oh. You mean you make it all yourselves?"

"Well...no, sir. In fact, not. Naturally we buy through the trade. There are certain suppliers...but all of the very highest..."

"Yes." Caspar was happy again. "That's what I mean. The person who buys from the trade. I wish to speak to him."

The man was now quite confused. "You are speaking to him, sir. That is... er...I happen to be...in beds, that is. Beds are...er...my...er..."

"Then," Caspar spoke like a magician promising marvels, "I have a bed to show you!" He walked to the side entrance, poked his head out, and beckoned his porters to bring the bed in. "Your name, pray?" he asked the man.

"Ah...that...ah...Vane, sir. Mister Alfred Vane. At your service." In bewilderment he watched the porters march in and begin to assemble the bedstead.

"There, Mister Vane," Caspar said. "Cast your eyes over that, if you will. Have you ever seen its like?"

Vane pinched his lip between thumb and forefinger; he was beginning to collect his wits. He smiled. "Is this a joke, sir? Some jest you and your good brothers and sisters have devised to beguile these hot days?" He appeared ready to join the joke and share a good laugh.

"Not at all," Caspar said. "I happen to be sole British agent—a great stroke of luck really—for this new French bed. You know my family has connections in the French iron business, I suppose?"

The man's smile broadened. "I'm sorry, sir." He chuckled. "I'd like to go along with this. But, you see, I happen to know where that particular bed was made, and it was about eighty miles from the French coast."

"As I said," Caspar cut in, desperately trying to recapture the initiative—and trying to smother the terrible feeling that the whole scheme was coming badly unstuck. "France, you see."

"No, sir! Eighty miles *this* side of the French coast. Shoreditch, in fact. Just down the road here, as you might say. Bankrupt stock, that is. And deservedly so in my opinion." He looked more closely at the bedstead. "Oh, yes—this is an old friend!"

Caspar's stomach fell out of him. His heart gave a painful thump. He was suddenly at a loss for words.

Mr. Vane smiled conspiratorially. "What is it, sir? A wager? I'll play along if you'll see me all right at the end of the day. You want me to buy it off you?"

"What d'you mean—'see you all right'?" Caspar asked. All his confidence had gone, but he did not know why.

The man laughed and shrugged and put his head on one side and waved contemptuously at the bedstead. "Well, sir, I can't sell rubbish like that; but if your porters will carry it off to the scrap merchant and you want me to pretend I've bought it, and if you'll see my books balance at the end of the week...well, I've no objection to playing along. Lady Stevenson is a most esteemed customer of ours."

"But what's wrong with it?" Caspar pleaded. "It looks a jolly good bed to me."

Vane's patience showed the first signs of unravelling. He spoke much more briskly, with little deference to Caspar's social rank. "For a start, sir, these tubes." He gripped one of the uprights that marked the four corners of the bed and pointed to the other three. "They should be cast and they're not. They're lapped. It's rubbish."

Caspar knew the terms and their meanings but the man assumed he did not. "There should be no seam in them. That's just thin folded sheet lapped on itself in a tube, the way you'd make a tube out of a sheet of paper."

"It's strong enough, though, isn't it?" Caspar asked, running his finger up and down the joint. It did feel rough, come to think of it now.

Vane watched. A slow grin spread over his face. "Yes!" he said. "I see you can feel it."

"But I can file that off and repaint it."

Vane was already shaking his head. "When that left the foundry—or, rather, the tinker's back yard, for that's where it was made—it was as smooth as a baby's...ah..." He suddenly remembered who Caspar was. "I don't know what they used for brazing compound, but it was badly adulterated. With phosphorus, I shouldn't wonder."

"Is that bad, Mr. Vane?" Caspar asked.

"As bad as can be, sir. Those corner posts will 'bloom' like that—as we call it—until it's all powder. Then they'll fall apart. No, sir. That bedstead's not fit for more than simple scrap. That's why I can't buy it from you."

"Very well," Caspar said, trying to recover some face. "I shall find another buyer."

Vane merely laughed. "Not in this trade you won't, sir! Those beds have been hawked all over London this year and more past. Try Timbuctoo." But when he saw Caspar's face he took pity on the lad. "What is your interest, sir, if I may be so bold as to inquire?"

So Caspar told him. Everything. From the moment his mother showed him the sample bed to the moment he walked into Avian's shop. "Is it really so hopeless, Mr. Vane?" he asked. "Is it all rubbish, or just those four tubes at the corners? The brass bits look fine and the other smaller bars aren't rough."

Vane looked at the bed again. "I don't think it was all made in the same place," he said, feeling it critically. "That's solid bar, so you've no problem there. And the brass is good," he allowed reluctantly. "That'd have some scrap value, I'd think. A shilling, perhaps."

"So," Caspar said, his hope rekindling, "if I could cut those corner posts out and replace them I'd have quite a good..."

"Not a hope, sir," Vane interjected. "Believe me, if it could have been done economically, it would already have been done. No, sir...if you'll pardon my saying so—this bears out the old adage that Society and Trade shouldn't mingle. If I may make so bold, my advice would be, cut your losses and stick to your own side of things."

Caspar held his temper against this impertinence. He even managed a smile. "Believe me, Mr. Vane, I intend to solve this problem. And I intend to sell these bedsteads and I intend to do it at a profit. Thank you for your help."

He nodded at his two porters and began to leave the shop.

Whether from genuine admiration or from a long eye on his own self-interest, Vane walked after him and halted him in the doorway. "In that case, sir, may I he even bolder and tender one more piece of advice?"

Caspar smiled. "I am already too much in your debt in that direction I fear, Mr. Vane, but...please?"

"If you are going to sell, sir, yourself I mean, in person, you cannot do it as the Honourable Caspar Stevenson. A buyer has to look down on a salesman, if you take my meaning, sir. That'll be your difficulty, sir. A gentleman can never disguise he's a gentleman." He stood back and became the deferential shop servant again. "Thank you for your custom, Mr. Stevenson, sir," he said aloud.

Moments later, out in the street, Caspar heard a female voice calling his name: "Mr. Stevenson? Mr. Stevenson, sir?"

He turned to see a lady in her middle years walking awkwardly behind him. Her whole attitude declared that she was ready to be snubbed. He thought he recognized her and took off his hat. "I apologize, madam," he said. "You have the better of me, though I seem to recollect...er..." Her clothes were good but almost threadbare.

She made a little curtsy. "No, you do not know me, sir. I was waiting in Avian's to see Mr. Vane. Then I heard him say your name and he assures me you are Lady Stevenson's son?"

"That is correct. And how may I be of service?"

"Please! Put up your hat, sir." Her hand rose to her throat. "Oh dear! I'm all a-flutter!" Her gloves were much darned. She was genteel but obviously in poverty. How ironical, he thought, if she were about to touch him for money—she who probably had some minuscule income, and he over a hundred pounds down the hole, as it now seemed.

"You are a customer of Avian's, Mrs....?"

"Mrs. Abercrombie, sir. Oh no, not I! The truth is I do a little writing for *My Lady's Drawing Room Companion.* Do you know the journal, sir?"

"Ah..." Caspar wondered how rude it would be to admit he didn't.

She rescued him. "Of course not! It is not written *for* your sort of household but *about* it. In brief, we seek to tell people of middle rank how their betters live...what they eat, what books they read, what colours they are wearing this season, the decorations they are applying to their homes...and"—she looked over her shoulder at Avian's—"their furnishings."

"You ask shop assistants!" Caspar said, both amused and intrigued.

"Oh!" she said, all eager to dissociate herself from that class of person. "They are so vain—no pun intended—but they cannot help prattling on about the importance of their customers." She smiled. "Most useful to me, of course."

The idea of it fascinated Caspar. This day had lifted the cover on a world whose existence he had, until then, only lazily perceived: the working world. The myriads of things people found to do! The odd ways they got their money. What an idea—to flatter shop assistants into gabbling about customers and then write it all down and sell it to an editor! And then think of all the other people who lived off it—the chappies who set up the type and turned the printing presses, the porters and carters who got the magazine to the railway station...the railways themselves...the newsagent who sold it...and the rag-and-bone man who collected the waste paper...even the rag sorters who supplied the paper-makers. How much would it come to altogether? A hundred pounds, perhaps! So if his mother put pink chintz on all her chairs next spring, say, this whole vast machine would leap into action and it would be like sprinkling a hundred pounds over all those people! How much of it fell on Mrs. Abercrombie? he wondered. Precious little by the look of her.

"And you think I may help you in that way?" Caspar asked.

"I...oh dear!" she stammered, and looked about her, as if for a hole to dart into. "You see...it is so hard to get *reliable* information. And one does so hate to print lies. Especially about people one admires. But ten words about Lady Stevenson would be worth pages on almost anybody else except the queen."

She still looked as if she wished the ground would absorb her, but the mind at work beneath it all was in no way so flustered. He could see that. Something very tough and enduring was driving her.

He laughed self-deprecatingly, to put her more at ease. "I'd be very little use, I'm afraid, Mrs. Abercrombie," he said. "I just don't notice such things. If they spilled red paint all over the room, I might just twig it after a week or two."

"Ah, quite." She obviously thought he was letting her down lightly. She prepared to go.

"But give me your card," he said. "You never know."

She still thought he was letting her down lightly, but she gave him her card and thanked him most effusively.

Caspar watched her go, marvelling at the way that being-in-business could change a fellow. Normally he'd have sent her away very sharply for such impertinence. But now? You never knew. So you kept everything open and vague—and vaguely, superficially nice—until you did know. In fact, his feelings toward the woman were no more cordial now than if he had been sharper with her.

All she had done was to distract him from his own troubles for a moment. When he got hack to the barn he had hired from his mother and saw all four hundred bedsteads ranged there—four hundred heads, four hundred feet, eight hundred frame sides, and four hundred wire mats—his heart dropped to his boots.

What on earth was he to do with all that rubbish? "Worth a few shillings each," he remembered Vane's words. "Old friends...try Timbuctoo...fall to bits!" He kicked at the nearest frame. It scattered a few of its neighbours, like falling dominoes; but their inertia soon halted the movement. Inertia! God, how could he ever move this lot! And a hundred pounds—a hundred and five pounds, ticking away at twelve and a half percent. If he bought nothing else all year, his pocket money would just about pay the interest. Why had he not tried to beat Chambers down to eight per cent? Because he was so damn sure he could get rid of all the beds in a week, that's why. He'd even have agreed to fifteen percent. What a fool he had been.

His stomach churned over and over and over. It was like knowing you were due a chief beating, a House beating, and a Barn beating, one after the other. The fact that, at the moment, you were unscathed and comfortable—no pain, no between-strokes terror—it counted for nothing. Because you knew. You were already strapped down and the men with the hammers were all around you—as Bassett said.

Bassett! For a moment he thought of going to confront that fellow. How he must be laughing! He'd got shot of twenty quids' worth of rubbish at five times its price. But then he thought, why give that gobshite the satisfaction? No, he'd get out of this somehow. He looked again at his stockpile of garbage—all eleven tons of it—and thought again of the clock ticking away at twelve and a half percent. And he had not the faintest notion how to do it.

"How many did you sell, dear?" Nora asked at dinner that evening.

"Ah," Caspar said jovially. "I'm on my way to a very good sale at Avian's, don't you know. They say my price is too high. But I think if I stick out, they'll come up to it."

"Avian's!" Nora said delightedly. "If you can sell there, you'll have the entré at any furnishing shop you wish. Well done! Are you sure your price isn't too high?"

"I kept your Mr. Bassett down by staying firm. I'm sure they'll come round, especially as they imagine it's just a caper on my part, so I don't need the cash. They're very keen to get the bed—you can tell that by the way they look at it."

"Good, dear. I'm so pleased for you. And I don't think it'll do any harm if they stew on it a week or so. I want you to go to Connemara and bring Winifred here. I don't want her to travel unescorted."

"Winifred?"

"Yes. She's going to Bedford College for a year or two."

Caspar was overjoyed. At least one thing was going right—his father must have relented enough to allow Winnie to go to college. "Good for the pater!" he said. "Did you persuade him to have second thoughts?"

Nora smiled sourly. "I shall write to let him know as soon as he has gone to India," she said.

Her words started the churning inside him all over again. Stevenson had not relented. It was trouble, trouble piling up all around him. How long could he hold out? How long before he would have to go to his mother and confess what a muck he had made of it and ask her to bail him out? In a way, despite his troubles, it would be a relief to get back to Connemara for a week or so. He could enjoy a bit of riding.

Chapter 27

You must keep your toes in to the girth more, sir," McGinty told Boy. "You ride like an infantry adjutant, so you do. And as for you, Master Caspar, the less said the better. Your heart's not here this while. In love, is it?"

Caspar smirked, as if McGinty had found his secret. He was damned if he'd tell anyone here what his problems really were.

They thanked McGinty and left him to untack their ponies. Winifred, Boy, and Caspar, still in riding clothes, went to walk on the beach before lunch; there was plenty of time to change.

Except for the onshore breeze it would be as hot here as it had been in London all the fortnight he was there. The noon sun poured down on them, making their pace as short as their shadows.

"I think something has happened between the mater and the guvnor," Caspar said. "She said nothing to you about college before she left here?"

"Nothing," Winifred confirmed.

"And when did she write to you?"

"It was dated the tenth."

Caspar pricked his ears. "But that's the date—" he began.

They stopped because he had stopped, and they waited. Caspar did not know whether to tell them, especially—thump! That lead weight in the gut again. He decided to tell them, out of bravado, if nothing more. Thumbing his nose at fate, while he still had the chance.

"That's the date on which she told me—or as good as told me—I could go into business if I wished. Instead of the army. If I could prove I was capable. You see, I told Greaves I wasn't too keen on the army, and he went and blurted it all out to the mater. That's how it all happened." He turned to Winnie. "Same day as she wrote to you. So, something must be happening for her to..."

"Go into business!" Boy exploded.

"Why?" Winifred rounded on him. "Why d'you speak as though it's unthinkable, Boy? That's just like you. You don't think; you just respond. It's only unthinkable because a lot of people who have nothing whatever to do with us, and no concern for us, and no interest in our happiness, because they say so."

Boy dismissed her outburst with an impatient glance; it wasn't worth answering.

"I'll tell you how unthinkable it is, Boy," Caspar cut in. "Mother has set me a test. Through one of her business associates I have acquired certain goods, wholesale, which I now have to factor at a profit. If I do, if I'm successful, she will support me in whatever business venture I may wish to engage."

Boy sneered. "What is it? A packet of biscuits? Games?"

"I'm not telling you—or anyone. Except this: I have a loan for over a hundred pounds at…a London clearing bank and over ten tons of…goods, in a warehouse, waiting to be sold."

Or melted, he thought.

"Really, Steamer?" Winifred was delighted. "How exciting!"

"I don't believe it," Boy said, desperate not to believe it. "Our mother could never be so disloyal—not after what happened last time Papa was here. It would be downright treachery."

Caspar shrugged. "Believe it or not," he said. "It's nothing to me. The interesting thing is that she arranged it on the tenth. The same day as she wrote to Winnie."

"Yes, Boy," Winifred said. "You can't deny the letter. She certainly wrote that."

"I simply refuse to believe it," Boy said. "Our mother would never do that."

"You refuse to believe it!" Winifred sneered. She turned to Caspar. "He's been impossible ever since he failed to track down Mary Coen."

"Ah, she's been found," Caspar said lightly, not daring to look at Boy. "I forgot to tell you."

He hadn't forgotten, but to make a special point of telling Boy could have given the game away; after all, Caspar wasn't supposed to know anything had taken place between Boy and the girl.

"Where?" Boy asked, taking no trouble to conceal his anxiety. "What happened to her?"

"No one knows what happened to her," Caspar lied. "She won't say. She ran away to see the guvnor about something and she fell foul of…I don't know. Anyway, she's at Hamilton Place for the moment."

He was aware what a terribly thin story it sounded. Only Winnie swallowed it at its face value. Boy, he could see, was thunderstruck.

"She's come to no harm, fortunately," Caspar added quickly. "And she's as happy as a lark at Hamilton Place. I think she must lead a charmed life!"

"Have you seen her?" Boy asked, tense to breaking point. "Or is she just down in the sculleries?"

"I saw her. Very briefly."

"Did you talk to her?"

"About why she went?"

Boy's nostrils flared. "Of course!" His vehemence belied the calm, patrician anger in his face.

"Not really. She had some vague idea of a land where she'd be beautiful—or be thought beautiful."

"Oh, poor Mary," Winifred said.

"I told her we all thought she was beautiful and the land was here. Is here."

"Is she coming back, then? Here?"

"I doubt it," Caspar said. "It would be a poor example to the other servants."

"I see," Boy said. He appeared genuinely calm now. "Excuse me, you two. I have things to do."

They watched him out of earshot of low-pitched conversation; then Winifred said, "He's so moody. Do you understand him, Steamer?"

"He is in love with Mary Coen, you know, Winnie."

"Balderdash!" Winifred shook her head in vigorous disbelief. She didn't even want to consider that idea.

"He'll get over it now he knows she's safe," Caspar said with an air of closing the subject.

Winifred bent and picked up a round stone, which she bowled along the beach. It clanged against a wrought-iron gate half sunk in the sand. "Out!" she cried, and laughed. "I haven't managed all week when it was defended. Isn't that my luck!"

"What d'you mean?" Caspar hurled another stone overhand at the gate and missed.

"Yah!" Winifred taunted. "That's our wicket."

"Wicket!" Caspar laughed. "It's as wide as a barn, anyone could hit that." He threw another stone and missed, turning to clap his hand over Winifred's lips before she could utter a sound. She kicked his shin and made him let go.

"It's Clement's new game, called triple cricket—or 'tricket'. There's three batsmen at a time instead of one."

"Say—it's the old gate from the orchard," Caspar said. He began a run-up to leap it.

But as he was in mid-air, poised as it seemed above the "wicket," time came to a stop. He was looking down at the gate and saw that, where one of the stiles was broken, Clement or someone had replaced it with a straight piece of driftwood. It wasn't the mechanics of the arrangement that caught his eye but the rather beautiful juxtaposition of the wood, polished to a velvet sheen by the sand and bleached pale by sun and salt, against the black of the painted iron.

"Eureka!" he cried as he landed. It was the answer to his problem with the bedsteads. He couldn't replace the lapped tubing with proper cast tube—not without making a mess or going to an impossible expense. But he could do it in wood!

"Eureka! Eureka!" he cried in ridiculous glee. "Oh, Winnie—you're a genius! And Clement's a genius! And I am geniusissimus! I'll make your fortune, you'll see."

"Stop it," Winifred cried, laughing in delight at her leaping, mad, screaming brother. But when he did stop she picked up her riding habit and shouted, "Can't catch me!" And she ran along the beach as she hadn't run for years.

Caspar pretended not to be able to catch her until they were almost where the sand came hard against the rocks. Then he ran easily beyond her and stood, wild-eyed and panting, barring her way. For a while they were both too breathless to speak; then they sat on the rocks, sweating hard and wishing they hadn't exerted themselves so much.

"I'm going for a swim," Caspar said. He raced out of his clothes and dashed into the water—not into the sandy part, but into one of the rocky pools to the side of the beach. The lovely taste of the salt, the sting to the eyes, the nose-wrinkling water, the cool of it all—how sweet life was when all your problems were solved. He could turn the wood, and carve it, at Ingilby's.

Winifred watched him enviously, looking at the farmhouse, then took her clothes off, too, and ran to join him, luxuriating in the sudden cool of the water. She looked down at her body, shivering in a reticule of light cast upon it and the sandy bed of the pool by the restless water, and she saw with shame how brown she had grown this holiday, despite all her care.

Caspar squirted a mouthful of water at her. She splashed back with her hands. The sport petered out and they half-sat, half-lay in the pool, wanting nothing more.

"I'm glad you're back, Steamer," she said. "Boy's been dreadful, like a wet funeral. It's been frightful since the Thorntons went."

"I told you, Winnie, he's in love with Mary Coen."

"Piffle!"

"No, it's true. I know it. I saw them kiss."

"Eurgh!" Winifred said, without thought. "How could he!"

"Her scars, you mean? That wouldn't worry Boy."

Winifred hadn't meant that. She was thinking of all the things Boy had been able to talk about only in Latin and Greek—his disgust at fleshly love and his determination to enjoy only the purest and most spiritual union with his wife, whenever and if ever he got married. And then in a moment of rare insight (rare, for Winifred was a clever and rather literal-minded girl, not overgiven to empathy), she saw that if Boy ever slid back from his own high ideals, it would have to be with some girl as repellent as Mary Coen.

"Have you been in love yet?" she asked Caspar.

"No. I don't seem to need it."

"Nor do I. And if Boy's behaviour these last weeks is anything to go by, I'm glad. I'm going to try never to need it. I'm sure it's superior not to need it instead of being such a dreadful slave."

Caspar was unwilling to go all the way with that sentiment. "It could be useful," he said.

"How? I don't see how."

"Well, the guvnor's busy arranging what we're all going to do in life. You don't think he's going to stop there, do you! When he says 'All the girls are to marry,' he's already standing eligible middle-aged men up in rows in his mind." And, seeing the alarmed flush in Winnie's face, he began to warm to this theme. "You've got a line of railway-company directors to choose from." He pretended to introduce them. "Walrus-moustache, stinks of yeast—dipped too often in the beer. Councillor Winterbottom, carries a lot of importance—all of it in front of him, writes you shy poetry but can't ever manage a good rhyme. Viscount Lushington, chases foxes, can't string more than three words together unless he's on horseback; his mother, Countess Broodmare, has to come and swallow the key to the booze cupboard in despair of getting you in foal."

"Stop!" Winifred shut her eyes tight and put her palms over her ears. Horror and laughter vied with one another throughout Caspar's fantasy list; but with this last item she felt her gorge rise and heave. She was literally on the point of vomiting.

"That's when a touch of love could come in handy," Caspar said happily. She did not hear.

He could part turn the wood and do a bit of carving at the top—vine leaves or something. Then he could split it along the line of the carving, where it wouldn't show. Then poke one up in the top hole, left by cutting out the rotten bit of lapped tube, and poke the other bit into the bottom hole. Hey presto!

"Promise, no more?" Winifred asked, tentatively lifting one hand off her ear.

"Promise."

"What was all that eureka about?" she asked.

"Nothing." He grinned truculently. "Little problem solved, that's all."

She looked down at the water, at her breasts floating. "Old Steamer," she murmured. "He's all secrets! I think I've got cool enough." She stood in cascades of water and leaped out onto the rocks. Caspar joined her and they walked through the heat in a great arc designed to intersect their clothes the moment they were dry.

"Who's all secrets?" Caspar asked. "Or, rather, who isn't?"

"Clement said that the other day—'Steamer's all secrets.'"

"So's Boy. Look at him falling in love like that. And you, with your letter to Cheltenham. We're all 'all secrets.'"

"We used not to be."

"We're growing up, that's all."

"I suppose so."

They walked on in silence. The sea was no more than a faint lapping of the rocks. The waves, mere inches high, sounded like a distant tap being turned momentarily on-off, on-off at lazy intervals.

He could do the wood turning in mahogany and the carving in lime. That would make the join look deliberate.

"We mustn't grow apart, though, Steamer. Especially you and me. We are the ones who will mark out the way for the others. Boy won't. If Papa harasses and dragoons us into toeing his line, Clem and Abbie and the others will have no hope. It's up to us. Papa must lose."

"I will never do anything except business," Caspar said (marvelling to himself, for, only yesterday, a captaincy in a smart regiment would have seemed a wonderful haven from his problems with the bedsteads).

"Even if it means running away from home?"

"Even."

"And starting with nothing?"

"Mother would help."

"She might die meanwhile. She might change…make it up with Papa. That's what I mean, Steamer. We've got to promise this in *all* circumstances. Never wavering. Never deviating. You and me against Papa. Implacable, defiant, unwavering, not dreading his very worst! You doing what you want. I what I want. Promise?"

Caspar almost burst into excited laughter, seeing, at one and the same moment, how comic and how earnest it was. Two naked children hatching a plot on an empty beach; two young people, knowing exactly what they wanted in life and for all their lives. Which were they? And which should he do—laugh, or promise.

And bind his life?

"And whoever needs help will always find it from the other? Whatever is asked," Winifred added. "We shall stint each other nothing."

She ran before him and faced him, to stop him walking on, as if to say, *Not another pace until this is settled!* He was suddenly too moved by her earnestness to speak. Solemnly he stretched forth his hand and nodded, looking deep into her eyes.

Smiling, with a smile that bound him to her cause more than her words had done, she took his hand and shook it firmly. He saw that she was not only Winnie, whom he had always known; she was also a very handsome, appealing, and warm young woman. He was glad they were to be so close. He was also glad they were reaching their clothes because with that realization had come a new awareness of her femininity—her sex. Until that moment she had been merely his sister, with whom he, and all the others, had always bathed in the sea. His question, however, was answered: They may have begun this dip as two naked children; they ended as two young people.

"Now I'll tell you a secret," she said, skipping back to his side and letting him walk the remaining few paces to their clothes. "I wasn't being truthful when I said I hadn't been in love."

Caspar picked up her shift between his toes and passed it to her in his lifted foot.

"You won't laugh?" she asked.

"If I feel like it, I shall instantly think of the guvnor."

She smiled and then grew serious again. "I was in love. Very much. I think I still am."

"Who?"

"Nick Thornton."

She was studying Caspar intently for his reaction. When she saw his face fall, she said quickly, "But I will try to manage without it."

"Good!" Caspar said, greatly relieved.

"Don't you like him?"

"He wouldn't do for you at all."

She nodded as if she knew what he meant. "In many ways I despise him. Isn't that funny! It doesn't stop me loving him at all. Even despising him."

Caspar was afraid to add anything. Later, when they were walking back to the farmhouse, she returned to the subject. "I want you to know and understand exactly why I am not doing anything about Nick," she said. "It is a question of what I am rejecting. It is not Nick, believe it or not—never mind those things I said about despising him. And it is not..." She cleared her throat. "I'm sure you know what I mean. It is not—*eros*. It is not the thought of a physical union. I do not by any means reject that."

"What then?" For Caspar the tension of this conversation was becoming unbearable; he hated hearing Winnie confess to such feelings.

"Matrimony itself. The *state* of matrimony. That is what I am rejecting—what I must reject." She looked speculatively at Caspar. "If you really have never been in love yet, I wonder if you know the cost of it?"

"I'm sure you wouldn't pay that cost for something worthless."

"I hope so, Steamer. By heavens, I hope it doesn't prove worthless—to give up home for it if necessary, and certainly to give up the love of a father, and of a husband. My life had *better* be worth it."

"I'll go and see what Boy's doing, I think," Caspar said.

Chapter 28

When Boy heard what had happened to Mary Coen—or that small part of the story Caspar had vouchsafed—he knew he was to blame. Even Uncle Walter had said that when a decent girl, even a servant girl, got carried away by that terrible passion, it was an honourable man's duty to remember why men had been made the stronger of the two sexes. And if Uncle Walter, who was such a dreadful old reprobate himself, said that, surely Dr. Brockman would indorse the maxim a thousand times more strongly—except that chief never descended to such petty details of actual behaviour, preferring always to keep the boys' minds directed toward high and lofty principles of general application.

But Boy had failed even the lecher's injunction; he was worse even than Uncle Walter. His loathing for himself, for his own body, for the vile corruption of his sex, had never been stronger. If Mary were here now, how purely he would love her. But she would never come back here—back to the place where she trusted and was let so badly down.

He tried to think of chief meeting with Mary in that spot by the roadside. With what noble and elevated thoughts he would have filled those minutes or hours! How enriched Mary would have felt as they parted. Then, in compensation, he tried to repeat the scene with himself in the same noble role; but that other image slipped beneath his guard and plastered itself upon his mind. And, even worse, he gloated upon it still! Lovingly his mind's eye ran over her sweet nakedness. Lovingly his mind's fingers closed upon that warm softness of her breasts. Lovingly his mind's lips closed on hers in infinite tenderness. Lovingly he was overwhelmed again with that spicy heat of her, sank into her, luxuriated in her, strained flesh to flesh.

He was evil, evil, evil—to be able still to think this way, when he knew what it had done to her. There was no good in him anywhere. Not one redeeming feature. If his soul were now cast into the scales, the emptiness of space itself would be enough to outweigh it.

An image kept coming into his mind. Years ago McGinty had gelded two colts behind the turf house. Boy had not understood the process—or, rather, its purpose. And McGinty had said, "Isn't it called 'taking their burdens from them'? Sure they're little enough now"—and he threw the tiny lumps of gristle to the dogs—"but 'tis enough to ease them. When those fillies start givin' out the orders, these fellas'll not lift a nose out the bucket."

"Taking their burdens from them." That was the phrase which had really etched itself into him.

McGinty had said it with a nod and a leer. But in endless repetition in Boy's mind, the leer had vanished, leaving only a dark solemnity and, finally, the suggestion of an all-embracing sympathy. "Taking their burdens from them." It was a tender act of compassion. Taking their burdens from them!

What good were those burdens? They poisoned life. Think of all those marvellous days he and Winnie and Caspar and the others had enjoyed until he was about fourteen. The days free of burdens, full of light and sun and laughter and energy, and calm sleeps to close them.

Then the pimples. The dirty skin. The new smells. The hair. The troublesome voice. The awkward knees and elbows. The sinking stomach. The despairing of lovely girls. The haunted nights—whether passed in indulgence or in the anguish of denial. The terrors of insanity ever near. The self-loathing. The weakness. The ridden imagination. The haunted heart. The heaped conscience. The violated chunks of maiden in a thousand shameful fancies. The Babylon of his burdens.

The idea was there even before he felt the penknife in his pocket or rose to meet the act with an involuntary and joyful yes. And it was a joyful idea. There was no moment when it was not there, nor another moment when it was. Instead a great, expanding, unmeditated joy filled him and he knew the idea had always been there, forming inside him. It did not occur to him. He finally achieved it.

He sat fully clothed in the shallows of the stream, knowing it was going to hurt and not caring. Of course it would hurt. It would be the worst pain he had ever endured—except that which he had endured spread through these last five years. He would endure this pain, and it would not endure.

The river was cold from mountain and lough. It would dull the pain to start with. It would stanch the blood and carry his corruption out to that great purifier, the sea.

He honed the knife on the pebbles until it gleamed; and still he went on honing, loving the purifying silver flash of its metal. It was clean. Steel was fine, clean, strong. He would be a man of steel soon; he would borrow its strength.

Then it occurred to him he should not do it here but just a little way up the hill. In that grove. The spirits of that grove, his own Eumenides, had seen the first act—his first and only act; now they should not be denied the finale. He would lay them all to rest. Those within and those who pressed all round him.

Singing *Dies irae, dies illa,* that greatest of all Christendom's penitential hymns, the hymn that had sweetened the lash of the flagellants' whips across medieval Europe, the hymn written by a proud lecher who was restored to grace and piety by castration, Boy set off up the hill to his and Mary's grove.

Rex tremendae majestatis,
Qui salvandos salvas gratis,
Salve me, fons pietatis!

Salve me! Salve me! How often had he cried that, thinking he could leave his salvation utterly to the mercy of God and not lift a finger himself. *Fons pietatis*—fount of piety. A more fitting word than "eunuch." He would soon be a fount of piety now. He knelt in prayer, in sweet communion with God until he shivered with joy at what he was to do. It would not be a pain. It would be an ecstasy.

Carefully he undressed, folding each garment and piling them in a ritual fashion that seemed to flow spontaneously from his very heart. And all the corruption in him, too, seemed to have fled back to its source between his thighs. The rest of him was dry and cool and serene. So different from his generative organs! They were clammy and foetid. Noisome outlaws.

He knelt and sat on his heels, forcing his testicles up. They lay like sacrificial brutes on the altars of his thighs. Unable to pity them now, impatient merely to be rid of them, he picked up the knife and worked it firmly into the grip of his thumb and two writing fingers. There was not a tremor in him. His heart beat not one pace above normal. He neither smiled nor frowned.

Without haste, but with no reluctance, he spread his scrotum and pinned a testicle between the index and middle fingers of his left hand. He saw the knife carry in an arc across his thigh and up until it was level with his eyes. He made the sign of the cross.

He did not see Caspar run across the grove. Nor did he feel the rabbit punch with which Caspar felled him. When he came to his senses again he was fully dressed in his wet clothes and the knife was nowhere to the seen.

"Why?" Caspar asked.

Boy rolled over on his stomach and hid his face. But Caspar was merciless. He turned his brother over and pinned him supine. "Why?" he repeated.

Boy shook his head. Caspar raised his fist and smashed the ground elder just to one side of Boy's face. "Why?" He raised his fist again.

Boy took advantage of it to squirm out from under—he was much bigger and more burly than Caspar, anyway. But once he was free he ran no farther than the leaning tree. The Eumenides, whom he could not fight, still pinned him to this spot more firmly than ever Caspar would.

"I don't know!" he said.

Caspar, who had begun to run after him, halted when he did. He now stood a few paces at Boy's back. "You do know. You're too frightened to say her name."

"It's me," Boy said, so quietly that Caspar hardly caught it.

"Mary Coen," Caspar said.

"She's only the very last, the very latest…thing."

"You think it was what you did. It wasn't. It was Nick."

Boy turned and faced him then, his mouth open in unwilling half-belief. "I debauched her…" he began.

Caspar laughed bitterly. "You just want to hurt yourself," he said. "I can't think why."

Boy's hands, clutching the leaning trunk, grew tense. The tendons rippled under the skin. "I want to purify myself," he told Caspar. His tone was almost conversational.

"Like *that*?"

"It seemed the only way."

Caspar gave a little laugh, to ease the moment in which he walked nearer Boy. "I'm glad we've arrived at the past tense."

"Where's my knife?"

"I threw it away."

Boy knew his brother was lying; Caspar was incapable of throwing something of such value away.

"There's nothing," Caspar went on, "no supposed crime or sin could be so bad as to warrant that. You would have"—he deliberately broke his voice back into a high falsetto—"ruined your who-o-ole life!"

Boy looked askance at him, thinking it an odd time and subject for joking. Then he saw Caspar was not joking. "Why d'you say it like that?" he asked.

"That's what it does to you. Didn't you know? Your voice breaks back again to treble."

Boy gulped. A sweat flushed his entire body. Everyone would have known! He closed his eyes and shivered.

"Did you really not know that?" Caspar asked.

Boy shook his head.

Of course, Caspar thought, remembering how Boy would always walk away from any group that began telling dirty jokes, of course he wouldn't know. "Dear me! *Quae peccamus juvenes ea luimus senes.*" It was one of Brockman's favourite Latin maxims: The sins we commit in youth we pay for in old age. "Most of us are happy to let the bill mount up." Caspar laughed. "I can't think of anyone but you who would want to pay in advance—and then shut the door on the delivery!"

Even Boy laughed, though a shade more grimly than Caspar. "How do other people…I don't know…tolerate it? How do you tolerate it?"

"Tolerate what?"

"Well—you know. You know the fiending that goes on at school. All the time. All the time! And that street in York. And everywhere. All over the place. And all around us. On and on and on. Everybody. All the time! How do they tolerate it? Why isn't everybody mad?"

Caspar raised his eyebrows, not quite knowing how to reply. "Most people feel mad because they think it's passing them by. It's always the other fellow who gets enough."

Boy breathed out in vehement disappointment, as if to say it was no good trying to explain it to Caspar.

"Well!" Caspar said, not wanting to lose contact with Boy nor to let him slip back into self-despair. "What is there to tolerate? Why should people go mad?"

"You know."

"I do not—come on, let's go out on the road. These flies are a damn nuisance."

They walked out to the hot dusty highway and strolled homeward at snail's pace. "That academy," Boy said. "You know—the one Brockman always warns us about."

Caspar stifled a sigh of dismay. "What academy?" he asked. "Where is it? Everbody knows that he just makes that up. We've even made expeditions to find it. You ask de Lacy and Causton and Moncur. You'd know, too, if you didn't turn your back and walk away whenever anyone says a rude word."

"But it's near Fiennes. Chief wouldn't lie."

"How near?"

"Less than ten miles, he always says."

"Right!" Caspar said, as if Boy had just trapped himself. "Now we've walked or ridden everywhere around Fiennes, wouldn't you say? There's not been very much in the way of building since the Romans left. Nor before. So it would be hard to slip in an extra building without anyone twigging it. Do you know of any building like the one he describes so graphically? Bars at the windows? Screams lifting the roof day and night? Mastiffs in the grounds? Locks on the gates? There isn't one—not in *twenty* miles. I'm saying it doesn't exist at all. Chief is a liar."

"Stop!" Boy cried.

"Honestly, Boy, it's not only me that says this. I'm not claiming any special wisdom. Everyone at school knows it's all just a sort of parable. He doesn't really expect you to believe it. Not literally."

"But it's true. I know it's true in my own life. I've proved it. Why does he say it if it isn't true?"

"He's like all those parsons who preach charity. Just see what happens to the poor beggars who take them literally and call to the vicarage for a crust to eat! I don't know why chief says it. I mean, I don't know why he bothers to say it—especially when any boy, with no more apparatus than his own body, can put the lie in his mouth in two months flat. Of all the pointless exercises we indulge in at Fiennes, chief's dirty talks are the worst."

"You just don't like him. That's all."

"I do not! He's vain. He's a prig. He's a self-righteous tyrant. You think he's so friendly! You can't grasp the fact that he merely patronizes you, and all his other clique of pharaohs. He's incapable of befriending anyone or anything. There's no warmth in him to kindle it."

"He's been jolly good for Fiennes," Boy said in a placatory tone. Caspar's passionate onslaught was a bit overwhelming.

"Hah! Napoleon was 'jolly good' for France, I daresay. It doesn't stop him being the worst shit since Genghis Khan."

"Anyway, he's not the only one who says it. All the books say it. Anyone who writes or speaks at all on morality says it. You can't explain that!"

Caspar ostentatiously closed his eyes and counted down his passion. "I would have thought," he said in tones deliberately measured. "I would have thought *that* the most obvious thing of all. No one preaches against the folly and sin of dancing on the top of church spires, do they! Parsons don't waste half an hour's good ranting time denouncing the eating of human flesh, do they! A fasionable West End sermonizer never warns his audience not to bugger the sheep, does he! The point, oh wise wise brother, is that if your trade is to stop mankind enjoying itself, you'd better choose something that all the people are doing as much as they can all the bloody time!"

Boy stared at him in horror. "You are the Devil," he said, meaning every word.

Caspar became heated again. "And I say the Devil is that man who, having decided upon his line of argument, tells any lie to support it and deludes the ignorant and credulous to the degree that…who delude people like *you* into such monst…—into such a terrible mutilation as you were about to do."

"Brockman does not lie," Boy said gently. Caspar's evident anger frightened him.

"He lies. He says self-pollution (as he calls it) makes you weak. It saps your judgement and vigour. It weakens your sight. Well"—he looked away and braced himself to say it—"I won the fives finals after three…acts. And in a week of twelve. I won the school junior steeplechase within an hour of two. And look at me—is there a single pimple or blotch on my skin? Am I deaf at all? Are my teeth falling out? Do I stare and stammer? Do my feet shuffle? Do I fail to look people in the eye? Is my mind dull? Am I always scratching at pocket billiards? Eh? Lie upon lie upon lie. He will stop at nothing. And all that two-faced, sanctimonious shit about 'Truth'! *He* is the Devil."

Caspar laughed then, having boiled off all his steam. He reached out and took Boy's arm, exactly as chief was wont to do. His imitation of chief's voice was also exact. "Give him up, m'boy, I implore you! Give him up while you yet have time!"

Boy had to laugh at that; the tone was precisely caught. But all of Caspar's contempt for the man was there, too, and, for a moment, Boy was allowed to glimpse his beloved chief directly through Caspar's eyes. It clashed so violently with the view he had formed over so many years that he was thrown back into confusion.

Caspar, seeing that hesitation, steeled himself to make his final and most unwilling revelation. "I'll prove it to you," he promised, "when we get back to the farmhouse."

When they arrived, he went up to his box and rummaged around for a time. He came down again with something concealed in the palm of his hand. He took Boy out to the turf house and then—still not satisfied with its seclusion—took him down to the centre of the hot, deserted beach. The other children were all out, riding the long circuit past Ballyconneely.

"Here," Caspar said, at last revealing what was in his hand: a small diary for the year 1857.

Boy recognized it at once. About eighteen months ago he had, to his shame, tried to read Caspar's diaries and found them all to be in some kind of code, part-mathematical, part-symbolic.

Caspar opened it at random, looked at it, then clasped it to his chest; he was now regretting the impulse that had brought him and his diary to this point. Boy waited.

Caspar took a deep breath. "I'll show you," he said. "Easter. Confirmation lecture…that's the full, guided tour of Inferno, isn't it?"

Boy nodded.

"See the squiggles?" He pointed to marks just below the dateline for each page, something like a tilde: ~. "Each of those is one of Brockman's 'acts of abomination'. One a day for ten days. This is an experiment, you see. And here are things you can measure. P is for 'pulse'—normal, normal, normal… and so on. Temperature I couldn't take, but, anyway, no fever. SH is standing on hands, length of time. That tests balance and strength, you see. At least three minutes every day. Could have gone on for hours. W is running up and down Whernside—no staving. And look at the times! I beat Brockman every day. So either he was hard at it himself or he's lying."

The next ten days were each marked ~ ~ . "See! No change in anything. V, by the way, is veins in the eye—looking for bloodshot eyes, you see. I forgot that the first week. That's the number of veins I could count in the lower half of my left eye. Doesn't change much, does it!"

Now that Caspar was launched into it, he became as proud of these performance records as an engine designer would be of a new locomotive. Grinning, he turned the page. "Then…" he said. Each of the next eight days was distinguished: ~ ~ ~.

He waited until Boy, who stared down at the book in complete impassivity, had absorbed the decorations before he said, "And still no really measurable change!"

"You stopped," Boy said pointing to the last two visible days.

"I got bored," Caspar said. "But look."

Every day of the following week danced with: ~ ~ ~ ~.

"And there's one of my fastest times ever up and down Whernside. After I had spat in chief's eye twenty-eight times." He turned over two pages quickly, and showed Boy a spread devoid of squiggles, though all the other measurements were there. "Here's where I..."

"Why did you turn over two pages?" Boy asked.

"Nothing," Caspar said. "It wasn't part of these tests."

"I don't believe you."

Caspar looked at the sky and, whistling, turned back a page. The early days of the spread bore random assortments of single, double, or treble squiggles. The Friday and Saturday were blank. Sunday was all but obliterated under: ~ ~ ~ ~ ~~~~~~~~~~~~

"Chee-rist!" Boy said. "That *must* have done something."

"It gave me blood blisters!"

"More than that."

"Yes. I can safely say that is over the limit. Fourteen a day would probably produce some of the effects Brockman predicts. But not four. Anyway"—He turned forward to the squiggle-free pages again—"here we are, as virgin as Brockman could wish. And no change—once we've recovered from the excesses of that Sunday."

Boy was disappointed. "No change at all? There must be."

"Except by here I felt decidedly irritable and shivery. And here"—he turned over and pointed to ~ ~ —"I broke down!" He grinned through lazy, half-closed eyes at the memory. It was bravado, put on for Boy.

"Let's see the rest," Boy said.

But Caspar snatched away the book. "No! The rest is not part of those tests. It's private. And don't you ever look in these now you know that code. Promise?"

Boy promised.

"But I'll tell you this, Boy. If every time I spit in Brockman's eye it's a shovelful on my grave, and if we're talking about the navvy shovel, I've got twenty-six cubic yards heaped up already!"

He laughed then, suddenly seeing it as a picture. "Hey!" he said. "I'm going to be a *real* pharaoh at this rate!"

Boy was not persuaded by Caspar's demonstration—at least, not completely and not all at once. He had lived too long and too faithfully, despite all his backsliding, by that other code. But at least it put enough doubt in his mind to prevent him from returning to the idea of self-mutilation as a way of relinquishing his burdens. It did not seem impossible that he might, in time, even borrow a little of his brother's skepticism and try some less ambitious experiments. After all, four or five years ago, before chief's lectures, it had never seemed to do him much harm. Perhaps when you did it knowing that it harmed you, it really did do so. But what if you did it knowing it was harmless? Like Caspar? Perhaps it really would be harmless. It was an exciting thought.

Of course, he still admired the man who had done so much for Fiennes, who was such a superb sportsman, who had such a great mind, who taught so supremely well, who always had time for any youth with any problem—who was, in short, such an example of moral, mental, and muscular vigour. But Brockman had undoubtedly lied. If what Caspar said was true, and if the other fellows had searched for that place and failed to find it, then Brockman had allowed a lie to go forward in defence of a truth. He had prostituted truth and turned it into a lie.

And so, for Boy, the real and immediate casualty of this affair was his worship of Brockman. The man had ceased to be a god.

Chapter 29

When Nora asked Roxby why he had never married, he patted his naked body the way a man pats all his pockets in search of coin. When it produced no apparent discovery, he turned his hands palm outwards and shrugged. "No idea," he said.

The charade had drawn Nora's attention to his body. A poor thing compared with John's. A poor performer, too. "Be serious," she said.

She was beginning to emerge from the euphoria of her rebellion against John. Fear was creeping in at all sorts of edges. There were things she could wish had been done differently or not at all. Roxby was one. She had spoiled a pleasantly flirtatious relationship—which in ten years, had never strayed beyond propriety—and what had she got in return? A pocketful of dust. A poke full of dust! She doubted she could bear having him in her bed one more time.

"If I were serious, you wouldn't believe it," he said.

"Try."

"Why've I never married?"

"Yes."

"It would be monstrous unfair on the lady." He looked at her, sizing her up for a swift confession. "I'm too bloody fickle, Nora. Take us. Here I am, wondering how to break it to you that I want to be off…" He sighed.

"And deciding to do it brutally," Nora said, not showing the faintest trace of her delight.

"You're not saying you've grown to love me!" he was stung into responding.

"I…" she began. And then she had to laugh, unable to keep up her pretence of shock and rejection.

"Thank God for that!" he said and at once got up and began to dress himself.

"One extreme to the other! You don't have to be quite so swift—now, that *is* brutal."

He sat down and made a feeble attempt to caress her with one limp hand. She caught it and flung it away petulantly. "Oh, go on then!" she said.

In the end her sense of relief triumphed over all the other stray feelings his going engendered. "But why would it be un*fair*?" she asked.

"I told you—too fickle. The number of times I've lain with Jenny or Minnie or Belle or Joyce..."

"Too boastful!" Nora interrupted. "Never mind fickle." She rose and began to dress, too.

"Nora, I'm going back over ten years—it's hardly excessive. My point is that I lie with one and dream of the other—even with you. And I know you're worth a hundred of any of them."

At last she saw what he was driving at, and it made her laugh. She could not believe he was so naïve. "Dear boy!" she said. "There's wives and there's wives, you know."

"Meaning?" He had discovered a grease mark on his waistcoat and was trying to shift it with a fingertip loaded with spit.

"I know half a dozen who would be delighted with an inattentive husband."

"I know a hundred!"

"You don't."

"What? Wives? Most of them, I..."

"No! Not wives, you idiot. Would-be wives. Unmarried girls. They'd carry a few children for you and be glad not to see you about the place too often. All they want is to have their own rank instead of one borrowed from their parents. You don't know anything about Society, do you! You have no idea how girls arc hemmed in and watched over if they're not married."

"Young girls?" He was interested now.

"I didn't say young."

"Oh! And the expense, too." He abandoned the grease mark, which was now like a bull's-eye in a large, wet target.

"There are some who would bring quite a tidy dowry."

"Who?"

"Dodo Kems, for one."

"She's foreign."

"She was born in England."

"All her people are foreign."

"All her people are worth several hundred thousand."

That silenced him. "Could you invite her to your first dinner next Season?" he asked at length.

"Fickle!" Nora laughed loudly. "You're as predictable as yesterday!"

She was glad when he was gone. She hoped she would be able to marry him off comfortably to some selfish, understanding, rich girl; it would suit Rocks to have a proper establishment of his own. And she might then be able to resume her former relationship with him; that would be impossible while he remained single.

Then she dismissed him completely from her mind. She had to go back to Maran Hill now and face one of the hardest Friday-to-Mondays of her life. She had to see John, who would be off to India on the Tuesday. For her children's sake she would have to pretend she knew nothing of The Bitch (as she now called Charity to herself). She wanted Winifred well settled in at college and she wanted Caspar to have fought his way to profit over the obstacles she had engineered. But she wanted these problems settled before John could stand everything on its head. So she had to be her old pleasant, unsuspecting self to him for a few days yet. She would have to ignore that unpleasantness outside the India Office. He certainly would; she was sure of that.

She had a more pressing reason, too, for remaining on terms with John: Young Roxby had been a mite careless once or twice this past week.

She covered the twenty-six miles from London by carriage, thinking it would be cooler than the train and more restful. Also she needed a little sleep—something Roxby had eroded deeply, and not altogether pleasurably.

On Highgate Hill she had one last look back at her Wolff properties—serried row upon row of furnished tombs that made her shiver. How could people want to live in them! But they did. And that's why the houses were there. For herself, she would almost prefer the thatched hovel she grew up in.

She fell asleep soon after and did not wake until Nanette tapped her gently on the knee just as they were approaching the gate lodge at Maran Hill. "Mrs. Bagot's doing the gate," she told Nora.

Nora put her head out of the window. "Where's Bagot?" she asked.

"Took 'is lordship to the station, my lady," she said.

"Botheration!" Nora said when she was inside the carriage again. "I hate dining alone. I hope he's not late back."

Even worse news awaited her when she arrived at the house: a letter left by John to say that he had been called away to the North but would try to be back on Sunday, the day after tomorrow.

Nanette unpacked. Nora ate in lonely silence, read fitfully, slept fitfully, got up early and went for a ride while it was still cool, looked at the household accounts, went through the linen and furnishings with the housekeeper, discussed the management of the coppices and coverts with the gamekeeper, looked over the horses and tack with the head lad, saw two of the farm tenants—who had expected to see John—went over the home farm with the bailiff and decided on sites for two new cottages, fell exhausted into bed and slept right through, barely arriving at church in time for matins. Country life was exhausting.

When she arrived back from church there was still no message from John. The whole of Sunday passed without sign of him.

Sleep did not come so easily that night. Lately John had taken to saying that their congress exhausted him—a man of forty-nine! If they had only the one night together and he was off to India next day, he might pass it in continence with her. He kept talking about the "hush of life" and a lot of phrases that would suit Arabella's bookshelves better than his lips. Well, she would have to *make* him do it; that was all there was to it.

First thing Monday morning she sent to the station to see if any message had come from him. The stationmaster sent back word that a telegraph had come down from Ingleton to expect Lord Stevenson off the six o'clock train that evening. That was bad—travel was another thing that brought on an attack of "hush of life." And Ingleton? He must have been to see Dr. Brockman.

By mid-morning the long-heralded break in the weather came. For over a week the blistering sun had shared the sky with ominous piles of cloud, brooding, purple masses that threatened rain but never delivered it. That morning the skies opened and even the greedy, parched gravel of the drive, unable to absorb the torrents, became a shallow strip of lake for a time.

After the heat it was refreshingly cool. Nora stood among the pillars of the portico and luxuriated in it. The smell of the earth, newly wet, was one of life's great, free pleasures; another was to stand, dry as toast and cool at last, only inches from those sheets of falling water.

If the children were here, they would be out there, standing in it, getting soaked to the skin, holding their faces to the sky and letting it batter them.

Or would they? The younger ones would—even Caspar, who already seemed more mature than Boy. Winifred wouldn't, though. That serious young woman. Nora tried to think of herself at Winifred's age. She had married John at eighteen; and in knowledge of the world she had already been middle-aged compared with Winifred. What, in giving so much to their children, had they failed to give them? How could Winifred, for all her cleverness, write a stupid letter like that to Miss Beale and then sit and wait for John to come down on her like a ton of organized fury! And how could Caspar, who had so much native shrewdness and presence of mind, fall for that trick with the beds—making the sample perfect and the rest rubbish? Had he even noticed yet that the sample was different? What was lacking in the children? There was a softness there, which did not come from her, and certainly it didn't come from John.

Still the rain fell. Would she go out and dance in it? If she weren't the lady—the tone setter—of this grand house, if all the servants had the day off, would she stand out there and let it beat down on her face and soak her to the skin?

She would! Even worse, she'd take her clothes off and dance in it, if she were all alone out here. There was still that in her. In a way, that's all Roxby had been to her—a brief, supposedly safe dance in the forbidden. She chuckled at the comparison: He was certainly wet enough!

Her thoughts hopped back to the children. Were they worth her rebellion against John? Or would she poison her relationship with him only to have Winifred and Caspar go sour on it all—Winifred meekly marrying, and Caspar taking to the army with all the gusto he was now putting into selling beds? Caspar must by now have found that the beds were worthless; had it changed his mind about going into business? How she wished he were less secretive... no, not really. If he was to go into business he would need that faculty. What she was really asking for was a mother's privilege of sharing in every part of her children's lives; and, to the extent that they were no longer children, she could no longer share.

There was another reason for wanting to share more of Caspar's present struggle: It was exactly the sort of venture she would have loved. To be utterly honest, she would love it still. She who now controlled nearly ten million pounds' worth of property and investment, Stevenson's and Wolffs', would love to be selling those four hundred beds! She still thought back with a special thrill to those days when she had set up the first Stevenson shop for the navvies on that first railway contract.

That shop had made a thousand pounds profit in its first year. It had been a real thousand, too. She had seen it in the bank—glittering golden piles of it. Now the gross profit on Stevenson's and Wolffs' came to more than a thousand a day;

and it meant very little. Figures on paper, nothing to the guts. Well…be honest, she thought. It meant being able to stand here in the middle of several hundred acres spanning the loveliest valley in Hertfordshire; it meant being able to hold the best salon in London; it meant wielding an influence that some of the highest ladies in the land envied; it meant all the carriages, horses, clothes, food, hunting, servants, entertainment she wanted. And it meant never having to worry about paying for it all. But it lacked the thrill of standing like David before the Goliath of some money citadel and coming away with the glittering piles—as Caspar would now have to stand. She wanted to do it for him. Failing that, she wanted to live it through him.

Knowing Caspar, she knew she could do neither.

She came back indoors and tried to play at the piano, but found herself unable to concentrate. John's impending arrival hung over the day. Like rain clouds, she thought. Most of her, she realized, had been glad he was not here on Friday. A whole weekend with him would have been more damping than this rain—a weekend of lectures on the children's duty to him and Society, his duty to the Empire, her duty to…No, he was too sensible for that, and her social influence was too important to let him antagonize her so directly; but their duty, oh yes—their duty to the firm, to all their people, to the country, to history…It was endless. Good thing they hadn't made him a duke—he'd have devoted his whole life to achieving his own deathbed canonization.

No, that was unfair. He was more complex than that. Despite all his talk there was a wily, self-serving cynicism at work beneath it. Look at the way he had shut up about her flouting of convention as soon as he realized what influence she was coming to have. And some of the things he did for friends in government would never feature in his biography either! Funny—Young John had inherited the idealism, Caspar the worldliness. Was the one any good without the other? If Caspar did get the business and failed to develop his father's idealism—that strange, mystical, loving, almost feudal sense of identity he shared with everyone who was a "Stevenson man"—what would become of the firm? What had young Bassett said?—"I wouldn't like to work for him!"

Perhaps, after all, she was wrong to push so hard for Caspar? "Stevenson men" were different from other men; they were more than just employees. They felt bound to John, and he to them, by a contract that had no legal terms—in fact, that transcended legal terms. For instance, if John was on a site and a new winding bucket was brought into use for winding men up and down a shaft, he would be in the first party to use it. He was the first "Stevenson man" in a diving suit. In the Crimean railway he had worked more under fire than anyone. The same was true of all his deputies—not because John would dismiss them for behaving otherwise, but because that was the spirit they had imbibed. But Caspar? "I wouldn't like to work for him!" Few men had ever said that about John.

Then again, perhaps she was reading too much into one throwaway remark, spoken half in jest anyway.

When John arrived, "hush of life" was written all over his face, in the very stoop of his walk. It tested Nora's sense of the ridiculous as she ran through all the repertoire of a grande horizontale to seduce her own husband, the undoubted father of eight of her children and, she hoped, the undoubting father of a possible ninth.

Meat, madeira, music, the melting glance—all her strategy foundered in his "Oh dear!" as, hand in hand, they climbed the stair to bed.

"You wouldn't leave me six months, comfortless!" she said.

He groaned. "I'll do my best for you. But don't expect too much for my part."

In the early days he had often called their love "a mountain"—meaning something grand and inspiring to dominate the whole land, not this long, weary trudge up an interminable scree.

And not all her wiles could raise him even to the most perfunctory performance. It maddened her because physically he was still the only man for her. Just to lie on him, even when he was impotent like this, and run her lips over his ear and feel his breath on her neck and his marvellous hands caressing her could turn her inside out. She trembled to be united with him once more. But there was nothing to unite with. Just the dead horse you couldn't flog.

Experience had taught her it was no good trying to arouse an interest that wasn't there. Her only hope now was to ambush him.

"We have to accept this," he sighed as she drew away from him. "It's the legacy of growing old."

It was possibly true, she thought; but she wished the sigh with which he said it had not been so contented.

In the small hours she awoke to see him standing in his nightshirt looking out of the window. The skies had cleared and it was bright moonlight.

"What?" she asked.

"There's a vixen yapping out there." He came back to bed.

She didn't want him to go straight back to sleep, so she said, "You never told me exactly what this inquiry in India is all about."

He chuckled, but without humour. "Not the most honourable thing," he said. "D'you really want to know?"

"It would be an odd wife who didn't. Whatever it is will deny me your company for six months."

"During which we'd probably meet a dozen times!"

"Curiously enough, John, I still quite enjoy those times."

"Can't think why," he said mournfully, "when I fail you like this."

Hope fled from her then and she lay back on her pillow with a sigh.

"It's not really an inquiry," he said after a silence. "We all know what's happened. We have to manage the inquiry so that something quite different appears to have happened."

"No doubt it's all tied up with honour," she said.

"It has everything to do with honour." Her sneer must have prompted him to explain it all. "The Political Branch has burned its fingers. It played a dangerous game, which, had it succeeded, would have extended English influence to a wide part of the Frontier, would have contained Russia more securely, and would have brought peace and relative prosperity to people who now lead lives that are impoverished, warlike, and rather short. I mean, it was worth doing if it had succeeded."

"But it didn't."

"Quite. And the Political Branch cannot possibly shoulder the blame. In the first place, no one knows (I mean no one can prove) that they were involved. In the second place, the Frontier peoples look upon us as bluff, hearty soldiers—simple souls with little imagination. Good targets for their local idea of sport, which is to hold ambush parties. They have no idea how devious and all-pervading the Political Branch is. And they must never find out—until we have them where we want them."

"But how will you stop them? I mean, what are you specifically going to do?"

"The Political Branch have selected a 'bluff, hearty soldier—a simple soul with little imagination' but an unbounded love for England, and I have to fix the blame upon him."

"John!" She sat bolt upright. "I think that is the most disgraceful thing I ever..."

"Oh, he will know it—in the end. He is, after all, a full colonel. In the end he will knowingly accept the blame. That will be my second task. First I hold the inquiry, where his protestations of innocence will seem most genuine, being true. Then, when we have found him guilty, on evidence that is at this moment being meticulously fabricated by the Political Branch, I must persuade him that, while most soldiers hope to sacrifice their lives for their country, on some the demands fall even more severely: They are asked to sacrifice their honour and go on living."

Nora felt quite sick at this flat recitation of treachery. "Why you?" she asked. "I cannot imagine you involved in this vile affair."

"Nor can anyone else. That is precisely why. I am known for my unflinching honesty. My probity is unassailable."

"But it could all fall to bits, John. The whole truth could still come out."

"Then I would be discredited," he said. "It is not only the simple colonel who is being called upon to make sacrifices for his country. But let us not despair, my love. At least I may certainly hope for a viscountcy out of it in five or so years' time. The poor colonel may look forward only to disgrace and obscurity." He laughed coldly. "If heaven did not already exist, we would have to invent it, just to encourage people like him."

It was small wonder, she thought, that he could not perform. How importunate she must have seemed to him for pressing so; he was a true brick for having tried. She must just hope she was not pregnant, that was all.

By the time that she knew beyond doubt that she was, indeed, pregnant again, she no longer cared. In fact, she welcomed it with a satisfaction that was almost savage; she wanted a child that John could be certain was not his. Because, two days after he had left for India, the Brockmans had sent on a parcel containing a pair of socks and some handkerchiefs that John's man had overlooked. The letter accompanying them had begun: "When Lord Stevenson left here on Saturday afternoon last…"

She didn't need to guess where he had been from Saturday night to Monday afternoon, nor the true reason for his inability to perform. Even his telegraph from Ingleton had been an arranged bit of duplicity.

She might just have forgiven him if he had spent three nights with her and one with The Bitch; at least, she would have tried to persuade herself to accommodate to it and to preserve a limping sort of love for him. But she would never forgive him the sense of priorities he had revealed. He had spared her the barest polite minimum of his time; and he had arrived so spent out as to make even that seem like a slap in the face.

She wrote to him then, the frostiest letter she could contrive, telling him that Winifred would be staying at Hamilton Place—"*my* Hamilton Place," she added in her only direct reference to her knowledge of The Bitch's existence (but it was enough, she thought)—and would be going to college this autumn and for the next two years. She added that she thought all future meetings between them should be by prior arrangement only. She ended by saying that she was enclosing another letter of the kind she might have written in other circumstances.

The other letter told him, in terms that any adoring wife might use, that she was expecting her ninth baby. She relished the deliberate ambiguity of it. *Let him stew six months*, she thought.

Chapter 30

"Hey—we're in Upper dorm, Steamer," Causton said. He made an obscene gesture. Upper dorm belied its name in one respect: it was just six steps above ground-floor level. The other dorms—Incubator, Squint, and Middle—were all one or two floors above. The thing about Upper dorm, so rumour had it, was that you could shin out after lights-out and be away wenching and boozing in the town in minutes. Blenheim, the House in which Boy was the new head pharaoh and Causton and Caspar the newest recruits to the buckdom of Upper dorm, was built on the drained bog that had so recently separated Fiennes from Langstroth. From the windows of Upper dorm Caspar could look out across a small stretch of garden directly into what had been his and Boy's mess in Purse's house, four years ago. It was hard now to remember what the bog had looked like; Blenheim and Ramilles and Malplaquet had been there for ages, it seemed.

But that room did not belong entirely to his past. It was from there, he hoped, that he was going to manage to sell his worthless stock of iron bedsteads.

"These look like the only two spare beds," Caspar said. "Which do you want?"

"Heuargh! The one nearest the window, clod!" He made the obscene gesture again.

"Good old Causton!" Caspar told him. "Say one thing for you—you know how to crack a good joke! And crack it. And crack it...Help!"

Without warning Causton attacked him—what was called a bollock fight: one hand guarding your own jewels, the other plundering your oppo's. They fought and pushed without resolution until they collapsed; self-conscious that, as bucks, they could no longer be accused of and thrashed for "ragging."

"*Pax*?"

"*Pax*."

It was nice to be back at school. The grown-up world was exciting, but it wasn't fun.

"Moncur was saying on the train that chief is going to give up School football and go in for Rugby football," Caspar said.

"He would! School football was nice brutal chaos. Chief'll ruin everything."

"It's so we can play other schools."

"And thrash them! *Bam*! *Bam*!" Causton beat clouds of dust and lint out of his blankets. Suddenly he stopped. "I say, Steamer. I had a pullet this hol."

"So did I. What was yours like?"

"Most obliging—I said sit and she lay!"

Caspar joined his laughter and together they went out to look at the new crop of roes. Like true veterans they agreed it was a crying shame there was no drumming in anymore. Old School was an already fading memory. The fabric of it was all still there, transformed into the new assembly hall; the old dorms had already been sliced up into classrooms. You could stand in them and say "My bed used to be here," but it didn't mean anything. The common room in each of the three new houses was called "the Barn" in sentimental memory, but the sweet disorder of that ancient institution had died with the closing of the Old School: no more Olympic games, no tramp fires, no grilling of chops, no tales of adventure, mystery, and terror around the smoky inglenooks (one of which now housed an organ). Boys could even be heard regretting the passing of the cramped, cold, damp cupboards in which they had done their studies.

None of them could express it precisely but all shared a sense of something lost in their transfer to these cold, healthy barracks; all felt that they were the last of a breed that had known what a school could truly be—when the boys formed one vast, independent camp and the masters a small beleaguered band, set well apart from real school life.

Now, under Brockman, the school was reaching deeper and yet deeper into the boys' lives. Unsupervised hours had all but vanished. Only divinity and Latin theme were now taught in public school; otherwise classes had shrunk to thirty boys and the masters kept them all at it, not just the saps. Evening hours were passed entirely in supervision, either under masters or under pharaohs. And even the free hours of the day were being insidiously eroded by sports that, while not exactly compulsory, were increasingly "expected." Cricket and the School's own football game (soon, as rumour said, to be replaced by Rugby football) had always been there. Now there was an ever-swelling number of newcomers. Fives had been first, then fencing, last spring it had been various Graeco-Roman games. All had begun as private enthusiasms of a master or a small group of boys, and all had swiftly joined that unofficial list of "done things." If you did not take part, you were vaguely suspect, you were letting something down—the school, the House, yourself. Solitary pleasures like horse riding and carpentry, which had enjoyed if not official encouragement then a warm tolerance at least, were the most suspect of all. They took a boy outside that all-embracing, dawn-to-dusk reach (indeed, dawn-to-dawn reach) of the school's machinery. "Machinery! Machinery!" Brockman was always saying it.

The dwindling band of Old Scholars, Caspar and Causton among them, of course, pitied the "new pots," who now could never experience school life as it should be, and who instead must pass under the yoke of saintly hypocrites like Brockman to be cowed, broken, and remoulded in the new Fiennes pattern. It was not a school; it was a factory. Machinery, machinery indeed!

"There's a young man who's grown!" Mrs. Ingilby called out when she saw Caspar coming down the lane.

"Good evening, Mrs. I. And you're still bright as a button!" Caspar said. Actually it was not true. The woman had a worried furtive look. He soon discovered why.

Ingilby himself was even worse. Not once did he look Caspar in the eye, pretending to be busy concentrating on a simple tenon joint that could not possibly be occupying more than a quarter of his mind.

"I'm right busy this time, Mr. Caspar. Lord knows when I've been busier, see thou. I doubt I s'll have time nor temper for teaching thee this while."

Caspar laughed. "I won't say I'm half your equal, Mr. Ingilby, though that's my cack-handedness, not your teaching, to blame. Even so, I'm sure I might give you a *hand*."

It was an old joke between them, but this time it did not even raise a smile.

"They say there's to be a new carpentry classroom at yon school o' thine. Happen thou could go there instead."

"Happen I could!" Caspar sneered. "I prefer here."

"Nay, I'm too ruined down with work, see thou. We s'll give it a miss this term, eh?"

"But, Mr. Ingilby…" Caspar was half pleading, half laughing. "I've really learned all you can teach—you said as much last term. I'm no make compared to you, but all I need is practice. I'll work for nothing," he blurted out, thinking that would surely change Ingilby's mind. He knew he was worth as much as any average journeyman carpenter.

Ingilby turned away. "Be off now," he barked.

And nothing Caspar said would make him speak again. When Caspar at last turned to go, he saw Mrs. Ingilby standing at the yard door. "Come inside," she whispered as he passed.

"What's happened?" Caspar asked. "I've never seen him like this. Is it something I've done?"

"It was Lord Stevenson," she said. "He come up here two weeks back and told Ingilby to have no truck with you. He isn't to let you cross the threshold of that workshop."

Caspar was thunderstruck. He could say nothing. Why had his father done this mean thing? Because of that disagreement in Connemara? No—his father was many things, but not vindictive, and certainly not in that petty way.

"Lord Stevenson said as how you was to go in the army and he didn't want you hand-labouring like this."

"But why should Mr. Ingilby take any notice of such an absurd request?" Caspar asked indignantly. "He's a free carpenter—his own master. He's not a Stevenson man any more."

"It's the pension, you see, master. He'd get the pension stopped on us."

"Never!" Caspar began. Then, seeing the woman's face, he asked, "Did my father say that?"

She nodded, lowering her eyes.

So! Ingilby had put up some resistance. His father would never have been reduced to making such a despicable threat otherwise. Of all the mean, scabby tricks!

"You rely on the pension?" he asked. "I thought…" He pointed with his eyes toward the workshop.

"The work?" she said wearily. "Nay, there's little enough o' that. They want him to teach at this new workshop in school. 'Demonstrator' they call it." She brightened. "Eay—think o' that! Ingilby a teacher in a great school the like o' yon! Without that and the Stevenson pension every meal 'ud be cat-collop and chimpings in this house, see thou."

Caspar was never one to waste time bemoaning a loss. His fury at Lord Stevenson for this piece of meanness would find its scope at the proper time, but that was not now. He had to salvage what he could; and he had to have enough turning and carving to convert a hundred of his beds during the Christmas holidays.

He went back across the yard to the door of Ingilby's workshop. How inviting and homely it looked now that he was forbidden there! His anger at his father flared again briefly.

"Mr. Ingilby," he said, "I know what has happened here and I will not ask you to risk angering my father in any way. But I presume he did not forbid you to undertake other work? Outside work?"

Ingilby, relieved that the pressures were off him, came smiling to the door. "Nay. That he did not."

"It so happens, you see, that I met a man this holiday, a fellow called Bassett, who works for Lady Stevenson. He owns a company by the name of The Patent Hygienic and Artistic Bed Company—have you heard of them?"

Ingilby shook his head. Caspar was tense with amazement at himself; this whole story was occurring to him about half a second before he spoke it, yet his tone suggested it was all stale, tedious background information that had to be trotted out before he could get to the point.

"Well, we were talking about a new bed he has designed. It looks like a cast-iron bedstead—in fact, it is a cast-iron bedstead except for the four corner posts. Now they are to be made in wood—turned and carved, you see?"

Ingilby nodded.

"One of his problems—it happened with his last design: that was for an *all*-wooden bed—one of his problems is that the furniture-making quarter of London is all small and crowded and on top of itself. You can't keep anything secret there, see. Things get copied overnight. So he was going to have these wooden corner posts made in France. However..." He drew in a deep, proud breath and smiled his broadest. "I said bugger that! London tongues may rattle like Eskimo teeth. A Yorkshireman knows how and when to keep a secret—especially if there's a goodly bit of clink at the end o' the road. The short of it is, Mr. Ingilby, my friend Mr. Bassett is willing to commission you to turn and carve four hundred corner posts between now and the first week in December..."

"Nay! I'd never do it!" Ingilby interrupted.

"You and Thomas would."

Thomas was the eldest boy, the one who had first brought Caspar here.

"Nay. He's to stay in school and better himself."

"He wouldn't be the first bright lad to be taken out of school when the family fortunes demanded it. Thirty pounds, Mr. Ingilby—thirty pounds is what you're turning away. Plus ten pounds for materials. Between now and December—think! A lot of money."

He could see Ingilby was thinking furiously. It was a lot of money.

"Have ye a drawing?" he asked.

Caspar took a sheet of paper from his pocket and showed Ingilby the profile he wanted to have turned in mahogany. "And if you'll open the big door and drag your bench half out here, I'll carve you the top part as a pattern in half an hour. Just so's I don't set foot inside—as Lord S. forbade."

He shouldn't have brought up the reminder. Ingilby almost turned the whole idea down then and there. He could see fear in the man's eyes, fighting with his desperate want of those thirty pounds. As he watched the man's struggle, Caspar prepared to say: "Remember, Mr. Ingilby, I will one day be running Stevenson's. What will happen to your pension then if you fail me now!"

Fortunately he did not have to say it. But an hour later, all the way back to school, he kept thinking of those words and turning over with shame the knowledge that he would have said them if it had been necessary. Business can be cruel, he realized; until then he had not been sure he could match its cruelty.

He was late for lockup and had the misfortune to be caught by Brockman, who was just leaving Blenheim, no doubt after some talk with Greaves, Caspar's housemaster.

"Where have you been, m'boy?" he asked sternly. He always pretended to hold a fair trial before he hanged you.

"I went for a walk, sir, and didn't notice the time I'm afraid. Is it after lockup?" The empty playing fields alone were an answer.

"Mustn't turn into a dreamer, m'boy. Your father was here just before he went to India, and asked us to make sure you shape into an alert and zealous man, fit for the queen's commission. Report yourself to your Head of House. Say I said you were to have six of the best. At once."

"Sir!" Caspar, sensing that Brockman was about to grip his arm and say something manly and soul-bracing, barked out his acceptance and turned on his heel. He did not see chief staring after him with a worried frown.

The shite! Caspar was thinking. *He knows Boy is the new Head of House. He could at least have said "your brother."*

Chief had one thing to his credit: He had abolished all bare-bottom swishings. Everyone kept on his trousers now. It was amazing what a cushioning even the thinnest worsted made.

Boy, so lost and pitiful in the formless outer world, was in his element here as Head of House. Every hour of the day and night had its prescribed pattern. Every rule governing behaviour was written down. Now it was not mere spoken tradition that said only pharaohs could wear their shoes laced ladder-fashion, it was House Rule 79…and so on for a hundred and eighty-two other regulations, ranging from expulsion offences, such as wenching, down to the deliberately vague catchall: "A breach of Common Sense is a breach of House Rules." In this structured world Boy was king. Aloof, unbending, respected, feared—the very best type of Fiennes man.

"Well we'd better beat you then," Boy said, as calmly as if he were making the most casual arrangement. "Go and call all out of the Barn." He and Caspar were alone in the head pharaoh's study.

Caspar chuckled. "Doesn't the incongruity of all this strike you?" he asked.

"I don't see any."

"After what you and I went through? Is what happened this summer no more real to you than this—this bit of idiocy?"

"You're not funking it, are you?" Boy was horrified.

Caspar closed his eyes in resignation. "Boy!" he said. "I'm talking about contrasts. I'm talking about the real world and the real rules out there—and this…" No word sufficient to convey the stupidity of it occurred to him.

"These rules are real, too—as you'll soon find out, my lad," Boy assured him. He was very impartial—it was exactly the way he would have spoken to a new pot down for his first beating. Boy went to the corner cupboard and selected a cane. He swished it once or twice, not threateningly—just as he would have swished it had he been alone in the room. "Good," he said. Then, turning again to his brother, asked, "What are you waiting for?"

"The impossible, I suppose," Caspar said, and he went to call all out of the Barn.

For Caspar it was nothing. Six years of being flogged had taught him almost total indifference to the momentary pain of it. Indeed, he was hard put not to laugh at Boy, who could only be a "Fiennes man," never a man; who, in the world of men, would always be Boy.

Caspar went straight from the beating to his study, where he wrote to Bernard Bassett, asking him as a favour to get some trade cards and a letterhead printed, saying The Patent Hygienic & Artistic Bed Company and an address of convenience at some small shop near Bassett's office, and to write back to Caspar on one of the sheets, appointing him agent and asking him to "get wooden corner posts made as we discussed." He also wrote to his bank asking for a further fifty pounds to be made payable at the West Yorkshire and Dales bank in Langstroth, saying that, after wide discussion with buyers in the trade, he had detected a market for a new design in beds and that, by the happiest chance, the beds he had bought were uniquely suited for adaptation. With the money, he explained, he would be able to adapt a quarter of his stock by the new year—the sale of which would pay off a hundred pounds of his borrowings.

He had no idea that his mother was the Machiavelli behind the entire operation, but he was sure that both Bassett and Chambers reported everything back to her. He didn't think Chambers, alone, would advance another penny; but these two snippets might just make his mother curious enough to make her tell Chambers to go ahead on her account. That, as he saw it, was his gamble. To his mother he merely wrote that he had had the most marvellous idea for his beds and, although it would delay his selling efforts for a while, it would certainly double his profits in the long (but not so very long) run.

To his father he wrote not at all.

Ten days later, with Ingilby's workshop in full operation and turning out ten to twelve corner posts a day, and with an accommodation for fifty pounds safely lodged at the bank in Langstroth, his plans took further shape. He wrote to Mary Coen, asking her to write back quickly and let him know what changes his mother was making at Hamilton Place in preparation for her winter season. Two days later he had her reply—new furniture from Watson, Bontor…new paperhangings by Trollope & Sons…new lamps from Miller & Co…and so on, all minutely described. Caspar copied it all out and sent it to Mrs. Abercrombie, the lady who wrote for *My Lady's Drawing Room Companion* and who had given him her card outside Avian's furniture shop. When his revived beds were ready, he wanted to use her again—getting her to write an article to puff the beds up in some way. A few days later she wrote back an embarrassingly effusive letter saying that she had been at her wit's end and that he saved her life, quite literally. Caspar was pleased for that. He was even more pleased at the fuss made over these trivia in *My Lady's Drawing Room Companion.* His mother, in one of her letters, mentioned "these very distressing revelations in that revolting periodical" but it was not until the Christmas holidays that he got to hear what a furore it had caused in Hamilton Place. By then his whole view of the world had undergone a profound transformation.

Chapter 31

IN THE MIDDLE OF THE PREVIOUS SUMMER TERM GREAVES HAD INSTITUTED A Fiennes Mathematical and Philosophical Society, which had at once become known by the vulgar as "Sapsoc." Members met twice a week in the evenings to listen to Greaves reading from scientific papers (a special *exeat* from the restrictions of lockup being granted for the purpose); then they would assemble again after Sunday chapel to discuss the notions they had been presented with at the evening meetings.

The summer meetings of Sapsoc had been thinly attended. But autumn had swelled the ranks. There was a new feeling in the air at Fiennes as in the world in general. Science was no longer a mere provider of wonders and curiosities; it was beginning to assemble large systems of thought that explained life and the universe in solid and intellectually satisfying ways.

This was apparent from the very first meeting of the autumn term, when Greaves read Professor Thomson's papers stating the laws of conservation and dissipation of energy, together with Clasius's classic statement of the Law of Thermodynamics.

"You see, gentlemen," he said, "the First Law, as we may call it—Professor Thomson's law—states that you cannot get something for nothing. Energy cannot be created; it cannot be destroyed. It may only change its form—light may turn into heat, sound may turn into heat, and so on. But no new energy is made. No energy is lost. But wait! 'Not so,' says Clasius. 'Energy may not be lost, but it can become unavailable. We may know it is there, but be unable to get at it, unable to use it.' Thomson says you can't get something for nothing. Clasius says you cannot even get back all your investment. After any transaction involving energy, some of it is forever unavailable. It has gone to join a vast pool that will one day be lowest grade—a pool that is ever-growing, a pool that will one day be the entire universe. Yes! The universe *is* running down! Its end is one universal bath of the lowest grade heat evenly spread. No light, no dark. No hotter, no cooler. No moving, no still. No centre, no outside."

To his hearers it seemed marvellous. Theirs was surely the ultimate privilege, to be sitting drinking cups of tea in a small drawing room in a remote Yorkshire dale, while comprehending—in a sense, overseeing—the (comfortably distant) fate of the universe. Caspar's contribution to the discussion was to point out that if the natural order was to even out concentrations and rarefactions of energy and make, instead, one level miasma, wearing down the peaks (so to speak) and filling the valleys, then mankind was always working counter to the natural tendency, always making and exploiting bigger concentrations and differentials.

As an example, he took steam engines, which had begun by working only with atmospheric pressure at about fourteen pounds an inch. Now there were engines working at hundreds of pounds an inch. In the future they would have engines working at thousands or even tens of thousands of pounds to the inch. Mankind, working in this way, would, he suggested, turn the world into the one shining exception to this pessimistic rule of universal running down.

Greaves said it was an interesting comment but he did not wish the discussion to take on a purely utilitarian, not to say industrial, tone; he wished them instead to concentrate on the grandeur of the philosophical scheme that linked so many distinct discoveries and ideas into one simple set of universal laws. Caspar privately thought that his own notion of mankind thumbing its nose at universal laws had far more grandeur.

But all these ideas were swept aside in the third week of term when Greaves began serial readings of the newly published *On the Origin of Species by Means of Natural Selection*, by Mr. Charles Darwin. It stunned his hearers; there was no doubt in any of their minds that they were listening to a profoundly revolutionary text. Being an elite of boys with strong interests in natural history and science, they all knew something of the earth's history as the geologists had revealed it. They knew the world was vastly older than the six thousand-odd years calculated by Archbishop Ussher. They knew the rocks and sediments and glacial deposits—even the water-eroded caverns that twisted through the limestone under their very feet—were evidence of processes that had consumed tens of millions of years, perhaps even hundreds of millions. They knew the different strata contained fossil relics, evidence not of one universal flood but of thousands of separate extinctions spanning aeons of time. They knew that the sheer number of species was already uncountably vast and, if one added extinct species, too, showed minor variations and similarities that amounted to caprice—a sheer display of virtuoso talent—if one assumed each to be the result of a separate and deliberate act of creation.

But this lumber of knowledge lay about in different attics of their minds, so to speak, half glimpsed and rarely dusted off. Not until Darwin's words fell upon their ears did they put all these notions together and see that they were but distinct parts of one and the same puzzle. Life had continuously evolved from life. Those fossils were not dead. Their legacy—the first eye, the first bone, the first brain—survived and changed eternally. That one eternal thread of change locked all of life's myriad forms into a single web of unending endeavour—to survive, to triumph, to multiply.

For Caspar these ideas were a transfiguration. It was suddenly clear to him why life was such a struggle—not his life, everyone's life: in obedience to universal law. A thousand forms were competing for a hundred places; most of them must lose. And even the winners were not safe, could not rest. Others were waiting, always, to wrest the laurels from them and send them down into that dark limbo into which they once sent their vanquished. Success and failure, riches and poverty, abundance and scarcity, privilege and deprivation...even such imponderables as optimism and pessimism, hope and despair—these were all mere aspects of one universal law of life: *survive!*

Throughout history there had been people to rant against these inequalities, advocating their abolition. Suddenly it was brilliantly clear that such abolition was possible only by abolishing life itself. One could pass a law banning shadows but the only way to carry it into effect was to extinguish all the lights.

He did not, however, offer these views to Sapsoc at large. Once bitten was twice shy, and he was not going to have Greaves accusing him of proposing that the modern capitalist was the most advanced form of life on earth (even though, thanks to Darwin, he now considered that to be most probably true).

The great thing about all this, in his view, was that it gave a single frame of reference to everything. From a narrow point of view you could look upon his struggles to make a success of this little business his mother had devised as mere greed at work, or vanity. But take a broader and altogether grander view, and you could see it as the working of a universal law through him. If life had any morality, it had to be derived from life itself, from life's own operations;

it could never be imposed from outside by mere thought or wish. You had to look at what was actually happening—had happened from the beginning until now—and derive all your rules from that.

And the two greatest rules, sanctified by all of history and prehistory?

Survive.

Succeed.

They justified everything. Even (or, perhaps, especially) the impending battle with his own father.

Chapter 32

THE REST OF THE FAMILY ENJOYED THEIR CHRISTMAS AT MARAN HILL. CASPAR stayed alone at Hamilton Place, leaving early for the ice-cold barn out in rural Holloway, returning late after fitting out a dozen or so beds with their new wooden corner posts. Even Christmas Day he spent out there. But on the afternoon of Boxing Day the last bit of lapped tubing had been sawn out and the last wooden replacement was in and given its final coat of boiled linseed oil. One hundred of his bedsteads had been transformed.

Weary but by no means exhausted, he threw wide the barn doors and let in a flood of thin December sunshine. It was a revelation, even to him, the author of the transformation. Not only were these beds unique, they were uniquely handsome. If they didn't sell at between two and three pounds each, he had learned nothing that very first day in the business. He had turned what was mere bravado, in his letter to his mother, into living, gleaming fact. He looked at the hundred he had transformed and could not quite grasp or believe that he had done it. Not even the aching muscles of his back, the ice in his boots; the sensationless fingers stuck onto his painful hands, not all of these together could quite convince him that the achievement was his.

He found a farmer with a hangover in need of fresh air, and persuaded him, for a modest fee, to cart one of the beds in to Hamilton Place. He wanted the story he was about to give to Mrs. Abercrombie to be at least superficially true. By the time they arrived at Hamilton Place, the sun and the farmer's hair-of-the-dog whisky had restored Caspar to all his vigour.

Mrs. Jarrett was annoyed at having to cope with this single member of the family. Everything was shrouded. The servants were all on board wages. Caspar's presence, though only from late each night to early each morning, consumed a quite disproportionate amount of the household's limited resources.

And especially on Boxing Day, when there was traditionally a grand ball in the servants' hall. So she was doubly annoyed when Caspar returned early with a strange bedstead and asked her to arrange for it to be put in his room in place of his present bed.

"What d'you think of it?" he asked her.

It was, she had to allow, a very handsome bed.

Then, suddenly, she didn't mind his coming home early at all. It answered another of her problems—the ghastly-looking Coen girl, who would have ruined any ball. She could be put to looking after Master Caspar—and if any girl was safe with a young man, it was Coen! Serve him right, too, for interfering in the summer like that. He'd have to look at her awful disfigurement all supper. Anyway, she'd suspected the girl as the source of that monstrous article in the *Companion*, so it would serve her right to miss the ball. She made Coen carry the bed up and arrange it in Caspar's room, crippled foot or no; there was no reason why anyone else should stir themselves.

Caspar, to loosen the knotted muscles of his back and shake the farmer's whisky from the channels of his head, went for a long ride in the park and then back home for a hot bath. In the meantime his room had been transformed. Mary had not only seen to the bed, she had filched decorations from downstairs and decked out the whole room, even hanging little swags of tinfoil around the paraffin-oil lamps. A soft, warm light suffused every corner. Mrs. Jarrett came in and looked at it with a surprising approval. The prettier the room, she went away thinking, the more it'll show her up.

Mary purloined a lot of edible delicacies from downstairs, too. She put them out while Caspar was behind the screens, taking his bath. His eyes went wide in greedy delight when he came out again and saw the table.

"I'll never manage all that! You'd better pull up a chair and feed yourself, too, Mary."

"Merciful hour, sir, I daren't do that!"

"It'll be all right if I say so."

"No, sir. That Mrs. Jarrett, she'd only take it out on me after, so she would. I'll empty your bath while you eat, and put coals on the fire."

"You'll do as you're bloody well told!" Caspar laughed, making her grin at the naughtiness of it. "I've been alone all week and I've always liked talking to you. If you're worried about Mrs. Jarrett, go and shut the door at the end of the passage. When it opens it squeals like a banshee; then she can't surprise us."

Mary went and closed the door. Then she sat down opposite him and ate with as much relish as he did, and she told him what a rumpus there'd been in the house after that article in the *Companion*, and how they'd questioned every servant one by one, and how the eyes nearly fell out of her when she saw it—wasn't everything she'd told him in it! And she was sure Mrs. Jarrett suspected her. And declare to God she'd never help him again! But she laughed when she said it.

They soon finished off the wine that had been intended for him alone, so she went down for more. She came back with two bottles and a dish of chestnuts for roasting. The mood changed. Her mood changed. Before, all the while they had been eating, she had been guardedly effusive, remotely warm. A single squeal of the farther door would have been enough to freeze her back into the proper servant girl.

But now she moved about the room completely at her ease. She put a pan of nuts on the trivet, where they would roast without burning. Then she poured him a glass of wine, then one for herself. All the while she looked at him with an odd, knowing smile.

"Are they having fun down there?" he asked.

"Sure they think they are," she said, and went to look at the chestnuts. "Soon be done. Wouldn't you sit by the fire here and I'll peel them for you?"

He picked up the wine bottle and turned toward the fireplace. "Ah, go on—quench that light," she said, involuntarily raising a hand to her scars. He almost obeyed but then, feeling very bold, he walked straight to her. She watched him, half smiling, half fearful, until it was too late to back away. Gently he kissed the scarred half of her face as he had wanted to last summer. She stood rigid and shivering, as if it were an initiation.

"Why d'ye do that?" she asked. Her breath made his neck tingle.

"You're a grand girl, Mary," he said, not pulling back yet. "I know why Boy fell in love with you. I think I could love you a bit, too. I'm sure any man who got to know you well would do the same—and never even see those things."

"God love you," she said.

A chestnut exploded. Then he went and put out the light.

He sat on the chair, she between his knees in the firelight, peeling chestnuts and popping them hot between his lips with her sinuous fingers.

"You eat too," he told her.

She ate a few, and she drank a lot of wine. "How is Boy?" she asked at last. It seemed natural for her head to fall dreamily to his lap.

Caspar chuckled grimly. "I barely see the fellow. It's hard to explain. We live in the same house at the same school, and we hardly talk together. He's the head boy, you see—the quare fella. I'm one of the bad boys." It seemed natural for his fingers to steal in among her hair and begin caressing her scalp and neck. Girl skin was lovely.

She shivered and buried her face on his thigh. It was some time before he realized she was crying. Her voice fell between his legs and bounced back, strangely altered and remote, from the floor. "God, I love him. I love that fella. I think of him every night and I weep my heart out my eyes till the throat on me hurts like a lodged nail. And where's the good of it!"

He squeezed her shoulder and said, "No good!"

Her weeping redoubled. "Aren't I the one that knows it," she said. "Wasn't it me told him the same!"

Caspar was crying now, too—not having the faintest idea why. "Let me hold you," he said. "I can't bear you to feel so alone."

She slid herself up into his lap, put her arms around his neck, and lay so still he thought she'd gone to sleep.

It was marvellous to want nothing of her—to feel this pity and to know it was pure pity, to feel protective and not to wonder would it pay well.

"Go on," she said.

"What?"

"Anything you want."

He was about to tell her how altruistic his sympathy was when she added, "You'd never know the good it is to me, feeling wanted."

But when he began to caress her she said, "Will I stay the night?"

"D'you want to?"

"Do you really love me a bit?" she asked. She pulled away from him then, so that she could see his face by the firelight as he answered.

Only the pretty half of her showed. Damp with tears. The rest was black as ink. It changed her, subtly. She was just a pretty girl, not Mary; he knew he did not love either of them. Not this pretty girl. Not Mary. And, though he wanted her, and he wanted her company this night more than anything, he told her the truth.

She breathed an immense sigh of relief. "Then I'll stay," she said. Her smile was radiant.

He looked at her in bewilderment. "You mean if I had lied—if I had said I loved you, you wouldn't have stayed?"

"I would not." She was serious again.

"Why ever not?"

"Isn't there enough pain already in it?" she said.

She stood up then and went to his now-cool bath, where she dipped a flannel and partly wrung it out. Then she came back to the fire and undressed—not provocatively but just as if he were not there. She held the flannel until it steamed in the heat of the fire, then she rubbed herself all over with it.

"Servant's Turkish bath," she said solemnly.

The sight of her hypnotized him. The delights he had dreamed of all these years, the joys he had so briefly sampled last summer in York…now…here…soon…all night! A terrifying congestion gripped his throat. She was gorgeous. *A woman's body is a glorious thing,* he thought. He could not rightly grasp each passing second. Everything floated as in a dream.

She refilled her glass and came to sit on his lap, sharing it with him, sip for sip. When it was gone, she said, "Will I go to bed? This is fierce uncomfortable!"

He followed her, shedding everything on him between the chair and the bedside. But when they were in bed—his stupendous new bed—a strange coyness affected them both. They could kiss, clasp, explore each other with their hands and lips, he could lie on her, she on him, they could entwine their limbs about each other…but they both fought shy of that final penetration. Caspar thought it the oddest thing; but he could not speak of it. Their minds had become spectators of bodies that spoke in an urgent, direct, but silent language. And not the obvious animal language, either.

When he spent himself into space it was like that kind of tickling which hovers between the intensest pleasure and pain; he heard his throat chuckling in a suit for mercy. Forked high on his thigh, she said his name again and again and then achieved an ecstasy that filled him with astonishment and envy. It left her limp and bathed in sweat, broken in every joint.

Several times that night they stirred into semi-wakefulness and rediscovered all those preliminary delights while still fighting shy of the final consummation. He knew he felt closer to her then than he would if they had gone all the way.

Just after dawn he awoke to find her dressed and clearing out the ashes.

"Mary?" he said; the word fought for birth through thickets of phlegm.

"I'll bring you your shaving water in a moment, sir," she said.

"Mary!" This time it was stronger.

She turned and smiled at him. He was closer to loving her then than at any time. He patted the bed.

She swilled the ash from her hands in his bathwater and, wiping them on her pinny, came and sat beside him. He stroked her bare, damp arms and smiled up at her.

"Aren't we mad, now," she said, "to be making such a fuss of love."

"Are we?"

"When liking's so warm and love is such pain."

"I don't know." He wanted to hear about love from her, to know not what love was like, but what *her* love was like.

"I'd sooner marry a man I liked than a man I loved," was all she could say.

He gave her arms the slightest tug, but it was enough to pull her face down to his. He kissed her so softly they barely touched. "I like you, Mary. There's no one else I feel so nice with as you."

She laughed and stood up. "Yet!" she said and went back to the grate.

He wanted to ask her then if she would be his mistress. Not now, but when he had left school. He didn't really want to join that herd of bachelors who swilled around Piccadilly and Soho, getting a taste for the wild oats they would then continue to sow after marriage. Even as he thought it, he realized that was not it, not with her. He wanted her in that way, of course—how could he deny it! But also he could talk to her. He realized with something of a shock that she was the only person he knew with whom he could *talk*. Even from Winnie he had to keep back some things; but with Mary, given time, he knew there was nothing they could not talk about.

Perhaps when he knew her a little better, he could ask her. The act of asking her would itself be something he could look forward to. And the idea that there might be someone in the world he could really talk to was very exciting.

Especially as it had nothing to do with love.

Chapter 33

Abercrombie's card bore a printed address (or "direction," as his mother always insisted on calling it) in Fitzroy Square. But this had been scratched out in ink and another address written below it: Basement, 6 Cleveland Street.

The move was small in geographical terms but half a world away in terms of social cachet, as Caspar saw the moment he entered Cleveland Street. It proved to be one of those hybrid London streets compounded out of the district that surrounded it. There were houses for artisans and tradesmen who served the West End. Rooms for the living-out servants, window cleaners, and knife grinders who made a living in Bloomsbury. Rooms for City clerks. Small shops. And the inevitable sprinkling of brothels.

Number six had no basement—at least, none that was visible from the front. It was a tobacconist and confectioner's shop with a handsome bow window. Caspar went inside.

"Mrs. Abercrombie?" he asked the man behind the counter. "Does she live here?"

The man was very old. His head, disproportionately large, seemed to float in the gloom. Stray reflections of it moved in long, pale pencils of light on the sides of the glass jars around him, like ghost acolytes. He shook his head. "No," he said solemnly.

"I was given this address."

"She died last night."

"Died!"

"Or over Christmas anyway. You can't be sure, this cold." It was the tone in which he had discussed the weather with customers for over seventy years.

"Oh, Lord!" Caspar said. His whole strategy depended on getting a free puff in the *Companion*; and now it was ruined.

"What's it to you, young sir?" the man asked.

"Did she say anything..." Caspar began, and then had to fight a terrible impulse to laugh.

A joke had gone around Fiennes last term:

> Asclepius [to Crito]: Where's Socrates?
>
> Crito [who has been weeping all night]: He's dead! He swallowed poison last night.
>
> Asclepius: Damn! Bother it! [Hoping against hope] I don't suppose he said anything about that chicken he owes me?

Caspar hadn't found it very funny—too far-fetched, he thought. Yet there he was, actually halfway through asking: "Did she say anything about an article for *My Lady's Drawing Room Companion*?" when the memory of the joke hit him. Only a small attack of intense throat-clearing saved him.

The man was looking at him in bewilderment.

"The editor sent me around for her copy," he explained. "It's late."

He could see the man disbelieved him, and Caspar knew why: Anyone who looked less like an office boy or printer's devil would be hard to imagine.

He glanced down at his clothes and gave a light laugh. "Oh! My uncle is the editor. The office boy didn't come in today. I'm just helping."

The man shrugged then. What was it to him? Her rent was covered and the parish would bury her. "Go down and see," he said, nodding toward the passage that led from the side of the shop into the back regions of the house. "They're laying her out now."

It was almost pitch black. He stumbled and groped his way toward the balustrade that guarded the downward flight of stairs, the only feature he had recognized in the brief sweep of light before the shop door had closed again behind him. The darkness accentuated the smells of tobacco and spice and twist and confections...and another smell, which at first he thought was the black odour of a damp basement. But as he descended the stairs he thought it might instead be the smell of death. Suddenly he had to fight a fear of going into that room.

He knocked at one door. Silence. A laugh came from behind another door. He knocked there.

"Wait, my darlin'!" a woman's voice cried out. She laughed again.

He tapped at the third door. After a while a naked filthy child of about five opened it. Inside he glimpsed such a scene of degradation as he did not know existed. The floor was awash in excrement. There were perhaps a dozen people inside. He could not tell, for the only light and air came in where two bricks had been knocked out of the wall, high up near the ceiling. He pulled the door quickly shut and held his nose and mouth as he stumbled toward the only remaining door.

It was from this basement that the once-genteel Mrs. Abercrombie had told the world how lived My Lady Stevenson and the Duchess of Wherever and Viscountess Whatnot in their gilded palaces! He knocked at what had been her door.

"Yus?" a coarse female voice cried.

He waited out of respect.

"Yus!" The cry was petulant. He went in.

Mrs. Abercrombie, a pauper, was obviously due no very great respect. She lay, for the most part naked, on a dirty deal trestle that was not one of the room's furnishings. In fact, the room had very few furnishings: a mattress and blankets on tea chests in the corner. A big box trunk, open and almost empty. It held a few items of patched and faded clothing, well rummaged about by the two drunken crones who were now sitting in a giggling stupor beside the corpse.

"If you come fer the writin' desk, my lovely, you're too bleedin' late! *'E* got 'is thievin' 'ands on it." She nodded at the ceiling.

He looked around the rest of the room and saw it was completely bare. At least Mrs. Abercrombie had had a window—all three square feet of a window. There was nothing in the way of paper. If there had been, it would have gone by now. The only hope was that it was in the writing desk, if she had written any copy at all.

He looked at her corpse; it was almost a skeleton already.

"She was starved," he said, more to himself than to the women.

"Yus, but it wasn't that what done for 'er," one of them croaked.

"No," the other cackled. She showed no teeth. "'Twas the cold, see."

He began a silent prayer for her soul but the woman who had spoken first suddenly sprang up and whipped away the threadbare shift that half covered the corpse. "'Ere!" she cackled. "Want to see if she can still wink at yer?"

And, howling with helpless, drunken laughter, the two old hags tried in vain to pry apart those cold shanks of thighs, locked in rigor.

Caspar fled to the sane, mean world that began at the stairhead; the mad laughter pursued him all the way.

"Yes," the old tobacconist said in the same conversational tone as before. "It's the Other Nation down there, young sir. She had no right there, either."

Then Caspar saw he was holding an envelope between his fingers. "Would this be what you were sent for?" he asked.

With relief Caspar walked to the counter, but the man clutched the envelope to him. "What would be the name of the periodical again?" he asked.

"I told you," Caspar said, his heart beginning to race. "*My Lady's Drawing Room Companion*."

The man looked and pieced it out, syllable by syllable. Caspar felt sure he would then hand over the letter, but he looked up and said, "And the address, sir?"

Oh, Lord! Caspar thought. *What was the bloody address!* He had seen it. "There's two," he said, playing for time. "The printer's, and the office. Which has she put?" He did not expect the man to answer.

Think, think, think! It was a part of London he'd never been to. Near the Strand—that was the picture he had. And a tree. That was a picture, too. It came to him suddenly and he almost shouted it out.

"Wych Court, is it?" he asked in careful carelessness. "Or the other one?"

Mercy! The man handed him the envelope, and then snatched it back. "Is she due any pay for it?" he asked.

Caspar prepared to face him down. He had already purloined the writing desk; he wasn't getting any more—not without working for it. "What would the cheapest respectable funeral cost?" he asked.

"As a favour?" the man said. "I know an undertaker as'd do one for a tenner."

That probably meant he could get one done for five.

"I'll see what my uncle says," he said, pointing at the envelope. "That may be worthless old rubbish." Still the man would not let go. "And we'll never know unless I get it to him in time for this issue, will we?"

That finally persuaded the man.

"Get those two hags out of her room at once," Caspar said. "I'll be back this afternoon."

He found he could not forge her writing well enough to pass inspection, so he wrote the whole thing out again in as close a hand as he could manage. She must have been very cold and weak, he thought. And he personally wouldn't have given tuppence for the information—a thin gruel of tittle-tattle. At the end he tacked his own nugget:

> There was a time when every article in our households had a voice. To those with ears to hear, it spoke of its maker, for in those halcyon times no line divided artist from craftsman. How different are these

days of ours, when artists who have been no nearer to our Birmingham iron foundries than the ticket office of Euston station mould sprays and wreaths and ferrous tributes to be poured out in limitless repeats by ironfounders who, though they may yearn to add a touch here, a fillip there, may not deviate one hairsbreadth from that which the remote artist has dictated.

Worst to suffer are those intimate articles never seen on public display, most especially that abomination, the French cast-iron bedstead. Leave it in a hotel in Dover, and it greets you next night in Reading, next in Macclesfield, next in Clitheroe...Dumbarton...John O'Groats. And think not, gentle reader, to escape to Iceland, for the man who so sprinkled the bedchambers of this fair land of ours with his deadening uniformity is even now in ballast for Reykjavik, you may be assured.

How fortunate we are, then, that among those emporia which are universally acknowledged as leaders in taste and elegance there is at least one, Avian's by name, where they are prepared to reverse this dispiriting trend. How fortunate, too, that we have at least one noted manufactory of beds, The Patent Hygienic & Artistic Bed Company, where the artist works beside the craftsman, and both have their voice. The result is a bed that is sturdy cast iron in its utilitarian parts and elegant hand-carved wood and wellfound brass in its artistic *achievements*. [Caspar italicized the word to give it an heraldic ring.]

Are we equally fortunate in our arbiters of excellence? It is they, the great ladies who lead London Society, who, by their patronage (or lack of it), will breathe life upon, or crush, this tender flower of artistic revival among the leviathan outpourings of smoky industry. It seems the question is already answered, for Lady Stevenson of Hamilton Place ("Of course," I hear you say) has installed the very first of these new beds in her son's room, and more, we understand, are to follow. And this, *mirabile dictu*, is before the beds have even appeared at Avian's! Other noted furnishers, we understand, hold the manufactory in siege for their supplies.

He bought a day suit off a surprised footman of about his own build, had a cab brought around to the back door, and set off for Wych Court. It was early afternoon.

Wych Court was in a seedy part of town, not quite Holborn, not quite Inns of Court, not quite Fleet Street. But it was quite the best centre for secondhand books, quite the worst for dirty books, and quite the liveliest for editorial offices of journals and magazines. If Grub Street had an heir in modern London, it was here, just north of the Strand.

Caspar told the cabbie to wait. Then he ran upstairs to the *Companion* offices and, putting on his cockiest Yorkshire, asked for the editor. It was a superfluous question. The editor sat on a six-inch dais in lordly isolation, three feet from his assistant, on the right, three feet from his clerk, in front of him, and three feet from his copytaster, to his left. The whole office was half the size of Caspar's bedroom.

"Mrs. Abercrombie's copy," Caspar said. "She's sorry she's late, but..."

The editor groaned. "Put it there," he said pointing to a deep basket on the clerk's desk. He had the face of a henpecked eagle, fierce from a distance, hesitant when seen closer to.

"Nay," Caspar said. "She wants an answer and some money at once. It's very hot is this. And if ye don't buy it, I'm to take it on to the *Realm*."

All four looked at him with open mouths. They were obviously finding it difficult to believe that Mrs. Abercrombie had issued orders so peremptory—or even that she had issued orders at all. The editor began to splutter in a high-pitched whine. "She...she...she what!"

"Mrs. Abercrombie?" the assistant said.

"I don't believe it!" the copytaster added.

Caspar looked at the clerk, who just grinned back at him encouragingly.

"Are ye going to read it or aren't you?" Caspar asked impatiently. "She's very badly and I'm to get her physic on the way home."

"Hot?" the editor asked. "What does that mean...*hot*?"

"You just read it."

At least he looked at it. "That's not her hand," he said.

Caspar swallowed. "I told you," he said "She's badly. She spoke it out and I took it down. Except the last bit," he added defensively. "She just told me, like, what she wanted and I wrote it meself."

The man flipped through the sheets. "Usual rubbish," he said to his assistant. Then Caspar saw his eye get caught by the addition. He read a few lines, darted a sharp look at Caspar, resettled himself in his chair, and read again from the top.

The clerk pulled a face that said *Good for you!*

The editor finished and looked at Caspar with the deepest suspicion. "You wrote that?" he asked.

"Aye," Caspar said belligerently. "What's wrong wi' it?"

"Yorkshire tyke like you!"

"Oh ah!" Caspar said. "Just because we don't talk soft, like you, you all think we've no education up there."

"Where did you get yours, may I ask?"

"Sheffield Wesley College."

The Sheffield Wesley College had taken a whole-page advertisement in *White's Directory for Leeds, 1853*. It being out of date and Nora having no further use for it, the book had hung in string-looped sections in the boghouse at Quaker Farm last summer, to be used as lavatory paper. Caspar, thinking the prospectus for this school made it sound a much more progressive place than Fiennes, had torn off the page and kept it. He could have told this man everything about the Sheffield Wesley College.

But the pat assurance of his answer seemed to satisfy the editor.

"If she's so sick, how did she get this information?" he asked next.

Caspar fidgeted with weary impatience—like, he hoped, a man deciding to go to the *Realm* instead. "She told me where to go and I went out and got the information for her," he said.

"Where?"

"You may not believe me, sir," he said with light sarcasm, "but I went directly to Avian's and this Patent Bed place out in Holloway. I'm well known for being devious."

The man suppressed a smile. "Whom did you see at Avian's?"

Caspar looked at the ceiling. "Mr. Vane…" he said, counting off his thumb and raising a finger as if he were about to begin a list. But the editor held up a hand.

"Very well, lad. Very well. I just had to make sure. Now let me tell you something: If you can find out things like this and write about them in this manner, then you are wasting your time running errands for stupid ladies who can't put two words together without boring the world to tears. You could put that Wesley College education of yours to work and make a very decent living, for a lad your age." He looked again at the paper. "Did you really write this?" he asked.

Caspar nodded, hoping it didn't show—the way his hair was bristling.

Dramatically the editor separated the sheets containing Caspar's writing from the rest, crossed out the two words 'we understand' from the final sentence (for even editors must justify their existence), passed them to his clerk, and said: "Rush that down to Turner's. Set and print, word for word, tomorrow's issue.

Make sure it's in tomorrow's issue, now. Cut Spring Fashions from the bottom. *Shift! Shift!*"

When the clerk ran out, the editor turned, still with that dramatic largesse, to Caspar and said, "Now, lad, I'm going to astonish you, I'm going to pay you five pounds for what you brought here today. That's fifty shillings for what it's worth and fifty shillings to encourage you to…"

"Ten pounds," Caspar said. He was only thinking of giving Mrs. Abercrombie a decent burial, but he saw in the other man's eyes that he was going to get it. The fight that was coming was pure commercial sparring.

For five minutes they argued, Caspar feeling absolutely in his element. It was only when he threatened to go to the *Realm* with all his future discoveries that the editor reluctantly agreed to ten pounds.

"Make up your mind to it," Caspar told him. "It'll be twenty next time—and even more in future!" His mother had dozens of friends, and he could sell them one by one! "And the stuff'll be a lot better than this rubbish about beds." He listed three or four grand ladies he could sell right now if he wished. It was enough. He knew he'd get his twenty and more. What on earth had he been worrying about beds for! Why hadn't he seen the possibilities when Mrs. A. had come to him first! Time to sharpen up his instinct for business—if he had one.

He went home via the tobacconist in Cleveland Street and handed over seven pounds; he was damned if he would pay ten for a five-pound funeral. The man was surprised to see Caspar in his working-class clothing but it shook him into accepting the seven instead of the ten. Caspar put that fact away, too: A dramatic change could unnerve people and make them accept things they would otherwise reject.

He told the man he would come to the funeral, which was to be tomorrow at St. Marylebone's—that was to prevent fraud between him and the undertaker. Caspar had no intention of actually turning up. Then he went home, had a bath, read a few papers, and waited for Mary to come, though there had been no arrangement.

The house was long silent by the time she came tiptoeing down the corridor and stole into his room.

"I'd given you up," he said, delighting in the feel and warmth of her.

"I had to wait till I was sure they were all asleep."

"I mean I thought you might not want to."

"Ah, ye were so careful of me last night, don't I know I'm safe? And sure I like it too."

Again he wanted to ask her to wait and be his mistress in two or three years; but still he fought shy of the words. Anyway, it was so lovely to hold her slim, graceful body and to know it would always be there for him.

She was gone before he awoke.

In the end he went to the funeral, where he was the sole mourner. He and another man, someone from the undertaker's, easily managed the coffin between them. By the time he had tipped everyone, from vicar to sexton, there was none of his—her ten pounds left. He was glad then to have seen her go properly, even though half of him kept reminding the other half that the Mrs. Abercrombies of this world and those other basement dwellers were the inevitable and essential victims of progress. He had to keep wiping those pictures from his mind. It was the only time he ever envied Brockman his gift for ignoring all concrete and down-to-earth considerations and sticking exclusively to lofty, abstract ideals.

Then, the Stevenson office being so near (and his father so far), he dropped in to see the people he had known from his childhood up. Among them was a new face—a man introduced as Ewart Hodge, a production engineer from the Stevenson steelworks at Stevenstown. He had come to London to report on a new Swedish improvement to the Bessemer system of steelmaking. He ended up taking Caspar to a pub for lunch and filling half his afternoon with steelman's talk.

He left Caspar in no doubt that the future in steel lay elsewhere than in the furnace shed or the hearth. "The big, bold man with the burn scars on his hands and face," he said, holding forth his own pitted fists, "has gone as far as his nose and eyes can take him. Now it's the turn of the man with the microscope and the bottles of chemicals. This Swede now, fellow called Göransson, very clever. He's shown how to make any grade of steel—*any* grade—by stopping the Bessemer converter at the proper moment during the blow. But he's using that Bergslagen ore, see—no phosphorus. So what are we going to do with our phosphoric ores, eh?" He winked. "The fellow with the test tubes is your man to tell you."

And though Caspar was merely filling in time until the *Companion* came out, he left that pub, where Ewart Hodge was still quenching his vast steelman's thirst, with his enthusiasm for industry fired to a new high. He saw it all so clearly. War, the soldier's trade, was increasingly being reduced to minor skirmishes, where civilization clashed with primitive and barbarous peoples. Among the civilized peoples themselves war was perhaps already becoming outmoded. After all, war was no more than an extreme form of competition; and did not trade and industry now offer a much more effective and direct means for countries to compete?

He could imagine the history books of the future with their descriptions of the Great African Steel War, in which England triumphed over France and Sweden in the race to capture the vast steel market of a Europeanized Africa. Or, perhaps, the triumph was over America—Hodge said that in three or four centuries America might become a serious commercial rival to England. The winners would get the markets; the losers would have to buy sub-licences or come to private arrangements with victorious English companies. That was civilized war! No one would die or be executed or imprisoned. Mass starvation and poverty would be just the natural, inevitable kind—not the exceptional kind that followed traditional wars.

Soldiers would become no more than colourful policemen who kept backward or disgruntled people in order; otherwise they would be sort of national toys kept for ceremonial occasions. The officers would all be the youngest sons of the aristocracy. How grand he felt to be on the crest of history's leading wave! How dull his father was to think that the army offered any sort of future to men of ambition. Only half-men like Boy, who needed rules and discipline so badly he'd been prepared to sacrifice his manhood for them, could find a niche there.

But how to persuade first Boy and then his father to see such an obvious truth?

His intention, once he was sure the item had appeared in the *Companion*, had been to go out at once to Maran Hill and tell his mother everything—to stop her from storming into Wych Court or Avian's demanding apologies, denials, and damages. But as soon as he opened the issue and leafed through it with fingers so trembling he could hardly control them, as soon as he read the item—which was word-for-word as he had written it—and seen what a "splash cut" they had made of it, portrait of Lady Stevenson and all, he knew he had to secure his sale with Avian's first. That would be his peace offering to his mother.

Or would it? Lordy, it was a rather dreadful thing he had done, he was just beginning to realize. A little item tucked at the end of a column was one thing, but this whole-page splash! Should he go to her at once and throw himself on her mercy? No—no! Businessmen didn't behave like that; mercy was not in the business lexicon.

No. He should go at once to Avian's and make a contract. But for that he would need a bed, or several beds, as samples. So he would have to go to the barn in Holloway first. Then he remembered Mr. Vane's warning about not trying to sell anything as the Honourable Caspar. Very well—he would go as the Yorkshire Tyke. "Caspar who? Never heard of him!" That would be fun.

When he got down from his cab in Hamilton Place at four o'clock that afternoon it was already dark. He was aware of a girl's figure under one of the gas lamps but he was very close to her before he recognized she was Mary. She was crying.

"Oh, Master Caspar!" she said, in a torrent of words and sharp inhalations. "I've been dismissed. And not a penny in wages, she says. Would you ever go and tell her 'twasn't me who told that paper anything? Sure she'll not even heed me."

The article! And Mrs. Jarrett—nasty, suspicious old harridan.

"I'll tell her," he said. "You come back inside with me."

At first she would not but, in the end, he persuaded her she could not stay out in the cold. He took her into the drawing room and sent a footman for Mrs. Jarrett.

"Sit down," he told Mary, pointing to a seat behind him, against the wall.

"No!" She shook her head in fear.

"Do as I say," he commanded. "When she comes in she'll tell you to stand up. I will agree with her and speak sharply to you. We don't want her to think there is"—he fanned his fingers—"between us."

Smiling, she sat.

"Get up, you baggage!" Mrs. Jarrett said the moment she entered the room.

Guiltily Caspar rose, looking with a mixture of fear and surprise at the housekeeper. She at once became flustered. "Goodness, Master Caspar—I didn't mean to address you."

Caspar looked behind him. "Oh! Quite so—how dare you, Coen!" He sat and faced Mrs. Jarrett, who remained standing. "Now, Mrs. Jarrett," he said. "I understand you have accused this woman of writing some article in…"

"Not writing, sir. I don't suppose she *can* write."

"I can so," Mary said.

"Be silent, woman!" Caspar barked, not looking around.

"But she must have spoken to that Abercrombie person."

"Why 'must have'?"

Mrs. Jarrett smiled the smile of the supremely confident. "Because, sir, no other servant knew that bed was there. They were all busy in servants' hall. She carried it up alone."

"*You* knew it, though."

She drew angry breath. "You are not, I trust, suggesting, sir..."

"And *I* knew it."

"Or that..." Doubts assailed her.

"Quite so, Mrs. Jarrett. It was, in fact, I who wrote that article. *And* the one back in October."

"But I don't understand."

He had been too clever. He should have said it straight away, humbly begged her pardon, and smoothed the whole thing over. It might just have worked. But he had humiliated her, and she was not going to forgive it. He was now in the position of a raw subaltern who had tried to use his theoretically senior rank against the regimental sergeant major. He would be lucky to escape intact himself. There was no hope left of saving Mary.

He saw Mrs. Jarrett's face harden.

"So you will, of course, reinstate Coen," he said quickly. "You were right to suspect her. And to dismiss her. Not one breath of criticism can be levelled at you—and certainly no apology is called for."

It was a good rearguard action but it was too late. He had done the damage already.

"I will not reinstate her, sir."

"But I think you must."

"And if you are wise, sir, you will not press it."

What could Caspar do but—with sinking heart—insist on knowing her reason?

"I happen to know, sir, where she spent last night."

Caspar knew his own face betrayed nothing, but he heard Mary's gasp from behind him.

"And," she went on, "knowing that, I have the strongest of suspicions about the previous night, too."

Caspar made his mind up at once. Of course, he could not continue to sit there and bandy words with the woman. "That will be all," he told her. "Kindly see that a coach is brought to the door in fifteen minutes."

She smiled in thin-lipped triumph. "Certainly, sir. I trust I shall hear no more of Coen."

"You shall," Caspar said vehemently. "By God, you shall. You leave me no alternative but to take Coen to my mother now and explain it all."

"No!" Mary called out.

Mrs. Jarrett looked not the least worried. "And ask her to choose between a son—a mere boy, who debauches servants and writes scurrilous articles about her—and a housekeeper who has given nearly twenty years' faithful service and managed this most difficult house, without causing complaint, for five? I think not, sir! I think not. The contest is too uneven."

It was bluff and counterbluff. Caspar smiled with an assurance he did not by any means feel. But that fact made him wonder if Mrs. J. was as confident as she seemed. "That is not quite the choice my mother faces. Coen, as you know, enjoys Lord Stevenson's most zealous protection. Lady Stevenson will have to balance his anger against your act of injustice. An even contest, would you say, Mrs. Jarrett?"

It threw her off balance. He pressed home the advantage, thinking he could see her next point. "You may object on the grounds that my mother is not widely noted for her fear of Lord Stevenson. But she does not like to have the battleground and weapons forced upon her."

It almost convinced her. If Mary had not been there…if he had smiled just a little…if…if…But she gathered herself together and breathed deeply with decision. "I would happily explain to Lord Stevenson my reason. A man of his moral rectitude would not, I think, be amused at his son's cavorting with this slut of a woman. I believe his protection would wither on the spot." She turned, unwilling to argue more. "I want her out of this house in five minutes."

"At least give her the wages due," Caspar said. It was an admission of defeat.

She neither paused nor hesitated in her progress to the door. "Not a farthing!"

Caspar turned, expecting to see Mary dissolve again in tears. But she was smiling broadly.

"Aren't you worried?" he asked. "She's got us, you know."

"She thinks she has. But Lord Stevenson'd understand. He'd not be too hard on you."

Caspar pulled a face of ultimate incredulity. "He'd murder me!"

Still she smiled. "Why would he do that—and him with a woman of his own up the other Hamilton Place? Sure he'd pat you on the back and buy you a drink! Fierce pleased he'd be."

Caspar stared, open-mouthed. "What are you saying?"

"The truth!" And she told him what had happened when Mrs. Thornton had brought her back here, and how Lady Stevenson had been so interested in the other Hamilton Place it had started her thinking, and how, one afternoon off, she had consulted a map, gone to the other house, spoken with one of the servants, and had all her suspicions confirmed.

To Caspar it was an extraordinary mixture of worldly wisdom (the suspicion and its confirmation) and naïveté (her idea of Lord Stevenson's response). He questioned her minutely then, to be sure there was no other explanation.

"Does my mother know?" he asked at length.

"She left this house that day looking fierce like a lady who's bent on finding out," Mary said. "Or she'd never have started me thinking."

A footman came in—the one whose day suit Caspar had bought—and told him the carriage was ready. Caspar asked him to go up to the bedroom and bring down the small leather bag beside the bed. It contained, in fact, his working-class outfit, day suit and all. When the man came hack, Mrs. Jarrett came into the drawing room behind him.

"Ah, Bowles," Caspar said to the footman. "I'd be most obliged if, as a favour to me, you'd carry Miss Coen's bag down to the carriage. I'd be most awfully grateful, don't you know."

The man gritted his teeth and nodded. "As you ask it so particular, sir," he said, picking up Mary's bag.

Caspar was amazed that a million-volt spark did not leap from Mrs. Jarrett and frizzle up himself and Mary as they swept past her into the hall. She looked as if she had easily generated such a charge.

"A petty triumph, I'm afraid," Caspar told Mary, still in Mrs. Jarrett's hearing. "She won every other round."

He did not know why he added these conciliatory words. Certainly he still felt bitter toward the woman. But, somehow, his concession seemed to make this stupendous new secret about his father just a little bit safer from anybody's penetration.

"Drive up to the Marble Arch," he told the coachman.

As soon as they were inside, she turned and kissed him. "God love you," she said. "You're a real man, so you are. D'you know that?"

"Why on earth? A man would be some help to you in a situation like this. What are you going to do now?"

Could he tell her about his hope of keeping her one day? Wait! It didn't have to be "one day." If he made enough money on this bed business, or selling his mother's friends, couldn't he offer to keep her at once? What did it cost to keep a woman? He was twitching with excitement. She needn't ever leave him now! He needn't fear losing her. He would never have believed that was such a magical thought, but it was.

"Sure I don't know," she said. "I'll go now to the Catholic Girls' Night Refuge and I'll start worrying tomorrow."

"Where's that?"

"In Seymour Place, up near the Marble Arch—didn't I think that's what you were meaning?"

"No. I was just going up to Avian's, the furniture place. I wonder, do they shut at ten? Or would it be nine tonight?"

"Sure, I don't know. Ten, I would think, if they're like the other shops."

"Never mind. Either way I've got plenty of time." His mind was now refocussed on the business of the evening. He decided to tell her nothing for now. Make a bit of money first. Show her. Nothing to convince a person like the sight of real coin.

"Furniture?" she said. "Would that be anything to do with them articles you wrote?"

He chuckled. "You're quick, Mary. I'm going to make a little fortune out of it. That's what. And then..."

"What?" she asked, fired by his excitement.

"You'll see."

He gave her a pound and left her off at the Night Refuge, saying he'd call for her again tomorrow and she was to do nothing until she had seen him again. Then he sent the coach back home; he wanted no tale carried to Mrs. Jarrett of where he had gone.

He took a cab out to Holloway, found his farming neighbour—now quite sober and not nearly such good company—and took him to the barn to load up three or four beds. While at the barn, too, he changed into Yorkshire Tyke. The farmer demanded an extortionate four shillings but Caspar was in no mood to argue. This was his big night. All the way out he had thought—pleasurably, comfortably—of Mary, and all the things he would be able to tell her and share with her once she was securely his. But she did not even cross his mind on the way back. He was full of the two dozen ways he was going to make the sale of sales to Mr. Vane.

Arrived at the back entrance to Avian's, he sent in his trade card, on which he had written Aloysius Abercrombie. From the speed with which Mr. Vane responded Caspar knew the *Companion* article had already made its mark at the shop.

It was dark enough in the street for Caspar to be identified by his clothes rather than his face and voice. "I've a crow to pick with you an' all," Vane said in an accent quite unlike the one Caspar had heard him use before. "Aloysius

Abercrombie!" Vane spoke the name with pedantic scorn, making Caspar think his disguise had already been penetrated. But it had not, for Vane added, "I s'pose she's your aunt."

"Aye," Caspar said, thrilled at sounding so Yorkshire and un-Honourable. "As a matter of fact she is. But it wasn't 'er sent me 'ere. It were Lady What-d'ye-call-'er…Stevenson."

Vane paused, uncertain. "*She* sent you?"

"Aye. I should 'ave bin 'ere yesterday and all, but I only 'ad five beds then, and she snapped up the lot. But they've let this new lot through customs. I've bin badgering them all day…"

"Wait now, wait," Vane said; it was overwhelming him. "Your aunt is Mrs. Abercrombie? And Lady Stevenson sent…"

"Was."

"Was what?"

"*Was* my auntie. She died yesterday. But that's got naught to do with this. You wait till you see these beds of yours, Mr. Vane." He deliberately slowed to a hushed reverence. "They are something very special. Where d'you want them?" Caspar skipped to the cart through the flood of light from the open door—but not quick enough.

Vane suddenly sprang after him, caught him by the shoulder and spun him round. "Well, I'm a Dutchman!" he said and burst into laughter.

Caspar had to remind himself that this was no childish let's-pretend; come what may, he was Aloysius Abercrombie. He could not fly for refuge back to the Hon. Caspar. He stared at Vane in puzzled good humour.

"These beds," Vane said, laughing. "They wouldn't have lapped corner posts made of old gas pipe, by any chance?"

Caspar looked puzzled. "D'ye mean the famous Shoreditch Four Hundred?" he chuckled in disbelief. "Do you know about them? Nay! Surely no one 'ad the neck to offer them up West?"

Vane, still amused, nodded. "One young fool did," he said.

"'E'd have to be more'n a fool," Caspar said.

"Ah! But I think he's learned a lot since then." Vane laughed and shook his head in disbelief. "Did anybody ever tell you," he asked tendentiously, "what a truly remarkable resemblance you bear to the Honourable Caspar Stevenson?"

Caspar's jaw dropped. He looked for justice from the surrounding night. "I'm a bit out of concert with that young man," he grumbled. "You're the second person who's said that today. And the first, believe it or not, was…"

"Oh, I'm going to believe it!" Vane promised with a huge wink.

"...was that young gentleman's mother. She kept turning me around like a baked potato and saying 'Incredible!' and 'I don't believe it!' Here!" He brightened. "Do I really look like him? I mean close enough to gull his tailor?" He looked down disparagingly at his threadbare suit. "I could just fancy a nice new outfit. You don't know who his tailor is, do ye?"

That sent Vane off into another paroxysm of laughter. But he obviously understood nothing was going to shake Caspar from his Yorkshire pose, so he pretended to play along: He rubbed his hands, he patted Caspar on the back, he guffawed—he was Second Citizen wanting to play Hamlet.

Until he saw the bed.

They carried it into the shop and set it up. And he fell silent. He looked at it. He walked away and looked at it. He came close up and looked at it and felt it. He ran his hands over the carving, felt the join, tested the surface with his thumb and fingertips, looked to see how it had been fitted, looked from above, looked from below.

At last he looked at Caspar and for a moment Caspar knew the man genuinely doubted he was the Honourable gentleman.

"Two quid," Caspar said, striking while the admiration was hot.

Vane sneered. "Do the screws a good turn, matey!" he said. "I grant they're not rubbish any more, but I still couldn't sell them above a pound. No—fourteen bob's the highest I could go. But I'll take half a dozen," he added as a bright concession.

For an instant Caspar glimpsed a wearisome vista of—what was four hundred divided by half a dozen?—seventy such visits to seventy shops in seventy towns until he was seventy-times-seventy screaming with boredom. Rigorously he closed his mind on the thought, looked at Vane, saw him as Fool, as Mortal Enemy, as Goldbag—as everything predatory man has ever despised or coveted. Then he knew he was going to win. Even Vane knew it—or so Caspar told himself as he looked into the man's eyes.

"Mr. Vane," he said. "You don't seem to have grasped what I've done for this shop." He saw a lady approaching them, obviously interested in the bed. Vane had his back to her. Caspar—to Vane's bewilderment—dropped whatever he had been about to say and began speaking, still to Vane, but entirely for the woman's hearing. "Ye see, Mr. Vane, there will only ever be three hundred of these beds." (That was a fast decision, he thought, as he mentally sold off a hundred for scrap. Three hundred sounded ten times more exclusive than four hundred.) "The moulds for the iron have already been broken. The templates for this"—he fingered the wood lovingly—"are burned. I burned them meself. These beds can never be repeated. They are what we call a 'limited edition.' And look at that carving—that was done by a real artist in wood!"

The woman was intensely interested. Caspar could see that without even looking at her directly. Vane drew breath to counterattack but she cut in: "Vane!"

He spun around. "Why, Mrs. Trumpington! I do beg your pardon."

"Forgive me for wandering into these regions of your shop but—ah—that bed—is that the one people are talking about so suddenly? I have just come from Lady Fry's, where it was all 'Artistic Beds.'"

Vane was now torn in half. He knew well enough that there might be a splendid market in these beds and he didn't want to talk it down. But he didn't want to talk it up in front of Caspar and certainly not before a price was set.

"They are very new, madam," he said defensively. "In fact, this is the first we've had in the shop."

She frowned. "But I thought—"

Caspar cut in with a light laugh. "We keep getting forestalled, madam. People keep buying them at the back door, the minute they're unloaded."

"People?"

"Aye. Lady Stevenson's housekeeper, a Mrs. Jarrett so I believe, took five!"

"Hmm!" She advanced the last, vital two feet and touched the bed. She touched it in such a loving way that both Vane and Caspar knew—Vane by experience, Caspar by an instinct he was that night discovering—she was sold. "How much, might I inquire?"

Vane made the fatal error of consulting Caspar with his eyes (meaning *Be quiet*) as he drew breath to say nineteen and eleven.

"Three pounds, madam," Caspar said, leaving Vane glad his own face was momentarily turned away from Mrs. Trumpington. He froze in fury.

Caspar saw the lady wince. He put just a little hint of patronage in his voice as he added, "They are, after all, intended for a very select group of customers, madam. Perhaps madam should also know," he added, inventing as he went along, "that my company—I represent the makers—have decided to sell these beds only through Avian's, and, moreover, that every purchaser will also receive a certificate guaranteeing that the bed they bought is one of a limited edition of three hundred—which, I assure madam, is a mere handful in a market where even ten thousand is modest. So this bed is for people who will sleep happier in the knowledge that—er—there are only two hundred and ninety-nine others like them in the world. Of course…" He gave a disparaging laugh. "Mr. Vane and me—we're very happy to sleep in a bed like ten thousand other beds. Glad to have a bed at all, Mr. Vane and me."

There, he thought, looking at her with a smile that masked a deep contempt, put yourself one side or other of *that* line!

"I'll take two," she said very firmly. "Will you please deliver tomorrow."

Vane let out a long-pent breath and broke into a broad smile. "Certainly, madam," he said. "With the very greatest pleasure."

"And I," Caspar said, "will personally select two that match in every particular. Being as it's a handmade, artistic product, there is naturally some slight variation between one and another, taken haphazard. The artist's 'handwriting,' we call it."

Mrs. Trumpington thought she was being very clever. "No!" she commanded. "Make sure there is some slight difference—but not apparent to the casual glance. I'm sure I should like to point out this 'handwriting' to people."

When she had gone, Vane looked at Caspar a long while in silence. Caspar was determined not to speak first. "Well," Vane said, "since I know who you are, I'm sure you know who she is."

Caspar shrugged a gesture of ignorance; in fact, he truly did not know.

"A great friend of the Ruskins, that's who."

"Ah! And if the first seven of three hundred are snapped up by Lady Stevenson and one of the Ruskin circle, can you still think you have no market? Even at three pounds?"

"Two pounds to you," Vane said firmly.

Caspar was going to argue but he saw from Vane's face that he had nudged his luck as far as it would go.

They went back outside to carry in the remaining four beds. "There's ninety more finished," Caspar said. "And with what you're going to pay me tomorra, I can get the other two hundred done."

Vane grinned. "And the other hundred?"

"I'll sell them for scrap."

Vane shook his head. "You'll sell them to us, Yorky my lad. *We'll* sell them for scrap. I never trusted the old aristocracy much. But if you're the new kind, I'd trust you as far as I could throw that horse."

"Two shillings apiece," Caspar said. It was double their value but he had no other way of clawing back some of Avian's monstrous fifty percent profit. (His own two-hundred-percent profit, by contrast, struck him as most reasonable, considering the work and the risk.)

Vane conceded with a laugh.

"And Avian's can get those certificates printed, of course," Caspar concluded. "I shan't bother with them now."

Next morning he paid into a new account in a new bank seven hundred and ten pounds—which was a hundred pounds more than he had expected. Mr. Avian himself had asked, in purely conversational tones, if The Patent Hygienic & Artistic Bed Company had plans for other part-handmade, part-industrial products. Caspar was on the point of telling the truth (that he never wanted to see another bed outside a bedroom in his life) when it struck him that the man's tone was just too conversational.

Hastily he changed his mind and said he had many ideas for future productions, which naturally he could not divulge, but he could say that the next bed Avian's would sell would be a most handsome affair in cast iron and *marble*. And, he added (being quite used by now to thinking a split second ahead of his galloping Yorkshire tongue), what's more—the marble would not only be hand carved, but hand chased in brass.

Ten minutes later, he had signed a document parting him forever from The Patent Hygienic & Artistic Bed Company and binding him to do that which he fervently longed to do—forget beds (as vehicles for anything but sleep or dalliance) for the next five years. For this Mr. Avian had reluctantly coughed up the extra hundred.

Caspar paid off his debt of £165. 4*s*. 7*d*. to Chambers's bank; he drew out £14. 15*s*. 5*d*. to have something to rattle; and he left £460 to earn interest at two percent. The remaining £70 he mentally discounted—that would have to go to the joinery that supplied the corner posts for converting two hundred more beds. Young Thomas Ingilby could return to school this coming term.

Yet he felt oddly deflated as he walked along Seymour Street to see Mary at the Night Refuge. Business had consumed his morning and he had had to go home to change back into Honourable clothing. It was past two o'clock before he reached the Marble Arch.

He ought to feel excited. His mother would have been satisfied with fifty pounds, profit. Bassett would have been astonished at any profit at all. And here he was with a net profit of over four hundred pounds and yet feeling rather damp and dispirited. He almost wished he hadn't sold all the beds. He'd rather like to be going into another furniture shop now and doing the whole thing all over again. Then he thought he knew why he was feeling like this: He ought to be going to see his mother and making his peace with her. He ought not to be chasing after Mary. Why, then, did he not turn at once and go to King's Cross?

The maid who answered the door asked him to wait for the Reverend Mother. He stood in the lobby, twitching his kneecaps alternately in a growing excitement: Mary was here! He would take her out for a walk in the frosty sunshine in the park, and slowly—teasingly—he would tell her everything. And then they'd go and find a room for her to rent and he'd pay three months down and give her enough for the half year in advance, and then what stupendous joys they would discover all afternoon, all evening, all night. He could see his mother tomorrow.

The folded letter was in his hands before he realized the Reverend Mother had placed it there. Not one to waste words, she turned and walked back up the passage. *The Hon. Caspar Stevenson*, was all it said. He opened it.

"If you don't mind, sir," the maid prompted, holding open the door.

He floated into the street.

My darling,

I fear for love it is such a pain. I love Boy (God between him and all harm). And you love me and do not see it. And no good can come out of it. So I must go, which I do not easily or lightly but terrible weary of suffring. Do not fret for me. I know where to go now to find that land where I would be beautyfull. I fret for you and pray the hurt will heal which it must and one day you will love who loves you back. And will be lucky to have you as careful of her as you were of me. I never liked man more than you. I could love you and fear for that. Thank you for the pound which helps me on my misery way. — Mary

PS—God love you.

One reading left him hollow. A second filled that emptiness with an ache of such intensity that any real pain, however severe, would have relieved it. A third brought anger: at the beds, at his mother, at business—at the world, for filling his days with trivia while this fuse had been sizzling—at Mary for misunderstanding, for not waiting to hear—at himself for giving her the money that let her escape, for not telling her more.

But that she should imagine he was in love with her! It was monstrous. Preposterous. Outrageous. Little Mary Coen. He in love with her? Hah! He marched across Oxford Street (almost stampeding a herd of long-horned cows being driven in toward Smithfield market) and set off into Hyde Park.

A fog was building in the slow, cold air. Already you could look directly at the sun, a pink disc hanging in the frozen grey sheets that swirled sluggishly among the bare black branches of the trees. He felt drab to his very soul.

All he'd wanted to do was keep her as his mistress. To sleep with her. Was that love!

He fumed at her presumption and stupidity all the way through the park. He walked straight past Hamilton Place, feeling too upset to go in.

Down through Green Park he went. Above was an arch of clouds as black as a catafalque.

"That land where I would be beautyfull!" Hadn't he told her she was beautiful? What more did she want? What land, anyway? He wanted to talk with her too. He wanted to go to bed with her and talk with her. But was that love?

On into St. James's Park he stamped, and, though it was the narrowest of the three parks, the fog was by now so thick he almost lost his way. He had intended to go down to the Thames. It smelled only faintly on cold days like this, and the sight of water was always, somehow, soothing. But he realized that even if he reached the river walls, he would hardly be able to see his own feet, let alone the water, so he turned around and—more slowly—began to creep home. The dark of the cloud was a premature night.

That big, empty house. With that hateful woman, Jarrett. If he lived a century, he'd never forgive her.

It was a lot of fuss to be making over a girl, when all he wanted was to be in bed with her. And hold her. And caress her. And kiss that sweet…that sweet… He broke down then. Yes, damn her—he loved her! Why hadn't she told him that before!

He was leaning against a damp tree, weeping into the crevices of its bark, frightening himself with the discovery of love. He was tortured by vivid pictures of the little room he hadn't rented, the warm oil lamps that had never shone on him and her, the hot muffins and tea she had not prepared, the glowing firelight that had not gilded her glorious nakedness, that tender and ultimate joy they had never consummated, and, above and beyond all, the millions of marvellous thoughts and words and secrets they had not shared, the billion warm smiles that time now denied him.

These he thought of while the cold reached into his bones, while the snow and the dark fell all around him, while he stared into the infinite crow-blacked tree an inch from his eye. Where was she? he asked the blackness. He'd give all his money to have her here, now, and tell her of these stupendous revelations that had him racked and skewered. Money was nothing.

Chapter 34

That was the term he lost interest in school. Whatever he did, he did it perfunctorily, with sufficient effort to scrape by. His teachers noticed it and told Brockman. His fellows noticed it, too, and, in passing, carried the gossip to the House pharaohs, to Boy, to Enderby, the new housemaster, and so—again—to Brockman.

His mother had been delighted at his success with the beds, though he told her he had made only a hundred pounds' profit. He would not tell her where he banked; and she knew it was not with Chambers. She would never find it, either, however many spies she sent out, for she did not even know of the existence of "Aloysius Abercrombie."

She had wondered aloud what had happened to Mary and thought it a pity Mrs. Jarrett had acted so hastily. Caspar said nothing. He did not show her the letter nor mention the mysterious "land where I would be beautyfull" nor the fat fella Mary had told him about last summer. Had he been less of a secrets-keeper he would have told his mother these things, and she would have explained them, and he might have saved Mary as Arabella had done the previous summer.

But he did not mope and weep. He was too young and vital for that. And the hurt lay too deep. So, to his fellows, he was just "Steamer"—very much as before, except for being a little quieter, tamer…less fun.

To him, school was much worse; "less fun" wouldn't cover the tenth of it. Greaves had gone and, with him, all stimulus to mathematics. The new fellow, Enderby, was competent enough. But he didn't inspire them nor stretch their minds; nor did he constantly tie maths in with science and the natural world nor with philosophy and the world of the mind. With Greaves you always felt that maths was the source of all physical and intellectual discovery—its source, its sinew, and its bone. That joy was gone, too; and the world was drab.

Every night he thought of Mary—and anything from a dozen to a hundred times a day. It was like picking the scab off a wound; the hurt would never heal. By day it was usually her scarred face, so appealing, so gentle-eyed, so *beautyfull*, that rose before him, making him curl up and wince. At night it was her sinuous body, her soft warmth, that enveloped him. He repeated endlessly in his mind everything he could remember of their times together—the music that had overwhelmed her, the roasting chestnuts and wine, the spicy warmth of her, the feel of her damp hands next day, her hair tumbling down as she leaned above him—the curtains of cinnamon-coloured hair that enveloped him, her kiss as soft as gossamer, and—what had she said?—" I weep my heart out my eyes till it puts a nail in my throat"...something like that. He knew exactly what she had meant.

And yet the wound did, inexorably, heal. By the Easter holidays people around him were saying he was his old self again. His masters were quite harsh in their end-of-term reports, though. All spoke of his slackness and lack of effort. Only Brockman, surprisingly to Caspar, was mild. "Your son," he wrote, "has such a nimble mind and such intellectual gifts that I feel sure this term has marked a mere pause in a development that has always delighted his masters. Some minds may forge, or plod, steadily forward. Others, more mercurial, go in sprints, from which they must, perforce, occasionally rest. I hope it is so with him. He must prove it so next term."

Nora took up these points with him late one afternoon when he was returning to Thorpe Old Manor after a day out with Lord Middleton's hunt (which, after thirteen years' resistance, had finally admitted the Stevensons in '55). It had been a glorious day. The Yorkshire wolds provided one of the best countries in foxhunting England, especially when the sun was bright as summer and the air still crisp with a memory of winter. Today had been such a day. They had found at three draws and enjoyed two marvellous chases, the last one of full twelve miles to a death in midfield. Caspar had stayed on terms to the end. Now he was hacking his spare mount homeward, leading the day's two exhausted warriors behind him.

The way led over a high, tree-lined ridge, the crest of the wold between Leavening and Thorpe. The trunks laid purple bars of shadow over the sun-rich grass and mud. Caspar thought, ritually, *Mary would love this*, and the idea hardly twitched within him. He was even able to feel glad of it and to vow that he would be much more careful next time he fell in love—if ever. He wanted to return to his former notion that falling in love was optional.

Coming down off the ridge, he saw his mother waiting for him at the manor gate. Now that her baby was due she never went more than half a mile from the house. Lord Stevenson had wanted her to stay in London, near the best medical men; but she had insisted that the child should be Yorkshire born and so had disregarded him. To Caspar, his father's failure to be here was just one more cause for contempt of the man; he'd be in London with that mistress Mary had found out. It was now fairly clear that his parents could preserve only the thinnest cordiality between them. He thought his mother had taken it all very nobly. He kept a special smile for her these days.

"You obviously had a good chase," she said.

He leaped down and gave the horses to Willett, the groom, who had come up the lane with Nora and now left her to Caspar's care.

"Nanette?" Caspar asked, looking around.

"I sent her back to make some tea."

He folded her arm around his. "You shouldn't drink tea, you know."

"I won't. I wanted to talk with you."

"Ah!"

They began to walk back down the drive.

"Willett didn't rake this before breakfast. I meant to speak to him," Caspar said.

"Don't change the subject."

"Oh, I wasn't aware we had a subject."

"Well, we have: you. And your school report."

Caspar laughed. "I must say you've been marvellous about it until now. Don't spoil it."

"I kept your father from your throat only by promising to speak to you myself. What went wrong last term?"

"What went wrong was that Greaves went. And since maths is all that really interests me—at least, in the Fiennes menu—I'm beginning to feel that school is pretty shent."

"Your father is a great believer in Fiennes."

"Yes! My father is a great"—he bit off the sentence—"many things," he pretended he was going to say. It deceived neither of them.

"What would you prefer to do?" she asked, pausing.

He pressed her arm. "Come on. Must keep moving or you'll get cold."

She loved the way he was so protective of her—much more so than Young John, who seemed embarrassed more than pleased at her pregnancy.

"D'you really want to know?" he asked.

"Of course, darling."

"I'll tell you, first. Then I'll tell you where they teach it." And he rattled off for her all the things they taught at Sheffield Wesley College, from land surveying and navigation, through French and German, to chemistry and metallurgy—and, of course, mathematics.

To Nora, as to Caspar, it sounded quite splendid.

"I'll tell you another splendid thing," he said. "I quote: 'Discipline is enforced by uniting firmness and kindness. Should anyone be refractory, he is taken apart and reasoned with.' What about that, eh!"

"Is there still so much thrashing at Fiennes?" she asked. "You boys never talk about it nowadays."

"No. Very much less than it was. I suppose each boy gets an average of twenty a term, cane or slipper."

"Still," Nora said, "with four hundred boys and three terms that's twenty-four thousand lashes. It does seem excessive."

"I got more than twenty last term. Boy gave me ten of them. He's very hard."

Nora sighed. There were some things about the male animal she would never understand. "Where is this other paragon of a college?" she asked.

"Not too far south of here," he said.

She thumped his arm in her frustration. "Can you never answer a question! Secrets—always secrets!"

He laughed. "Sheffield Wesley College. I'll tell you another thing—it's an extension of London University. I could go and take a degree from there. I was thinking of paying my own fees if the guvnor didn't agree."

"You mean move there? Now?"

"Yes."

"Your hundred pounds won't last too long."

Caspar cleared his throat. "As a matter of fact, it's four hundred. Over."

And then he told her the full story of The Patent Hygienic & Artistic Bed Company. They reached the house before he had finished.

"Do you remember Tip and Puck?" she interrupted him. "I still expect them to come dashing out to meet me, barking away. D'you remember? Dear old things!"

He saw a tear trembling in her eye and patted her arm comfortingly.

She made him come into her business room, on the ground floor, where she had had a bed made up to save the fatigue of the stairs. There he finished the full tale of last December's commercial triumph.

She thought a long time and then looked at him, almost in fear. "You have the money, then. You also have a head for business—well I always thought as much. But you probably have a better head than anybody in this family."

His smile almost split his cheeks.

"I'm not telling you that in order to swell it," she said, still solemn. "But to get you to see why it might be a disaster for you to go to this Sheffield College. I can see the short-term attractions, of course. And I don't belittle them. But you would be doing your father's work for him. You would be cutting yourself off without a penny."

He drew breath to speak; then the thought got home to him.

Nora went on, hoping she was saying what he had been about to say. "You may not mind. You could probably start from nothing and build something even bigger than Stevenson's now is. You might not—because everyone in business needs luck. We've seen some very astute people ruined and no fault of their own. But, given luck, I'm sure you'd do well. Yet just think, Caspar—Stevenson's has a book value of four million. As a going concern, goodwill included, it must be worth all of six. Think what you could do with that! You would start as the richest man in England."

Caspar giggled almost in terror—these were seditious thoughts he had never dared embrace so openly. "I wouldn't own it, surely?" he asked.

"Who cares!" she said. "I don't own the Wolff Fund, but I control it, absolutely. I don't care if the man in the moon owns it as long as I have unfettered control. Don't you see!"

He saw. His heart raced. "What about Boy, though?"

She looked away. "Why d'you think I'm saying all this to you? It's for Young John's sake, too, you know. I'm very worried. In my view he would be one unholy tragedy for the firm—and for himself, if he took charge." She seemed about to say more, but no words came.

"Convince the guv'nor!" he said.

"You and I will never do that. Your father is hourly expecting to turn into Julius Caesar—or the North Star." She studied his reaction and smiled as if his calm response had confirmed something for her. "But you might persuade Young John."

He tried to sound as if the idea was just occurring to him. "I think Boy should not go up to University, you know. I think he should be given one contract to manage from start to finish. I believe he would then persuade himself."

Nora, smiling, shook her head. "He must be over twenty-one, or Stevenson will find every excuse under the sun for him. So he must go to Cambridge. And then he must be allowed to persuade himself. And above all, you must be there to pick up the pieces. If you have meanwhile shunted yourself onto the Sheffield branch line…no hope."

He nodded, too grateful to her for words.

"You know why I am doing this for you, I hope," she said. "It is not because I love you or admire you more than I do Young John. Never let yourself think that. I do this for his sake, too, as I said. He has a far stronger sense of duty than you have—in fact. I don't believe you have any. But he would quite literally kill himself before he'd admit defeat. So don't think I'm your ally and his enemy. Ever."

She saw him biting his lip, hating himself for having thought it. Touched, she added: "I'm also doing this because I believe you have something even your father and I don't have. The ability to think ahead. Your father can think two months ahead if he's forced to it. I can think two years, with difficulty. I believe (and it may be no more than a mother's touching faith in her son) but I believe that anyone who can keep secrets the way you can must be able to think very far ahead. I hope so, anyway—because that's half of what all this is about."

He rose to go then, saying he hoped it was true. He didn't want to hear any more.

"Oh, you can prove it," she said, springing the trap. "You can go back to school and leave it in two years' time with every honour and prize and exhibition going. You can please your father in every way. You can turn into the golden boy of the family. Because, Caspar, five years from now—or whenever it may be—you will need all that goodwill capital in his bank. You will need to draw it all."

He laughed, thinking he could surely go now, but she pressed on: "Have you told me everything about your poor performance last term? There was no other reason?"

He faced her uncertainly. "If you were speaking Latin, mater, I'm sure that would be what they call a 'question expecting the answer no.' " He knew she had been far too offhand when she had discussed Mary's dismissal with him that time.

"And you would be right," Nora said.

"Mrs. Jarrett told you, then? I mean, told you more than you said she did?"

"Oh, Caspar! You have this trick of saying and not—saying. What 'more' did Mrs. Jarrett tell me?"

"About Mary Coen."

"And…? And…? I'll strangle you one day!"

"And me."

Nora sighed out a vast relief. "At last!" she said. And she waited.

Caspar told her, then. Everything. It hurt much less than he had feared. He even showed his mother Mary's letter. He could see she was close to tears by the time he had finished. "You aren't angry?" he asked in surprise.

"I am," she said, without sounding it. "Of course I am. But I'm glad she meant so much to you. A lot of young men of your class simply forget that servant girls are people. They use them quite shamelessly. I would be—I would be more than angry, I would be heartbroken if any son of mine behaved like that. Never forget, even if they are not servants of ours or of the company, they are all people. Your father never forgets it. I try not to. And so must you."

He was struck by the way she said "young men of your class," not "our class." It reminded him that she had come up from quite humble origins. But how humble? He remembered that dreadful basement in Cleveland Street—what the tobacconist had called the Other Nation. Had her life been that bad? "You never talk much about when you were young, do you, mater," he said. "I often wonder what it was like. Where you lived, and so on."

"Best forgotten," she said. "There's too much future to think about."

Chapter 35

She called the new baby Sefton without even consulting John. She was making it very clear to him, in every way she could, that the child was not his. But he seemed to realize what she was at and went out of his way to deny her the satisfaction of his anger. She wondered if—as part of the famed "hush of life"—he had become unaccountably weak. Or perhaps he just didn't care? She'd served all his purposes; now she could go her ways. Neither explanation seemed very likely. The most probable reason, she realized glumly, was that he was playing some sort of deep waiting game. He was still a man to watch, and never to underestimate.

He made one or two attempts at reconciliation, but so frostily that she thought he was really trying her mood. For her part, these attempts merely strengthened her resolve that, until he turned The Bitch out into the streets where he had first found her—and where she belonged—and until their bastards were in the workhouse, there would be no reconciliation. She treated his attempts as that sort of male sentimentality which wants to keep its cake and eat it.

Naturally he would come to some of her salons and dinners, just as before—they would keep up appearances in public. And naturally, too, they would always meet to deal with the business. Too many people—too many thousands of people—depended on Stevenson's for them to put personal rancour above so much trust. Nora was aware that, for her at least, there was a certain amount of dishonesty in this. She was, in part, using the business to keep a tenuous line between John and herself. And because that line was there and had to be kept intact, she could afford the luxury of rejecting him completely in her private life. Any other wife, not having the business to cushion such indulgence, might have swallowed part of her hurt and responded to his overtures and so, step by step, have hoped to win him back.

Half of her suspected that was what she ought to be doing. But the other half set her jaw stubbornly against it. She was not "any other wife" and if it took twenty years for him to learn that—never mind. Learn it he would! She would never, never go on her knees for him.

In June of that year, when Sefton was just a month old, John had to go to Canada to head a commission whose main purpose was to unruffle a lot of colonial feathers over the debacle of the Grand Trunk Railway. He was an obvious choice since Stevenson's had refused to have anything to do with the railway from the outset. And now the main contractors, Sir Morton Peto, Tom Brassey, and Edward Betts, were all in deep money troubles over it. John had kept clear of the project as soon as he discovered that the entire railway was to be engineered to English standards—very costly and very permanent works everywhere. English standards were appropriate to England, where lines were short, population dense, traffic high, and return on capital was quick. None of that was true of Canada. What Canada needed was temporary works of a much lower standard—built to last ten years instead of a thousand—whose improvement could then be paid for out of revenue. America had proved it could be done. They even laid track held in place by nails! And generally they worked to standards that would turn an English engineer's hair white in less than a mile. But the Canadians, being still British, knew better; and they employed English engineers.

Well, they were better. They were also bankrupt. And voters were now being presented with the bill. So Lord Stevenson must preside over a commission to reconcile as many conflicts as possible, as speedily as might be, as tactfully as only he knew how, and as cheaply as the civil servants who accompanied him could manage.

Before he left he said something about time healing the wounds. Nora, determined that no mention of The Bitch would ever pass her lips, said nothing.

Caspar's final remarks of that Easter holiday conversation left a deeper impression on Nora than her response at the time had suggested. Perhaps, she thought, that was the elusive something which was lacking in all her children: a knowledge of their parents' backgrounds. Not head-knowledge but heart-knowledge. Her experience, and John's, spanned the whole range of England's two nations. In the years before they met, she had choked in cotton mills, he down sewers. They had lived during those times in the meanest slums. At the other extreme, they had been at the Palace and had been presented to the queen—as, next autumn, Winifred and Young John would be presented.

The children could not really comprehend it. To them poverty was the standard of life enjoyed by the servants. Well, Caspar didn't think that any longer. But look what a shock the discovery had been to him. The more she thought about it, the more convinced she became that the children must see for themselves those places she had known.

She said nothing to them, but that summer on their way to Ireland, instead of travelling straight through Manchester on the loop line between the Manchester & Leeds and the Liverpool & Manchester, they all got out at Victoria and were ushered, bewildered and excited, into two waiting coaches. Sefton, of course, was still with his wet nurse back at Thorpe. The four next youngest, Abigail, nearly fourteen now, Hester, Mather, and Rosalind, now eight, were with the servants in the second coach. Nora and Nanette were with the four older children in the lead: Winifred, nineteen, Boy, Caspar, and—just turned fifteen—Clement.

Abigail was furious at being put with the children.

"Why should I?" she asked fiercely.

The others rounded on her and chanted her eternal complaint: "I can't help being younger than you four!"

"Well I can't!" she screamed.

"No," Clement said, "but you can help behaving younger than the *other* four!"

Everyone laughed except Abigail, who sat glowering in the corner of her coach, breathing stertorously through flared nostrils.

Out they drove, through Chorlton on Medlock, Greenheys, Longsight, Levenshulme, Heaton Chapel, and Cringle Fields to the outskirts of Stockport. What all those names had once meant to her!

"All this was green fields when I was young," Nora said.

"Mother's got her property-buying face," Winifred teased.

"No." Boy laughed. "It's got too dirty. She's going to sell it."

Nora wondered how to make them understand what these scenes meant to her—and ought to mean to them. Caspar watched her from the dark of the diagonal corner. Winifred returned to her tales of the trivial naughtinesses that passed for wrongdoing in Bedford College. Boy capped each tale with a head-pharaoh's-eye view of similar peccadilloes at Blenheim. Caspar tried to remember the formula for compound interest, which his mind kept muddling with exponential logarithms. He knew his money had earned £5 8*s.* since December but he could not, in his head, remember how he had arrived at the sum. Anyway, he knew that to collect interest, even at two percent, was better than to pay it. Some time about last November that twelve and a half percent had really made him sweat. In ten years his £460 would be worth £561 15*s.*

At Stockport, Nora made the coachman turn left up a winding lane south of the stinking river Tame. "To Brinnington," she said. It was not far now. How curious, she thought, that Winifred should talk of property buying. The first property she had ever bought, out of the profits on the original Stevenson shop, lay just a few miles farther south at Alderley Edge. A hundred acres for a thousand pounds. If she still had it, the land would now be worth almost forty times that, what with all the fine houses that had been built out there since. But she had been forced to sell it when John's foolhardiness had nearly bankrupted Stevenson's (though only she and he knew it was that bad) back in 1849. Even worse, he had offered her back the value of all her properties when the firm was right side up again, and she had refused because (oh, irony of ironies!) the money they represented might drive a wedge between herself and him. Well, John wasn't the only fool in this family. Over a quarter million that would have been.

The coachman told her they were near Brinnington. She looked out and thought he must be making a mistake. All these mean terraces and hovels? It couldn't be! True, her family had lived in a hovel hereabouts, but it had been one of a row of only five, near the spring. All the rest was pasture and copse. This terrible sprawl must have obliterated them.

Or had it? She leaned far out of the window, seeking Brinnington Mount.

Relief! It was still too far away. Their hovel—"o'il" they had called it (or "pig coit" when the mud was at its slushiest)—was still some way along this lane.

Winifred was the first to realize what their mother was at. "Mama!" she cried in delight. "Is this where you used to live? When you were poor?"

Nora's smile was answer enough.

The young people looked out at the dreary townscape with new eyes.

"Good Lord!" Boy said.

Caspar, who had been trying to remember his compound interest sums, had just recalled with satisfaction that if his investment were left untouched for a hundred years, his grandchildren would get about £3,400; the news that these were the famous slums his mother's family had been reduced to was apposite: if he could go back a century to that profligate old squire, her great-grandfather, and tell him the power of compound interest, what a difference it would have made to his mother's life! Why were people so shortsighted? If everyone was compelled by law to invest just one pound at two percent, and if it was left untouched for two thousand years, the whole world could retire and live off the interest.

As soon as he arrived at this notion he realized there was something wrong with it. The mathematics? Surely not. But if the mathematics was right, everything else had to be right. Mathematics was the key. That's what it was for—to help you get everything else right. Some more thought was needed.

"Stop here," Nora said.

They had left the last straggle of houses behind. The fields were beginning to assume a remembered pattern, though they were all smaller than she had expected. She got down, helped by Caspar, who had leaped ahead of her.

"There were five 'o'ils' somewhere here," she said. "I don't suppose they'll be more than little mounds now. Look for some rough, low banks, sort of squarish, in a row. On this side."

About twenty yards farther along, the straggling hedgerow gave out to a large, weed-strewn patch of unfenced land. "About here?" Winifred asked. She held her mother's other arm.

"I think it is," Nora said, trying to put more conviction into it than she felt.

"There are some remains of earthworks up here," Boy called from a little way into the common.

"What a wretched place," Abigail told the world from the depths of the second coach. "Why have we been brought here, I'd like to know?"

They picked their way—all except Abigail, who, for the moment, refused to dismount from the coach—to the centre of the rough patch Boy had found. "I thought somehow it was nearer the lane," Nora said.

"What did you do all day, Mama?" Hester asked.

Nora stood in what had, presumably, been their hovel and looked around. What had she done? What had she not done! And how to begin to tell them, these plump, bright-eyed, rich children who looked so alien in this new context. In her mind's eye she saw her own little brother and sister, Wilfred and Dorrie, "not enough fat on 'em as'd grease a gimlet," as they used to say—"all skin an' gursley." How the old words came back. "Gursley!" She'd call it "gristle" now, but it wasn't the same. "Gristle" was what you reprimanded the chef for not removing; "gursley" was what you were glad to eat, just as you were glad to eat anything.

"What did we do?" she repeated aloud, trying to put a little laugh into it. "I used to chase crows for tuppence a day in those fields over—well, in the fields that used to be there. And I remember once, I must have been sixteen, in that terrible winter of thirty-six, when there was no work for forty miles, all of us went out at dead of night and—you see the field up the hill there?" They nodded, following her pointing finger. "That was in turnips. And we went up there to dig some up."

"Stealing?" Boy said, aghast.

She looked at him a long while before she nodded. "Aye," she said. "Cabbaging, we used to call it."

"You said turnips," Clement said.

"Never mind; it was just a way of speaking. Anyway, the ground was so hard with the frost that we only got out one before they put the dogs in the field. One frozen turnip between six of us! And it was the only food we'd had in two days."

"It was still stealing," Boy said.

"When you've listened to a two-year-old sister and a three-year-old brother whimpering with hunger for two days, Young John, the voice that tells of property sounds thin and far away."

"Mama!" Boy protested. "Do you know what you're saying!"

Nora answered very gently, and all the more convincingly for it. "I know exactly what I'm saying, my boy. My purpose in bringing you here is for you to know it, too."

Boy was about to reply that stealing could never be right. No circumstances could ever excuse breaking a commandment. But one look at his mother's face and he kept a troubled silence.

"We used to wash wool down there, too," she went on. "Let me see, our dad's loom would've been here, and my brother and me, we'd sit on the floor here and tie and untie the marches and knee shafts when our dad wanted to change the shedding. Of course, he'd be doing the rinks at the same time—up here." She mimed it until their bewilderment became plain. Then she laughed. "Never mind," she said. "I suppose all you really wanted to know is if we had time to play. Well—precious little. Everything we did had to be for money."

"Just like now," Abigail said, condescending to join the group. "I think you must have been mad to live here."

Nora told them then the one thing she had been determined not to tell them. The fact that the hovel was reduced to such insignificant contours made it easier. "After our dad died," she said, "I was left to look after the two young ones. Did you see that big mill near where we left the highway? There's a thousand looms in there and I tended two of them for ten bob a week. If you have difficulty imagining what hell is like..." She did not finish the sentence. "Anyway. The door of this o'il fell away." She stood where the threshold must have been. "I put a tea chest here. It was stout enough to keep little Wilf and Dorrie in, but it didn't keep Tom o' Jones's boar out. And when I came home from the mill that night, I found Wilf's arm up here in the rafters. Just the one arm."

She went to the place and almost sculpted the arm in the empty air. She had no idea how to go on; she had forgotten, even, why she had begun the story. The most of her was back there, twenty-two years ago, reliving the horror of discovering the arm, which had been shaken up there from the ravening jaws of a hungry boar. She stood with her own arms raised and frozen.

Boy came forward and gripped her elbow until she relaxed. She returned to them, smiling to show that it was a long time ago. "And little Dorrie," she said, in the conversational tones of someone winding up a tale, "was bitten by rats the following week, took badly from it, and died." She pointed at the far corner. "Over there." She turned to Abigail with a smile. "And that is why, my dear, I shall not apologize if we seem excessively mercenary to you."

Abigail tossed her head and stalked away back to the coach. The other children were glad of Nora's smile; without it the story they had just heard would have been quite insupportable. Nora, now regretting having said anything, decided she would travel back to the station with the younger ones and cheer them up again.

The coachman looked at the open drain between the land and the common and decided they could not cross it. "Go on farther," Nora told them. "I think there's a big open space up the end there where you can turn."

"Tell us some of those funny sayings you used to use," Mather said when she was settled and the carriage was moving down toward the turning place.

It was a game they hadn't played for years; she wondered if they would remember the dialect of her youth—the words she had taught them for fun.

"Down in merlygrubs?" she said.

"Depressed!" Abigail cried. She had always loved those northern words. The others all smiled in anticipation of her next question.

Nora was delighted they were taking to it so well; she had at once regretted telling them of Wilf and Dorrie. This would take the taste away.

"And a cat doesn't purr, it…what?"

"It three-thrums!" Abigail giggled.

"Don't answer them all, popsie," Nora cautioned. "What's a ne'er-do-well?"

"A shuffletoppin'," Mather said with glee.

"I liked 'glumpy and gloarin,'" Hester said. The memory was coming back to her. "That meant 'sullen and staring.'"

She glanced at Abigail and giggled. Abigail pouted and stuck out her tongue.

"And feeling 'wemmley and cocklety,'" Mather said. "What did that mean, Mama?"

"Sick and unsteady," Abigail said.

"I didn't ask you. Mama, tell her I wasn't asking her."

But Nora heard none of them for there, outside the carriage window, was the very hovel she had been telling them about—the last of the row of five. Those mounds in the field must have been something else, some earlier hovels. And another family must have moved into this one and kept it in some sort of repair; although it was now deserted, it still had a recently inhabited look about it. They all did. They were all pretty much as she remembered them.

A little way farther on they came to the turning place. On the way back she knew she could not simply drive past her old home, not having come all this way.

"Stop," she told the coachman when they were once again level with the derelict hovels.

It was quite a while before the other, leading coachman realized they had stopped. Meanwhile Nora had descended alone and alone had walked into the place that had once been "home" to her and six others. The one-room homes of the very poor are almost interchangeable even when they are occupied. Deserted, only geography distinguishes one from another. The families who had lived here between her departure and this day had left no mark she could swear was not hers or her family's. It was like stepping back twenty-two years. No! It was like eliminating those intervening years and having that terrible past come smashing through all the defensive tricks of time and memory.

The space that had held Wilf's arm could not be safely mimed in empty, open air; for there was the very rafter where it lodged. Yesterday, as it were. And there was the exact corner in which Dorrie had complained of being "wemmley" and where she had lain, swallowing air and vomiting and turning her eyes up inside her head. Nora was appalled that those terrible images had such power over her still. Of all the regrets in her life, the chances denied to little Wilf and baby Dorrie were the deepest and most searing.

A hand slipped through her arm, making her start.

"You mustn't fret, Mother." Abigail's voice. "It was so long ago. And you have all of us now, you know."

She heard herself laughing! Not in humour. And certainly not at Abigail's attempt to comfort her. But out of sheer relief at the truth of what Abigail had said. And how curious, she thought, that, of all her children, those words meant most to her when they came from Abigail's lips—sharp-tongued, selfish, self-destructive young Abigail, who could yet be softer and more loving than any of them.

She squeezed her daughter's hand. "I do," she said. "Indeed and indeed, I do."

They walked back outside. "I'm glad I came," she added as they went back to the coach. "I'm sure it won't haunt me now as much as before."

Boy came running back along the lane. "I say, are you all right?" he called.

"I am now," she shouted back. "Let's all go and eat."

It was a splendid lunch, in the directors' buffet of the Manchester & Leeds at Hunt's Bank. During the course of it Caspar told his mother that if all the Stevensons for the next five hundred years left his £460 untouched, it would be worth over ten million pounds and would yield nearly a quarter of a million each year!

When Nora laughed, as if she thought it were just a nice fancy, he swore to her that he would never touch the money. He would set the first example.

It was a promise he was to break the very next day.

Chapter 36

THEY MET UP WITH THE THORNTON CHILDREN—NO WALTER OR ARABELLA this time—on the quayside at Liverpool. After they had all gone aboard and run along the corridors and up and down the companionways and round the decks, and been in their cabins, and swung the lamps in their gimbals, Nick winked at Caspar and sauntered upon deck. Caspar, of course, followed.

"Who has a tale to tell-oh?" Caspar said, grinning already with anticipation.

"I have a tale to tell-oh! A tale of tail." He pronounced it "tayill" to make the pun clear.

Caspar rubbed his hands and leaned on the rail. They watched the nets full of luggage being hauled aboard.

"Tell me, Steamer, d'ye know what a Dipsas is? Or a Manticora? A Wyvern? A Simurgh? Eh?"

"Female grotesques, aren't they?" Caspar giggled.

"Indeed, old son. And your humble servant is here to tell you of them. Oh, and more! You know I was in Paris last Easter."

"You sent me a card."

"So I did. Well, I think that before a fellow marries and settles down he ought to do those things he won't be able to do so easily afterwards."

"You! Getting married?"

"Course not. But there's so many of 'those things,' don't you know."

They both laughed heartily.

The seamen began to lash the canvas over the open mouth of the luggage hold. The officer of the gangway looked at his watch every few moments. At last he called "All ashore that's going ashore," and the cry was taken up throughout the ship.

"Well," Nick said. "Before I went, didn't I overhear my mater telling Mrs. Cornelius about this strange house in Paris, in the Cours des Coches, where they keep half a ton of female grotesques. Wait! Having seen them, I revise that: a ton and a half of female grotesques, for gents whose taste for the normal has been dulled by overstimulation."

Caspar, on cue, laughed and waited to hear more, begging for it with his eyes and wet lips.

"'Course that don't apply to me. But since I don't think I'll ever succumb to overstimulation (quite the reverse—can't get enough!), I thought this year's as good as nineteen-hundred so why not; I'll be dead of spermatorrhoea by then, anyway. So along I go to Cours des Coches and lo and behold! There it is. I tell you, my mater could do the best fem guide in Europe. Big, swell place. Lots of plush. Lots of gilt. But—les girls! Christ, you never saw such things. Things! All dressed up like little virgins and brides. One was a nun—well, you'd expect that, wouldn't you, in a papist heaven like France. But you wouldn't expect a nun with tusks and a big scaly bump on her forehead, would you! An elephant woman all in black. She couldn't talk either—only go *hneuyrghhneuyrgh*, like a peke with asthma."

"Did you shag her?" Caspar asked in horrified fascination.

"You wait!" He was so confident of Caspar's interest now he did not look at him.

The last of the non-passengers went ashore and the seamen began to make the crane ropes fast to the gangway. Others went forward and aft to loosen the ropes and hawsers to the quayside bollards.

"There was one there I didn't see at first. But when I did, I knew I had to take her. I'd waited too long." He glanced briefly at Caspar. "Guess."

"How can I!" Caspar laughed. "I've never been within ten miles of..."

"But you have of *her*. It was that slavey of yours at Quaker Farm—the one we watched Boy screwing. You remember! With the ghastly face and the splendid tits."

Caspar felt every muscle in him go rigid. The gooseflesh on his arms rose against the material of his shirt. By supreme effort of will he managed to kill every sound or gesture that might distract Nick. Fortunately, Nick was now well launched and needed no question, nor even laugh, to prompt him into further revelation.

"As soon as I saw that loathsome half-face and remembered that glorious body I knew it had to be her."

They tested the knots to the gangplank.

"She didn't know me, though. Too drunk. Terrible stink of wine. It was all a bit of a washout, in fact. Too bloody weepy. As soon as I got into her she broke out in tears. The froggy fellow who runs the place said a lot of his clientele adore that and are willing to pay extra for it."

The seamen on the quayside signalled that the knots were firm and the men at the steam winch took a bite on the capstan.

Caspar could stand no more of it. He'd heard all he needed to know. "How much money have you, Nick?"

"Wait! You haven't heard how…"

"How much!" He eyed the coil of rope that had to be wound through before the gangplank lifted. It was dwindling fast.

"Two quid. But…"

"Give it me."

"I say…"

"Give it me!"

Awestruck, Nick handed it over.

"I'm going to get Mary Coen out of there," he said, already moving down the companionway. "Tell my mother what you've just told me. Twist it to suit yourself. Ask her for your two quid back."

The rope was all gone. The strain was on the gangplank now. He wasn't going to make it!

Then a cook came out and tapped one of the seamen on the shoulder—one who was holding the rope tightly bitten to the capstan. He let it go partly slack and the rope merely held its place, neither winding nor unwinding. Some kind of argument followed. Caspar leaped down the next companionway in two frog jumps. Then, without pause, he rushed out along the gangplank, which was by now being hauled up again, and jumped the eight-foot gap between the end of it and the quayside, landing in a sprawl.

"Hey, Steamer!" came Nick's cry from far above.

Caspar looked up.

"She's not worth it. But the elephant woman is!"

Caspar hated himself. How, he thought, loving Mary as he did, could he still laugh at Nick?

He had only enough cash to travel third to London—a nightmare of a journey on wooden seats. Fortunately third-class carriages were no longer open to the skies.

He arrived in Hamilton Place at dawn, forced himself to sleep until midday, drew out twenty pounds, caught the lunchtime train to Dover and was in Paris by eleven o'clock that night. Luckily it was at last possible for English people to travel in France without a passport, an item Caspar had, in any case, forgotten in his anxiety.

He paused long enough to book into a small *hôtel garni* in the Rue du Helder at fifteen francs, or twelve shillings, a day—which he thought extortionate but had no time to argue down.

At Hamilton Place he had borrowed his mother's Murray and had since found Cours des Coches on the map tucked in the back-cover pocket. It was just over half a mile away, a cul-de-sac running west from the Rue de la Madeleine, just north of the Faubourg St. Honoré.

As he walked down the Boulevard des Italiens, toward La Madeleine, he decided he would have to pretend to be an interested client of this dreadful house. An outraged young lover would probably be left on the pavement. So would an employer seeking a runaway servant. Was 450 francs enough? He ought to have drawn out more perhaps. Too late now.

For the first time, he began to think of Mary. Mary as he loved her. Mary as she was last Christmas. Until now his mind had shied away from all those particulars; she had been almost an abstract—as if Nick had said "Your country is in danger." He knew he had not dared to think of the real, particular Mary until he was this close to her.

And now that he was so close, now that he dared, a terrible foreboding overtook him. He remembered what Nick had said: "drunk...terrible stink of wine...crying all the time...customers like it."

What sort of ruins was he going to pick up?

Did he care? He decided he did not. Whatever had become of Mary he would collect the bits and take her home.

Would he marry her? He wouldn't have to.

But if that was the only way? It was hard for him to think of it. He would have to do all those things his mother cautioned against—leave Fiennes (where he was now following her advice to become the golden boy) and either finish his own education in Sheffield or be done with it and go out to earn his own—and her—living.

But if there was no other way? It would mean giving up four million at least. And, with Mary, he could never have any place in Society. It was giving up a lot.

But if there was no other way? He would. He did not decide it. He realized it. He was still a prisoner of her gentleness and her ghastly beauty. Besides, he comforted himself, a lot of people led very agreeable lives outside Society. Doctors, clergymen, teachers, lots of people with very successful small businesses. Their lives were probably a lot happier than those of people in Society.

The doorknocker on the house in the Cours des Coches took the form of a femal icthyogryph—as if to be a mermaid were not already deformity enough. It was a long time being answered. But the girl who came was both young and dainty. She held the door only part open, on a long chain.

"*Votre carte de visite, s'il vous plait, monsieur?*" she asked.

"I beg your pardon!" Caspar gasped. Somehow he assumed that the last thing anyone would mention or ask for in such a place was an honest name.

"*Monsieur est anglais?*"

"Yes…er…je cherchez…je lookez for…"

She smiled prettily—and contemptuously. "Monsieur may speak English. Monsieur must comprehend that only gentlemen of refinement are admitted 'ere."

Reluctantly Caspar handed in his card: Mr. Caspar Stevenson. Bang went half his strategies. The girl shut the door and silence fell once more.

After another interminable wait the chain was removed and the door swung open to reveal a portly man ravaged by ancient smallpox pits. "Welcome in, milor'!" he said with a bow. "César Calignani's choice of female pulchritude is yours."

"Lookin' forward to this, what!" Caspar said as he came in.

They walked down a long, carpeted corridor. Caspar saw the names on the doors—the names Nick had listed. The walls were hung with gothic paintings of grotesque females in obscene situations; little niches held sculptures of a similar nature. Plush and gilt were everywhere.

"Some of our beauties cannot even waddle upstairs," Calignani said. "These are their boudoirs."

"That girl who answered the door…" Caspar began.

Calignani laughed. "You like that touch? You are a man of refined wit, sir, despite your youth. Yes, many of my visitors do not see the exquisiteness of it—as an act of the wit."

His accent was better than his vocabulary.

They came to the centre of the house, a kind of large lounge full of sofas and ottomans where the choice was made. The pretty girl was ready with two glasses of brandy.

"My compliments, milor'," Calignani said. "Our selection of *belle tournure* is at this hour somewhat diminished. Many of my choicest dainties have retired for the night with their ardent paramours. But"—he waved his hand around the dimly lighted room—"we still have the grandmother, the bald one, the little—tcha! It's better *en français, oui: La Grand'mère, La Tête-chauve, La Minime, La Grasse-grasse, La Courbée, La Mère l'Oye…"*

Caspar looked around the sorry collection of hopeful freaks with more pity than revulsion. "I have a particular taste," he said. "I hear from a friend that you have a red-headed girl here, half of whose face is perfect, the other half completely…"

Calignani held up his hand. "*La Répandreuse, oui?*" he asked.

"I don't know her name."

"Always she weeps."

"Ah! Now that sounds like her."

"*Hélas*, monsieur, she is no more."

It was a while before Caspar could say the word: "Dead?"

"No, no, no. She is no more here."

His excellent English was obviously a patter that lasted only from door to lounge room.

"Oh!" Caspar's relief was enormous. "Some other house?"

The man laughed. "For her? There is no other house but Calignani's."

"But where is she, then?"

"I cannot tell you that, milor'."

"But you *do* know?"

"Of course I know." Calignani looked at him suspiciously. Caspar dropped all pretence. "But please tell me," he begged. "I wish to marry her. Truly I do."

Something communicated directly from ardent youth to jaded old ruin. Calignani saw something there whose existence he had forgotten. His beady, avaricious eyes softened for a moment. "You cannot," he said. "She is married now."

"Who to?" Caspar was growing desperate.

"Of course I cannot tell you. He is a frequent visitor here. He is an aristocrat—enough!"

"Please tell me! All I want is to speak to her. I just want to be sure she is happy—please?"

Calignani looked around the lounge. "Nothing here will do instead?" he asked.

"Is she happy?"

"She loves music, hein?"

"I…yes, I think she did."

"I am told she is often at concerts and the opera. They call her *La Veuve*—because of the dark veils, you see. 'The widow,' I think." He spoke to a gilded Corinthian column, near Caspar. "You sure there is nothing here for you?"

Caspar knew he would get no more out of the man. "I'm sorry," he said.

"Too early." The man chuckled.

Caspar looked at him in surprise. It was well past midnight.

"Forty…fifty years too early. We wait! What about Garence? Does she interest you?" He put his hand through the arm of the pretty girl.

Caspar looked at her. Of course she interested him! Any other night—any other time. "Tomorrow…or tomorrow," he said.

Calignani tightened his grip on the girl. "Thank the good God for *l'amour*," he said, parading his relief. "I am lonely too, tonight." He pulled the girl to him. She laughingly imitated a cat, purring and rubbing herself against him.

"I must pay you for my brandy," Caspar said. "At least I must do that."

But the man let go of the girl and swept Caspar back into the corridor. Caspar's last glimpse of the girl showed the smile falling from her face like a discarded mask. "The women of this trade have a saying," he told Caspar. "*Payer c'est oublier*—to pay is to forget. I will not let you pay, and then you remember this brandy, this scene, this house, many years. And when you are old and nothing excites anymore, then you think perhaps it's time to come back to Cours des Coches. I am dead perhaps. These…*filles*…are gone. But *la service* it's immortal." He saluted and laughed. "You come back—oh, yes!" He took the empty brandy glass from Caspar's fingers and pulled it away, level and slowly, as if a thread already united himself and the young man.

As Caspar crossed the threshold back into the street, Calignani gripped him by the shoulder. "Mary Coen," he said. "She is now a comtesse! Either she is happy or she is a fool. That's good for you, yes?"

Caspar smiled. "I suppose it is," he said.

When he went to bed that night he truly intended to go home the following day. But the pigeons awoke him just after dawn and he spent two sleepless hours in bed reconciling himself to the fact that he was not going to leave Paris until he had seen Mary Coen and assured himself that she was happy in her new life—if, indeed, it was not all a figment, the sort of tale any brothel keeper might use for putting off the importunate.

All the sensible, rational parts of him were already condemning this whole venture. Surely, they said, he had got over Mary Coen very nicely until Nick had come along? His response had not been from rekindled love but from mere fellow feeling, the thought of Mary drinking herself nightly into oblivion and weeping so. Not love, surely. He wasn't making that mistake again, was he?

He could listen to those inner voices quite calmly. But he could not yet pay them much heed. Something in him—call it foolish, call it what you would—something had to see her.

One look in the *Almanac de Gotha* convinced him of the impossibility of tracing her through the list of comtes he found there. Music—that was his only hope: Mary's love of music. Had it survived the booze and the land where she was "beautyfull"?

The season was not in his favour. True, the Conservatoire concerts were over. So were the Concerts Philharmoniques established by M. Berlioz. But that still left a lot of summer promenade concerts. Caspar spent that first evening dashing from Musard to Herz to Ste. Cécile, and all the other first-class public salons. At each he searched frantically for a heavily veiled woman. At each he was disappointed. But at the Union Musicale he had one small stroke of luck—enough to make him prolong his search by at least a few days. One of the attendants there took him aside and asked him to cause less stir. Caspar explained he was looking for "La Veuve." The man's response made it plain that such a person did, at least, exist, and that she frequented concerts often enough to be remarked upon.

It was not until lunchtime on his third fruitless day that he remembered reading of the open-air concerts at the Pré Catalan in the Bois de Boulogne. Murray's dismissed it as "vastly over-rated by the Parisians, who speak of it as perfection." Caspar saw he had read this carelessly the first time. The judgement referred to the Pré Catalan as a garden—not to the quality of the music that was presented there. He decided to spend the afternoon at the place.

He saw no one in widow's weeds. That evening he telegraphed his bank to send more money. He also wrote to his mother, telling her the bare outlines of his search and stressing the visits he was making to the Palace of Industry and the Louvre—which he did at a brisk, nonstop walk next morning.

That afternoon he was once again at the Pré Catalan and once again seeing no widow, as at all the concert halls the previous evening. The widow existed but could not be found. It was, he realized, a statistical problem. The most tiresome and inelegant way to solve it would be to blanket-cover every concert, every evening. He had to find her pattern by inquiry. He had to match it. Then the other part of his mind told him if that was all he was doing—reducing the whole thing to a mathematical game—he might as well complete the journey to Connemara and play it on the beach with stones. It would be a great deal cheaper.

At that moment an urchin put a note in his hand and waited for a reward. Caspar read it before parting with any money:

Darling Caspar,

I was in the coach behind you here yesterday. And again today.

He looked around. There was no coach.

I will give this to a gamin and I will go. You are a big risk to me. If you are foolish, I will say I do not know you and so. Come back tomorrow and walk past the carriage. I will pretend to recognize you and call you over. You must behave like it's no big meeting. Yawn, look at your watch, and etc. Whatever we say. If you get talking hot, I will have to drive away. Please do this whatever you think if you have any regard to me altogether.

Mary (La Comtesse d'Auvreuil)

PS—God love you.

Next day he left much too early. At the Porte Maillot he stopped the cab and decided to walk the remaining three kilometres through the Bois. He ran the gauntlet of a long line of *putains*; some of these Paris girls were glorious creatures. But even as he looked at them, admiring them, lusting for them, he knew he would never actually go with any of them. He looked and admired as a male animal. But as Caspar he knew he would always be thinking of the coarseness of people like Nick; the commercial thing would ruin it—the public commercial thing. What he really wanted was Mary. A mistress. Like his father had.

They were still setting out the seats when he arrived despite his leisurely stroll through the Bois. The first of the musicians were just uncasing their instruments. In the baking August sun he had to endure almost forty-five minutes of music, walking up and down past the carriages, having no idea which, if any, she was in. But at last she put him out of his misery.

A carriage window went down. "Mr. Stevenson?" It was her voice.

For her sake he turned, frowning with slight annoyance.

"Over here," she said.

Scowling he walked to her coach. She was still concealed in the dark. It was a low-slung landaulette, so they were more or less on a level.

"No need to overdo it," she said. "The quare fella has no English."

That must mean the coachman.

Caspar took off his hat. "Why, it's Miss...Miss...?"

"Miss Coen, as was. Now La Comtesse d'Auvreuil."

He took the gloved hand she pushed out through the window and kissed it. Nothing about it was Mary, for which he was profoundly glad.

He stood back. "Tedious weather."

"It is the count's day to go to—that place. Don't name it!"

"I was there. Nick told me."

"Nick?"

"Nick Thornton. He saw you there."

She clearly had no memory of it.

"Could you lift your veil?" It was so frustrating to have to make these heartfelt requests in the tones he normally used with people he barely knew.

"Better not. Why did you come?"

"You know why I came." He yawned.

"Then you know why I cannot change anything now."

"Are you happy, Mar...Madame?"

"I can do no harm to you here. I can do no harm to Boy."

His fake yawn induced in him a real desire to yawn. Paradoxically, because it was genuine, he did his best to smother it.

She laughed. "That was much better! Yes, I am happy. I go to many concerts and the opera. I learn the piano. I learn to sing. I'm fierce happy altogether. Tell Boy that."

"I will. What about your man, the fella with the title?"

"That's no business of yours."

"Of course. I had better go."

"But I'll tell you. He never touches me if that's what...He's very old. I have a dress like actresses wear, to change quickly. We sit in our box in the Opera and pull the curtains to a crack. And I sit and watch the stage, naked as a babe, while he spends the whole evening putting jewels and bangles on me and moving the candelabra round to look at me."

"The 'land where you'd be beautyfull'," he said with a light, despairing laugh. "You found it at last."

"It is so," she said. "You can't have every dream come true. Or where would be the use of heaven?"

Chapter 37

"I TAKE IT WE'VE HEARD THE LAST OF MARY COEN?" NORA ASKED WHEN CASPAR had come back to Quaker Farm.

"You take no such thing. The comte is old and she is young. And so am I." Caspar was teasing, but his mother swallowed it.

"Caspar! You can't still be thinking along those lines."

"It's not every man who boasts a mistress who outranks his own mother, socially!"

She saw he was joking then and changed her tone at once. "Oh! A mistress—now, that's quite another matter."

"I see," Caspar said, his smile hardening. "Mistresses are all right."

The smile faded from Nora's lips. She returned to reading the financial journal on her lap. "By the way," she said, ultra-conversationally, "did our new comtesse tell you how she came to make her first visit to Paris?"

"She did."

"In detail, I mean?"

"In *every* detail."

Nora's frown darkened, though she was still pretending to be more absorbed in her reading. "It's not a tale for wide currency."

Caspar laughed, desperately wanting to provoke her into joining him. "Oh, mater—I wasn't even going to tell *you*!"

"That's right, popsie," she said, still with her eyes on the page, and still not smiling. "I'm sure I never want to hear it."

Caspar sighed and stood up; that was a hornet's nest! "I'll go along the beach and meet the others coming back."

"They might take the road."

"I'll have to chance that."

∽

Winifred and Nick, at least, were returning from their outing by way of the beach.

"Steamer!" Nick called and spurred his horse into a gallop, pulling short only inches from where Caspar unflinchingly held his ground. Nick looked worried, until he saw Caspar smiling; then he grinned.

"As I was saying before you rushed off, I had the elephant woman instead. I hope you took my advice, young 'un."

Caspar was holding a string of seaweed he had picked up idly as he walked. He swung it at the horse, making Nick forget everything except trying to control the beast.

Winifred came trotting up then, forcing them to drop the subject. "Hello, Steamer."

"Hello yourself, Winnie."

"Nick, be a good angel and take my horse on back to the stables. I would hold some converse with this imperfect knight."

Caspar winked at Nick, who leaned over to take Winifred's reins. "See what happens when you give them too much education!" They all three laughed.

"Swim?" Caspar asked as they watched Nick ride away. He didn't sound too keen on the idea himself.

Winifred smiled. "Young ladies of Bedford College do not go swimming *à la peau nue* with young gentlemen from Paris." She took his arm and looked at him appraisingly. "Big grown-up boy—where did you get the money?"

Caspar suppressed a smile, knowing that Winifred could have no idea why he had gone to Paris. "You remember what I was telling you—just about here, in fact—this time last year? Mama's commercial test for me?"

"Oh, I hoped it was that. So—it was a success?"

"Unh-huh."

"A big success?"

Caspar whistled through his smile.

"I'm more glad than I can say," Winifred told him. "If you had failed, everything would have crashed down."

He frowned, puzzled. Her clutch on his arm was fierce. "You don't realize, do you. You are the keystone of all our hopes. Not just of yours. Mine, too. And even Boy's—though he'd never admit it. And because we are blazing the path, the hopes of all the others, too. Was it a really big success, Steamer? Would it *astonish* Father?"

"It astonished me."

"Astonish me then, Steamer."

He looked at her, wondering if he should. "A hundred pounds profit on a hundred and fifty invested," he said.

It astonished her—and that, after all, was exactly what she had asked him to do.

"Good," she said in the tone of someone laying aside the first item on the agenda and taking up the second. "Now, Steamer, I want you to help me with mathematics this summer. It's something Bedford and I are not too good at."

"Why do you want to be good at maths?"

"Because I can foresee a situation where, if we teachers don't prepare ourselves, girls' schools will teach languages and music—they will teach mere *accomplishments*. And boys' schools will teach money-earning things like mathematics and science."

"What's wrong with that?" Caspar asked in surprise.

"Well, of course it's wrong."

"Surely you wouldn't train ladies to go out and work. Like men, I mean!"

She grinned belligerently at him. "Oh, Steamer. When we have vanquished the Common Enemy, I can see battle royal between you and me. You have a lot of education yet to undergo."

"Start now, then."

"No. First the Common Enemy."

Caspar laughed. They had reached the last sand bar before the harbour. The tide was at full ebb and they could just squeeze around the head of the stone breakwater.

"You haven't a leg to stand on—that's why you're keeping quiet," he sneered.

She pushed him over into the damp sand and ran around the breakwater, thinking he would hotly pursue. Moments later she crept back and peeped around the stones. Caspar was still sitting in the sand. He looked up at her in mock admiration. "I am deeply impressed," he said, "by the rigorously intellectual nature of your argument. You have quite won me over."

Winifred laughed and came to help him up. As she dusted the sand off him she said: "You're so much older than Boy."

"I always have been."

She became serious again as they walked up the shelving, seaweed-anchored sand of the harbour floor. "You know, Steamer, we talk glibly of this battle we've got to fight—and quite soon now, I'd think...a year or two. And we always talk as though the winning were certain. But I sometimes think we haven't a hope. Lord Stevenson and Society and all that terrible dead weight—they are so strong. So...strong. Do you really think we can have our puny way against them? Really?"

He hated what he was about to say, but he knew it had to be said. "Don't rely absolutely on me, Winnie. You must have another plan up your sleeve—one without me. I'm the man who takes the chances when they duck up. I met a fella on the boat back from France, an American. He's absolutely certain they're going to have a civil war soon. He says there's going to be fortunes made over there in arms and ammunition. He got me so fired up, I tell you, I damn near—excuse me—took an entirely different ship out from Liverpool. So listen well—if I get impatient, or if I see a chance that's far too good to miss..."

He left the rest unsaid.

"I see," Winifred said bleakly.

They were almost back at the door before she added: "I suppose it's as well to know it."

Part Three

1862–63

Chapter 38

"HAPPY CHRISTMAS, DARLINGS! HAPPY CHRISTMAS," NORA WAS SAYING IT early this year in the hope that it might come true. Already it had one thing in its favour—it was the first Christmas for years that everyone was home. Today she was meeting Young John and Caspar off the train from Cambridge. While the porters sorted out their boxes, the two young men, not eager to exchange one cramped carriage seat so immediately for another, walked up and down the platform with their mother.

"I have no dinners and no salons for fifteen days," she said. "How blissful! This is going to be a very family Christmas."

Her two sons squeezed her arms, making a tight, smiling group.

Fresh snow had fallen in the night and the sun had not yet melted its edges, so the whole world was wonderfully sharp-edged to the eye and crisp to the warm and well-shod foot.

"I say," Boy cried, hitting and rubbing his gloved hands together, "isn't this splendid! Let's walk down the hill—the carriage can catch us up." Clouds of vapour wreathed his mouth. "D'you feel up to it, mater?"

Nora took jocular offence at his solicitude and stalked off through the station arch. The young men trotted after her. "Catch us up!" Caspar shouted to the coachman.

The station had to be built near the top of the northern ridge of the Maran valley, whose sloping sides were too steep for railway works. Trains soared across it on the mammoth Welwyn Viaduct, whose towering, hundred-foot arches had been put there by John Stevenson in the late forties. The way down to the hamlet of Digswell led through snow-shrouded lanes and fields, but there had already been enough traffic to and from the station on the hill to flatten the snow upon the road.

Nora looked around with more than passing curiosity. "While we're alone," she said. Then she paused and began a new sentence. "You know your father has been expecting to be raised from baron to viscount for some time now?"

They nodded.

"Well"—she spoke as if promising great treasure—"he's done even better than that. Of course, it's to be kept absolutely…"

"An earl!" Boy said excitedly.

"Sssh!" the other two rounded on him.

"What territory?"

Nora laughed. "Of course he wanted to be the Earl of Yorkshire, but they said 'too big'; and he couldn't be Earl of York, because there's already a duke. So he thinks he'll settle for 'Wharfedale.' I think it sounds quite distinguished—'The Right Honourable, the Earl of Wharfedale, K.G.B., G.C.S.I.'—don't you?"

"That means *I'll* be Lord Stevenson, now!" Boy said.

"And your sisters will be Lady Winifred, Lady Abigail, and so on."

"It's not fair!" Caspar pretended to sulk. "The rest of us just stay Honourables. But seriously—why does he need to take a territorial title? It's so feudal. He could just be Earl Stevenson. Which would be much more honest."

"Well, it won't ever concern you, Steamer," Boy teased. "You want a title, you'll have to go and earn one of your own."

Caspar stalked his brother like a stage villain. "You are shu-hure of living so lo-o-ong?"

Boy ran off in heroically proportioned terror and vaulted a gate into a field. Caspar followed and stood on the near side of the gate, glowering at him. Neither was sure whether to carry the tomfoolery any further. Nora rescued them by telling them to grow up—this minute.

"An earldom!" Boy said when he and Caspar had rejoined her. "I thought he might he raised from baron to viscount—but to go all the way up to earl!"

"Yes, he didn't expect it," Nora said. "He's obviously made himself more useful to Whitehall than he thought."

"Or than *we* thought," Caspar said.

"Mmm," Nora said.

Boy said nothing.

"Is the guvnor home now?" Caspar asked.

"No, he's coming on Christmas Eve, with some guests. It's all to be a bit of a surprise. Winifred's home already."

"And is she well?" Boy asked. They were just passing the point where the bridle path left the lane.

"Isn't it glorious!" Nora said. "I'm almost tempted to walk along the bridle path." She spoke as if she meant it, too.

"Oh, let's!" Boy said excitedly.

Nora considered it. "No," she said reluctantly. "I have too much to do."

Boy looked longingly at the path. "Would you think me terribly discourteous, mater, if I walked home?"

"Not at all, dearest. You, too, Caspar, if you wish." Unseen by Boy she plucked at Caspar's sleeve. "I shouldn't mind in the slightest."

"I'll keep you company," Caspar told his mother.

Boy kissed Nora, said it was going to be a marvellous Christmas, and set off up the bridle path slashing at every twig within reach of his cane. The other two watched him, all that hearty, muscular enthusiasm wrapped in a long coat, topped by a tall, shiny stovepipe of a hat—vigour stark in black and white.

"What do the others say of him?" Nora asked. "I try to imagine what others say about each of you and it's so hard."

"That you couldn't hope for a more steadfast friend. That he'd drive himself to his grave if that were the only way to win. That he'd never do anything underhand or mean or dishonest. He's the golden boy of St. John's—as you know, I suppose."

"But?"

Caspar looked sidelong at her. "What d'you mean: 'But'?"

She pushed him playfully. "It was the most thunderous unspoken 'but' I ever heard!"

He shrugged. "Well—you know Boy! He is just so simple and trusting. He takes the whole of Christianity for gospel. One of the dons said Boy would subscribe to a *hundred* and thirty-nine articles if you asked him kindly."

"D'you believe that?" She was annoyed that Caspar could so neutrally report this light mockery of her eldest son.

"No. I think you'd also have to tell him everybody else had already done it."

She breathed out angrily, though her anger was not so much at Caspar as at the probable truth of what he had said. Boy turned and waved back at them just before he passed out of sight into a dip in the path. They waved back.

"Come on, or you'll get cold," Caspar told her. They walked the remaining fifty yards or so to the bottom of the hill. "I remember," he went on, "when I was, oh, nine, I suppose, someone who had pleaded not guilty had been hanged for murder, and I felt wretchedly miserable because this man had said he hadn't done it, and yet they'd gone and hanged him." He laughed at his former innocence. "I don't say Boy is quite as simple-minded as that—but very nearly. D'you know,"—he turned to Nora as if he feared she did not quite believe him—"he told me only the other day that if everybody in the world would only keep the commandments and love his neighbour, all the world's problems would be solved!"

"Very well, dear," Nora said testily. "You've made your point."

Caspar laughed a rounding-off laugh. "The trouble is he's absolutely right—by definition almost. No one can disprove it."

The carriage, which had taken a different route with a gentler gradient, was waiting just around the corner. As Caspar helped her to board he said, "I noticed when he asked how Winnie was, you didn't answer. Is she not well? I thought that since the guvnor let her take the post at Cheltenham…"

Nora held up her gloved hand. "It's not that. She'll tell you."

"Serious?" He climbed in behind her.

"It's growing. She wants to start her own school. In London."

Caspar laughed in astonishment. "I'll say one thing for us—we do nothing by halves!"

Nora did not share his mirth. "It's most inconvenient," she said. "I thought we could solve the problem of you three piecemeal. I thought she was settled, despite all the argument about taking no salary. I thought, that's Winifred out of the way. Because, believe me, the problem of you and Young John will have to be resolved very soon now." She tapped with her fingers on the carriage window sill. "And I'm not ready. And you're not ready." She looked sharply at him. "Or are you? What do you really think of Cambridge?"

"Ghastly!"

She smiled in relief. "I know you can't put much in your letters."

"Frightful. It's school all over again, only worse. At school the masters made some attempt to keep their little feuds among themselves; I mean, there was some sort of social division between boys and masters. At college, since almost all the undergraduates are socially superior to the dons, there's none, so all that petty backbiting is out in the open. The dons are monks really. I feel stifled after one term there. They have this great reputation for wit, and really, you know, it's all just rudeness, what you and I would call rudeness, dressed up in ecclesiastical trappings. How Boy can stick the course and go back for an extra half I can't fathom." He looked out of the window and laughed dourly. "Well—of course, I can."

"Your father has invited Caroline Sherringham and her aunt to stay for Christmas," Nora said. "He wrote to tell Young John about it."

Caspar caught her tone, which warned there was more in it than met the eye. He thought a while. "Dynasties?" he said at last.

"Well...the Sherringhams have no son. But they do have one of the biggest ironworks in the whole of South Wales."

"Oh, Lord!" Caspar said, feeling sick within. "If he marries the Sherringham girl before he proves he's not the man for Stevenson's that would tear up the whole ticket!"

"Only from your point of view," Nora said.

He looked sharply at her.

"Well, darling, these things have to be faced. I'm not in a conspiracy with you to get you Stevenson's at all costs. I will only work to get you Stevenson's if, at the same time, I am saving your brother from the shock of discovering his unsuitability to the world of business. If anything comes of this dynasty thing, he will have to have the firm; and then I shall have to ignore your ambitions and throw all my energies into saving Young John from himself and seeing that we get good managers in where and when they're needed."

Caspar sat tensely, biting his lip, deep in thought.

"It may come to nothing," Nora said, without much hope.

"I was prepared to accept 'Stevenson Brothers,'" Caspar told her with a sigh. "I would have welcomed just the iron and steel part of the business—which I think are being grossly neglected." He clenched his fists in frustration. "But if Boy marries the Sherringham girl, that would be out of the question."

"Then perhaps *you* must dazzle her instead," Nora suggested.

Caspar stared at her, unable to see whether or not she was joking. "D'you know," he said, astonished at himself, "I don't believe I could. The merger of the two businesses is absolutely right, I'd feel it would be wrong to spoil it."

Nora laughed. "Has it never struck you how very like your father you are. In some ways you think exactly like him!"

Boy walked briskly along the snow-bright path, breathing the sharp morning air, thinking he must be just about the happiest person going. As the eldest son of an earl he'd have the courtesy rank and title of viscount—and, of course, he'd take his father's barony, Baron Cleveland, also as a courtesy title. "Lord Stevenson,"

he'd be called—Lord Stevenson, Baron Cleveland. How marvellous! It was the crowning of a very happy year.

He had stayed up at Cambridge not to study but to try to establish a university Rugby football team. With more and more public schools switching to the Rugby version of the game, university football had changed even in the short while he had been up. Men from different schools used to go away to any spare bit of waste ground and scratch together a couple of sides to play their old-school version of the game. By and large they still did, but there was an increasing number of men from other schools which, like Fiennes, had switched to Rugby and it was becoming possible to pick an all-university team to play Oxford.

At least, it would have been possible if the college authorities had been just halfway decent about letting men go away for their matches. In one game Cambridge, away to Oxford, had turned up with eight men out of the fifteen missing; the "Cambridge" team that won that particular match had actually had a majority of Oxford men playing for it! Still, the whole Rugby venture had been eminently worthwhile. He would like to have stayed to see the year out, but the serious world now called.

And when the serious world contained such attractions as, on the one hand, the management of a large railway contract for Stevenson's, and, on the other, the courting of a lovely girl like Linny Sherringham—with (as his father's letter had made clear) the blessing of both sets of parents—its call was not too hard to obey.

He was especially glad about the Stevenson contract, which was to build the major part of the Cockermouth, Keswick, & Penrith Railway—through the Lake District, some of the loveliest landscape in the country. He was due to start in January, so he had to get his wooing of Miss Sherringham over and done with this Christmas.

The thought of it didn't worry him particularly. He knew her well. In fact, they had both been presented at court on the same day, and that always welded a special sort of bond between people. Not many others, he knew, would call her "lovely." Her face was rather too long, her lips a little too thin, her eyes slightly too close together. But she was a serious and dutiful girl with a great reputation for piety, of a rather low-church kind; and, to Boy, that counted more than physical attraction. He had always been determined to lead as chaste a marriage as was consonant with the need to have children. Now, with so pious a wife as Linny Sherringham to share his life, he was doubly determined to exercise his baser self only when they wanted children. He coloured at the very thought of it but told himself firmly that it would be necessary.

Perhaps it wouldn't be necessary for a year or two, though. They would need some time to settle down in the enjoyment of each other's company and tastes, as well as to build up the sort of joint piety their conjugal life would demand. Anyway, he would tell her these things—in a properly reticent fashion—this vacation. It would rest her mind greatly to know she wasn't going to be yoked for life with the average sensual sort of brute.

For most of that walk his thoughts dwelled joyfully on the positive aspects of his future with this paragon of a wife. They would build a large house somewhere, in the Midlands probably—about a hundred rooms—with its own chapel and chaplain, and, with his help, they would try to walk with God in everything. Theirs would be the perfect village. Poverty would be unknown there. So would every kind of indulgence and excess. It would become a centre of Christian temperance and vigour. A beacon—a pharos, in Brockman's sense—in an increasingly ugly and materialistic world. Linny and their daughters would daily visit the poor and needy, the sick and disabled, with nourishing baskets of food and words of cheer. The hale and fit would all be found work about the estate or, farther afield, in Stevenson's. Above all, their own frugal, pious, and industrious example would percolate down to all their tenants and servants, making one hive of industry, sobriety, and happiness. He was sure that he, with Linny at his side, would represent a new and more noble kind of master and landlord, one who stood at the very opposite pole from the drunken, dissolute, swashbuckling squire of barbarous Georgian days.

He could not wait to begin. He saw himself having very little to do with Stevenson's. It was one of the largest undertakings in the country and could hardly grow larger now; certainly he had no ambitions to see it get any bigger. In short, it could more or less run along of its own momentum, with an occasional prod from a general manager. This test of his father's was just a way of showing everybody how well he could manage if he had to.

The contract up in the Lake District had him more worried than his courtship of Miss Sherringham. Time and again he had asked his father to spell out the most basic rules about managing a contract of that size, and all his father could say was things like: "Keep an ear to the ground. Listen for grumbles among the men—especially between the different trades." That was all very well, but it didn't tell you what to do. All his father could say there was, "Use your Stevenson instinct!"

Another thing his father said was: "Keep a close eye on all your costs. Do anything to avoid going over your allowance." But in the next breath he'd say:

"Never fear to spend boldly to avoid a disaster." Well, where did that leave you! In fact, the guvnor was very fond of contradictory advice. He'd say: "In thirty years of railway building we've met and solved every problem. Never fear to ask the main office for advice; and never fear to listen to the man with the shovel. There's more native sense in a navvy camp than in ten books on engineering." But he would also tell Boy to use his own initiative and not go crying to head office at every turn—and also to learn to sort out the chatterbox workman, "all gas and gob," from the true tradesman.

In short, all he had to do was be a parsimonious bold-spender, who heeded the advice of navvies that he sent away with a flea in their ears and, when he was in real trouble, to use an instinct he had not yet proved himself to possess.

His mind shied away from such difficulties and focused again on the far more alluring prospect of a spiritual union with Linny Sherringham.

Chapter 39

In these snows they hunted more for a good ride than in the hope of a kill. Most people, once they had winded one good hunter, retired, glad of the exercise, but already looking forward to the hot punch, the mulled ale, the spiced frumenty that awaited their return.

All the Stevenson children joined the hunt that afternoon of Boy's and Caspar's return; even baby Sefton, just two and a half years old, was sat upon a little Shetland pony and allowed to watch them away from one draw. But by half past three, with evening falling quickly and no prospect of a good chase, the hunt broke up and they all came home—a grand sight, Nora thought, as she watched them trotting down the long drive, all in their pink and black against the driven white of the snow.

Clement, who was supposed to have squired Abigail over the jumps, was annoyed that she had always sneaked ahead of him in the last few yards—most dangerously—and taken the fence before him. All the way down the drive he kept trying to cut in on her, sharply enough to make her horse shy up. But his horse and hers were such friends that they simply arched their necks and leaned inward, head upon head, in a most loving way. Abigail, knowing full well what Clement was at, kept saying it looked so pretty and how kind of Clement, thereby adding to his fury. Abigail, a world expert at fury herself, affected not to notice.

Hester and Mather tried to get their ponies to walk in perfect step with each other; but the only aids they had to mark out the timing of the pace—hands, heels and voice—carried quite different connotations to their mounts, who, accordingly, halted, trotted, shouldered in, piaffed, and tossed their heads in growing confusion and alarm.

At last Mather's pony, near to home and tired of this muddle of commands, took the bit in its jaws and bolted. Boy and Winifred had to gallop up, one on each side, and seize a rein apiece to pull it to a halt. It was a display of concerted horsemanship of which Nora felt proud, though she would have a sharp word to say to young master Mather.

When they had dismounted and were walking back across the yard Winifred suddenly remembered something. "Oh, Steamer," she called, "come and see what you think of Diana's left fore. I think the shoe has spread."

For form's sake she lifted the hoof and for form's sake Caspar looked at it. "We've got to talk," she murmured.

He looked around. "Up in the hayloft."

They took a lantern up. Caspar sprawled across some bales. Winifred was too restless to sit.

"Caroline Sherringham will be here in an hour or two," she said.

"There's nothing we can do about it."

Still Winifred paced about, saying nothing.

"You might think more clearly if you sat down," he told her.

She obeyed, with a reluctant sigh. "D'you think she's right for him?" she asked.

"I hardly know her. She just seems a nice, ordinary, rather plain young girl."

"Hah!"

"Am I wrong?"

"You ought to take more interest in people, Steamer. You only show an interest if you think they'll be some help to you. Or threat."

"Even that's hard enough."

"Yes—well, you see the disadvantage now. Linny Sherringham is a very real threat. And you know nothing about her. Nice! Ordinary!"

"Ah! Then you enlighten me."

She looked angrily at him. "Damn you!" she said.

"Why so?" Her outburst startled him, made him sit up.

She stood again and went to adjust the lamp wick. "There are some things one hardly discusses about…people. Especially girls." She was shivering with nervousness. "Of our class…you know."

He was now as embarrassed as she. "You mean…Linny is…"

She clenched her fists and turned to him, squaring up. "Let's not pretend, shall we? I've taught a term in a girls' school of the highest class. It would be crass to pretend."

"Pretend what?" He did not want her to say it.

"Oh, Steamer!" She stamped a foot. "We all know that people are supposed to be one thing when they are really another. I mean, Boy acts like a saint in grade-one marble. That's his public face. But he may in reality be the most terrible old reprobate."

"Not him!" Caspar said heavily.

"Are you sure?" She seemed a little disappointed. "Do you know him so well as to be absolutely sure?"

"Believe me."

She slumped. "Oh dear!"

"Why?"

"You see the difficulty, Steamer. I mean, you're a very different character, different sense of humour, and so on. But on that subject, that particular subject… you do know what we are talking about, don't you?"

He blushed and nodded.

"On *that* subject, Steamer, you seem the same as Boy. And so do Nick and Father—and all the men one meets. Yet it can't be, can it."

"Can't it?"

She sighed, knowing how hard it was going to be to make Caspar forthcoming—yet how important it was, too. "I'll put it the other way: How do girls seem to you?"

He coughed once. "Attractive?"

"Caspar!"

When she used his real name she was angry.

He grew angry then, too. What right had she to force him into this most distasteful conversation? But, if she insisted, he'd show her. "We are taught," he said, "that the sexual passions of girls of good class…that *is* what we are talking about, isn't it, Winnie? Sex?"

"Yes." In the gloom of the single lantern he could not read her face.

"Say it."

"Sex," she said. There was no tremble in her voice.

"We are taught that their—you know—passions are not awakened until they marry. And even then…" He was so hot and embarrassed that he had to pause. "Why on earth are we discussing this?"

"And even then," she finished it for him, "it needs a considerate and understanding husband to quicken it?"

"Something like that."

She sat down, deflated, on the haybales facing him. "Oh, Steamer. How did we get into such confusion?"

"You started it."

"Not us, silly. People in general. Society."

"Confusion?"

"Well! Are all you men the way you behave toward us? You say Boy is a saint. Are you? Is Father? Is Nick? Is his father?"

Caspar shrank into himself, like a trapped animal. "Why should I answer?" he asked.

"Because we should know the truth. Because it's important—especially now."

At last her meaning—the particular point she was trying to make—penetrated that thick crust of protective idealization. "You mean...Linny is prone to..."

"I mean Linny. I mean me. I mean nine out of ten of the girls I teach. I mean if you truly think our passions are hidden even from ourselves until considerate and understanding people like you give us a new name, you are living in a world of delusion."

He sat dead still, bolt upright, looking at her, trying to assimilate this new information.

"Steamer," she said, made uncomfortable by his silence and his fixed stare, "do you really mean that you thought it was any different? You? So worldly wise?"

"All right." He nodded firmly. "I accept it. I accept the fact of it—and your rebuke. I'd still like to know how you know it of Linny Sherringham."

"Because of what she still thinks I didn't see her doing with Nick when we played hide-and-go-crush at Palace Gate last Christmas."

Caspar gave an involuntary laugh. "Well! With *Nick*!" Then he saw how agitated she had become and he stopped. "I'm sorry," he stammered. "I thought that was all over with. I mean, I thought it was nothing anyway."

She shook her head; he fancied he saw tears filling her eyes.

"You see?" she said quietly. "He has never ventured the faintest impropriety with me. And yet—three seconds in that cupboard with Linny and..."

"But then he can have no respect for her. And he must have enormous respect for you."

"Why d'you say it like that? Is he such a reprobate?"

"He...has his moments."

"I suppose she made him do it, really. She took his hand and placed it...here." She touched her breast. "I saw that."

"Why on earth are we talking about all this, Winnie? Is there any point?"

She beseeched the ceiling for strength. "With Linny practically on our door-step? About to be thrown to Boy? Linny, who will probably behave the way men are supposed to behave—and Boy, who (if you're right) will behave the way we women are supposed to? The irresistible force of Linny and the immovable object of Boy? Is there any *point*?"

Caspar laughed; all tension had gone, now. "I suppose so."

"I must say, though, that was not my fear when I raised the topic. I was..."

"What topic was that, Winnie?" he teased.

"Sex," she said firmly and deliberately.

This time he laughed.

"My fear," she went on, "was that the irresistible force would meet the irresistible object. You'd better be right about Boy or a lot of sour hopes will be dashed."

"We'd better go," he said.

She took his arm as they crossed the dark stable yard.

"Winnie," he said. "About you and Nick—would it help at all if I dropped a hint? I'd be very tactful."

She squeezed his elbow. "Bless you, Steamer, I know you would—but, no, thanks."

"Don't you...wouldn't you like to marry him?"

"Of course I would." He heard the strain in her voice. "But I told you, years ago. I want to teach. I want to do something about the deplorable state of female education in this country. And I could not do it as a married woman. It is not Nick I reject. Nor male companionship. It is the state of marriage. I want to possess my own school. How could I do that if it became my husband's property and all its income was really his? I could not expose it to such danger. I have to sacrifice something. So it had better be...all that."

Caspar laughed and shook his head. "One term at Cheltenham and you want your own school!"

They were inside the big house now, approaching the grand staircase—grand only because, in 1812, the owner of Maran Hill had commissioned one of England's greatest architects, Sir John Soane, to remodel the house. Soane, with his exquisite taste, had fitted what looked like a great sweeping stair into what was really quite a small well in the heart of the house. Despite that, it was easy going and Caspar and Winifred swept up without slackening their pace.

"Miss Beale is so wrong," Winifred said.

"Of course!"

"No, I'm serious, Steamer—though I know you'll side with her. She is set against any form of competitiveness. We have no examinations. No top or bottom of the class—or middle. No competitive sports. We play no other schools. Everything is co-operation. All help each other. Community spirit!"

Caspar looked at her open-mouthed. "Why on earth should I agree with that! It's the very opposite of what I think education should be."

Winifred sprang the trap. "For *girls*, Steamer?"

"Ah...yes, I see."

"She says that a girl's nervous constitution is too delicate to face competitive examinations And in any case, since her girls may always look to the protection of a man—a husband, a father, a brother—their roles will always be domestic. Their natures must be trained to be co-operative, subordinate, uncompetitive, submissive."

They had reached the door of his bedroom; hers was at the other end of the passage.

"There's a lot in that," he said.

"I knew you'd agree," she sneered. "But that's why I want to start my own school. On quite different lines."

"But you can't answer her argument."

She shook her head pityingly. "I suppose," she said, "if it were the law—and the universal custom—that all bed knobs were to be painted red, you're the sort of person who would conclude that bed knobs were inherently red."

"I thought we'd left that topic behind," he said.

At first she did not understand. Then she saw it and gave him a withering look. "Sometimes, Caspar," she said as she walked off down the passage, "you are not grown-up at all."

He laughed. All the same, he thought as he went in to dress for dinner, it was an odd image for her to choose, especially after all that insistence that girls' minds weren't so very different from boys' minds.

Chapter 40

THEY KNEW THAT LT.-GEN. (RETIRED) SIR CHARLES D'O. REDVERS, BT., G.C.S.I., of the Indian Army, and his wife, of Malvern, were to be guests that Christmas. That, after all, was why they were standing within the portico, watching the two carriages pull around the sweep this cold Christmas Eve morning. (Nora would have no truck with the modern fashion for waiting indoors and letting a major domo bring your visitors in to you.) But in a thousand guesses they would never have arrived at the identity of John's other invitee.

As soon as the carriages pulled to a halt John leaped out and handed down Lady Redvers to present her to Nora. Sir Charles followed. He had the stiff stoop of an old commander. Two piercing eyes of an astonishingly pale blue stared out at the world from beneath paper-thin curtains of eyelid, sloping down in the special way that separates the English upper class from all other human species, in that it derives from a lifetime of unflustered and superior inspection of the world. When Caspar was presented to him, the folds momentarily lifted.

"Hmphf nycum prah long talk with you, young fellow," he said. "Hmwah!"

"Indeed, sir. I look forward to it keenly."

"Hyeurm earn, what! Yes."

But Caspar barely heard him, for John's other guest, now descending from the carriage, hat in hand, was—quite unmistakably—Blenkinsop!

"Look!" Boy whispered fiercely in Caspar's ear.

"I see," Caspar whispered back over his shoulder.

Nora could not help overhearing this exchange but she had no time to pursue it, for John was already bringing this most unprepossessing man to her. The name Mr. Michael Blenkinsop meant nothing. The incident had been so long ago.

Caspar turned on his heels and ostentatiously walked indoors; Boy hesitated and then followed.

John, of course, was stunned—and then angry. The anger was uppermost in his voice as he apologized to Blenkinsop and strode into the house after his two uncouth sons. Nora went to show Sir Charles and his wife the house and their rooms; Winifred—perforce—played hostess to Blenkinsop.

Caspar and Boy had gone straight into the gun room, whose door opened below the grand stair. Caspar stood in the open door, waiting for his father. John strode into the room and shut the door behind him.

"How dare you!" he said to Caspar.

"That *person* is not welcome here, sir," Caspar answered.

"Have a care, young man. Have great care. That person is to be your brother-in-law."

"No!" Boy called out.

"I'll hang for him first," Caspar said evenly.

John looked in astonishment at Boy. "You've surely never even met him," he said.

Caspar, too, rounded on Boy. "Yes. You stay out of it. What happened was between Blenkinsop and me."

John turned back to Caspar. "So—you obviously do know him."

"Very well indeed, Father. As a sodomite. As a liar. As a coward. As a cheat. As a man capable of overlooking debts of honour. Yes, I know *him*."

John was now white with rage. "Those, sir, are monstrous slanders on a man who is not here to challenge..."

Caspar was already walking to the door.

"Stay when I'm talking!" John thundered.

"I'll fetch him here," Caspar said, delighted he could remain so cool and firm. It was a long time since he and his father had crossed swords so openly. He had always lived in dread of it; so far it was more exhilarating than frightening.

"You will do no such thing," John commanded. "I will not have a guest of mine exposed to such insults."

"Are you saying, sir, that you do not believe me? Do you accuse me of saying these things without cause?" Caspar was very firm.

John saw where he had allowed himself to be manoeuvred. He could either call his son a liar or he could allow a guest of his to be blackguarded under his own roof. He appealed to Boy. "What do you know of this?"

Caspar levelled a trembling finger at his brother but said nothing. Boy shifted uneasily. "It is for Caspar to say, sir."

"But you agree with him?"

Boy did not flinch. "I would add to his list, sir. As, indeed, could he."

John faced the two of them. "Now, see here. Mr. Blenkinsop is a guest of mine. I cannot entertain any accusation against him while he is under my roof…"

"I'll throw him out, gladly," Caspar said. "Then you can listen freely!"

"Caspar!" Boy said.

"It's a pity you're not as young as your behaviour suggests," John said. "I'd send you to your room for two days. As I was saying—Mr. Blenkinsop is my guest, and while he is under my roof I must ask you to withdraw your accusations against him, whether or not they have any foundation."

He looked expectantly at them both.

"I will agree," Boy said, "with the greatest reluctance and on condition there is no question of his marrying any of ours—Winifred, I suppose you mean?"

"This is still my house. I make the conditions here." He turned to Caspar.

"What is the alternative?" Caspar asked.

John had to think. In his mind there had been no provision for an alternative. "You will be sent alone to Thorpe," he said. "And spend Christmas there."

"I accept," Caspar said instantly and left the room.

"But wait!" John called after him—fruitlessly. He turned back to Boy. "I asked the general especially for his sake. Is it really so bad? I can't think how you appear to know Mr. Blenkinsop so well."

"We don't know him since he left Fiennes."

John frowned. "Fiennes? But he was at Uppingham. I have his father's word for that. His father is a close friend of mine, I may add."

Boy turned and casually began to finger the chain that held all the guns padlocked. "I will pick my words with care, Father. I think it very likely that Blenkinsop completed his schooling at Uppingham; for it certainly was not complete when…er…*circumstances* arose that made it impossible for him to return to Fiennes in the spring of eighteen fifty-five."

"Fifty…but that was nearly eight years ago! You must have been…"

"And you see how it still rankles! With both of us. I think it would be best if you put it to Blenkinsop that he should become unwell—or be called home on urgent family business."

"I will not!"

"I'm sure you will find him accustomed to complying with requests for his discreet disappearance—or non-appearance."

"I'll do no such thing! He is my guest."

Boy snapped the chain taut with a vicious tug. He turned to face John. "Then I must tell you, sir, that unless you do, I will not sit at table with him and I shall tell my mother and sister our reasons and, ladies though they are, they will find it hard to be civil to him."

John thought back over the list Caspar had recited. Sodomite…cheat…liar. Was it wise to dig? His sons obviously felt very deeply about it. Nevertheless he was master of this house.

At that moment Caspar came back in, grinning from ear to ear. "Panic over," he said.

Neither of them could even guess what he meant.

"Blenkinsop didn't recognize me, of course. But I asked him…a certain question, and he said, 'Good God! *That* Stevenson!' and remembered an aunt he was supposed to meet off a boat from Switzerland."

"Switzerland?" John asked, disoriented. "Boat?"

"Remembered he'd forgotten to sow next year's radishes. I don't know. Anyway, he's round in the stable yard hopping around in a frenzy while they get the tumbrel harnessed again."

John started toward the door. "I must go and see him."

But Boy got there first. "And say what, pater? He's bound to write. Let that seal it, eh?"

John thought a long while. The tension became almost unendurable, but at last he turned away from the door and began to pace the room, still in silence. On his third traverse he halted at the window and looked out at the white world. Boy was sure his father was thinking of that marvellous snowbound Christmas here, sixteen years ago, when Abigail was born and their mother had nearly died; then, when she came back from the gates of death, all the children and their father had gone racing down the hill on a toboggan Uncle Walter had made. Boy, too, longed for the return of the happy, innocent family they had known then; he was sure his father was thinking the same at that moment. Caspar was also certain his father was thinking of a happy, obedient little family—not this one, but the one Mary Coen had told him of, the one with that Charity woman. They would still be young, obedient, and adoring; the guvnor would like that.

In fact, John was thinking of neither of these things. He was coming to terms with his astonishment at the degree of opposition his sons had found it possible to mount and maintain—especially Caspar. He knew he ought to squash it very firmly, and at once. But could he—when Caspar had shown himself quite willing to go and spend a lonely Christmas in Thorpe? Besides, there were obligations too, to the general and to the Sherringham girl.

"Listen," he said, turning at last from the window. He even managed a smile as he went toward them and put his arms around their shoulders. "We'll hold this in abeyance until after Christmas. You"—he squeezed Caspar—"know why the general's here. And you"—he squeezed Boy—"know why the Sherringham girl is here. So go to it, both. And go to it well. If well enough, perhaps we may even ignore this deplorable incident."

Boy basked in this return of goodwill. Caspar wondered how long it had been since that particular hand and arm had caressed that other woman.

"Perhaps," Caspar said to Nora when he explained it to her later, "it was as well we were arguing over what proved to be an empty casket. At least he knows how determined I will be. And Boy. Boy surprised me."

"Boy will surprise you all one day," Nora said with great conviction.

"He obviously hasn't surprised Linny Sherringham yet."

"Have *you*?" Nora did not expect an answer. "Would you really have gone to Thorpe on your own?" she went on.

"No." Caspar was very matter-of-fact. "I would have left home for good."

"You and your five hundred pounds!"

"Five hundred and thirty-two."

"Where?"

"America, probably. Make something out of their war. I met an American on the boat a few years ago. He said you could make a fortune in guns over there."

"This Blenkinsop thing meant as much as that to you?"

Caspar did not like her implication that it was a trivial affair. "Matter of principle," he said gruffly.

She smiled fondly at him. "Your father imagines Young John is the one in his image. But really it's you. If you were prepared to cut yourself out of the family rather than eat at the same table as Mr. Blenkinsop, perhaps yon can understand why he will not easily yield up the firm to anyone but Young John. I mean—his stubbornness, perhaps you can understand that."

Caspar, seeing exactly what she meant, nodded gloomily. He turned to leave.

"Going to America might not be such a bad thing at that," Nora mused. "It's a big enough and shocking enough thing to do—enough to move that mountain of stubbornness."

Caspar, now on his way out by the door, paused. "If I went, I'd go for good," he said. "No games."

Boy and Caroline Sherringham were allowed more licence at this time than either had enjoyed before or would be allowed again, whether or not they became engaged. They could even wander alone into the drawing room together, provided the door was left open and provided it was not too long before the notes of the piano began their tinkling reassurance to the straining ears in nearby rooms.

Caroline proved adept at producing Chopin-like melodies with hands that had a life of their own; the rest of her could then engage in the most animated conversation about anything under the sun and moon. Of course, there was never the slightest question of their really being alone together for more than a few minutes.

After Christmas dinner, Boy left his father with Caspar and the general and went to turn the pages of Caroline's music. The drawing room being occupied by Nora and the aunt, with Lady Redvers and Winifred being momentarily expected, Caroline decided she would like to try some harpsichord pieces. The pianoforte was in the drawing room, the harpsichord in the adjoining library. And since the instrument had less range of expression than the piano, it was even easier to leave her hands to their own devices on the keyboard.

"You may sit beside me, Mr. Stevenson," she said. "This seat is quite wide."

He obeyed, uneasy that he could not do so without pressing his hipbone to hers—or was it to her stays? Or the hoops or whatnots of her ballooning dress? He felt weak at the proximity of her. Girls were so different. Frightening. A girl in all her silks, gleaming and dainty, with such soft skin, so porcelain white, was so frighteningly alien. He tried to move his hip away from hers, blushing to think that she might imagine he welcomed the pleasure.

His success in putting half an inch between them was short-lived; she merely spread herself more and left him with half a buttock uncomfortably lifted onto the raised wooden edge of the bench.

"You could try this left-hand part," she said. "It's very easy. No—wait! I'll get into C, and then you can do it in C, G, and F. The same notes in each."

With speed and ease she modulated the key down to C major. Then Boy took over her left-hand part.

"Now F...now...back to C!" she said. "You see! Easy—I'll call them out."

In the drawing room, Miss Lascelles, the aunt, smiled to herself.

The new left hand on the harpsichord was unmistakably heavy and male.

"Can you tell fortunes?" Linny asked, holding the palm of her free hand upright.

"No," Boy said. "Surely it's all superstition." His right hand stayed resolutely clenched on his thigh.

"Here," she said. "I can." And she grabbed his free hand and spread it. "F," she said. "G. Good! I see a life full of adventure and acts of great daring. C again."

"I trust not!" Boy said uncomfortably. "I was rather hoping for a quiet life. And a good one, of course."

"A man should be daring. G," she said. "C."

"He can be morally daring. Spiritually daring, too. Ouch—sorry!" He had got into B natural instead of C.

Outside Nora and the aunt avoided each other's eyes.

"Not with shoulders as big as yours," she said. "Can you change C-F-A?"

"I'll try. What have my shoulders to do with it, Miss Sherringham? That wasn't half bad, was it!"

"Then back A-F-D. You, dear Mr. Stevenson, are obviously…don't take your hand away…obviously designed for action and acts of daring. Like your father. And your hand says it, too. F. See here…the strength and depth of that line? The Duke of Wellington had a line like that, you know. F sharp to A sharp. Now down to G—and that puts us in a minor key, remember. I'm a great believer in all the things our hands can tell us." She stroked the palm of his hand with her nails. "Aren't you?"

"There are," he said in a warm and eager voice, "forms of belief that are more important."

"Well," the general said, "it was on the fifth of April, eighteen forty-two, you worn 'em?"

"Sir?" Caspar asked.

"You born then?"

"No, sir. A year later."

"Goo' go'. Strorn'ry. Well, the Khyberees had the pass blocked. Stones…mud…bushes…never saw a hike, mnhmn tjah. Hort?" He looked expectantly at Caspar.

"The port is with you, my boy," John said.

"Oh—sorry!" Caspar wondered how long this nightmare could go on. It went on:

"Ha ha soldiers. British hool-uhhuna man great discipline. Haddthoro…honour myself to lead one party. Up scarlahinahoul. 'N turls, tell you. Got furla win shootin all round. Scattered pfff!" For some reason he then put a pineapple in the centre of the table. "General Pollock!" he said. He lifted the cloth and stood two empty wine bottles underneath. "Vloo m'nah tjichar—there!" He pointed to two other wine bottles and, in the same grandiloquent sweep of his hand, to Caspar and the cloth on his side.

Caspar lifted the cloth and pushed his two wine bottles under. "The Khyber Pass!" he said as understanding dawned.

"Strackly! 'N turls!" The general beamed. He reached past John and pushed the fruit bowl to the end of the table. "Slade! No—pwartah say? Sale! Sale under siege, erha." He strung a handful of nuts and figs down the Khyber Pass, saying, "Convoy ah hrunns haharition, 'n turls. Must get through."

Wineglass by finger bowl, plant pot by tangerine, the obscure geography of that remote corner of the empire as it had appeared to one of its military servants in the heat of the ambush of the fifth of April, in the year before Caspar was born, was re-created on the damasked table at Maran Hill.

Step by barely intelligible step, the Khyberees were massacred, the fort of Ali Musjid retaken, Jellalabad relieved, and Muhammad Akbar's force of six thousand defeated. "Gobba two strn'drds by whally—not to henchman four guns. What? Most excitin' dayyer ahife—hwa! I'll say. 'N turls."

He was breathing heavily, as if he had just run in with the news of the relief of Jellalabad. He looked excitedly at the remains of the four bottles and for a moment Caspar feared he was about to repeat the whole episode.

"Ah—what trade, general, is carried through the pass?" he asked quickly. "What would be its annual value?"

"Hnurgh? H'aid? Hotch no idea—snot. Snot soldier's bizzis. 'N turls."

John, acutely aware that the conversation had taken a not altogether happy path, said, "Shall we rejoin the ladies?" He hoped Young John had fared better.

On the way out the general lurched against the table. At the far end, Jellalahad fell heavily to the floor, smashed to pieces, and strewed its fruit and nuts far across the carpet. "Hneurygh, swami massingham," the general said. "Yes—'n turls."

"I see," Linny Sherringham was saying at that moment. She had just stopped playing. Even her lips were drained of blood. "Yes, I think I see." She stood up. "Well, Mr. Stevenson, do not think me insensitive to the honour you have..."

"I think it fair to add...I'm sure I may safely add, in strictest confidence...that Lord Stevenson is to have an earldom conferred upon him in the new year."

"Yes. Ah…well, as I say, please do not think me insensitive to the honour you do me, but I fear I should prove quite incapable of living up to such towering ideals."

"But, Miss Sherringham, you would!" Boy pleaded. His world was slipping from his grasp. He could not understand it. All the while he had spoken of his dearest dreams, she had smiled in such sweet agreement.

"I am…" She looked at his troubled eyes and almost melted. He was so handsome—how *could* he be so holy? What a waste! "I am very ordinary in my devotions. Very ordinary, you understand. I could not spin them out above ten minutes a day. Four to get up with and four while the maid swirls the warming pan."

"That's only eight."

"And grace at meals."

"Oh, but you could," he insisted. "You would see. It is such a joy to give each moment to God. And to choose continence."

She held up a hand. "No more, please, Mr. Stevenson. I assure you I am not your match. I never could be." They had come to the door back into the drawing room. She turned and smiled sweetly. "There's an end, now. Had I deceived you into false hope, or put you off and let it dwindle and dwindle, I should have disliked myself so."

They went into the drawing room then. John, who had just arrived at the other door with the general, saw at once in Young John's face that the evening had not gone well for him either.

Caroline went up to her aunt, made some excuse about how fatiguing the harpsichord was, and retired from the company.

On her way upstairs she met Caspar coming down.

"Miss Sherringham," he said. "You look as if you'd lost a friend and found her foot."

The image was so unexpected it forced her to laugh, much against her true mood.

Caspar guessed at once that Boy had, in their mother's phrase, "surprised" Linny Sherringham. She wasn't pretty, he thought, but somehow he didn't mind. She was pleasant to be near. You felt she was a very straight, honest sort of a girl. No tricks. Nothing devious.

"May I come by?" she said, smiling as if she thought his blocking the stairhead were a game.

Until that moment it hadn't been, but he decided to make it so. He smiled, too, and shook his head. "House rule thirty-seven," he said. "Christmas Day, young girl unattached, young man unattached, stairhead, forfeit to pass."

She giggled. She put her hands behind her back and swirled, turning left, turning right. "What forfeit, stern sir?"

Her breasts were made very obvious by her movement; he thought of her taking Nick's hand like that and putting it there. "A leeetle, leeetle kiss," he said.

"No mistletoe?"

"House rule thirty-eight. Not needed."

Smiling would-be wickedly, she rose one step nearer him. She raised her lips. "I like your house rules."

"Of course you do," he whispered. "House rule thirty-nine requires you to like all the others."

"They get better as they go on."

Their lips met. She intended the kiss to be brief and humorous. But Caspar, suddenly realizing how long it had been since he had kissed a girl, put his arms about her and lifted her the one remaining step. His kiss was long and passionate.

At first she resisted. Then she stood passively and let him feel he was not stirring her. He broke.

"Don't," she said. She was not annoyed or frightened or disgusted. Her tone plainly meant *Don't spoil it.*

He let go of her, ostentatiously. "I believe it may thaw tomorrow," he said.

She laughed—and did not move impossibly far away either. "I'm dying to hear rule forty."

"There has to be a thaw before rule forty applies," he said. He licked his lips slowly.

She came near him and touched his face. "Don't be serious," she said.

He still smiled. "I imagine you've had quite enough seriousness for one evening?"

She blew a draught of air up over her face, as people do when they wish to mime heat or embarrassment.

"Now house rule forty-one…" he began.

"Yes?"

"Says you are free to go." He turned his palms to face her.

"In that case…" She came back to him and kissed him lightly and briefly on the lips. The effect on him was far more powerful than the crusher he had stolen. "What about rule forty?" she wheedled.

"You're getting warmer," he said.

"You're very different from your brother."

"Oh, there could be only one Boy!"

"I'm glad you're not like that," she said.

He nodded and smiled, unable for once to say anything.

She went along the passage to her room, which was also Winifred's. He ran after her but stopped short.

"Er…about house rule thirty-seven."

"Yes?"

"It applies, as I said, only to *un*attached females."

A slow smile spread over her face. "I'm so glad we didn't break it," she said. And when she reached her door, she turned, and added, "I don't like breaking the rules."

"Good night, Miss Sherringham."

"Good night, Mr. Stevenson."

He almost danced back downstairs. When he had told Winnie that Nick had had no respect for Linny Sherringham, he had got the boot on the wrong foot: She had no respect for Nick.

Later, on his way to bed, Caspar passed his father. He could not resist saying, "I think I understood most of what the general said, pater. But what was that *'n-turls* word he kept using?"

John stared at him long and hard. "I don't know," he said at last. "I'm afraid I just don't know."

When Caspar got back to his own room he found Abigail sitting on his bed.

"Have you been at my diaries again?" he asked at once. Abigail was utterly amoral and had always helped herself to anything she wanted, on the faintest whim. In mitigation it had to be said that she was equally careless of her own belongings and didn't at all mind if everyone borrowed everything of hers. Indeed, her brothers and sisters had proved as much by concertedly stripping her room of every personal possession one evening. She hadn't even noticed.

"No use," Abbie said. "It's all in code. Besides, now I'm sixteen I've given up all that sort of childishness."

"What are you doing here, then?"

"Bearding the lion in his den and other fearfully brave things, I suppose."

Caspar relaxed enough to smile. Abbie had lately taken to saying "clever" and "funny" things, some of which (on the principle that if you only throw enough darts, a few are bound to score high) actually were quite funny or clever.

"I know something about our father that you don't know," she said.

"I very much doubt that," Caspar answered, hoping to taunt her into an early revelation instead of suffering her usual cat-and-mouse dribble of fact and provocation.

"I followed him one day when he thought I was gone to Madame Tussaud's."

"Which way?" Caspar asked. The other Hamilton Place was not too far north of Madame Tussaud's.

She knew at once from his tenseness that she had struck gold. "Ah!" she said.

He cursed his impatience and resolved to box a bit more clever. "I see!" he sneered. "This is the usual pottage of trivia all tricked out à la Abbie to resemble a substantial meal—which it ain't!"

"Ah, but it is."

"Go to bed, Abbie. I'm tired."

"I followed him out to St. John's Wood."

Caspar let the light of far-off reminiscence flood his eyes. "You know," he said, "when I was your age I followed him to Dalmatia. The firm was doubling a single-track railway, as I remember, which we had first..."

"I followed him to Hamilton Place."

"The mater's house? What's so extraordinary about..."

"No! Another Hamilton Place."

"There isn't another Hamilton Place!" Caspar felt sick at these revelations; the last person to be entrusted with this kind of knowledge was Abigail. In one of her blind yet oh-so-calculating furies she would blurt it out in the most damaging possible way.

"There is, there is, there is," she crowed, bouncing all the while on his bed.

He sprang upon her and pinned her down with his hands around her throat. For a moment he experienced a genuine intention to strangle her; but it quickly passed.

Abbie, however, had sensed it, and the knowledge of where she had driven Caspar both delighted and awed her. It was real power.

"Listen," he told her, speaking vehemently. "You've stumbled on a grown-up secret and you've got to treat it like a grown-up."

"Don't pretend you know!" she said although she could tell that he did.

"I've known for three or four years and not even told Winnie or Boy. You're the only other one who knows." He let go of her and sat on the bedside.

"Who is she?" Abigail abandoned her now futile attempt to establish a superiority.

"Did you see her?"

"Yes—not to talk to. Just walking."

"I've never actually seen her. What's she like?" Now he could afford to let her have a superior moment.

"Pretty, I suppose. Who is she?"

"Her name's Charity. She's the girl who used to work at Aunt Arabella's and Aunt Sarah's."

"They've got children, you know—Papa and her."

"I know." He also knew that he must now try to get her to take an adult view of this business. "It is the main reason for this schism between him and the mater. She is very hurt by it—especially, I imagine, because he lets her call herself Charity Stevenson and so their bastard children are also called Stevenson."

"Have you talked to the mater about it?" Abigail desperately hoped he had; it was precisely the sort of secret she would love to share with her mother.

"Never!" Caspar said with all the urgency he could muster. "Even when I've seen her in tears and known it was that. Even though she knows I know. I've never..."

"How does she know you know?"

"Because the person who told me also told her."

"Who?" Abbie was turning belligerent again.

"A scullery maid we used to have. You wouldn't remember her. The point is, despite all this, I've never discussed it with her or tried to sympathize. It's her private..."

"I can't see why she worries." Abbie pouted. "They're not *real* Stevensons—only Stevensons by charity." Her wide eyes waited for him to laugh—as, of course, he had to. It was the sort of remark that he, after a term at Cambridge, longed to have the wit to invent. Then she laughed, too, in an entirely innocent delight, as if some barely conscious part of her brain had said it—as much to her surprise as his.

"Very good, Abbie," he said, growing serious again. "I hope you will one day be able to say it to the mater; it will cheer her up no end. I give my solemn promise I won't say it. But I also hope you will be grown-up enough about it to know when the time will be ripe—even if it means waiting for years and years. You will wait, won't you?"

She smiled and nodded with such sincerity that for once, despite all those years of shattered promises behind them, he found it possible to believe her.

"Oh, Abbie," he sighed. "What are you going to do in life, eh? That tongue of yours will unmarry you a thousand times before you've even one ring on your finger."

"Oh, I won't marry," she said with such a simple lack of drama that—coming from her—it rang like revealed truth.

"No," he said, catching her solemnity. "I imagine you won't."

"I'll be an artist," she said, "or a writer, and I'll lead a delicious life."

He sat cross-legged on the bed and took her hands in his, relishing a sibling intimacy they had never before gained. "Isn't it nice," he said, "to know exactly what you want to do!"

"Godlike!" she said.

Later, when she had gone back to her own room, he thought over this conversation. The events of this Christmas—despite all the horse rides and snowball fights and feasting and all the other family fun—were moving with a sort of doomed inevitability toward a grand, not to say lifeshaking argument between their father and Winifred and himself. Yet this little encounter with Abbie hinted at an endless succession of such battles as each child grew toward his or her majority. What would their father make of Abbie's wish to be a painter or writer!

Had his parents any inkling of what was coming along? He'd been so absorbed in his own problem—with an occasional glance at Winnie's—that he simply hadn't noticed Abbie. It was odd, too, that despite all the hateful, hurtful, odious things she had said and done to him—and to others, to be sure—ever since she had first drawn breath, it was hard not to love her and want to help and protect her. This hard shell she affected was a mask to a rather lost, rather frightened, eternal child. Of all his brothers and sisters she was the one to whom he felt most in bondage; and tonight, he thought, she had sensed it. What would she now make of it? He knew that if he won his own personal battle, and if she needed his help to win hers, he could never refuse it to her.

Chapter 41

FOR FORM'S SAKE IT WAS STILL BOY WHO SQUIRED LINNY SHERRINGHAM OVER most of her jumps that Boxing Day meet; but when his hunter went lame on him it was natural enough for him to retire and ask Caspar to take over his duties—Linny had spent most of the checks talking with Caspar, anyway. When Boy got home the general asked him—or told him—to make a two for billiards.

Twelve hours' absence from the port bottle had made a great improvement in the old man's intelligibility, to the extent that Boy was able to grasp about two words in three.

"Sign a hiss-spent youth, they say." The general guffawed as he took his break past the thirty mark. "Played a horfu' lot. Know that. 'N turls."

Boy played miserably.

"Turn ye down, hnuh huagh?" the general asked.

"It would seem so, sir." Boy rallied and smiled. After all, they were men together. It wouldn't do to make the whims of a woman so important.

"Lot o' that on the Frontier, 'n turls. Yes." His fifth break went to forty-five. "What what what!" he chirrupped.

"I didn't know we had womenfolk up there," Boy said.

"Hnuh? No Onona. Here! Womenfolk are here. Broken hearts are there." Down went the red with a smack. "Damn nuisance, 'n turls."

Boy laughed uncomfortably. "I don't think it's that bad in my case, sir. Faith, you know, is a great comfort."

The general put down his cue and looked at Boy in a mixture of astonishment and delight.

"I mean," Boy said, "I don't think I shall suddenly be appearing on the Frontier."

The general's delight faded. "Pity. Mmmmnh." He chewed his lips. "What we need. Men of faith. Men of vision. Not your brother—*trade!* Pshwah! Fortin hundrun, 'n turls." The sentence dissolved in a trembling whistle that subsided into normal, if somewhat loud, breathing.

"My brother, sir? Caspar?"

"'S fella. Trade! Hmh money." He pierced Boy with his eye "Faith!" he barked. "A Christian mission of sword, fire, and Bible, sir! Trade? Pshwaah!"

"What's it like out there, sir?" Boy asked. "I mean, what's it *really* like?"

The general took the cue from Boy's hand and laid it parallel with his own upon the table. "Khyber Pass," he said.

He picked the red from a pocket and put it at one end. "General Pollock," he said.

And while his eyes looted the room for troops, rocks, Khyberees, the Fort of Au Musjid, and a yet unbroken Jellalabad, he said, "Fifth of April, eighteen forty-two, you worn em?"

"Almost, sir," Boy said. "Just one month later."

"That's me boy." The general beamed. "Speak my language—wha! Yes, 'n turls."

Caspar did not love Linny Sherringham. At least, if what he had felt for Mary Coen had been love (and it had certainly been powerful enough to make him do many things contrary to his real nature), he was not in love with Linny. But they got on splendidly together, like people who had known each other a long time. He remembered Mary's words, about wishing to marry someone she liked rather than someone she loved—"Why do we fret over love when liking's so pleasant?" As his friendship with Linny ripened, he came to understand more and more what Mary meant.

Also—he could not ignore it—a marriage between himself and the eldest Sherringham girl would immeasurably strengthen his claim to part of the Stevenson business; especially his claim to the only part he really wanted—the iron and steel works. If he could control such works in Wales and the northeast, at Stevenstown, sheer geography would do half his selling for him.

But, and here was the core of his dilemma, he could not honourably court Miss Sherringham until he had at least a nod and a wink that the Stevenstown steelworks would come his way; and he could not—dared not—approach Lord Stevenson until he could be quite sure of bringing in the prize of Miss Sherringham. In a way he wished he did love her; then he would have no qualms about courting her, and to hell with the consequences.

If he had been just a little more adept at reading the social signs, he would have been that necessary bit bolder. For Aunt Lascelles was bending all the rules of chaperonage as far as they would go without actually breaking to ensure that her linnet came back with at least one Stevenson head in her trophy bag. If he had been less secretive, he would have told all to Winifred or his mother, either of whom would have assured him at once that he could count on at least one prong of his pincer attack on Stevenson's. But whenever they approached the subject with him, he was so evasive and casual that they would not risk the disloyalty such assurances entailed.

He did not even tell Linny enough to settle her mind. All he could say was that he was having problems reconciling his father's wishes and his own. "If I might go into Stevenson's," he said, "instead of the army, I would be able to make so many other firm arrangements." With that one enigmatic sentence, and a discreet squeeze of the arm as he spoke the word "firm," she had to be content.

"I think I never shall get to hear rule forty, Mr. Stevenson," she said with a sigh.

"But I promise you, Miss Sherringham, the very day—the very hour—I hear that my future and Stevenson's are to be linked, you shall hear rule forty. I shall shout it to you from the top of Sherringham's tallest chimney."

She laughed. "You promise?"

"My most solemn promise."

These hints seemed clear and satisfactory at the time. But when she retailed them to her parents—without the firm sincerity of his eyes to buoy them up—they seemed much thinner and more obscure.

"Poor John," Nora said in a voice as devoid of commiseration as she could make it. "Our sons seem to have misread their parts completely."

He had been complaining to her that Young John seemed to be spending all his time with the general, leaving Caspar to squire the Sherringham girl. And tomorrow they would all be gone.

Nora turned out the lamp on her bedside table. The other lamp still burned, on what would have been John's side of the bed if he still shared it with her.

"Even worse," he said, "all four of them seem to enjoy it thoroughly."

"So there's no one traitor! No one to blame."

"Oh," he said bitterly, "I know who to blame. The tradition of disobedience in this family is both ancient and deep."

"Disobedience to custom?" she asked. "Or to vows?"

The look on his face was so ambiguous, especially with the light behind him, that she could not tell if he was working up to a rebuke of her or a confession. She wanted neither—at least, she wanted to be independently sure of The Bitch's departure first. And even then he'd have some sentence left to serve. She turned her back on him.

His hand lifted the blanket.

"Save it," she snapped without moving. "You never know when you might need it."

Normally he would have walked off to the bed in his dressing room, exasperated at her coldness. It was a measure now of his anxiety that he overlooked her rebuff and stayed. "Those two boys," he said. "They were quite ready to defy me, you know."

"Those two what?"

He gave a puzzled snort. "They are hardly men."

She turned to him then, annoyed she had put out her lamp, leaving his face in darkness, hers in the light. "I thought I had grown weary of saying it, weary of warning you. I thought you had grown weary of listening. Those two 'boys'—or men—will not fit into your moulds. Young John is not by temperament or natural aptitude fitted for your shoes."

He cut in as she drew breath. "He will overcome both those drawbacks—if they exist, which has yet to be shown."

"And Caspar," she went on, unheeding, "has been fitted to take your place for the last four years. In fact, he'd run tight circles around you now."

She saw his fists clench but, without seeing his face, she felt lost. Was she trying to make him angry? Or listen to reason? Was he even in a mood to listen?

"Pure imagination," he said. He sounded angry, but under control. More cold, really. "I bring it up merely to tell you that I intend to teach them both a lesson in obedience. I will not tolerate this open opposition from them. I will not tolerate opposition of any kind. And I mean you, especially, to heed this. Young John will leave this week for the Lake District. Caspar will not be going back to Cambridge; he will have until March to find himself a regiment—or I shall find one for him. And I have written to Miss Beale informing her that Winifred's honorary services are no longer available. Winifred is to marry." He looked at her expressionless face. "Well?"

"Well what?" she asked.

Now he was silent.

She continued: "You said I was to heed. I am heeding. You want me to discuss it, too? You want to hear what an utter, pig-headed fool you are being?"

He stood abruptly. "Not really, thank you." He walked toward his dressing room. "But you keep out of it," he warned.

"Or what, John? Will you black my eyes? Will you smash my teeth down my throat? What other sanctions have you left, John? You've withdrawn everything else."

"I…?" he choked. "*I've* withdrawn?"

She faced him calmly. "Now you heed this," she said. "Until now I have played the very minimum part necessary to maintain the affections of a family whose true needs and interests you no longer care about. But if you persist in this headstrong and utterly destructive course, you will find me at every turn—sleeves rolled up and all."

He slammed his door behind him—and at once opened it again. "You will come off worst," he warned.

Five minutes later she had awakened Caspar. She talked with him for about twenty minutes.

Next day, on their way back from the station, where they had seen off their guests, Caspar singled out Winifred and spoke to her all the way home. After lunch, John called them all into the library. Caspar and Winifred took care not to sit facing squarely on to him; if anything, they formed a group like a round committee.

"We'll wait for your mother," John said.

The long case clock had a slow, deep, oily tick.

Nora came in with a piece of needlework—something they had not seen in her hands for years. Only John, who had seen so little of her anyway, found it unsurprising.

"Before you begin, Father," Caspar said, "I feel I would like to…"

"Before you begin, sir," John barked, not wanting to lose the initiative, "you will hear me out. This interruption of yours is quite characteristic of the insubordination you have all shown to me lately."

"Quite," Caspar said.

"And I have…" Winifred began.

"Will you keep quiet!" John roared. "You listen to nothing."

"I only want to…" Caspar was all conciliation.

"Quiet!"

"But, Papa, dearest..." Winifred was all sweetness and admiration

"No! No! No! You are here to listen. You are not here to speak. We've all heard quite enough of your wants, your aspirations, your hopes. Now you will listen to what has been decided. But first I want to say that your behaviour the other day, young John and Caspar, was utterly reprehensible. Whatever long-past grudge you held against Mr. Blenkinsop, it was appalling manners to impugn his honour to me while he was my guest. The manners of guttersnipes." He looked at Caspar. "I trust you now agree?" he asked.

"I had hoped that topic was closed, guvnor," Caspar answered.

"I told you upon what condition I would consider it closed."

For a while father and son stared at each other. "Well?" John prompted.

"We cannot reopen the topic, sir, without discussing Blenkinsop's character. And I will not do that with ladies in the room."

"So!" John said grimly. "You persist! You have not withdrawn your slur against my guest one whit."

"It seems, sir, that we both persist. You persist in believing me to be a liar without even inquiring as to..."

"Enough!" John said. "I have heard enough. It was my intention to give you two months to find a regiment. I now give you two weeks."

"Give me two hours—it makes no difference. I shall never join the service."

"Caspar!" Nora warned.

"It's no good, mater. It's already too fierce," he answered, as much as to say *Keep quiet now.*

John looked threateningly at Nora. "I told you," he said before turning back to Caspar. "If I say you will join the Swiss navy, sir, then you will join the Swiss navy," he said.

Caspar rose to go, calm as an ice cellar. "By your leave," he said.

"No, sir," John barked. "You do not have my leave. And you, miss"—he rounded on Winifred—"are not to return to Cheltenham. I have already informed your Miss Beale that your honorary services are no longer available..."

"I wish to found my own school," Winifred said quickly.

"You..." John began.

"But I am not prepared to discuss it in this atmosphere of rancour."

"Not prepared? Not *prepared*!" John shouted her down. "You do not seem to be aware, young madam—nor you, sir"—he turned back to Caspar—"that all your fine airs and graces—I want, I wish, I propose—all this grandeur is funded by generous allowances from me. You, young man, will find all your tradesmen's accounts are closed two weeks from today—and will remain so until you join your regiment. Your allowance will also cease, upon the same terms." He paused, seeing that Caspar was shaking his head with a sort of sad gravity.

"Look, guvnor, let's try at least to discuss this calmly. Eh?"

John gave the faintest, wariest of nods, banking his anger for the moment. "I won't be talked out of it," he warned.

"You are saying, in effect, that you will pay me to join the colours but not to do anything else?"

"Your allowance, and all other privileges, will cease unless you do my will."

"And in no circumstances will you entertain this idea of my taking over even part of the firm?"

"That does not even arise."

"Because it is to go to Boy?"

"May I ask the purpose of these rather fruitless…"

"Boy," Caspar interrupted, turning to his brother, "suppose someone came to you and told you he could land a tasty great contract for Stevenson's provided you greased his palm with a bribe?"

"I hope and trust I should know my duty," Boy said.

"There!" John turned triumphantly on Caspar as if he were routed. Caspar smiled. "I hope you'll both be very happy," he said, half to himself. Then, raising his voice, he went on in a firm, calm tone: "You have told me your wishes, sir. Now I will tell you exactly what I am going to do. I am going to my room to pack. Then, tomorrow, I shall leave this house for the last time. I will not go into the army. I shall go into business on my own account. And when Boy's 'knowledge of his duty' has brought your firm to its knees, I will buy out what is left and show you how it should be managed. All this I promise you."

"Caspar!" Nora called out angrily. "You burn every boat!"

"Exactly."

John laughed. Anyone who entered at that moment would have taken it for a most pleasant laugh. "You are very sure of yourself," he said.

Caspar stood to go. In equally pleasant vein he replied, "Not entirely without cause." He crossed the room to the door.

"Steamer!" Winifred pleaded.

He stopped and guiltily faced her. "Sorry, Winnie," he said. "Let's see what's in store for you." He sat—a very provisional gesture—near the door.

Winifred turned back to John. "I know you wish me to marry, Father," she said, "but I swear to you now by my most solemn oath that I never shall. You may disown me. You may throw me out of your house. I will not marry. I shall teach. And one day I shall be head of my own school, and it will be the best that…"

At that point John exploded. "God in heaven!" he roared. "Is there no obedience, no respect, no sense of duty in this family! You are going to bring my firm to its knees; and you are going to manage to acquire and run the best school in the world! Is this a new race we have bred? All must want—all must have—the best? What do you know of the world? Of life? Nothing! You are children. Yahoos screaming for superlatives. It is we who know the world and life, we, your mother and I. And it is we who will determine what you shall do. Within one month, sir, I guarantee you will be back on your knees, begging me to use my influence at the War Office on your behalf. And you, miss, before this twelve months is out, will be begging me for a husband. Now do not trifle with me"—his voice rose to a new pitch of fury as he saw her draw breath to argue—"I warn you, there is a way to make you *beg* me to get you married. Do not force me to use it. Bend now, willingly, for if you resist, I will break that proud and rebellious spirit before it poisons your whole life."

The strings of the harpsichord carried forth into the silence a hundred fading resonances of his anger. Boy then added his obbligato: "If only everybody did their duty, there would be no strife and we would be one happy family again. Why must we quarrel so?"

John smiled and nodded at him with a warmth that only Boy took to be wholehearted.

Nora, seeing no one else was going to speak, said, "I'm glad I was included a few moments ago, because I feel it's time I had my say."

"It's pointless, mater," Caspar said, and all his bitterness now came out into the open. "How can you argue about duty to family, and obligations, and respect, with *that* person, when you know and I know, full well, that he…"

"Caspar!" Nora almost screamed. The intensity of her voice frightened everyone, even herself a little. "Never…" she said, pointing a warning finger at him. The finger shook as she struggled to complete the sentence; but no words came. At length she drew breath, gathered herself with some effort, and, still looking at Caspar, said in a most casual, conversational tone, "This young man is well able to look after himself. When he goes from here, our firm loses one of the best—potentially one of the best—business brains I have ever seen. I fear not for him but for us." She turned to John then. "And I fear for you, too," she went on. "It is not in your nature to see ability wasted. If you have your way with these two young people, it would be the most monstrous waste of ability. And one day that fact would be borne in upon you. I think when this black storm has passed from you, the regret would be more than you could bear."

She relapsed into silence, though only moments earlier her whole attitude had been one of winding up to some climax. Her stillness took them all by surprise.

"Is that all?" John asked tendentiously.

She looked miserably at him and squared her shoulders. "Not quite. You must be saved from the worst of yourself. Winifred is of age. You have no further obligation to her. You may leave her to me now. I shall make sure her abilities are not wasted."

Boy was scandalized at this defiance. "Mother!" he said.

Caspar shouted at Boy to mind his own business—while he still had it. Before two words were out of his mouth, Winifred joined in, shrieking at both her brothers to be quiet. Meanwhile Nora was trying to add, above the shouting, that she would support Winifred and finance her school—and make sure it was profitable.

In the midst of the babel John rose and walked to the door. The move silenced them. Into that silence he said, "The prattle of self-will! Let it run while it may!"

Nora, seeing that old, implacable glint in his eye, was suddenly gripped by an immense though formless anxiety. He was planning some dreadful response to this defiance by Winifred and Caspar. And until she knew what it was, she could do nothing but pray that the "storm," as she called it, would lift from him before rather than after he did...whatever it was.

She had not long to wait, though she was not at home when the blow fell. The storm over John's mind was as black as ever when his carriage drew up outside Nora's Hamilton Place and he sent in word desiring Winifred to come out and see him. Winnie suspected nothing as she climbed into the carriage; the notion that she was being abducted by her own father never entered her head.

But while they were still on their way to London Bridge station John made it very clear that she was already beyond her mother's protection. In the calmest voice, a voice far more sad than angry, he told her how, two hours from now, while he and she were on their way to Folkestone harbour and the ferry to France, a message would be delivered to Nora advising her of Winifred's new, temporary residence at an *école corrective et tempérante* in Normandy—a place where recalcitrant daughters could be imprisoned until they came to their senses. Nora would doubtless bring on her necessary belongings when she went over there—as she certainly would—to try to get Winifred released. It would be a vain journey.

He was a little unnerved that Winifred made no reply, but he went on to explain that it was for her own good—that it was wicked of her to flout his authority and to want to work. Whoever heard of a teacher who was also the eldest daughter of an earl! Lady Winifred Stevenson, teacher of coal merchants' daughters—what did that sound like!

Still she said nothing; but those great, pitying eyes never left his face.

He told her, too, that the discipline in this French school would be harsh, the work arduous, the day long, the comforts few, and rest short. But she need not stay there one minute longer than she wanted. She had only to ask to see the matron and to tell her that she was ready to submit to his will and she would be on the next cross-channel ferry to England. He would be at the quayside to meet her.

And still she said nothing.

Not until their coach was drawing up before the gates of the rather grim fortress that was to be her home did she break her silence. He clearly had not seen the place before; even he was a little shaken at the sight of it.

"Dear, innocent Papa!" she said, gentle and unsmiling. "I'm sure it never once occurred to you that everyone in Society will assume I am pregnant." She deliberately chose a word considered too coarse for polite society. "Everyone will think that *that* is why you have put me away in here!"

She saw at once in his face that the thought had, indeed, never struck him. He had been too singlemindedly intent on getting her away from Nora and into some place where only her submission would buy back her freedom.

She saw the doubt wound him; then she poured on the salt. "Those ranks of elderly viragos who sit at the side of every ballroom, determining who shall and who shall not be eligible for whom—what do you think they'll make of it, Papa? Mr. Blenkinsop turned off at his very arrival. Me put in here within a fortnight. Now *there's* two and two to make forty! Not all the money nor all the influence of the great Earl of Wharfedale will find me a husband *then*—or not one the great Earl may be proud of."

"Be quiet!" he said angrily.

"And the longer you keep me here, the more you will confirm their suspicions."

"At least," he said, hoping to silence her by turning her own argument around, "it will stop your ideas of being headmistress in your own school."

"Not a bit of it," she said, as if she had expected him to say that—as, indeed, she had, for she had passed two-thirds of her long and silent journey imagining all the turns this last, vital conversation between them might take. "My girls are the daughters of the middle classes. Much more practical, down-to-earth people than your upper-class pishies. They look for *value*. Results! It's the class you ought never to have left." She gave a little laugh. "Why, they might even welcome the chance to patronize a lady against whom there was a little whiff of scandal!"

His anger was now more frightened than choleric. "You will not be here long enough," he promised. "This place will very quickly break you. You will submit."

Now she was serene. She even managed to look at him with compassion as she said the one word, "Never!"

She neither paused nor even looked back at him before she vanished through the gates. Even the wardresses—and what else could one call them—stood a little in awe of her calm and self-possessed dignity.

A bitterly cold dawn the following day found Nora and Caspar (who had not run away quite as swiftly as he had promised in the heat of that argument) hammering at those same gates for admittance. They were allowed to pass in her boxes, but neither threats nor pleas—nor money—could gain their own entry. The rules were clear: no visitors without the father's consent; no letters unless from the father or covered by a letter from him; and the girl herself might reply only through him.

Nanette, while all this was going on, found a back-door way of smuggling in a message to Winifred, telling her not to despair and to be sure that everything that could be done was being done to secure her early release.

Nora and Caspar went straight to the prefect of police. But it was obviously not the first time he had been disturbed at his breakfast by a distraught or angry mother. He was suave, bland, and utterly unhelpful.

Nora's own lawyer, who handled all the legal side of her Deauville properties, was no more forthcoming: There was no right of *habeas corpus* in France, he explained, and that was why such schools were placed here. A father's rights over an unmarried daughter, whatever her age, were paramount.

"It's why people need two parents," Caspar said bitterly when every potential line of action was shown to be fruitless. "If you and that man were still on speaking terms, this could never have happened."

And Nora, although they were standing in the middle of a crowded street in broad daylight, burst into tears. These last twenty-four hours had been too much for her.

Caspar was now intensely embarrassed. He had hit out at her unthinkingly, needing only to vent his own bitterness and sense of frustration; if his father had been there, Caspar would have killed him. "There, there," he soothed, slipping his arm about her shoulders and gripping her tightly. She turned inward to him and buried her face between his neck and shoulder, pushing off her bonnet. "I've been so little use to you," she sobbed.

It had been a hard pill to swallow—after so many years when her money had seemed to spell absolute power, she had now been forced to understand that all the money in the world was futile if the institutions of the state were ranged against it. She, the richest woman in England, could not legally retrieve her daughter from an institution into which any father could jettison that same daughter for as long as he pleased.

"Don't go to pieces now, mater," Caspar said. "You still hold the key for all of us. When we've beaten him, we're going to need you. And so will he."

She took heart then and found enough courage to expose her tear-reddened face to the day. "You are going to beat him, aren't you, darling!"

"Into the ground," he answered. Then, realizing the unintended implication of the metaphor, he quickly put a flat hand level with the side of his knee. "Up to here, anyway."

"What'll you do now?" she asked when they were once more in their carriage and on their way back to Dieppe.

"I have a head full of Latin and Greek, which must make it the second most useless organ this side of Rome, ancient or modern. So I suppose my first aim must be to fill it with something more practical."

She smiled for the first time since they had learned of Winifred's abduction. He was glad. In the long, lonely months that lay ahead he wanted her to remember him as jovial and confident; whenever doubts came, he wanted that brighter picture of himself to sustain her.

"What practical things?" she asked. "I mean, in particular."

"In particular? I'm sure I told you. Small arms and ammunition—a fairly portable skill, I think. And with all those buffaloes and Indians…"

"Do you know anything about the trade over there?"

He smiled and drew breath, like a conjuror about to top his act. "New York," he said, in a reading voice. "Trades Directory, eighteen sixty-two. Arms: ammunition, eight firms; Arms: armaments, four firms; Guns: pistol makers, twenty…"

Nora laughed. "Very well! Very well!" she said, holding up her hands to fend off this weight of information.

"No, you asked for it and you shall hear it to the end. Guns: pistols, importers of, twelve firms; Gunsmiths, nineteen; Military goods, twenty-seven; Percussion caps, six; Shooting galleries, five; Shot manufacturers, four."

Nora had laughed herself out before he finished, but her humour was restored. "I should have known better than to doubt that you understood what you were about," she said. But later, in a more serious mood, she asked if he didn't think the trade sounded a little overcrowded.

He puffed out his stomach and put his fingertips together in an imitation of a pompous businessman. "If, ma'am, I may summarize a lifetime in the trade, my advice is this: Never strive to be first; strive only to be best."

Again he made his mother laugh. "Oh, Caspar! I'm so glad we have you. You are going to help us all, aren't you? You won't run away completely and abandon us altogether?"

"Nay!" He laughed, becoming the Yorkshire Tyke once more—the Aloysius Abercrombie who had sold those beds and who now, in place of the Hon. Caspar, was going to learn all about guns. "Nay! I shall need to know th' terms afore I can answer that!"

This time Nora did not laugh quite so freely.

Two weeks later, living a day-long impersonation of Aloysius Abercrombie, he had vanished among the smoke of the forges and the clang of the engineering shops of the English Midlands—Birmingham, Coventry, Wolverhampton—an apprentice to fortune. And Winifred sat at the barred windows of her cell and drank deep of bitterness. She did not cry. Not once since the outer gate had shut behind her had she cried. Her soul filled with a quiet and abiding hatred of a world in which this outrage was possible. A male world—for, even without Nanette's smuggled letter, she understood well how powerless her mother now was. Night after night she sat at that window, renewing, reinforcing, resharpening her resolve that from the day of her release out of this odious place to the day of her final release from the larger imprisonment of being a female in such a world, she would work to end that monstrous domination of the regiments of men.

Beside her lay five letters from her father. Not one had she opened. Her own letters to him were calm, reasoned, and utterly damning. But she knew him; she knew he would hear the cry they suppressed.

Chapter 42

Boy heard nothing of Winifred's fate until, early in March, Caspar took a few days off from his new life and made the journey north to Cumberland to see him.

Boy had not made the expected mess of the Cockermouth, Keswick, & Penrith contract, yet his methods were as opposite to his father's as they could possibly be. John's system was to trust until trust was abused. Boy's was to trust nothing and no one.

At first, people—his engineers, tradesmen, and navvies—said it was only natural. He was sort of on trial. Of course he'd be strict, wouldn't he? Just wait and watch, though—he'll ease up and become a chip off his father's block.

They waited. They watched. And Boy did not ease up. Every inch of working had its deputy, foreman, ganger, timekeeper. Every yard of progress was charted minutely and pinned down to individual workers; no one here was ever going to be able to say, "It wasn't me, it was someone else did that bit." God help the man who showed late without damn good, copperbottom cause, or who got drunk, or brawled, or left early, or who did not pull his weight. Even calls of nature were rationed and charted. Two unpaid hours a week went on maintenance, when tools were cleaned, sharpened, tightened, and straightened; equipment repaired; staging checked and renewed; ropes respliced; and every nut, bolt, screw, clip, hinge, fastener, shackle, pin, and bracket checked and rechecked. If any nut showed the week's mud undisturbed by a spanner, someone got dismissed.

It was the safest, most orderly, smoothest running, soberest and most miserable working ever to go under the name of Stevenson. But work was hard got that spring and summer, so desertions were few.

John had regular reports from "friends" on the site, of course. At first he assumed, like everyone else, that his son was starting tight and would loosen up. And even when it became clear to him that Young John was, by nature, a disciplinarian of a very tough kind, he was still more relieved than worried. He laughed, indeed, to think how his greatest fear had once been that Young John would leave everything to his deputies and lie around reading poetry and the classics all day!

Even as Caspar rode along the line of the workings he could tell that everything—superficially at least—was as it ought to be on a Stevenson contract. His fierce disappointment told him how deeply he still longed to take over the firm instead of Boy. It was a longing his conscious mind and will had disavowed on that baleful day after Christmas when the whole family had fallen apart. If ever there was a moment when his resolve to go to America finally set firm within him, it was when he passed the neat piles of stores and the shipshape workings and sensed that military purposefulness which pervaded every site. At least as an organizer and manager of men and enterprise, Boy was not going to disgrace himself.

Boy seemed almost ashamed of being so glad to welcome Caspar to the seat of operations.

"What d'you think?" he asked when their greetings were over.

"Very impressive, Boy, I must say." Caspar nodded judiciously and looked around him again as if he thought some little out-of-place element might just have escaped his notice.

"You all thought I'd make an unholy mess, now didn't you?"

"I expected it. But I see I was wrong. There's no fear of that now."

"And you?" Boy asked. "Where have you been—and doing what?"

By now they had strolled away from the huts that comprised Boy's headquarters. The small and flimsy structures were dwarfed by the masses of Skiddaw Fell to the north and Grisedale Pike to the southwest. It was scenery of rugged grandeur, closer to God than to man. And today, when a whole landscape of clouds poured overhead, spanning peak to peak in one rolling roof of liberated white cliffs, it would have been easy to understand John's fears that Boy might lie around reading poetry and classics. It was a place in which to sit and invent new symphonies by Mozart and Beethoven; it was a place that did three-quarters of the inventing for you.

"I'm more worried about Winnie," Caspar said. "Has your father let her out yet?"

"Let her out!" Boy was too astonished at the words to take up the "your father."

"Have they not told you?"

"I've wondered about her and worried, I must say. I keep writing and she doesn't answer. But I've been so busy here. What should I have been told?"

"She's in a private jail in France. Your father's put her in there until she agrees to give in to him." Caspar could almost feel the coldness and stiffness invade Boy at his side.

"I'm sure it's in her best interests," Boy said. "Our father would never do anything so serious unless it were for the best in the long run."

"The mater says he regretted it as soon as he'd done it. Now he wants to get her out. Even the slightest gesture from her would do. But, of course, she's his daughter. She'd die first. And he'd die rather than just give in. So it's a matter of seeing which stiff neck breaks first."

"If you're going to talk in that disrespectful way, I wish you'd change the subject."

"Well!" Caspar gave a bitter laugh. "I suppose that answers the only question I really came here to ask—forlorn hope though it was from the start."

Boy looked curious. He obviously wanted to know exactly what Caspar had been going to ask; but he did not want to prolong a distasteful conversation.

"I was hoping to persuade you to use the fact that you are also, by courtesy, Lord Stevenson, to deceive the governess of Winnie's jail and get her out. I thought it might appeal to the romantic in you to break this impasse."

"You must be mad."

"I must be." He turned and began to stride back toward his horse, forcing Boy to follow. "I'm glad you're doing so well, Boy," he said. "I truly am. I hope, though, that you're never really put to the test. And I hope you will always be able to think of your father as you do now."

"What the devil are you talking about?" Boy asked angrily. Half his anger was at being forced to trot along behind Caspar.

"If you ever find out, you'll remember I said it." Caspar swung himself up onto his horse. "If I want to get in touch with you, I'll write to the London office. All this"—he glanced for one final, envious time at the encampment of huts—"has a depressingly temporary look."

"Where will you be?" Boy asked.

Caspar spurred his horse away at a canter. "America!" he shouted back over his shoulder.

Chapter 43

FOUR MONTHS LATER, WHEN CASPAR STEPPED OUT OF CASTLE GARDEN, Manhattan, and into the Battery, he knew more about small arms—their design, manufacture, and ammunition—than anyone in the world. At least, the proof that that was so would not have surprised him. It had certainly cost him enough to acquire this expertise; his capital had shrunk to just over £310—or, as he must now learn to think of it, $2,114.48 American. A miraculously revived Aloysius Abercrombie had haunted the small arms manufactories in and around Birmingham, first as a skilled stockmaker, then, by degrees, rivetter, lathe turner, reamer, general machinist, and temperer. Where he could bluff, he did; where he could not, he bribed or bought.

Actually, in the few humble moments of his day, those minutes before he sank into sleep, when he allowed himself briefly to contemplate the as-yet empty future not as a Stevenson heir but as an untried businessman of uncertain trade and no fixed address, in those moments he knew how thin his skill really was. He just had to hope it would not be tested too severely all at once.

Five pounds of his capital had gone on an immigrant ticket from Liverpool to New York. For the first few days he had regretted not paying the extra seven pounds and going second class; conditions in steerage had been really appalling. But then he realized they were actually slightly better than at Old School when he had first gone to Fiennes, especially once he had struck up a couple of friendships among his predominantly Irish fellow passengers. After that, he weathered the six-week passage with little sweat. Those shipboard friendships, though they had endured three thousand miles of ocean, did not survive thirty yards beyond the wide-open portals of Castle Garden. From there on they were all in competition.

His first call after finding rooms had to be at the National Bank of the Republic where the newly dead Aloysius Abercrombie's letter of credit should be awaiting the newly revived Hon. Caspar Stevenson. It was, and Caspar breathed a lot easier.

"Just visiting?" the cashier asked.

"Quite honestly, Mr. Ford, I don't know," Caspar answered. "I've not been on your soil an hour."

"You surely haven't." Mr. Ford grinned and stamped his heel on the bank's marble floor. "No soil here, sir. This island comprises—if I may so adumbrate—solid, living rock."

"I shall certainly stay a while."

"Take my advice, sir. This is no town to visit…"

"Oh, I was looking forward to…"

"I mean at this particular juncture in history, sir. If it would not seriously discommode you, my advice is to absquatulate forthwith and return in a month. Not to say two months, sir. Or three."

Caspar was not yet aware of the American instinct when faced with the demands of a formal situation (and what could be more formal than a meeting with an Honourable so early of a Monday morning!) to vanish in a cloud of learned-sounding polysyllables, like a squid into his ink (or, rather, a decacephalopod into his own nigrescent exudations). He could not make out whether or not the man was just trying to be jocular.

"Why at this particular time, Mr. Ford?"

"We are at war, sir."

"And have been for over two years, surely?"

"Ah!" Ford held up a finger and beamed as if Caspar had gone right to the heart of the matter. "Exactly so, young man. And we have used up all our patriots. The fodder for next month's cannon must he drafted, you see." He looked suddenly as if he feared all this might be boring the young gentleman.

"Go on," Caspar said, encouragingly. "I may say, I may tell you, Mr. Ford, for you seem a decent, discreet sort of a fellow"—Caspar leaned over the edge of the man's desk and lowered his voice—"I might, I just very well might, open a business in this city. So anything you may tell me, in the strictest confidence, you understand, would do more than satisfy an idle curiosity."

"A business, mmh? A business." He looked troubled.

"Is there something wrong, Mr. Ford?" Caspar asked.

Ford obviously decided to be frank with him. "We are, you understand, a very *Irish* city. I would think two out of every seven you meet here are of that…ah… Hibernian…ah…"

"Extraction?"

"Quite."

"Or 'eviction,' more like."

Ford pointed at him. "Doubly true, sir. Doubly true. Yes. And your Irishman, having shed his own troubles, is loath, you see, to shoulder those of the nigger slave. Especially when the freed niggers are pouring north and taking all the hod-carrying jobs at any wage."

"Ah! You mean the war is not popular here—the Union cause is not popular?"

"Indeed—and this draft is detested, sir. Detested. Especially since any man with three hundred loose dollars may buy himself immunity from the draft. So it will be the poor who will be coerced into uniform. And the poor are the Irish." He sighed. "No sir! I would not be a nigger in this town, not for all the money between here and Charlestown pier."

"Here" was the corner of Wall Street and Broadway.

"Nor," Caspar said, "by implication, an English aristocrat?"

Ford smiled impishly. "For all the money in Wall Street? I might. I just might at that!"

Caspar laughed. "Well, Mr. Ford, you are very encouraging. But, surely, New York is a big city? There must be room."

"Big?" Ford was surprised. "You come from London and you call this 'big'—New York? Why, it's but a village by comparison."

Caspar assumed the man was just showing a polite modesty; he did not yet understand how rare a commodity that was. "Surely," he said, "I have a map of the city—avenues nearly thirteen miles long, streets over two miles, numbered up to two hundred or more..."

He petered out as he saw the smile on Ford's face.

"You'll pardon me, sir, but maps of this city have looked like that since my grandfather's time. I think the first thing you've got to do is climb"—he took Caspar to the window and pointed to it—"Trinity steeple. Over three hundred feet, I believe. The tallest building in the city. And from there you may have a bird's-eye view of the entire built-upon area. An hour's stroll north of here there are cows in green fields!"

At first Caspar was disappointed but then he reflected that even an area five miles by two was a lot of stone and mortar; there must still be room for the founding home of America's greatest weapons manufacturer-to-be.

Ford, rightly sensing that Caspar did not yet want to discuss his business, left the matter of his bank's help vague—vague but positive. In parting he told Caspar of the Mercantile Library up in Astor Place, where he might glean a great deal of useful commercial information. Caspar thanked him and said he felt sure he would be back for more than the mere business of drawing out his weekly expenses.

For some reason the view from the top of Trinity steeple put him in mind of the tower at Thorpe Old Manor. He could not think why, for, physically, there was not one single point of similarity. Perhaps it was that both were places from which to survey the empires of fantasy. From Thorpe tower he had (in his mind's eye) looked down upon the whole range of the Stevenson empire and possessed it. Now, here, on Trinity steeple, a lump came into his throat at the memory.

He thought it extraordinary. All those stifling summer evenings and nights on the Atlantic when he had watched the water coil back in the slick wake behind the ship, had watched yard by yard the distance grow between him and all he had ever wanted—all that time he had felt more hopeful than downcast. Yet here, where the focus of those hopes was spread in a vast panorama at his feet, he thought instead of all those things his father's tyranny had denied him forever—for Caspar now had no thought of going home again except as a rich and independent businessman in his own right.

He shook his head, as if he might thereby dislodge these gloomy thoughts. He told himself that this nostalgia would serve no purpose. He reflected that most people probably felt this way an hour or two after the euphoria of landing. He needed a woman. Tonight he'd go out and find one. Or even hire one—why not? Heartened at the idea, he turned to take stock of his new empire.

And from those dizzying heights, he had to confess, it looked nowhere near as large as imagination (fed by that somewhat bombastic map) had painted it. The built-upon part of the city pushed up two fingers to the level of Central Park—one fat one between Sixth and Eight Avenues, one thin one on Third. Between and on either side the buildings dropped back to the low Thirties. To be sure, he could not number them so precisely from where he stood, but the general pattern was clear: New York was small.

After lunch he lay despondently on the bed he had hired in the least fly-infested room of twelve fly-infested rooms he had seen before resigning himself. The house was between Lispenard and Canal streets and had horse railways on both sides. If he opened the windows, the dust and cinders came dancing in on the merciless sunbeams; if he closed them, he stifled. It was certainly no city to be in during early July. Maybe he ought to go to the Mercantile Library that Ford had mentioned and look at directories going back over the last ten years. He hadn't been able to do that in England. There he'd see how the gun trade was growing. Or if it was.

Armed with this new resolve, he leapt up from the bed, regretted the exertion, and strolled at a much more leisurely pace out into air so hot and sticky you could almost bottle it. He could not face the idea of going back indoors, into a library especially. He'd do it tomorrow. Surely he'd earned this half day off?

He had it in mind to explore the edges of his new territory, and so set off up Broadway. After a mile or so, Astor Place, running diagonally northeast, offered some relief from the depressing monotony of the right angle and he took it. At Third Avenue he decided to ride a car uptown, but before he had gone four blocks north the track was blocked by a line of stationary cars as far as the eye could see. By Thirteenth Street he was back on the foot pavement; most of the people in the street were heading north. There was an air of suppressed excitement about them.

From Twentieth Street all the shops were shut. From the low Thirties the throng grew steadily more dense. In several places small crowds had collected around street orators who spoke to one purpose only—to damn the draft. But the crowds seemed curious rather than responsive. It was the same at Forty-sixth Street, where the press of people entirely blocked the highway. The centre of their interest was a three-floor wooden house guarded by a single line of frightened-looking policemen with drawn locust sticks.

Caspar learned from a man in the crowd that this was one of the draft offices. There were several competing explanations of what was happening, or going to happen, but the most popular among the bystanders was the belief that the leader of a local volunteer fire company called the Black Joke had been drafted, and the company had come to destroy the house and the wheel.

It soon became clear that the mob on the south side of the street was mostly of peaceful, curious sightseers, but on the north a much larger and very much less orderly mob was pouring down from the direction of Central Park. It did not take them long to drive the police indoors, and then out again by the back door; and very soon after, the Black Joke had set fire to the place. Within half an hour it was a heap of glowing cinders. Other fire companies were then, at last, allowed through to save the ashes.

Throughout, Caspar was astounded at the behaviour of the more respectable part of the crowd. They did not exactly laugh or cheer, but they treated it as a fairly everyday sort of spectacle—something to look at, shake the head and frown over, but not to be unduly upset by. Anywhere in England such scenes would be the talk of the country. The police and the military would have been there at once.

And every rioter would have been safely in chains within the hour. Clearly, he thought, life in America, even in its most civilized city, was going to be a shade more raw than in Tipperary.

The mood was less tolerant at Lexington Avenue, whither most of the rioters drifted once it was clear that the draft office would not be saved. Lexington was undeveloped beyond Forty-first Street, but at Forty-fifth there were two isolated houses on a vacant block and these became the next focus of the mob's anger. One person said a wounded policeman had gone into one of the houses, another that a draft officer lodged there, a third that it was occupied by Negroes.

Soon there was no window left whole in either house. The occupants—no wounded policeman, nor military person, nor anyone who was not white of skin among them—fled through the back yard and over the fields. Caspar felt, and could sense around him, a bitter anger as laughing, drunken louts and women looted both houses of all portable articles, even washstands and writing desks. Soon a slow curl of smoke came from one of the downstairs windows and, rather than face again the sickening sight of a property burning, unhindered, to its foundations, he turned west and made for Fifth Avenue in the middle of the island. People in the crowds had said there was now serious rioting all down the east and west sides. The mob was going for the weapons and ammunition in the Armory on East Twenty-second Street.

At Forty-second Street and Fifth Avenue, on the northern edge of the city, he came to the reservoir. Opposite were the smouldering remnants of what had once obviously been a fine, large building. There was a grim-faced man, a gentleman by his clothes, standing a little apart from the crowd. Caspar asked him quietly what the building was.

The man looked at him, sizing him up. "You are an Englishman, sir?"

"Caspar Stevenson, at your service."

"Bidwell Fox, sir, at yours." Both men bowed. "What it *was*"—Fox returned his gaze to the remains of the building—"is the Colored Half Orphan Asylum. What it *is* is the fruit of the corrupt and unbridled Democratic politics that has turned this city into the modern Sodom and Begorrah."

"And the children?" Caspar asked, appalled.

"All saved but one—a little girl of six. They battered her to death for the crime of nigritude. She hid beneath her bed."

He was obviously disgusted, yet in the heavy, bitter calm of his words Caspar detected a variant of that same acceptance of violence he had noted in the other, earlier crowd. It was dreadful, his tone implied, but it happened every day.

And now Fox even smiled ruefully, as if his seriousness had been a small breach of etiquette. "I see you have a stout cane there, Mr. Stevenson. And so have I." He firmly renewed his grip. "Back to back we should make a formidable pair. So, if it is your intention to return downtown..."

"Will it be so bad?"

"You never know. In this city you never know."

In fact, if Caspar had confined his wanderings to the middle of the island, south of Twenty-fifth Street, he would have remained unaware that any disturbance was taking place at all. Omnibuses were plying as usual the length of Fifth Avenue. Nevertheless the two men elected to walk; it would be less torrid out in the street than inside the cars.

Fifth Avenue was obviously the place to build his mansion once he had made his fortune, Caspar thought. There were houses here as fine as any modern London houses. While the two men strolled, Fox enlarged upon his theme of the destruction of New York by its Democratic politicians.

"The perpetrators of that outrage upon the Asylum were apprehended by the police, but you may be sure that even now there are Democratic politicians at the station houses demanding their release, Democratic magistrates are announcing that this war is unconstitutional, the draft is unconstitutional, and the murderers of coloured children are merely exercising their legal right to resist an oppressive government. And that scoundrel Archbishop Hughes is already passing out thousand-year indulgences. Oh yes! Jefferson Davis is king of New York, sir."

At Fifteenth Street he startled Caspar with a sudden, and obviously unpremeditated invitation to dinner. But of course Caspar was delighted to accept—he was learning so much about his new home city he would have been a fool not to, whatever his twenty years of drummed-in etiquette said to the contrary. He was doubly surprised that Fox intended them to dine in his own home. And trebly surprised to find that he quite liked this easy, affable intimacy on so short an acquaintance. In England you were taught to distrust any stranger until you had good cause to think better of him. Here, it seemed, the reverse was true. And why not? It was certainly working to his advantage.

The time drew on to eleven o'clock before he left his new friends, Mr. and Mrs. Fox, in their house in (no, *on*—he must remember that) *on* Irving Place.

Funny to think of a house being on a Street! Sort of perched, would it be? On stilts, perhaps? He giggled. Still, the English wasn't much better: in a street! On a river…in a river? When Americans heard English people saying their house is in such-and-such a street, they must have a picture of a house half buried among the cobblestones! He giggled even louder. Why was it so important anyway? Much more important to keep this bloody pavement still. Not "pavement." They had another word. Sideway? No. Gone! Ask tomorrow.

The rain, which began to fall in lovely, cooling bucketsful before he was halfway back to his lodging, helped to sober him. He was quite steady—without needing to take elaborate care to be so—as he went up to his room, where he hung up his clothes, towelled himself dry, and lay naked on his bed listening to the sheets of rain falling on the rooftops, streets, and…and *sidewalks*!

His achievement of the word sent him almost at once into a deep, smiling slumber. Twice in the night he got up to drink greedily; it saved him from a thick head next day. It was still raining hard, both times, so he felt not too bad about pissing straight out into the street. Onto the street? He chuckled. He pissed into. The piss went onto—surely?

Back in bed he remembered he was supposed to have had a girl. Never mind, he thought with a yawn. Time enough. Time enough. It wasn't so important.

Chapter 44

NEXT MORNING AT BREAKFAST THEY ALL ATE AT THE SAME TABLE LIKE ONE big family; indeed, the semi-permanent residents, who formed the majority, *were* one big family, and all highly tickled to be joined by an English aristocrat. There was no secret in how they came to discover him for what he was. Mrs. Axelschmidt, the German widow who owned and ran the house, had, she explained, unabashed, looked through his belongings and then gone up to the library to consult Debrett. Of course, the current edition did not mention the recently conferred earldom. And nor did Caspar.

When all the welcomes and introductions were through, they went back to their earlier topic—the riots of yesterday, which probably formed the only topic at every New York breakfast table that morning.

Caspar heard, but only half believed, that a great fire had destroyed Central Park and even the rain hadn't fully extinguished it; that Croton Reservoir had been breached, sending a wall of water down as far as Madison Square; that two Negroes had been hanged and mutilated by women on Clarkson Street in the Third Ward; that the Armory on Twenty-second Street had taken fire and collapsed with several hundred looters self-barricaded inside it; that the Irish were intent on driving the Yankees out of Manhattan; that the rioters were sure to try to break into the banks on Wall Street today; and that the inmates of a house of prostitution on Water Street had been savagely beaten for concealing a Negro servant girl.

The last item surprised him in that no one appeared embarrassed or flustered that such a place was mentioned by its proper name in mixed company. The girls at the table, too, several of whom worked in shops and private houses nearby, all seemed a very forthcoming, independent lot. Anyway—Water Street. He stored away the name.

The other information—about the intended looting of the banks of Wall Street—worried him deeply. His first action today, he decided, must be to get down to the Bank of the Republic, draw out all his money, and then leave the island by the nearest ferry. There must be plenty of safe places nearby, on Long Island or Staten Island or in New Jersey, where he could stay until the authorities had brought the mob in Manhattan to heel. He went south on Broadway, hurrying despite the oppressive heat that had already built up. The rain had stopped but the sky was still overcast in one even gray of eye-hurting intensity from horizon to horizon.

Broadway was jammed solid by a mob several blocks before Wall Street. This was a mob that had tried (and almost succeeded in) firing the *Tribune* offices in Printing House Square. The police had driven them along Park Row and on down Broadway, planning, no doubt, to keep them penned on the southern tip of the island. Seeing no possibility of getting forward by this route, Caspar looked at his map and cut eastward along Maiden Lane, thinking he could then go down William Street and come into Wall Street halfway along.

But no sooner had he turned south than a vast mob, many thousand strong, men and women of the most ruffianly kind, came pouring down the road behind him, from the slums and tenements of the Bowery and the Five Points district. Now he was securely wedged between two mobs—this one behind him and the one at the foot of Broadway. He had no choice but to make for Wall Street as fast as he could.

The street was already crowded. The authorities must have heard of the rumoured attack on the banks, for the police were there in force, making repeated club attacks on the mob. Many of the people trapped in the crowd were, like himself, respectable men on lawful business—and there were even one or two respectable women there, as well. Caspar was relieved to discover that the police did not rain their clubs down indiscriminately. For the moment he was safe from that quarter.

But the sudden inrush of new rioters from the Five Points and the Bowery changed the whole picture. Within minutes the police withdrew to the shelter of banks and houses in the portion of the street they had so laboriously cleared. At first he thought this move was either out of cowardice or represented a sensible regrouping before they launched a new attack. He soon saw that their reason was far more sinister.

For there, broadside on between the piers at the end of the street, was a frigate. She towered over the street. Every gunport was open, and from the black mouth of each peered a cannon. Hundreds of times, in imagination and fact, he had peered at the business ends of cannons without ever realizing what it would feel like if they were loaded and primed. He was terrified. Those guns weren't there as an empty threat. They were charged with canister and grape. At any moment, to judge by the speed of the police retreat, they would fill this street with whizzing balls of lead flying fast enough to cut right through a man. He had never felt so vulnerable. Every gun seemed to be aimed right between his eyes.

He did not panic. He could even, for half a second, appreciate the irony of it. All the things he had done in his life, all that he had learned, useless and useful, all his plans, his defiance of his father, and now he, Caspar, was here to make his fortune and show everyone, especially show his father and make him eat his words. All that was about to be cut to nothing by a cannonade fired indiscriminately to quell a mob whose quarrel was not even remotely connected with him! What a waste, he thought. What a waste of *me*!

Then he saw the girl and all thought of himself evaporated. He was not the only one to make the obvious connection between the sudden police withdrawal and the towering presence of that frigate with her guns pointing so as to rake the entire length of the street. All around him people were turning their backs to the ship and trying to flee up the street or out via the cross streets. The girl, afraid of getting caught up in the mob, was clinging to the brass knocker of one of the banks. Caspar knew he had to go to her rescue.

A respectably dressed man loomed out of the swirling crowd nearby. Caspar grabbed him by the arm and shouted: "That girl, sir! We must go to her assistance!"

The man looked incredulously at him, said "Shee-it!" (which Caspar was slow to interpret), wrenched free his arm, and vanished back into the mob.

Caspar began to feel desperate. The momentum of the crowd was carrying him farther and farther from the girl. He fought his way to the inner edge of the sidewalk and, curse by blow, struggled back upstream toward the girl. When he was still some yards from her he saw her hand torn free from the knocker. At once she was swept into the crowd and fell. He heard her scream.

Like a mad demon he fought and pummelled his way to where she was lying. She was being fearfully trodden and trampled. He bent to try to lift her, praying he would not be borne down, too. And at that moment there was a noise like thin ice breaking up along a river in thaw—a sort of skittering, clattering sound that seemed to come from the walls above and opposite. It passed, quicker than thought, up the street. The screams and the roar of the cannon were simultaneous. He realized then that the first sound had been the grapeshot scattering along the walls of the buildings. A man behind Caspar, a man who would have been shielded had Caspar not bent down at that moment, fell across him, bearing him down upon the unconscious girl. Caspar did not need to feel the hot blood pouring onto his neck and shoulder to know that the man was dead.

The mob had passed. Caspar risked looking up. Incredibly he saw that the shot had turned their panic into anger. They were looking at the fifteen or twenty dead who littered the street and they were actually turning and preparing to march on the ship!

With every ounce of strength he possessed, he hauled the girl out from beneath the dead man. It could only be moments before the sailors reloaded and fired a second salvo. He half-dragged, half-carried the girl down the street—the fifteen longest paces of his life—to the corner of Pearl Street. He just made it around the bend as the second cannonade rang out. Again it was preceded for a fraction of a second by that chilling, withering noise of shot skittering along the walls and pavement.

There were screams, of course, but something else—a great angry roar that curdled his blood and filled him with as much fear as had the sight of the frigate's guns. He was no more safe here than he had been in Wall Street.

He lifted the girl, fireman fashion, across his shoulders and stumbled up Pearl Street. He got no farther than Platt Street before his knees gave way under him. He took the skin off his cheek and left hand but managed to save the girl from a nasty crack. He struggled to his feet again and looked around for shelter. The first house in Platt Street, on the northern side, was open; later he was to learn that a Negro family had abandoned it in terror an hour earlier; at that moment it seemed as if Fate had decided to leave the horseshoes out of her fists for just one round. Too weak to lift the girl again, he dragged and rolled her up the five steps, through the front door, and into the passage.

A room opened to their right. He went in alone. It was empty but for a bed and some infested clothing and blankets. He pulled the mattress to the window with the half-formed idea that if they were surprised, they could at least have the slight hope of escape by it. When he went back to the passage she was beginning to stir.

He had only got her halfway to the mattress when she came around fully. She saw him. He smiled to reassure her, not knowing how ghastly the blood and the dirt from the street made him look. Her eyes went wide in horror; she drew breath to scream and then winced at the pain in her ribs. It allowed Caspar time to say: "You're safe. You've been hurt, but you're safe now."

He thought she fainted again, but it was just the pain. When it passed, she opened her eyes. Caspar meanwhile had found a can of water, which smelled fresh, behind the door. He dipped a clean handkerchief in it and came back and laid it on her brow. His words had only partly reassured her but this completed the job.

"Who are you?" she asked.

"Name of Caspar Stevenson, miss. From England. I came through Castle Garden yesterday."

She grinned. "My!"

"Yes. The guidebook says nothing about all this, you know. I shall have a very sharp word or two to say to the publisher—a Mr. Miller, I believe?"

She bit her lip rather than laugh.

"Sorry!" He hit his forehead with his clenched fist. "Look—can you struggle up onto the mattress if I bring it here?"

He pulled the mattress over from the window, arranging it to touch her so that all she had to do was a single roll. Seeing the contortion of her face in performing that one simple manoeuvre, he was glad she had been unconscious while he carried her.

"I'm going to pull it near the window," he said. "I must be able to watch the rioters."

"They're not rioters," she said with difficulty.

He could not understand why she said it but he didn't want to make her talk. He smiled down. "Of course not. It's the church picnic, just got a little out of hand."

"Wash your face," she whispered. It seemed a lot easier to whisper.

As slowly and gently as he could he dragged the mattress to the window and then went to dip his handkerchief in the water again to wash the blood and grime from his face.

"Better," she whispered. She sounded Irish, but then a lot of the Yankee accent sounded Irish to him.

All the same, when she said "better" it could almost have been Mary Coen. He smiled at her. What could he say that wouldn't start a conversation? Perhaps "yes" and "no" wouldn't tax her too much.

"Hungry?" he asked.

"No, thank you."

"Don't bother about please and thank you. Just say yes or no—or shake your head. Thirsty?"

"A bit."

He looked out into the street. It was full of rioters in angry groups; working up courage, perhaps, to return to Wall Street. He saw several muskets and revolvers plus one carbine, and almost everyone not so armed had a club or butcher's knife. Across the street was a fruiterer's; next to it, a wine and liquor shop. He described the scene to her. "Shall I risk going across for an orange or something?"

She winced with pain as she raised her hand to clutch his. "No!" she said urgently. "Not for me." Her hand was cold—on such a day as this, too; it must be the hottest day of the year.

He took off his jacket and draped it over her feet. She had nice, trim little ankles. He looked at her face then, just as a face, rather than as something to clean or to worry at because of the pain it registered. It was a very pleasant face, too. Strong. Good, clear features, generous mouth, deep-blue, vivacious eyes—not afraid—curly auburn hair, what he could see of it under her bonnet.

"Is it all still there?" she whispered, grinning. She was learning a way of talking that was not too painful.

"Was it so obvious? I'm sorry."

"It was quite an audit."

He told her what had happened back there in Wall Street. Then, having nothing else to say, he told her—or began to tell her—what had happened to him yesterday, until he saw it distressed her. So instead he told her about the voyage over. She liked that much better.

"What's happening outside?" she asked.

"They seem to have given up the idea of fighting for the moment. Except one another. They're just getting more drunk."

"Wouldn't you know it," she said bitterly. Then she smiled again. "Tell me about England, where you live and that."

"I've left all that behind," he said.

A police officer rode into the street and dismounted, tying his horse to a lamppost right outside the window. Caspar thought the man was either brave or amazingly foolhardy. The officer walked across the street and into the saloon. The rioters were too astonished to molest him, though several shouted at him and brandished their weapons. Caspar decided not to tell her about it. Tell her what, instead? What had she asked? England.

"My family has several houses, actually. There's Thorpe Old Manor up in Yorkshire..."

"Where's Yorkshire?"

"It's part of the north of England. It's bigger than Canada."

"But it can't be. All of England isn't bigger than New York State."

"I know it isn't. But Yorkshire's bigger than Canada, all the same."

She smiled. "I see. Go on."

He liked her; she caught his jokes quickly. The officer came out of the saloon while he went on speaking to her. Despite all that followed he did not once pause in his narrative nor betray his horror in his tone as he told her of the Old Manor, and Maran Hill, and Hamilton Place.

The officer was halfway back to his horse—sword in one hand, drawn pistol in the other—when a great thug of a man came running from the saloon brandishing a rifle above his head. He held it by the barrel, turning it into a club. He brought it down full force on the officer's neck and shoulder, dropping him at once. Immediately the whole crowd fell upon him, kicking him and thrashing him with clubs.

"Are you a 'sir'?" she asked.

"No, I'm not. I'm a commoner. But I have the courtesy title of Honourable. I met some people the other night—I mean last night—who said I should use it here. It would be good for business: The Honourable Caspar Stevenson. What do you think? I don't know your name, by the way."

"Dee Lane," she said.

Someone put a couple of twists of rope about the officer's ankles and groups of laughing men took turns dragging him up and down over the cobbles. He was still conscious and at one point he even attempted to rise.

"I think you surely should, Honourable," the girl said (pronouncing it "on-a-bull"). "It's cunning."

"Cunning?"

"Well—cute. Why do you have that title?"

"Because my father's an earl, actually."

A priest came into the street. The men paused in their game.

"You always say 'actually'," she said. "You said, 'We have several houses, actually' and 'My father's an earl, actually'."

"Do I?" He laughed.

The priest bent over and administered the last rites to the officer.

"Will you be an earl one day, Hon'able?"

"Only if my older brother dies before me. Or if I make a fortune and go back and give a lot of it away, I might be made an earl in my own right. Then"—he laughed—"I'd be *Right* Hon'able."

She closed her eyes and grinned knowingly. "Just like here," she said. "You mean pay the politicians."

The priest stood up and walked back among the throng to Pearl Street. Here and there he exchanged friendly words and greetings with the rioters. As soon as he had gone they began dragging the officer around again at the end of the rope. By now he appeared unconscious.

"No," Caspar said. "It's not as blatant as that. One founds libraries, alms houses, schools for mechanics, one endows colleges—that sort of thing."

"For heaven's sake!" She had spoken too violently; she winced and paused until the pain subsided. "You mean you do all that in your own name, and the pols, who've gotten nothing out of it for themselves, give you more honours? That doesn't line up."

"I suppose not. I've never thought of it, actually."

"Actually!"

Some women came with knives and began to slash at the officer's flesh. He was, beyond doubt, unconscious now. The women laughed a great deal and encouraged children to come and drop stones on the man. Some of the stones were very big and needed two or three children to lift them. He must have had several bones broken by it.

"Actually, Hon'able, what line of business are you going to make this fortune in, actually?"

"I don't know, act...—no, I mustn't say it!" He laughed. "I had thought of small arms and ammunition manufacture. But...oh, I don't know. With all this burning and destruction, and all those green acres up beyond Forty-fifth... perhaps building would be more sensible."

"Who do you know here?"

"Only people I've met. People at my lodgings, Mr. Fox, and..."

"No, no. I mean who do you—you know—*know*. Who will get you the work? Who'll protect you? That sort of 'know'."

The men came back out of the saloon and began dragging the body around again; the women ran whooping and shrieking after it with their knives until one, in her excitement, cut a lump off one of the others. Then they fought among themselves and the men had to come and separate them. They all went back into the saloon, leaving the body in the gutter. To his horror, Caspar saw the man was still moving.

If it weren't for the girl he'd risk going out and helping the poor fellow.

"I think I can protect myself, Miss Lane," he said. "And as for getting work, if the price is low enough and the quality is..."

She whistled—not in amazement. She whistled a tune.

"No?" he said.

"No," she confirmed.

"It's the land of opportunity, isn't it?"

"It was, Hon'able. It surely was. 'Land of opportunists' is more like it now."

"Get me work from where?" he asked. "And protect me from what?"

"Whom," she said. "Work from *whom*. Protect from *whom*. You need someone to talk to people who can put work your way." She crinkled imaginary money in her fingers as she said "talk." "And you need someone to protect you"—again the imaginary money—"from the gangs."

"I see." He looked at her. "How do you know all this, Miss Lane?"

"Family business, you could say." She clenched her eyes and tried to raise a hand to her forehead.

"Is anything the matter?" he asked.

"My head. Is it cut open—on top there?"

There was blood on her bonnet; he had thought it came from the dead man. "Shall I take it off and see?" he asked, being careful to keep any alarm out of his voice and face. He undid the strings and gently peeled off the material. The blood was fresh. "It looks as if you've grazed the skin. Does it hurt?"

"It's a terrible itch."

"But no headache?" He tried to sound very knowing.

"No."

"Even so, I think I'd better try and get a doctor to you. I'll risk going out."

Swift as a cat she grabbed his arm. "No! They'd kill you, Hon'able."

"They would not!" He laughed at the very notion—even though he was looking straight at the body of the police officer, not four yards from the window.

"They would. Believe me—I know. I'm all right. It's just a graze, as you say." She smiled. "Just wait. It'll cool off and then you can get word to my father." She held out a limp hand for him to grasp. "Tell me about your father, your people."

Three hours later Caspar realized he had said a great deal more than he would have believed himself capable of saying. It was not only that Miss Lane was such an encouraging listener, who smiled, who frowned, who melted in sympathy, who radiated understanding; it was not just that. His narrative had turned into a voyage of self-discovery, too. Never, not even to himself, had he been forced to connect all the different hopes of his father and mother and Boy and Winifred, and all the pressures of Society and convention into one single narrative. (Of course, he said nothing of Mary Coen—that was both private and irrelevant.) It helped, too, to explain it to a foreigner, who could not possibly be expected to understand the ins and outs of English Society. And while he was explaining them to her, his hair—though it had not literally stood on end—actually bristled on his scalp. For he realized he was coming to see his father's point of view. Not to share it, of course. But to see it as a plausible, even rational, alternative to his own: The demands of Society were the single most powerful force in England; Society was the source of all patronage; its members had access to all kinds of privileged information—much of it trivial gossip, to be sure, but not all of it; there was nothing Society could not arrange, conceal, promote, or kill, if it were so minded. To choose to be outside it was to suffer a kind of amputation; to flout it, even in some minor degree, was to risk that same cutting off; so to go against its demands and dictates you needed very good reasons. From his father's point of view were Boy, Winifred, and himself "good reasons"?

How odd, he thought, that he should have to come all this way and sit with this unknown, wounded girl in this filthy room, and all the bizarre circumstances outside, before he could even frame that question, let alone face it honestly.

The girl was quick to sense that he was not relating a string of history and stale conclusions; instead he was—not only *in* her presence but *because of* her presence—undergoing a private odyssey. She shared all of its excitement. The revelations of English Society as a holder and dispenser of power (a very different picture from the one promoted in the ladies' journals) caused her no difficulty. She seemed very familiar with all the mechanisms he outlined. But Caspar's revelation of himself kept the shine in her eyes, the smile on her lips, and on her tongue all those sympathetic little interrogatory words that help a narrative to flow and to flow.

So, three hours later, Caspar knew far more about his present situation. But he understood all the less why his response to his father had been so extreme. Did he regret having laid bare so much? He looked down at Miss Lane and found he regretted none of it. He knew how artfully she had probed and winkled to hear more, more, more, and he begrudged her not one word of it. He hardly dared admit the comparison yet, but he believed he could tell her all those things he had once promised himself he would tell Mary Coen. *Could* tell her? He had already told her, or begun to.

It bound him to her, he realized, in a unique way. If those ruffians broke in here now he would give his life to protect her—not, as it would have been in Wall

Street, out of the general demands of chivalry, but out of…not love. Surely not? Out of something unique. Some uniquely great liking that was not quite love.

His thirst was by now raging, and so, he felt sure, was hers. "I'll go upstairs," he said. "See if anyone up there can spare us some water."

He knocked on several doors and, though he was certain there were people within, he got no reply. He came back downstairs. Outside they were pouring oil over the officer's corpse; one of the men had just made sure it was a corpse. Clearly they were going to hang him to the lamppost and torch him. Caspar was just wondering what to do for the best when one of the men climbed the lamppost. He was two-thirds of the way up, and on a level with their window, when he happened to glance inside and see Caspar looking out. He dropped like a flag and called several other louts urgently to him. They had a shouted consultation, with many glances up at the window.

As soon as it was clear they intended to come in, Caspar told Miss Lane. She smiled. "Don't fret yourself," she said. "There's no harm in them."

He gave one snort of derision, threw a blanket over her, told her at all costs to stay still, and, over her feeble protests, went to the door. He had only just shut it behind him when the first of the thugs burst open the front door. Caspar didn't wait to argue or bluff it out but hurled himself at the fellow, leaping into the air and kicking out with both feet. He sent the man backward down the steps and projected himself, in reaction, halfway back up the passage.

"Hon'able!" he heard her cry.

"Be quiet, you stupid woman!" he shouted back.

He reached the door just before the second assault. There was no key. He had to try to hold it shut. It was soon clear he was not going to be able to keep them at bay for very long. They were battering at it with some sort of implement, a bench or a pole of some kind.

He would have to lead them away from this house, away from Miss Lane. He would open the door just in advance of one of their batterings and hope to take advantage of their confusion to leap out and get away. He counted the shuddering knocks to get the rhythm: one…two…three!

On the three he jerked open the door and stood aside. A shaft from a demolished cart just grazed his thigh. But the men at the other end fell sprawling up the steps. His yelp of agony added to the shock as he limped-jumped over them and on them, down the steps, and limped-ran toward Pearl Street. As he went he shouted, "Fetch the priest! Fetch the priest!" in the hope of adding to the confusion.

He made it into Pearl Street and almost reached John Street before he was brought down—not by any man, but by a stray dog as terrified as himself. Before he could rise again he was firmly in the grip of four of the rioters.

He gave no struggle, pretending to be only semi-conscious. If he was to make another run for it, they should be lulled into lowering their guard. The people, seeing his state, offered no immediate violence. Surrounded by skipping, chattering children—the same who had stoned the officer—he was carried feet first back toward Platt Street.

As they passed the house where he and the girl had taken refuge, the window he had used for a lookout was thrown up and a rioter poked his head out. "Go steady with him now, boys. He's all right, that one, so he is."

Their attitude changed at once. Their grip on him became gentler and more supportive. As they neared the front step he gave up his pretence of semiconsciousness and struggled to be allowed to stand. They did not resist.

"What is it?" one of his erstwhile captors asked a man at the top of the stairs.

"Isn't he with Joe Delaney's girl!" the man answered.

"If you've harmed her…!" Caspar shouted and ran at him up the steps.

The man, much bigger than Caspar, caught and held him easily. "If we've harmed her!" he laughed. "Boys, that's a good 'un. If *we've* harmed her! What about dem bastards wit' the guns?"

Further argument was cut short by the sudden appearance of Miss Lane herself at the doorway of the room. One man supported each arm.

"Miss Lane!" Caspar broke free from the giant and ran to her.

She levered herself out of the men's support and almost fell on him. "It's all right," she whispered through her pain. "These are friends."

"We'll see, shall we!" he said grimly. "Get a cart," he told the two men who had held her. "Horse cart, handcart, anything she can lie on." The two men looked for confirmation to the giant. "Damn your sides—move!" Caspar barked.

They ran past him and down the steps.

"And you—big fella—get the mattress from in there, or a clean one if you can find it, to cushion her." He heard the man go. "Are you…could you get more comfortable?" he asked her gently. "Do you want to sit down? Or lie down."

She made a little murmur of pain and kept her arms tight about him. He felt her head shake on his chest. The blood seemed to have stopped oozing from the graze on her scalp.

Once she was on the mattress—a brand-new one, looted from a shop, together with several luxurious covers—she became a great deal easier and more relaxed, until she turned her head and saw the ghastly, mutilated body of the police officer hanging from the lamppost. The cart began to move at that moment but her eyes were fixed upon the corpse until they were going north on Pearl Street and their refuge house cut off her view of it. Moments later it was put to the torch. They saw only the reflection of the flames in the windows around. The gleeful laughter followed them. The driver also laughing, told her all the things they had done to "dat dam fella." Throughout the narrative her eyes never left Caspar's face; he sat on the cart at her side, his legs dangling.

There were tears in her eyes as the man finished. She pulled her hand from beneath the covers and grasped Caspar's, giving it a squeeze. "God love you," she said, not understanding the sudden pain that clouded his eyes.

It was several hours before he was allowed into her bedroom—at her insistence—for a brief farewell. During that time he had come to terms with many surprises.

She was not "Dee Lane" but a Delaney. Leonora Delaney, known for short as "Laney" Delaney. Her father, Joe Delaney, was an important politician in the Fourteenth Ward—undisputed territory of the Bowery Boys, the Plug Uglies, the Dead Rabbits, the Shirt Tails, the Chichesters, the True Blue Americans, the O'Connell Guards, and all the other gangs whose blood ran as green as a shamrock leaf. His response to the appearance in his house of a young English aristocrat as the saviour of his daughter's life may be imagined. It took more swallowing than Joe Delaney could manage in the space of one evening, especially on top of a gruelling day spent in prying his constituents from the grip of the Yankee police, the agents of England.

He made no secret of his dislike for Caspar; so much so that when the man came down from his daughter's room and told Caspar to go up for a few minutes, Caspar could not help saying, "You surprise me, sir."

A grim smile of amusement showed briefly through the man's set features. "'Tis that girl is surprising me," he said. "But if I cross her, sure she'll only be worse."

Laney was bathed and bound and comfortable in a huge mound of a goose-down mattress. A pretty little mob nightcap covered the wound on her head, leaving her auburn curls loose about her face. Caspar's heart turned over. She was beautiful, he realized.

She held out a hand. He took it and sat beside her. An old woman—a grandmother?—sitting in the corner, and unnoticed by Caspar until then, put down her knitting, cleared her throat, and pointed to their linked hands. Reluctantly Laney let go of him. "She's mostly deaf," she said quietly to Caspar. "If you talk no louder than this, she can't follow."

"I've been pondering one or two things, Miss Laney," he told her.

She blinked prettily. "Yes, Hon'able?"

"You were in no danger from that mob—"

"Ah, ah!" she warned.

"All right—from that Sunday-school outing. They wouldn't have harmed a hair of your head."

"Did I say they would?"

"You let me believe it."

She shrugged her right shoulder and smiled. "God, you're so full of false beliefs, where would I begin? You believe our people have no good cause…"

He drew breath to interrupt, but she went on: "Of course you do. You're English, aren't you? Don't you damn us the minute you hear the brogue? You don't even listen once you hear that."

"Oh, come up!" he cajoled. "You know full well there's a difference."

"But you don't deny it."

"I do, as it happens. But you'd have to know me and my family and what we've done in Ireland a great deal better before I'd expect you to believe it."

She looked at him a long time then. "All right," she said. "I should have told you."

"Why didn't you?"

Again the silence. She drew breath. She almost spoke. "I'm not going to tell you," she said.

He smiled knowingly. She joined in. "We could talk so easily there, couldn't we," she said. It was partly a comment on their silence, partly the explanation she had just refused him.

"I'll tell you one thing," she went on. "If you're going to start in business here, you're going to need the help of men like Joseph Delaney. So what you did today won't…"

He laid a finger on her lip to silence her. The old woman stopped knitting. He took his hand away and, when the woman looked down again, he briefly kissed the finger that was still warm and wet from her.

"You don't need to say that," he told her earnestly. "If you said your father was my sworn enemy, I would still try and see you again. I am not to be bound to you by promises of help—you pick my nits, I'll pick yours. There is no need for that."

"I'm glad."

"So am I."

This time the silence was warm and easy.

"We're mad," he said at last.

"Of course we are." She spoke with her eyes shut. She seemed greatly at peace.

He left her then and came quietly back downstairs. Halfway down he was surprised by Joe Delaney's peremptory, "Is that the fella?"

He looked over the banister rail. Delaney was holding the arm of the man Caspar had kicked down the steps of the house in Platt Street. Behind them stood the giant. Caspar turned and ran back to the stairhead…how could he escape? Where?

"Come back, me boyo!" Delaney called, roaring with laughter. "We're not after you."

As if Caspar would believe him! He ran to the back of the house and threw open a casement window. His thigh was beginning to get muscle-bound where the cart shaft had grazed it—could he make it over the sill, let alone to the outhouse roof below? Even then, was there any way out of the back yard? Grunting with the pain, he lifted one leg out of the window. Already there were heavy footsteps on the stair.

He almost got the other leg over before his pursuer—the giant, not the man he had kicked—grabbed him back into the house, pinning him in a huge embrace.

"You're all right!" the voice said softly in his ear. "They mean you no harm now."

It sounded genuine enough. "I'll walk," Caspar said, pleased that the man let him go and made no attempt to stand near, where he could grab him if he ran again.

"Well," Delaney asked when Caspar showed again, "is it him?"

"Sure how would I know!" The kicked man laughed and held his hand flat near his knees. "Wasn't he so high when last I saw him. And me not much bigger." But he turned to Caspar. "Do you know Keirvaughan?" he asked.

"What if I do?"

"Does your father be having a farm there?"

"He might."

"John Stevenson?"

"That's my father's name."

"Who took a big estate at Keirvaughan and paid the passage and eighty dollars each to three hundred families?"

There was no point in denying it further. "He did so," Caspar said in the man's own vernacular. "And made going farms for the twenty who were left behind."

The kicked man turned to Delaney. "'Tis the very same," he said.

Delaney was one big grin, from political ear to political ear. "Young man!" he said. "Don't I owe you the grandest apology that ever man gave or got?" He turned to the giant, who had overtaken Caspar on the stairs. "A drop, Michael," he said. "That fella's as dry as a stone and much too sober for my liking." He beamed the full six inches of his smile back to Caspar. "*Fáilte romhat!*" he said, waving at the room beyond. "*Fáilte romhat.*"

His cheerfulness was so sudden and so complete that Caspar instantly knew him as a man never to be trusted. But he would certainly be useful. In so many ways.

"*Sláinte!*" Caspar said when the malt was in his hand.

It was his second night in New York and the second night in a row that he ended up drunk. This was one hell of a city for liquoring up a stranger.

That same evening the *Great Eastern* sailed from Liverpool, outward bound for New York. Among her passengers were the Countess of Wharfedale and her daughter Lady Winifred Stevenson.

Chapter 45

ALTHOUGH BOY ORGANIZED AND MANAGED HIS RAILWAY WORKING MORE effectively than even his father had dared to hope, he at last did something that really worried John. A Councillor Ericson, on one of the local councils, had done a great deal to ensure that Stevenson's got the contract; it was the sort of "oil of angels" that went on all the time. And of course John had shown appropriate gratitude—or had thought it appropriate. Ericson had believed otherwise. He felt he should have had double, and he came, and said so to Boy.

Boy had naturally refused to believe his father could be involved in any such underhanded business and had sent in a full report to the chief constable of Lancashire. After that it had taken John a great deal of behind-the-scenes work to keep the whole affair quiet and get it dropped. When this was safely done in mid-May, John asked his son to come down to London for a "half-term report." Somehow the young man had to be made aware what sort of a world he was now moving in.

They spent the morning going through the books.

"Even your mother says they're impeccable; and there's no higher praise possible," John told him.

They also went through the daily log and the progress sheets—Boy, in effect, talking his father step by step through the project and John just nodding and smiling and finding nothing to disagree with or even to criticize, except in the mildest way.

It made for a very pleasant lunch, especially for Boy, who was longing to hear all the family news at first hand. He had felt it would be wrong during business hours to talk family.

"How's Winnie?" was his first question. "She's stopped writing." He hoped his father would now take him into his confidence—after all, he, too, believed that Winnie should be disciplined.

"Er...she's at a school in France. She's very well. She writes to me several times a week."

The lie left Boy feeling betrayed. "Well, tell her to drop you just once in a while and think of sending me a line," he said coldly.

John nodded. He knew he was storing up future trouble in deceiving Young John like this. The fact was (as Winifred knew) the suppressed cry in each of her letters—her cold, damning, relentless, unanswerable letters—was tearing his heart out. He longed for some sufficient reason to bring her back home, but she gave him none. He had sent her there for falsely claiming she was submitting to his will; now she could repeat that claim—and make it a hundred times less sincere—and still he would release her. But he knew it was the very last thing she would now do.

What was wrong with these Stevenson children? All as stiff-necked, in their different ways, as a rusted weathercock! Winifred, who would not bend an inch; Caspar, who simply vanished rather than bow to his father's will; and now Young John, who had almost put a valued business friend in jail. Well, at least Young John was amenable to reason. He always saw sense in the end.

They decided to walk around the park rather than go straight back to the office. It was a fine afternoon. The whole of the first half of May had been rainless and sunny, though rather on the cold side. The turf underfoot was hard and springy. Fleecy clouds streaming overhead kept a satisfying interplay of light and shade dappled over the view.

"No news of Caspar," Boy said. All through lunch he had been dying to raise the topic but, having no idea how his father would respond, did not want to risk the awkwardness. Here, walking around in the open air, it would not be so sticky.

"No," John said.

Boy sighed. "I miss him, you know. He was always good company."

John grunted. He did not want to confess it, but he was missing Caspar, too. There was a hole in his landscape where that stubborn, self-possessed, ruthless face should have been.

Boy decided to risk a bit more. "I've often wondered, since—you know—whether the army would have been absolutely the thing for him." He was encouraged by his father's mildly interested expression. "I mean to say, guvnor, when a chap runs off like that, giving up everything, don't you know, rather than join the colours, it's bound to make one think a bit."

"He should have tried it at least," John said. "He could have purchased out after a year if it didn't suit. I'm not unreasonable. I wouldn't have jibbed at that."

"Oh, quite, sir. One hesitates to say this, not just because he's one's own brother, but about any man behind his back—but there's something not quite up-and-down about Caspar. Don't you feel it?"

"In what way?"

"One always feels he's holding something back from one. Never giving the full account—only the necessary account. And one feels he wouldn't be above picking and choosing his truths, and…and helping them to fit his case. That wouldn't really do in the army, would it."

"The army is very big, my boy. And in the upper…"

"But it's founded on honour, pater. It is honour alone that distinguishes the soldier from the slaughterer."

"True. Yes. But there are times and places…and, ah, circumstances…where different kinds of honour, different levels of honour might conflict."

"Are there, pater?"

"For instance, where the honour of your country might require you to sacrifice your own honour."

"I find that hard to imagine. What sort of honour would feed upon dishonour? I would not own that country. Anyway, what I was going on to say—about Caspar—was that, if he had been in charge of this railway of mine, I believe he might not have reported that wretched Ericson to the police."

"Ah! Now…"

"I don't say he'd have any dealings with the scoundrel. Of course, that would be unthinkable. But he wouldn't have pursued the matter. That's what I'm getting at, you see."

"Let's sit down," John said.

Boy sighed with contentment. He had dreaded today and now he could not imagine why. It was perfect. "I think heaven will be very like Regent's Park," he said.

John was silent a while. "D'you ever wonder why heaven is perfect, Young John?" he asked.

His son laughed in embarrassment. The answer was so obvious.

"I mean," John said, "with all eternity before them, they can afford to be perfect and stay perfect, can't they! They would be fools not to."

Boy began to feel worried. That was not the answer which seemed so obvious to him.

"But look at this city. Look at this country. Think of the few who have power and money, and the millions who have neither—who are consumed from dawn to dusk merely with the problems of keeping body and soul together. And look how short life is, even for the man who lives a century! It's never long enough. It's nearer to hell than to heaven, what?"

"I suppose so, guvnor. Are you talking about Original Sin or something?"

John cleared his throat. "I'm trying to say that you've led a very privileged and sheltered life. I'd just like you for a minute to imagine you had nothing. A little test, if you like. Let's say we exchange your clothes with that verminous heap of a man lying under that tree there. Now! There's London. Here's you. No money. No food. No home to go to. No friends to call upon. What d'you do?" He laughed. "It's a bit like what Caspar's doing, I suppose."

"Except that he has money."

"Has he? But your mother assures me she is not…"

"He has his own money. I thought you knew."

"What d'you mean—his own money?"

"Oh. Well, a couple of years ago, when he was always going on and on about wanting to be in business. I don't know much about it. Mama lent him a hundred pounds as a sort of test and he doubled it in a few months—paid her back and kept the rest."

"The devil he did!" John tried to sound annoyed but his pride was uppermost.

"Of course, I didn't hear a word of it from him. Winnie told me. Anyway, Caspar isn't in poverty—wherever else he may he. And as to your test, I'm afraid I don't quite grasp it, pater."

John sighed. "No. It's too roundabout, isn't it. What I'm saying is that your mother and I both began life very much in the sort of situation I was asking you to assume."

"I know," Boy said, and, lowering his voice, he added: "She said they used to steal! They took a turnip from a field once. I was so ashamed for her."

"Even though it was their only way of staying alive?"

"But it wasn't. There were workhouses then, surely? Anyway, I'd sooner die than steal."

"Of course you would. Yes, of course you would. And great credit it does you. But the world, you see, is not so simple. And Stevenson's—the firm, I mean, as distinct from us as people—Stevenson's is of this world. Very much so."

Boy drew breath to speak but John spoke on, a little louder, and silenced him. "The firm has to do things, sometimes, that you and I, as people, would shrink from doing—would 'die rather than do,' d'ye see? Just as with countries, you know. People in charge of countries have to do things on behalf of those countries they would never do on their own behalf."

Boy was rigid with tension. "What sort of things, sir?"

John paused. "For instance, we have to seek help from people—help, information, influence, a good word in the right ear—that sort of thing. And, of course, we have to pay for it."

"People?" Boy was shivering. "You mean people like Councillor Ericson."

"*Many* people like Councillor Ericson. Many, many people."

There was a long silence. "I see," Boy said at last.

"We have been doing it for so long—from the beginning, in fact. I had to pay over a thousand pounds on our very first contract to a man who is now a bishop! We forget, you see. And then you come along and—with different standards."

Boy stood up, anguish in every line of his face. His hands took independent life. He walked away, but not far. John did not follow. He watched his son struggling to come to terms with these new ideas.

Boy kicked at a pebble in the grass and missed. He stooped and picked it up, weighing it. He clenched his fist around it and, at last, dashed it back to the ground. He came back to his father. "Different standards?" he said, his voice barely under his control. "But I thought they were *your* standards. Your motto for your earldom: *Sit sine labe decus*—Let honour be spotless. I believed that of you!"

"They are my standards," John said quietly.

Boy looked puzzled. "But how...I mean, how can that be?"

"My personal standards. They are the standards, the very highest, by which I would regulate my personal life. But, as you must have learned even in these last few months, any man in charge of the fortunes of others has responsibilities, duties, obligations that make it impossible for him to apply those personal standards as rigorously as he would like."

"No, pater. I can honestly say I haven't learned that."

"Then you're a fool, Young John! The whole contract exists only because of Councillor Ericson's help and our payment for it."

Boy stood rigid; his voice was back under control—very icy control. "I'd rather be a fool than a scoundrel, sir." He expected his father to become angry, but John was most placatory.

"Please try to distinguish between personal and business morality. Business has its rules. Everyone knows it ways. Everyone plays by them. You cannot come into the business world and apply the rules of some Utopia—some far-off, future, heavenly state. Believe me, Stevenson's has a deserved reputation for being among the most honest and straight-dealing firms. And so we are—where it matters. We never do shoddy or dangerous work. We don't pad out our costs.

We don't let people down on dates and deliveries. We shoulder responsibility honestly for our few mistakes and put them right at our expense. We pay our people on time and in coin of the realm. We give pensions…injury compensation. We don't seek legal ways out of responsibilities that are morally ours. I could go on and on like this. Believe me, a list like that puts us amoung a very small and select group of employers in this country. In the world."

"But…" Boy began.

"But," John cut in, "if we turned ourselves into Utopia and Co., we very soon wouldn't be in existence. D'you understand that? We would not be here to extend these very considerable benefits to our customers and servants."

Boy sighed.

"D'you see?" John pressed.

"I do. I do see. It's very hard to swallow though."

John stood and gripped him by the shoulders. "I know, my boy. I'm sure it is. But remember: I am not talking about personal, individual behaviour, only company behaviour. In our personal lives *Sit sine labe decus* is always the motto."

Boy nodded glumly, but John knew it was now only a matter of time before he grew up and joined the world at large. "Tell you what, my boy," he said. "You stay out here and think about it. Walk around for an hour or so. Get used to these ideas—they've come as a bit of a shock, I can see. Let them rattle around a bit. Then come back to the office and see me."

Boy took more than an hour to come to terms with the new morality, but he was just about reconciled to it as he went back across the Marylebone Road and into Nottingham Place. He was on the doorstep of the office, still deep in worried thought, when a messenger boy came up to him with a letter.

"Lord Stevenson?" he asked. "Would he live here, sir?"

"Yes?" Boy said. "I am Lord Stevenson."

"Ah." The lad still clutched the letter. "That would be the name of John Stevenson? I was to put it particular into his hands."

"Yes, yes." Boy was excited now for of course this was the promised message from Caspar. He felt it in his bones. He gave the lad a sixpence and took the letter. "Lord Stevenson, Nottingham Place," was all the directions it bore.

It never crossed his mind that the letter was for his father. In that case, Caspar—or anyone—would have put "The Rt. Hon. the Earl of Wharfedale" on the envelope. With trembling fingers he opened it.

"Hamilton Place," it was headed. But not Caspar's hand at all. An illiterate hand, in fact. Who was writing to him from his mother's house?

"My darling darling..."

He gulped. A hoax?

"Little Ormerod is coughing very bad and the doctor dispairs of him. I know I am not to write or communicate with you like this but seeing as he is your flesh too I..."

Boy froze. It was a letter to his father! He wondered again if it was a hoax. Who was little Ormerod? There were no babies at Hamilton Place.

"Any reply, sir?" the lad asked.

"Was one expected?"

"No, sir. The lady said as you'd probably go straight out there."

"Out there?"

"Yes, sir." The lad was surprised that he was surprised.

"I'll go at once," Boy said. On impulse he thrust the letter back into the lad's hand and said, "Take this inside. Go to the second floor and say Lord Stevenson said the earl was to read this, too." He made the fellow repeat the message before he let him go.

Then he went back up to the Marylebone Road and hailed a cab.

"Are there two Hamilton Places in London?" he asked.

"Yes, sir. One up west, one out in the briars."

"Take me to the second one."

All the way out he searched desperately for some innocent explanation of those few words he had read, but none occurred to him. Honour forbade him to read further, once he had realized his mistake, but it did not prevent him from finding out things for himself.

He got down at the corner of Hamilton Place. A maidservant ran up to him. "Oh, sir—are you the doctor, sir?"

Boy hid his annoyance at being taken for a tradesman. "Young Ormerod, is it?"

Relief flooded the girl's face. "Oh, yes, sir—do hurry, sir."

She ran ahead of him to the house. When they reached the gate, he said, "I am not the doctor, you understand. Not in person. But he must be here soon. Go back and wait for him."

"But, then—who are you, sir?" the girl asked.

He pushed past her, past the sign that read HAMILTON COTTAGE. "My name is Stevenson," he said. He did not knock but walked straight indoors.

Charity came running downstairs, filled with relief, for only the doctor or John would come in unannounced like that. Boy held up a hand before she could speak. "I am Lord Stevenson," he said. And when the bewilderment showed, he added, "I am the earl's eldest son. I'm afraid your letter was delivered to me in error."

She sank to the stairs, buried her face into her hands, and began to weep bitterly, as if a long, hard struggle had ended against her.

At that moment John came bursting indoors. He took in the scene at once, hardly pausing. He came straight to Boy and grabbed his shoulder, so hard that Boy cried out in pain. John was shivering with rage. "You...you shit!" he spat into Boy's face. "You sanctimonious little piece of shit! Get out of this house!"

He thrust Boy back along the hall with such force that he went full smack into the stained-glass doorway. The light grip of the lead gaskets barely slowed his progress, but, by the same token, neither did the glass and metal damage him much beyond a few scratches to his fists. He ended up on the gravel footpath surrounded by little sherds of coloured glass and twisted fingers of lead. The doctor picked his way over him without pause or word.

Boy rose slowly to his feet, dusted himself down, picked up his hat, dusted that down, and limped out to find a cab and go to his club.

From there, after a good hot bath, he wrote to his father's club:

Dear Lord Stevenson, I realize it was perhaps a little unfeeling of me to go to Hamilton Cottage at such a time, but I regard your behaviour to me there as unspeakable and unforgivable. After all your fine words on personal honour this afternoon, to accuse me of being sanctimonious is, sir, an outrage on truth and on honour itself. But I say no more of that. It is not to me that you will one day have to account for your behaviour, but to One infinitely more qualified to judge how well you can reconcile it to your own choice of motto. When that day comes, I trust I shall have been spared and will be spared further, long enough to remove the tarnish on our name and that motto at least.

There can now be no question of my undertaking the career you chose for me. By your behaviour and your words you have released me from all filial obligations to please. I now feel free to follow my own preference, which, out of duty to you, I confessed to no one, and barely dared to own even to myself. Tomorrow I shall attend upon General Sir Charles Redvers and ask him to use his good offices to secure me a captaincy in an Indian regiment. It may surprise you to learn that I shall not offer him payment for this help; nor will he expect it.

I shall pass my life among men for whom "honour" is not a mere counter to be exchanged for commodities, services, and pleasures at whim. I will, you may be sure, breathe no word of the whore and the bastard for whom you have bartered yours.

I renounce what claim I may legally have to the firm and to my inheritance of it; but I look to you to support me in the army in the only style to which you have let me grow accustomed. You know it is impossible for an officer to live honourably without an income.

I have the honour to remain, sir,

Yours sincerely,

John Stevenson.

Chapter 46

It was past midnight before John arrived at the other Hamilton Place—Nora's house. At least she did not refuse to see him; she must realize how serious it was to bring him here at such an hour.

She did not, of course, know that he had waited to be sure little Ormerod was past the crisis before he had come.

"Young John has gone," he said as soon as he was in her bedroom.

"Gone?" She sat up and pulled a shawl around her. She could think of nothing to say beyond this repetition of his words. Earlier that night she had given an important dinner—one of the most important of her life, for it had been graced by a royal duke. John had not been invited. The dinner had been a success, but as always she now felt drained and deflated. "What d'you mean—gone?"

"He's left the firm. He won't work for us. I mean, he won't have anything to do with the firm. He wants no part of it, he says."

"But why?"

"Because of the 'oil of angels.' Because he cannot reconcile it with notions of honour he learned—at Fiennes, I suppose. He certainly never learned them from us. There's an irony for you, if you want to gloat!"

"John! It's far too serious for anything so petty-minded."

"Oh, I wouldn't blame you. You never wanted them to go to Fiennes. I was the one who insisted, wasn't I!" He sat heavily beside her on the bed. "Not a blunder but a boomerang!" He lowered his face into his hands and she suddenly realized that he was weeping. Not violently or ostentatiously. More like a man who was exhausted.

She wanted to hold him then and to comfort him. Even more, she wanted him to hold her. To comfort her—to more-than-comfort her. The muscles of her thighs and back twitched into rigidity while she longed for him as she had not longed in years.

But she was too proud and stubborn to make any actual move. And he was too defeated, and too fearful of her, to make himself even more vulnerable.

She let his weeping pass off and then asked, in a voice much calmer than she herself felt, "What will he do instead?"

"Go into the army." He had to clear his throat twice before he could complete the sentence.

"He told you that?"

"He wrote to me."

"Wrote? That's not like him."

"Isn't it? I don't know what's like him and what's not like him. I don't know what any of them are like. Obviously."

An evasiveness in his tone and gesture made her feel certain that he had told her very little of what had really passed between himself and their son. Something quite dreadful must have happened for Young John to write to his father instead of saying it, whatever it was, man to man.

John looked at her wistfully. "You're being uncharacteristically mild."

Nora thought well before she answered. Then, seeing no point in being soft, she said, "Mild? With my eldest daughter in prison, my eldest son run off to India, and my next son vanished God knows where—all because you know what's best for them. I wouldn't exactly say I'm mild, John. I'm just praying you'll know what's *worst* for the other six, so that I'll have some children left me in my old age."

John nodded. "You're right," he said. "I deserve that."

"You deserved it! And more. You've ruined our family. It will never recover from what you've done."

Her ferocity startled even herself. Her fear that she would capitulate to him—beg him to come into her bed—was too deep for her to grasp or to relate to the savagery of her outburst.

He fell upon her feet, trying to clutch at them through the counterpane. "Don't," he begged. "You're saying nothing I haven't said to myself a hundred times already this evening, before I came here."

She pulled her feet away, leaving him to scrabble at empty material. "Why did you come here, John? Just to snivel and wipe your nose on my bed linen?"

He sat up and looked at her briefly but could not face her gaze. Eyes downcast, he said, "Don't, Nora. Please don't. I came here to…of course…say I was wrong. I was wrong. I was wrong. And to ask you what I must do now to make it right? Or as right as it can be made. Are you sure you don't know where Caspar is?"

"Why?"

"I want him. I need him. I mean, the firm needs him. Did he really make a hundred profit on a hundred you lent him?"

She smiled, for the first time. "Who told you that?"

"Young John. This afternoon. He said Caspar told Winifred and she told him."

She shook her head, still smiling. "Oh, Caspar! Always making things secret! In fact, he made over five hundred pounds on it. By the most outrageous piece of business: clever, and just a little…" She waved her fingers doubtfully, suggesting that the language had not yet coined the right word for what Caspar had done. She looked at John. "It was exactly what you would have done at his age."

John nodded ruefully. "D'you know what he's doing now? Where he is?" When Nora hesitated, he added, "I only want him back. I want him for Stevenson's."

"He's somewhere in the Midlands, I think. His last letter to me—and he doesn't write often—was from Wolverhampton. But, knowing Caspar, I'd say that's a certain sign he's nowhere near Wolverhampton in fact, but only went there to post his letter. As to what he's doing—he's acquiring those skills that Fiennes seems to have neglected to impart. I hate to lay the curse on him again, but he is very like you."

"Can you get in touch with him?"

"I've already been trying. He talked most about going to America—but, of course, with him it's just as likely to be a sign he has no intention of going there at all. And what about Winifred?"

"I'll give you a letter. Will you…go to her?"

"Tomorrow." She did not take her eyes off him. Every time he looked up at her he stared directly into those pools of accusation. "Is that all, John?" she asked. "Do your confessions stop there? Is that all you want back? Just Winifred and Caspar?" She could not make it plainer than that.

He looked at her. He stretched forth his hands. "Nora."

She clutched the shawl to her, for fear of obeying that almost overpowering urge to surrender to him. "What, John?"

"Oh, Nora!"

"What?"

Still he held his hands out to her. "It's not easy…I…"

She had to shut her eyes. "You are trying to tell *me* that it's not easy?"

He fumbled for her body through the counterpane. "I know what you'll ask of me. And I can't!"

She leaped from the bed and backed on tiptoe against the wall. "Can't?" she roared in one long rising note.

He bowed his head and clutched the counterpane to his lips. "I can't," he whispered into it.

"Then either you leave this room, or I will."

His eyes sought hers, begging for mercy. "But Sefton…" he said.

"Yes?"

"I've owned him as my son. Never by word or gesture have I suggested…I've owned him, Nora."

She saw the justice of it. And he caught the hesitation in her gaze. His eyes lit up.

She shivered. Oh, how delicious it would be to run to him now! To feel his arms about her again—to surrender to all that mountainous strength—to be his. To belong! To belong again.

She took a step toward him. He smiled. It was going to be all right! It was going to be marvellous! She held her arms forward to him, feeling suddenly shy of his touch. The shawl fell from her. His hands came up to take hers. He was lost in wonder and adoration—he could not believe it.

"You may support them," she said in the gentlest, most loving tone. "And her. Provide for her. Make sure they are well launched. But you'll never see them again, will you?"

To her horror the light and joy fled from him at once. "You…bitch!" he said. "I told you you'd ask it. And I said I couldn't. And you pretended you weren't going to. You trapped me."

She backed away, appalled at his words. "You thought I'd ask *that*!" Her voice rang out. "That? I'll tell you what I was going to ask. I was going to ask you to throw them into the street. Damn you to hell—I was going to *insist* you do it!" She had second wind now. Her fury possessed her utterly. "What? You thought you could come creeping into my bed one night a month—and into hers for the other night—or however many it is you can manage these days? Thought I'd just lap that up, did you? Well, if she's still the whore she was when you found her, I'm surprised your feeble and infrequent little pokes can satisfy her. Are you sure they do, John?"

He turned and left the room.

"How many of her bastards did you truly sire?" she shouted after him. "How many do you merely 'own'?"

Then she ran to the bed and pulled the pillows over her head so that no one could hear her howling and howling and howling, at the thought of all she had so nearly regained—all that was now forever lost to her.

Her only comfort—and it did not occur to her for many hours—was the thought of that much greater loss, if she had yielded on what John had imagined were her terms.

Chapter 47

When Nora and Winifred took rooms at the Park Avenue Hotel, she knew she had just two hours to find Caspar if she wanted to surprise him. Her portrait was too often in the magazines, and the Great Ship Company (owner of the Great Eastern) was too solicitous of her welfare as a distinguished passenger for her to hope to slip into Manhattan unnoticed. Within two hours, she estimated, her arrival would be recorded in one newspaper or another. It would be a shame if, having traced him here despite all the attempts he had made to cover his tracks, she was to be cheated of the prize: the look on his face when he saw her.

She knew that Caspar's secrecy was not directed specifically against her but was turned against the world in general. He had not tried to cover his tracks—that had been natural to him. On the contrary, to leave an open trail that all could follow would have called for some overpowering reason. All her probings of the London banking system—open and clandestine—had drawn a blank. She had known then that Caspar was using another name. And there the trail ran out, until she had remembered that furniture shop he had dealt with. Mr. Vane had at once supplied the name Aloysius Abercrombie, which, at the end of May, turned up in a London bank as a transferrer of some funds to the Hon. Caspar Stevenson at the National Bank of the Republic in New York, corner of Broadway and Wall Street. Thither she and Winifred were now bound. Their mere nine days under steam had enabled them almost to outstrip Caspar, condemned by the vagaries of windpower to a six-week voyage.

They spent the first part of the drive, south from Madison Square, like all visitors, looking, absorbing. Nora, from time to time, glanced anxiously at her daughter, who was so quiet since her release from that "school." Nora had expected anger, she had been prepared for bitterness, she had even thought that Winifred might have gone a little wild and abandoned in celebration of her freedom. This range of expectation was, she wryly reflected, a measure of her ignorance of her own daughter and of the directions in which she had been maturing these last few years. For Winifred had returned to her family with none of these moods upon her; instead there was a cold and calm determination. The object of that determination she had not yet revealed, not even on the voyage out, when there had been nine brisk, warm, leisurely days to expand into, days for both of them to heal their many inner wounds. But there was no mistaking the fact that, beneath that reserved though sunny exterior, Winifred now nursed an aim of such all-consuming importance that it left no room for the shallow and obvious responses of anger or bitterness. She was even warm to her father and managed to suggest that she owed him some debt for having incarcerated her in that place. Nevertheless, Nora did not entirely trust this, to her, unnatural calm; she was still watchful for signs of the outburst she felt sure had to come.

"Fine houses, Mama," Winifred said. "If Caspar's seen these, you'll have a job to lure him back home."

"Six million pounds?" Nora said.

"And his father's welcome—don't leave that aside."

"But he detests his father."

Winifred's smile said she knew better.

"I wonder if you're right," Nora said. After a silence, she went on: "Isn't it strange how you can work for years to make a certain thing happen? And then, when you're actually in sight of it, you wonder?"

"Wonder if you're right?"

"Mmmm."

"You mean about Caspar and Stevenson's?"

"D'you think he's right, popsie?"

"He's very different from Papa. I know you think they're very alike. But I don't."

"He's practical. He's avaricious. He's good with people. He's out for himself..." Nora's list petered out into silence. She was provoking no response in Winifred.

"I like Steamer, Mama," she said at length, as a kind of insurance against what was coming next. "He is good with people. He is good company. There's no one I'd rather be shipwrecked like Robinson Crusoe with." She laughed. "But he couldn't run away then, could he! He couldn't desert me and follow his own star. And that's the point. Papa is good with people, too. But Papa also cares about them. If Papa took up someone, he'd never, never desert them—no matter *what* it cost him."

Nora looked in alarm at her daughter. Did she know? Was she trying to excuse, in this roundabout way, John and The Bitch? One glance showed she was not. In all innocence Winifred had said to Nora the one thing that—give or take a bitter year—might ultimately reconcile her to John's continued infidelity.

Winifred went on developing her point: "Steamer isn't like that. I'm not blaming him any more than I'd blame a man for being colour-blind. It's not a thing you can develop at will, I think. But Steamer will be the greatest friend to a person as long as there's utility in it, as well. When that's gone, or is used up, it's a brick wall made of smiles and words but nothing more."

Nora drew sharp breath. "That's very harsh, dear."

"It would be if he could help it. But, as I say, I think he is just like that. So—to turn your question around—do you think Stevenson's needs someone like that for its next phase of...growth? Hardly growth...perhaps just to stay where it is. I don't know. What d'you think yourself?"

The thought had occurred to Nora even as Winifred was speaking. "It connects," she said, "with one thing I've always thought about him. And that was why I believed he, rather than Young John, should take over. I've always felt that, once he became really familiar with the business, he'd be able to do what your father's never done and what I find I can't do—which is to say: '*There* is where the business should be ten years from now.' While you were talking about him it occurred to me that 'there' might be a very different place from where the firm is now. So perhaps we do need a man like Caspar—a man who can go on encouraging people, praising them, and so on, for what they're doing now; and all the while the other half of his mind is preparing to drop them, finish off their work, switch to the new direction or whatever it may be. Someone who truly cared about people, like your father, someone less secretive couldn't do it."

Winifred's mouth was open and dry. "Isn't that awful, Mother?"

"It's an awful responsibility. Do we want Stevenson's to go that way? What if all the other, nicer ways lead back down into the pit? Wouldn't it be better for Stevenson's to go under rather than turn into that sort of firm? Oh, Winifred! We have two minutes to decide!"

Winifred closed her eyes as if in prayer. "I wish I were more of a fatalist," she said. "I wish I believed these things were out of our control...that some great Spirit of History was just wafting us all along like a great river. I wish it didn't matter who was in charge or what he was like or what he did."

"You're wishing to be a Marxist," Nora said, amused.

"Am I? Theirs must be a splendid religion. We could say 'to hades with it, let Steamer take over, history will sweep him on willy-nilly'."

"Instead, what do we say?"

"I say we don't really know enough about Steamer to be sure he'd be like that. So we can't play God with him and the firm."

Nora laughed, mostly in relief. "We can't even play that other god—the Spirit of History."

The driver announced that they had arrived.

On her card, which simply said "The Countess of Wharfedale," she added in pencil, "the mother of the Hon. Caspar Stevenson," and sent it in. The head cashier, Mr. Ford, came running out, snatched off his hat and stood bareheaded before the carriage door.

"Mr. Ford?" Nora asked before he could introduce himself; she had prepared this well before she left. "I have greetings for you from Mr. Bidwell, the Wells, Fargo man in London. And also from Mr. Adams of Chambers's Bank—who was here last autumn?"

"Indeed, madam, I recollect the gentleman with…ah…the warmest, that is to say, the most cordial and amicable sentiments. And to be sure, Mr. Bidwell is a colleague these venerable years. Yes, indeed. And may I be permitted to extend to your ladyship and…er…" He waved amicably at the air in Winifred's direction.

"Winifred, dear, this is Mr. Ford, the chief cashier of New York's most important banking house. Lady Winifred Stevenson, who is the elder sister of that…'scallawag,' I believe you would say?"

"Not if they are successful, ma'am." Ford's eye twinkled. "I doubt if we would call the Honourable Caspar by that particular adumbration."

"Oh?"

"Have you not seen his new offices?"

"New offices, Mr. Ford? But how long has he been here?"

"Little short of two weeks, ma'am." He sounded surprised she did not know.

"Our letters, you see, Mr. Ford, have passed each other on the Atlantic. We cannot find his office. Nor do we know his business. Nor his prospects. Nor his associates…for my part, I believe 'scallawag' is a somewhat *mild* term."

Ford glanced nervously around. A copy of *Gilbart on Banking*, propped against the window from inside, was signal that his sanctum had been tidied, cleaned, and burnished by twenty fevered hands, and it was safe to invite Lady Stevenson and her daughter inside. Which he then did.

Half an hour later, refreshed with iced lemonade, they left for Caspar's office, the Uptown Construction Company on Baxter and Canal Streets, firmly in *down*town Manhattan.

"Isn't that typical of Steamer, Mama!" Winifred said when they were back in the cab. "He even throws people off the scent about where his company is located."

During that half hour they had learned all they thought they needed to know about Caspar, the Fourteenth Ward, Joe Delaney, Miss Laney Delaney, and the prospects for a construction company with such connections.

"I must say," Nora told Winifred, "I never imagined we'd glean so much so soon. Can you imagine how many weeks it would have taken to find all this out in London!"

"I wonder if all Americans are as fond of talking about other people. It's like Ireland, isn't it?"

"It's useful. Caspar will revel in it."

"I was just thinking that. And if he's found a girl, and a good business, and has fallen on his feet the way Ford was saying...well! We won't see him back in England."

"We'll see about that!" Nora answered, with far more confidence than she felt.

The Uptown Construction Company was in no position to start business. In fact, its position, as Nora and Winifred pushed through the quarter-open front door and wandered hesitantly up the rickety stairs, was on its knees, scrubbing the floor and bawling "Rule, Britannia" at the top of its cracked, unmelodious voice.

"Caspar!" Nora called out in horror.

He dropped the scrubbing brush, turned, and stood, all in one swift movement. "Holy Mother of God!" he shouted in parody-Irish. "Laney, would ye ever look who it is!"

Laney came out of hiding from behind a tall cupboard. She, too, had a scrubbing brush in her hand, which she at once dropped.

"Mater!" He came forward and embraced her warmly. "And Winnie, too!"

"Hello, popsie!"

"Hello, Steamer."

"Darling—no! I mean, mater and dear sister, may I have the honour to present Miss Leonora Delaney, known to all as Laney Delaney. Darling, this is my mother, Lady Stevenson, and my sister, Lady Winifred."

Laney wiped her hand carefully. "The cleanest hand in the Fourteenth Ward," she said as she offered it. "Welcome to you both, ladies. And welcome to the future-greatest construction company this city has ever seen."

As Nora shook the proffered hand she thought she had never heard territory or relationships so adroitly and swiftly marked. No wonder Caspar had nearly introduced them to her, instead of the proper way around.

"I see it is a hive of industry already," Nora said. She decided to scratch at the girl a little to see what she was made of—also to see how Caspar responded. "And how democratic you have already become, my dear. Does Miss Delaney work for you?"

"I work like a charm," she said brightly and tickled Caspar in the ribs.

"She works like a charm," Caspar confirmed, grinning. "But I say! What are you doing here—both of you? Winnie, I'm so glad you're free!"

"Why were you singing 'Rule Britannia,' Steamer?"

"Singing?" Laney sneered.

He smirked. "I thought it was Laney's father coming up. I just like to add a bit of variety to his life. All he hears are those dreadful jigs and Fenian songs." He ducked a loose, playful punch from the girl.

"Besides, she's not supposed to be here. The doctor said she must rest."

"Yes, I've heard all about that from the wonderful Mr. Ford."

"It seems I owe your son my life, Lady Stevenson. Those Yankees were firing grapeshot into civilian crowds when he carried me to safety."

Caspar cleared his throat. "Not to mention those Irish rascals!"

"No," Laney said, pursing her lips together. "Don't!"

Caspar turned to his mother, with that especially serious face he wore only when joking, and said, "You know how our bruises go red, white, and blue? Well"—he pointed to a bruise on her forearm—"look! Orange and green."

"Hon'able!" Laney was really annoyed. "I'm trying to tell your mother how grateful I am and how rightly proud she can be of you."

Caspar shrugged, chastened.

"Lady Stevenson, your son showed the sort of bravery that, on a battlefield, earns the big medals."

"Big as tombstones," Caspar said. "Some of them."

Laney turned on him, flaring with anger. "You're impossible today," she cried. She left his side and went to the window. It was the sort of move that usually precedes a struggle not to cry.

Nora thought the girl was nowhere near to tears; but it had been a neat hit of social engineering. Now she had to take the girl's part—women together, aren't men brutes, that sort of thing.

"Miss Delaney," she said, "we English have acquired the most unnatural habit of banishing our young males to remote schools at a very tender age. The result is that they can never accept praise or commendation from a woman, however well deserved. Nevertheless a good kick, aimed where it won't blind them, will serve wonderfully instead."

She did not expect Miss Delaney to make a sudden rush at Caspar and, giggling like a schoolgirl, try to kick him on the shins. She certainly didn't expect Winifred, who had rationed her laughs to one a day since her release, to join in, braying like a jackass. She almost found herself joining them as Caspar shrieked and hopped and skipped about the empty office. Until that urge took her she had not realized what aggressive feelings Caspar could arouse in people—even in people who loved him. Perhaps, she thought, especially in people who loved him.

For Caspar it was long-ago, faraway Mrs. Purse again; the girls were careful to miss him by inches and to falter when he looked like being cornered.

"*Pax!*" he cried. "I surrender. I surrender."

Both girls stopped, breathless, glad of the excuse. They looked at each other, a little hesitantly, and then, without thought, flung their arms around one another and embraced.

"Steamer, you've met your match at last," Winifred said, still smiling at Laney.

"Say!" Laney said. "His name's Caspar. You call him Steamer. I call him Hon'able." She turned on Caspar. "Who *are* you?"

Caspar grinned. "All things to all women," he said.

"Well!" Nora used her come-to-order voice. "We have obviously called on this busy firm at a most inconvenient time. So what I propose is that we"—she linked her arm with Winifred's—"should invite its two principals to the dinner rooms of the Fifth Avenue Hotel at seven o'clock this evening." She looked around with mock asperity. "At least they have chairs there."

Everyone laughed and agreed that would be splendid. As Nora was going down the stairs Laney ran to the landing above her and said, "Lady Stevenson,

I'm sure you have many family and personal things to say to your son. I will come at seven. But he will be there at six."

Nora had to admit it was beautifully done. With supreme grace and confidence, with the gentlest of smiles, with the softest voice and the most considerate words, Miss Delaney had allowed Caspar to be alone with his mother.

"A charming girl," Nora said when they were back in the coach. "A very nice girl indeed. Yes!" She looked at Winifred. "And what does that smile mean?"

"You don't see it, do you?"

"See what?"

"Yourself! She is you. She is so exactly you, my hair stood on end. It is quite uncanny."

Nora felt winded. "How can you say so? What possible resemblance is there?"

"If you can't see it, I can't make you see it."

"Name one point of resemblance!" Nora was bewildered at Winifred's air of utter certainty.

"Everything. Simply everything."

"A girl from an Irish-American slum and one of the leaders of London Society? Everything?"

"Think, Mama dear! Those hovels you took us to—at Stockport. And now think of the circles Miss Delaney just ran around you and me. Can you imagine anything that would leave her at a loss?"

For Nora it was as if the carriage seat and floor were sinking away beneath her. She suddenly saw how right Winifred was, and she marvelled that no hint of such an idea had occurred to her at the time. But now that she, too, was convinced of it, she had the most uncanny feeling of having gone a ghostly circle to meet herself.

"Thank God Caspar had the luck to find her," Winifred went on.

"Can you imagine anyone else being able to control him? She is exactly what he needs. And Stevenson's."

As soon as he heard that Boy had joined the army, Caspar asked, "Have you come to bring me back?"

"D'you want to come back?" Nora asked. She and Caspar were alone in a corner of the hotel lounge, drinking these newfangled "cocktails." Winifred, tactfully, was still dressing with the help of Nanette.

Caspar put on a broad, quizzical smile to mask anything his face might otherwise reveal. "What's the betting? At Stevenson's, I mean. What odds are you giving, mater?"

"Don't play games, Caspar."

"All right. I don't think I will come back to England." And when she showed surprise, he added, "You started from nothing. You know what an excitement it is to fight your own way up."

"It is when you succeed, popsie."

Caspar scratched his cheek. "I see that point."

"So—do you want to come back?"

"I would make big changes."

"We would expect it."

"We?"

"Your father assures me he would expect it. Of course you would not be given a free hand for some time."

Caspar laughed. "You make it sound so attractive. I have a very free hand here."

"If you are coming back, I don't want there to be any misunderstandings."

How odd, she thought, to be bargaining and manoeuvring with her own son, exactly as she would with a stranger. But that was exactly what made Caspar right. You could never have talked with Young John like this; and that, by the same token, was what had made him wrong.

"There would be the problem of Laney," he said in a voice made carefully neutral.

"You no doubt mean the problem that she is far too good for you?"

His face lit up. "D'you mean that? Truly?"

"I mean it so sincerely, Caspar, that I am thinking of making it a condition of your return that you bring her with you."

He was silent a while; obviously he had prepared for opposition on this point. The lack of it had disconcerted him. Some of the joy left his face. "Yet I don't know," he said. "We've stayed up late night after night talking about all our plans here. And she is New York. She's a New York girl to her very core. Don't be deceived by the Irish business. That's politics, pure politics—meaning very impure politics, of course. She breathes this place. She…this place…they're not…you can't…they're like *that*!" He clamped both his hands together, squeezing them white. "Take her away, put her in England, in English Society? I don't know."

"Are you saying she must decide for you?"

He pursed his lips and raised his eyebrows. "That's the size of it. She'd be deciding for herself, too. We aren't really so separate any more."

"Does she mean so much?"

His eyes twinkled as he nodded and smiled. Nora, shamefully, found she had to stifle a pang of jealousy that love was still abroad in the world, was there for the finding.

"It's hard not to be stupid about it," he said. "You know—to believe that something moved me at the very first, when I saw her in that mob on Wall Street. (Don't ever call it a mob when she's around, by the way.) Looking back, though, it's easy to think it." He was silent a while and then said, "She isn't out of my thoughts day or night. Everything I do, you know, I have to relate to her, do it for her. I think she's the most wonderful person who ever lived or breathed. If we each live to a hundred, it will not be long enough for me. And I don't care if I never make a fortune. I know we'll always get by. And as long as I am with her..." He had spoken all this into his dry martini. Now he looked up and saw, to his astonishment and dismay, that his mother was crying. "What did I say?" he asked.

She shook her head. "Nothing. Of course you...nothing."

"All I meant to show, darling," he said—he had never called her "darling" before; it made her reach out blindly and grip his hand. He gripped back his reassurance—"was that it won't be *her* deciding for *me*. There is no her and me anymore. Not where decisions like that are involved."

Nora was herself again by the time they all sat down for dinner. During the early courses her conversation was almost entirely with Laney. Winifred joined in from time to time, to prevent it from seeming an inquisition. Indeed it was a most thorough inquisition but, because Laney recognized she was in the hands of two experts and because she was on home territory and had nothing to conceal, it never appeared to rise above the level of the most aimless conversation. Caspar hardly took his eyes off her.

The give-and-take had let slip a good deal of information on the Stevenson side, too. Laney soon knew that Caspar was one of the heirs to a business worth thirty to forty million dollars, one of the biggest in England. She already knew that Caspar had run away because he had been intended for the army, and that his mother had opposed the notion and wanted him for the business. The question that shrieked in her mind was: Had Lady S. come to call him back? And there was a subsidiary: Would he go? A subsidiary to that: Would she be asked to go, too? And, so, like a hall of mirrors the questions bounced back and forth, only half-illuminating one another: Would she go, if asked? In what capacity?

The strongest theme in them all, like a common tint in the glass of every mirror, was money.

What was even one million dollars like, let alone thirty?

At last the main question had to be asked aloud: Was Caspar being asked to return home?

Nora could sense the anguished suspense behind Laney's calm words. She longed to say everything she had said to Caspar, but she still had to be sure of this girl—independently of anything he or Winifred had decided. "If he wishes to," was all she said.

Laney looked at Caspar. "Honey?" she asked.

"I said you would decide for us," he told her. "And we have a week to talk about it." He turned to Nora. "I suppose you are going back on the *Great Eastern*?"

"That was our plan."

"I think she sails again a week today. Friday. We will let you know before then, of course." He gripped Laney's hand above the cloth, in full view. Her return grip was even harder.

Chapter 48

Six days later, on the eve of the ship's sailing, Laney and Caspar again dined with the two ladies. They had met, in various combinations, almost every day. Laney had taken Winifred on a tour of Manhattan schools where, armed with a letter of introduction from Governor Opdyke, she was given royal receptions, and even her closest and most incisive questions were not only tolerated but answered at length. Caspar had squired his mother to a number of Wall Street banks, where she, already something of a legend in financial circles, greatly extended her acquaintance and influence. They were all out to solicit funds, of course; but she considered the American system for regulating bank activities to be even more slipshod than the English one, and so she ended up investing very little. "Profit isn't everything," she warned Caspar, who had been very impressed with the banking wealth so in evidence on Fifth Avenue.

During these and all other encounters they had studiously avoided broaching that central topic—will they, won't they? But the questions fairly buzzed around its periphery. By the time of that final dinner Caspar knew that he would have complete control of the iron and steel section within a year, and of the firm in another five—except for railways, harbours, docks, and dams, which would always be his father's. It sounded like a big exception, being more than half the firm, but Caspar was confident that, by his own efforts in the iron and steel division, he would soon reverse the balance. So that didn't worry him.

Laney knew that he would be building a very big country house of around two hundred rooms, with indoor servants numbering over a hundred, and with forty or so gardeners and groundsmen. She would be one of the leaders of Society, wherever the house was to be built, and she would have undisputed sway over the house, its contents, and its people. She could not believe it, of course. English people were noted for their reserve; it was well known they took five years to decide whether to try a different kind of knot in a cravat. How could they be offering her all this so swiftly?

"They're desperate, darling," Caspar told her. "In their hearts, for all that they like you, they are hating this rush. But also, they are Stevensons. They are not unused to quick decisions when the need strikes. My father proposed to my mother the day they met—I mean within twenty-four hours. And they were married inside three weeks."

That really impressed Laney.

Caspar wasted no time that final evening. As soon as they were seated he said, "We haven't been able to make up our minds."

Both ladies let out disappointed gasps.

"I know," Caspar said apologetically. "I said Laney would decide for us, but it didn't prove so simple. I think, on the whole, she is in favour of our coming."

Nora and Winifred began to smile again.

"But I," he went on, "am against."

"Why, popsie?" Nora tried hard to keep a querulous edge out of her voice.

"She's convinced she can manage the house, the people, the whole Society nexus."

"On her head!" Winifred said.

"Even in her sleep," Nora confirmed.

Caspar sighed.

"What Caspar's afraid of, Lady Stevenson, is that I will—both as an uncouth, cultureless American and, even worse, as an Irish-American—that I would be exposed to ridicule."

"She would suffer the cruellest jibes," Caspar said. "You know exactly the sort of thing people would say. People—English people, I mean—make blunders and gaffes all the time. And no one says a word. They treat it as a delightful chance to show how tolerant and magnanimous they all are. But just let Laney make the same mistake—let her seat a maid of honour to the queen above the daughter of a baron—and listen to the malice ring around the county all season!"

"But a maid of honour to the queen *does* sit above a baron's daughter," Winifred said.

"No, dear," Nora contradicted, "they rank just above wives of Knights of the Garter."

"You see!" Caspar said to Laney.

"I'd learn all that," she said scornfully. "Believe me—it's a whole lot easier than learning who's in, who's out in New York politics. At least an earl is always an earl and his wife stays his wife."

But Caspar shook his head. "Even people who've grown up among it"—his hands waved toward Winifred—"get it wrong. Just think"—he turned to his mother and sister—"of the difficulties in referring to dukes and marquesses who are also privy councillors! Even my own courtesy title, Honourable—think who that covers! Here's a 'Mr. Robinson and the Honourable Mrs. Robinson,' let's say. Now those titles alone tell the three of us straight away that he's the son of a knight, at best, married to the daughter of a baron or viscount. But 'The Honourable Mrs. *Peter* Robinson'? Tell me within two seconds who she might be—because that's often all the time you have?"

Nora shook herself, as if she had felt mesmerized. "Wait!" she said. "What are we discussing these trivialities for? We are Stevensons. We don't give half a rupee for these petty things. I call all the men who come to my salons and dinners by their surnames. 'Dreadful!' say the books. But I do it." She turned to Laney. "Don't listen to this nonsense from my son. If you have our sort of money, keep a good cellar, employ the best of chefs, help the right people, and keep your heart in the right place, it'll only take you five or six years to convert any Englishman into a kind and decent fellow. Or Englishwoman. Perhaps ten years in her case."

"Cunning," Laney said.

"Cunning?" Nora echoed.

"She means cute," Caspar explained.

"Cute?" Nora said, just as bewildered as before.

"You see." Caspar laughed. "Already we speak a different language. All right, mater. I'll tell you the truth, now. I've gone too far down this furrow I'm ploughing. I can't let go and start something else. I love"—he looked at Laney—"this city. It's raw, it's crude, it's provincial, but it has something London has already lost. I don't know what, exactly, but something. Our future, Laney's and mine, is here. If she were English, if she were someone like Linny Sherringham, I might think twice. But I won't expose her to that. I won't cripple her, when here she…she is queen. She is a star in the sky here."

"And Laney?" Nora asked.

Laney looked at Caspar. "Whithersoever thou goest…" she began. And then, too happy to sustain that solemnity, she looked at Winifred, her eyes sparkling, then at Nora, and said simply: "I goest!"

When she saw Nora's disappointment, she added, "Don't be glum, Lady Stevenson. The ocean's only nine days broad now. Why, once it took that long to get to Boston. And with one son in India and the other here, we're going to be a world family. Just you see."

Chapter 49

Next morning, to their surprise, Caspar came alone to join them for breakfast. "Where's Laney?" Winifred asked.

"She's gone to Brooklyn on some errands for her father. I think it's just tact on her part. That's why she made a real proper goodbye last night."

"Well, it's nice to see you, anyway," Nora said. "I thought we wouldn't see you until the pier. After luncheon, I mean."

"I came to ask you something."

"Ah." They waited while he assembled the question. It took a lot of breath.

"What if I bought the iron and steel works—the whole of Stevenstown—from the firm?"

"With what money?"

He smiled. "That's always the second question—as a great London financier once said to me! Let's finish the first. You see, what I'm afraid of is throwing Laney to the lions right at the top of Society. If all we had was one little old ironworks—one *cheap* little old ironworks—hem hem—we could start there in exactly the same way as here. We could grow toward the top."

"Oh yes, Mama!" Winifred said. "Wouldn't that be marvellous!"

"And I would lend you the money?" Nora asked.

"If the guvnor wouldn't give it." He bit his lip and raised his eyebrows like a clown, as if to say "Aren't I impudent!"

"Poor boy—you're desperate for that part of the firm, aren't you," Nora said. "I'm afraid, popsie, it's a horse that won't run—won't even start, in fact. Your father never would agree to it." When Caspar looked downhearted, she added, "Would you? In his position?"

He nodded sourly. "No."

Winifred drew breath to speak but he stood and walked swiftly from the room, as if he could not face them and his failure at the same time.

"I sometimes think that to have a free choice is the most terrible burden in the world," Nora said when she and Winifred were alone once more.

At eleven o'clock, when they were taking a little rest from their packing, Caspar came back again. This time there was a sheepish grin on his face.

"Sorry about that little scene," he said. "It's a bit of a shock to see things as the guvnor sees them. Anyway"—he thrust an envelope into Nora's hands—"I haven't been idle since. There's all my thinking about the future of Stevenstown and the steel industry. It may be a bit of a muddle but it's all there. If you get the right sort of man in charge, it could dwarf the rest of the firm in ten years. Pick him very carefully. Promise me that?"

Nora laughed at his solemnity.

"Promise!" he shouted. He was quite angry.

When she had promised, he calmed down a little and took to pacing about the room, poking his fingers idly into drawers and boxes.

"I don't think I'll come to the pier," he said. "I'll say goodbye now. No—not goodbye. Au revoir. We'll come to England next summer. See you all."

He kissed Nora, who clung to him in open disbelief of his promise. "You will, popsie, won't you?"

"You'll have to send me the money," he said, more in his old and true character. "I'm not going to dig into my company for years."

After he had gone, Winifred nearly burst into tears. "Poor old Steamer," she said. "He's so torn. I hate to see him like that."

Caspar sat alone at the stairhead of the offices of the Uptown Construction Company. Where is Laney? he wondered. She ought to have been back by now. He wanted her to be with him. Now.

He wanted to know it was worth his giving up so much. He wanted to touch her. He wanted her voice to raise the tingle on his neck. He wanted the smell of her here. Oh, there were so many things he wanted.

Above all he wanted to escape from the dreadful logic of this call to go home. For he had not been honest, either with Laney or with his mother and sister, in saying that he would not expose Laney to the ridicule of Society. The complete truth was that he would not expose himself and Stevenson's to the risks of such ridicule. He could not honourably go back and shoulder six millions-worth of responsibility—all that capital, all those trusting, loyal people—he could not saddle it with the burden of a girl from a Fenian-American slum quarter, no matter how bright or lovely or talented.

To take the firm in the directions he knew it had to go next, he needed to build that vast palace and become the confidant of royalty, no less—perhaps even the moneylender to royalty; international royalty, too, not just English. What use would Laney be there? A thundering liability—the fact could not be blinked away.

In those surroundings, possessed of those aims, he needed a wife to the manner born. He needed—Linny Sherringham.

Where was Laney?

Linny...Laney! So near in sound. Such worlds apart in meaning.

The more he thought of all the things his refusal to return had cost him, the more desperately he needed to be with Laney and renew the ardour that alone justified what he had done.

It wasn't only the loss of the stately palace, whose massive walls and windows and turrets he could see so clearly in his mind's eye—surrounded by its terraces and fountains, its flowing lawns, proud peacocks, sweeping cedars, and carefully tended shrubberies and woods—it was not just the loss of this that plagued him. He saw, too, the yet-to-be-built bays and sheds of Stevenstown steel mills—the converters and open-hearth furnaces that his father would neglect to commission, the forges and rolling mills, the cable winders and wire drawers, and all the other new-world-pioneering machinery that would make Stevenson's synonymous with steel. All those things he had put in his notes to his mother.

Please, Laney, please come soon, he begged the silence. *Let me touch you and so own this city.*

In a more abstract way he also saw (much as he could "see" the shape of a mathematical idea) the business as it might be in twenty years' time. Even as it was at present, the firm was perfectly placed to move into shipbuilding and big land-engineering projects—especially big bridges. Didn't New York need bridges! If there were a bridge to Brooklyn, Laney would be back by now. The chances the firm was throwing away! If only they acted properly now, then in twenty years one ship in ten in the world—in the *world!*—could have the words Stevenson Clyde...Stevenson Belfast...Stevenson Tyneside...embossed on her stern. Stevenson New York? Well, he chuckled to himself, it was hardly the same thing.

But if he had Laney, it would do. It would just about do.

Unaccountably he also thought of young Abigail. Not to see her for years—that, too, would be a loss, he realized.

He stood and went to the window, looking alternately at the two roads that might bring her from one of the Brooklyn ferries. *Laney? Oh, God, do come! Do come soon! Without you it's all loss.*

The farewell at the pier didn't seem like a farewell at all. The ship was built for four thousand passengers. Only a few hundred were sailing in her. Nora and Winifred waved half-heartedly at other passengers' farewell wishers, pretending that somewhere in that thin crowd stood Caspar and Laney.

"They'll do marvellously, Mama!" Winifred said. "One day we'll laugh at ourselves for being so sad."

Just at that moment, as the gangway was being wheeled from the ship's side, they saw Caspar—and they both knew at once that it could be none other—come bursting through the pier gates and run, vaulting bags and trolleys, scattering porters and pier workers, right to the foot of the gangway. The company was so eager for passengers that the men pushed the gangway back against the side of the ship and reopened the door at its head. Caspar, sweating and breathless, ran up.

Because she had already cast off for'ard and was drifting to an angle with the pier, he had to leap a fair gap at the top, but, with the help of two sailors, he just made it. Nora and Winifred had meanwhile come running down to the entry deck.

"Caspar!" they both cried as he picked himself up.

He was too out of breath to speak. His face was pure torment. Both read the agony there as he looked from one to the other and back again.

The first officer came up. "Madam," he said apologetically to Nora. "We must sail. If this gentleman is a visitor, I fear..."

"Sail! Sail!" Caspar shouted hysterically. "I am a passenger."

"Oh, Caspar..." his mother began.

But he turned and ran up the companionway to the top deck. They followed at their own fastest pace and arrived to see him clutching the rail and looking out at New York as if he were about to jump back off the ship at any moment.

Nora was on the point of going forward to him when Winifred clutched at her arm. She shook her head at her mother. "Leave him," she said.

As the vast ship gathered speed and turned to leave Manhattan astern, Caspar walked crabwise along the rail until he was at the very back of the ship. *I could still jump it,* he kept saying to himself. *I could swim that far.* All the time he felt his muscles twitching to obey that impulse, while his spirit—that tyrannous spirit—all avarice, forbade them to do more than merely twitch.

Long after it had become truly impossible to leap into the water and swim ashore, he went on saying to himself: *You could! You could!* Bitter tears of self-hatred soaked his cheeks. What a rotten, rotten man he was!

Only then did Nora and Winifred dare to approach him.

"Steamer?" Winifred said hesitantly.

They saw him stiffen. "I couldn't do it," he said. "In the end—when I had to choose—I couldn't say no to Stevenson's."

Nora came near him, too shy to touch. "But all those things you said about Laney…"

He flung himself upon her, bending at the knees to become a child in stature. "They're all true," he howled. "They're all still true. Oh my God, my God, my God—how am I going to live without her? I've done a terrible thing."

"What did she say?" Winifred asked.

"I didn't…I left her a letter," Caspar said and broke down completely.

Nora was weeping now, and so was Winifred. They stood clinging together for what little comfort there was, a windswept group, alone at the stern, while the last faint lines of the Long Island shores slipped below the horizon.

None of them knew—and it was to be many years before even Caspar learned—that Laney never read his letter. She was already lying dead in Bellevue Hospital while he wrote it. The cause of death was given as "subdural hemorrhage following a recent blow on the skull." The doctor did not like to open her to confirm the diagnosis; all the evidence of those who saw her collapse on the street supported it. And there was the still-healing scar on her scalp. There had been many proofs in the aftermath of the draft riots that human cranial bones are no match for clubs, paving stones, and boots. Hers was not the first cranial hemorrhage he had seen that week.

Caspar's letter was found by the woman who was sent in, days later, to clean up the offices of the Uptown Construction Company. Though barely literate, she could make out enough to know the letter would only distress Joseph Delaney. She kept it a week, and then she burned it.

Joe Delaney, even in the depth of his grief at the loss of the most wonderful and treasured daughter ever granted to a man, had time to reflect bitterly on Caspar's desertion, without so much as a word to all the people who had helped him. He assumed Caspar had heard of Laney's death and had just cut away and run for England. But then, Joe had always known that an Englishman's honour was not a coin for universal tender.

Chapter 50

Day after day Caspar wakened thinking joyfully of Laney, and only then remembering. It was the morning fist-between-the-eyes. His body, which ached with unfulfilled love for her, was merciless. It prepared him to bump into her around every corner—even here on the ship. The rational cry of *Impossible!* was no medicine against the visceral depths of all that pain. Even his nose strained to pull the scent of her from out of the salt on winds from the Azores and Africa. Love does not know what "impossible" means.

Even now he could not look at the ocean without stiffening against an impulse to leap into it. It was still partly his desire to swim and swim and swim until he was back in Manhattan; but now, too, the impulse was confused with a blind desire for oblivion, a release from this intolerable hurt.

Nora, who so recently had felt that same hurt herself, was more hesitant in comforting Caspar than was Winifred, who had had the merest brush with the pangs of unfulfilled love. Perhaps, obscurely, Nora realized that if she said "It will pass—however painful, it will pass," Caspar would see through the half-truth to the lie at its core. It would never pass; it might be overlaid; it might diminish; but it would never completely pass. But Winifred could say those same words and her innocence would cleanse them of double intentions.

He never responded beyond a smile, a squeeze of the hand, and a shrinking back into himself. But on the sixth day out, with two-thirds of the voyage done, he surprised her at the ship's rail. It was a bright, sunny day on a calm sea whipped to little white horses by a pleasant breeze.

"Well, Winnie," he said with jovial effort as he joined her, "that's quite enough of me. Tell me about yourself. What did you do in prison?"

And she was so pleased to see even a shadow of the old Caspar return that she told him everything—of the school she had planned down to the last detail of the smallest classroom, of its organization, its scope, its curriculum, the aims its girls would have when they left, their assault on the walled and medieval City of Man.

"But I won't be happy," she said, "until I can call it the West London College for Girls and Boys. Just like in America, where boys and girls sit in the same classroom and learn the same lessons from the same teacher."

Caspar certainly heard enough to shock him out of his despondency; but he was not so apoplectic as he would have been a year earlier.

"You've seen the result," Winifred risked saying. "Surely you won't say it's unnatural or injurious?"

He closed his eyes but remained outwardly calm. She moved until she was pressed against him, arm to arm. "Oh, Steamer, you must go back for her. If you don't, you'll hate yourself forever."

"I couldn't go back for her. I could never look her in the eyes again."

"You must take the very next ship from Liverpool."

"No."

He was so decided, so calm, that she turned to him in surprise.

He spoke to the ocean. "Did it ever strike you—I don't suppose it did—how like our mother Laney is?"

"Is she?"

"They're sisters. In all essentials."

"Isn't that the highest possible..."

"Not," he cut in, "for a firm that's already the size of Stevenson's. Not for the second generation. Don't you see it? You remember the house I described to her? That big house? She'd die. She couldn't walk into something she hadn't helped build up. The mater couldn't have done so, either."

"You don't *need* that house, Steamer. You need her so much more."

His calm was beginning to frighten her.

"I don't need it," he said. "But Stevenson's does. The firm and the family. There's nine of us. There could be—sixty, seventy, eighty of our children. The firm can't absorb them all. Even our father's patronage and influence wouldn't place them all and marry them all. So we must not just penetrate the very, very, very top of Society. We must become it. We shall have to be on Christian-name terms with royalty. Not in order to do any better, you understand, not any better for our children. Just to make sure they enjoy the prospects we nine share now. That big house is only the first of the things we're going to need. But without it we can't even think of getting the others."

"It sounds very cold, very calculating, very…"

"Very far seeing?" he said.

"Yes. Mama said you have that ability."

"It won't be so bad. It will have its compensations. But Laney Delaney has no place in such a world. I could not destroy her by trying to force her into it."

Winifred felt sick. "Steamer," she asked quietly, "when did you think all this out?"

He considered that question a long time. "I don't know how to answer that," he said finally. "As soon as you and the mater turned up, I knew I was going to be cajoled into coming back. I suppose it didn't take more than five minutes to realize I couldn't bring Laney, too. But then I intended to turn down the offer—as I did, in fact. I didn't decide to come back." His voice took on a bitter edge. "I let *this*"—his heels stamped at the deck of the ship—"and *that*"—he waved at the ocean—"make it irrevocable for me. I'll marry Linny Sherringham. She goes with the job, you could say."

By now, Winifred was so appalled she could barely rise above a whisper. "But then you think just like our father. He wouldn't disagree with a word you've said."

"Hah!" The bitterness was absolute. "The wormwood and gall of this last year has been the slow realization that the guvnor has been absolutely right. Every step of the way. Except that he should have sired me before Boy."

"Oh, Caspar!" she shouted as she ran away. "You are such a clever fool!"

They called briefly at Cork, which allowed Caspar to kit himself out in new clothes and return his borrowed ones to the First Officer.

When they docked at Liverpool, John was on the pierside. He had come with only one question on his mind—and his binoculars had answered it while the *Great Eastern* was still out in the tideway.

The delight on his face was huge as he ran up the gangway, the moment it was in position. He had eyes only for Caspar.

But in those final yards a doubt—almost a shyness—seemed to possess John.

"Guvnor!" Caspar called out. He advanced with outstretched hand, a huge smile where no such smile had been for nine year-long days.

Reassured, John strode toward him again, so that they almost collided. Too close for a handshake, they embraced, and then again. Then John, radiant in his joy, caught his son by the shoulders and held him off for an arm's length inspection. He glanced swiftly and slyly over Caspar's shoulders at the unsmiling face of Winifred.

"I decided I couldn't fight all the Stevensons and win. They're too tough."

"Oh, don't say that, Guv'nor," Caspar answered. "I've just joined your side."

John laughed uproarious delight. "Think we can keep them in their place?" he asked. "You and I, together?"

"Better than that," Caspar replied, and he, too, looked over his shoulder to smile at Winifred. "First we'll *find* them a place. *Then* we'll keep them in it!"

Laughing together, they went down the gangplank, not even noticing that the ladies were left behind.

"Sometimes," Nora said, looking at the two black-coated backs and the tall, shiny hats of her husband and son, "sometimes it would be rather nice to be a god."

About the Author

Malcolm Macdonald is the author of thirty novels, including the bestselling Stevenson Family Saga, *Rose of Nancemellin*, and *Hell Hath No Fury*. He was born in England in 1932, and currently lives in Ireland.